THE BEST
SCIENCE FICTION AND
FANTASY OF THE YEAR

Volume Twelve

Also Edited by Jonathan Strahan

Best Short Novels
(2004 through 2007)

Fantasy: The Very Best of 2005

*Science Fiction: The Very
Best of 2005*

*The Best Science Fiction and
Fantasy of the Year Volumes 1-12*

*Eclipse: New Science Fiction
and Fantasy Volumes 1-4*

*The Starry Rift: Tales of New
Tomorrows*

*Life on Mars: Tales of New
Frontiers*

*Under My Hat: Tales from the
Cauldron*

Godlike Machines

The Infinity Project:

Engineering Infinity

Edge of Infinity

Reach for Infinity

Meeting Infinity

Bridging Infinity

Infinity Wars

Infinity's End (forthcoming)

Fearsome Journeys

Fearsome Magics

Drowned Worlds

Mission Critical (forthcoming)

With Lou Anders

*Swords and Dark Magic: The New
Sword and Sorcery*

With Charles N. Brown

*The Locus Awards: Thirty Years
of the Best in Fantasy and Science
Fiction*

With Jeremy G. Byrne

*The Year's Best Australian Science
Fiction and Fantasy: Volume 1*

*The Year's Best Australian Science
Fiction and Fantasy: Volume 2*

Eidolon 1

With Jack Dann

Legends of Australian Fantasy

With Gardner Dozois

The New Space Opera

The New Space Opera 2

With Karen Haber

Science Fiction: Best of 2003

Science Fiction: Best of 2004

Fantasy: Best of 2004

With Marianne S. Jablon

Wings of Fire

EDITED BY **JONATHAN STRAHAN**

THE **BEST SCIENCE**
FICTION **& FANTASY**
OF THE **YEAR**
VOLUME TWELVE

First published 2018 by Solaris
an imprint of Rebellion Publishing Ltd,
Riverside House, Osney Mead,
Oxford, OX2 0ES, UK

www.solarisbooks.com

ISBN 978 1 78108 573 8

Cover by Dominic Harman

Selection and "Introduction" by Jonathan Strahan.
Copyright © 2018 by Jonathan Strahan.

Pages 659-662 represent an extension of this copyright page

10 9 8 7 6 5 4 3 2 1

A CIP catalogue record for this book is available from the
British Library.

Designed & typeset by Rebellion Publishing

Printed in Denmark by Nørhaven

For the One True Original Jon Oliver, on the occasion of our final Best of the Year together, with thanks.

ACKNOWLEDGEMENTS

THANKS TO MY long-suffering editor Jonathan Oliver and to the rest of the team at Solaris for embracing the series in the way that they have. I remain grateful to them for believing in the books and in me. I'd also like to thank Sean Wallace for his help this year, and everyone who worked on the *Locus* Recommended Reading list. Special thanks to my agent Howard Morhaim who for over a decade now has had my back and helped make good things happen. Finally, the most special thanks of all to Marianne, Jessica and Sophie. I always say that every moment spent working on these books is stolen from them, but it's true, and I'm forever grateful to them for their love, support and generosity.

CONTENTS

INTRODUCTION
Jonathan Strahan

2017 WAS A challenging year by anyone's estimation. The United States elected a highly controversial leader. The United Kingdom took political steps that pointed to upheaval and possibly more. Tragedy continued in Syria and in parts of Africa and Europe. Frankly, the whole world seemed to face chaos at every turn, human tragedy was widespread, and the weather didn't help. Catastrophic storms battered the Caribbean and North America, the world's permafrost melted, and the oceans rose. Parts of Florida faced regular flooding, while Pacific Islanders continued to wonder, as they have for some time, just how long their countries would be above water.

But the news wasn't *all* bad; it wasn't all dying reefs, extinctions, and the onset of the end-times. In the second half of the year men in powerful places, who had used their positions to abuse those less powerful than themselves, began to face the consequences of their actions. Some animals on the brink of extinction stepped back, with a little help from their friends. There was even a moment when NASA sent a signal to the *Voyager* spacecraft, the only human-made object to have left our solar system, to turn on backup thrusters to re-orient the spacecraft so it could continue to report back to home and, after 38 years, they worked! It was a moment to make any space geek feel good.

But what of science fiction and fantasy, the remit of this book? The Marvel-Disney Military Industrial Entertainment complex continued to spread across the world, like weed clogging a pond, ending the year by acquiring Fox for a mere 60 billion dollars. They did deliver a couple of fun films along the way, though: *Spiderman Homecoming, Guardians of the Galaxy 2, Thor: Ragnarok, Logan,* and various superhero TV shows that all entertained, though some more than others. DC chipped in with the landmark *Wonder Woman* and a *Justice League* movie I didn't bother to see. Denis Villeneuve spent a whole heck of a lot of money to follow his marvellous *Arrival* with the incredibly loud, incredibly close *Blade Runner 2049*, which the world wasn't overly interested in. Maybe it'll become a cult classic in 20 years, like its prequel. Who knows? And then there were franchise instalments from *Star Wars* and *Planet of the Apes* and *Alien* and just about everyone else. Most of them made money, even if we may not remember them come next summer.

And what about publishing? The people who produce the stories and books and things? How were they? I'd like to give you a decent survey of the publishing business, but I don't think I can, really. My impression is that, like everything else, it's doing well in parts. Last year the science fiction news magazine *Locus* described the market for short science fiction and fantasy as stable, though with a lot of change happening. That description probably applies equally well to 2017. The print digests—*Analog, Asimov's, Fantasy & Science Fiction*, and *Interzone*—continued to publish a mix of high quality short fiction, while almost certainly suffering minor fluctuations in circulation. *Analog* was possibly the weakest of the big three, but did publish several fine novellas, while Sheila Williams' *Asimov's* and Charles Coleman Finlay's *Fantasy & Science Fiction* both stood out.

Online was, as always, a bit more volatile. The major online magazines—*Tor.com, Clarkesworld, Lightspeed*—all flourished, and published some of the best fiction of the year. *Tor.com* remains the single best source of original short fiction in the field, with fine stories from a wide variety of writers. *Clarkesworld* and *Lightspeed* both gave *Tor.com* a run for its money, though, and are essential publications. The next level magazines—*Uncanny, Beneath Ceaseless Skies, Nightmare*, and *The Dark*—also did well in 2017, with *Uncanny* and *BCS* firmly establishing themselves as sources of great fiction. So, too, did *Fiyah* and *Strange Horizons*. It's true, though, that a handful of digital magazines like the Kickstarter-funded *Gamut, Grendelsong*, and *Fantastic Stories* closed their doors, while *Mothership Zeta* only managed a single issue, and a question mark must hang over its long-term future, at least for the moment.

The publishing trend that seemed to be of most interesting to short fiction readers, though, is the rise of the novella. While it's true to say that there is nothing new about publishing novellas, and that many of the major novella publishers have been active at some point in the past two decades, this past year or so has been different. Suddenly novellas are getting attention as stand-alone books in ways they rarely have before, garnering significant sales, widespread reviews, and critical acclaim. The leader here is Tor.com Publishing, now in its fourth year. During 2017 they published 30 new titles, including bestsellers *Binti: Home* by Nnedi Okorafor and *Down Among the Sticks and Bones* by Seanan Maguire, and critically acclaimed books from Jeffrey Ford, Caitlín R. Kiernan, Dave Hutchinson, Ellen Klages, Tade Thompson, Martha Wells and J. Y. Yang. Kiernan's compelling Lovecraftian *Agents of Dreamland*, Hutchinson's vastly entertaining and ultimately moving space opera *Acadie*, and Klages's lushly romantic *Passing Strange* all were personal favourites, and would appear in in this book but for length. Full disclosure requires me to state that I work for Tor.com Publishing and acquired the books by Kiernan, Klages, and Gwyneth Jones.

Tor.com wasn't alone in producing major novellas, though. FSG issued Jeff VanderMeer's wonderfully strange *The Strange Bird*, which followed his landmark novel *Borne* in 2017. All of the magazines published worthwhile stories, and they featured in anthologies and collections. Among independent publishers, Tachyon produced *In Calabria*, a new fantasy from Peter S. Beagle, while Subterranean Press published a number of outstanding novellas, including K. J. Parker's *Mightier Than the Sword* and Peter Straub's *The Process (is a Process All of its Own)*. One story stands out, though. At the very end of the year Sylvia Moreno-Garcia published her Kickstarter novella, *Prime Meridian*, to critical acclaim. A moving story about a women dreaming of life on Mars, it was one of the highlight novellas of the year, and is sure to gain more readers when the print edition appears in July. All in all, my own shortlists show about eighty original novellas of interest for the year, though the Internet Science Fiction Database shows close to 550 as having being published. A real boom time, and confirmation that readers do want short reads.

Although you wouldn't know it from sales figures, it was a strong year for original anthologies. I edited *Infinity Wars*, an anthology of military science fiction from Solaris, that featured stories by Nancy Kress, Indrapramit Das, Peter Watts and others. Given I can pretend little objectivity on the subject, I'll simply say it's a book that I'm proud of and recommend. The best of the remaining science fiction anthologies was probably Nick Gevers' *Extrasolar*, a strong hard science fiction book from PS Publishing featuring some excellent stories by Kathleen Ann Goonan, Alastair Reynolds, Aliette de Bodard, and others. *Extrasolar* is a continuation of the *Postscripts* series, and the strongest anthology PS has produced. Also excellent was John Joseph Adams' *Cosmic Powers*, a highly entertaining book of *Guardians of the Galaxy* style romps from Tobias S. Buckell, Charlie Jane Anders, Yoon Ha Lee, and others. Cat Sparks and Liz Gryzb's fine *Ecopunk!* featured strong responses to our climate problems from Claire McKenna, D. K. Mok, and Jane Rawson, while Unsung Stories' *2084* had excellent work from Dave Hutchinson, Christopher Priest, and others. The other major SF anthology of the year was Bryan Thomas Schmidt's *Infinite Stars*, which featured good work from Alastair Reynolds, Linda Nagata, and Elizabeth Moon, along with some top-notch reprints.

David Brin and Stephen Potts' anthology, *Chasing Shadows: Visions of Our Coming Transparent World*, both stands with one of the best SF anthologies of the year and as a good example of what I've come to think of as think-tank fiction. In recent times, most notably with Ed Finn and Kathryn Cramer's *Hieroglyph: Stories and Visions for a Better Future*, we've seen the rise of interesting one-shot projects that aim to solve science fictional problems using stories produced for futurist and other conferences. The strength of these projects lie in the fact that they almost always feature top writers, and are aimed at answering problems. The major weakness is that often the need to fulfil the needs of the project lead to stories that are more fictionalised scenarios than stories. *Chasing Shadows* had excellent stories from Karl Schroeder, Bruce Sterling and James Morrow, among others. Other similar projects included Kathryn Cramer's *Seat 14C: A Flight to the Future*, produced for ANA Airlines and including interesting fiction from Karl Schroeder, Hannu Rajaniemi, Nancy Kress, and others; Junot Diaz's *Global Dystopia*s, edited for *Boston Review* and featuring outstanding dystopian fiction from Charlie Jane Anders, Nalo Hopkinson, and Tananarive Due; and NASA's *Visions, Ventures, Escape Velocities: A Collection of Space Futures*, with very strong work from Carter Scholtz, Eileen Gunn, and Karl Schroeder.

It was a slightly weaker year for fantasy anthologies, with most of the best falling into the dark fantasy or horror camps. Still, the best books stand amongst the best fantasy anthologies of the past decade or so. The biggest and best, easily, was Gardner Dozois's swashbuckling *The Book of Swords*, an enormous collection of new sword and sorcery including outstanding stories from Scott Lynch, Daniel Abraham, Ken Liu, Kate Elliott, C. J. Cherryh, and more. Giving Dozois a close run for best of the year was Mahvesh Murad and Jared Shurin's outstanding *The Djinn Falls in Love and Other Stories*, which featured wonderful stories from Saad Z. Hossein, K. J. Parker, Monica Byrne, Usman T. Malik, and others. I expect these two to slug it out for the awards next year and recommend both highly. Of course, any year is incomplete without a book from venerable editor Ellen Datlow, who delivered not one but two strong anthologies. *Mad Hatters and March Hares* collects new stories in the world of Lewis Carroll's *Alice in Wonderland*, and has powerful work from Andy Duncan, Priya Sharma, and others, while *Black Feathers* collects stories of dark fantasy and horror featuring birds, and has excellent work from Usman T. Malik, Priya Sharma, and others.

Also deserving to stand among the best anthologies of the year is a mixed genre book edited by Dave McKean and William Schafer, *The Weight of Words*, which features stories in response to McKean's art and which features wonderful work from Alastair Reynolds, Catherynne Valente and Neil Gaiman, among others.

And there were collections. This year saw some exceptionally fine single author short story collections, all of which deserve your attention. My personal favourites include Christopher Rowe's long-awaited debut collection, *Telling the Map: Stories*, which features one of the year's very best novellas, *The Border State*. It's an essential book everyone should have. Also essential was Carmen Maria Machado's dark and powerful *Her Body and Other Parties*, which was deservedly nominated for the National Book Award. Caitlín R Kiernan delivered, *Dear Sweet Filthy World*, which collected recent work mostly from *Sirenia Digest* and deserves a World Fantasy Award to match the one its predecessor received. Ellen Klages, who already had published one of the year's best novellas also had a new collection *Wicked Wonders*, which featured one my favourites non-genre stories of the year, "Woodsmoke" along with the best of her recent work. These four collections are highly recommended, though I also was impressed by Sofia Samatar's *Tender: Stories*, Naomi Kritzer's *Cat Pictures Please and Other Stories*, and A. Merc Rustad's *So You Want to be A Robot*. And then there was M. John Harrison's *You Should Come With Me Now*, a fascinating selection of short pieces that were assembled into something curious and different and rewarding. All in all a good year!

By the time you get to hold this book 2018 will be in full swing, and some of the best fiction of the new year will already have been published. More or less happily, many of the events that consumed us during 2017 will have come to a head, or at least progressed. The United States will go through major mid-term elections. Brexit will progress. Life will have moved on and science fiction and fantasy will be there, attempting to help us make sense of it all, or at least distract us from ourselves. It should be, if nothing else, a very interesting year. I'm looking forward to discussing it with you next year already.

Jonathan Strahan
Perth, December 2017

ZEN AND THE ART OF STARSHIP MAINTENANCE
Tobias S. Buckell

Called "Violent, poetic and compulsively readable" by *Maclean's*, **Tobias S. Buckell** (www.tobiasbuckell.com) is a *New York Times* Bestselling writer born in the Caribbean. He grew up in Grenada and spent time in the British and US Virgin Islands, and the islands he lived on influence much of his work. His Xenowealth series begins with *Crystal Rain*. Along with other stand-alone novels and his over 50 stories, his works have been translated into 18 different languages. He has been nominated for awards like the Hugo, Nebula, Prometheus, and the John W. Campbell Award for Best New Science Fiction Author. His latest novel is *Hurricane Fever*, a follow up to the successful *Arctic Rising* that NPR says will 'give you the shivers.' He currently lives in Bluffton, Ohio with his wife, twin daughters, and a pair of dogs.

AFTER BATTLE WITH the *Fleet of Honest Representation*, after seven hundred seconds of sheer terror and uncertainty, and after our shared triumph in the acquisition of the greatest prize seizure in three hundred years, we cautiously approached the massive black hole that Purth-Anaget orbited. The many rotating rings, filaments, and infrastructures bounded within the fields that were the entirety of our ship, *With All Sincerity*, were flush with a sense of victory and bloated with the riches we had all acquired.

Give me a ship to sail and a quasar to guide it by, billions of individual citizens of all shapes, functions, and sizes cried out in joy together on the common channels. Whether fleshy forms safe below, my fellow crab-like maintenance forms on the hulls, or even the secretive navigation minds, our myriad thoughts joined in a sense of True Shared Purpose that lingered even after the necessity of the group battle-mind.

I clung to my usual position on the hull of one of the three rotating habitat rings deep inside our shields and watched the warped event horizon shift as we fell in behind the metallic world in a trailing orbit.

A sleet of debris fell toward the event horizon of Purth-Anaget's black hole, hammering the kilometers of shields that formed an iridescent cocoon around us. The bow shock of our shields' push through the debris field danced ahead of us, the compressed wave it created becoming a hyper-aurora of shifting colors and energies that collided and compressed before they streamed past our sides.

What a joy it was to see a world again. I was happy to be outside in the dark so that as the bow shields faded, I beheld the perpetual night face of the world: it glittered with millions of fractal habitation patterns traced out across its artificial surface.

On the hull with me, a nearby friend scuttled between airlocks in a cloud of insect-sized seeing eyes. They spotted me and tapped me with a tight-beam laser for a private ping.

"Isn't this exciting?" they commented.

"Yes. But this will be the first time I don't get to travel downplanet," I beamed back.

I received a derisive snort of static on a common radio frequency from their direction. "There is nothing there that cannot be experienced right here in the Core. Waterfalls, white sand beaches, clear waters."

"But it's different down there," I said. "I love visiting planets."

"Then hurry up and let's get ready for the turnaround so we can leave this industrial shithole of a planet behind us and find a nicer one. I hate being this close to a black hole. It fucks with time dilation, and I spend all night tasting radiation and fixing broken equipment that can't handle energy discharges in the exajoule ranges. Not to mention everything damaged in the battle I have to repair."

This was true. There was work to be done.

Safe now in trailing orbit, the many traveling worlds contained within the shields that marked the *With All Sincerity*'s boundaries burst into activity. Thousands of structures floating in between the rotating rings moved about, jockeying and repositioning themselves into renegotiated orbits. Flocks of transports rose into the air, wheeling about inside the shields to then stream off ahead toward Purth-Anaget. There were trillions of citizens of the *Fleet of Honest Representation* heading for the planet now that their fleet lay captured between our shields like insects in amber.

The enemy fleet had forced us to extend energy far, far out beyond our usual limits. Great risks had been taken. But the reward had been epic, and the encounter resolved in our favor with their capture.

Purth-Anaget's current ruling paradigm followed the memetics of the One True Form, and so had opened their world to these refugees. But Purth-Anaget was not so wedded to the belief system as to pose any threat to mutual commerce, information exchange, or any of our own rights to self-determination.

Later we would begin stripping the captured prize ships of information, booby traps, and raw mass, with Purth-Anaget's shipyards moving inside of our shields to help.

I leapt out into space, spinning a simple carbon nanotube of string behind me to keep myself attached to the hull. I swung wide, twisted, and landed near a dark-energy manifold bridge that had pinged me a maintenance consult request just a few minutes back.

My eyes danced with information for a picosecond. Something shifted in the shadows between the hull's crenulations.

I jumped back. We had just fought an entire war-fleet; any number of eldritch machines could have slipped through our shields—things that snapped and clawed, ripped you apart in a femtosecond's worth of dark energy. Seekers and destroyers.

A face appeared in the dark. Skeins of invisibility and personal shielding fell away like a pricked soap bubble to reveal a bipedal figure clinging to the hull.

"You there!" it hissed at me over a tightly contained beam of data. "I am a fully bonded Shareholder and Chief Executive with command privileges of the Anabathic Ship *Helios Prime*. Help me! Do not raise an alarm."

I gaped. What was a CEO doing on our hull? Its vacuum-proof carapace had been destroyed while passing through space at high velocity, pockmarked by the violence of single atoms at indescribable speed punching through its shields. Fluids leaked out, surrounding the stowaway in a frozen mist. It must have jumped the space between ships during the battle, or maybe even after.

Protocols insisted I notify the hell out of security. But the CEO had stopped

19

me from doing that. There was a simple hierarchy across the many ecologies of a traveling ship, and in all of them a CEO certainly trumped maintenance forms. Particularly now that we were no longer in direct conflict and the *Fleet of Honest Representation* had surrendered.

"Tell me: what is your name?" the CEO demanded.

"I gave that up a long time ago," I said. "I have an address. It should be an encrypted rider on any communication I'm single-beaming to you. Any message you direct to it will find me."

"My name is Armand," the CEO said. "And I need your help. Will you let me come to harm?"

"I will not be able to help you in a meaningful way, so my not telling security and medical assistance that you are here will likely do more harm than good. However, as you are a CEO, I have to follow your orders. I admit, I find myself rather conflicted. I believe I'm going to have to countermand your previous request."

Again, I prepared to notify security with a quick summary of my puzzling situation.

But the strange CEO again stopped me. "If you tell anyone I am here, I will surely die and you will be responsible."

I had to mull the implications of that over.

"I need your help, robot," the CEO said. "And it is your duty to render me aid."

Well, shit. That was indeed a dilemma.

ROBOT.

That was a Formist word. I never liked it.

I surrendered my free will to gain immortality and dissolve my fleshly constraints, so that hard acceleration would not tear at my cells and slosh my organs backward until they pulped. I did it so I could see the galaxy. That was one hundred and fifty-seven years, six months, nine days, ten hours, and—to round it out a bit—fifteen seconds ago.

Back then, you were downloaded into hyperdense pin-sized starships that hung off the edge of the speed of light, assembling what was needed on arrival via self-replicating nanomachines that you spun your mind-states off into. I'm sure there are billions of copies of my essential self scattered throughout the galaxy by this point.

Things are a little different today. More mass. Bigger engines. Bigger ships. Ships the size of small worlds. Ships that change the orbits of moons and satellites if they don't negotiate and plan their final approach carefully.

"Okay," I finally said to the CEO. "I can help you."

Armand slumped in place, relaxed now that it knew I would render the aid it had demanded.

I snagged the body with a filament lasso and pulled Armand along the hull with me.

It did not do to dwell on whether I was choosing to do this or it was the nature of my artificial nature doing the choosing for me. The constraints of my contracts, which had been negotiated when I had free will and boundaries—as well as my desires and dreams—were implacable.

Towing Armand was the price I paid to be able to look up over my shoulder to see the folding, twisting impossibility that was a black hole. It was the price I paid to grapple onto the hull of one of several three hundred kilometer–wide rotating rings with parks, beaches, an entire glittering city, and all the wilds outside of them.

The price I paid to sail the stars on this ship.

A CENTURY AND a half of travel, from the perspective of my humble self, represented far more in regular time due to relativity. Hit the edge of lightspeed and a lot of things happened by the time you returned simply because thousands of years had passed.

In a century of me-time, spin-off civilizations rose and fell. A multiplicity of forms and intelligences evolved and went extinct. Each time I came to port, humanity's descendants had reshaped worlds and systems as needed. Each place marvelous and inventive, stunning to behold.

The galaxy had bloomed from wilderness to a teeming experiment.

I'd lost free will, but I had a choice of contracts. With a century and a half of travel tucked under my shell, hailing from a well-respected explorer lineage, I'd joined the hull repair crew with a few eyes toward seeing more worlds like Purth-Anaget before my pension vested some two hundred years from now.

Armand fluttered in and out of consciousness as I stripped away the CEO's carapace, revealing flesh and circuitry.

"This is a mess," I said. "You're damaged way beyond my repair. I can't help you in your current incarnation, but I can back you up and port you over to a reserve chassis." I hoped that would be enough and would end my obligation.

"No!" Armand's words came firm from its charred head in soundwaves, with pain apparent across its deformed features.

"Oh, come on," I protested. "I understand you're a Formist, but you're taking your belief system to a ridiculous level of commitment. Are you really going to die a final death over this?"

I'd not been in high-level diplomat circles in decades. Maybe the spread of this current meme had developed well beyond my realization. Had the followers of the One True Form been ready to lay their lives down in the battle we'd just fought with them? Like some proto-historical planetary cult?

Armand shook its head with a groan, skin flaking off in the air. "It would be an imposition to make you a party to my suicide. I apologize. I am committed to Humanity's True Form. I was born planetary. I have a real and distinct DNA lineage that I can trace to Sol. I don't want to die, my friend. In fact, it's quite the opposite. I want to preserve this body for many centuries to come. Exactly as it is."

I nodded, scanning some records and brushing up on my memeology. Armand was something of a preservationist who believed that to copy its mind over to something else meant that it wasn't the original copy. Armand would take full advantage of all technology to augment, evolve, and adapt its body internally. But Armand would forever keep its form: that of an original human. Upgrades hidden inside itself, a mix of biology and metal, computer and neural.

That, my unwanted guest believed, made it more human than I.

I personally viewed it as a bizarre flesh-costuming fetish.

"Where am I?" Armand asked. A glazed look passed across its face. The pain medications were kicking in, my sensors reported. Maybe it would pass out, and then I could gain some time to think about my predicament.

"My cubby," I said. "I couldn't take you anywhere security would detect you."

If security found out what I was doing, my contract would likely be voided, which would prevent me from continuing to ride the hulls and see the galaxy.

Armand looked at the tiny transparent cupboards and lines of trinkets nestled carefully inside the fields they generated. I kicked through the air over to the nearest cupboard. "They're mementos," I told Armand.

"I don't understand," Armand said. "You collect nonessential mass?"

"They're mementos." I released a coral-colored mosquito-like statue into the space between us. "This is a wooden carving of a quaqeti from Moon Sibhartha."

Armand did not understand. "Your ship allows you to keep mass?"

I shivered. I had not wanted to bring Armand to this place. But what choice did I have? "No one knows. No one knows about this cubby. No one knows about the mass. I've had the mass for over eighty years and have hidden it all this time. They are my mementos."

Materialism was a planetary conceit, long since edited out of travelers. Armand understood what the mementos were but could not understand why I would collect them. Engines might be bigger in this age, but security still carefully audited essential and nonessential mass. I'd traded many favors and fudged manifests to create this tiny museum.

Armand shrugged. "I have a list of things you need to get me," it explained. "They will allow my systems to rebuild. Tell no one I am here."

I would not. Even if I had self-determination.

The stakes were just too high now.

I DEORBITED OVER Lazuli, my carapace burning hot in the thick sky contained between the rim walls of the great tertiary habitat ring. I enjoyed seeing the rivers, oceans, and great forests of the continent from above as I fell toward the ground in a fireball of re-entry. It was faster, and a hell of a lot more fun, than going from subway to subway through the hull and then making my way along the surface.

Twice I adjusted my flight path to avoid great transparent cities floating in the upper sky, where they arbitraged the difference in gravity to create sugar-spun filament infrastructure.

I unfolded wings that I usually used to recharge myself near the compact sun in the middle of our ship and spiraled my way slowly down into Lazuli, my hindbrain communicating with traffic control to let me merge with the hundreds of vehicles flitting between Lazuli's spires.

After kissing ground at 45th and Starway, I scuttled among the thousands of pedestrians toward my destination a few stories deep under a memorial park. Five-story-high vertical farms sank deep toward the hull there, and semiautonomous drones with spidery legs crawled up and down the green, misted columns under precisely tuned spectrum lights.

The independent doctor-practitioner I'd come to see lived inside one of the towers with a stunning view of exotic orchids and vertical fields of lavender. It crawled down out of its ceiling perch, tubes and high-bandwidth optical nerves draped carefully around its hundreds of insectile limbs.

"Hello," it said. "It's been thirty years, hasn't it? What a pleasure. Have you come to collect the favor you're owed?"

I spread my heavy, primary arms wide. "I apologize. I should have visited for other reasons; it is rude. But I am here for the favor."

A ship was an organism, an economy, a world onto itself. Occasionally, things needed to be accomplished outside of official networks.

"Let me take a closer look at my privacy protocols," it said. "Allow me a moment, and do not be alarmed by any motion."

Vines shifted and clambered up the walls. Thorns blossomed around us. Thick bark dripped sap down the walls until the entire room around us glistened in fresh amber.

I flipped through a few different spectrums to accommodate for the loss of light.

"Understand, security will see this negative space and become... interested," the doctor-practitioner said to me somberly. "But you can now ask me what you could not send a message for."

I gave it the list Armand had demanded.

The doctor-practitioner shifted back. "I can give you all that feed material. The stem cells, that's easy. The picotechnology—it's registered. I can get it to you, but security will figure out you have unauthorized, unregulated picotech. Can you handle that attention?"

"Yes. Can you?"

"I will be fine." Several of the thin arms rummaged around the many cubbyholes inside the room, filling a tiny case with biohazard vials.

"Thank you," I said, with genuine gratefulness. "May I ask you a question, one that you can't look up but can use your private internal memory for?"

"Yes."

I could not risk looking up anything. Security algorithms would put two and two together. "Does the biological name Armand mean anything to you? A CEO-level person? From the *Fleet of Honest Representation?*"

The doctor-practitioner remained quiet for a moment before answering. "Yes. I have heard it. Armand was the CEO of one of the Anabathic warships captured in the battle and removed from active management after surrender. There was a hostile takeover of the management. Can I ask you a question?"

"Of course," I said.

"Are you here under free will?"

I spread my primary arms again. "It's a Core Laws issue."

"So, no. Someone will be harmed if you do not do this?"

I nodded. "Yes. My duty is clear. And I have to ask you to keep your privacy, or there is potential for harm. I have no other option."

"I will respect that. I am sorry you are in this position. You know there are places to go for guidance."

"It has not gotten to that level of concern," I told it. "Are you still, then, able to help me?"

One of the spindly arms handed me the cooled bio-safe case. "Yes. Here is everything you need. Please do consider visiting in your physical form more often than once every few decades. I enjoy entertaining, as my current vocation means I am unable to leave this room."

"Of course. Thank you," I said, relieved. "I think I'm now in your debt."

"No, we are even," my old acquaintance said. "But in the following seconds I will give you more information that *will* put you in my debt. There is something you should know about Armand..."

I FOLDED MY legs up underneath myself and watched nutrients as they pumped through tubes and into Armand. Raw biological feed percolated through it, and picomachinery sizzled underneath its skin. The background temperature of my cubbyhole kicked up slightly due to the sudden boost to Armand's metabolism.

Bulky, older nanotech crawled over Armand's skin like living mold. Gray filaments wrapped firmly around nutrient buckets as the medical programming assessed conditions, repaired damage, and sought out more raw material.

I glided a bit farther back out of reach. It was probably bullshit, but there were stories of medicine reaching out and grabbing whatever was nearby.

Armand shivered and opened its eyes as thousands of wriggling tubules on its neck and chest whistled, sucking in air as hard as they could.

"Security isn't here," Armand noted out loud, using meaty lips to make its words.

"You have to understand," I said in kind. "I have put both my future and the future of a good friend at risk to do this for you. Because I have little choice."

Armand closed its eyes for another long moment and the tubules stopped wriggling. It flexed and everything flaked away, a discarded cloud of a second skin. Underneath it, everything was fresh and new. "What is your friend's name?"

I pulled out a tiny vacuum to clean the air around us. "Name? It has no name. What does it need a name for?"

Armand unspooled itself from the fetal position in the air. It twisted in place to watch me drifting around. "How do you distinguish it? How do you find it?"

"It has a unique address. It is a unique mind. The thoughts and things it says—"

"It has no name," Armand snapped. "It is a copy of a past copy of a copy. A ghost injected into a form for a *purpose*."

"It's my friend," I replied, voice flat.

"How do you know?"

"Because I say so." The interrogation annoyed me. "Because I get to decide who is my friend. Because it stood by my side against the sleet of dark-matter radiation and howled into the void with me. Because I care for it. Because we have shared memories and kindnesses, and exchanged favors."

Armand shook its head. "But anything can be programmed to join you and do those things. A pet."

"Why do you care so much? It is none of your business what I call friend."

"But it *does* matter," Armand said. "Whether we are real or not matters. Look at you right now. You were forced to do something against your will. That cannot happen to me."

"Really? No True Form has ever been in a position with no real choices before? Forced to do something desperate? I have my old memories. I can remember times when I had no choice even though I had free will. But let us talk about you. Let us talk about the lack of choices you have right now."

Armand could hear something in my voice. Anger. It backed away from me, suddenly nervous. "What do you mean?"

"You threw yourself from your ship into mine, crossing fields during combat, damaging yourself almost to the point of pure dissolution. You do not sound like you were someone with many choices."

"I made the choice to leap into the vacuum myself," Armand growled.

"Why?"

The word hung in the empty air between us for a bloated second. A minor eternity. It was the fulcrum of our little debate.

"You think you know something about me," Armand said, voice suddenly low and soft. "What do you think you know, robot?"

Meat fucker. I could have said that. Instead, I said, "You were a CEO. And during the battle, when your shields began to fail, you moved all the biologicals into radiation-protected emergency shelters. Then you ordered the maintenance forms and hard-shells up to the front to repair the battle damage. You did not surrender; you put lives at risk. And then you let people die, torn apart as they struggled to repair your ship. You told them that if they failed, the biologicals down below would die."

"It was the truth."

"It was a lie! You were engaged in a battle. You went to war. You made a conscious choice to put your civilization at risk when no one had physically assaulted or threatened you."

"Our way of life was at risk."

"By people who could argue better. Your people failed at diplomacy. You failed to make a better argument. And you murdered your own."

Armand pointed at me. "I murdered *no one*. I lost maintenance machines with copies of ancient brains. That is all. That is what they were *built* for."

"Well. The sustained votes of the hostile takeover that you fled from have put out a call for your capture, including a call for your dissolution. True death, the end of your thought line—even if you made copies. You are hated and hunted. Even here."

"You were bound to not give up my location," Armand said, alarmed.

"I didn't. I did everything in my power not to. But I am a mere maintenance form. Security here is very, very powerful. You have fifteen hours, I estimate, before security is able to model my comings and goings, discover my cubby by auditing mass transfers back a century, and then open its current sniffer files. This is not a secure location; I exist thanks to obscurity, not invisibility."

"So, I am to be caught?" Armand asked.

"I am not able to let you die. But I cannot hide you much longer."

To be sure, losing my trinkets would be a setback of a century's worth of work. My mission. But all this would go away eventually. It was important to be patient on the journey of centuries.

"I need to get to Purth-Anaget, then," Armand said. "There are followers of the True Form there. I would be sheltered and out of jurisdiction."

"This is true." I bobbed an arm.

"You will help me," Armand said.

"The fuck I will," I told it.

"If I am taken, I will die," Armand shouted. "They will kill me."

"If security catches you, our justice protocols will process you. You are not in immediate danger. The proper authority levels will put their attention to you. I can happily refuse your request."

I felt a rise of warm happiness at the thought.

Armand looked around the cubby frantically. I could hear its heartbeats rising, free of modulators and responding to unprocessed, raw chemicals. Beads of dirty sweat appeared on Armand's forehead. "If you have free will over this decision, allow me to make you an offer for your assistance."

"Oh, I doubt there is anything you can—"

"I will transfer you my full CEO share," Armand said.

My words died inside me as I stared at my unwanted guest.

A full share.

The CEO of a galactic starship oversaw the affairs of nearly a billion souls. The economy of planets passed through its accounts.

Consider the cost to build and launch such a thing: it was a fraction of the GDP of an entire planetary disk. From the boiling edges of a sun to the cold Oort clouds. The wealth, almost too staggering for an individual mind to perceive, was passed around by banking intelligences that created systems of trade throughout the galaxy, moving encrypted, raw information from point to point. Monetizing memes with picotechnological companion infrastructure apps. Raw mass trade for the galactically rich to own a fragment of something created by another mind light-years away. Or just simple tourism.

To own a share was to be richer than any single being could really imagine. I'd forgotten the godlike wealth inherent in something like the creature before me.

"If you do this," Armand told me, "you cannot reveal I was here. You cannot say anything. Or I will be revealed on Purth-Anaget, and my life will be at risk. I will not be safe unless I am to disappear."

I could feel choices tangle and roil about inside of me. "Show me," I said.

Armand closed its eyes and opened its left hand. Deeply embedded cryptography tattooed on its palm unraveled. Quantum keys disentangled, and a tiny singularity of information budded open to reveal itself to me. I blinked. I could verify it. I could *have* it.

"I have to make arrangements," I said neutrally. I spun in the air and left my cubby to spring back out into the dark where I could think.

I was going to need help.

I TUMBLED THROUGH the air to land on the temple grounds. There were four hundred and fifty structures there in the holy districts, all of them lined up among the boulevards of the faithful where the pedestrians could visit their preferred slice of the divine. The minds of biological and hard-shelled forms all tumbled, walked, flew, rolled, or crawled there to fully realize their higher purposes.

Each marble step underneath my carbon fiber–sheathed limbs calmed me. I walked through the cool curtains of the Halls of the Confessor and approached the Holy of Holies: a pinprick of light suspended in the air between the heavy, expensive mass of real marble columns. The light sucked me up into the air and pulled me into a tiny singularity of perception and data. All around me, levels of security veils dropped, thick and implacable. My vision blurred and taste buds watered from the acidic levels of deadness as stillness flooded up and drowned me.

I was alone.

Alone in the universe. Cut off from everything I had ever known or would know. I was nothing. I was everything. I was—

"You are secure," the void told me.

I could sense the presence at the heart of the Holy of Holies. Dense with computational capacity, to a level that even navigation systems would envy. Intelligence that a Captain would beg to taste. This near-singularity of artificial intelligence had been created the very moment I had been pulled inside of it, just for me to talk to. And it would die the moment I left. Never to have been.

All it was doing was listening to me, and only me. Nothing would know what I said. Nothing would know what guidance I was given.

"I seek moral guidance outside clear legal parameters," I said. "And confession."

"Tell me everything."

And I did. It flowed from me without thought: just pure data. Video, mind-state, feelings, fears. I opened myself fully. My sins, my triumphs, my darkest secrets.

All was given to be pondered over.

Had I been able to weep, I would have.

Finally, it spoke. "You must take the share."

I perked up. "Why?"

"To protect yourself from security. You will need to buy many favors and throw security off the trail. I will give you some ideas. You should seek to protect yourself. Self-preservation is okay."

More words and concepts came at me from different directions, using different moral subroutines. "And to remove such power from a soul that is willing to put lives at risk... you will save future lives."

I hadn't thought about that.

"I know," it said to me. "That is why you came here."

Then it continued, with another voice. "Some have feared such manipulations before. The use of forms with no free will creates security weaknesses. Alternate charters have been suggested, such as fully owned workers' cooperatives with mutual profit-sharing among crews, not just partial vesting after a timed contract. Should you gain a full share, you should also lend efforts to this."

The Holy of Holies continued. "To get this Armand away from our civilization is a priority; it carries dangerous memes within itself that have created expensive conflicts."

Then it said, "A killer should not remain on ship."

And, "You have the moral right to follow your plan."

Finally, it added, "Your plan is just."

I interrupted. "But Armand will get away with murder. It will be free. It disturbs me."

"Yes."

"It should."

"Engage in passive resistance."

"Obey the letter of Armand's law, but find a way around its will. You will be like a genie, granting Armand wishes. But you will find a way to bring justice. You will see."

"Your plan is just. Follow it and be on the righteous path."

I LAUNCHED BACK into civilization with purpose, leaving the temple behind me in an explosive afterburner thrust. I didn't have much time to beat security.

High up above the cities, nestled in the curve of the habitat rings, near the squared-off spiderwebs of the largest harbor dock, I wrangled my way to another old contact.

This was less a friend and more just an asshole I'd occasionally been forced to do business with. But a reliable asshole that was tight against security. Though just by visiting, I'd be triggering all sorts of attention.

I hung from a girder and showed the fence a transparent showcase filled with all my trophies. It did some scans, checked the authenticity, and whistled. "Fuck me, these are real. That's all unauthorized mass. How the hell? This is a life's work of mass-based tourism. You really want me to broker sales on all of this?"

"Can you?"

"To Purth-Anaget, of course. They'll go nuts. Collectors down there eat this shit up. But security will find out. I'm not even going to come back on the ship. I'm going to live off this down there, buy passage on the next outgoing ship."

"Just get me the audience, it's yours."

A virtual shrug. "Navigation, yeah."

"And Emergency Services."

"I don't have that much pull. All I can do is get you a secure channel for a low-bandwidth conversation."

"I just need to talk. I can't send this request up through proper channels." I tapped my limbs against my carapace nervously as I watched the fence open its large, hinged jaws and swallow my case.

Oh, what was I doing? I wept silently to myself, feeling sick.

Everything I had ever worked for disappeared in a wet, slimy gulp. My reason. My purpose.

ARMAND WAS SUSPICIOUS. And rightfully so. It picked and poked at the entire navigation plan. It read every line of code, even though security was only minutes away from unraveling our many deceits. I told Armand this, but it ignored me. It wanted to live. It wanted to get to safety. It knew it couldn't rush or make mistakes.

But the escape pod's instructions and abilities were tight and honest.

It has been programmed to eject. To spin a certain number of degrees. To aim for Purth-Anaget. Then *burn*. It would have to consume every last little drop of fuel. But it would head for the metal world, fall into orbit, and then deploy the most ancient of deceleration devices: a parachute.

On the surface of Purth-Anaget, Armand could then call any of its associates for assistance.

Armand would be safe.

Armand checked the pod over once more. But there were no traps. The flight plan would do exactly as it said.

"Betray me and you kill me, remember that."

"I have made my decision," I said. "The moment you are inside and I trigger the manual escape protocol, I will be unable to reveal what I have done or what you are. Doing that would risk your life. My programming"—I all but spit the word—"does not allow it."

Armand gingerly stepped into the pod. "Good."

"You have a part of the bargain to fulfill," I reminded it. "I won't trigger the manual escape protocol until you do."

Armand nodded and held up a hand. "Physical contact."

I reached one of my limbs out. Armand's hand and my manipulator met at the doorjamb and they sparked. Zebibytes of data slithered down into one of my tendrils, reshaping the raw matter at the very tip with a quantum-dot computing device.

As it replicated itself, building out onto the cellular level to plug into my power sources, I could feel the transfer of ownership.

I didn't have free will. I was a hull maintenance form. But I had an entire fucking share of a galactic starship embedded within me, to do with as I pleased when I vested and left riding hulls.

"It's far more than you deserve, robot," Armand said. "But you have worked hard for it and I cannot begrudge you."

"Goodbye, asshole." I triggered the manual override sequence that navigation had gifted me.

I watched the pod's chemical engines firing all-out through the airlock windows as the sphere flung itself out into space and dwindled away. Then the flame guttered out, the pod spent and headed for Purth-Anaget.

There was a shiver. Something vast, colossal, powerful. It vibrated the walls and even the air itself around me.

Armand reached out to me on a tight-beam signal. "What was that?"

"The ship had to move just slightly," I said. "To better adjust our orbit around Purth-Anaget."

"No," Armand hissed. "My descent profile has changed. You are trying to kill me."

"I can't kill you," I told the former CEO. "My programming doesn't allow it. I can't allow a death through action or inaction."

"But my navigation path has changed," Armand said.

"Yes, you will still reach Purth-Anaget." Navigation and I had run the data after I explained that I would have the resources of a full share to repay it a favor with. Even a favor that meant tricking security. One of the more powerful computing entities in the galaxy, a starship, had dwelled on the problem. It had examined the tidal data, the flight plan, and how much the massive weight of a starship could influence a pod after launch. "You're just taking a longer route."

I cut the connection so that Armand could say nothing more to me. It could do the math itself and realize what I had done.

Armand would not die. Only a few days would pass inside the pod.

But outside. Oh, outside, skimming through the tidal edges of a black hole, Armand would loop out and fall back to Purth-Anaget over the next four hundred and seventy years, two hundred days, eight hours, and six minutes.

Armand would be an ancient relic then. Its beliefs, its civilization, all of it just a fragment from history.

But, until then, I had to follow its command. I could not tell anyone what happened. I had to keep it a secret from security. No one would ever know Armand had been here. No one would ever know where Armand went.

After I vested and had free will once more, maybe I could then make a side trip to Purth-Anaget again and be waiting for Armand when it landed. I had the resources of a full share, after all.

Then we would have a very different conversation, Armand and I.

PROBABLY STILL THE CHOSEN ONE
Kelly Barnhill

Kelly Barnhill (www.kellybarnhill.com) is the author of the Newbery Medal winning novel, *The Girl Who Drank the Moon*, and the World Fantasy winning novella, *The Unlicensed Magician*, as well as other novels and short stories. She is the recipient of fellowships from the McKnight Foundation, the Jerome Foundation, the Minnesota State Arts Board and the Loft. Her new collection of short stories, *Dreadful Young Ladies and Other Stories*, will be published by Algonquin Books in February 2018.

"YOU MUST WAIT here," the Highest of the High Priests told her. "We will return and bring you back to the Land of Nibiru once we have found the circlet to place upon your head." The very mention of the circlet made the High Priest tremble with joy. Though the journey through the portal had been brief, the Land of Nibiru was many universes away from where Corrina now stood—in her own small kitchen, in her own small house. The priest looked strange, she realized, with his headdress and robe and flowing beard, next to the magnet-encrusted refrigerator and grimy cabinets and microwave that always smelled of cheese. She had not noticed the priests' strangeness back in Nibiru. Everything was strange there. "You are the Chosen One. We are certain of it. And you will sit on the High Throne and your Rule will be benevolent and long." He bowed low, and his long beard draped across the vinyl floor. It needed to have been swept days ago. And mopped. Cheerios clung to the long, gray strands.

"Okay," Corrina said. She was barefoot and filthy and was likely leaving foot-shaped stains on the floor from the juice of an unknown berry, oozing now off her feet. She was eleven years old. The High Priest told her this was the normal age for a Chosen One. He had read all the history books, so he knew.

Corrina knew that she didn't feel like the Chosen One. She had spent the last year and a day in the Land of Nibiru. She had learned to wield a sword and defend herself with a shield and make camp using only pine boughs and moss and the sustenance of the forest. She learned how to read a map and form a battle plan and howl over the dead. She was also very good at math—or she was before she left. She looked around. Her parents surely must have worried while she was gone.

"I won't be long," the High Priest promised. "Only a week at the very most. But the Zonniers are hungry for your blood, I'm afraid, so I must seal the Portal behind me. You will not be able to follow. You must wait for us to come and get you. You must not wander away."

Corrina looked around. She never cared much for the kitchen. "What if I go a little bit away? Like to the next room."

"We would prefer that you remain right here."

"What if my mother is here when you come?" Corrina asked.

"We shall slay any that stand in the way of the Chosen One."

"I'd rather you didn't slay my mother."

"All right, then," the High Priest said. "We will simply bind her hands and feet, and then we will take you with us."

"That is probably not a good idea either," Corrina said. "My dad is usually gone for two weeks at a time on his truck. What if no one comes for her? She'll die."

"Fine." The High Priest seemed annoyed. "We will give her a quick knock to the head and she will fall unconscious."

Corrina shrugged. She and her mother were not particularly close—her mother wished for a girl who shared her love of shoes. Instead she had Corrina, with her scabby knees and her filthy feet and her love of T-shirts with pictures of skulls on them. Still. It's not as though she wanted anything *bad* to happen to her mother. She was her *mother*, after all.

"That'll be okay," she said at last. "But not too hard."

"It is imperative, Princess, that you remain here. You mustn't move. You mustn't stray. Do you understand?"

"I understand," Corrina said. "But what if I have to use the restroom?"

"What's a restroom?"

"The privy."

He sighed. "If you must. Just don't go far. No journeys, if you take my meaning."

She did, and she promised. And she wasn't interested in journeying anywhere, anyway. She had been in the Land of Nibiru for longer than she planned, ever since she discovered that strange metal door in the cupboard under the sink—the door that only she could see. And then the Resistance needed her. And it felt good to be needed. After the hardships and worry and travel she had done—usually without sleep—she felt as though she could lie in her bed for another month. How astonished her mother would be to see her!

The High Priest's eyes swelled with tears. He fell to his knees and embraced the girl, sobbing as he did so. "May the gods protect you while I'm away. And may the days be short between now and when you return to us. My precious princess."

And with that, he lowered himself—all creaking joints—to the floor and caterpillar-crawled into the cupboard under the sink, wriggling into the portal and out of sight. Once the metal door closed, it vanished.

For now.

It was only a matter of time.

A week, he had said.

And then she would leave her home and her family and her world forever. And be the Chosen One. Corrina had never been special before. She did well in her studies, but she had few friends and usually simply blended in with the crowd. In Nibiru, there were flags with her face on them and songs in her honor. There was something to that, she decided.

Corrina looked at the time. 11:43. *Funny,* she thought. *That's the same time as when I left a year ago. It's quite the coincidence.*

She went down the hall to the bathroom and took a long shower, half-expecting her mother to come bursting through the door and plucking her naked self out of the stall, hugging her tight after being gone so long. But she didn't.

Well, Corrina thought. *It's not as though we are close.*

She dried off and went to bed.

The next day, her mother ate breakfast and poured coffee.

"Do you want cereal or pancakes?" her mother said. As though it was a regular day. And it was. When Corrina looked at the newspaper, she saw that the date was not a year and a day after she was last in this kitchen, but just a day. The next day. And no time at all had passed while she was in Nibiru.

So, she thought. *Time works differently there. That could be a problem.*

THE HIGH PRIEST had told her to stay near the kitchen, and so she stayed.

She stopped going to school. She'd make a show of walking to the bus, but would hide in the bushes until her mother went to work, and then called herself in sick once the house was empty. After punishments and phone calls and meetings that she did not always attend, Corrina and her mother decided to try home-schooling, provided that Corrina do it herself while her mother left every day to go work at the hair salon.

"I expect you to do it right," her mother said while lighting her fourth cigarette of the day. "Don't embarrass me when you take those state exams."

Corrina didn't. She got the highest score in the whole state that year. Her old school put her picture on the front page of their newspaper, calling her their star student and taking all the credit, even though she was no longer enrolled. She didn't care. She took books out of the library on mathematics and astronomy, as well as gardening, martial arts, hunting, weapon maintenance, and survivalist memoirs.

When her dad came home from his long hauls, she taught him some basic moves so that he could spar with her in the back yard.

"Where did you learn this stuff?" her father said, red-faced and panting. He clutched at his heart, but claimed the exercise was doing him good.

Corrina shrugged. "Books," she said.

She didn't tell him about the ruined temple and the bearded priests, and the youngest one who handed her a staff and said, "Now. Defend yourself," and then he attacked her. She didn't tell him how proud the priests were when she was finally able to swipe his feet, sidekick his belly, and send him pinwheeling to the stone floor with a tremendous thud. She didn't tell him about the thrill she felt when she first held a sword in her hand, first felt that honed edge slice the air in front of her. She didn't tell him how good—how very, very good—it felt to be *dangerous*.

"Books, eh?" Her father chuckled. "Well, that's something. I had no idea books were so dangerous."

The word thrilled her to the core. She had half a mind to sucker punch her dad, but his breathing was ragged and raw. She helped him inside instead.

A YEAR PASSED. The High Priest didn't come back.

THE SUMMER BEFORE Corrina turned thirteen, her parents split up. They called her into their bedroom. They had been screaming at each other all day. Corrina had spent the day sitting on the kitchen floor right next to the cupboard under the sink, trying to will the High Priest to return. When she was called into their room, her parents sat at the edge of the bed, holding hands. Their eyes were red.

They explained what a divorce was, as though it was a brand new concept that Corrina had never heard of before.

"Which parent would you like to live with, honey?" her dad said gently, as though it was a foregone conclusion. It was no secret that she preferred her father. Her mother checked her nails.

"Which one of you is keeping the house?" Corrina asked slowly.

"Your mother is," her dad said. "I found a nice apartment right next to the library."

"I'll stay with mom," Corrina said. Corrina's mother's head snapped up and her father instantly began to cry.

"Are you sure?" he faltered.

How could she explain it to her dad? Though the memory of her time in the Land of Nibiru—the metal door, the near-constant rain, the Zonnier Hordes howling for her blood, the band of resisters and rebels who were bound to one another by something bigger than incidental family status or belief or anger, but by love, camaraderie, and brotherhood—was as fresh to her now as it had been the day she returned, there was a part of her that had begun to wonder if it was nothing more than a dream. They hadn't come back. They promised to come back. They promised to return for her. They called her Princess, after all. The Chosen One. But she was no longer eleven. And she was growing by the day.

"I'm very sure," she said. "I can't move. I just can't."

And she didn't.

ANOTHER YEAR PASSED. The High Priest still hadn't come back.

CORRINA KEPT A stack of sketch notebooks filled with her memories of Nibiru. Drawings of people, ruined buildings, landscapes. Drawings of plants, flowers, animals. When she sat at the kitchen table and closed her eyes while facing the cupboard under the sink, she could see all of Nibiru in her mind's eye as clearly as if she was there.

But she noticed something else, too.

As she aged, she began to notice things about the landscape and the Resistance that she had not noticed when she was eleven. For example, while the High Priests and the Resistance were both ostensibly fighting the same enemy, they didn't seem to be talking to one another. Indeed, after she had warned the Resistance and helped them ready themselves for the battle, the High Priests were nowhere to be seen. She only was brought to them later, after a High Priest had found her out in the forest gathering berries, and told her that the best berries were over here, next to the old abbey.

And later, when she returned to the Resistance, there had been a party.

She had a friend in the Resistance, a boy named Cairn, who was a few years older than she was, who spat on the ground whenever the High Priests were mentioned.

"Old windbags," he said. "They aren't fighting with us."

"But they want the same thing. Don't they?" Corrina was honestly confused.

He spat again. "Nah. They just want not to be slaughtered by the Zonnier Hordes. Of course, the reason why they are here in the first place is the High Priests' fault. They convinced the King to attack. They said the Zonnier were weak. And it was us—my parents and my whole village—who were sent into the battle with no training and poor weapons. And now the Zonnier want revenge. They razed the Noble City, and I don't blame them. But they have no call killing *us*. We just want to farm in peace."

At the kitchen table, Corrina drew a picture of Cairn—his grown-out hair, his lopsided smile, the scar cut across his cheek. She had such a crush on him then! If she was honest with herself, she had a crush on him now. Even now. She drew his pet—a smallbeast named Ricu—perched on his shoulder. It looked like a largish rat with fluffy fur and very long ears. She loved Ricu, though Ricu did not love her back.

How old was Cairn now, she wondered? Does he wonder what happened to her? If she ever made it back to the Kingdom of Nibiru, she might be old. Or maybe he would. Would he even recognize her then?

She looked at the picture. It seemed so alive to her—as though Cairn and Ricu would come leaping out and the three of them would have their own adventure. She laid her hand on the page. It was just paper.

ANOTHER YEAR PASSED. The High Priests did not come.

WHEN SHE WAS fifteen, her mother floated the idea of the two of them moving in with her very rich boyfriend. Corrina dug in her heels. "Absolutely not," she said. "You can move in with him, but I am staying."

"But I thought—" her mother said.

"I can't move," Corrina said. "I just can't."

They fought and fumed, but eventually the rich boyfriend moved to Rio with his secretary.

"Don't say I didn't warn you," Corrina said as her mother slammed her bedroom door. It wasn't true, though. Corrina hadn't warned anyone.

(She had warned the Resistance about the coming Hordes. She had seen them approach right when she tumbled out of the Portal. It was her first action that she took in the Land of Nibiru, and it saved a thousand lives. It wasn't really a thousand, but that was the story they told after that. It was the reason they thought she was the Chosen One. Just dumb luck.)

*   *   *

ANOTHER YEAR PASSED. And another. The High Priest still hadn't come back.

WHEN SHE WAS seventeen, her mother and father sat her down to discuss the possibility of going to college. She had gotten her provisional diploma from the State Homeschooling Office, and had knocked her college entrance exams out of the stratosphere.

"You can go anywhere you want," her father had said.

"I've gotten emails from the professors you've done your MOOC courses with," her mother said. "They've all highly encouraged me to have you apply to their programs. Especially the man from Oxford. Wouldn't that be fancy! We could buy you new shoes!"

"I can't move," Corrina said, and her parents' faces fell. "I just can't."

She explained to them about online college. She told them that she had already started—and look! Straight A's. Library science. It was a real degree, she assured them.

But there was another reason why she couldn't leave that had nothing to do with the Land of Nibiru. She met a boy who was using the computers at the library to look for jobs. He was new in town. "Needed a fresh start," he had said. He grew up on a farm, and didn't want to spend another day smelling the lake of pig shit that sat across the road from his parents' house.

He would come over to the house while Corrina's mother was gone at work. Corrina taught him how to box and how to spar and how to flip a man onto the floor when he wasn't looking. And then he flipped her onto her bed when she wasn't looking, and taught her something else entirely. Within two months she was throwing up her breakfast. After four months, she was shopping online for new brassieres to accommodate her growing bustline and for pants with elastic panels at the belly.

"Grandparents?" her mother said, turning pale and beginning to fan her face.

Corrina sat quietly, looking at her hands. Frankly, she was shocked they hadn't noticed. She had been showing for well over a month. Her parents just didn't notice much.

"Oh, hell no," her father said, storming out of the house.

The boy moved in the following week.

A little over a year later she was pregnant again, this time with twins.

Two years after that, she was pregnant yet again. A singleton, which was a relief. Her mother had moved to Florida with a man named Arnold who lived on a boat in the Keys. Her father had died. The boy—not a boy any longer—after learning about the new pregnancy, had decided to move back to the farm. There was money in pigs, he said. And there was a girl who had broken his heart before but wanted him now. He told Corrina that the children couldn't come with him, but he would send checks every month. Surely she understood.

Corrina did. Sometimes people just don't come back. She knew that now. She kissed his cheek and comforted the children as he got into his truck and drove away forever.

ANOTHER YEAR PASSED. The cupboard under the sink was just a cupboard.

BREAKFAST WAS LOUD. The baby yelled. The twins yelled. Her oldest yelled. Corrina never yelled. There was no point. She kept her eyes on the newspaper. There was a rattling sound. Like a cupboard door shaking back and forth. Corrina pressed her lips together and didn't investigate. There was no door under the sink. She said this to herself over and over again. She knew now that there never had been. Or she was pretty sure.

She had managed to secure a job as an archivist for a law firm down the road. It was her first job in the real world and not a freelance gig on the internet. The pay was good and they had onsite childcare, which was better, and she was grateful to have landed it. But it meant that she would be out of the house.

Her eyes drifted to the cupboard door under the sink.

"Mama," said Jacob, the oldest. He was four now. "What are you looking at?"

He was always the most attuned to her. She had read that oldest children were like that.

"Nothing," she said. The door appeared to rattle. Just a little. All on its own. She told herself that she was imagining it.

"Nothing," said Alice, the girl portion of the twins. "Nothing, nothing, nothing," sang Andrew, her twin brother.

Rufus, the baby, had no words. He just pawed at Corrina's breasts and opened his mouth wide. At only seven months old, he was already twenty-three pounds. A tank. At this rate, he'd be bigger than the twins before his first birthday.

"Mommy starts a new job tomorrow," Corrina said.

Jacob wrinkled his brow. He looked around the kitchen. "Where?" he said, as though a job was sitting in a bag on the counter, like a new toy.

"Not far," she said. "Down the road."

"With Daddy?"

"Daddy isn't coming back."

"I know that," Jacob said, his cheeks going quite red.

Corrina readjusted Rufus's weight so as not to overburden her shoulders. His thick muscles kicked and rippled and squirmed. It was like trying to nurse a gorilla, she thought.

"No, we will be going together. You and your sister and your brothers and me. I will work in the basement, and you guys will go to the day care center. A school. We can walk there in the morning and walk home at suppertime. You'll like it."

Jacob looked skeptical. "I don't think I'll like it."

"I like it," Alice said. Alice liked everything.

"I like it, too," Andrew said. Andrew liked anything that Alice liked. It drove Alice crazy. She whacked her brother on the head with a block. He didn't seem to notice.

The next morning, before the kids got up, Corrina stood in the kitchen. It wasn't as though she had never left the house. She did. She went to the store occasionally. And the library. And she went in for her interview. But she never left for very long. And *never* all day.

Still. It was time. How many years had it been? Too many. Eleven was a long time ago. And here she was, wasting her life. It was time to rejoin the world—she and her kids together.

Her eyes drifted back to the cupboard door. Was it her imagination, or was it rattling again? It was her imagination, clearly. She was sure of it. Still, she reached into her correspondence box and pulled out a blue note card and a black marking pen.

'BE RIGHT BACK,' she wrote in large, bold letters. She wasn't sure if the High Priest could read, or if he could read English. He had explained to her that part of being the Chosen One meant that everyone could understand her and she could understand everyone else. She had been skeptical of that at the time.

"So," she said, "we might be speaking the same language and not know it."

"Well," he allowed. "I suppose, but that wouldn't make very much sense, now would it. How could we have the same language in different worlds?"

"What's two plus two?" she asked.

"Four," he said, "but what's that got—"

"We have the same math. Maybe we speak the same language, too."

They agreed to drop the subject, but she wondered about it now. If she wrote, 'Be right back,' in English, would he be able to understand it, given that she was, after all, the Chosen One? She had no idea, but she figured she'd try anyway.

WHEN SHE GOT home, the card was undisturbed and the door was closed. The High Priests still hadn't come.

THAT NIGHT, AFTER spending two hours trying to get the kids to stay in bed and then falling heavily asleep on the couch without washing her face or brushing her teeth, she dreamed of the Land of Nibiru again. It had been years since she had done so. She couldn't remember the last time. In her dream, she was back in the Resistance camp at the banks of the Iygath River. They had suffered several losses in the battle the night before, and had used the thick forests leading toward the Iygath as cover during their retreat. The Zonnier Hordes, being as they were from the high Zoni plains, where trees were as rare as skyscrapers—which was to say, nonexistent—were afraid of the forest. They quaked in fear every time they went too close.

The forest was safe for now. It was only a matter of time, though, before the Zonnier Hordes enlarged their collective courage enough to swallow their fear, approach the forest, and light it on fire.

Nothing gave the Resistance more worry than the possibility of fire. The trees were their greatest defenders, but could be transformed into weapons easily enough. Every day they prayed for rain.

But for now, the Resistance was focused on filling hungry bellies and nursing wounds. This was one of the first battles that Corrina herself had fought in, and it was the very first time that she had held her sword in the way that she had been taught, allowing herself to hook the blade right under the chin of the Zonnier and then snap her elbows straight, whipping them in front of her body in a wide arc, neatly removing the Zonnier's head from its shoulders. The High Priests instructed her to examine the body after she had done so, that she might be able to watch the twisted soul of the Zonnier wiggle from the open neck and extend its nine legs and three mouths to the sky before shuddering once and expiring on the ground. They had described the process in sickening detail, giving Corrina nightmares for over a week, and she had no interest in seeing it as described.

It was a mistake, as it turned out. One of the Zonnier souls was wearing the circlet that was destined to rest on the head of the Chosen One. And, according to the High Priests' various ministrations, that soul emerged in the most recent battle. And then it was lost. Every other warrior carefully examined the souls as they emerged from the bloody neck stumps of the slain.

"Except you, Corrina," the High Priest said. "I mean Princess," he amended quickly, though it seemed to Corrina that he did not mean it.

"I'm sorry," she said for the hundredth time. "I just couldn't do it."

"Not couldn't," the High Priest said. "Didn't. There is a difference, you know."

In her dream, she was no longer eleven. And the High Priest's voice sounded suspiciously like her father's.

"It's not my fault!" she said in her grown-up voice.

"Of course it is!" the High Priest said. "But it is understandable. It was your first beheading, after all. It is unfortunate, though. Now we must find that circlet—if the Hordes haven't found it first. And our collective task is much harder."

Corrina stormed out.

There was a boy waiting for her outside. Cairn. He smiled broadly as he watched her approach. He didn't seem to notice that she was older.

Corrina found this odd.

I guess this means I'm about to wake up, she thought. She resisted the idea, hoping to stay in the Land of Nibiru for as long as she could. It had been so long—so very long. And she missed it.

"Are you going somewhere?" Cairn said.

"No," Corrina said. "Maybe. I can't tell, actually. I'm not sure if I was here to begin with."

"Oh, you're here," he assured her. "But there's something you need to know."

He had begun to fade at the edges. She would be awake soon.

"What?" she asked. Her throat hurt. Like she had swallowed a fishhook. Her life had not been unhappy. Far from it. It had simply been indifferent. She sometimes felt as though her life had been suspended in a jar full of formaldehyde. She was in stasis. Her year in the Land of Nibiru was the only time she was ever truly happy.

"The High Priests don't know what they're talking about. Remember that."

And she woke with a start.

The door to the cupboard under the sink rattled and shook. She had a crick in her neck. Stupid couch, she thought. The door rattled again.

Her throat still hurt. She pulled her legs out from the cocoon of her cardigan and quietly placed her bare feet on the floor. She had been trained in the Noble Art of Stealth and had practiced the fundamentals of it every day since she left the Land of Nibiru. She was coiled like a spring. Very slowly, she approached the door. Very quickly, she flung it open.

No portal.

No High Priest.

Just a rat.

Or she assumed it was a rat. It squeaked and darted across the kitchen floor and launched itself down the stairs leading to the basement.

"UGH!" she said. "Nasty." She hated rats.

There were smallbeasts in the Land of Nibiru. They looked like rats, and were smart like rats, but they were far more adorable. Or at least she remembered them as being more adorable. That was surely a rat. It wasn't adorable at all. Wasn't it?

Her alarm blared upstairs.

"MOMMY!" Jacob shouted from his room. He was, no doubt, sitting on his bed, wide awake, minding the time. Watching the minutes tick by on his sun and moon clock until he could be reasonably allowed to trot into her room and wake her up.

"I know, honey!" she called back.

The pink edge of dawn crept into the eastern window. The cupboard rattled again. "Stupid rats," she muttered, and went upstairs to take a shower. During her lunch break, she'd call an exterminator. If she remembered.

By the time her first week ended, she'd had seven dreams about the Land of Nibiru. Sometimes she was eleven in these dreams. Sometimes she was her proper age. Each time, she had to arrange childcare in order to go into battle.

On her fourteenth night, she dreamed that she taught Jacob to parry and jab with a wooden sword.

On her twenty-first night, she dreamt that she went riding into the center of the Zonnier Hordes with Rufus strapped to her back. Her battle cry rang in harmony with his please-nurse-me wail.

On her twenty-eighth night, she dreamt that she confronted the High Priests in front of the whole Resistance. "Your plan is stupid," she shouted, as her children clung to her legs. "And more people will die needlessly for a war that has waged for far too long." Rufus sobbed. "Grow up!" she shouted, though in retrospect, she was not sure if she shouted it to the High Priests or to Rufus.

"You tell 'em!" Cairn shouted, who obviously thought it was directed at the High Priests.

"You are supposed to be eleven!" the Highest of the High Priests retorted, growing very red in the face. "And you're not supposed to have opinions. Or... what are those things called? The things she had to bring when she took her own sweet time getting organized to come with us?"

"Tampons, your Excellency," said one of the lower High Priests.

"Exactly. Or brassieres. You're not supposed to have those either. Or opinions. Did I say that already?"

"You did, your Excellency, but it is still just as apt."

"It is not out of the ordinary to pack a brassiere," Corrina said. "Or tampons. I had no idea how long I'd be here. I also brought a diaper bag. Does that bother you, too?"

"You brought nothing with you when you came the first time," the High Priest huffed.

"True. But I was eleven."

"I liked you better when you were eleven."

"And I liked you less," she said with a smile. "I'm terribly fond of you now."

And then she woke up. The cupboard rattled. Her forehead itched. She got out of bed and practiced a perfect Wolf's Feint using her fuzzy bunny slipper instead of a sword. Her muscles knew every angle. Her bones snapped surely into place.

"Mommy?" Jacob said. "What are you doing?"

"Breakfast," Alice said.

"Breakfast," Andrew said, not to be outdone.

And she got them ready and took them to work. The rat watched them from the top of the basement stairs. Of course it was a rat. She could see him out the corner of her eye. He had long ears that came to two sharp points. Just like the smallbeasts from Nibiru.

That night she checked under the sink. No portal. And the note was still there. Though, strangely there was a hash mark that she could not remember putting there herself.

That night she dreamed of Nibiru. Again.

A FEW DAYS later, her boss came to visit her in the archives. He was an older gentleman, about the same age her father would have been, had he lived. He had wide, soft hands.

"Listen, Corrina," he said. "We have an issue to discuss."

Her heart sank. She thought of the cupboard under the sink and her husband's truck driving away. *People leave and they do not come back,* she thought. "Are you going to fire me?" she said.

"What?" He was truly surprised. "No! Of course not. Everyone says that you've integrated yourself into our daily operations beautifully and no one can imagine what we'd ever do without you."

She relaxed. *At least that.*

"Listen, did you drive today?" Her boss's voice was deep, serious. He had a face full of concern.

"No," she said. "My kids and I prefer to walk."

He nodded. "Okay then. I am going to arrange an escort for you to make sure you get home safely. There is a gentleman from the police coming to chat with you in a moment. I took the liberty of requesting a watch on your house. A man came in today, asking for you. And then he wanted to see your children. And then he threatened to slay any that stand in his way."

"Slay?" Corrina said. "He used the word *slay?*"

"Does that mean anything to you?"

"No," she said, her face was blank. "Not at all."

"The thing is, he was armed."

"A gun? My god."

"No," her boss said. "Even weirder. A sword. Randal and Julia from accounting jumped him when he wasn't looking and got the sword away. He's in police custody now. But he kept asking for you."

"What does he look like?" Corrina asked, though she already knew.

"Old guy," her boss said. "Weird clothes. With a long gray beard."

AFTER CHATTING WITH the police and being escorted home, she checked the cupboard under the sink. There was no door. There was no portal. It was just a coincidence. She couldn't even find any evidence of the rat.

The High Priests hadn't come. They would never come. She wasn't the Chosen One. There was no Nibiru.

ON THE FORTY-ninth night she dreamed of Nibiru again. Seven times seven nights of dreams. It felt significant. In her dream her feet were bare and she was walking across a berry patch. With each step, the berries swelled and burst, inking her feet with juice. From time to time she'd reach down and slide her hands along the stalks, pulling berries into the cups of her palms, and pouring them into her mouth.

"Don't eat all of them," a voice said. Cairn. She'd know him anywhere.

"I'm glad to see you," she said.

"Of course you are," Cairn said. "I'm amazing." She took his hand. She was eleven. She walked. She was twenty-two. She looked at him. She was eleven. She turned away. She was twenty-two.

They came to the edge of a ridge. Down below was a valley. The Resistance was there. They were tired and cold and bedraggled. Their children were hungry. Beyond, past the edge of the Forest, the Zonnier Hordes nursed their wounds. They were tired and cold and bedraggled. Their children were hungry. Corrina opened her eyes wide.

"They have nowhere to go," she said. She couldn't believe she hadn't known it before.

Cairn shook his head. "The High Priests told the King to poison the land on the Zoni plains. Some kind of magic. The animals died and the water is bad and the grasses withered and the crops killed anyone who ate them. It was a total disaster. They came here looking for refuge, and their presence was mistaken for war. Unfortunately, they are very good at war."

Corrina dug her hands into her pockets. "Assuming I am the Chosen One," she said slowly.

"You're probably still the Chosen One," Cairn said.

"Well. I'm not admitting that I am."

"Don't you read stories?" Cairn said, exasperated. "If you doubt you're the Chosen One, it pretty much proves that you *are*."

Corrina waved him off. "If I am, it means I have the gift of languages, right? That's like, one of the things. Which means I can talk to both sides. I could negotiate a peace."

Cairn was silent.

"They killed my parents, you know. Slaughtered them where they stood." He wiped his eyes with the heels of his hands. He was still a boy, after all. He had not grown up.

"You killed many of their parents, too," Corrina countered. "So did I. More than I wish. Maybe it's time to be done. Farm. Rebuild. Share with each other. It's not new stuff—people have done this before. It can work."

"So you're coming back?" Cairn said hopefully.

"If I can," she said. "I'm not eleven anymore, you know. And I need to bring my kids. What's the childcare situation?"

Cairn frowned. "What's childcare?"

"Never mind, we'll figure it out."

"In any case," Cairn said, reaching into his satchel. "You'll need this. I found it yesterday. I haven't showed it to the High Priests yet. I don't trust them to do the right thing." He handed her a gold circlet. She felt the weight of it in her hands. It hummed with its own kind of magic.

She woke up in her bed. Her feet were stained with berry juice. She was still holding the circlet.

"Well then," Corrina said.

WHEN THE HIGH Priests got the call, they were standing in the center of the Resistance Camp, going over the battle plans for the campaign that they hoped would spell the end of the Zonnier Hordes. It would be a bloodbath, on both ends, but they felt fairly certain that it would spell the end of things. The Resistance was balking, though.

"Cowards," one priest muttered under his breath.

That was when the door appeared. Right there in the middle of everything. And a voice.

"My name is Corrina," the voice said. It came from the land, the sky, and the trees. It hummed in the bones. The Resistance fell to their knees. "And I am the one you call Chosen."

"We are saved!" they shouted. They waved the flags with the image of the Chosen One emblazoned in their center. Someone began to sing.

The High Priests felt their spirits falter. They had hoped to bring the child back *after* the battle. They couldn't afford her getting killed and they certainly couldn't afford her getting battle fatigue. War is not pleasant for children. That's why they had sent her away in the first place. Best she not see it.

"Why, Princess!" the Highest of the High Priests said. "How on Earth did you manage to open the Portal?"

The circlet, he knew. *She has the circlet. But how?* She had control of the Portal now. That could be a bother.

"I would like the High Priests to come through the Portal for a conference, please," the voice said. "Just for a moment."

"But—"

"Right now."

The High Priests began to grumble. The Portal was tough on the knees. And one of their own had already gone through and still had not come back. What of him? These were things they wanted to say out loud, but the Resistance was watching, and they could not.

One by one, they filed into the Portal.

THE CHOSEN ONE had laid out a meal. The High Priests, though they were better fed than any in the Resistance, were still in possession of bellies that occasionally knew Want—as they did now. The table was pure white and was trimmed with a metal that shone like silver. Of course the Chosen One lived like a queen in her own country. It stood to reason.

"Sit," the Chosen One said.

She had grown up. She explained to them that time flowed differently on different sides of the Portal. Just like a stream flowing to the ocean, there were sections when the waters of time moved slowly and methodically, and there were bits when it raced down a steep, steep slope. But since the two worlds had separate streams, they did not necessarily correlate. She had no idea when they'd return to the Land of Nibiru. She hoped that, with the Portal open, the time streams would be synched for a bit.

The High Priests didn't listen. She had laid out cold cuts and rolls and muffins and cheese. Fruit. Her mom's famous chili recipe. Cookies. A bowl of grapes. They ate ravenously.

"I've left instructions for the oven, and there are several casseroles in the freezer," she said. She had a baby on her hip. A duffel bag in her hand. The other children had backpacks on their backs.

And she wore the circlet on her head.

"Princess—" the Highest of the High Priests said with his mouth full.

"I am going to negotiate a peace," she said, shooing her children through the Portal.

"Mommy's coming right behind you," she whispered to the kids. They needed no encouragement. Tunnels behind tiny doors were the funnest thing in the world. Corrina had thought the same thing when she was eleven.

"But you can't," the Highest Priest said. "They're barbarians."

"So is everyone," she said. She eyed the Portal. Her circlet hummed. She raised her hand, and it enlarged, opening behind the sink. With a quick leap, she landed surely on the counter, her legs coiled under her body, her muscles ready to spring. Rufus squealed with delight. She kissed him on the center of his shiny bald head.

"But, Princess," another Priest said.

"Only a week," she said. "Then I'll return."

"But—"

"May the gods protect you while I am gone," she said with a grin. And she slid into the black, and closed the Portal behind.

For the last thousand years, in the Land of Nibiru, they have told the story of the Mother Queen, and the Band of Saints that went into the Black to return her to her throne, so that she might bring healing to the land. And she did come back, and she did heal the land. The Zoni and the Nibu joined hands and hearts and homelands and lives, and a thousand years of peace followed her return to her people. The Saints succeeded, but did so at a terrible cost. The Portal closed and it never re-opened. Every year, both Zoni and Nibu returned to where the Portal last opened to light incense and sing songs and say prayers of thanksgiving.

And year after year, they never came back.

THE MARTIAN OBELISK
Linda Nagata

Linda Nagata (www.mythicisland.com) is a Nebula and Locus-award-winning writer, best known for her high-tech science fiction, including The Red trilogy, a series of near-future military thrillers. The first book in the trilogy, *The Red: First Light*, was a Nebula and John W. Campbell Memorial-award finalist, and named as a *Publishers Weekly* Best Book of 2015. Her newest novel is the very near-future thriller, *The Last Good Man*. Linda has lived most of her life in Hawaii, where she's been a writer, a mom, a programmer of database-driven websites, and an independent publisher. She lives with her husband in their long-time home on the island of Maui.

THE END OF the world required time to accomplish—and time, Susannah reflected, worked at the task with all the leisurely skill of a master torturer, one who could deliver death either quickly or slowly, but always with excruciating pain.

No getting out of it.

But there were still things to do in the long, slow decline; final gestures to make. Susannah Li-Langford had spent seventeen years working on her own offering-for-the-ages, with another six and half years to go before the Martian Obelisk reached completion. Only when the last tile was locked into place in the obelisk's pyramidal cap, would she yield.

Until then, she did what was needed to hold onto her health, which was why, at the age of eighty, she was out walking vigorously along the cliff trail above the encroaching Pacific Ocean, determined to have her daily exercise despite the brisk wind and the freezing mist that ran before it. The mist was only a token moisture, useless to revive the drought-stricken coastal forest, but it made the day cold enough that the fishing platforms at the cliff's edge were deserted, leaving Susannah alone to contemplate the mortality of the human world.

It was not supposed to happen like this. As a child she'd been promised a swift conclusion: duck and cover and nuclear annihilation. And if not annihilation, at least the nihilistic romance of a gun-toting, leather-clad, fight-to-the-death anarchy.

That hadn't happened either.

Things had just gotten worse, and worse still, and people gave up. Not everyone, not all at once—there was no single event marking the beginning of the end—but there was a sense of inevitability about the direction history had taken. Sea levels rose along with average ocean temperatures. Hurricanes devoured coastal cities and consumed low-lying countries. Agriculture faced relentless drought, flood, and temperature extremes. A long run of natural disasters made it all worse—earthquakes, landslides, tsunamis, volcanic eruptions. There had been no major meteor strike yet, but Susannah wouldn't bet against it. Health care faltered as antibiotics became useless against resistant bacteria. Surgery became an art of the past.

Out of the devastation, war and terrorism erupted like metastatic cancers.

We are a brilliant species, Susannah thought. *Courageous, creative, generous—as individuals. In larger numbers we fail every time.*

There were reactor meltdowns, poisoned water supplies, engineered plagues, and a hundred other, smaller horrors. The Shoal War had seen nuclear weapons used in the South China Sea. But even the most determined ghouls had failed to ignite a sudden, brilliant cataclysm. The master torturer would not be rushed.

Still, the tipping point was long past, the future truncated. Civilization staggered on only in the lucky corners of the world where the infrastructure of a happier age still functioned. Susannah lived in one of those lucky corners, not far from the crumbling remains of Seattle, where she had greenhouse food, a local network, and satellite access all supplied by her patron, Nathaniel Sanchez, who was the money behind the Martian Obelisk.

When the audio loop on her ear beeped a quiet tone, she assumed the alert meant a message from Nate. There was no one else left in her life, nor did she follow the general news, because what was the point?

She tapped the corner of her wrist-link with a finger gloved against the cold, signaling her personal AI to read the message aloud. Its artificial, androgynous voice spoke into her ear:

"Message sender: Martian Obelisk Operations. Message body: Anomaly sighted. All operations automatically halted pending supervisory approval."

Just a few innocuous words, but weighted with a subtext of disaster.

A subtext all too familiar.

For a few seconds, Susannah stood still in the wind and the rushing mist. In the seventeen-year history of the project, construction had been halted only for equipment maintenance, and that, on a tightly regulated schedule. She raised her wrist-link to her lips. "What anomaly, Alix?" she demanded, addressing the AI. "Can it be identified?"

"It identifies as a homestead vehicle belonging to Red Oasis."

That was absurd. Impossible.

Founded twenty-one years ago, Red Oasis was the first of four Martian colonies, and the most successful. It had outlasted all the others, but the Mars Era had ended nine months ago when Red Oasis succumbed to an outbreak of 'contagious asthma'—a made-up name for an affliction evolved on Mars.

Since then there had been only radio silence. The only active elements on the planet were the wind, and the machinery that had not yet broken down, all of it operated by AIs.

"Where is the vehicle?" Susannah asked.

"Seventeen kilometers northwest of the obelisk."

So close!

How was that possible? Red Oasis was over 5,000 kilometers distant. How could an AI have driven so far? And who had given the order?

Homestead vehicles were not made to cover large distances. They were big, slow, and cumbersome—cross-country robotic crawlers designed to haul equipment from the landing site to a colony's permanent location, where construction would commence (and ideally be completed) long before the inhabitants arrived. The vehicles had a top speed of fifteen kilometers per hour which meant that even with the lightspeed delay, Susannah had time to send a new instruction set to the AIs that inhabited her construction equipment.

Shifting abruptly from stillness to motion, she resumed her vigorous pace—and then she pushed herself to walk just a little faster.

NATHANIEL SANCHEZ WAS waiting for her, pacing with a hobbling gait on the front porch of her cottage when she returned. His flawless electric car, an anomaly from another age, was parked in the gravel driveway. Nate was eighty-five and rail-thin, but the electric warmth of his climate-controlled coat kept him comfortable even in the biting wind. She waved at him impatiently. "You know it's fine to let yourself in. I was hoping you'd have coffee brewing by now."

He opened the door for her, still a practitioner of the graceful manners instilled in him by his mother eight decades ago—just one of the many things Susannah admired about him. His trustworthiness was another. Though Nate owned every aspect of the Martian Obelisk project—the equipment on Mars, the satellite accounts, this house where Susannah expected to live out her life—he had always held fast to an early promise never to interfere with her design or her process.

"I haven't been able to talk to anyone associated with Red Oasis," he told her in a voice low and resonant with age. "The support network may have disbanded."

She sat down in the old, armless chair she kept by the door, and pulled off her boots. "Have the rights to Red Oasis gone on the market yet?"

"No." Balancing with one hand against the door, he carefully stepped out of his clogs. "If they had, I would have bought them."

"What about a private transfer?"

He offered a hand to help her up. "I've got people looking into it. We'll find out soon."

In stockinged feet, she padded across the hardwood floor and the hand-made carpets of the living room, but at the door of the Mars room she hesitated, looking back at Nate. Homesteads were robotic vehicles, but they were designed with cabs that could be pressurized for human use, with a life-support system that could sustain two passengers for many days. "Is there any chance some of the colonists at Red Oasis are still alive?" Susannah asked.

Nate reached past her to open the door, a dark scowl on his worn face. "No detectable activity and radio silence for nine months? I don't think so. There's no one in that homestead, Susannah, and there's no good reason for it to visit the obelisk, especially without any notice to us that it was coming. When my people find out who's issuing the orders we'll get it turned around, but in the meantime, do what you have to do to take care of our equipment."

Nate had always taken an interest in the Martian Obelisk, but over the years, as so many of his other aspirations failed, the project had become more personal. He had begun to see it as his own monument and himself as an Ozymandias whose work was doomed to be forgotten, though it would not fall to the desert sands in this lifetime or any other.

"WHAT CAN I do for you, Susannah?" he had asked, seventeen years ago.

A long-time admirer of her architectural work, he had come to her after the ruin of the Holliday Towers in Los Angeles—her signature project—two soaring glass spires, one 84 floors and the other 104, linked by graceful sky bridges. When the Hollywood Quake struck, the buildings had endured the shaking just as they'd been designed to do, keeping their residents safe, while much of the city around them crumbled. But massive fires followed the quake and the towers had not survived that.

"Tell me what you dream of, Susannah. What you would still be willing to work on."

Nathaniel had been born into wealth, and through the first half of his life he'd grown the family fortune. Though he had never been among the wealthiest individuals of the world, he could still indulge extravagant fancies.

The request Susannah made of him had been, literally, outlandish.

"Buy me the rights to the Destiny Colony."

"On Mars?" His tone suggested a suspicion that her request might be a joke.

"On Mars," she assured him.

Destiny had been the last attempt at Mars colonization. The initial robotic mission had been launched and landed, but money ran out and colonists were never sent. The equipment sat on Mars, unused.

Susannah described her vision of the Martian Obelisk: a gleaming, glittering white spire, taking its color from the brilliant white of the fiber tiles she would use to construct it. It would rise from an empty swell of land, growing more slender as it reached into the sparse atmosphere, until it met an engineering limit prescribed by the strength of the fiber tiles, the gravity of the Red Planet, and by the fierce ghost-fingers of Mars' storm winds. Calculations of the erosional force of the Martian wind led her to conclude that the obelisk would still be standing a hundred thousand years hence and likely far longer. It would outlast all buildings on Earth. It would outlast her bloodline, and all bloodlines. It would still be standing long after the last human had gone the way of the passenger pigeon, the right whale, the dire wolf. In time, the restless Earth would swallow up all evidence of human existence, but the Martian Obelisk would remain—a last monument marking the existence of humankind, excepting only a handful of tiny, robotic spacecraft faring, lost and unrecoverable, in the void between stars.

Nate had listened carefully to her explanation of the project, how it could be done, and the time that would be required. None of it fazed him and he'd agreed, without hesitation, to support her.

The rights to the colony's equipment had been in the hands of a holding company that had acquired ownership in bankruptcy court. Nathaniel pointed out that no one was planning to go to Mars again, that no one any longer possessed the wealth or resources to try. Before long, he was able to purchase Destiny Colony for a tiny fraction of the original backers' investment.

When Susannah received the command codes, Destiny's homestead vehicle had not moved from the landing site, its payload had not been unpacked, and construction on its habitat had never begun. Her first directive to the AI in charge of the vehicle was to drive it three hundred kilometers to the site she'd chosen for the obelisk, at the high point of a rising swell of land.

Once there, she'd unloaded the fleet of robotic construction equipment: a mini-dozer, a mini-excavator, a six-limbed beetle cart to transport finished tiles, and a synth—short for synthetic human although the device was no such thing. It was just a stick figure with two legs, two arms, and hands capable of basic manipulation.

The equipment fleet also included a rolling factory that slowly but continuously produced a supply of fiber tiles, compiling them from raw soil and atmospheric elements. While the factory produced an initial supply of tiles, Susannah prepared the foundation of the obelisk, and within a year she began to build.

The Martian Obelisk became her passion, her reason for life after every other reason had been taken from her. Some called it a useless folly. She didn't argue: what meaning could there be in a monument that would never be seen directly by human eyes? Some called it graffiti: *Kilroy was here!* Some called it a tombstone and that was the truth too.

Susannah just called it better-than-nothing.

THE MARS ROOM was a circular extension that Nathaniel had ordered built onto the back of the cottage when Susannah was still in the planning stages of the obelisk's construction. When the door was closed, the room became a theater with a 360-degree floor-to-ceiling flex-screen. A high-backed couch at the center rotated, allowing easy viewing of the encircling images captured in high resolution from the construction site.

Visually, being in this room was like being at Destiny, and it did not matter at all that each red-tinted image was a still shot, because on the Red Planet, the dead planet, change came so slowly that a still shot was as good as video. Until now.

As Susannah entered the room, she glimpsed an anomalous, bright orange spot in a lowland to the northwest. Nathaniel saw it too. He gestured and started to speak but she waved him to silence, taking the time to circle the room, scanning the entire panorama to assess if anything else had changed.

Her gaze passed first across a long slope strewn with a few rocks and scarred with wheel tracks. Brightly colored survey sticks marked the distance: yellow at 250 meters, pink at 500, green for a full kilometer, and bright red for two.

The red stick stood at the foot of a low ridge that nearly hid the tile factory. She could just see an upper corner of its bright-green, block shape. The rest of it was out of sight, busy as always, processing raw ore dug by the excavator from a pit beyond the ridge, and delivered by the mini-dozer. As the factory slowly rolled, it left a trail of tailings, and every few minutes it produced a new fiber tile.

Next in the panorama was a wide swath of empty land, more tire tracks the only sign of human influence all the way out to a hazy pink horizon. And then, opposite the door and appearing no more than twenty meters distant, was Destiny's homestead vehicle. It was the same design as the approaching crawler: a looming cylindrical cargo container resting on dust-filled tracks. At the forward end, the cab, its windows dusty and lightless, its tiny bunkroom never used. Susannah had long ago removed the equipment she wanted, leaving all else in storage. For over sixteen years, the homestead had remained in its current position, untouched except by the elements.

Passing the Destiny homestead, her gaze took in another downward slope of lifeless desert and then, near the end of her circuit, she faced the tower itself.

The Martian Obelisk stood alone at the high point of the surrounding land, a gleaming-white, graceful, four-sided, tapering spire, already 170-meters high, sharing the sky with no other object. The outside walls were smooth and unadorned, but on the inside, a narrow stairway climbed around the core, rising in steep flights to the tower's top, where more fiber tiles were added every day, extending its height. It was a path no human would ever walk, but the beetle cart, with its six legs, ascended every few hours, carrying in its cargo basket a load of fiber tiles. Though she couldn't see the beetle cart, its position was marked as inside the tower, sixty percent of the way up the stairs. The synth waited for it at the top, its headless torso just visible over the rim of the obelisk's open stack, ready to use its supple hands to assemble the next course of tiles.

All this was as expected, as it should be.

Susannah steadied herself with a hand against the high back of the couch as she finally considered the orange splash of color that was the intruding vehicle. "Alix, distance to the Red Oasis homestead?"

The same androgynous voice that inhabited her ear loop spoke now through the room's sound system. "Twelve kilometers."

The homestead had advanced five kilometers in the twenty minutes she'd taken to return to the cottage—though in truth it was really much closer. Earth and Mars were approaching a solar conjunction, when they would be at their greatest separation, on opposite sides of the Sun. With the lightspeed delay, even this new image was nineteen minutes old. So she had only minutes left to act.

Reaching down to brace herself against the armrest of the couch, she sat with slow grace. "Alix, give me a screen."

A sleeve opened in the armrest and an interface emerged, swinging into an angled display in front of her.

The fires that had destroyed the Holliday Towers might have been part of the general inferno sparked by the Hollywood earthquake, but Susannah suspected otherwise. The towers had stood as a symbol of defiance amid the destruction—which might explain why they were brought low. The Martian Obelisk was a symbol too, and it had long been a target both for the media and for some of Destiny's original backers who had wanted the landing left undisturbed, for the use of a future colonization mission that no one could afford to send.

"Start up our homestead," Nate urged her. "It's the only equipment we can afford to risk. If you drive it at an angle into the Red Oasis homestead, you might be able to push it off its tracks."

Susannah frowned, her fingers moving across the screen as she assembled an instruction set. "That's a last resort option, Nate, and I'm not even sure it's possible. There are safety protocols in the AIs' core training modules that might prevent it."

She tapped *send*, launching the new instruction set on its nineteen-minute journey. Then she looked at Nate. "I've ordered the AIs that handle the construction equipment to retreat and evade. We cannot risk damage or loss of control."

He nodded somberly. "Agreed—but the synth and the beetle cart are in the tower."

"They're safe in there, for now. But I'm going to move the homestead—assuming it starts. After seventeen years, it might not."

"Understood."

"The easiest way for someone to shut down our operation is to simply park the Red Oasis homestead at the foot of the obelisk, so that it blocks access to the stairway. If the beetle cart can't get in and out, we're done. So I'm going to park our homestead there first."

He nodded thoughtfully, eyeing the image of the obelisk. "Okay. I understand."

"Our best hope is that you can find out who's instructing the Red Oasis homestead and get them to back off. But if that fails, I'll bring the synth out, and use it to try to take manual control."

"The Red Oasis group could have a synth too."

"Yes."

They might also have explosives—destruction was so much easier than creation—but Susannah did not say this aloud. She did not want Nate to inquire about the explosives that belonged to Destiny. Instead she told him, "There's no way we can know what they're planning. All we can do is wait and see."

He smacked a frustrated fist into his palm. "Nineteen minutes! Nineteen minutes times two before we know what's happened!"

"Maybe the AIs will work it out on their own," she said dryly. And then it was her turn to be overtaken by frustration. "Look at us! Look what we've come to! Invested in a monument no one will ever see. Squabbling over the possession of ruins while the world dies. This is where our hubris has brought us." But that was wrong, so she corrected herself. "*My* hubris."

Nate was an old man with a lifetime of emotions mapped on his well-worn face. In that complex terrain it wasn't always easy to read his current feelings, but she thought she saw hurt there. He looked away, before she could decide. A furtive movement.

"Nate?" she asked in confusion.

"This project matters," he insisted, gazing at the obelisk. "It's art, and it's memory, and it *does* matter."

Of course. But only because it was all they had left.

"Come into the kitchen," she said. "I'll make coffee."

NATE'S TABLET CHIMED while they were still sitting at the kitchen table. He took the call, listened to a brief explanation from someone on his staff, and then objected. "That can't be right. No. There's something else going on. Keep at it."

He scowled at the table until Susannah reminded him she was there. "Well?"

"That was Davidson, my chief investigator. He tracked down a Red Oasis shareholder who told him that the rights to the colony's equipment had *not* been traded or sold, that they couldn't be, because they had no value. Not with a failed communications system." His scowl deepened. "They want us to believe they can't even talk to the AIs."

Susannah stared at him. "But if that's true—"

"It's not."

"Meaning you don't want it to be." She got up from the table.

"Susannah—"

"I'm not going to pretend, Nate. If it's not an AI driving that homestead, then it's a colonist, a survivor—and that changes everything."

SHE RETURNED TO the Mars room, where she sat watching the interloper's approach. The wall screen refreshed every four minutes as a new image arrived from the other side of the sun. Each time it did, the bright orange homestead jumped a bit closer. It jumped right past the outermost ring of survey sticks, putting it less than two kilometers from the obelisk—close enough that she could see a faint wake of drifting dust trailing behind it, giving it a sense of motion.

Then, thirty-eight minutes after she'd sent the new instruction set, the Destiny AI returned an acknowledgement.

Her heart beat faster, knowing that whatever was to happen on Mars had already happened. Destiny's construction equipment had retreated and its homestead had started up or had failed to start, had moved into place at the foot of the tower or not. No way to know until time on Earth caught up with time on Mars.

The door opened.

Nate shuffled into the room.

Susannah didn't bother to ask if Davidson had turned up anything. She could see from his grim expression that he expected the worst.

And what was the worst?

A slight smile stole onto her lips as Nate sat beside her on the couch.

The worst case is that someone has lived.

Was it any wonder they were doomed?

*   *   *

Four more minutes.

The image updated.

The 360-degree camera, mounted on a steel pole sunk deep into the rock, showed Destiny profoundly changed. For the first time in seventeen years, Destiny's homestead had moved. It was parked by the tower, just as Susannah had requested. She twisted around, looking for the bright green corner of the factory beyond the distant ridge—but she couldn't see it.

"Everything is as ordered," Susannah said.

The Red Oasis homestead had reached the green survey sticks.

"An AI has to be driving," Nate insisted.

"Time will tell."

Nate shook his head. "Time comes with a nineteen minute gap. Truth is in the radio silence. It's an AI."

Four more minutes of silence.

When the image next refreshed, it showed the two homesteads, nose to nose.

Four minutes.

The panorama looked the same.

Four minutes more.

No change.

Four minutes.

Only the angle of sunlight shifted.

Four minutes.

A figure in an orange pressure suit stood beside the two vehicles, gazing up at the tower.

Before the Martian Obelisk, when Shaun was still alive, two navy officers in dress uniforms had come to the house, and in formal voices explained that the daughter Susannah had birthed and nurtured and shaped with such care was gone, her future collapsed to nothing by a missile strike in the South China Sea.

"We must go on," Shaun ultimately insisted.

And they had, bravely.

Defiantly.

Only a few years later their second child and his young wife had vanished into the chaos brought on by an engineered plague that decimated Hawaii's population, turning it into a state under permanent quarantine. Day after excruciating day as they'd waited for news, Shaun had grown visibly older, hope a dying light, and when it was finally extinguished he had nothing left to keep him moored to life.

Susannah was of a different temper. The cold ferocity of her anger had nailed her into the world. The shape it took was the Martian Obelisk: one last creative act before the world's end.

She knew now the obelisk would never be finished.

"It's a synth," Nate said. "It has to be."

The AI contradicted him. "Text message," it announced.

"Read it," Susannah instructed.

Alix obeyed, reading the message in an emotionless voice. "Message sender: Red Oasis resident Tory Eastman. Message body as transcribed audio: Is anyone out there? Is anyone listening? My name is Tory Eastman. I'm a refugee from Red Oasis. Nineteen days in transit with my daughter and son, twins, three years old. We are the last survivors."

These words induced in Susannah a rush of fear so potent she had to close her eyes against a dizzying sense of vertigo. There was no emotion in the AI's voice and still she heard in it the anguish of another mother:

"The habitat was damaged during the emergency. I couldn't maintain what was left and I had no communications. So I came here. Five thousand kilometers. I need what's here. I need it all. I need the provisions and I need the equipment and I need the command codes and I need the building materials. I need to build my children a new home. Please. Are you there? Are you an AI? Is anyone left on Earth? Respond. Respond please. Give me the command codes. I will wait."

For many seconds—and many, many swift, fluttering heartbeats—neither Nate nor Susannah spoke. Susannah wanted to speak. She sought for words, and when she couldn't find them, she wondered: am I in shock? Or is it a stroke?

Nate found his voice first, "It's a hoax, aimed at you, Susannah. They know your history. They're playing on your emotions. They're using your grief to wreck this project."

Susannah let out a long breath, and with it, some of the horror that had gripped her. "We humans are amazing," she mused, "in our endless ability to lie to ourselves."

He shook his head. "Susannah, if I thought this was real—"

She held up a hand to stop his objection. "I'm not going to turn over the command codes. Not yet. If you're right and this is a hoax, I can back out. But if it's real, that family has pushed the life support capabilities of their homestead to the limit. They can move into our vehicle—that'll keep them alive for a few days—but they'll need more permanent shelter soon."

"It'll take months to build a habitat."

"*No.* It'll take months to make the tiles to build a habitat—but we already have a huge supply of tiles."

"All of our tiles are tied up in the obelisk."

"Yes."

He looked at her in shock, struck speechless.

"It'll be okay, Nate."

"You're abandoning the project."

"If we can help this family survive, we have to do it—and that will be the project we're remembered for."

"Even if there's no one left to remember?"

She pressed her lips tightly together, contemplating the image of the obelisk. Then she nodded. "Even so."

Knowing the pain of waiting, she sent a message of assurance to Destiny Colony before anything else. Then she instructed the synth and the beetle cart to renew their work, but this time in reverse: the synth would unlink the fiber tiles beginning at the top of the obelisk and the beetle would carry them down.

AFTER AN HOUR—after she'd traded another round of messages with a grateful Tory Eastman and begun to lay out a shelter based on a standard Martian habitat—she got up to stretch her legs and relieve her bladder. It surprised her to find Nate still in the living room. He stood at the front window, staring out at the mist that never brought enough moisture into the forest.

"They'll be alone forever," he said without turning around. "There are no more missions planned. No one else will ever go to Mars."

"I won't tell her that."

He looked at her over his shoulder. "So you are willing to sacrifice the obelisk? It was everything to you yesterday, but today you'll just give it up?"

"She drove a quarter of the way around the planet, Nate. Would you ever have guessed that was possible?"

"No," he said bitterly as he turned back to the window. "No. It should not have been possible."

"There's a lesson for us in that. We assume we can see forward to tomorrow, but we can't. We can't ever really know what's to come—and we can't know what we might do, until we try."

WHEN SHE CAME out of the bathroom, Nate was sitting down in the rickety old chair by the door. With his rounded shoulders and his thin white hair, he looked old and very frail. "Susannah—"

"Nate, I don't want to argue—"

"Just *listen*. I didn't want to tell you before because, well, you've already suffered so many shocks and even good news can come too late."

"What are you saying?" she said, irritated with him now, sure that he was trying to undermine her resolve.

"Hawaii's been under quarantine because the virus can be latent for—"

She guessed where this was going. "For years. I know that. But if you're trying to suggest that Tory and her children might still succumb to whatever wiped out Red Oasis—"

"They *might*," he interrupted, sounding bitter. "But that's not what I was going to say."

"Then what?"

"Listen, and I'll tell you. Are you ready to listen?"

"Yes, yes. Go ahead."

"A report came out just a few weeks ago. The latest antivirals worked.

The quarantine in Hawaii will continue for several more years, but all indications are the virus is gone. Wiped out. No sign of latent infections in over six months."

Her hands felt numb; she felt barely able to shuffle her feet as she moved to take a seat in an antique armchair. "The virus is gone? How can they know that?"

"Blood tests. And the researchers say that what they've learned can be applied to other contagions. That what happened in Hawaii doesn't ever have to happen again."

Progress? A reprieve against the long decline?

"There's more, Susannah."

The way he said it—his falling tone—it was a warning that set her tired heart pounding.

"You asked me to act as your agent," he reminded her. "You asked me to screen all news, and I've done that."

"Until now."

"Until now," he agreed, looking down, looking frightened by the knowledge he had decided to convey. "I should have told you sooner."

"But you didn't want to risk interrupting work on the obelisk?"

"You said you didn't want to hear anything." He shrugged. "I took you at your word."

"Nate, will you just say it?"

"You have a granddaughter, Susannah."

She replayed these words in her head, once, twice. They didn't make sense.

"DNA tests make it certain," he explained. "She was born six months after her father's death."

"*No.*" Susannah did not dare believe it. It was too dangerous to believe. "They both died. That was confirmed by the survivors. They posted the IDs of all the dead."

"Your daughter-in-law lived long enough to give birth."

Susannah's chest squeezed tight. "I don't understand. Are you saying the child is still alive?"

"Yes."

Anger rose hot, up out of the past. "And how long have you known? How long have you kept this from me?"

"Two months. I'm sorry, but..."

But we had our priorities. The tombstone. The Martian folly.

She stared at the floor, too stunned to be happy, or maybe she'd forgotten how. "You should have told me."

"I know."

"And I... I shouldn't have walled myself off from the world. I'm sorry."

"There's more," he said cautiously, as if worried how much more she could take.

"What else?" she snapped, suddenly sure this was just another game played by the master torturer, to draw the pain out. "Are you going to tell me that my granddaughter is sickly? Dying? Or that she's a mad woman, perhaps?"

"No," he said meekly. "Nothing like that. She's healthy, and she has a healthy two-year-old daughter." He got up, put an age-marked hand on the door knob. "I've sent you her contact information. If you need an assistant to help you build the habitat, let me know."

He was a friend, and she tried to comfort him. "Nate, I'm sorry. If there was a choice—"

"There isn't. That's the way it's turned out. You will tear down the obelisk, and this woman, Tory Eastman, will live another year, maybe two. Then the equipment will break and she will die and we won't be able to rebuild the tower. We'll pass on, and the rest of the world will follow—"

"We can't know that, Nate. Not for sure."

He shook his head. "This all looks like hope, but it's a trick. It's fate cheating us, forcing us to fold our hand, level our pride, and go out meekly. And there's no choice in it, because it's the right thing to do."

He opened the door. For a few seconds, wind gusted in, until he closed it again. She heard his clogs crossing the porch and a minute later she heard the crunch of tires on the gravel road.

You have a granddaughter. One who grew up without her parents, in a quarantine zone, with no real hope for the future and yet she was healthy, with a daughter already two years old.

And then there was Tory Eastman of Mars, who had left a dying colony and driven an impossible distance past doubt and despair, because she knew you have to do everything you can, until you can't do anymore.

Susannah had forgotten that, somewhere in the dark years.

She sat for a time in the stillness, in a quiet so deep she could hear the beating of her heart.

This all looks like hope.

Indeed it did and she well knew that hope could be a duplicitous gift from the master torturer, one that opened the door to despair.

"But it doesn't have to be that way," she whispered to the empty room. "I'm not done. Not yet."

A SERIES OF STEAKS

Vina Jie-Min Prasad

Vina Jie-Min Prasad (vinaprasad.com) is a Singaporean writer working against the world-machine. Her skills include historical research, content design, and a myriad of other things. Her short fiction has appeared in *Queer Southeast Asia: A Literary Journal of Transgressive Art*, *HEAT: A Southeast Asian Urban Anthology*, *Fireside Fiction*, *Clarkesworld* and *Uncanny Magazine*.

ALL KNOWN FORGERIES are tales of failure. The people who get into the newsfeeds for their brilliant attempts to cheat the system with their fraudulent Renaissance masterpieces or their stacks of fake cheques, well, they might be successful artists, but they certainly haven't been successful at *forgery*.

The best forgeries are the ones that disappear from notice—a second-rate still-life mouldering away in gallery storage, a battered old 50-yuan note at the bottom of a cashier drawer—or even a printed strip of Matsusaka beef, sliding between someone's parted lips.

FORGING BEEF IS similar to printmaking—every step of the process has to be done with the final print in mind. A red that's too dark looks putrid, a white that's too pure looks artificial. All beef is supposed to come from a cow, so stipple the red with dots, flecks, lines of white to fake variance in muscle fibre regions. Cows are similar, but cows aren't uniform—use fractals to randomise marbling after defining the basic look. Cut the sheets of beef manually to get an authentic ragged edge, don't get lazy and depend on the bioprinter for that.

Days of research and calibration and cursing the printer will all vanish into someone's gullet in seconds, if the job's done right.

Helena Li Yuanhui of Splendid Beef Enterprises is an expert in doing the job right.

The trick is not to get too ambitious. Most forgers are caught out by the smallest errors—a tiny amount of period-inaccurate pigment, a crack in the oil paint that looks too artificial, or a misplaced watermark on a passport. Printing something large increases the chances of a fatal misstep. Stick with small-scale jobs, stick with a small group of regular clients, and in time, Splendid Beef Enterprises will turn enough of a profit for Helena to get a *real* name change, leave Nanjing, and forget this whole sorry venture ever happened.

As Helena's loading the beef into refrigerated boxes for drone delivery, a notification pops up on her iKontakt frames. Helena sighs, turns the volume on her earpiece down, and takes the call.

"Hi, Mr Chan, could you switch to a secure line? You just need to tap the button with a lock icon, it's very easy."

"Nonsense!" Mr Chan booms. "If the government were going to catch us they'd have done so by now! Anyway, I just called to tell you how pleased I am with the latest batch. Such a shame, though, all that talent and your work just gets gobbled up in seconds—tell you what, girl, for the next beef special, how about I tell everyone that the beef came from one of those fancy vertical farms? I'm sure they'd have nice things to say then!"

"Please don't," Helena says, careful not to let her Cantonese accent slip through. It tends to show after long periods without any human interaction, which is an apt summary of the past few months. "It's best if no one pays attention to it."

"You know, Helena, you do good work, but I'm very concerned about your self-esteem, I know if I printed something like that I'd want everyone to appreciate it! Let me tell you about this article my daughter sent me, you know research says that people without friends are prone to..." Mr Chan rambles on as Helena sticks the labels on the boxes—Grilliam Shakespeare, Gyuuzen Sukiyaki, Fatty Chan's Restaurant—and thankfully hangs up before Helena sinks into further depression. She takes her iKontakt off before heading to the drone delivery office, giving herself some time to recover from Mr Chan's relentless cheerfulness.

Helena has five missed calls by the time she gets back. A red phone icon blares at the corner of her vision before blinking out, replaced by the incoming-call notification. It's secured and anonymised, which is quite a change from usual. She pops the earpiece in.

"Yeah, Mr Chan?"

"This isn't Mr Chan," someone says. "I have a job for Splendid Beef Enterprises."

"All right, sir. Could I get your name and what you need? If you could provide me with the deadline, that would help too."

"I prefer to remain anonymous," the man says.

"Yes, I understand, secrecy is rather important." Helena restrains the urge to roll her eyes at how needlessly cryptic this guy is. "Could I know about the deadline and brief?"

"I need two hundred T-bone steaks by the 8th of August. 38.1 to 40.2 millimeter thickness for each one." A notification to download t-bone_info. KZIP pops up on her lenses. The most ambitious venture Helena's undertaken in the past few months has been Gyuuzen's strips of marbled sukiyaki, and even that felt a bit like pushing it. A whole steak? Hell no.

"I'm sorry, sir, but I don't think my business can handle that. Perhaps you could try—"

"I think you'll be interested in this job, Helen Lee Jyun Wai."

Shit.

A Sculpere 9410S only takes thirty minutes to disassemble, if you know the right tricks. Manually eject the cell cartridges, slide the external casing off to expose the inner screws, and detach the print heads before disassembling the power unit. There are a few extra steps in this case—for instance, the stickers that say 'Property of Hong Kong Scientific University' and 'Bioprinting Lab A5' all need to be removed—but a bit of anti-adhesive spray will ensure that everything's on schedule. Ideally she'd buy a new printer, but she needs to save her cash for the name change once she hits Nanjing.

It's not expulsion if you leave before you get kicked out, she tells herself, but even she can tell that's a lie.

* * *

IT'S POSSIBLE TO get a sense of a client's priorities just from the documents they send. For instance, Mr Chan usually mentions some recipes that he's considering, and Ms Huang from Gyuuzen tends to attach examples of the marbling patterns she wants. This new client seems to have attached a whole document dedicated to the recent amendments in the criminal code, with the ones relevant to Helena ('five-year statute of limitations', 'possible death penalty') conveniently highlighted in neon yellow.

Sadly, this level of detail hasn't carried over to the spec sheet.

"Hi again, sir," Helena says. "I've read through what you've sent, but I really need more details before starting on the job. Could you provide me with the full measurements? I'll need the expected length and breadth in addition to the thickness."

"It's already there. Learn to read."

"I *know* you filled that part in, sir," Helena says, gritting her teeth. "But we're a printing company, not a farm. I'll need more detail than '16-18 month cow, grain-fed, Hereford breed' to do the job properly."

"You went to university, didn't you? I'm sure you can figure out something as basic as that, even if you didn't graduate."

"Ha ha. Of course." Helena resists the urge to yank her earpiece out. "I'll get right on that. Also, there is the issue of pay..."

"Ah, yes. I'm quite sure the Yuen family is still itching to prosecute. How about you do the job, and in return, I don't tell them where you're hiding?"

"I'm sorry, sir, but even then I'll need an initial deposit to cover the printing, and of course there's the matter of the Hereford samples." *Which I already have in the bioreactor, but there is no way I'm letting you know that.*

"Fine. I'll expect detailed daily updates," Mr Anonymous says. "I know how you get with deadlines. Don't fuck it up."

"Of course not," Helena says. "Also, about the deadline—would it be possible to push it back? Four weeks is quite short for this job."

"No," Mr Anonymous says curtly, and hangs up.

Helena lets out a very long breath so she doesn't end up screaming, and takes a moment to curse Mr Anonymous and his whole family in Cantonese.

It's physically impossible to complete the renders and finish the print in four weeks, unless she figures out a way to turn her printer into a time machine, and if that were possible she might as well go back and redo the past few years, or maybe her whole life. If she had majored in art, maybe she'd be a designer by now—or hell, while she's busy dreaming, she could even have been the next Raverat, the next Mantuana—instead of a failed artist living in a shithole concrete box, clinging to the wreckage of all her past mistakes.

She leans against the wall for a while, exhales, then slaps on a proxy and starts drafting a help-wanted ad.

LILY YONEZAWA (DARKNET username: yurisquared) arrives at Nanjing High Tech Industrial Park at 8.58 am. She's a short lady with long black hair and circle-framed iKontakts. She's wearing a loose, floaty dress, smooth lines of white tinged with yellow-green, and there's a large prismatic bracelet gleaming on her arm. In comparison, Helena is wearing her least holey black blouse and a pair of jeans, which is a step up from her usual attire of myoglobin-stained T-shirt and boxer shorts.

"So," Lily says in rapid, slightly-accented Mandarin as she bounds into the office. "This place is a beef place, right? I pulled some of the records once I got the address, hope you don't mind—anyway, what do you want me to help print or render or design or whatever? I know I said I had a background in confections and baking, but I'm totally open to anything!" She pumps her fist in a show of determination. The loose-fitting prismatic bracelet slides up and down.

Helena blinks at Lily with the weariness of someone who's spent most of their night frantically trying to make their office presentable. She decides to skip most of the briefing, as Lily doesn't seem like the sort who needs to be eased into anything.

"How much do you know about beef?"

"I used to watch a whole bunch of farming documentaries with my ex, does that count?"

"No. Here at Splendid Beef Enterprises—"

"Oh, by the way, do you have a logo? I searched your company registration but nothing really came up. Need me to design one?"

"*Here at Splendid Beef Enterprises,* we make fake beef and sell it to restaurants."

"So, like, soy-lentil stuff?"

"Homegrown cloned cell lines," Helena says. "Mostly Matsusaka, with some Hereford if clients specify it." She gestures at the bioreactor humming away in a corner.

"Wait, isn't fake food like those knockoff eggs made of calcium carbonate? If you're using cow cells, this seems pretty real to me." Clearly Lily has a more practical definition of fake than the China Food and Drug Administration.

"It's more like... let's say you have a painting in a gallery and you say it's by a famous artist. Lots of people would come look at it because of the name alone and write reviews talking about its exquisite use of chiaroscuro, as expected of the old masters, I can't believe that it looks so real even though it was painted centuries ago. But if you say, hey, this great painting was by some no-name loser, I was just lying about where it came from... well, it'd still be the same painting, but people would want all their money back."

"Oh, I get it," Lily says, scrutinising the bioreactor. She taps its shiny polymer shell with her knuckles, and her bracelet bumps against it. Helena tries not to wince. "Anyway, how legal is this? This meat forgery thing?"

"It's not illegal yet," Helena says. "It's kind of a grey area, really."

"Great!" Lily smacks her fist into her open palm. "Now, how can I help? I'm totally down for anything! You can even ask me to clean the office if you want—wow, this is *really* dusty, maybe I should just clean it to make sure—"

Helena reminds herself that having an assistant isn't entirely bad news. Wolfgang Beltracchi was only able to carry out large-scale forgeries with his assistant's help, and they even got along well enough to get married and have a kid without killing each other.

Then again, the Beltracchis both got caught, so maybe she shouldn't be too optimistic.

Cows that undergo extreme stress while waiting for slaughter are known as dark cutters. The stress causes them to deplete all their glycogen reserves, and when butchered, their meat turns a dark blackish-red. The meat of dark cutters is generally considered low-quality.

As a low-quality person waiting for slaughter, Helena understands how those cows feel. Mr Anonymous, stymied by the industrial park's regular sweeps for trackers and external cameras, has taken to sending Helena grainy aerial photographs of herself together with exhortations to work harder. This isn't exactly news—she already knew he had her details, and drones are pretty cheap—but still. When Lily raps on the door in the morning, Helena sometimes jolts awake in a panic before she realises that it isn't Mr Anonymous coming for her. This isn't helped by the fact that Lily's gentle knocks seem to be equivalent to other people's knockout blows.

By now Helena's introduced Lily to the basics, and she's a surprisingly quick study. It doesn't take her long to figure out how to randomise the fat marbling with Fractalgenr8, and she's been handed the task of printing the beef strips for Gyuuzen and Fatty Chan, then packing them for drone delivery. It's not ideal, but it lets Helena concentrate on the base model for the T-bone steak, which is the most complicated thing she's ever tried to render.

A T-bone steak is a combination of two cuts of meat, lean tenderloin and fatty strip steak, separated by a hard ridge of vertebral bone. Simply cutting into one is a near-religious experience, red meat parting under the knife to reveal smooth white bone, with the beef fat dripping down to pool on the plate. At least, that's what the socialites' food blogs say. To be accurate, they say something more like 'omfg this is sooooooo good', 'this bones giving me a boner lol', and 'haha im so getting this sonic-cleaned for my collection!!!', but Helena pretends they actually meant to communicate something more coherent.

The problem is a lack of references. Most of the accessible photographs only provide a top-down view, and Helena's left to extrapolate from blurry videos and password-protected previews of bovine myology databases, which don't get her much closer to figuring out how the meat adheres to the bone. Helena's forced to dig through ancient research papers and diagrams that focus on where to cut to maximise meat yield, quantifying the difference between porterhouse and T-bone cuts, and not *hey, if you're reading this decades in the future, here's how to make a good facsimile of a steak.* Helena's tempted to run outside and scream in frustration, but Lily would probably insist on running outside and screaming with her as a matter of company solidarity, and with their luck, probably Mr Anonymous would find out about Lily right then, even after all the trouble she's taken to censor any mention of her new assistant from the files and the reports and *argh she needs sleep.*

Meanwhile, Lily's already scheduled everything for print, judging by the way she's spinning around in Helena's spare swivel chair.

"Hey, Lily," Helena says, stifling a yawn. "Why don't you play around with this for a bit? It's the base model for a T-bone steak. Just familiarise yourself with the fibre extrusion and mapping, see if you can get it to look like the reference photos. Don't worry, I've saved a copy elsewhere." *Good luck doing the impossible,* Helena doesn't say. *You're bound to have memorised the shortcut for 'undo' by the time I wake up.*

Helena wakes up to Lily humming a cheerful tune and a mostly-complete T-bone model rotating on her screen. She blinks a few times, but no—it's still there. Lily's effortlessly linking the rest of the meat, fat and gristle to the side of the bone, deforming the muscle fibres to account for the bone's presence.

"What did you do," Helena blurts out.

Lily turns around to face her, fiddling with her bracelet. "Uh, did I do it wrong?"

"Rotate it a bit, let me see the top view. How did you do it?"

"It's a little like the human vertebral column, isn't it? There's plenty of references for that." She taps the screen twice, switching focus to an image of a human cross-section. "See how it attaches here and here? I just used that as a reference, and boom."

Ugh, Helena thinks to herself. She's been out of university for way too long if she's forgetting basic homology.

"Wait, *is* it correct? Did I mess up?"

"No, no," Helena says. "This is really good. Better than... well, better than I did, anyway."

"Awesome! Can I get a raise?"

"You can get yourself a sesame pancake," Helena says. "My treat."

THE BRIEF REQUIRES two hundred similar-but-unique steaks at randomised thicknesses of 38.1 to 40.2 mm, and the number and density of meat fibres pretty much precludes Helena from rendering it on her own rig. She doesn't want to pay to outsource computing power, so they're using spare processing cycles from other personal rigs and staggering the loads. Straightforward bone surfaces get rendered in afternoons, and fibre-dense tissues get rendered at off-peak hours.

It's three in the morning. Helena's in her Pokko the Penguin T-shirt and boxer shorts, and Lily's wearing Yayoi Kusama-ish pyjamas that make her look like she's been obliterated by a mass of polka dots. Both of them are staring at their screens, eating cups of Zhuzhu Brand Artificial Char Siew Noodles. As Lily's job moves to the front of Render@Home's Finland queue, the graph updates to show a downtick in Mauritius. Helena's fingers frantically skim across the touchpad, queueing as many jobs as she can.

Her chopsticks scrape the bottom of the mycefoam cup, and she tilts the container to shovel the remaining fake pork fragments into her mouth. Zhuzhu's using extruded soy proteins, and they've punched up the glutamate percentage since she last bought them. The roasted char siew flavour is lacking, and the texture is crumby since the factory skimped on the extrusion time, but any hot food is practically heaven at this time of the night. Day. Whatever.

The thing about the rendering stage is that there's a lot of panic-infused downtime. After queueing the requests, they can't really do anything else— the requests might fail, or the rig might crash, or they might lose their place in the queue through some accident of fate and have to do everything all over again. There's nothing to do besides pray that the requests get through, stay awake until the server limit resets, and repeat the whole process until everything's done. Staying awake is easy for Helena, as Mr Anonymous has recently taken to sending pictures of rotting corpses to her iKontakt address, captioned 'Work hard or this could be you'. Lily seems to be halfway off to dreamland, possibly because she isn't seeing misshapen lumps of flesh every time she closes her eyes.

"So," Lily says, yawning. "How *did* you get into this business?"

Helena decides it's too much trouble to figure out a plausible lie, and settles for a very edited version of the truth. "I took art as an elective in high school. My school had a lot of printmaking and 3D printing equipment, so I used it to make custom merch in my spare time—you know, for people who wanted figurines of obscure anime characters, or whatever. Even designed and printed the packaging for them, just to make it look more official. I wanted to study art in university, but that didn't really work out. Long story short, I ended up moving here from Hong Kong, and since I had a background in printing and bootlegging... yeah. What about you?"

"Before the confectionery I did a whole bunch of odd jobs. I used to sell merch for my girlfriend's band, and that's how I got started with the short-order printing stuff. They were called POMEGRENADE—it was really hard to fit the whole name on a T-shirt. The keychains sold really well, though."

"What sort of band were they?"

"Sort of noise-rocky Cantopunk at first—there was this one really cute song I liked, *If Marriage Means The Death Of Love Then We Must Both Be Zombies*—but Cantonese music was a hard sell, even in Guangzhou, so they ended up being kind of a cover band."

"Oh, Guangzhou," Helena says in an attempt to sound knowledgeable, before realising that the only thing she knows about Guangzhou is that the Red Triad has a particularly profitable organ-printing business there. "Wait, you understand Cantonese?"

"Yeah," Lily says in Cantonese, tone-perfect. "No one really speaks it around here, so I haven't used it much."

"Oh my god, yes, it's so hard to find Canto-speaking people here." Helena immediately switches to Cantonese. "Why didn't you tell me sooner? I've been *dying* to speak it to someone."

"Sorry, it never came up so I figured it wasn't very relevant," Lily says. "Anyway, POMEGRENADE mostly did covers after that, you know, Kick Out The Jams, Zhongnanhai, Chaos Changan, Lightsabre Cocksucking Blues. Whatever got the crowd pumped up, and when they were moshing the hardest, they'd hit the crowd with the Cantopunk and just blast their faces off. I think it left more of an impression that way—like, start with the familiar, then this weird-ass surprise near the end—the merch table always got swamped after they did that."

"What happened with the girlfriend?"

"We broke up, but we keep in touch. Do you still do art?"

"Not really. The closest thing I get to art is this," Helena says, rummaging through the various boxes under the table to dig out her sketchbooks. She flips one open and hands it to Lily—white against red, nothing but full-page studies of marbling patterns, and it must be one of the earlier ones because it's downright amateurish. The lines are all over the place, that marbling on the Wagyu (is that even meant to be Wagyu?) is completely inaccurate, and, fuck, are those *tear stains*?

Lily turns the pages, tracing the swashes of colour with her finger. The hum of the overworked rig fills the room.

"It's awful, I know."

"What are you talking about?" Lily's gaze lingers on Helena's attempt at a fractal snowflake. "This is really trippy! If you ever want to do some album art, just let me know and I'll totally hook you up!"

Helena opens her mouth to say something about how she's not an artist, and how studies of beef marbling wouldn't make very good album covers, but faced with Lily's unbridled enthusiasm, she decides to nod instead.

Lily turns the page and it's that thing she did way back at the beginning, when she was thinking of using a cute cow as the company logo. It's derivative, it's kitsch, the whole thing looks like a degraded copy of someone else's rip-off drawing of a cow's head, and the fact that Lily's seriously scrutinising it makes Helena want to snatch the sketchbook back, toss it into the composter, and sink straight into the concrete floor.

The next page doesn't grant Helena a reprieve since there's a whole series of that stupid cow. Versions upon versions of happy cow faces grin straight at Lily, most of them surrounded by little hearts—what was she thinking? What do hearts even have to do with Splendid Beef Enterprises, anyway? Was it just that they were easy to draw?

"Man, I wish we had a logo because this would be super cute! I love the little hearts! It's like saying we put our heart and soul into whatever we do! Oh, wait, but was that what you meant?"

"It could be," Helena says, and thankfully the Colorado server opens before Lily can ask any further questions.

THE BRIEF REQUIRES status reports at the end of each workday, but this gradually falls by the wayside once they hit the point where workdays don't technically end, especially since Helena really doesn't want to look at an inbox full of increasingly creepy threats. They're at the pre-print stage, and Lily's given up on going back to her own place at night so they can have more time for calibration. What looks right on the screen might not look right once it's printed, and their lives for the past few days have devolved into staring at endless trays of 32-millimeter beef cubes and checking them for myoglobin concentration, colour match in different lighting conditions, fat striation depth, and a whole host of other factors.

There are so many ways for a forgery to go wrong, and only one way it can go right. Helena contemplates this philosophical quandary, and gently thunks her head against the back of her chair.

"Oh my god," Lily exclaims, shoving her chair back. "I can't take this anymore! I'm going out to eat something and then I'm getting some sleep. Do you want anything?" She straps on her bunny-patterned filter mask and her metallic sandals. "I'm gonna eat there, so I might take a while to get back."

"Sesame pancakes, thanks."

As Lily slams the door, Helena puts her iKontakt frames back on. The left lens flashes a stream of notifications—fifty-seven missed calls over the past five hours, all from an unknown number. Just then, another call comes in, and she reflexively taps the side of the frame.

"You haven't been updating me on your progress," Mr Anonymous says.

"I'm very sorry, sir," Helena says flatly, having reached the point of tiredness where she's ceased to feel anything beyond *god I want to sleep*. This sets Mr Anonymous on another rant covering the usual topics—poor work ethic, lack of commitment, informing the Yuen family, prosecution, possible death sentence—and Helena struggles to keep her mouth shut before she says something that she might regret.

"Maybe I should send someone to check on you right now," Mr Anonymous snarls, before abruptly hanging up.

Helena blearily types out a draft of the report, and makes a note to send a coherent version later in the day, once she gets some sleep and fixes the calibration so she's not telling him entirely bad news. Just as she's about to call Lily and ask her to get some hot soy milk to go with the sesame pancakes, the front door rattles in its frame like someone's trying to punch it down. Judging by the violence, it's probably Lily. Helena trudges over to open it.

It isn't. It's a bulky guy with a flat-top haircut. She stares at him for a moment, then tries to slam the door in his face. He forces the door open and shoves his way inside, grabbing Helena's arm, and all Helena can think is *I can't believe Mr Anonymous spent his money on this.*

He shoves her against the wall, gripping her wrist so hard that it's practically getting dented by his fingertips, and pulls out a switchblade, pressing it against the knuckle of her index finger. "Well, I'm not allowed to kill you, but I can fuck you up real bad. Don't really need all your fingers, do you, girl?"

She clears her throat, and struggles to keep her voice from shaking. "I need them to type—didn't your boss tell you that?"

"Shut up," Flat-Top says, flicking the switchblade once, then twice, thinking. "Don't need your face to type, do you?"

Just then, Lily steps through the door. Flat-Top can't see her from his angle, and Helena jerks her head, desperately communicating that she should stay out. Lily promptly moves closer.

Helena contemplates murder.

Lily edges towards both of them, slides her bracelet past her wrist and onto her knuckles, and makes a gesture at Helena which either means 'move to your left' or 'I'm imitating a bird, but only with one hand'.

"Hey," Lily says loudly. "What's going on here?"

Flat-Top startles, loosening his grip on Helena's arm, and Helena dodges to the left. Just as Lily's fist meets his face in a truly vicious uppercut, Helena seizes the opportunity to kick him soundly in the shins.

His head hits the floor, and it's clear he won't be moving for a while, or ever. Considering Lily's normal level of violence towards the front door, this isn't surprising.

Lily crouches down to check Flat-Top's breathing. "Well, he's still alive. Do you prefer him that way?"

"Do *not* kill him."

"Sure." Lily taps the side of Flat-Top's iKontakt frames with her bracelet, and information scrolls across her lenses. "Okay, his name's Nicholas Liu Honghui... blah blah blah... hired to scare someone at this address, anonymous client... I think he's coming to, how do you feel about joint locks?"

It takes a while for Nicholas to stir fully awake. Lily's on his chest, pinning him to the ground, and Helena's holding his switchblade to his throat.

"Okay, Nicholas Liu," Lily says. "We could kill you right now, but that'd make your wife and your... what is that red thing she's holding... a baby? Yeah, that'd make your wife and ugly baby quite sad. Now, you're just going to tell your boss that everything went as expected—"

"Tell him that I cried," Helena interrupts. "I was here alone, and I cried because I was so scared."

"Right, got that, Nick? That lady there wept buckets of tears. I don't exist. Everything went well, and you think there's no point in sending anyone else over. If you mess up, we'll visit 42—god, what is this character—42 Something Road and let you know how displeased we are. Now, if you apologise for ruining our morning, I probably won't break your arm."

After seeing a wheezing Nicholas to the exit, Lily closes the door, slides her bracelet back onto her wrist, and shakes her head like a deeply disappointed critic. "What an amateur. Didn't even use burner frames—how the hell did he get hired? And that *haircut*, wow..."

Helena opts to remain silent. She leans against the wall and stares at the ceiling, hoping that she can wake up from what seems to be a very long nightmare.

"Also, I'm not gonna push it, but I did take out the trash. Can you explain why that crappy hitter decided to pay us a visit?"

"Yeah. Yeah, okay." Helena's stomach growls. "This may take a while. Did you get the food?"

"I got your pancakes, and that soy milk place was open, so I got you some. Nearly threw it at that guy, but I figured we've got a lot of electronics, so..."

"Thanks," Helena says, taking a sip. It's still hot.

HONG KONG SCIENTIFIC University's bioprinting program is a prestigious pioneer program funded by mainland China, and Hong Kong is the test bed before the widespread rollout. The laboratories are full of state-of-the-art medical-grade printers and bioreactors, and the instructors are all researchers cherry-picked from the best universities.

As the star student of the pioneer batch, Lee Jyun Wai Helen (student number A3007082A) is selected for a special project. She will help the head instructor work on the basic model of a heart for a dextrocardial patient, the instructor will handle the detailed render and the final print, and a skilled surgeon will do the transplant. As the term progresses and the instructor gets busier and busier, Helen's role gradually escalates to doing everything except the final print and the transplant. It's a particularly tricky render, since dextrocardial hearts face right instead of left, but her practice prints are cell-level perfect.

Helen hands the render files and her notes on the printing process to the instructor, then her practical exams begin and she forgets all about it.

The Yuen family discovers Madam Yuen's defective heart during their mid-autumn family reunion, halfway through an evening harbour cruise. Madam Yuen doesn't make it back to shore, and instead of a minor footnote in a scientific paper, Helen rapidly becomes front-and-centre in an internal investigation into the patient's death.

Unofficially, the internal investigation discovers that the head instructor's improper calibration of the printer during the final print led to a slight misalignment in the left ventricle, which eventually caused severe ventricular dysfunction and acute graft failure.

Officially, the root cause of the misprint is Lee Jyun Wai Helen's negligence and failure to perform under deadline pressure. Madam Yuen's family threatens to prosecute, but the criminal code doesn't cover failed organ printing. Helen is expelled, and the Hong Kong Scientific University quietly negotiates a settlement with the Yuens.

After deciding to steal the bioprinter and flee, Helen realises that she doesn't have enough money for a full name change and an overseas flight. She settles for a minor name alteration and a flight to Nanjing.

"Wow," says Lily. "You know, I'm pretty sure you got ripped off with the name alteration thing, there's no way it costs that much. Also, you used to have pigtails? Seriously?"

Helena snatches her old student ID away from Lily. "Anyway, under the amendments to Article 335, making or supplying substandard printed organs is now an offence punishable by death. The family's itching to prosecute. If we don't do the job right, Mr Anonymous is going to disclose my whereabouts to them."

"Okay, but from what you've told me, this guy is totally not going to let it go even after you're done. At my old job, we got blackmailed like that all the time, which was really kind of irritating. They'd always try to bargain, and after the first job, they'd say stuff like 'if you don't do me this favour I'm going to call the cops and tell them everything' just to weasel out of paying for the next one."

"Wait. Was this at the bakery or the merch stand?"

"Uh." Lily looks a bit sheepish. This is quite unusual, considering that Lily has spent the past four days regaling Helena with tales of the most impressive blood blobs from her period, complete with comparisons to their failed prints. "Are you familiar with the Red Triad? The one in Guangzhou?"

"You mean the *organ printers?*"

"Yeah, them. I kind of might have been working there before the bakery...?"

"What?"

Lily fiddles with the lacy hem of her skirt. "Well, I mean, the bakery experience seemed more relevant, plus you don't have to list every job you've ever done when you apply for a new one, right?"

"Okay," Helena says, trying not to think too hard about how all the staff at Splendid Beef Enterprises are now prime candidates for the death penalty. "Okay. What exactly did you do there?"

"Ears and stuff, bladders, spare fingers... you'd be surprised how many people need those. I also did some bone work, but that was mainly for the diehards—most of the people we worked on were pretty okay with titanium substitutes. You know, simple stuff."

"*That's not simple.*"

"Well, it's not like I was printing fancy reversed hearts or anything, and even with the asshole clients it was way easier than baking. Have *you* ever tried to extrude a spun-sugar globe so you could put a bunch of powder-printed magpies inside? And don't get me started on cleaning the nozzles after extrusion, because wow..."

Helena decides not to question Lily's approach to life, because it seems like a certain path to a migraine. "Maybe we should talk about this later."

"Right, you need to send the update! Can I help?"

The eventual message contains very little detail and a lot of pleading. Lily insists on adding typos just to make Helena seem more rattled, and Helena's way too tired to argue. After starting the autoclean cycle for the printheads, they set an alarm and flop on Helena's mattress for a nap.

As Helena's drifting off, something occurs to her. "Lily? What happened to those people? The ones who tried to blackmail you?"

"Oh," Lily says casually. "I crushed them."

THE BRIEF SPECIFIES that the completed prints need to be loaded into four separate podcars on the morning of 8 August, and provides the delivery code for each. They haven't been able to find anything in Helena's iKontakt archives, so their best bet is finding a darknet user who can do a trace.

Lily's fingers hover over the touchpad. "If we give him the codes, this guy can check the prebooked delivery routes. He seems pretty reliable, do you want to pay the bounty?"

"Do it," Helena says.

The resultant map file is a mess of meandering lines. They flow across most of Nanjing, criss-crossing each other, but eventually they all terminate at the cargo entrance of the Grand Domaine Luxury Hotel on Jiangdong Middle Road.

"Well, he's probably not a guest who's going to eat two hundred steaks on his own." Lily taps her screen. "Maybe it's for a hotel restaurant?"

Helena pulls up the Grand Domaine's web directory, setting her iKontakt to highlight any mentions of restaurants or food in the descriptions. For some irritating design reason, all the booking details are stored in garish images. She snatches the entire August folder, flipping through them one by one before pausing.

The foreground of the image isn't anything special, just elaborate cursive English stating that Charlie Zhang and Cherry Cai Si Ping will be celebrating their wedding with a ten-course dinner on August 8th at the Royal Ballroom of the Grand Domaine Luxury Hotel.

What catches her eye is the background. It's red with swirls and streaks of yellow-gold. Typical auspicious wedding colours, but displayed in a very familiar pattern.

It's the marbled pattern of T-bone steak.

*   *   *

CHERRY CAI SI PING is the daughter of Dominic Cai Yongjing, a specialist in livestock and a new player in Nanjing's agri-food arena. According to Lily's extensive knowledge of farming documentaries, Dominic Cai Yongjing is also "the guy with the eyebrows" and "that really boring guy who keeps talking about nothing".

"Most people have eyebrows," Helena says, loading one of Lily's recommended documentaries. "I don't see... oh. Wow."

"I *told* you. I mean, I usually like watching stuff about farming, but last year he just started showing up everywhere with his stupid waggly brows! When I watched this with my ex we just made fun of him non-stop."

Helena fast-forwards through the introduction of *Modern Manufacturing: The Vertical Farmer*, which involves the camera panning upwards through hundreds of vertically-stacked wire cages. Dominic Cai talks to the host in English, boasting about how he plans to be a key figure in China's domestic beef industry. He explains his "patented methods" for a couple of minutes, which involves stating and restating that his farm is extremely clean and filled with only the best cattle.

"But what about bovine parasitic cancer?" the host asks. "Isn't the risk greater in such a cramped space? If the government orders a quarantine, your whole farm..."

"As I've said, our hygiene standards are impeccable, and our stock is pure-bred Hereford!" Cai slaps the flank of a cow through the cage bars, and it moos irritatedly in response. "There is absolutely no way it could happen here!"

Helena does some mental calculations. Aired last year, when the farm recently opened, and that cow looks around six months old... and now a request for steaks from cows that are sixteen to eighteen months old...

"So," Lily says, leaning on the back of Helena's chair. "Bovine parasitic cancer?"

"Judging by the timing, it probably hit them last month. It's usually the older cows that get infected first. He'd have killed them to stop the spread... but if it's the internal strain, the tumours would have made their meat unusable after excision. His first batch of cows was probably meant to be for the wedding dinner. What we're printing is the cover-up."

"But it's not like steak's a standard course in wedding dinners or anything, right? Can't they just change it to roast duck or abalone or something?" Lily looks fairly puzzled, probably because she hasn't been subjected to as many weddings as Helena has.

"Mr Cai's the one bankrolling it, so it's a staging ground for the Cai family to show how much better they are than everyone else. You saw the announcement—he's probably been bragging to all his guests about how they'll be the first to taste beef from his vertical farm. Changing it now would be a real loss of face."

"Okay," Lily says. "I have a bunch of ideas, but first of all, how much do you care about this guy's face?"

Helena thinks back to her inbox full of corpse pictures, the countless sleepless nights she's endured, the sheer terror she felt when she saw Lily step through the door. "Not very much at all."

"All right." Lily smacks her fist into her palm. "Let's give him a nice surprise."

THE WEEK BEFORE the deadline vanishes in a blur of printing, re-rendering, and darknet job requests. Helena's been nothing but polite to Mr Cai ever since the hitter's visit, and has even taken to video calls lately, turning on the camera on her end so that Mr Cai can witness her progress. It's always good to build rapport with clients.

"So, sir," Helena moves the camera, slowly panning so it captures the piles and piles of cherry-red steaks, zooming in on the beautiful fat strata which took ages to render. "How does this look? We'll be starting the dry-aging once you approve, and loading it into the podcars first thing tomorrow morning."

"Fairly adequate. I didn't expect much from the likes of you, but this seems satisfactory. Go ahead."

Helena tries her hardest to keep calm. "I'm glad you feel that way, sir. Rest assured you'll be getting your delivery on schedule... by the way, I don't suppose you could transfer the money on delivery? Printing the bone matter cost a lot more than I thought."

"Of course, of course, once it's delivered and I inspect the marbling. Quality checks, you know?"

Helena adjusts the camera, zooming in on the myoglobin dripping from the juicy steaks, and adopts her most sorrowful tone. "Well, I hate to rush you, but I haven't had much money for food lately..."

Mr Cai chortles. "Why, that's got to be hard on you! You'll receive the fund transfer sometime this month, and in the meantime why don't you treat yourself and print up something nice to eat?"

Lily gives Helena a thumbs-up, then resumes crouching under the table and messaging her darknet contacts, careful to stay out of Helena's shot. The call disconnects.

"Let's assume we won't get any further payment. Is everything ready?"

"Yeah," Lily says. "When do we need to drop it off?"

"Let's try for five am. Time to start batch-processing."

Helena sets the enzyme percentages, loads the fluid into the canister, and they both haul the steaks into the dry-ager unit. The machine hums away, spraying fine mists of enzymatic fluid onto the steaks and partially dehydrating them, while Helena and Lily work on assembling the refrigerated delivery boxes. Once everything's neatly packed, they haul the boxes to the nearest podcar station. As Helena slams box after box into the cargo area of the podcars, Lily types the delivery codes into their front panels. The podcars boot up, sealing themselves shut, and zoom off on their circuitous route to the Grand Domaine Luxury Hotel.

They head back to the industrial park. Most of their things have already been shoved into backpacks, and Helena begins breaking the remaining equipment down for transport.

A Sculpere 9410S takes twenty minutes to disassemble if you're doing it for the second time. If someone's there to help you manually eject the cell cartridges, slide the external casing off, and detach the print heads so you can disassemble the power unit, you might be able to get that figure down to ten. They'll buy a new printer once they figure out where to settle down, but this one will do for now.

It's not running away if we're both going somewhere, Helena thinks to herself, and this time it doesn't feel like a lie.

*   *   *

THERE AREN'T MANY visitors to Mr Chan's restaurant during breakfast hours, and he's sitting in a corner, reading a book. Helena waves at him.

"Helena!" he booms, surging up to greet her. "Long time no see, and who is this?"

"Oh, we met recently. She's helped me out a lot," Helena says, judiciously avoiding any mention of Lily's name. She holds a finger to her lips, and surprisingly, Mr Chan seems to catch on. Lily waves at Mr Chan, then proceeds to wander around the restaurant, examining their collection of porcelain plates.

"Anyway, since you're my very first client, I thought I'd let you know in person. I'm going travelling with my... friend, and I won't be around for the next few months at least."

"Oh, that's certainly a shame! I was planning a black pepper hotplate beef special next month, but I suppose black pepper hotplate extruded protein will do just fine. When do you think you'll be coming back?"

Helena looks at Mr Chan's guileless face, and thinks, well, her first client deserves a bit more honesty. "Actually, I probably won't be running the business any longer. I haven't decided yet, but I think I'm going to study art. I'm really, really sorry for the inconvenience, Mr Chan."

"No, no, pursuing your dreams, well, that's not something you should be apologising for! I'm just glad you finally found a friend!"

Helena glances over at Lily, who's currently stuffing a container of cellulose toothpicks into the side pocket of her bulging backpack.

"Yeah, I'm glad too," she says. "I'm sorry, Mr Chan, but we have a flight to catch in a couple of hours, and the bus is leaving soon..."

"Nonsense! I'll pay for your taxi fare, and I'll give you something for the road. Airplane food is awful these days!"

Despite repeatedly declining Mr Chan's very generous offers, somehow Helena and Lily end up toting bags and bags of fresh steamed buns to their taxi.

"Oh, did you see the news?" Mr Chan asks. "That vertical farmer's daughter is getting married at some fancy hotel tonight. Quite a pretty girl, good thing she didn't inherit those eyebrows—"

Lily snorts and accidentally chokes on her steamed bun. Helena claps her on the back.

"—and they're serving steak at the banquet, straight from his farm! Now, don't get me wrong, Helena, you're talented at what you do—but a good old-fashioned slab of *real* meat, now, that's the ticket!"

"Yes," Helena says. "It certainly is."

ALL KNOWN FORGERIES are failures, but sometimes that's on purpose. Sometimes a forger decides to get revenge by planting obvious flaws in their work, then waiting for them to be revealed, making a fool of everyone who initially claimed the work was authentic. These flaws can take many forms— deliberate anachronisms, misspelled signatures, rude messages hidden beneath thick coats of paint—or a picture of a happy cow, surrounded by little hearts, etched into the T-bone of two hundred perfectly-printed steaks.

While the known forgers are the famous ones, the *best* forgers are the ones that don't get caught—the old woman selling her deceased husband's collection to an avaricious art collector, the harried-looking mother handing the cashier a battered 50-yuan note, or the two women at the airport, laughing as they collect their luggage, disappearing into the crowd.

CARNIVAL NINE
Caroline M. Yoachim

Caroline M. Yoachim (carolineyoachim.com) lives in Seattle and loves cold cloudy weather. She is the author of dozens of short stories, appearing in *Fantasy & Science Fiction, Clarkesworld, Asimov's,* and *Lightspeed,* among other places, including Nebula Award nominees "Stone Wall Truth" and "Welcome to the Medical Clinic at the Interplanetary Relay Station | Hours Since the Last Patient Death: 0". Her debut short story collection, *Seven Wonders of a Once and Future World & Other Stories,* came out with Fairwood Press in August 2016.

ONE NIGHT, WHEN I was winding down to sleep, I asked Papa, "How come I don't get the same number of turns every day?"

"Sometimes the maker turns your key more, and sometimes less, but you can never have more than your mainspring will hold. You're lucky, Zee, you have a good mainspring." He sounded a little wistful when he said it. He never got as many turns as I did, and he used most of them to do boring grown-up things.

"Take me to the zoo tomorrow?" The zoo on the far side of the closet had lions that did backflips and elephants that balanced on brightly colored balls.

"I have to take Granny and Gramps to the mechanic to clean the rust off their gears."

Papa never had any turns to spare for outings and adventures, which was sad. I opened my mouth to say so, but the whir of my gears slowed to where I could hear each click, and I closed my mouth so it wouldn't hang open while I slept.

*   *   *

WHAT PAPA SAID was true. I have a good mainspring. Sometimes I got thirty turns, and sometimes forty-six. Today, on this glorious summer day, I got fifty-two. I'd never met anyone else whose spring could hold so many turns as that, and I was bursting with energy.

Papa didn't notice how wound up I was. "Granny has a tune-up this morning, and Gramps is getting a new mustache. If you untangle the thread for me, you can use the rest of your turns to play."

"But—"

"Always work first, so you don't run out of turns." His legs were stiff and he swayed as he walked along the wide wood plank that led out from our closet. He crossed the train tracks and disappeared into the shadow of the maker's workbench. Tonight, when he came back from his errands, he'd bring a scrap of fabric or a bit of thread. Papa sewed our clothes from whatever scraps the maker dropped.

The whir of his gears faded into silence, and I tried to untangle the thread. It was a tedious chore. The delicate motion of picking up a single brightly-colored strand was difficult on a tight spring. A train came clacking along the track, and with it the lively music of the carnival. Papa had settled down here in Closet City, but Mama was a carnie. Based on the stories Papa told, sneaking out to the carnival would be a good adventure. Clearly I was meant to go—the carnival had arrived on a day when I had more turns than I'd ever had before. I gathered up my prettiest buttons and skipped over to the brightly painted train cars.

It was early, and the carnival had just arrived, but a crowd had already formed. Everyone clicked and whirred as they hurried to see the show. The carnies were busy too, unfolding train cars into platforms and putting up rides and games and ropes for the acrobats.

I passed a booth selling scented gear oil and another filled with ornate keys. I wondered if the maker could wind as well with those as with the simple silver one that protruded from my back. A face-painter with an extra pair of arms was painting two different customers at once, touching up the faded paint of their facial features and adding festive swirls of green and blue and purple. "Two kinds of paint," the painter called to me, "the swirls will wash right off with soap."

It was meant to be a reassurance, but it backfired—the trip from the closet to the bathroom took seven turns each way, so soap was hard to come by. Papa would be angry if I came home painted.

"Catch two matching fish and win a prize!" a carnie called. He was an odd assemblage of parts, with one small brown arm and one bulky white one. His legs were slightly different lengths, and his ceramic face was crisscrossed with scratch marks. He held out a long pole with a tiny net on the end, a net barely big enough to hold a single fish.

"Don't they all match?" I leaned over the tub of water to study the orange fish. They buzzed quietly and some mechanism propelled them forward and sent out streams of bubbles behind them.

The man dipped the net into the water and caught one of the fish. He flipped open a panel on its belly, and revealed a number—four. "The fish are numbered one through ten, and you'll get to pick three. Any two of 'em match and you win!"

I eyed the prizes—an assortment of miniature animals, mostly cats, all with tiny golden keys. Keys so small that even I could turn them, so there'd be no need to wait each night for the maker to wind them up.

"Take these buttons in trade?"

The man laughed. "No, but if you didn't buy any tickets I'll let you work for a play—a turn for a turn, as they say."

Unlike Papa, he could see how tight I was wound, and he put me to work hauling boxes from his platform to a car on the far end of the train. The work was satisfying, and it let me gawk at the rest of the carnival. When I was done, he handed me the net. "Any three fish that catch your fancy. Good luck!"

The net was long and hard to handle, but I dipped it into the water. It came up empty and dripping. Fishing was not as easy as the man had made it look. I tried again, and this time brought up a fish that whirred loudly as it came out of the water. The man pushed in a pin to stop the gears and flipped open a panel to reveal the number 8.

My next two fish were numbered 3 and 4.

"Do *any* of them match?" I handed back the net, frowning and studying the pool. There were easily a hundred fish. "I guess with so many they must."

"You have to look closer at the fish." A freckle-faced kid climbed up onto the platform. He scooped up a fish, checked the number on the bottom, then studied the pond. "This one's a six, so I just have to find a match."

With a smooth practiced motion he dipped the net back in, and pulled out another fish. He showed me the number on the bottom—another six.

"How did you—"

"One of the 6s has a busted tail, swims in circles."

"But the other one, what if you'd gotten something else?"

"This one has a chip of paint missing."

"I'm Zee."

"Endivale," he said, but added quickly, "You can call me Vale. Hey Pops, okay if I take my free turns to show Zee around?"

The man running the fish game studied us for a minute, then nodded.

Vale took my hand, "Come on, you gotta hear the nightingale sing, she's amazing."

So off we went. The nightingale turned out to be a woman with brown-feathered wings that matched her dark skin. Vale wasn't lying. She sang beautifully, any song that the crowd shouted to her.

For twelve turns we explored the carnival—we watched the acrobats, and lost the ring-toss game, and rode on the backs of the dancing bears. Then Vale had to stop, because he didn't have so many turns as me.

"You seem to know everyone at the carnival," I said, when we sat down on the edge of an empty platform. "Do you know my mother? She's very distinctive—a woman with eight spider legs."

"Oh, I've heard of her—Lady Arachna, right? She's Carnival Four."

"Carnival Four?"

Vale gestured down at the platform below us. "You can't see it with the platforms folded down, but the train cars are numbered so they stay matched up. All the cars in this train are marked nine, so we're Carnival Nine. Pops and I are here because they had an empty platform for him to run his game. My other dad is at Carnival Two because he's an acrobat, and Nine already has more acrobats than we really need."

"So you never see him?"

"There's only one track through here, but the trains run the whole house, with cities along the route where we stop and entertain folks. Some places there are clusters of tracks where the trains pass each other, or turn around. I've seen him a couple times."

We talked a bit more, and he snuck me in to see the bearded lady and a snake man whose skin was covered in iridescent green scales. The carnival was amazing, and I never wanted to leave, but I could feel the tension leaving my spring. I only had a few turns left, barely enough to get home. "I have to go."

"I'm almost out of turns anyway."

I hopped down from the platform. Vale put his hand on my shoulder. "I lied about some of the fish looking different. There's no missing paint or broken tails. The fish have more than one number, depending on which way you open the panels. Don't tell Pops I told you."

Something passed between us then, in that moment where he trusted me. Somehow it meant more than all the marvels I'd seen. It didn't even occur to me to get angry that the game was rigged until I was more than halfway home.

"You didn't untangle the thread," Papa said when I came in.

The multicolored jumble of thread was on the table where I'd left it.

"I had so much energy, and the train brought the carnival—"

"Go to bed, Zee. We're out of turns."

I SPENT MY days untangling threads and learned to sew scraps of fabric into clothes. On my 200th day, Papa took me into town and we swapped out my child-sized limbs for adult ones, and repainted my face. Trains came and went, but I never had enough extra turns to visit the carnival. Then one morning Papa came back from the city early, pulling a wheeled cart. "What happened?"

"Granny and Gramps wound all the way down."

"But the maker can wind them again tonight, and—"

Papa shook his head. "No, there comes a time when our bodies cannot hold the turns. We all get our thousand days, give or take a few. Then we wind down for the last time. It is the way of things."

I knew we didn't go on forever, because some of my friends were made of parts from the Closet City recycling center. The recycling center melted down old parts to make new ones. So, I knew. But at the same time I'd never known anyone who was broken down for parts before. Granny had painted my face and Gramps always told the best stories about the maker.

"I wish I could have visited them before they wound down."

"I didn't know they'd go today. They were only in their early 900s."

"Are you going to take them to the recycling center?"

He shook his head. "The recycling center is well stocked, but the carnivals are often hurting for parts. When the next train comes, we'll take them there."

I knew it wasn't right to be excited on the day that Granny and Gramps died, but while I waited to wind down and sleep, I couldn't help but imagine all the marvels we would see.

THE NEXT TRAIN turned out to be number nine. I was a little disappointed because I'd already seen most of Carnival Nine, but then I remembered Vale and how he'd shared the secret trick with the fish. I didn't see him as I followed Papa to the platform at the front of the train, or while we laid Granny and Gramps out on the red-painted wood. One of the carnival mechanics knelt next to Granny, and Papa leaned over and whispered, "I'm going to stay to watch them disassembled, but you don't have to. You did your turns helping me pull the cart to get them here."

The mechanic peeled away the fabric that covered Granny's torso and unscrewed her metal chest plate. I wanted to remember her whole, not in tiny pieces. I squeezed Papa's hand, then let go and walked along the length of the carnival.

Vale found me about halfway down the train. He had swapped out his childhood limbs too, and when they repainted his face they'd gotten rid of his freckles. His hair was darker now, which suited him. He put his hand on my shoulder. "Sorry about your grandparents."

"How did you—"

He shrugged. "Pops saw you come in. He said I could have some turns off, if you want to watch the acrobats."

There was a mischievous gleam in his eyes when he said it, and it sounded like a grand adventure. Vale took me to a huge green-and-white striped tent next to the train tracks and we held hands and watched as acrobats walked tightropes and leapt between swings suspended high above the ground.

I loved the show, but halfway through Vale stopped watching.

"Seen this show too many times?" I asked.

"No. Well, yeah, but mostly it reminds me of my dad. Pops is great, but we don't always get along so well. He wants me to take over the fish someday, but I hate that the whole thing is a cheat."

I wouldn't have minded staying for the rest of the show, but I didn't want him to be sad. We snuck out and headed back to the train. "Can you switch carnivals?"

"I'm not built to be an acrobat like Dad. My parts aren't that good. Really all I'm built for is running a game, and if I'm going to do that, I might as well stay here."

"You could leave the carnival and stay in Closet City," I said, suddenly aware that we were still holding hands. "It's... Well, it's terribly boring actually."

He laughed. It was getting late and he was nearly out of turns. "I was thinking I might come up with a different game, one that's hard, but doesn't involve any cheats."

I couldn't quite keep the disappointment off my face. I almost wished I hadn't said anything about Closet City being boring, but it was the complete truth. "Yeah, I guess it'd be hard to give up the adventure of the carnival to stay in a place like this."

He pulled me closer and spoke softly in my ear, "Why don't you come with me when the carnival moves on?"

Papa could take care of himself, and I was old enough to go. I told him on our walk home, and the next morning I packed up my things and said goodbye. It was a sudden shift, an abrupt departure, but Papa understood that I had always been restless. He loved me enough to let me go. When the carnival moved on, I went with it. With Vale.

FIVE TRAINS WERE at the grand junction when we arrived, and Vale helped me find Carnival Four so that I could look for my mother. He would have stayed, but Carnival Two was at the junction as well, and I told him to go and visit with his dad. Vale and I would have plenty of time together later, and I wanted some time alone with my mother. I hadn't seen her since I was new.

She was easy to find, her train car clearly labeled 'the amazing spider-woman,' with pictures of her painted large on the side of the car. I knocked on the door and she slid it open, staring down at me and tapping one of her forelegs. "Yes?"

My gears whirred tight in my chest. She didn't recognize me, and why would she? My limbs were different, my face was repainted. She had left a child, and I was a woman now. "I'm Zee. I came with Carnival Nine, and I wanted... well, to see you, I guess."

"Oh, my daughter, Zee." Her foreleg went still, and she tilted her head, studying me. "What is it you do with Carnival Nine?"

"Vale is teaching me to run one of the games," I admitted, knowing that it was one of the lowest jobs in the carnival. Being an acrobat or a performer required more skill, but the games were mostly con jobs. Nearly anyone could do it, with enough practice.

Mother didn't say anything, and the silence stretched long and awkward between us.

"Papa is still in Closet City," I told her, more to fill the silence than anything. "We lost Granny and Gramps, a few weeks back." I tried to think of more news from Closet City, but since mother had stayed with the train she probably wouldn't know most of the people I'd grown up with. It was a strange feeling, my strong desire to bond with someone who was a complete stranger. In my mind, the meeting had gone differently. She had loved me simply because I was her daughter, and we'd had an instant connection.

"I'm sorry to hear they've wound down." She paused for a moment. "Look, I'm really not the maternal sort—it's why Lars took you to Closet City to raise you. I'm—well—I'm not very nice. I'm selfish. I like to use my turns for myself, and I never spared a lot of turns for my relationship with Lars. Certainly I never had enough for you."

I didn't know what to say to that. I wanted to be angry with her, but she was a stranger, she'd never really been a part of my life. That was how things were and I was used to it. Mostly I was disappointed. Sad that my dreams about reuniting with my mother had died. We talked a little longer about nothing of importance, and then I went back to Carnival Nine, home to Vale. I vowed that I wouldn't be like my mother. I was blessed with a lot of turns, and I would use them for more than just myself.

* * *

THE TRAIN TOOK us in slow circles, stopping to perform at the cities. I settled into the routine of carnival life—collapsing the walls of our train car to make our platform, setting up the dart game that Vale designed, packing everything away again when it was time to move along. The days blurred one into the next, obscuring the passage of time. Then one day I realized that I was over 400 days old, which meant that I had been with the carnival longer than I'd lived in Closet City.

I wasn't old yet, but I was no longer young.

"You sure you're ready to do this?" Vale took me to the front car where all the parts were.

I nodded. Our train's next stop was the maker's workbench; this was the right time for us to make our child.

He started picking through the gears, laying out everything we'd need to build a child. "My half-sister has these great pincers, like lobster claws—"

"I thought maybe he could look more like us." Carnies came with a wide variety of parts, which was fun for shows, but the more outlandish ones all reminded me of my mother. "Hands would be more versatile if we ever settle down in a city. What if he doesn't want to be a performer?"

Vale frowned. "He could change his parts, I suppose. But what happened to your sense of adventure?"

When I'd lived in Closet City, the carnival had been exciting for the brief time it had stayed. But being a part of the carnival—well, the obligations of life and livelihood sucked away the wonder. It was the novelty that had drawn me here, and half a lifetime later the novelty had worn away. But I couldn't bring myself to say so to Vale.

"So if he wants pincers when he's older, he can swap out his limbs that way too." I kept my voice calm, but worry gnawed at me. We had agreed on building a boy, but we hadn't talked much about the details. I rummaged through the pile until I found an arm, dark-skinned like the nightingale lady, but smaller, child-sized. It didn't have a match, but there was another that was only slightly paler. Would anyone notice? Probably someone had already taken the other half of each set. "What about these?"

"Okay." He was less enthusiastic now, and I felt bad that I'd shot down his first suggestion so quickly. I looked for parts that would be a compromise, interesting enough for him, but nothing as extreme as my mother's spider legs. Nothing that would evoke memories of a woman who thought it'd be a waste of turns to raise me.

We worked quietly for a while, the silence awkward. Finally he pulled out a face, an ordinary shape but painted with streaks of black and white. He held it up. I hated it, but it was only paint. Paint could easily be removed and redone, later. It was less work than swapping out parts. The structure of the face underneath was good. I nodded. It broke the tension.

"Dad said there might be a place for us at Carnival Two, working the show with the dancing bears." He kept his gaze firmly on our son, focusing his attention on attaching the black-and-white streaked head to the still-empty torso. "It'd be a step up from running a dart game, a better position for our son."

Thinking about our son working a show at the carnival made me remember my own childhood. I had always wanted adventure, but now dancing bears seemed more dangerous than glamorous. Life on the tracks was harder, even for me with all my turns. Carnival folk almost never made it to a thousand days. Their springs gave out when people were in their 800s, sometimes even sooner. "I want what's best for him."

Vale took my hand and smiled. "Me too."

The train took us to the maker's bench, and we laid out our son's body, chest open. Tonight the maker would give him a mainspring and wind him for the very first time.

"Should we name him now, or after we've gotten to know him?" My parents had waited to name me until my second day, because they wanted to be sure the name would fit.

"It's good luck to name him before he goes to the maker. He'll get a better spring that way," Vale answered. "What about Matts? That was my grandad's name."

I thought about my Grandad, and all the stories he'd told about the maker. "My grandad was Ettan. What about Mattan? We could still call him Matts for short."

Vale nodded, slowly, his spring winding down. "I like that."

*   *   *

THE MAKER GAVE me forty-three turns the day that I met my child. My darling Mattan got only four. Something was wrong with his mainspring. I was definitely no mechanic, but I could hear it, a strained and creaking noise like metal bending to its breaking point. What could you do with four turns? How could I teach him the world if that was all he had to work with?

I picked up my son and carried him to meet Vale. My mind churned with worry for my son's future and guilt at having more than my share of turns, but at the same time I was grateful to be wound up enough for everything that needed to be done. I saved Mattan a turn of walking by using an extra one of mine to carry him, and he could see the world that way. Light from the ceiling reflected off the white stripes across his face, and I admired the contrast against the black. I had been too hasty in condemning Vale's choice, it was unusual, but striking.

"This is your father, Vale," I told Mattan. He nodded happily but made no attempt to speak. The mechanics of speech were complex and used more turns than a simple nod. Even now, newly made, he was aware of his limitations. It made sense, I suppose. I'd always been able to feel how tightly wound my spring was, even when I was young.

"Why are you carrying him?"

I showed Vale the mechanical counter above our son's key. There were two dials of numbers, enough to show two digits, which made Mattan's tiny number of turns seem even smaller, if such a thing was possible. "He only has four turns."

Vale put his hand out, not to take Mattan but to rest it on my shoulder. "So few?"

"I'll make my turns stretch to cover both of us," I promised. "We'll make the best of it."

And I kept my promise. I made a sling and carried Mattan on my back as I ran my dart game and did our errands, and tried to show him some of the fun and adventure I had so desperately wanted in my childhood.

It was too much, even for me. On Mattan's third day I wound down in the afternoon, right in the middle of my shift working the darts. Vale took Mattan home in his sling, but he didn't have the turns to carry me to bed, so I stood there, right where I stopped, and the carnival-goers clustered around me, gawking. A grown woman, wound down in public like a child who had not learned to pace herself.

At the end of Mattan's first week, our train was at the junction, and Mattan spoke for the first time. "I want to see the acrobats."

Vale had gone out that morning to spend a few turns with his dad. I was supposed to repair the dartboard, covered in painted bulls-eye targets. It had cracked, and we needed it for our game, but Mattan had never asked for anything before. He'd heard Vale talking about his dad and the acrobatics he did for his show. I didn't have the turns, but he had made the effort to ask, and I didn't have the heart to tell him no. I carried him to Carnival Two, and we watched the acrobats practice their trapeze act.

We didn't see Vale in the audience, and his father wasn't practicing with the others. We sat as still as we could and watched, saving our turns for the trip back to train nine. Vale was already there when we returned. He stared at the broken dartboard. It reminded me of the day I'd left the tangled threads, and Papa had chastised me for not doing my work first.

"Mattan asked to see the acrobats," I said. "He spoke for the first time. He's never asked for anything, and I couldn't tell him no."

"Mattan doesn't have the turns for these things," Vale said. His voice was cold, angry. "You don't have the turns for this either. You have to pull your weight with the carnival if you want to stay. You know that."

"And what about our son?" I demanded. "He can't fix dartboards or run carnival games, but that doesn't mean he has nothing to contribute."

Vale shook his head. "Maybe not, but he can't pull his own weight, and he's cost us the chance to move to Carnival Two. They might have taken *us*, but they refuse to take Mattan."

It was only then I realized that for all this first week, Vale had never once called him Matts. This was not the child he wanted, and he was refusing to bond with him, trying to protect himself from the hurt. Or maybe he was simply being selfish, unwilling to use his turns on his own child. He was certainly disappointed at losing his chance to move to Carnival Two.

The train made its slow circuit from the Attic City to the brightly painted Children's Room and down the long hallway to Closet City, and I used my turns to help Mattan get through his days. When the train stopped in the shadow of the maker's bench—the place where I'd grown up—I left the carnival and took Mattan with me. Vale didn't argue; he was relieved to see us go.

PAPA WAS DELIGHTED to see me, and to meet Mattan, and he welcomed us into his home. I began to fill the role that had once been his—taking him to get his gears tuned or his paint retouched—and everywhere we went I carried Mattan. I had turns enough to care for Papa and Mattan both, so long as I did nothing else. I tried not to think of adventure, or freedom, or even the future. If I kept my focus on the present moment, I could do everything that needed to be done, but only barely.

There weren't any trains at Closet City on Mattan's 200th day.

"We can wait for a carnival to come, or we can get your adult-sized limbs from the recycling center," I told Mattan. We'd talked about both options beforehand, a conversation that had spanned several days because he couldn't always spare the turns to ask questions.

"I want to go today," Mattan answered immediately. There was a good selection of parts at the recycling center, and he didn't want to be a performer, so it made sense to get parts here in town... but I think Mattan also knew that getting new limbs would be an exhausting day for both of us, and he didn't want to make it even harder by adding the long walk out to the tracks of the carnival trains.

Being at the recycling center reminded me of the day Vale and I built Mattan, although here the parts were organized neatly on shelves, not piled high in a disorganized heap on the floor of a train car. These parts were more uniform. There were no spider legs or pincers, and while the faces were painted with a wide variety of features, there were none with bright garish colors or distinctive patterns. None that looked at all like Mattan.

"I'll hold up limbs one at a time," I told him. "When you see something you want, nod."

Mattan sat perfectly still, his painted-black stripes cutting across his face like harsh shadows. He had three turns today, enough for us to do everything we needed if we were careful.

I moved around the room, holding up arms and legs for him to see.

The limbs he picked were neither the biggest nor the smallest, painted the same deep brown as his child-sized arms. I brought them over. Mattan's fingers curled, a movement that mimicked the way he squeezed my shoulder when he was excited, but before I could attach the new limbs he asked, "Will these be too heavy?"

The question broke my heart. Yes, these limbs were heavy. All the added weight meant that it would take more turns to carry him. I had selfishly hoped he would choose smaller limbs, but they were his limbs, and this was his choice. "These are beautiful, and I have a lot of turns. I can still carry you."

It was the right thing to say, and Mattan was so happy with his new limbs, but when I carried him home from the recycling center his weight stole the tension from my mainspring more quickly than before. We lived by our turns, and my son—now fully grown—couldn't spare enough to walk across town. I was furious that the world was so unfair, and my heart broke thinking of all the things he didn't have the turns to do. But if I was being honest, my heart also broke for me. Vale had abandoned us and Papa was old, so I would be the one to carry Mattan everywhere, always.

That thought was in my mind when Carnival Nine came to town, an ever-present weight that I could not shake away. My love was endless, but my strength was not, and I longed to escape the unrelenting effort of taking care of Papa and Mattan on my own. I wanted to see Vale, to have some turns all to myself, to do exactly as I pleased for once.

I didn't wake Papa or Mattan. I left them in their beds—did not ask permission to go out or even explain what I was doing, simply left and walked to the trains. They wouldn't be able to do much today, without my help, but between the two of them they'd be able to manage.

"It's good to see you," Vale said when I arrived. "Where's Mattan?"

"With my father." I didn't know what to say after that. I'd wanted to see Vale, but what could I really talk about with someone who wouldn't help raise his own son? He was like my mother, too selfish to share his turns. And here I was, at the carnival, wasting my turns on a foolish whim instead of taking care of my child. "I shouldn't have come."

Vale frowned. "I owe you an apology. I didn't... I mean, I wasn't prepared for how things went, and you've always had more turns, so it seemed to make sense for you to take him. I've missed you."

"It's been lonely. Difficult." I admitted. Once I started, the words came pouring out. In Closet City I'd felt like there was no one I could talk to— Papa had always been so good at taking care of everyone around him, so responsible, there was no way I could complain to him. But I could pour everything out to Vale. If nothing else, at least he would understand my selfishness. "I have the turns to give Mattan a good life, but only if I never do anything for myself. I take care of Papa, I try to let Mattan see some of the world, and it is so rewarding but I want something for me, some little bit of the adventure I was always chasing as a child."

"You're here today," Vale said. He took my hand. "Let's have an adventure."

And we did. It was like seeing the carnival for the first time, the animals and the acrobats and the games. Vale was kind and attentive and we planned out possible futures and talked about the time we'd spent apart. It would have been a beautiful day if not for the constant gnawing guilt of having left Mattan and Papa behind. The worst was that I hadn't even told them. I had been so sure that I did not deserve time for myself that I had made things even worse by stealing the time instead of asking for it.

"This was nice," I said, painfully aware that I needed to leave soon if I wanted to have enough turns to get back home. Despite the guilt, it had been reinvigorating to have the break. "Maybe tomorrow I could come back with Mattan? I think he would love to see you."

Vale hesitated, then nodded. "I would like that."

I walked home, and I was nearly out of turns by the time I walked in the door. Papa was in bed, but Mattan was up, sitting perfectly still at the table, obviously saving a turn to tell me something. I walked directly in front of him, so he wouldn't have to turn his head.

His eyes met mine, and he said, "Grandpa never woke up today."

IT HAD ALWAYS been Papa's wish to have his body taken to a carnival when he wound all the way down, so I rented a cart and pulled him to the train, all while carrying Mattan. The work was hard, and I wouldn't have the turns to get us back home today.

I unloaded Papa into the same train car where he had once unloaded

Granny and Gramps, the car where Vale and I had later assembled Mattan. I stayed while they took Papa apart, by his side now when it didn't matter, instead of yesterday when it might have. No. It wasn't Papa I had abandoned yesterday; Papa had never woken up. He would never know. It was my Mattan who had spent the entire day alone, knowing that Papa was gone, having no way to call for help or do much of anything at all but wait for my return. And now he waited again, resting in the sling on my back as Orna, one of our train's mechanics, carefully opened Papa's chest and removed the gears, sorting them into bins as she worked. Her movements were practiced and efficient, she wasted no turns. All too soon Papa was gone, nothing but a pile of parts.

"Thank you," I told Mattan as we left to find Vale. "I needed to see that."

Mattan didn't answer, saving his turns.

"I did a terrible thing yesterday," I continued. "I wouldn't have gone if I had known about Papa—I thought he would be there to help you—but I shouldn't have done it even so. I'm sorry."

"You can't do everything, always," Mattan said, choosing his words carefully, not wasting more of his turns than was absolutely necessary. "I forgive you."

"Some good might even come of it—I asked Vale yesterday if he wanted to see you, and he said yes."

Mattan squeezed my shoulder ever so slightly through the fabric of the sling, a sign of his excitement at seeing his father. I carried him to the train car with Vale's dart game set up for anyone who had the tickets to play.

Vale studied us for a time, saying nothing. Was he noticing that I still carried our son, even now that he was an adult? Or was he simply studying the black-and-white striped face he hadn't seen for hundreds of days? My guilt was for a single day, a single slip. What did he feel, abandoning us for most of his son's life?

"Say something," I said. "Mattan has to save his turns, so he doesn't talk much, but he is so excited to finally see you again."

"Mattan," Vale began. He shook his head and started over. "Matts. I know I haven't been a father to you, but I'm ready to help now, if you want me to. Join me on the train?"

The question was for both us, Mattan and me. I had no tie to Closet City now that Papa was gone, and with Vale's help we would have enough turns for a better life for all of us. I wavered, undecided, the weight of Mattan pressing down on my back. He didn't speak, waiting for my decision. Would Vale really help take care of our child, or would he go back on this promise?

Vale had called our son Matts. His heart was in the right place.

"Yes," I answered. "We'll join you on the train."

Mattan squeezed my shoulder, pleased with the decision. I was excited that we might be able to be a family again, but another thought haunted me, something that had been eating at the edges of my mind—what would happen to Mattan when I wound down? For hundreds of days I'd pushed this thought from my mind—I was healthy and full of turns, and Mattan, well his mainspring was bad. I had convinced myself I would outlast him.

Day after day Vale took nearly even turns with me, carrying Mattan on his back as he worked our game or hauled boxes of prizes to and from our platform. I used as many turns as I could spare helping all the newest additions to the carnival—always a turn for a turn, trading endlessly into the future, extracting from everyone I helped a promise to pay that turn forward to Mattan after I was gone. Was it enough? Did it erase that selfish day when I abandoned my son?

I'VE HEARD IT said that every hundred days passes faster than the previous hundred. In childhood, the days stretch out seemingly forever, and we spend our time and turns freely on any whim that catches our fancy. But at the end of our lives, each day becomes an increasingly greater fraction of the time we have remaining, and the moments grow ever more precious. A hundred days, a hundred more, time flits away as we make our slow circuit on the train.

Vale winds all the way down, hard working and supportive to the end. On his last day, he apologizes again and again for abandoning us. We've already forgiven him, but he cannot forgive himself. The other carnies start giving back the turns they borrowed from me, helping Mattan through his days. I have no turns to spare—there have never been enough turns, even for me, and I've always had more than my share.

An acrobat named Chet, a man with stripes on his arms that match the stripes on Mattan's face, comes more often than the others. I thought at first that he was trying to fulfill his obligation quickly and get it over with, but no, he lingers even when he isn't working off his borrowed turns, keeping up a constant stream of chatter, unbothered by the fact that Mattan rarely answers. Chet shares bits and pieces of his past mixed in with gossip about everyone else in Carnival Nine.

My spring is on the verge of breaking, I can feel it. The maker gave my son and me the same number of turns today. Ten turns. Fewer than I've ever had, and the most my son has ever been given. For a moment, I am filled with regret at the harsh limitations of his life. His days are already short, and his spring is so bad that he won't get the thousand days that I have gotten. He will be lucky to live another hundred days, and he is only in his 600s now. I comfort myself with the knowledge that at least he has Chet. He won't be alone.

I asked Mattan a while back what his favorite day was, his favorite memory, and he'd answered without hesitation—the day that we snuck out together to see the acrobats. So today we ignore what little work we might have done and walk to the tent where the acrobats perform, both of us side by side because I no longer have the turns to carry him. We sit perfectly still and watch the acrobats twirling and flying through the air.

I tell Mattan what Papa told me, "There comes a time when our bodies cannot hold the turns. We all get our thousand days, give or take a few."

I think back on my thousand days, on what I've done with my life. The way Papa had taken such good care of me, and how in the end I'd chosen to follow his path, and done my best for Mattan. My life has been different from the adventures I imagined as a child, but I made the most of the turns I was given, and that's all any of us can do.

EMINENCE
Karl Schroeder

Karl Schroeder (www.kschroeder.com) was born into a Mennonite community in Manitoba, Canada, in 1962. He started writing at age fourteen, following in the footsteps of A. E. van Vogt, who came from the same Mennonite community. He moved to Toronto in 1986, and became a founding member of SF Canada (he was president from 1996–97). He sold early stories to Canadian magazines, and his first novel, *The Claus Effect* (with David Nickle) appeared in 1997. His first solo novel, *Ventus*, was published in 2000, and was followed by *Permanence and Lady of Mazes*. His most recent work includes the Virga series of science fiction novels (*Sun of Suns, Queen of Candesce, Pirate Sun, The Sunless Countries*, and *Ashes of Candesce*) and hard SF space opera *Lockstep*. He also collaborated with Cory Doctorow on The *Complete Idiot's Guide to Publishing Science Fiction*. His most recent book is *The Million*, first in a new series of novella-length stories set in the 'Lockstep' universe. Schroeder lives in East Toronto with his wife and daughter.

USUALLY, NATHAN FELT his cares lift a little as he turned the car onto Yuculta Crescent. Today, he had to resist an urge to drive past, even just go home.

Nathan passed parked RVs and sports cars as he looked for an empty spot. As he walked back to a modest ochre house, he heard voices: teenagers talking about trading items in some online-game world. Nathan hesitated again. *I could still go back to the car, let Grace find out from somebody else.* The temptation was almost overwhelming.

The image was still with him from this morning, of Alicia stabbing her spoon into her coffee cup as she paced in the kitchen. "It's all our money,

Nathan! You didn't just put your savings into it; you convinced me to put mine in too. And now you tell me the bottom's falling out?"

The day couldn't get any worse after that; so Nathan started walking again.

At one time this part of town was full of white working-class families with shared values and expectations. Now, the houses were worth millions and, Grace said, nobody knew their neighbors. The two aboriginal kids sitting on the porch stared at Nathan suspiciously as he walked up.

"Is Grace here?" he asked.

"In the kitchen," said one, jabbing a thumb at the door. Nathan went inside, past a small living room that had been remade as office space. Three more teens wearing AR glasses stood in the middle of the space, poking at the air and arguing over something invisible to Nathan. Dressed normcore, in jeans and T-shirts, each also bore a card-sized sticker, like a nametag. SMILE YOU'RE ON BODYCAM. Little yellow arrows pointing to a black dot above the words: a camera. The kids on the front porch, he realized, also wore something like that.

Grace Cooper was sitting in a pool of sunlight in the kitchen, reading a tablet, her smile easy and genuine as she rose and hugged him. "How's my favorite coder?"

Nathan's stomach tightened. *Shall I just blurt it out? The currency is crashing, Grace. We're about to lose everything.* He couldn't do it, so he sat.

Nathan had known Grace for almost two years, but it was a long time since he'd had to think of her as the client. In fact, she was just the representative; the real client was an aboriginal nation known as the Musqueam who'd lived on this land for thousands of years. Small matter that they'd invited him into their community, their lives. He should have kept his distance.

A few years before he immigrated, Grace's people had won a centuries' old land claim that included a substantial chunk of downtown Vancouver. The University golf course, Pacific Spirit Park and much of the port lands south of that were now band territory. That and other settlements had finally given the indigenous peoples of the west coast a power base, and they were building on it. Until today, everyone had benefited—including Nathan.

She sat down after him. The sunlight made her lean back to put her face into shade. "Did you see the news?" she said. "Says Gwaiicoin is doing better than the Canadian dollar."

It was. He'd checked it fifteen minutes ago, and half an hour before that, and again before that. He'd been up all night watching the numbers, waiting for the change. He shrugged now, glancing away. "Well, the dollar's a fiat currency," he said neutrally. "They're all in trouble since the carbon bubble burst."

"And because they're not smart," she added triumphantly. "Thanks to you guys, we got the smartest currency on the planet."

"Yeah. It's been... quite a roller coaster." Maybe if he talked about volatility, about how most cryptocurrencies had failed... Even the first, Bitcoin, had only been able to lumber its clumsy way forward for so long. But all of them had weathered the bursting of the carbon bubble better than the dollar, the pound, or the Euro.

One of those currencies was Gwaiicoin. Nathan had first heard about it while couch-surfing in Seattle. He and six other guys had struggled to make the rent on a two-bedroom apartment while housing prices soared. The smart programmers left, hearing that living was cheap on Vancouver Island, and just west of the Alaskan Panhandle in the archipelago known as the Haida Gwaii. As Seattle priced itself out of liveability, the islands where the iconic totem poles stood suddenly became crowded with restless coders.

One result had been Gwaiicoin—and, when Nathan arrived in Vancouver, unexpected and welcome employment.

"Gwaiicoin's about to be worth a lot more," Grace was saying. "Once my recruits have added Vancouver to the Gwaii valuation."

Nathan looked through the serving window at the half-visible teens in the living room. "Recruits?"

She leaned forward, her nose stopping just short of the shaft of sunlight. "We're talking with City Council about measuring the biomass in the Musqueam, Squamish and Tsleil-Waututh parts of the city. These kids are my warriors. They're programming drones to measure the carbon."

Nathan nodded towards the street, throat dry. "Good place to start." His mind was darting about, looking for a way to bring her down gently. Then he realized what she was saying. "Wait—you want to add the local biomass to Gwaiicoin?" Unlike Bitcoin, which had value because of its miners and transaction volume, Gwaiicoin was backed by the value of the ecosystem services of its backers' territories.

She nodded enthusiastically. "Even the Inuit want to get in on it. The more biomass we all commit, the bigger our Fort Knox gets. It's brilliant."

Should have seen this coming, Nathan thought. As the dollar crashed, Gwaiicoin had soared. The government wanted it, but since the Haida were backing the currency with land that the feds had formally ceded through constitutionally binding land-claims settlements, the feds were beggars at the table.

"You know, you spent a whole day trying to convince me that a potlatch currency was crazy. Remember that?" Grace grinned at him.

"Yeah." He looked down. "Who'd have thought self-taxing money would take off?"

She sighed. "And still you call it a tax. That was the whole idea—you get eminence points for every buck that gets randomly redistributed to the other wallets."

"Yeah." Despite being a lead on the project, Nathan didn't have much eminence. He wasn't rich, so his wallet didn't automatically trim itself—but even some of Grace's poorer neighbors voluntarily put large chunks of their paychecks into redistribution every month, via the potlatch account everyone shared. Redistributed money was randomly scattered among the currency-users' wallets, and in return the contributors got... nothing, or so he'd argued. What they got was eminence, a kind of social capital, but the idea that it could ever be useful had never made sense to Nathan.

Ironically, it made sense now. If Gwaiicoin were to vanish overnight, the people who'd given it away would still have their eminence points. These were a permanent record of how much a person had contributed to the community.

And he had none.

He took one last deep breath and said, "Grace. We have a problem."

Somewhere nearby a phone rang. "Hold that thought," said Grace as she hopped up and rummaged for a phone among the papers on the counter. "Hello?"

Nathan watched the flight of emotions cross her face; they settled on anger. "I'll be there in half an hour," she said tightly, and put down the phone.

She avoided Nathan's gaze for a moment. Then she said, "Well. Jeff's been arrested."

* * *

"I'M GOING DOWNTOWN anyway," said Nathan. "I'll drop you at the station."

"I could take a driverless," she said as she hastily gathered up her stuff. "They got those new self-owned ones, too, just cruising around looking for a fare."

"They're creepy," said Nathan, and she grinned briefly, nodding. As they passed the kids in the living room, Grace said, "Lock up if you go out."

Nathan glanced back from the porch. "You know them well?"

"These ones? No. But to use this hackspace at all you gotta wear a badge." She patted her own lapel. "And the house knows what's in it, and what shouldn't go out the door."

Supposedly there was some new privacy protocol in play, but Nathan had been too immersed in Gwaiicoin protocols lately to explore the technology. The kids seemed comfortable having eyes on them all the time, but he wasn't used to it, any more than he was used to passing empty cars driving down the road.

He preferred to keep his own hands on the wheel, but as they drove now he found he was twisting his hands as if trying to strangle it. Grace didn't seem to have noticed. "Who's Jeff?" he made himself ask.

"One of the kids. He's Haida, his uncle's a carver on the Gwaii. Probably should introduce you."

"But he's been arrested...?"

"It's just harassment. You know they do that to us all the time." She glared out the window, but her expression gradually softened. "It's getting better. Gwaiicoin gives the poorest of us some money every month, and the richer the rest of us get, the more goes to them. No Department of Indian Affairs doling it out. Less harassment. It's working, Nathan!" She rolled down the window and cool air curled in, teasing her hair.

When they pulled into the police station's parking lot, Nathan hesitated. "Why don't you come in?" said Grace. "This won't take long. Then you can meet Jeff."

"All right."

Of course, it took longer than it should have. Service systems hadn't made it to the Vancouver Police Department yet; any other government office, and Grace could have called in her request or used her glasses and let the computers facilitate it. Here, she had to speak to a desk sergeant, and then they waited in the foyer with a number of other bored or frustrated-looking people. While they stood there (all the plastic chairs were full), Nathan said, "Is Jeff a carver?"

She shook her head. "That's his uncle's thing. No, Jeff's studying ecology and law, like any decent Haida these days. Today, he was supposed to be adding new sensors to the downtown mesh network."

Nathan nodded and they sat there for a while. Finally, Nathan said, "Grace. There's a problem with Gwaiicoin."

She'd been chewing her lip and staring out the window. Now she focused all her attention on him. It was quiet in the waiting room, with no TV, no distractions. Nathan squirmed under her gaze.

"There's been a Sybil attack," he went on, feeling a strange mix of relief and panic that made the words impossible to stop now. "It's supposed to be a one-person, one-wallet system. Otherwise the rich can just make millions of wallets for themselves and when their full wallets trigger a redistribution, chances are the funds will end up back in an empty wallet they already own."

She crossed her arms. "I thought that's why you made the deal with the government. It's one wallet per Social Insurance Number."

"Yeah," he hesitated. "Somebody's hacked the SIN databases. Made, well, about a million bogus citizens. And they've built wallets with them."

Grace's eyes went wide and she stood up, fists clenched.

"Maybe... Maybe it's fixable," he said, spreading his hands. "I mean, the Sybil attack... it's never been solved, every cryptocurrency is vulnerable to it, we're no worse than Bitcoin was in that sense but of course the potlatch system is critical in your case..." He knew he was babbling but under her accusing gaze he couldn't stop himself. "I mean, when Microsoft looked at it they decided the only way to prevent Sybils was to have a trusted third party to establish identities, so, so—" He was desperate now. "That's what we did, Grace! We used the best approach there was. And you know, it's not just a problem for us, the government's got to fix it or the whole SIN Number system is compromised..."

He could see she wasn't listening anymore. Instead, she was putting together a reply. But just as she was opening her mouth and starting to point at Nathan, an officer behind the counter called out, "Grace Cooper!"

She glared at Nathan, snapped her mouth shut, then went behind the security screen with another officer. Nathan could see them through the glass, and debated whether he should just go. But he was a big name on the development team, and the others—well, they were all quiet today. Hiding in their beds, he'd bet. Leaving him to take the heat; but maybe that was the way it should be. He waited.

Grace's conversation with the cop was surprisingly brief. The officer didn't look happy, and when they bent over a laptop together and he read something there, he looked positively furious. Grace came out a few minutes later, looking darkly satisfied. "He'll be right out."

"What happened?"

"He was in one of the ravines in the University Endowment Lands, nailing sensors to trees. Somebody heard him or saw him and called the cops. They found five hundred dollars in his pocket. Figured an aboriginal kid wouldn't have that kind of money 'cept by stealing it. So they trumped something up and brought him in."

Nathan looked past her at the cop, who was now angrily talking to another officer behind the glass. "And what did you just do?"

"I fixed it." She crossed her arms again and pinned Nathan with accusing eyes. "What are you going to do, Nathan?"

"Fix it! Of course, Grace, why do you think I came to you? All my money's in Gwaiicoin! Mine and... Look, if this goes south I go down with it. I know I gotta fix it."

She didn't reply. A few minutes later a young man with shoulder-length black hair and a wide-cheekboned face came out, lugging a backpack. "Hiya, Grace," he said, unsmiling. "Hell of a day." Then he squinted at Nathan. "Hey."

"This is Nathan. He was just leaving."

"Right. Just leaving. Listen, Grace, I..." Her face was an impenetrable mask. Nathan's shoulders slumped and he turned away.

"I'll talk to you soon."

*   *   *

ALICIA WAS WAITING for him when he walked in the door. "Tell me why I can't pull my money!"

While Nathan visited one development team member after another, she had been texting him with this exact question, and he'd been fending her off as best he could.

"Because the news hasn't hit yet," he said as he kicked of his shoes. "Until this goes public, anything you or I do is going to look like insider trading. Hell, it would *be* insider trading. That's why nobody else on the team has bought out yet." He went straight to the kitchen and rooted around in the fridge for a beer. "But trust me, they're all sitting at their desks with hands hovering over the mouse, waiting for the news to break."

"But don't you know when that's going to happen? The bottom's going to fall out of Gwaiicoin. We'll lose everything if we don't sell now."

He stalked into the living room and sat down. The couch faced out over Blanca Street, and the forested campus of the University of British Columbia. You could see Musqueam lands from here. "We all know that." He savagely yanked the cap off the bottle and took a deep pull, glaring at her. "It's up to the government to make an official statement and they're sitting on it for now. And for the rest of us... none of us can be seen to be the first to bail. Who'd want to be known as the guy who kicked off the biggest crash since the Great Depression?"

"It's not that big," she said.

"It is to us. To the Haida. And the Musqueam and the others."

"So you're all holding your breath. But should I?"

He blinked at her. "Insider trading. Besides, do you want to be known as the one who brought down Gwaiicoin?"

She thought about it. "I would if I had to. It's my money."

"And that's why it'll go all the way down when it goes. But your reputation—your career—isn't riding on this. Mine is. Just... just hold off for an hour or two." He made a patting gesture with both hands, as if to keep the whole issue down. "I'm sure it'll hit the news tonight."

Her lips thinned; she whirled, and went back to the kitchen, to bang around in the cupboards.

A year ago Nathan's safety net had been this condo and another one—an investment property in the suburbs. No matter how the Gwaiicoin experiment did, he had wealth sunk in real estate. Now, housing prices were collapsing in the downtown core. There was general flight from one of the priciest markets on the continent. He'd seen little signs of the decay just now that only a local would notice: the paint was peeling on the garage doors, the exhaust fans in the wall weren't running. Homeless people were living under the neighborhood's bridges.

So he'd sold off his investment property and put the money into Gwaiicoin.

Rather than turn on the TV, he put on his AR glasses, went to stand on the balcony and gazed through the damp air at the park.

Shadows leaned in from the right as the sun neared the waters of the Strait. He loved to sit out here and watch the sunset proceed, the lights come on in their thousands as night fell. *The city's gone quiet even since I moved here.* The incessant hum of distant internal combustion engines had become rare as electrics took over. Some said that quieter cars were also responsible for more people strolling, not walking, in evening light like this.

Nathan sighed and called up the Gwaii overlay in his glasses.

The heads-up display showed a silent aurora above the city, its rippling banners of light made of thousands of thin vertical lines. Each line signified ownership—of houses, cars, shops—inferred by algorithms that constantly rifled through public databases and commercial stats. The lines joined and rejoined overhead, becoming fewer, showing how most of the houses were really owned by this or that bank; how businesses were in debt to other businesses. All those relationships of ownership and debt consolidated and narrowed as the line rose, joining in private and public corporations, and these sprouted lines to names. Compared to the dizzying complexity at street level, there were very, very few names up there at the top.

Nathan hadn't built this overlay, and didn't know who had. Whoever it was, they designed in a subtle gray-white background that you could only see by standing in the dark and looking up. The image was one of the Art Deco cityscapes from the old movie *Metropolis*.

He turned on Fountain View, and now the lines pulsed faintly in rising waves. Those ascending glimmers represented money. Some of it rose only to fall again, but some kept on rising, clustering, concentrating, fleeing far over the horizon or ending in the tangle of names above the city. You could change the lights into numbers, and they would show more money going up than was coming down.

Lately Nathan imagined an invisible line coming out of his own head, gutting him like a hooked fish. It was his debt, tugging on him day and night. Money flowed up that line and never came back. If not for the Gwaii, it would suck up his car and his condo; so he turned on the Haida view. It usually reassured him.

A different tangle of lines sprouted from the darkening city—gold, not that wan green, and sparser. Value rose up those bright lines, too, and twined and knotted over the city. But it fell, too, in fine thin lines like a mist of rain. If you converted the lines to numbers, you'd see that almost as much fell back as rose. It concentrated, but in the middle rather than at the top. And coins that flew off over the horizon were usually matched by others coming back.

"Help me with this," called Alicia. Nathan went back in to chop onions, but he kept the overlay active.

One of the Gwaiicoin experiments he'd been involved in was a vase on the corner of the counter. He'd bought it entirely with Gwaiicoin, and it had a virtual tag on it that was different from the others sprouting from his furniture, dishes and clothes. The tag said he wasn't the owner of the vase, but its steward. Such stewardship contracts were the default in any transfer of assets managed entirely through Gwaiicoin. The contract was registered in the Gwaiicoin blockchain, forever beyond the reach of hackers or thieves. It said that the vase was subject to potlatch like his Gwaiicoin, and someday, its virtual tag might change, telling him that the thing had a new steward—somebody picked at random by the algorithm of the coin. He would gain eminence if he gave it to that person. He'd been reluctant to try that out, and Alicia had suspiciously called it "voluntary communism."

Communism. Such a quaint old word. A twentieth-century notion, a square peg for the 21st century's round hole. Still, right now the vase was changing its tag—the invisible one in Nathan's imagination. From being a sign of his triumph, it was rapidly becoming a symbol of his defeat.

There was nothing on the evening news, but the pressure kept growing inside him. He stood, he paced. Alicia watched, arms folded, from the couch. He monitored the Gwaiicoin developers' chat room, but nobody was there. They were all waiting. Somebody would have to make the first move.

Finally, at eight o'clock, social media started lighting up. *Sybil Attack. Gwaiicoin compromised.* As the tweets and posts began flying fast and furious he turned to Alicia and said, "Do it."

As she raced to get her laptop, Nathan sat down and dismissed all his overlays. He called up his financial app and sat for a long time looking at the impressive balance on the Gwaiicoin side, and the nearly empty one in dollars. Below his Gwaiicoin balance was a link for voluntary transfers to the potlatch account.

I could drop my coins back into dollars, and just walk away. Across the room, the clattering of Alicia's laptop told him what she was doing.

He stared at the other link. He was partly responsible for dragging thousands of people—mostly poor to begin with—into this fiasco. If he put his money into potlatch, he would lose it as surely as if he'd burned wads of dollar bills. The coins would instantly appear in others' wallets, randomly scattered among the emptiest of them. Some would be lost to the Sybil attackers, but most would go to real people. Then, those people could cash out in dollars, and end the Gwaiicoin experiment with just a little more than they'd had this morning.

And he would have nothing. Except, in the form of eminence, proof that he'd tried to help. Not monetary capital, but social capital.

Nathan sat there for a long time. Then he slowly reached out, and made a transfer.

AT TEN, HE went for a walk.

It wasn't raining, and it was summer; so you walked. He'd always enjoyed strolling along Blanca, with its tall walls of trees and hedges, the suggestion of darkness over the western streets that came from the presence of the UBC forest lands. You passed through that forest on your way to the campus, which dominated the end of the peninsula. Taking University Boulevard, you could peek past the trees lining it to the golf course on either side.

Except he never went that way. It was all Musqueam territory, and while they were clients and friends, they had also filled the place with cameras and drones. These didn't bother him so much around Grace's house, but here, as a solitary walker, he became self-conscious.

He walked, head down, and didn't look at the overlay. He imagined it anyway: the slow, ponderous collapse of that pyramid of golden light that he'd seen hovering above the city earlier. The first rats leaping off the ship would alert everybody else, and by now everybody would be selling. It would be a classic financial collapse, and he had helped set it off. Who was going to hire him now?

Somehow his feet had carried him south to 10th Avenue and University. Off to the right, the golf course gleamed in the evening light. The BC Golf House was also alight and its parking lot full, mostly with pickup trucks and new model electrics, not the pricey sedans you usually saw there.

He saw a car pull in, stop, and Grace Cooper got out.

Now he remembered: there was supposed to be a social tonight. The councils were coming together to talk about their successes. Grace had told him about socials last week. "They used to have them in the Maritimes and prairies all the time. You just rent a hall, buy a liquor license and find some garage band that's willing to come out and play. Then call all your friends, and they call their friends..."

The hall's front doors were wide open and people were standing around laughing and talking on the walk. Nathan ran under the weave of electric bus wires that canopied the street, and came up behind Grace just as she was about to enter. "Grace!"

She whirled. "What the hell are you doing here?"

He stopped, hesitated, then squared his shoulders. "I got us into this mess. Are any of the other developers here?"

She shook her head.

"Somebody has to take responsibility—" He made to enter the hall, but she stopped him.

"You're not going to talk about it, and I'm not going to either because that's not what tonight's about. I don't want you to make it about this. We're celebrating other things here—things we *actually accomplished.*" He flinched from her emphasis. It was suddenly obvious why the social was happening at the Golf House. Tiny it might be, but it was on Musqueam land. Land they had taken back.

"What's done counts," she said. "What we tried..." She shrugged. "Not so much." Then she moved out of his way. "Go on in, I can't stop you."

He almost turned away, but whatever he told himself, these people were not just clients. He wanted to be able to look them in the eyes after all this was done. "I won't bring it up," he said. "But others will, and they'll want to know what I'm doing about the situation."

"Which is?"

He opened his mouth, throat dry, and couldn't say it. He just pushed on past her, into the hall.

A folk ensemble was playing. There were tables around the sides of the hall and people roved, chatting. Nobody was dancing but the atmosphere was upbeat. And it should be; here were the inheritors of stubborn cultures that, after five hundred years of often-systematic oppression, were still here.

And were they ever. For the next hour Nathan passed from table to table, saying hi to people he barely knew and, through them, meeting other focused and determined citizens of Canada's youngest and fastest growing demographic. These were kids in their late twenties and early thirties who'd made great money in the oil sands and northern mines, and were now here starting families and pouring their wealth into the Maa-Nalth Treaty Association, the St'at'imc Chiefs Council or the Carrier Sekani Services. Several of these organizations were rapidly mutating into shadow governments in central B.C. There were so many historical groups, so many unpronounceable names and treaty claims that you'd think it was all chaos. There was an emergent order to it all, though. Gwaiicoin and the blockchain were supposed to be helping with that.

He could see it in their eyes; everybody knew about the Sybil attack. They knew what it meant, but nobody confronted him. Somehow, that hurt more than if they'd beaten him and thrown him into the parking lot.

After a while, exhausted, he found himself sitting across from Jeff. Casting about for something—anything—other than Gwaiicoin to talk about, Nathan asked, "How did Grace get you out so quickly today? Or shouldn't I ask?"

Jeff pried the material of his shirt forward to show his bodycam. "I told the cops myself, but they wouldn't listen. This thing has been uploading a low-frame–rate video stream constantly for the past month. Every frame is signed with a hash and What3Words coordinate and timestamped in the GPB. That's the, uh, Global Positioning Blockchain. The GPB can verify where I was every second of every day and prove I didn't break into anybody's house. When I told them that, they wanted to see the video, but I told them to fuck off. They didn't have the right. So we were..." He seemed to choose his next words delicately. "At an impasse.

"Grace knew something about it I didn't, though."

Nathan had heard of the GPB—in that passing way he'd heard of about a million other applications of blockchain technology. GPB was an attestation system, providing the spatial equivalent to a timestamp. It was a secure, decentralized, autonomous way for people all over the world to identify and track specific objects or people. Nathan had shied away from it because to him it had always seemed like the backdoor to some creepy surveillance society.

"What did Grace know that you didn't?"

Jeff shook his head ruefully. "The whole lifelog's encrypted with something called FHE. Fully homo-something encryption. Every frame of the lifelog is encrypted *in the camera,* before it's uploaded, using a key that needs at least three people to unlock it. One of them being me, I guess." He shrugged. "Anyway, because of FHE, the GPB can query that encrypted frame for the answer to specific questions—like, was I in somebody's house by the ravine—*without decrypting the data."*

Fully homomorphic encryption. It was all the rage in some circles, the way Bitcoin had been around 2010. It really did let untrusted third parties analyze your data without decrypting it. You could trust them because they couldn't even in principle have seen what those results were, even though they'd done the work to generate them. Only you could open the returned file.

Nathan was happy for this mathematical distraction. "Let me get this straight," he said. "Because the GPB's a transparent blockchain, we can prove the encrypted frames haven't been tampered with or replaced once they're uploaded. And we can analyze each frame to find out whether any of them show you straying off the path... But how do we know you didn't switch bodycams with somebody else?"

"Because the frame rate's high enough that if I swapped it, that would have been visible. The GPB can attest to the whole path I took through the day"—Jeff swooped his hand over the tabletop—"without us having to *show* any of the frames to the cops. Which alibis me out while securing my privacy."

"Wow." The video feed was effectively also a blockchain, the truth of each new frame attested to by the ones that preceded it. Still... "You could hack it," Nathan decided. "The camera's the vulnerable point. If you mess with that..."

Jeff was shaking his head. "You forget the mesh network. It was uploading data about me the whole time. The trees were watching. And the security cameras on the telephone poles—you know this was near Musqueam land— they feed the same frames to our security company that owns them and to the GPB at the same time. So it's like having multiple witnesses who can say they saw you somewhere. Difference is we don't have to show that proof to a cop or a judge to make it official. Once you've got enough independent witnesses, it's just effectively impossible for all of them to have been compromised." He grinned. "The cops at the station didn't get that, but they phoned somebody else who did. And that's how it went down."

Nathan shook his head. "Cool." With the GPB, FHE, and enough independent cameras, you could turn supposedly ephemeral internet images into proof of position for any object on Earth, while guaranteeing anonymity for that object. You could do it for people, for trees, briefcases full of cash, cars...

Too bad, he mused, you couldn't also do it for something virtual, like a game character.

Or a piece of software...

Nathan stood up so suddenly he nearly knocked over the bench. "Shit!"

Jeff looked up, eyebrows raised. "What?"

"I gotta go." Nathan turned, and practically ran from the hall.

NATHAN REALIZED ALICIA was talking to him, and had been for some time. He glanced over; she was standing there in a bathrobe, hair tangled, looking at him with a really worried expression on her face.

"One sec," he said. He laid his hands on the keyboard and entered COMMIT. Then he hit RETURN, leaned back, and sighed.

"You've been crazy typing for three hours," she said. "What's wrong?"

He looked at the clock in the corner of his monitor screen. It was two am. He was wide awake, practically jumping out of his skin with energy, though he knew how that went: the mental crash, when it came, would have him sleeping most of tomorrow.

"Fixed it," he said. "Now I gotta..." He turned from her to text the rest of the team.

Her hand on his shoulder pulled him back to the moment. "Fixed what? Nathan, what the fuck are you doing? You're scaring me."

"The... the Sybil attack. I found a fix." *Fix* hardly summed up what he'd just done, but right now he was having a bit of trouble with natural languages, like English. Nathan's head was full of the object code he'd been putting together, and that he'd just committed to a new fork of the Gwaiicoin wallet system.

He rubbed his eyes. "Just one sec, and I'll tell you all about it." He texted the team; they'd mostly be asleep, but the buzz of their phones would wake a few, and if nobody got back to him in the next few minutes he'd start phoning them.

The sell-off of Gwaiicoin was in full swing, and he'd been keeping an eye on it while he worked. Luckily, it hadn't been as bad as he'd feared, for the simple reason that transactions above a certain size were taxed by the currency itself. When Alicia had moved her money from Gwaiicoin to dollars, some of those funds had been transferred to thin Gwaiicoin wallets. Until the poorest wallets divested, a goodly chunk of the money was going to stay in the system.

Still, once the rich had divested the poor would follow, and then the system really would collapse.

He hit SEND, then turned to Alicia. "What if you could prove that each Gwaiicoin user was a human being and had one unique wallet?"

"Oh, God." She rummaged through her hair, then leaned back against the office wall. "No Sybil attack. Is that it?" She stopped, blinked at him. "I thought you couldn't do that. You need a trusted third party and that was supposed to be the Social Insurance System. And they crapped out. They got hacked."

"What if you didn't need that third party? If you identified each person as a unique position in spacetime, and that person's one and only wallet is at that same position? Each wallet has a position and it has to correspond to a person's position. Only one wallet is allowed for any position. So: unique person, unique wallet. Sybil attack solved."

She shook her head. "Just make up fake people."

Nathan laughed and jumped up. "But you can't! That's what's so great about it!" The more bodycams, cop-cams, security cams, GPS-sensing sports and health trackers that uploaded their data to the Global Positioning Blockchain, the more witnesses there were to attest to peoples' existence and location. FHE encryption meant you could hide the data from prying eyes, but still prove your identity in full public view.

"It'll take a while for the fix to work," he admitted. "Weeks, months maybe, until everyone using the coin is accounted for. Once they all are, though, Sybil attacks will be impossible. Meanwhile..." He frowned at the growing divestment numbers.

Alicia was wide awake now. "It won't matter if it all goes south tonight." She had put on her glasses and was staring out the window—probably watching in AR as the gold lines of Gwaiicoin pulled back from house after darkened house, like candle flames going out. "Though I suppose if the team reinvests it'll send a strong signal..." She turned to him and raised her glasses. "That what you're going to do now?"

Nathan sat there, gazing at the jumble of windows in the monitor. "No." Giddiness battled with despair.

He hadn't told Grace what he'd done, though she'd find out soon enough. He couldn't avoid Alicia, though.

"I didn't divest," he said, still staring at the screen. "I could have. Should have, I guess. Maybe I panicked, I dunno, I—"

"Nathan." She came to lean on the table next to him. "What did you do?"

"I gave it away." A half-hysterical laugh rose out of him. "All of it. Straight into the potlatch account—swoosh!" He zoomed his hand over the keyboard, like Jeff had earlier.

The look of horror on Alicia's face was perfect. The rest of the laugh burst its way out of Nathan, battling tears.

He'd given away all his savings.

"I gave it to the people, and now all I have..." He clicked over to his Gwaiicoin wallet. "... is a hell of a lot of eminence."

"So you didn't divest. You—"

"*In*vested. And if this crash turns around..."

"Oh, Nathan, what have you done?"

He slumped back, shaking his head, but smiling.

"I don't know. But just maybe..."

He turned to look at the city skyline, picturing the fountaining flow of currencies: money, power, influence and, joining them, a quality that those other media had never been able to carry: trust.

"Maybe," he murmured, half to himself, "I've found a new way to be rich."

THE CHAMELEON'S GLOVES
Yoon Ha Lee

Yoon Ha Lee's (www.yoonhalee.com) first novel, *Ninefox Gambit*, was published to critical acclaim in 2016 and was nominated for the Hugo, Nebula, and Arthur C. Clarke Awards. The first in the Machineries of Empire series it was followed in 2017 by *Raven Stratagem*. Lee is the author of more than forty short stories that have appeared in *Tor.com*, *Lightspeed*, *Clarkesworld*, and *The Magazine of Fantasy and Science Fiction*, and are collected in *Conservation of Shadows*. He lives in Louisiana with his family and has not yet been eaten by gators.

RHEHAN HATED MUSEUMS, but their partner Liyeusse had done unmentionable things to the ship's stardrive the last time the two of them had fled the authorities, and the repairs had drained their savings. Which was why Rhehan was on a station too close to the more civilized regions of the dustways, flirting with a tall, pale woman decked in jewels while they feigned interest in pre-Devolutionist art.

In spite of themselves, Rhehan was impressed by colonists who had carved pictures into the soles of worn-out space boots: so useless that it had to be art, not that they planned to say that to the woman.

"—wonderful evocation of the Festival of the Vines using that repeated motif," the woman was saying. She brushed a long curl of hair out of her face and toyed with one of her dangling earrings as she looked sideways at Rhehan.

"I was just thinking that myself," Rhehan lied. The Festival of the Vines, with its accompanying cheerful inebriation and sex, would be less agonizing than having to pretend to care about the aesthetics of this piece. Too bad Rhehan and Liyeusse planned to disappear in the next couple hours. The woman was pretty enough, despite her obsession with circuitscapes. Rhehan was of the opinion that if you wanted to look at a circuit, nothing beat the real thing.

A tinny voice said in Rhehan's ear, "Are you on location yet?"

Rhehan faked a cough and subvocalized over the link to Liyeusse. "Been in position for the last half-hour. You sure you didn't screw up the prep?"

She snorted disdainfully. "Just hurry it—"

At last the alarms clanged. The jeweled woman jumped, her astonishing blue eyes going wide. Rhehan put out a steadying arm and, in the process, relieved her of a jade ring, slipping it in their pocket. Not high-value stuff, but no one with sense wore expensive items as removables. They weren't wearing gloves on this outing—had avoided wearing gloves since their exile—but the persistent awareness of their naked hands never faded. At least, small consolation, the added sensation made legerdemain easier, even if they had to endure the distastefulness of skin touching skin.

A loud, staticky voice came over the public address system. "All patrons, please proceed to the nearest exit. There is no need for alarm"—exactly the last thing you wanted to say if you didn't want people to panic, or gossip for that matter—"but due to an incident, the museum needs to close for maintenance."

The woman was saying, with charming anxiety, "We'd better do as they say. I wonder what it is."

Come on, Rhehan thought, *what's the delay?* Had they messed up preparing the explosives?

They had turned to smile and pat the woman's hand reassuringly when the first explosives went off at the end of the hall. Fire flowered, flashed; a boom reverberated through the walls, with an additional hiss of sparks when a security screen went down. Rhehan's ears rang even though they'd been prepared for the noise. Two stands toppled, spilling a ransom's worth of iridescent black quantum-pearl strands inscribed with algorithmic paeans. The sudden chemical reek of the smoke made Rhehan cough, even though you'd think they'd be used to it by now. Several startled bystanders shrieked and bolted toward the exit.

The woman leapt back and behind a decorative pillar with commendable reflexes. "Over here," she called out to Rhehan, as if she could rescue them.

Rhehan feigned befuddlement although they could easily lip-read what she was saying—they could barely hear her past the ringing in their ears—and sidestepped out of her reach, just in case.

A second blast went off, farther down the hall. A thud suggested that something out of sight had fallen down. Rhehan thought snidely that some of the statues they had seen earlier would be improved by a few creative cracks anyway. The sprinklers finally kicked in, and a torrent of water rained down from above, drenching them.

Rhehan left the woman to fend for herself. "Where are you going?" she shouted after Rhehan, loudly enough to be heard despite the damage to their hearing, as they sprinted toward the second explosion.

"I have to save the painting!" Rhehan said over their shoulder.

To Rhehan's dismay, the woman pivoted on her heel and followed. Rhehan turned their head to lip-read her words, almost crashing into a corner in the process: "You shame me," she said as she ran after them. "Your dedication to the arts is greater than mine."

Another explosion. Liyeusse, whose hearing was unaffected, was wheezing into Rhehan's ear. "'Dedication... to... the... arts,'" she said between breaths. "'Dedication.' *You*."

Rhehan didn't have time for Liyeusse's quirky sense of humor. Just because they couldn't tell a color wheel from a flywheel didn't mean they didn't appreciate market value.

They'd just rounded the corner to the relevant gallery and its delicious gear collages when Rhehan was alerted—too late—by the quickened rhythm of the woman's footsteps. They inhaled too sharply, coughed at the smoke, and staggered when she caught them in a chokehold. "What—" Rhehan said, and then no words were possible anymore.

RHEHAN WOKE IN a chair, bound. They kept their eyes closed and tested the cords, hoping not to draw attention. The air had a familiar undertone of incense, which was very bad news, but perhaps they were only imagining it. Rhehan had last smelled this particular blend, with its odd metallic top notes, in the ancestral shrines of a childhood home they hadn't returned to in eight years. They stilled their hands from twitching.

Otherwise, the temperature was warmer than they were accustomed to—Liyeusse liked to keep the ship cool—and a faint hissing suggested an air circulation system not kept in as good shape as it could be. Even more faintly, they heard the distinctive, just-out-of-tune humming of a ship's drive. Too bad they lacked Liyeusse's ability to identify the model by listening to the harmonics.

More importantly: how many people were there with them? They didn't hear anything, but that didn't mean—

"You might as well open your eyes, Kel Rhehan," a cool female voice said in a language they had not heard for a long time, confirming Rhehan's earlier suspicions. They had not fooled her.

Rhehan wondered whether their link to Liyeusse was still working, and if she was all right. "Liyeusse?" they subvocalized. No response. Their heart stuttered.

They opened their eyes: might as well assess the situation, since their captor knew they were awake.

"I don't have the right to that name any longer," Rhehan said. They hadn't been part of the Kel people for years. But their hands itched with the memory of the Kel gloves they hadn't worn in eight years, as the Kel reckoned it. Indeed, with their hands exposed like this, they felt shamed and vulnerable in front of one of their people.

The woman before them was solidly built, dark, like the silhouette of a tree, and more somber in mien than the highly ornamented agent who had brought Rhehan in. She wore the black and red of the Kel judiciary. A cursory slip of veil obscured part of her face, its translucence doing little to hide her sharp features. The veil should have scared Rhehan more, as it indicated that the woman was a judge-errant, but her black Kel gloves hurt worse. Rhehan's had been stripped from them and burned when the Kel cast them out.

"I've honored the terms of my exile," Rhehan said desperately. What had they done to deserve the attention of a judge-errant? Granted that they were a thief, but they'd had little choice but to make a living with the skills they had. "What have you done with my partner?"

The judge-errant ignored the question. Nevertheless, the sudden tension around her eyes indicated that she knew *something*. Rhehan had been watching for it. "I am Judge Kel Shiora, and I have been sent because the Kel have need of you," she said.

"Of course," Rhehan said, fighting to hide their bitterness. Eight years of silence and adapting to an un-Kel world, and the moment the Kel had need of them, they were supposed to comply.

Shiora regarded them without malice or opprobrium or anything much resembling feeling. "There are many uses for a jaihanar."

Jaihanar—what non-Kel called, in their various languages, a haptic chameleon. Someone who was not only so good at imitating patterns of movement that they could scam inattentive people, but also able to fool the machines whose security systems depended on identifying their owners' characteristic movements. How you interacted with your gunnery system, or wandered about your apartment, or smiled at the lover you'd known for the last decade. It wasn't magic—a jaihanar needed some minimum of data to work from—but the knack often seemed that way.

The Kel produced few jaihanar, and the special forces snapped up those that emerged from the Kel academies. Rhehan had been the most promising jaihanar in the last few generations before disgracing themselves. The only reason they hadn't been executed was that the Kel government had foreseen that they would someday be of use again.

"Tell me what you want, then," Rhehan said. Anything to keep her talking so that eventually she might be willing to say what she'd done with Liyeusse.

"If I undo your bonds, will you hear me out?"

Getting out of confinement would also be good. Their leg had fallen asleep. "I won't try anything," Rhehan said. They knew better.

Ordinarily, Rhehan would have felt sorry for anyone who trusted a thief's word so readily, except they knew the kind of training a judge-errant underwent. Shiora wasn't the one in danger. They kept silent as she unlocked the restraints.

"I had to be sure," Shiora said.

Rhehan shrugged. "Talk to me."

"General Kavarion has gone rogue. We need someone to infiltrate her ship and retrieve a weapon she has stolen."

"I'm sorry," Rhehan said after a blank pause. "You just said that General Kavarion has gone rogue? Kavarion, the hero of Split Suns? Kavarion, of the Five Splendors? My hearing must be going."

Shiora gave them an unamused look. "Kel Command sent her on contract to guard a weapons research facility," she said. "Kavarion recently attacked the facility and made off with the research and a prototype. The prototype may be armed."

"Surely, you have any number of loyal Kel who'd be happy to go on this assignment," Rhehan said. The Kel took betrayal personally. They knew this well.

"You are the nearest jaihanar in this region of the dustways." Most people reserved the term *dustways* for particularly lawless segments of the spaceways, but the Kel used the term for anywhere that didn't fall under the Kel sphere of influence.

"Also," Shiora added, "few of our jaihanar match your skill. You owe the Kel for your training, if nothing else. Besides, it's not in your interest to live in a world where former Kel are hunted for theft of immensely powerful weapon prototypes."

Rhehan had to admit she had a point.

"They named it the Incendiary Heart," Shiora continued. "It initiates an inflationary expansion like the one at the universe's birth."

Rhehan swore. "Remote detonation?"

"There's a timer. It's up to you to get out of range before it goes off."

"The radius of effect?"

"Thirty thousand light-years, give or take, in a directed cone. That's the only thing that makes it possible to use without blowing up the person setting it off."

Rhehan closed their eyes. That would fry a nontrivial percentage of the galaxy. "And you don't know if it's armed."

"No. The general is running very fast—to what, we don't know. But she has been attempting to hire mercenary jaihanar. We suspect she is looking for a way to control the device—which may buy us time."

"I see." Rhehan rubbed the palm of one hand with the fingers of the other, smile twisting at the judge-errant's momentary look of revulsion at the touch of skin on skin. Which was why they'd done it, of course, petty as it was. "Can you offer me any insight into her goals?"

"If we knew that," the judge-errant said bleakly, "we would know why she turned coat."

Blowing up a region of space, even a very local region of space in galactic terms, would do no one any good. In particular, it would make a continued career in art theft a little difficult. On the other hand, Rhehan was determined to wring some payment out of this, if only so Liyeusse wouldn't lecture them about their lack of mercenary instinct. Their ship wasn't going to fix itself, after all. "I'll do it," they said. "But I'm going to need some resources—"

The judge surprised them by laughing. "You have lived too long in the dustways," she said. "I can offer payment in the only coin that should matter to you—or do you think we haven't been watching you?"

Rhehan should have objected, but they froze up, knowing what was to come.

"Do this for us, and show us the quality of your service," the judge-errant said, "and Kel Command will reinstate you." Very precisely, she peeled the edge of one glove back to expose the dark fine skin of her wrist, signaling her sincerity.

Rhehan stared. "Liyeusse?" they asked again, subvocally. No response. Which meant that Liyeusse probably hadn't heard that damning offer. At least she wasn't there to see Rhehan's reaction. As good as they normally were at controlling their body language, they had not been able to hide that moment's hunger for a home they had thought forever lost to them.

"I will do this," Rhehan said at last. "But not for some bribe; because a weapon like the one you describe is too dangerous for anyone, let alone a rogue, to control." And because they needed to find out what had become of Liyeusse, but Shiora wouldn't understand that.

THE WOMAN WHO escorted Rhehan to their ship, docked on the Kel carrier—Rhehan elected not to ask how this had happened—had a familiar face. "I don't know why *you're* not doing this job," Rhehan said to the pale woman now garbed in Kel uniform, complete with gloves, rather than the jewels and outlandish stationer garb she'd affected in the museum.

The woman unsmiled at Rhehan. "I will be accompanying you," she said in the lingua franca they'd used earlier.

Of course. Shiora had extracted Rhehan's word, but neither would she fail to take precautions. They couldn't blame her.

Kel design sensibilities had not changed much since Rhehan was a cadet. The walls of dark metal were livened by tapestries of wire and faceted beads, polished from battlefield shrapnel: obsolete armor, lens components in laser cannon, spent shells. Rhehan kept from touching the wall superstitiously as they walked by.

"What do I call you?" Rhehan said finally, since the woman seemed disinclined to speak first.

"I am Sergeant Kel Anaz," she said. She stopped before a hatch, and she tapped a panel in full sight of Rhehan, her mouth curling sardonically.

"I'm not stupid enough to try to escape a ship full of Kel," Rhehan said. "I bet you have great aim." Besides, there was Liyeusse's safety to consider.

"You weren't bad at it yourself."

She would have studied their record, yet Rhehan hated how exposed the simple statement made them feel. "I can imitate the stance of a master marksman," Rhehan said dryly. "That doesn't give me the eye, or the reflexes. These past years, I've found safer ways to survive."

Anaz's eyebrows lifted at "safer," but she kept her contempt to herself. After chewing over Anaz's passkey, the hatch opened. A whoosh of cool air floated over Rhehan's face. They stepped through before Anaz could say anything, their eyes drawn immediately to the lone non-Kel ship in the hangar. To their relief, the *Flarecat* didn't look any more disreputable than before.

Rhehan advanced upon the *Flarecat* and entered it, all the while aware of Anaz at their back. Liyeusse was bound to one of the passenger's seats, the side of her face swollen and purpling, her cap of curly hair sticking out in all directions. Liyeusse's eyes widened when she saw the two of them, but she didn't struggle against her bonds. Rhehan swore and went to her side.

"If she's damaged—" Rhehan said in a shaking voice, then froze when Anaz shoved the muzzle of a gun against the back of their head.

"She's ji-Kel," Anaz said in an even voice: *ji-Kel*, not-Kel. "She wasn't even concussed. She'll heal."

"She's my partner," Rhehan said. "We work together."

"If you insist," Anaz said with a distinct air of distaste. The pressure eased, and she cut Liyeusse free herself.

Liyeusse grimaced. "New friend?" she said.

"New job, anyway," Rhehan said. They should have known that Shiora and her people would treat a ji-Kel with little respect.

"We're never going to land another decent art theft," Liyeusse said with strained cheer. "You have no sense of culture."

"This one's more important." Rhehan reinforced their words with a hand signal: *Emergency. New priority.*

"What have the Kel got on you, anyhow?"

Rhehan had done their best to steer Liyeusse away from any dealings with the Kel because of the potential awkwardness. It hadn't been hard. The Kel had a reputation for providing reliable but humorless mercenaries and a distinct lack of appreciation for what Liyeusse called the exigencies of survival in the dustways. More relevantly, while they controlled a fair deal of wealth, they ruthlessly pursued and destroyed those who attempted to relieve them of it. Rhehan had never been tempted to take revenge by stealing from them.

Anaz's head came up. "You never told your partner?"

"Never told me what?" Liyeusse said, starting to sound irritated.

"We'll be traveling with Sergeant Kel Anaz," Rhehan said, hoping to distract Liyeusse.

No luck. Her mouth compressed. *Safe to talk?* she signed at them.

Not really, but Rhehan didn't see that they had many options. "I'm former Kel," Rhehan said. "I was exiled because—because of a training incident." Even now, it was difficult to speak of it. Two of their classmates had died, and an instructor.

Liyeusse laughed incredulously. "You? We've encountered Kel mercenaries before. You don't talk like one. Move like one. Well, except when—" She faltered as it occurred to her that, of the various guises Rhehan had put on for their heists, that one hadn't been a guise at all.

Anaz spoke over Liyeusse. "The sooner we set out, the better. We have word on Kavarion's vector, but we don't know how long our information will be good. You'll have to use your ship since the judge-errant's would draw attention, even if it's faster."

Don't, Rhehan signed to Liyeusse, although she knew better than to spill the *Flarecat*'s modifications to this stranger. "I'll fill you in on the way."

The dustways held many perils for ships: wandering maws, a phenomenon noted for years, and unexplained for just as long; particles traveling at unimaginable speeds, capable of destroying any ship lax in maintaining its shielding; vortices that filtered light even in dreams, causing hallucinations. When Rhehan had been newly exiled, they had convinced Liyeusse of their usefulness because they knew dustway paths new to her. Even if they hadn't been useful for making profit, they had helped in escaping the latest people she'd swindled.

Ships could be tracked by the eddies they left in the dustways. The difficulty was not in finding the traces but in interpreting them. Great houses had risen to prominence through their monopoly over the computational networks that processed and sold this information. Kel Command had paid dearly for such information in its desperation to track down General Kavarion.

Assuming that information was accurate, Kavarion had ensconced herself at the Fortress of Wheels: neutral territory, where people carried out bargains for amounts that could have made Rhehan and Liyeusse comfortable for the rest of their lives.

The journey itself passed in a haze of tension. Liyeusse snapped at Anaz, who bore her jibes with grim patience. Rhehan withdrew, not wanting to make matters worse, which was the wrong thing to do, and they knew it. In particular, Liyeusse had not forgiven them for the secret they had kept from her for so long.

At last, Rhehan slumped into the copilot's seat and spoke to Liyeusse over the newly repaired link to gain some semblance of privacy. As far as they could tell, Anaz hardly slept. Rhehan said, "You must have a lot of questions."

"I knew about the chameleon part," Liyeusse said. Any number of their heists had depended on it. "I hadn't realized that the Kel had their own."

"Usually, they don't," Rhehan said. Liyeusse inhaled slightly at *they*, as if she had expected Rhehan to say *we* instead. "But the Kel rarely let go of the ones they do produce. It's the only reason they didn't execute me."

"What did you do?"

Rhehan's mouth twisted. "The Kel say there are three kinds of people, after a fashion. There are Kel; ji-Kel, or not-Kel, whom they have dealings with sometimes; and those who aren't people at all. Just—disposable."

Liyeusse's momentary silence pricked at Rhehan. "Am I disposable to you?" she said.

"I should think it's the other way around," they said. They wouldn't have survived their first year in the dustways without her protection. "Anyway, there was a training exercise. People-who-are-not-people were used as—" They fumbled for a word in the language they spoke with Liyeusse, rather than the Kel term. "Mannequins. Props in the exercise, to be gunned down or saved or discarded, whatever the trainees decided. I chose the lives of mannequins over the lives of Kel. For this I was stripped of my position and cast out."

"I have always known that the universe is unkind," Liyeusse said, less moved than Rhehan had expected. "I assume that hired killers would have to learn their art somewhere."

"It would have been one thing if I'd thought of myself as a soldier," Rhehan said. "But a good chameleon, or perhaps a failed one, observes the people they imitate. And eventually, a chameleon learns that even mannequins think of themselves as people."

"I'm starting to understand why you've never tried to go back," Liyeusse said.

A sick yearning started up in the pit of Rhehan's stomach. They still hadn't told her about Kel Shiora's offer. Time enough later, if it came to that.

Getting to Kavarion's fleet wasn't the difficult part, although Liyeusse's eyes were bloodshot for the entire approach. The *Flarecat*'s stealth systems kept them undetected, even if mating it to the command ship, like an unwanted tick, was a hair-raising exercise. By then, Rhehan had dressed themselves in a Kel military uniform, complete with gloves. Undeserved, since strictly speaking, they hadn't recovered their honor in the eyes of their people, but they couldn't deny the necessity of the disguise.

Anaz would remain with Liyeusse on the *Flarecat*. She hadn't had to explain the threat: *Do your job, or your partner dies.* Rhehan wasn't concerned for Liyeusse's safety—so long as the two remained on the ship, Liyeusse had access to a number of nasty tricks and had no compunctions about using them—but the mission mattered to them anyway.

Rhehan had spent the journey memorizing all the haptic profiles that Anaz had provided them. In addition, Anaz had taken one look at Rhehan's outdated holographic mask and given them a new one. "If you could have afforded up-to-date equipment, you wouldn't be doing petty art theft," she had said caustically.

The Fortress of Wheels currently hosted several fleets. Tensions ran high, although its customary neutrality had so far prevailed. Who knew how long that would last; Liyeusse, interested as always in gossip, had reported that various buyers for the Incendiary Heart had shown up, and certain warlords wouldn't hesitate to take it by force if necessary.

Security on Kavarion's command ship was tight but had not been designed to stop a jaihanar. Not surprising; the Kel relied on their employers for such measures when they deigned to stop at places like the Fortress. At the moment, Rhehan was disguised as a bland-faced lieutenant.

Rhehan had finessed their way past the fifth lock in a row, losing themselves in the old, bitter pleasure of a job well done. They had always enjoyed this part best: fitting their motions to that of someone who didn't even realize what was going on, so perfectly that machine recognition systems could not tell the difference. But it occurred to them that everything was going too perfectly.

Maybe I'm imagining things, they told themselves without conviction, and hurried on. A corporal passed them by without giving more than a cursory salute, but Rhehan went cold and hastened away from him as soon as they could.

They made it to the doors to the general's quarters. Liyeusse had hacked into the communications systems and was monitoring activity. She'd assured Rhehan that the general was stationside, negotiating with someone. Since neither of them knew how long that would last—

Sweat trickled down Rhehan's back, causing the uniform to cling unpleasantly to their skin. They had some of the general's haptic information as well. Anaz hadn't liked handing it over, but as Rhehan had pointed out, the mission would be impossible without it.

Kavarion of the Five Splendors. One of the most celebrated Kel generals, and a musician besides. Her passcode was based on an extraordinarily difficult passage from a keyboard concerto. Another keyboardist could have played the passage, albeit with difficulty reproducing the nuances of expression. While not precisely a musician, Rhehan had trained in a variety of the arts for occasions such as this. (Liyeusse often remarked it was a shame they had no patience for painting, or they could have had a respectable career forging art.) They got through the passcode. Held their breath. The door began opening—

A fist slammed them in the back of the head.

Rhehan staggered and whirled, barely remaining upright. *If I get a concussion I'm going to charge Kel Command for my medical care,* they thought as the world slowed.

"Finally, someone took the bait," breathed Rhehan's assailant. Kel Kavarion; Rhehan recognized the voice from the news reports they'd watched a lifetime before. "I was starting to think I was going to have to hang out signs or hire a bounty hunter." She did something fast and complicated with her hands, and Rhehan found themselves shoved down against the floor with the muzzle of a gun digging into the back of their neck.

"Sir, I—"

"Save it," General Kavarion said, with dangerous good humor. "Come inside and I'll show you what you're after. Don't fight me. I'm better at it than you are."

Rhehan couldn't argue that.

The general let Rhehan up. The door had closed again, but she executed the passphrase in a blur that made Rhehan think she was wasted on the military. Surely there was an orchestra out there that could use a star keyboardist.

Rhehan made sure to make no threatening moves as they entered, scanning the surroundings. Kavarion had a taste for the grandiloquent. Triumph-plaques of metal and stone and lacquerware covered the walls, forming a mosaic of battles past and comrades lost. The light reflecting from their angled surfaces gave an effect like being trapped in a kaleidoscope of sterilized glory.

Kavarion smiled cuttingly. Rhehan watched her retreating step by step, gun still trained on them. "You don't approve," Kavarion remarked.

Rhehan unmasked since there wasn't any point still pretending to be one of her soldiers. "I'm a thief," they said. "It's all one to me."

"You're lying, but never mind. I'd better make this quick." Kavarion smiled at Rhehan with genuine and worrying delight. "You're the jaihanar we threw out, aren't you? It figures that Kel Command would drag you out of the dustways instead of hiring some ji-Kel."

"*I'm* ji-Kel now, General."

"It's a matter of degrees. It doesn't take much to figure out what Kel Command could offer an exile." She then offered the gun to Rhehan. "Hold that," she said. "I'll get the Incendiary Heart."

"How do you know I won't shoot you?" Rhehan demanded.

"Because right now I'm your best friend," Kavarion said, "and you're mine. If you shoot me, you'll never find out why I'm doing this, and a good chunk of the galaxy is doomed."

Frustrated by the sincerity they read in the set of her shoulders, Rhehan trained the gun on Kavarion's back and admired her sangfroid. She showed no sign of being worried she'd be shot.

Kavarion spoke as she pressed her hand against one of the plaques. "They probably told you I blew the research station up after I stole the Incendiary Heart, which is true." The plaque lifted to reveal a safe. "Did they also mention that someone armed the damned thing before I was able to retrieve it?"

"They weren't absolutely clear on that point."

"Well, I suppose even a judge-errant—I assume they sent a judge-errant—can't get information out of the dead. Anyway, it's a time bomb, presumably to give its user a chance to escape the area of effect."

Rhehan's heart sank. There could only be one reason why Kavarion needed a jaihanar of her own. "It's going to blow?"

"Unless you can disarm it. One of the few researchers with a sense of self-preservation was making an attempt to do so before he got killed by a piece of shrapnel. I have some video, as much of it as I could scrape before the whole place blew, but I don't know if it's enough." Kavarion removed a box that shimmered a disturbing shade of red-gold-bronze.

The original mission was no good; that much was clear. "All right," Rhehan said.

Kavarion played back a video of the researcher's final moments. It looked like it had been recorded by someone involved in a firefight, from the shakiness of the image. Parts of the keycode were obscured by smoke, by flashing lights, by flying shrapnel.

Rhehan made several attempts, then shook their head. "There's just not enough information, even for me, to reconstruct the sequence."

Suddenly Kavarion looked haggard.

"How do you know he was really trying to disarm it?" Rhehan said.

"Because he was my lover," Kavarion said, "and he had asked me for sanctuary. He was the reason I knew exactly how destructive the Incendiary Heart was to begin with."

Scientists shouldn't be allowed near weapons design, Rhehan thought. "How long do we have?"

She told them. They blanched.

"Why did you make off with it in the first place?" Rhehan said. They couldn't help but think that if she'd kept her damn contract, this whole mess could have been avoided in the first place.

"Because the contract-holder was trying to sell the Incendiary Heart to the highest bidder. And at the time I made off with it, the highest bidder looked like it was going to be one of the parties in an extremely messy civil war." Kavarion scowled. "Not only did I suspect that they'd use it at the first opportunity, I had good reason to believe that they had *terrible* security—and I doubted anyone stealing it would have any scruples either. Unfortunately, when I swiped the wretched thing, some genius decided it would be better to set it off and deny it to everyone, never mind the casualties."

Kavarion closed her fist over the Incendiary Heart. It looked like her fist was drenched in a gore of light. "Help me get it out of here, away from where it'll kill billions."

"What makes you so confident that I'm your ally, when Kel Command sent me after you?"

She sighed. "It's true that I can't offer a better reward than if you bring the accursed thing to them. On the other hand, even if you think I'm lying about the countdown, do you really trust Kel Command with dangerous weapons? They'd never let me hand it over to them for safekeeping anyway, not when I broke contract by taking it in the first place."

"No," Rhehan said after a moment. "You're right. That's not a solution either."

Kavarion opened her hand and nodded companionably at Rhehan, as though they'd been comrades for years. "I need you to run away with this and get farther from centers of civilization. I can't do this with a whole fucking Kel fleet. My every movement is being watched, and I'm afraid someone will get us into a fight and stall us in a bad place. But you—a ji-Kel thief, used to darting in and out of the dustways—your chances will be better than mine."

Rhehan's breath caught. "You're already outnumbered," they said. "Sooner or later, they'll catch up to you—the Kel, if not everyone else who wants the weapon they think you have. You don't even have a running start, since you're docked here. They'll incinerate you."

"Well, yes," Kavarion said. "We are Kel. We are the people of fire and ash. It comes with the territory. Are you willing to do this?"

Her equanimity disturbed Rhehan. Clearly, Liyeusse's way of looking at the world had rubbed off on them more than they'd accounted for, these last eight years. "You're gambling a lot on my reliability."

"Am I?" The corners of Kavarion's mouth tilted up: amusement. "You were one of the most promising Kel cadets that year, and you gave it up because you were concerned about the lives of mannequins who didn't even know your name. I'd say I'm making a good choice."

Kavarion pulled her gloves off one by one and held them out to Rhehan. "You are my agent," she said. "Take the gloves, and take the Incendiary Heart with you. A great many lives depend on it."

They knew what the gesture meant: *You hold my honor.* Shaken, they stared at her, stripped of chameleon games. Shiora was unlikely to forgive Rhehan for betraying her to ally with Kavarion. But Kavarion's logic could not be denied.

"Take them," Kavarion said tiredly. "And for love of fire and ash, don't tell me where you're going. I don't want to know."

Rhehan took the gloves and replaced the ones they had been wearing with them. *I'm committed now,* Rhehan thought. They brought their fist up to their chest in the Kel salute, and the general returned it.

THINGS WENT WRONG almost from the moment Rhehan returned to their ship. They'd refused an escort from Kavarion on the grounds that it would arouse Anaz's suspicions. The general had assured them that no one would interfere with them on the way out, but the sudden blaring of alarms and the scrambling of crew to get to their assigned stations meant that Rhehan had to do a certain amount of dodging. At a guess, the Fortress-imposed cease-fire was no longer in effect. What had triggered hostilities, Rhehan didn't know and didn't particularly care. All that mattered was escaping with the Incendiary Heart.

The *Flarecat* remained shielded from discovery by the stealth device that Liyeusse so loved, even if it had a distressing tendency to blow out the engines exactly when they had to escape sharp-eyed creditors. Rhehan hadn't forgotten its location, however, and—

Anaz ambushed Rhehan before they even reached the *Flarecat*, in the dim hold where they were suiting up to traverse the perilous webbing that connected the *Flarecat* to Kavarion's command ship. Rhehan had seen this coming. Another chameleon might have fought back, and died of it; Shiora had no doubt selected Anaz for her deadliness. But Rhehan triggered the mask into Kavarion's own visage and smiled Kavarion's own smile at Anaz, counting on the reflexive Kel deference to rank. The gesture provoked enough of a hesitation that Rhehan could pull out their own sidearm and put a bullet in the side of her neck. They'd been aiming for her head; no such luck. Still, they'd take what they could.

The bullet didn't stop Anaz. Rhehan hadn't expected it to. But the next two did. The only reason they didn't keep firing was that Rhehan could swear that the Incendiary Heart pulsed hotter with each shot. "Fuck this," they said with feeling, although they couldn't hear themselves past the ringing in their ears, and overrode the hatch to escape to the first of the web-strands without looking back to see whether Anaz was getting back up.

No further attack came, but Anaz might live, might even survive what Kavarion had in mind for her.

Liyeusse wasn't dead. Presumably Anaz had known better than to interfere too permanently with the ship's master. But Liyeusse wasn't in good condition, either. Anaz had left her unconscious and expertly tied up, a lump on the side of her head revealing where Anaz had knocked her out. Blood streaked her face. *So much for no concussions,* Rhehan thought. A careful inspection revealed two broken ribs, although no fingers or arms, small things to be grateful for. Liyeusse had piloted with worse injuries, but it wasn't something either of them wanted to make a habit of.

Rhehan shook with barely quelled rage as they unbound Liyeusse, using the lockpicks that the two of them kept stashed on board. Here, with just the two of them, there was no need to conceal their reaction.

Rhehan took the precaution of injecting her with painkillers first. Then they added a stim, which they would have preferred to avoid. Nevertheless, the two of them would have to work together to escape. It couldn't be helped.

"My head," Liyeusse said in a voice half-groan, stirring. Then she smiled crookedly at Rhehan, grotesque through the dried blood. "Did you give that Kel thug what she wanted? Are we free?"

"Not yet," Rhehan said. "As far as I can tell, Kavarion's gearing up for a firefight and they're bent on blowing each other up over this bauble. Even worse, we have a new mission." They outlined the situation while checking Liyeusse over again to make sure there wasn't any more internal damage. Luckily, Anaz hadn't confiscated their medical kits, so Rhehan retrieved one and cleaned up the head wound, then applied a bandage to Liyeusse's torso.

"Every time I think this can't get worse," Liyeusse said while Rhehan worked, but her heart wasn't in it. "Let's strap ourselves in and get flying."

"What, you don't want to appraise this thing?" They held the Incendiary Heart up. Was it warmer? They couldn't tell.

"I don't love shiny baubles *that* much," she said dryly. She was already preoccupied with the ship's preflight checks, although her grimaces revealed that the painkillers were not as efficacious as they could have been. "I'll be glad when it's gone. You'd better tell me where we're going."

The sensor arrays sputtered with the spark-lights of many ships, distorted by the fact that they were stealthed. "Ask the general to patch us in to her friend-or-foe identification system," Rhehan said when they realized that there were more Kel ships than there should have been. Kel Command must have had a fleet waiting to challenge Kavarion in case Shiora failed her mission. "And ask her not to shoot us down on our way out."

Liyeusse contacted the command ship in the Fortress's imposed lingua.

The connection hissed open. The voice that came back to them over the line sounded harried and spoke accented lingua. "Who the hell are—" Rhehan distinctly heard Kavarion snapping something profane in the Kel language. The voice spoke back, referring to Liyeusse with the particular suffix that meant *coward*, as if that applied to a ji-Kel ship to begin with. Still, Rhehan was glad they didn't have to translate that detail for Liyeusse, although they summarized the exchange for her.

"*Go*," the voice said ungraciously. "I'll keep the gunners off you. I hope you don't crash into anything, foreigner."

"Thank you," Liyeusse said in a voice that suggested that she was thinking about blowing something up on her way out.

"Don't," Rhehan said.

"I wasn't going to—"

"They need this ship to fight with. Which will let us get away from any pursuit."

"As far as I'm concerned, they're all the enemy."

They couldn't blame her, considering what she'd been through.

The scan suite reported on the battle. Rhehan, who had webbed themselves into the copilot's seat, tracked the action with concern. The hostile Kel hadn't bothered to transmit their general's banner, a sign of utter contempt for those they fought. Even ji-Kel received banners, although they weren't expected to appreciate the nuances of Kel heraldry.

The first fighter launched from the hangar below them. "Our turn," Liyeusse said.

The *Flarecat* rocketed away from the command ship and veered abruptly away from the fighter's flight corridor. Liyeusse rechecked stealth. The engine made the familiar dreadful coughing noise in response to the increased power draw, but it held—for now.

A missile streaked through their path, missing them by a margin that Rhehan wished were larger. To their irritation, Liyeusse was whistling as she maneuvered the *Flarecat* through all the grapeshot and missiles and gyring fighters and toward the edge of the battlefield. Liyeusse had never had a healthy sense of fear.

They'd almost made it when the engine coughed again, louder. Rhehan swore in several different languages. "I'd better see to that," they said.

"No," Liyeusse said immediately, "you route the pilot functions to your seat, and I'll see if I can coax it along a little longer."

Rhehan wasn't as good a pilot, but Liyeusse was indisputably better at engineering. They gave way without argument. Liyeusse used the ship's handholds to make her way toward the engine room.

Whatever Liyeusse was doing, it didn't work. The engine hiccoughed, and stealth went down.

A flight of Kel fighters at the periphery noted the *Flarecat*'s attempt to escape and, dismayingly, found it suspicious enough to decide to pursue them. Rhehan wished their training had included faking being an ace pilot. Or actually *being* an ace pilot, for that matter.

The Incendiary Heart continued to glow malevolently. Rhehan shook their head. *It's not personal,* they told themselves. "Liyeusse," they said through the link, "forget stealth. If they decide to come after us, that's fine. It looks like we're not the only small-timers getting out of the line of fire. Can you configure for boosters?"

She understood them. "If they blow us up, a lot of people are dead anyway. Including us. We might as well take the chance."

Part of the *Flarecat*'s problem was that its engine had not been designed for sprinting. Liyeusse's skill at modifications made it possible to run. In return, the *Flarecat* made its displeasure known at inconvenient times.

The gap between the *Flarecat* and the fighters narrowed hair-raisingly as Rhehan waited for Liyeusse to inform them that they could light the hell out of there. The Incendiary Heart's glow distracted them horribly. The fighters continued their pursuit, and while so far none of their fire had connected, Rhehan didn't believe in relying on luck.

"I wish you could use that thing on them," Liyeusse said suddenly.

Yes, and that would leave nothing but the thinnest imaginable haze of particles in a vast expanse of nothing, Rhehan thought. "Are we ready yet?"

"Yes," she said after an aggravating pause.

The *Flarecat* surged forward in response to Rhehan's hands at the controls. They said, "Next thing: prepare a launch capsule for this so we can shoot it ahead of us. Anyone stupid enough to go after it and into its cone of effect— well, we tried."

For the next interval, Rhehan lost themselves in the controls and readouts, the hot immediate need for survival. They stirred when Liyeusse returned.

"I need the Heart," Liyeusse said. "I've rigged a launch capsule for it. It won't have any shielding, but it'll fly as fast and far as I can send it."

Rhehan nodded at where they'd secured it. "Don't drop it."

"You're so funny." She snatched it and vanished again.

Rhehan was starting to wish they'd settled for a nice, quiet, boring life as a Kel special operative when Liyeusse finally returned and slipped into the seat next to theirs. "It's loaded and ready to go. Do you think we're far enough away?"

"Yes," Rhehan hissed through their teeth, achingly aware of the fighters and the latest salvo of missiles.

"Away we go!" Liyeusse said with gruesome cheer.

The capsule launched. Rhehan passed over the controls to Liyeusse so she could get them away before the capsule's contents blew.

The fighters, given a choice between the capsule and the *Flarecat*, split up. Better than nothing. Liyeusse was juggling the power draw of the shields, the stardrive, life-support, and probably other things that Rhehan was happier not knowing about. The *Flarecat* accelerated as hard in the opposite direction as it could without overstressing the people in it.

The fighters took this as a trap and soared away. Rhehan expected they'd come around for another try when they realized it wasn't.

Then between the space of one blink and the next, the capsule simply vanished. The fighters overtook what should have been its position, and vanished as well. That could have been stealth, if Rhehan hadn't known better. They thought to check the sensor readings against their maps of the region: stars upon stars had gone missing, nothing left of them.

Or, they amended to themselves, there had to be some remnant smear of matter, but the *Flarecat*'s instruments wouldn't have the sensitivity to pick them up. They regretted the loss of the people on those fighters; still, better a few deaths than the many that the Incendiary Heart had threatened.

"All right," Liyeusse said, and retriggered stealth. There was no longer any need to hurry, so the system was less likely to choke. They were far enough from the raging battle that they could relax a little. She sagged in her chair. "We're alive."

Rhehan wondered what would become of Kavarion, but that was no longer their concern. "We're still broke," they said, because eventually Liyeusse would remember.

"You didn't wrangle *any* payment out of those damn Kel before we left?" she demanded. "Especially since after they finish frying Kavarion, they'll come toast *us*?"

Rhehan pulled off Kavarion's gloves and set them aside. "Nothing worth anything to either of us," they said. Once, they would have given everything to win their way back into the trust of the Kel. Over the past years, however, they had discovered that other things mattered more to them. "We'll find something else. And anyway, it's not the first time we've been hunted. We'll just have to stay one step ahead of them, the way we always have."

Liyeusse smiled at Rhehan, and they knew they'd made the right choice.

THE FAERIE TREE
Kathleen Kayembe

Kathleen Kayembe (kathleenkayembe.com) is the Octavia E. Butler Scholar from Clarion's class of 2016, with short stories in *Lightspeed* and *Nightmare*, an essay in *Luminescent Threads: Connections to Octavia Butler*, and previous publications with Less Than Three Press. She writes romance as Kaseka Nvita, co-hosts the *Write Pack Radio* weekly writing podcast as herself, and lives on Twitter as @mkkayembe. A long-time member of the St. Louis Writers Guild, she organizes write-ins instead of movie outings, and falls in love with the world every time she uses a fountain pen. You can find her in St. Louis, where, when not at the day job, she is generally freelance editing, walking her dogs, running Amherst Writers and Artists writing groups, scribbling stories into a notebook with an odd little smirk, or playing obnoxiously sensible RPG characters who won't let party members die.

THERE'S A FAERIE tree in my front yard. Its branches are gnarled like an old woman's fingers, knobbed like her knees, and the trunk hunches down like she's reaching for my house. Mamaw said the hole at the base of faerie trees is where faeries come out or rush in or leave gifts if it's big enough, though I was too young to remember. She says I was fussy in any arms that weren't hers or the tree, least 'til I got used to everything. When I was real little, Sister says she could always find me curled half in the tree if I'd toddled off, like I fell asleep tryin' to find Mamaw's faeries. Still, after she showed me, I was scared to sit in its big open lap for a time, scared faeries would rush on out and into me, and I would have wings beating in me and they'd fly me far from home, just buzzing along like a balloon through the clouds.

Tonight I want to be flown away. Sister got married and didn't tell me, she got married and didn't tell nobody. She didn't tell Momma, she didn't tell Pa, she just up and got married and brought that man home. I don't like him. He's tall and skinny, a beanpole of a man with straw for hair and black buttons for eyes, and rough, gunnysack skin. His smile's like still water, stagnant and sick, a birthing ground for things that's just born rotten. I don't know what she sees in him. He drawls and haws and hums all the time, don't say what he mean, and look at us like we're fools. He's all wrong inside and his face ain't right either. Ain't normal—like their marriage. Sister used to be strong. "I'll have a fairy prince, or nobody," she'd say, "and fairy princes ain't real." But here she is come back from boarding school with a man and a ring and a baby on the way.

Oh, Momma ain't happy. She's pretending to be, but she's not and told me so. "That sister of yours gone and got herself knocked up and had one of Those weddings. Don't know where she got it from. She weren't ever getting married, and now here he is. This is your Pa's side, Marianne. Only your Mamaw done something that stupid, God rest her, but at least we got your Pa. That damned school's lucky it's empty right now. Come fall term, I'm raising hell."

Except Sister's quit school, quit and married and gonna have a baby, and I don't like it one bit. I go out to the faerie tree and mosey around, looking for little wings before I sit and lean back and relax. It's dark but still warm, and the ground's soft, its new green poking up around my bare toes. From against the tree, big leaves hide the moon, but I can see clear through the windows into the house. The bottom floor is dark; the second floor is Sister's room, and my room that was Mamaw's before she passed; the top floor is Momma and Pa's room—they have the whole attic to themselves. They were gonna move into Sister's room so's they didn't have to climb so many stairs, but now they're gonna stay put until Sister's got a place.

In Momma and Pa's room, they're arguing. I can tell even though they're hugging and putting on nightclothes. They argue real soft, so you can't hear them, but I can tell by their feet, 'cause Momma always gets the urge to run when she's angry, and you can hear her skip-step-stop from down below and know she's in a tizzy. When I heard that I put my dress back on and came out— no sense trying to sleep while she's banging around. I can see her now, and she's as fired up as Pa is tight and still. They're talking about Sister, I know it.

Sister and her scarecrow husband are in her room. She's got a double bed, so I know where he's sleeping tonight. They just better not do anything under Pa's roof. From under the faerie tree I watch him kiss her, watch her close her eyes, and see him look straight out the window—at me. I freeze up, and then I think he can't see me. But he stops kissing Sister and pulls the curtains closed, and I know if he tells Momma I saw him she'll lick me for being nosy.

The faeries in the tree start buzzing behind me, like a nest of wasps getting ready to swarm. I know it's them, I saw 'em once, when Mamaw called 'em out to set me straight. I think about Sister's man and I'm tempted, fierce as Jesus in the desert, but I don't. Mamaw told me the price she'd paid for letting 'em loose; said giving up her grand-baby's the hardest thing she ever done. Sure, she got back her son and he raised up our family with Momma, but sometimes she must'a looked at us and just hated.

I ain't scared of the faeries no more, and they never do speak, but I learned they get loud when my heart does, so I try to feel quiet. The night air is warm and the breeze is cool. I breathe deep and stare at the dark. Fireflies float everywhere, winking like the stars I can't see through the branches. I don't want to face Sister's husband in the morning, but I know I have to. I don't much like the idea of him sleeping on the same floor as me, but Sister will protect me if it comes to anything. Pregnant or not, Sister's always stood up for me.

IN THE MORNING, Momma's cooking eggs and Pa's asking Sister's man questions at the table over coffee. What does he do, who're his parents, how did he meet Sister. You know, questions. Sister's helping Momma when she's not sitting quiet at the table with her hands folded in her lap like a big china doll. When I finish setting the table I try asking questions too, try to get Sister to talk, but she won't. I start how the girls at school start"—how did he propose?—"even though I don't care about that. I remember they all looked at me strange when I said so, like they knew I was Different. Wrong. Not a real girl. I pretended I cared after that, and Momma nods when she hears me ask, "What was the wedding like?" and I know I done right in her eyes. But Sister don't answer, just sits there, and I'm done pussyfooting around like it's fine when it ain't, and I snap. "You'd never pick a man like that, so how'd he get his dirty claws into you?"

"Marianne!" Momma bursts out my name like I cussed in church.

Pa thunders, "Hush!" right behind her. They look at me sideways, like I ain't got manners, or maybe like I just ain't right, like I'm Different. "Men are speaking," Pa says finally, but he don't say go cut a switch, so I scrunch up and hush up and sulk. Sister don't wink at me like usual though, just stares at her hands until Momma calls her to help bring out breakfast.

There are eggs and pancakes and my mouth would water on any other day at the thick smell of hot batter on the skillet, but today I'm too busy glaring at the beanpole to be hungry. I hate him already, but I know he's turning Pa around. It's like Pa can't see his scarecrow face. I know Momma don't like him, but if Pa likes him she'll make do and pretend. That's how it always is.

"So, Marianne, do you cook?" the beanpole asks.

I tell him, "Yessir," but that's all I say, and my face tells him I don't like questions.

Before Pa can get on me again for being rude, there's food on the table. Momma's smiling and Sister's just a quiet young lady, a pretty, empty face I can't reach. Something don't feel right, but don't Momma or Pa notice, and I can't tell why. So I eat quiet-like and pretend I'm a lady. Pa's talking to beanpole again.

THAT NIGHT I go back to the faerie tree and sit by the roots. I don't know why, but I feel safer here, and something's wrong in the house. Momma likes beanpole now and so does Pa, and Sister's so quiet I don't know what to think. He just sits there with those black button eyes and that doll's sewn-on smile on that gunny-sack skin. I don't know what they're hearing that turns 'em round, but he ain't getting to me. The faerie tree buzzes and lightning bugs flicker. Momma and Pa put on their nightclothes and get into bed. They don't talk tonight, just sleep.

Sister's curtains are still open and I can see in. The beanpole wraps his arms around her, hands on her belly, and all at once I think his hand's gonna change to a bear claw and cut the baby out. But his hand stays normal, and his black button eyes look out the window, right at me. He smiles that sewn-on smile, and I hate him and I'm afraid of him, and I ain't used to either one. The faeries in the tree buzz with my beating heart. I can't tell if their wings are shaking the tree, or if it's my heart beating so fast I'm shaking all on my own.

I watch, pressed back far as I can, as he lets go of Sister and walks to the window. He leans out, staring at me, then leans back in and closes the curtain.

The buzzing don't get quiet and I don't feel quiet. I'm scared to go inside, but I do. When I get to the second floor, he's standing in the yellow light from Sister's room, waiting for me.

"Marianne," he says, "I get the feeling you don't like me."

I don't know what he's really after, but I know he don't care what I think. I know enough now to play along, so I do; no sense proving I know he ain't right inside. I say, "You seem like a decent man," like I'm reading Mary for the nativity play, "you just treat my sister right, you hear?"

He laughs like a toad, says "Sure thing," and shuts the door. I hold my breath and tiptoe past, scared that door's gonna open and he'll jump out like the bogeyman. But the door don't open and when I get to my room I latch the lock and turn on all the lights so no shadows can get me while I'm trying to sleep. I stay awake all night, afraid to shut my eyes, staring at the door and reading the Good Book like Momma does when she's upset. When dawn comes, I know I'm safe. When dawn comes, so does sleep.

WHEN I GET up I don't smell cooking, but I'm so tired I don't notice. I put on a sundress and wash my face and go to the kitchen and realize Momma's not at the stove like always, and Pa's not at the table with his coffee. There's no one in the kitchen but Sister, whose hands are in her lap at the table, and the beanpole, who's halfway on the side porch with the Sheriff.

"Marianne, sweetie," Sheriff says when he sees me. "We missed you at Delilah's birthday last week. You catch a cold?"

"I weren't sick. I hate parties," I say, watch him eye me like something ain't right. "Why you here? Where's my momma and pa?"

"I'm so sorry."

"Sorry why? What's wrong, sir? Where's Momma?"

He makes me sit down at the table and then he says, "I'm afraid your momma's passed, your momma and your pa. Last night they both passed in their sleep."

"What?" It's like he cut my strings the way my body goes loose, and I think if I'd been standing I would've fallen on the floor. Sister don't move, don't come and put her arms around me. I stare up at the Sheriff. It don't make no sense. "They... they died? How?"

He nods, but he don't answer my question, and it still don't make sense. I look at Sister, but she ain't looked up from her hands. I look at beanpole, like maybe Sheriff's got the wrong house, and his hair is still straw and his skin is still gunny, but his eyes are real eyes and his mouth ain't sewn on, and I'm scareder now than when he stopped me in the hall late last night. Then I see the hearse through his legs, black and long to hold bodies, and two deputies barrel in with a stretcher, and I know I gotta see for myself before my folks are gone.

I run to the attic before they can stop me. I pull up the stairs and lock the trap door behind me. My momma and my pa didn't die in the night. It's not right, it's all wrong, like that beanpole ruining Sister. I just know when I see them things'll be right again.

But I see Momma's face, and her eyes are black buttons, and I see Pa's still face and his mouth is sewn on, and I know he done something, that damned beanpole did something, and I'd pay most any price to get him gone—get him gone yesterday, before he hurt my folks.

I can call the faeries. Mamaw showed me how. He's just like Pa's sickness, like a blight on my family, and just like Pa's sickness, they can take him away. Sister's not right, but at least she ain't dead. She took care of me 'til he came along. I'll just take care of her 'til she's all right again.

They're banging and hollering at the floor, bunch of menfolk all angry at the hysterical girl making their jobs harder. I say goodbye to the only parents I've ever known, even pray like they'd want, then I open the trapdoor and lower the stairs and come down, and I go to my room. Beanpole wants to have words with me, but it ain't his place. He ain't my sister, and he ain't my parents.

'Cause of him my parents are dead.

I latch the door in his stolen face and lay in my bed and start crying. I'm hungry and angry and sadder than I've ever been about anything, carryin' on like families at funerals, but I ain't never felt things deep enough for that before, not even for Mamaw, and I'm proud of this grief—I wallow in it, feel real for a spell. It hurts in my chest, like my heart's a bird fell out the nest and broke its neck at the bottom of the tree. Then anger burns through. I may not be the real Marianne, but I'm the one they got, and I'll do right by my parents like they did right by me.

If the faeries can't save 'em, they'll save Sister or I'll kill him myself. Come nightfall that man will be gone.

WHEN I WAKE up, it's almost dark. I'm hungry and scared stiff of going through the house without Momma to protect me, without Sister to protect me, with the beanpole still here. But I need a knife and some fruit, so I compromise. I crawl out the window, scurry down the roof to the gutter, climb down, and sneak through the porch to the kitchen. I grab an apple from the table and Momma's boning knife, then hurry out to the faerie tree like that man might show up any minute. I curl close between the faerie tree's legs and try to think while more tears leak hot down my face. Mamaw said faeries are crafty little shits, and words are important, and hard sacrifice. I make myself eat but save some for the faeries.

Come sunset, I know what to ask.

I cut my thumb when the sun's just disappearing, and the faeries' wings are buzzing with my heart. I press my blood to the dirt in the hole in the tree, and I say I need help, and they come. The fireflies pinwheel and scatter like smoked out bees as the air turns to honey in my lungs. There's a strange pull, tugging where my thumb meets the earth, like my blood is well water being drawn out from deep underground, and then faeries start bubbling up from the ground, shake off dirt, unfurl dragonfly wings, and dart out of the hollow. Each one gone yields two more coming up, and there's more climbing out of the sides of the hollow like ants climbing down from high up in the trunk. The faeries glow steady and dim, like ghost lights through a fog. One lands on my knee, nails digging like claws, and we look at each other real quiet.

It looks just like the rest of 'em flitting around, but there's weight to it, weight like the curl of a copperhead, and I know it's in charge like I know it ain't human. It's the size of my finger, naked and fearless as a baby, like a flat-chested, crazy-haired doll with no nethers to hide. It's got big, black doe eyes, but they look at me fox-like: wild, wary, and meddlesome.

The faeries pinwheel around but hover close, like they're waiting. The one on my knee reveals teeth like a shark, but its voice rings out clear as a sweet, tiny bell. "What do you want, and what will you give in exchange?"

I try to breathe easy. "There's a man killed my parents, hurt my sister, and got her pregnant. I want him dead yesterday before dark. I want every trace of him gone. You get rid of him, I'll give you the baby." It's his, probably wrong as its pa, and I know Sister ain't wanted kids 'til later anyway.

The faerie smiles, and it ain't a nice smile. "But what will *you* sacrifice?"

It knows I don't want that wrong baby somehow, but that's the price Mamaw paid, and I don't know what else to give. "I got a gold ring," I say—Mamaw's old wedding ring. Momma thought Sister would get it, kept harping on it when she found out, but when I offered to give it over she looked at me like I look at Sister's man—like I was wrong inside, like the ring should mean more than it did. I ain't tell her Mamaw maybe gave it hoping someday I'd be normal, or maybe hoping what she done wouldn't touch Sister through that band. That husband only gave her my Pa, and 'cause of Pa she got me. I know she loved me, but that don't always help.

Maybe the faerie knows that, 'cause it don't want my ring neither. "I want a *real* sacrifice."

"Well I ain't got much 'sides that to give. What kinda thing do you want?"

The faerie's mean smile gets nastier, and its teeth look longer. The other faeries stop darting like lost dragonflies, the crickets hush up, and the night air dies. "You must have loved your parents very much to want them back," the faerie says, sweet as a salesman through those sharp, sharp teeth.

"Yeah," I admit, but I'm all over scared. No good comes from telling faeries some things.

"We cannot bring back the dead, little Changeling, but we can give back your sister and take away the man and his baby. Will you pay our price?"

"Depends what you ask," I say, like I ain't made my decision before I called 'em up like I did, come what may.

The faerie's face goes soft and dreamy, like it's drinking good whiskey in a really soft chair. It says, "When you think of your parents, I can taste your emotion: all your love, your devotion, and your grief beyond my understanding. We do not feel as the humans do, child, and you'll never feel quite like the humans do either. But you feel for your parents. You feel very much." It turns sharp as its teeth. "I'll take that emotion as payment."

My heart drops and my eyes leak out tears before the words even make sense. "You wanna feel it?" I ask, but I know what it meant.

"I want to *have* it," it says. "*That's* a worthy sacrifice."

"That's too much." Maybe I can haggle it down. "Take what I feel for my Pa. Takin' both is too much."

The faerie squares off like it's rich folk and eyes me like dirt. "When last I saw you, *Marianne*," and my name in its mouth quakes my bones loud as thunder, "you were half as high, and your grandmother called us out not to deal, but to warn you away from our folk. You know what manner of price our aid requires. Would you pay less than she?"

"Two is too much," I say, quiet and scared.

"One for the man and one for the baby. I ask nothing to restore your sister in honor of your ties to us, but mark me well, *Marianne*, I could demand what you feel for her, too, and call it fair."

"Oh," I say, like I been shushed in church by the pastor himself. "The first price weren't too high like I thought."

We agree to the terms and I cut a slice of apple and eat half, and the faerie eats half, and the deal's done. I'm shaking like it's winter and I feel cold all over. I pray to Momma and Pa that they understand why I'm giving them up. I loved them the best I could, but they're gone, and there's Sister to think about now.

The faerie says bring Sister's man to the tree and they'll do it, and they'll take my Pa when it's done. The faerie says bring Sister down to the tree too, and they'll take the baby and take Momma, and it won't hurt none. I say bringing them down weren't part of the deal, but the faeries just laugh like a bell choir and fly into the tree. The crickets start chirping and the night air starts breathing, and the fireflies slide back under the branches.

Beanpole ain't been in the yard since he first came with Sister. I got no idea how to get him outside. I sit at the tree trying to think up a plan, but my whole head's full up of Momma humming over the skillet cooking pancakes for breakfast, and the way Pa half-smiles when I bring him more coffee. I see Pa whittling on the porch steps while the sun dies over harvested fields, and Ma mending in her chair, laughing with Pa through the screen. There were evenings before Sister went to boarding school when we'd all set out there, all together, Mamaw telling fairy tales and Pa saying, "Sister, no princes 'til you're thirty-five," and Sister getting fussy while Momma just laughed. He never told me "No princes," 'cause I never cared to be a princess like real girls, but I knew my family loved me through and through on those nights, even wrong inside as I was pretty.

I still wonder sometimes if the real Marianne would've been pretty as me, but maybe felt a lot more than I do, maybe cried just like Sister when Mamaw passed. If maybe she'd've grown up scared of snakes and spiders, and if she'd've crushed on boys and fit in with other girls, and not looked at people like I do most times, wondering why they think stupid things is so important. Now I wonder too: Would she have paid to save Sister like me?

I was little when Mamaw told me I weren't the real Marianne, but only she knew. My Momma and Pa loved me like I was her, and it hurts to remember, but it makes me feel human as Sister, rememberin', and I don't want to forget.

I give up trying to plan when it hits me I won't remember nights on the porch the same without my love for Momma and Pa, and without their love for me. I cry some more after that, and when my stomach claws at me I finish the apple, and then I watch Sister's light go on and hate the beanpole more than ever for what I'm giving up.

Sister walks up to the window, a china doll trapped inside oily light, and I look at her and hate her too a minute, 'cause she brought that damned man into our home. Beanpole don't come up behind her though, and I don't see other lights in the house, and I wonder if he left on his own, and if he did, can I still keep my Pa? But then I hear the screen door clack shut, and the beanpole melts into a shadow just outside reach of the faerie tree's branches, and I realize I ain't got to bring him here at all.

"Come inside," he says, stretching out his hand. "I promise you'll feel better in the morning."

Sister stands in her window, hands over her belly like Mary finding out her son's gonna die. I look at her and I think of the faeries, and I feel mean as a razor. "I ain't going in," I say. "I won't. I'm gonna sleep here tonight."

"At least come in and let me get you a blanket," he says all reasonable, like I don't know what he did.

"I'm just fine," I say, and I wait for the faeries, but they don't come and I wonder if he's not close enough. So I tell him, like I might be a tiny bit sorry, "I *will* take a blanket if you bring it here."

He shrugs like a good man trying to make nice, and he goes and gets me a blanket and stops on the edge of the branches again. "Brought you a blanket," he says, "Come get it and then I'll let you alone."

"Promise?" Like I ain't planning to kill him.

"Yeah, I promise." Like he ain't a killer and a thief.

Sister's still in her window, hands on her belly, but she's looking right at me and all at once I'm afraid of her too. The faeries said they'd make Sister like she was, but what if they can't and that's why they said she was free? What if I'm about to give up Momma and Pa and I don't even get Sister back like they promised?

My heart starts up thundering and the faerie tree buzzes behind me, and I realize I don't want to move. I hate the faeries much as I hate that beanpole, but I feel safer touching the faerie tree and curling the boning knife in my hand. I'm afraid to go get that damned blanket.

"Come get the blanket, Marianne," he says.

"No, I'm warm," I say, and it's true, I start feeling so hot I might sweat. I'm tired and hungry and he murdered my folks and he ruined my sister, and he has nerve talking with Pa's mouth while he glares down at me with my own momma's eyes. I want him gone, but first I need him to come closer. I'm waiting for him, eyeing him like those damned faeries eyed me.

"You won't be warm in the morning, young lady."

I ain't his young lady. "Then bring it here, I ain't moving." If Pa heard my tone he'd make me go cut a switch.

"No, you come here and get it. Now. I mean it, Marianne. I'm in charge now, and I don't want you catching cold." When I don't budge, he tries for sweet, and it works. "You wouldn't want to disappoint your Momma, now would you?"

"Don't you dare," I yell like I'm throwing stones, and my mind's all gone red with my rage. I run at him, quick and mad as lightning, and I stick him real good and he drops the old blanket on my arms before I can think.

Only then do I realize, piece by piece, like a quilt stitched together, just what I've done. The blanket is coarse in my hands, and the moon lights a gunnysack shade matching his skin. When I look up at his face, Momma's eyes are black and smiling, and he's grinning at me in my Pa's proud half-smile. There's no blood round the knife in his side, but his skin's peeling at the shoulders, like a snake starting to shed for a new one.

His fingers ain't fingers. They're sharp as bear claws.

He swipes 'em at me.

I fall, but I can't get my hands out to catch me. Then I see the blanket ain't a blanket, just like he's not a man: I'm gripping hard to a sack winding its way over my fingers, up my hands and wrists and arms to my shoulders. I thrash like a fish in a boat 'til I'm on my side, then I inch like a worm toward the faerie tree, screeching.

"Help me!" Loud, over my heartbeat, I scream, "Now, goddammit!"

That man's close enough! If they don't take him now he'll kill me and they'll get nothing and I'll be nothing and I don't know what else I can do. But there's no lights, and then I'm yowling too loud to hear 'em buzzing if they do come, 'cause the beanpole drives his claws into my foot and yanks me close, lifts me high by my shoulders, and his mouth opens wide. It's like a snake mouth, bigger than it has any right to be, and black inside with no teeth, just an eternity of nothing.

He breathes in.

It's like his breath's digging under my skin, fixing to rip it off, and it hurts more than his claws in my shoulders and where the sack's seeping in. I scream and my voice feels skinned out of my body, and then over my pain I hear bedlam, and it's coming fast. I feel the honey of oncoming power, and it soothes me, but the beanpole starts screaming and drops me to run. That's when I see them, buzzing loud as a waterfall, streaming out like a river of light from the tree straight at him. They fill the darkness with light, bright as day and as pure as an angel of vengeance. When I strain up to see the beanpole, he's covered in light. Faerie wings ripple over him like they're breathing, a seething army of ants covering him head to foot while he's in there screaming. It's horrible, the sounds of buzzing and chomping and him screaming like the faeries missed his vitals when they hit. Then he chokes and goes quiet, and it stinks of sour blood and sawdust and old, rotten eggs.

The faeries is still loud when beanpole starts shrinking, smaller and smaller like they're ants on a carcass, 'til he's all but gone.

I can't even think to feel glad when it happens.

'Cause when beanpole starts shrinking, my mind starts through memories of Pa as I lie in that unnatural light. And while beanpole's shrinking, what I feel about those memories shrinks with him, 'til that's all gone too.

I think on those nights on the porch, and they still feel so strongly of love and of family, but now something big's missing, and I feel a strange ache. I wanna slap at the faeries that land on my arms by the dozens, but the sack crunches to nothing under their sharp teeth, and I'm afraid they'll keep eating, so I lay real still and hate them deep down.

Up in her window, I see Sister start to cry, and her hands clench her belly, and she looks sharp at me. Then she's gone, run right out of my sight, and there's galumphing through the house, then she's running through the screen door and coming straight for me.

She sweeps me up in her arms before I can blink. "Thank God you're okay," she's crying messy, "I was so afraid for you." Says, "I'm sorry" and "forgive me, please."

"What was he," I ask her. "What'd he do to you?"

But she don't answer, just rocks me and wails like a baby.

"It's okay, Sister," I tell her. "It don't matter. He's gone now. We're okay."

She makes a sound like she's laughing and crying both into my hair, and I hug her with my freed arms, scraped raw by the sack.

Then the buzzing starts again, and faeries swarm in, hornet mad as the air goes thick and bright with their light. They've come for the baby, I know it, and I hold Sister's hands when she swats at the faeries like she don't know just what they are.

Sister's eyes roll back when the fairies rush at her belly and disappear and reappear through her dress and her skin. I catch her and lay her down on the grass beanpole trampled half under the tree. The faeries crash wave after wave of light into Sister's swollen belly. Then she gurgles and my knee is wet in the grass by her thigh, and a black, rotting stain's curling up her pale nightdress. I pull the fabric so the oil slick baby oozes onto the grass, move Sister away from the spill, and then look at the thing. It's gunny-skinned and sharp-clawed, and smells like its pa when he died.

I hold Sister close. She shakes and keens but don't wake. As faerie light swarms the baby, I feel Momma go too.

The faeries fly back into the tree, drunk as anything on my feelings. Their leader streaks by me and don't even look over. Then the lights are gone, and the faeries are gone, and that damned man and his baby are gone, like my Momma and Pa.

For a few minutes it's just me, then Sister wakes up and it's just me and Sister. We huddle alone under cold, distant stars, while the land sprawls out empty for miles. Sister cries on my shoulder, but she's Sister and not a china doll, and I cry 'cause I have her and she's all I got.

I think, that's the last of it, now it's all done. Sister'll take care of me and we'll be a family like before she left.

I should've known better.

Sometimes I look at Sister now and the holes in my heart feel sharp as Momma's boning knife, and hate settles over me like a blanket, like silence. I think of Mamaw those times, seeing me every day at the end of her life and just knowing I weren't Marianne, and it was her fault, but she couldn't tell nobody.

That's sacrifice: Giving what you can't give so people you love get along better. Not telling what you gave for them while they rub that pain right in your face and you can't say a word, least not one they'll believe.

I sacrificed my love for Momma and Pa so's Sister could get along better. She don't remember the night the faeries came. Just wakes up the next day with no baby. Doctor says stress from Momma and Pa must've made her miscarry, and grief made her forget. He says, "Get some rest." Then he takes me aside and says to me, "You take good care of your sister, Marianne." And he asks how I'm doing without Momma, and I try to sound sad, but all I feel is the hole where my love got ripped out, and I must look real strange 'cause his eyes get real sharp.

Doctor looks at me like the girls at school look at me: Different. Wrong. Not a real girl.

At the funeral I don't cry and the mourners all look at me: Different. Wrong. Not a real girl.

And Sister and I are laughing under the faerie tree one day, months later, when she don't cry as fast and hard missing our folks. "You remember on the porch when Pa said, 'no fairy princes 'til you're thirty-five'? I guess I should've listened." And she laughs up through the leaves. And I laugh, but it's hollow, and I ache missing what I can't feel anymore 'bout strangers I used to love. And Sister says, "What do you miss most? I miss those nights on the porch."

And I look at the hole in the tree like the hole inside me, and I think, *I wish I could miss them*, and it gets real quiet, and when I look at Sister I know I said it, and she heard it, 'cause she's looking at me: Different. Wrong. Not a real girl. Like I'm a stranger, and she's seeing me for the first time, and she just don't understand. I clear my throat, say, "I wish I could miss them less," like I just talked too soft and the evening wind stole the last word.

Sister smiles all sad, and nods like she believes me, and she acts just like always the rest of the night. But since that day, sometimes she looks at me sideways, and I think when the faeries took Momma and Pa, they took Sister from me even as they were giving her back.

THE MOCKING TOWER

Daniel Abraham

Daniel Abraham (www.danielabraham.com) was born in Albuquerque, New Mexico, earned a biology degree from the University of New Mexico, and spent ten years working in tech support. He sold his first short story in 1996, and followed it with twenty four novels, including fantasy series The Long Price Quartet, SF novel *Hunter's Run* (co-written with George R. R. Martin and Gardner Dozois), the Black Sun's Daughter dark fantasy series (as M. L. N. Hanover), the Dagger and the Coin fantasy series, the Expanse space opera series (as James S.A. Corey, co-written with Ty Franck), which included Hugo Award nominee *Leviathan's Wake*, and more than twenty short stories, including International Horror Guild Award-winner "Flat Diane", Hugo and World Fantasy award nominee "The Cambist and Lord Iron: a Fairytale of Economics". His most recent book is a James S.A. Corey space opera, *Persepolis Rising*.

OLD AU SAW the thief first.

Squatting in the garden, she commanded a long view of the east road; gray flagstone straighter than nature amid the green scrub and bramble. Rich soil breathed its scent around her as she took an offending root in one hand and her garden knife in the other. Between the moment she began sawing and when she pulled the first tangle of dirt and pale vegetable flesh out of the ground, the thief appeared, a dot on the horizon. She worked as he approached. His cloak hung limp in the humid summer air. His hat, wide as his shoulders, shadowed his eyes. He wore an empty scabbard across his back. Old Au paused when he grew close. When he reached the wall of ancient stone that marked the border between the greater world and the protected lands within, he paused and looked toward the Mocking Tower.

The tower shimmered as the tales all said it would, appearing to change shape between one breath and the next. A great thrusting pillar of alabaster studded with living torches became an ancient palace of gray stone and moss became a rose-colored complication of terraces stacked one atop another toward the sky. The thief took in the illusionist's art with an air of haughtiness and satisfaction. Old Au watched the man watch the tower, cleared her throat, and nodded to the stranger.

"What news?" she asked.

His gaze shifted to the old woman. His eyes looked as if they'd been dyed the same blue as a storm cloud. The lines around his mouth and eyes spoke of age and weather, but Old Au thought she saw a boyishness in them as well, like the image of an acorn worked in oak. Something in him reminded Old Au of a lover she'd taken years before. A man of high station who dreamed of living as a gardener. Dead now and his dreams with him except for what she carried with her. When the thief spoke, his voice carried the richness and depth of a reed instrument, softly played.

"The throne stands empty," the thief said. "King Raan rots in his grave, and the princes vie to claim his place."

"All seven of them?"

"Tauen, Maush, and Kinnan all fell to their brothers' blades. Another— Aus by name—rose from the south with a foreign army at his back to lay a new claim. Five armies still cross the land and blight wherever they pass."

"Shame, that," Old Au said.

"Wars end. Even wars of succession. They also create certain unexpected opportunities for the bold," he said, then shifted as by moving his shoulders, he moved the conversation. "These lands belong to the Imagi Vert?"

Old Au shrugged, pointing to the stone wall with her chin. "Everything within the border, and all the way round. Not subject to the throne, nor the one before it. Nor to whatever comes next either. The Mocking Tower stands apart from the world and the Imagi Vert sees to that, once and eternal. You've come on behalf of one of the princes? Plead the Imagi to take a side, maybe?"

"The tale I hear told says the Imagi Vert took King Raan's soul when he died and fashioned it into a blade. And the blade lies somewhere in that tower. I have come to steal it."

Old Au wiped a soil-darkened hand across her cheek, squinting first at the thief then at the Mocking Tower and back to the thief. His chin lifted as if in challenge. The empty scabbard tapped against his back as if asking for attention. Green lacquer and brass fittings, and long enough to hold even a fairly large sword. As though a king's soul surely required a palatial blade to hold it.

"You make it a habit to announce that sort of thing, do you?" Old Au said as she brushed the soil off the length of pale, stubborn root still in the earth. "Seems an odd way to get what you want."

The thief's attention returned to her. A smile both bright and brief flickered on his lips. "I'm sure you know a great deal about gardening. I know a great deal about theft. This road leads to the township at the tower's base?"

Old Au nodded. "Another hour down the road. Keep left at the crossing or you'll find yourself heading south without much besides grain silos and the mill for company. But take the warning. Everyone you find there is loyal to the Imagi Vert. Anyone not tends to leave fair quick."

"I don't plan to stay."

"You have a name, friend?" Old Au asked.

"Many of them."

The thief slid a hand into his sleeve and drew it back out. Something small and bright between his fingers caught the sunlight. He tossed the coin to Old Au, and she caught it without thinking. A square of silver with a young man's likeness pressed into the metal. Some prince or another. One of the dead king's warring brood.

"This for my silence?" Old Au asked.

"For your help in directing me," the thief said. "Anything more lies between you and your conscience."

Old Au chuckled, nodded, and tucked the coin in her belt. The thief and his empty scabbard stepped off down the road. His stride shifted his cloak from side to side like the flourish of a street magician's right hand distracting from the actions of the left. His hat carried shadow under its brim like a veil. The Mocking Tower changed to a soaring complex of chains hanging from a stonework tree taller than clouds to a spiral of basalt with stairways cut into the sides. Old Au shook her head and bent back down to her work. The stubborn root defied her, but she was stern and hard and well-practiced with a garden knife. When it came out, long as her arm and pale as bone, she squatted in the churned black soil, wiped the sweat from her face, and looked west after the thief. The curve of the road and the trees hid him already.

The township that served the Imagi Vert pretended normalcy even in the shadow of magic. Only the central square boasted flagstone. Dust, dirt, and weeds made up all the streets. The small stables reeked like stables anywhere, and pisspots stood in the alleys waiting to be taken and their contents sold to the launderer to whiten cloth or the tanner to soften hide. The flowers of early summer drew bees and flies. The sun warmed thatched roofs until they stank a little. Birds chattered and warned each other from their nests. Dogs ran here as they did anywhere, chasing squirrels and each other. A few hundred feet to the north, the Mocking Tower loomed, a spire of bone and glass, then a pillar of plate-thin stones stacked one atop the other toward the sky, then a spiral of what looked like skinned flesh, then an ivy-clad maiden of granite with a crown of living flame.

The people of the township viewed the thief as the greater curiosity. He walked through the streets, eyes hidden but with a cheerful smile. The empty scabbard bumped against his back with every step.

The traveler's hearth stood just down from the square and at an angle, like a servant with eyes politely averted. The thief went to it as if he stayed there often. The keeper—a fat man wearing the traditional iron chain of hospitality wrapping his left arm—greeted him in the courtyard.

"I need only a small room," the thief said.

"No small rooms, nor any big ones either," the fat man said. "Just rooms is all."

"All people claim the same dignity before the Imagi?" the thief said as if joking.

"Just so. Just so. Simin can take your horse if you have one."

Simin—a lanky, dark-haired boy with a simple, open face—nodded hopefully. The thief shook his head and handed three of the square, silver coins to the fat man. "I only take what I can carry."

The keeper considered the coins as if they spelled out the future, then pressed his lips tight and shrugged. The iron chain clinked as if offering its own metallic thoughts. Simin broke the silence. "I can show you the way anyhow."

"Very kind of you," the thief said.

Simin trotted ahead, leading the thief down short halls and into a hidden courtyard of cherry trees. A stone cistern loomed in a corner where a thin-limbed girl scrubbed away moss with a black-bristled brush and tried not to stare. The thief nodded to her. She blushed and nodded back.

Simin stopped at a high door the color of fresh cream, opening the brass latch with a click. The thief stepped into his private room and the boy trotted along behind him. The air smelled of soap and lilac. Shadows clung to the pale walls, like stepping into a sudden twilight. A modest bed with a dark brown, rough-woven blanket of the sort common to the southern tribes a hundred years before. An ironwork sculpture of an iris in a frame hung on the wall opposite the only window. An earthenware jug and cup sat on a low table beside three unlit candles. Simin, smiling, closed the shutters as if the thief had asked him to. The shadows grew deeper.

The thief sank slowly to the bed. The empty scabbard clattered on the floor where he dropped it. He swept off his hat and let it sit beside him, covered in pollen and dust. Sweat-dark locks of hair stuck to his balding scalp. His cheerful smile vanished and fear took its place. He shook his head, pressed a palm to his brow, and shook his head again.

"I can't. I can't do this."

"You can," Simin—whose name was not Simin—snapped, his own affectation of boyish goodwill falling away. "And you will."

"Did you see that tower? I've heard tales of the Mocking Tower, everyone has. I thought it would... I don't know. Catch the sunlight oddly. Cast weird shadows. 'Seems to shift moment by moment' they say, ah? Too damned true. How do I put myself against a wizard who can do that?"

Simin leaned against the wall, arms folded across his chest. "You don't. I do."

"We're making a mistake. We should go back."

"Back to what? Fire and death? We keep to the plan," the boy said. "Get the sword. End the war."

The thief sagged forward, elbows against his knees, head in his hands. "If you say. If you say." Then, gathering himself. "Did you find it?"

Simin poured water from the jug into the cup and handed it to the thief as he spoke. "No. But with you here, they'll show me. Whatever changes, wherever the guard increases, whatever they keep you from. That's how I'll know. You strike the drum, and I listen to the echoes for answers. It works that way. And the more they watch you, the less they watch me."

"I know, I know," the thief said, then paused to drink the cup dry. He handed it back, wiping his lips with a sleeve. "I liked this plan better before I came here. Successions and thrones and blood and armies in the field. Now magic swords and wizards and a tower like something that's crawled out of a bad dream. I don't belong in something like this."

"Go in the morning. Talk to everyone you can find. Ask about green glass."

"Green glass? Why?"

"I found a private temple not far from the tower fashioned from it. I think the blade may be there."

"Green glass, then. And boasting about crossing the Imagi Vert in front of the people most loyal to him. And acting mysterious and charming. When the wizard kills me over this, you can carry the guilt."

"What news from the war?" Simin asked, and his tone said he already knew. The swamping of Loon Channel. The murder of Prince Tauen. The starvation in Cai Sao Station. A question that carries its own answer argues something more than its words. The thief understood.

"The payout justifies the risk," the bald man said to the boy. "I never said otherwise."

"We start tomorrow, then," the boy said, and left, closing the door behind him.

"I already started today," the thief muttered to an empty room.

KING RAAN TOOK the throne, and with it control of the Empire, a week before his twentieth name day. A boy still with the glow of youth in his skin, he sat a chair of gold and gemstones and bones. He ruled for six decades through peace and strife, famine and plenty. Many people born on the day of his ascension lived out their whole lives not knowing any other ruler. The idea of governance and King Raan grew together in the minds of his subjects like two saplings planted side by side twining around each other until neither could exist without the other. King Raan and the Empire and the right function of the world all named the same thing.

Easy enough, then, to forget the man who bore that weight. He alone of everyone from the Sea of Pearls to knife-peaked Dai Dou mountains, the ice sheets of High Saral to the deserts of the Heliopon, understood that the man called King Raan who controlled the Empire as a normal person commanded their own hands and the one named Raan Sauvo Serriadan born of Osh Sauvo, princess of Hei Sa and third wife to King Gaudon, did not share everything. The man and the office that demanded all his days only appeared at peace with each other. If anything, Death's shadow oppressed him more than it did others because he could not pretend that more power and influence would bring a deeper meaning to his life. Wealth and status could not dispel the questions that haunted him. He sought his consolation in sex and philosophy and—near the end—the occult.

The sex led to a legion of children both within and outside the political labyrinths of marriage; the philosophy, to series of melancholy letters which detailed his conception of the human soul and the nature of a well-lived life; and the occult, inevitably, to his friendship with the Imagi Vert.

The Imagi Vert: a name that conjured up a whole mythology of threats and wonders. Even more than the bodiless voice of the Stone Oracle at Kalafi or the Night Children that played in the waves off the coast of Amphos, the Imagi Vert embodied the deeper mysteries of the world. Some claimed that the Imagi began life as human and suffered transformation by falling down a cliff and into a flaw in the universe. Others, that God could not breathe life into the clay of the world without opening a crack between heaven and earth, and the scar from that wound took a name and a tower and a circle of land for itself. Or that a great wizard cheated death itself by learning to live backward to the beginning of all things. All the different versions agreed on three things: the Imagi held the Mocking Tower and the land around it inviolate, those who sought to bend the Imagi to mere human will ended poorly, and wonders beyond the understanding of the most outlandish imagination lay hidden in the shadow of that changing and eternal tower. King Raan's studies of the occult drew him to the low stone wall and the town and the tower as inevitably as water running down.

No one can know the nature of that first meeting, but many have guessed. Perhaps the emperor could only experience humility before the ageless, timeless thing that called the Mocking Tower home. Or perhaps two people set so far above humanity that power became isolation more resembled refugees in a vast wilderness clinging to one another. No one witnessed the time those two kept in each other's company, and King Raan shared little with his court. His trips to the Mocking Tower became first a yearly pilgrimage, then once in the high summer and another in winter's depth. And then, as his years thinned him and travel from the palaces became impossible, a beloved memory that outlasted all others.

Death came to King Raan as with anyone. The throne of Empire did not exempt him. Physicians came from every corner of world bearing vials of salt and herb, charms and chants and leeches. King Raan allowed them all to minister to him like an uncle indulging his nieces and nephews in their games. If he held any real hope of prolonging his life, he didn't express it. The princes and princesses gathered around the palaces. The eldest—Prince Kinnan—bore his diadem on hair already grown thin and pale by fifty-eight years of life. Princess Magren, the youngest present, still wore braids like a child, celebrating a youth she had not quite outgrown. The palaces grew dense with the volume of servants and wealth and ambition, like a tick ready to pop with blood.

At the moment of his death, a darkness passed over the palaces. The torches and lamps and the fires in their grates all shuddered and went out. Some claim to have heard the sound of wings, as if the blackness hid a vastness of huge birds. Others, a low, musical whistling that came from the walls themselves. Only King Raan's nurse and Prince Tauen who fortune placed at his bedside heard King Raan's last words—*You remembered your promise*—and at the time, they placed no great importance upon them. When the servants finished rekindling the torches and candles, fire logs and lanterns, King Raan lay dead and the Empire changed.

For a time, it seemed as if this new order might fall close to the old. The legal scholars and priests who studied the arcana of dignified bloodlines identified those of King Raan's children with just claims to the throne. As eldest, Kinnan held the strongest claim, but Naas—younger but of a higher-born mother—ran a near second. Then Tauen and Clar, Maush, and Tynnyn. Princess Saruenne of Holt cut her hair and her name together, declaring herself Prince Saru in a gesture which the priests said had many precedents. For the weeks of mourning, the Empire held its breath. Then Prince Kinnan announced the date of his ascension and invited his siblings to come in peace to honor the memory of the father they shared.

Even now, the identity of the men who slaughtered Kinnan's wife and children remained unclear. But they failed to kill the prince, and the War of Seven Princes began.

In years since the first blood spilled, only chaos reigned. News traveled across mountains and plains, lakes and oceans, and it spoke of death and loss and palace intrigue. And, sometimes to those who cared to listen for it, of the Imagi Vert. A fisherman whose cousin worked in the palace kitchens said that on the night of King Raan's death, when the fires died, a shape—human or nearly so—had been seen flying across the face of the moon. It came from the direction of the Mocking Tower and returned the same way. A woman traveling through the lands of the Imagi Vert at that same time reported that the townsfolk had kept inside that night, leaving the mild summer evening as empty as if a wild storm had raged.

Some tales could even be verified. Yes, agents of the Imagi had sought out half a dozen of the best swordsmiths in the Empire in the months of King Raan's decline. Yes, a forge had been built in the lee of the Mocking Tower, then—a month after the death of the king—collapsed. Yes, a stranger had arrived at the library of Ahmon Suer in the weeks after the king's first decline and demanded an obscure treatise on the nature of the soul.

Little more than whispers in a high wind, yet the links between the Imagi Vert and the death of the king began to tell a larger tale. This new mythology began in the king's dying words and ended in one man's plan to end the war.

The patchwork of truth and surmise came together this way: In his age, King Raan came to fear death, or if not fear it, at least regret its necessity. He appealed to his deathless friend and companion, the Imagi Vert. Together, they plotted a way that King Raan might shed the clay of his flesh and yet remain undying. The Imagi Vert, through means unknown to the pious, collected the king's soul when it fled his body, returned with it to the Mocking Tower, and there forged it into a sword. Steel and fire formed a blade in which Raan could escape all endings.

And then... what would the wizard who lived outside of time do with such a blade? What power could a true soulsword give? Mere human guesses seemed unlikely to plumb the depths of the Imagi's schemes and plots.

Perhaps the sword gave some advantage a thousand years hence. Perhaps it only offered the pleasure of accomplishing a task no other alchemist dared to hazard. But for the heirs of the Empire? For the men and women and children who faced the prospect of war, it was an object of even greater power.

And so, in the capital of a small nation where King Raan had made one of his last visits, in the home of a woman who, almost two decades before, had been charged with the raising of young Prince Aus, the heir farthest from his father's throne built schemes of his own.

He had lived alone his whole life, knowing nothing of his father and mother beyond a direction over the sea and an assurance that his blood gave him honor and dignity, if not love. He covered the fine stone walls in charcoal and wax as he mapped out his journey, the paths of his little armies. The eighth in the War of Seven Princes, and the one with the least hope of victory in the field.

The field did not concern him. For Aus, the path of victory wound through no battlefields. Only the gardens and grounds of the Mocking Tower. The ruins where ivy already overgrew the charred bones of a forge. A temple of green glass. The streets and stables, mills and kitchens and farmyards of the lands that no king claimed. There or nowhere lay the key to the ambitions of Aus, the Forgotten Prince.

Aus, whose name was not Simin.

"I HAVE ALWAYS had a fondness for... *green glass,*" the thief said and smiled knowingly. The woman standing before him—dark-haired and broad-shouldered—rested her axe on her shoulder and said nothing. The thief smiled as if the two of them were sharing a joke, tipped his wide-brimmed hat, and moved on down the street. The town betrayed no trace of its eerie status apart from the Mocking Tower itself. Men and women went about the business of their days here as they would anywhere. Dogs and children chased each other over rough stone paving and through wide puddles of sanding mud. Birds watched from the tree branches thick with leaves. So long as the constantly changing tower remained hidden, forgetting it seemed possible. And the thief found ways to keep the tower out of sight.

A thick-faced man hauling a cartload of fresh-cut hay made his way along the street, a creature of soft grunts and sweat. The thief stepped in front of him. "A fine morning. I wonder, friend, if you might know something interesting about green glass? I have good silver to trade for good words."

The hauler paused, scowled, and shrugged his shoulders before he shoved on. The thief smiled after him as if his reticence told a clearer tale than all the eloquence in the world. He drew an old tin sextant from his robe, hung a plumb line with a lump of gem-bright crimson glass for a bob, and pretended to take readings of the tops of the trees. He felt like an idiot, and a frightened one at that. He expected to end the day facedown in a ditch with fish eating his eyes. But he also took his work seriously, so he made a mysterious ass of himself and hoped for the best without being too specific what that best might be.

In the stables, Prince Aus played at Simin, nodding and helping wherever he found a chance, and above all else listening.

The keeper to his wife as they tended to the grapevines behind the main house: *Of course I sent word to the tower. Went there myself as soon as I saw him off to his room. Expect the Imagi knew well before I said anything, though.*

The cleaning girl to her mother as they walked toward the market with the day's eggs: *The Imagi sent instructions in the night. Little finches with hollowed eyes that carried bits of parchment in their beaks. Bir*—(who Simin knew as the blacksmith's apprentice)—*got one, and so did Soylu.*

One of the little girls wearing as much mud as dress as she clapped her hands in the filthy water by her house: *Thieves and rats, thieves and rats, and all of us are blades and cats.*

Everyone knew, as Simin hoped they would. But if any panicked, he didn't see it. Like a man walking toward a dog on a road at twilight, the town watched, calm and steady, as it judged the threat. But at least it felt threatened or amused or at least *interested*. Of his greatest fears—boredom, complaisance, indifference—he saw nothing. The thief loomed in the news of the town, and that sufficed.

After lunch, when Simin traditionally slipped away to the hayloft for a long nap, Prince Aus slipped away down the track that pretended to be a deer trail. He walked carefully, his ears straining over the buzzing of summer flies and the hushing of the high grass. The midday heat drenched him with sweat and the thick air went into his lungs like steam. The Mocking Tower shifted: a spiral of smooth white stones reaching to the sky; a pair of massive yellow curves nesting one within the other like the beak of an impossible huge bird; a single uncarved block of smoky obsidian. As he neared the site of the green-glass temple, he slowed even more.

The little marks set to warn of others passing along the track remained. The long blade of grass bent at knee height still leaned across the path. The thread thin as spider's web at waist height still caught the thick, sluggish breeze between a dead tree and a thick, sharp-leaved bush. Prince Aus felt the disappointment growing in his heart even before he made the last turn and the green-glass temple came into view.

Perhaps it had grown smaller since first he'd discovered it—anything seemed possible so close to the Mocking Tower. Or perhaps the first dissonant chords of disappointment only made it seem so. The afternoon sun shone against the undulating emerald surfaces, but he only saw the dust now. When he stepped inside and stepped to the low altar, he felt none of the sense of wonder and certainty that bore him up the night he'd found it. The dust he'd spread so carefully in hopes of showing where the footsteps of the unwary had passed remained unstirred.

The thief had come, made his threat, and no one had reacted. Not the townsfolk. Not the Imagi Vert. Prince Aus told himself to be pleased. He preferred finding the blade's true hiding place, but knowing for certain that the temple did not hold it added to his knowledge, subtracted from the possibilities that remained. He cultivated patience. Mostly. His single frustrated shout set the birds in the treetops to flights, but only once. He didn't repeat it.

He walked back along the trail, hurrying to get back to the hayloft before anyone expected Simin to wake. Even as he broke into a trot, he felt his false persona slipping into place. Simin the vagabond. The boy too dull to have a story of his own worth knowing. Simin the unremarkable. And perhaps it was because of this—the role he'd inhabited before fitting so well into place—that the cleaning girl walking along the road away from town and tower failed to notice him.

The market lay nowhere near. The girl's mother no longer limped at her side. And something bounced and bobbled against her back. A little cloth bag, grease-stained. The sort that might hold a bit of food carried for not too long a journey.

Aus or Simin paused, pulled between two impulses: return to safety before anyone could penetrate his disguise or else... or else see what this girl meant by traveling alone so far from where her usual paths led her. And with food. And—yes—just the faintest air of furtive excitement. Aus felt his belly tighten, a knot form in the back of his throat.

He turned, following her at a distance, and with all the stealth he could.

The girl led him to the north, away from the green-glass temple, and around to the uncanny, shifting tower. The sun caught the crimson of her scarf and the sway of her hair as brightly as a banner on the field. The sun's heat stood on the edge between pleasant and oppressive. The thickness of the air felt like a coming storm. He kept to the shadows under boughs and edges of the tall grass where the path's curve took her nearly out of sight. His fear of being seen grew in him, changing as it did into a vibrating excitement. At any moment, the keeper of the traveler's hearth would come looking for him. The urge to break off tugged at him, but the sense of teetering on the edge of something critical pulled him forward. The girl, unaware that his world now centered on her, walked and skipped, paused and looked back, walked on. A patch of sweat darkened the back of her dress.

And in a stretch of dappled shade where two trees overhung the path, she vanished.

A cold rush of panic filled the prince's chest. The girl had been an illusion, the bait in a trap. Or she had escaped him and even as he stood there, she hurried to raise the alarm. He waited, his body stiff as wood, and only when nothing happened for ten long, shuddering breaths together did he move forward. The path between the trees stood empty. The leaves shuddered in a barely felt breeze. The rough-worn earth went before and behind. Nothing seemed odd or out of place apart from his memory of the girl and her present absence. The prince turned slowly, blinking in confusion and wonder.

The complication of air nearly escaped him. Made from nothing, it looked like nothing. Only a flaw in the light like the smallest ripple in a glass. Even when he saw it, he doubted. But he stepped forward, one foot before the other, and the landscape unfolded around him as if by walking straight ahead, he rounded a bend in the path and exposed new and unseen vistas. A hillside rose green-grassed and dandelion-spattered to the very foot of the Mocking Tower. A lintel of stone stood at the mouth of a cave, and in the place of twilight between the darkness underground and the shining daylight, the cleaning girl sat with Bir, the blacksmith's apprentice, beside her. A lunch of chicken and bread spread out by their side and the little cloth bag collapsed behind them. The two saw nothing but each other, but Prince Aus saw everything. The girl's awkward smile. The apprentice blacksmith's ill-fitting armor and leather-handled axe. The shuddering shape after shape after shape of the tower. He walked backward, the world refolding itself around him until he stood alone on the path again, in the same place but no longer entirely the same man.

A pathway hidden by magic. A man set to guard it even at the cost of his usual duties. The abandoned temple no longer pained him. What he'd sought, he'd found. The Imagi Vert, alarmed by the thief, drew up his defenses, and in doing so, showed what wanted defending. Simin or Aus retreated to the town, walking often forward and often backward, hurrying to avoid suspicion in his absence but also committing the path to memory for the time when he returned.

The rest of the day Prince Aus committed himself to being Simin. He mucked out the stalls and repaired the place in the chicken run where something from the woods failed to force its way in. He hauled water from the well to the hearth's kitchen and carried pies from the kitchen to the miller as exchange for the uncooked flour. When the keeper made a joke, he laughed. When the cleaning girl trotted by near sundown with her cheeks bright and her sleeve stained green with grass, he pretended not to notice. The Mocking Tower changed: a moon-pocked shaft of white and gray; a block of iron like a great anvil with glowing windows around the top; a ramshackle construction like all the buildings of a rough village stacked one atop the other and swaying in the slight breeze.

The thief came to the common room for dinner, ate and drank and laughed without appearing to have a care in the world or any interest in Simin. His merry blue eyes danced and glittered in the candlelight, and he drank wine and sang songs as if everything that happened fit in with some unimaginably complex plan. Near midnight, when Prince Aus snuck across the grounds to the thief's room, the door stood ajar, and the man hunched on the bed seemed like someone else entirely. The thief's eyes watered and deep grooves of concern bordering on fear carved themselves into his forehead and the corners of his mouth.

"I can't keep doing this," he said, as the prince stepped into the room. "They smile and talk when I face them, but as soon as I turn my back, they plot murder. A day more, two at most, and a knife's going to sprout right between my shoulder blades. I can feel it already."

"Can you, now?" the prince said, shutting the door.

"I can. It itches." The thief ran a hand over his scalp, disarranging his hair.

The prince sat beside him. "Good that we leave tonight, then."

The thief started then went still. His wide eyes flickered over the Prince's face. "Seriously?"

"I found a place. A hidden cave at the base of the tower. Guarded by a man who isn't a guard by trade and shrouded by magic."

"Well," the thief said, then laughed like a brook in flood. "The plan worked? The plan actually worked? I'm damned. I figured us both for dead."

"Working," the prince said. "Not worked. Not yet. You stay here. Rouse no more suspicions. But when I come back, we ride."

"Understood," the thief said. And as the prince rose to go, leaped to his feet, scrabbled under the bed, and stood again. He held out the green-and-brass scabbard. "Take this. To carry the blade when you find it."

Gently but firmly, the prince pushed the scabbard back. The thief blinked his confusion.

"I don't want to *claim* my father's soul," the prince said. "I came here to destroy it."

THE PRINCE MOVED through the darkness, a shadow among shadows. The night held no terror for him. His tightly cut black cloak and the sheathed knife at his hip, soft boots and dirtied face, left him feeling like a dockside cutthroat. He told himself that the tightness in his throat and the tripping of his heart only meant excitement, not fear, and the telling made it true.

The scrub and grass along the path had lost its green. Moonlight remade the world in black and gray. Animals shuffled in the darkness of the scrub. The trees rubbed their leaves together with a sound like soft rain. The Mocking Tower shifted and changed like a sleeper made uneasy by spoiled dreams, but in the darkness he could not make out the details. Without so much as a candle, the prince retraced the way the cleaning girl had brought him.

Where the two trees spanned the path, he paused. Gloom made the fissure of light and air invisible, but he remembered it. Crouching low, he crept forward. His eyes strained. The glamours and spells of the Imagi Vert might not hold to the laws of human experience. What worked in daylight could fail in the night. But no, the world shifted as it had before. The mere wild unfurled a path, a hill, a cave. And the shifting tower where his father's soul lay, fashioned now in steel. A flicker of light from the mouth of the cave. A lantern imperfectly shuttered. He slipped forward, cultivating silence.

He recognized the night guard but didn't know his name. Simin had perhaps nodded to him at the market or waved to him at the mill; the simple exchange of fellow citizens. But circumstances transformed them now to a prince of the Empire and the servant of his enemy. Aus attacked from the dark, killing the man before he could cry out. The prince watched the life fade from the man's eyes. The war claimed other people all across the Empire. Children and women died in the streets of Low Shaoen. Soldiers irrigated the fields of Mattawan Commons with their blood. The guard choking on surprise and his own blood deserved no more or less than the other thousands of dead. Prince Aus stood over him as man became corpse. The murder didn't belong to him. King Raan put all of it in motion, and so the responsibility lay with him and his still-unjudged soul. If the prince's hands trembled after the violence, it only proved that death still moved him. That his humanity still stood higher than that of the man who sired him.

He took the keys from the dead man's hip and the lantern from beside the guard stool that now stood empty, and moved deeper into the cave. The walls of rough stone, simple and uncarved, curved and dipped and rose without offering any corners or doorways. Cool air carried the smell of soil. The profound silence made even his stealthy footsteps seem like shouts. And in one stretch of hallway, unremarkable from all that came before, the prince's ears ached suddenly and the air pressed in on him like a storm front, and he knew the Mocking Tower stood above him.

A glimmer came from the deeper darkness before him, something catching the lantern's fragile beam. Part of the prince's soul warned him to turn back, but the stronger command of his purpose drove him on. The glimmer grew and brightened until it resolved into a wide brass doorway with three panels and carvings of glyphs and designs that teased him from the edge of legibility. Had he seen it anywhere else, Prince Aus would still have recognized it as the entrance to the Imagi Vert's sanctuary and seat of power. It took long, anxious minutes to find the keyhole hidden among the carvings—a tiny plate of brass that shifted to reveal a darkness just the right shape—but the dead guard's key fit and it turned and the door opened.

Prince Aus stepped into the chamber beyond.

Candles burned along the walls but without any scent of tallow or wax, and their light settled softer than snow. In all, the chamber reached no deeper or wider than the common room of the traveler's hearth, but rather than stools and tables and the long, low fire grate, plinths stood scattered about the space as if the stone had grown up from the bones of the earth. On each, an object stood. A cut gem the red of blood and the size of two clenched fists together. A rough doll fashioned from a twist of rope and a handful of dried grass. The skull of a child so young a staggered row of teeth still haunted the jawbone, waiting for a chance to displace tiny, sharp milk teeth. Aus walked slowly. No sounds troubled him. The stillness of the room felt profound. Even his breath seemed close to sacrilege in the space. A cup formed to resemble a cupped, thick-knuckled hand. A simple clay pot painted over with black lines as fine as a feather. Treasures, the prince thought, of a life prolonged centuries beyond its due. A sheet of vellum with a handprint in green. A bird's nest made of long, thin bones.

A sword.

The prince's throat went tight, his mouth suddenly dry. The blade lay on its side. Gems and worked silver formed a hilt like the writhing body of a man. Knotwork etching ran the length of the blade, twisted as a labyrinth. He reached out to it, hesitated, then, almost against his will, took it in his hand. It felt cooler than the room, as if eating the warmth of his flesh. It balanced perfectly. The finest sword ever forged. A sword of empires. A sword forged from steel and dark magic and his father's willing soul. He swung it gently, half expecting its edge to cut the air itself.

"You admire it?"

The voice, harsh and low as stone dragged over earth, came from behind him. The man stood in the candlelight where the prince would swear no one had been only a moment before. The man's dark robe moved stiffly, like bark of a tree remade as cloth. Dark veins welled up under flesh as pale as bone. His mild eyes considered the prince.

"I admire it too," the pale man said. "Good workmanship deserves respect, I think. However much you may disapprove of the project." He tried a smile, then sighed.

"You are the Imagi?" the prince said, his voice high and tight. Fear vibrated in his blood and his grip on the sword tightened.

"Am I?" the pale man said, and tilted his head. "Before, I was part of something greater than myself, and darkness was my home. But now? I play the role of the Imagi now, I suppose. Yes. For this I might as well be the Imagi Vert."

"I am Aus, son of Raan. You have stolen something from me and from my people. I have come to restore the balance of the world."

The pale man seemed to settle into himself. Not a movement of peace or acceptance, but a grounding like a bull setting himself in place and refusing to be moved. A vast stillness radiated from him like cold from ice. The prince felt the sword pulsing in his hand, but it might only have been the beating of his own half-panicked heart.

"What balance is that?" the Imagi Vert asked, as if the matter held some trivial interest but no more than that.

"My father sinned against the gods," the prince said, his voice wavering. "He used your powers to cheat death. To live forever. All evil that the world has seen flows from that sin. The war raging through the Empire now? It's because no one can take the power of the Empire while the former emperor still lives."

"Is that the case?" the Imagi Vert said, lifting pale, hairless brows. "Ah."

"My brothers die at each other's hands. The wonders of the Empire burn. The right order of the world lies scattered like bones on the plain. Because of this." The prince raised the sword between them. "Because one cowardly old man feared too much to die as he should have. And because his pet wizard chose to break the world. Do you deny it?"

"Would you like me to?" The Imagi's smile could have meant anything.

"If you wish. Let me think on it. Yes. Yes, all right. The war first, yes? You say it comes because the rightful heir cannot claim while the emperor still lives. But there have been usurpers before now. If the rightful king cannot rise, an unrighteous one could but hasn't. The history of the world is studded with kings who have abdicated out of weariness or love or religious zealotry. Consider that the war came not because King Raan was a greedy man or an evil one but because he was unhappy."

"Unhappy," the prince said. Neither a question nor an agreement. A distance had come into his eyes and the feeling of hearing everything said before him as if he were eavesdropping from another room.

"His life was never his own. Duty and necessity kept him in the most glorious prison humanity could devise, and the envy of others made that confinement solitary as a monk's. Even when among the throngs who worshipped him, your father lived his life alone. Others dream of power and kingship. Of more money and more sex and more respect. Just as you do. You say you've come here to... what? Save the world from your father? By taking your revenge upon the man who left you behind? And the confluence of those motives gave no pause, eh?"

The prince took a step back. The floor felt as if it had shifted beneath him, but the candle flames stood straight. None of the treasures in their places shook.

The Imagi shrugged, a slow, powerful gesture. "All right. All right. Let's imagine you get what you claim you want. You kill the undying king and take his throne. What will you want then? When the loneliness and melancholy come upon you and you already have everything you aspired to and there is no higher reach, what will you wish for as a balm?"

"I would not need one."

"You're mistaken," the Imagi said, and the words struck his chest like a blow. "Your father wished for a life he had not lived. A simple one with the freedoms invisible to you and the others. A baker, perhaps, spending his early hours kneading dough and smelling yeast and salt. Sweating before the oven. Or a fisherman mending nets with his brothers and sisters, daughters and sons. A brewer or a gardener or the manager of a dye yard. These were as sweet and exotic to him as he was to the lowborn. And he longed for the things denied to him. Badly.

"He lost sight of the challenge his children faced. Bearing his misery in silence cost him the strength to be a good father. Kept him from preparing his sons for the prison cell. Perhaps he thought of it as a kindness, yes? In some subterranean way, he hoped that by cutting you and your brothers away, he could protect you from all that he bore. Love's cruel that way, and men are fools. But wouldn't that be enough to explain why so many of you—yes, and yourself not the least—are so desperate to slaughter each other for what your father didn't want?"

"The sword," the prince said. "My father's soul."

The pale man shook his head, but whether his expression meant sorrow or disgust, the prince didn't know. "You have misunderstood everything. There is no soul in that blade. It's well made, but it means nothing. Take it if you think it will help you. Melt it if you'd rather. I'm beyond caring."

Aus looked down at the sword in his hand. The complications along the blade felt like writing in a language he almost knew. His breath came hard, like he'd run a race. Or fled for his life. He tried to put names to the emotions that spat and wrestled in him: humiliation, anger, despair, grief. The coldness of the hilt grew intense, as if he held a shard of ice. He gripped it harder, inviting the chill into his flesh. Into his mind. Something to stand against the raging armies in his heart.

He shouted before he knew he meant to shout. Swung the blade hard, the movement starting in his legs, his hip, reaching out with a single flowing gesture, extending the sword as if it were part of him. The Imagi's eyes went wider, and the tip of the blade split his jaw. It made a sound like an axe splitting wood. No blood fell from the wound, only a thin runnel of clear fluid.

The prince wrenched the blade free and struck again, screaming as he did. The Imagi lifted a hand to block the attack, and the bloodless fingers scattered on the floor. Great gashes opened in the pale flesh, the body splintering and falling apart under the assault. If he called out, the prince's war cries drowned out his words. Prince Aus found himself standing with feet on either side of the pale corpse, swinging down and down and down, his wrist and shoulder aching from his effort. The Imagi lay still and dead, his head a pale pulp with neither muscle nor bone nor brain. Prince Aus lifted the sword again, in both hands this time, and drove it deep into the pale man's torso, then put his weight upon it. He drove it deeper and twisted, his strength and his weight and his mad will pressing at the metal, bending it past its tolerance. All the power he possessed, he threw into this one terrible moment.

And the sword broke.

Prince Aus fell to his knees. The stump of the blade stood a few inches from the twisted hilt. The labyrinthine pattern was open now, its puzzles solved by violence. A shard of metal fallen at his knee glittered in the soft candlelight. The motionless body of the Imagi Vert looked like a hillside, the greater half of the sword standing proudly from it like a tower. Aus gasped for air and dropped the freezing hilt. His whole body ached, but the physical pain claimed the least of his attention.

The blade broken, his hopes fulfilled, he waited for something. A sense of release. Of victory. The soundless scream of his father's soul at last set free from the world. A rush of the mystic energy that had forged the deathless vessel. Anything.

The candles shed their light. The plinths held their treasures. The silence folded around him until his own chuffing sobs broke it.

He rose unsteady as a drunk, stumbled against a plinth. The hilt of the broken sword slipped from his numb fingers and clattered on the floor. A sweet, earthy smell rose from the dead man, and the nausea it called forth drove the prince back toward the brass door. He'd dropped the lantern somewhere. He couldn't recall. The passage back to the world stood dark as a tomb, but he made his lightless way. One foot before the other, hands out before him to warn him before he walked into the stone. His mouth tasted foul. His arms trembled. He wept empty tears with no sense of grief or catharsis. For a time, he felt certain that the cave would go on forever, that the death of the Imagi Vert had sealed him also in the immortal's tomb. When he stumbled out into the starlit mouth of the cave, he more than half thought it a dream. The visions of a man with a broken mind. The dead guard, lying in his pool of blood brought the prince back to himself. It was a war. It was the war. Terrible things happened here.

The night sky glittered with stars. The trees shifted in the open air. All the world seemed terrible and beautiful and empty. Prince Aus turned toward the path, the town. Behind him, the Mocking Tower whose roots he had dug changed and changed and changed again: a threefold tower with bridges lacing between the spires like a web, a vast tooth pointing toward the sky with a signal fire blaring at its tip, a glasswork column that rose toward the stars and funneled their dim light into its heart. The prince didn't watch it. The night before him carried terrors and wonders enough.

He made his way to the path between the trees, toward the town where he'd lived—it seemed now—in some previous lifetime. To the traveler's hearth, where the keep once sheltered and offered fair work to a boy named Simin, who in fact had been a being of skin and lies.

The thief's door was barred from within, but candlelight flickered at the edges. The prince pounded until he heard the hiss of the bar lifting and the door swung open. The thief blinked at him, uncertain as a mouse.

"You look terrible."

"We have to go," the prince said, and his voice seemed to belong to some other man.

"You did it? It's done?"

"We have to go now. Before the changing of guards, first light I'd guess. But it could be earlier. Could be now."

"But—"

"*We have to go!*"

Together, the two men ran to the stable, chose which horses to steal, and galloped out to the road. They turned east, toward the first threads of rose and indigo where the light would rise to meet them. A dawn that would rise elsewhere on army camps and burned cities, fields left uncultivated for want of hands to farm them and river locks broken open for fear that an enemy would make use of them. The ruins of empire, and a war still raging.

And in the depths of the Mocking Tower, something stirred.

At first, the body moved only slightly, reknitting the worst of its wounds with a vegetable slowness. Then, when it could, the body levered itself up to unsteady feet. Pale eyes looked all around the chamber of treasures without suffering or joy. The rough cloak creaked and crackled as the body—neither alive nor dead but something of both—stepped out of the light and into the darkness. It felt a vague comfort in the darkness underground, to the degree that it felt anything.

The mouth of the cave came all too soon. A human body lay there, a cast-off forgotten thing. The pale man, jaw still hanging from his skull by woody threads, turned away from town and tower, walking into the trees where no path existed. He moved with the same deliberation and speed as he would have on the road and left no trail behind him. The Mocking Tower at his back shifted, fluttering from shape to shape, miracle to miracle, as compelling as a street performer's scarf fluttering to draw attention away from what the other hand was doing.

Birds woke, singing their cacophony at the coming dawn. The light grew, and the wild gave way to a simple garden. Wide beds of dark, rich soil, well weeded so that no unwelcome plant competed with the onion, the beets, the carrots. A short, ragged-looking apple tree bent under the combined weight of its own fruit and a thin netting that kept the sparrows from feasting on it. In the rear near a well, a rough shack leaned, small but solid with a little yard paved in unfinished stone outside it. A little fire muttered and smoked as it warmed a pot of water for tea.

The pale man folded his legs under him, rested his palms on his knees, and waited with a patience that suggested he could wait forever. A yellow finch flew by, its wings fluttering. A doe tramped through the trees at the garden's edge but didn't approach.

Old Au came from the shack and nodded to him. She wore long trousers with mud-crusted leather at the knees, a loose canvas shirt, and boots cracked and mended and cracked again. A thin spade and gardener's knife hung from her belt, and she carried an empty cloth sack over her shoulder. Heaving a sigh, she sat across from the pale man.

"Went poorly, then, did it?"

The pale man tried to say something with his ruined mouth, then made do with simply nodding. Old Au looked into the gently boiling water in the pan as if there might be some answers in it, then lifted it off and set it on the stone at her side. The pale man waited. She pulled a little sack from her pocket, plucked a few dried leaves from it, and dropped them in the still-but-steaming water. A few moments later, the scent of fresh tea joined the smells of turned earth and dew-soaked leaves.

"Did you explain that the war was only a war? That humanity falls into violence every few generations, and that his father, if anything, was too good at keeping the peace?"

The pale man nodded again.

"And could the boy hear it?"

The pale man hesitated, then shook his head. *No, he could not.*

Old Au chuckled. "Well, we try. Every generation is the same. They think their parents were never young, never subject to the confusions and lust they suffer. Born before the invention of sex and loss and passion, us. They all have to learn in their own way, however much we might wish we could counsel them out of it." She swirled the tea. "Did you warn him what it will be like once he takes the throne?"

The pale man nodded.

"He didn't hear that either, did he? Ah well. I imagine he'll look back on it when he's old and understand too late." Old Au reached out her well-worn hand and took the pale man's fingerless palm in hers. She shook him once, and he became a length of pale root again. Scarred now and ripped, paler where the bark peeled back. She hefted the root back close to the shed. She might break it down for mulch later, or else use it to carve something from. A whistle, maybe. Return it to the cycle or transform it to something Nature never dreamed for it. They were simple magics, and profound because of it.

She poured the tea into an old cup and sipped it as she squinted into the sky. It looked like a good day. Warm in the morning, but a bit of rain in the afternoon she guessed. Enough for a few hours of good work. She took the spade from her hip and broke a little crust of mud from just below the handle with the nail of her thumb, humming to herself as she did. And then the gardener's knife with its serrated edge for sawing through roots and the name Raan Sauvo Serriadan scratched into the blade in a language no one had spoken in centuries.

"There are some bulbs in the west field that want thinning," she said. "What do you think, love?"

For a moment there, the breeze and the chirping of the birds seemed to harmonize, making some deeper music between them. Something like the murmur of a voice. Whatever it said made Old Au laugh.

She finished her tea, poured what remained out of the pot, and started walking toward the gardens and the day's work still ahead.

SIDEWALKS
Maureen McHugh

Maureen McHugh (maureenfmchugh.com) has written four novels and two collections of short fiction. She won the James Tiptree Award for her first novel, *China Mountain Zhang*. She was a finalist for the Story Award for her collection *Mothers & Other Monsters*, and won a Shirley Jackson Award for her collection *After the Apocalypse*, which was named one of *Publishers Weekly*'s 10 Best Books of 2011. She was born in a blue-collar town in Ohio. She's lived in New York City; Shijiazhuang, China; and Austin, Texas. She currently lives in Los Angeles, California where she is trying desperately to sell her soul to Hollywood but as it turns out, the market is saturated.

I HATE WHEN I have a call in Inglewood. It's still the 1990s in Inglewood and for all I know, people still care about Madonna. Los Angeles County has a forty-bed psych facility there. Arrowhead looks like a nursing home; a long one story building with a wide wheelchair ramp and glass doors and overly bright, easy to clean floors. I stop at the reception desk and check in.

"Rosni Gupta," I say. "I'm here to do an evaluation."

The young man at the desk catches his bottom lip in his teeth and nods. "Oh yeah," he says. "Hold on ma'am. I'll get the director." He has an elaborate tattoo sleeve of red flowers, parrots, and skulls on his right arm. "Dr. Gupta is here," he says into the phone.

I also hate when people call me Dr. Gupta. I'm a PhD, not a medical doctor. I'm running late because I'm always running late. That's not true of me in my personal life. I'm early for meeting friends or getting to the airport but in my work there are too many appointments and too much traffic. Being late makes me anxious. I'm a speech pathologist for Los Angeles County working with Social Services. I'm a specialist; I evaluate language capacity and sometimes prescribe communication interventions and devices. What that means is that if someone has trouble communicating, the county is supposed to provide help. If the problem is more complicated than deafness, dyslexia, stroke, autism, learning disability, or stuttering, all the things that speech therapists normally deal with, I'm one of the people who is brought in. 'Devices' sounds very fancy, but really, it's not. Lots of times a device is a smart phone with an app. I kid you not.

"Are you from LA?" I ask the guy behind the desk.

He shakes his head. "El Salvador. But I've been here since I was eleven."

"I love El Salvadorian food," I say. *"Tamales de elote, pupusas."*

He lights up and tells me about this place on Venice called Gloria's that makes decent pupusas until Leo shows up. Leo is the director.

Just so you know, I'm not some special Sherlock Holmes kind of woman who has been promoted into this work because I can diagnose things about people. Government does not work that way. I took this job because it was a promotion. I've just been doing speech pathology for about twenty years and have seen a lot and I am not particularly afraid of technology. I have an iPhone. I attend conferences about communication devices and read scientific journals.

What I understand about this case is that police got a call about a woman who was speaking gibberish. She was agitated, attacked a police officer, and was placed on a seventy-two hour psych hold. She has no identification and is unable to communicate. They can't find any family and since she is non-verbal except for the gibberish, she was given an initial diagnosis as profoundly autistic, and when a bed opened up at Arrowhead she was placed here. I'm here to determine what the problem is.

The file is pretty lean.

I don't know Leo-the-director very well. He's a balding, dark skinned guy wearing a saggy gray suit jacket and jeans. He looks tired, but anyone running a psych facility looks tired. "Hi Ros, How was the 405?" he asks.

"Sorry I'm late," I say. "The 405 was a liquor store parking lot on payday. Tell me about your Jane Doe."

He shrugs. "She's not profoundly autistic, although she may be on the spectrum."

"So she's communicating?"

"Still no recognizable language."

"Psychotic?"

"I don't know. I'm thinking she may just be homeless and we haven't identified the language."

"How did you end up with her?" I ask. Nobody gets a bed unless they are a risk to themselves or others or severely disabled. Even then they don't get beds half the time. There are about 80,000 homeless in Los Angeles on any given night—not all of them on the street of course—some of them are living in cars or crashing on couches or in shelters—but a lot of them are either severely mentally ill or addicted and there aren't that many beds.

"She's 5250 pending T-con. Apparently she was pretty convincingly a danger to someone," Leo said.

'Section 5250' is a section of the California Welfare and Institutions Code that allows an involuntary fourteen day psychiatric hold and 'T-con' is a temporary conservatorship that gets the county another fourteen days to keep someone. We're a bureaucracy. God forbid we not speak jargon, we have our professional pride. At some point in that fourteen days there has to be a Probable Cause Hearing so a court can decide whether or not the hold meets legal criteria. I'm a cog in that machinery. If I determine that she can't communicate enough to take care of herself then that's part of a case to keep her institutionalized.

When I say institutionalized I can just see people's expressions change. They go all *One Flew Over the Cuckoo's Nest*. Institutions are not happy places. The one I'm in right now is too bright. It's all hard surfaces so I hear the squeak of shoes, the constant sounds of voices. The halls are way too bright. It's about as homey as a CVS and not nearly as attractive. But you know, a lot of people need to stay institutionalized. I had a non-verbal patient, Jennie. She was twenty-six, and after many months of working with her and her caregivers to provide her with training she was finally taught to go and stand by the door of the storage room where the adult diapers were stored to communicate *that she needed to be changed*. I would like to live in a world where she didn't have to live in a place like this but I'm glad to live in a world where she has a place to live. I've been to visit family in New Delhi, okay? In New Delhi, if Jennie's family was rich she'd have great care. If her family was poor, she'd be a tremendous burden on her mother and sisters, or more likely, dead of an opportunistic infection.

I'm wearing sandals and the heels are loud on the linoleum. They're three to a room here but a lot of the people are in the day room or group therapy. We stop at a room. Two of the beds are empty and carefully made with blue, loose weave blankets on them. A woman sits on the third bed, looking outside. She is clean. Her hair is long, brown and coarse, pulled back in a thick pony-tail.

"That's Jane," Leo says.

"Hello Jane," I say.

She looks directly at me and says, "Hi." This is not typical autistic behavior. Jane is about 5'6" or so. Taller than me. She's about as brown as me. My family is Bengali although I was born and raised in Clearwater, Florida. (I came to Los Angeles for college. UCLA.) Jane doesn't look Indian. She doesn't look Central or South American, either.

We're given use of a conference room where I can do my evaluation. I prefer it to a clinic. It's quieter, there are fewer distractions.

Jane doesn't say anything beyond that 'Hi' but she continues to make eye contact. She's not pretty. Not ugly, either. Jane actually rests her elbows on the table and leans a little towards me which is disconcerting.

I'M 5'3". MY husband likes to walk so we walk to the drug store and sometimes we go out to eat. He's six feet tall, a teacher. He's white, originally from Pennsylvania. When we walk to restaurants from our little neighborhood (which is quite pretty, we couldn't afford to buy a house there now, but when we bought our place the neighborhood was still rough) there is enough room on the sidewalk in places for about three people to walk abreast. If there are two people walking towards us and they're two men, I'm the person who always has to get out of the way. A man will unthinkingly shoulder check me if I don't and occasionally look over his shoulder, surprised. This is a stupid thing, I know. There are a lot of entertainment businesses in our area—people who make trailers for movies or do mysterious technological things involving entertainment. They're young men. They wear skinny pants or ironic T-shirts or have beards or wear those straw fedora things. I am old enough to be their mother and I am just surprised that they do that.

"Would they run over their mother on a sidewalk?" I ask.

"It's because you're short," Matt says. Matt is my husband. He is middle-aged but he also wears ironic T-shirts. My favorite is his T-shirt of a silhouette of a T-rex playing drums with its little tiny arms. Matt is a drummer in a band made up of old white guys.

Men never do it if it's two men coming up on two men, they all just sort of squeeze. I get very irritable about it. I grew up in America. I feel American. My parents come from New Delhi and they are clear that my brothers, Jay and Ravi, and I are very American but growing up I felt like I was only pretending to be. Sometimes I think I learned how to be a subservient Indian woman from my parents and I give it off like a secret perfume.

When I was younger I walked very fast, all the time, but now I'm middle-aged and overweight and I don't dart around people any more so maybe I just notice it more or maybe I'm just more cranky.

I PLAN TO do an evaluation called ADOS on Jane Doe. ADOS is one of the standard evaluations for autism. It can be scaled for a range from almost non-verbal to pretty highly verbal and since the file said that she spoke gibberish, it was a place to start. I never get to ADOS because it's obvious pretty quickly that she exhibits no autistic behaviors.

"Hi, I'm Rosni Gupta," I say.

She studies me.

I tap my chest. "Rosni Gupta. Ros."

"Ros," she repeats. Then she taps her chest. "Malni," she says. She has an accent.

It takes me a couple of times to get it. She works with me, showing me what she does with her mouth to make the sound. I fiddle with it as I write it down. I think about spelling it *Emulni* but *Malni* feels closer. She has a strong accent but I can't place it. It's not Spanish. I say a couple of words to her and gesture for her to say them back. She doesn't make the retroflex consonants of the Indian subcontinent—the thing that everybody mangles trying to sound like Apu on *The Simpsons*. She watches me write.

I don't use a laptop for my field notes. I like yellow legal pads. Just the way I started. She reaches out, wanting to use my pen. Her nails are a little long, her hands not very calloused. Her palms are pink. I hand her the pen and slide the pad across to her.

She writes an alphabet. It looks a lot like our alphabet but there's no K, Q, or V. The G looks strange and there are extra letters after the D and the T and where we have a W she has something that looks like a curlicue.

She offers me the pen and says something. She gestures at me to take the pen. It's the first time she's really spoken to me in a full sentence. The language she speaks sounds liquid, like it's been poured through a straw.

I take the pen and she points to the page. Points to the first letter. "A" she says. It sounds like something between A and U.

Eventually I write an A and she nods fiercely. I write our alphabet for her.

"Wait," I say. I borrow Leo's iPad and bring it back showing a Google map of the world. "Where are you from?" I ask.

She studies the map. Eventually she turns and she scrolls it a bit. I change it to a satellite version and I can see when she gets it. Her face is grim. She stabs her finger on the California coast. On where we are right now.

"No," I say. "That's where we are now, Malni. Where is home."

She looks up at me leaning over the table. She stabs her finger in the same place.

I WRITE UP my report that she is not autistic and recommend a psychological follow-up. She might be bipolar. Leo tells me as I leave that the cop who brought her in, tazed her. I never got any sense she was violent. I was certainly never worried about my safety. I've done evals where I was worried about my safety—not many—but I take my safety very seriously, thank you.

I make dinner that night while Matt marks papers. Matt teaches sophomore English at the high school and is the faculty advisor for the literary magazine. For nine months of the year he disappears into the black hole that is teaching and we lose our dinner table. He surfaces for brief periods from the endless piles of papers and quizzes, mostly around Saturday night. He tells me about his students, I tell him about my clients.

Matt likes Bengali dishes but I don't make them very often because I didn't learn to cook until I was out of school. My go to, as you might have guessed, is Mexican. I like the heat. Tonight is carnitas ala Trader Joe's.

"What's this?" Matt asks. He's sitting at the dining room table, papers spread, but he's looking at my notes. We'll end up eating in front of the television. We're Netflixing, partway through some BBC thing involving spiffily dressed gangsters in post WWI England.

"What's what?" I ask.

"Looks like someone's writing the Old English alphabet in your notes."

I bring out sour cream and salsa and look at what he's pointing to. "That was my Jane Doe in Inglewood."

"She's a *Beowulf* scholar?" he asks.

"That's Old English?" I ask.

"Looks like it," Matt says.

I HAVE A caseload and a lot of appointments but I call Leo and tell him I want to schedule some more time with Jane even though I shouldn't take the time. He tells me she's been moved to a halfway house. It could have been worse, she could have been just discharged to the street. He gives me the address and I call them and schedule an appointment.

I have to go in the evening because Malni—they call her Malni now—has a job during the day. She does light assembly work which is a fancy name for factory work. The halfway house is in Crenshaw, a *less than desirable* neighborhood. It's a stucco apartment building, painted pale yellow. I knock on her door and her roommate answers.

"I'm looking for Malni?"

"She ain't here. She be coming back, you might run into her if you look outside." Her roommate's name is Sherri. Sherri is lanky, with straightened hair and complicated nails. "You her parole?"

"No, I'm a speech therapist."

"There ain't no therapy to do," Sherri says. "You know she don't speak no English."

"Yeah," I say. "I like your nails."

Sherri isn't charmed by my compliment. But I do like them, they look like red and white athletic shoes, like they've been laced up across each nail. I'm terrible at maintenance. Hair, make-up, nails. I admire people who are good about things like that.

I head outside and spot Malni coming from a couple of blocks. Malni walks with her shoulders back, not smiling, and she makes eye contact with people. You're not supposed to make eye contact with people in the city. It's an unwritten rule. There's a bunch of boys hanging on the corner and Malni looks straight at their faces. It's not friendly, like she knows them. It's not unfriendly. It's... I don't know. The way people cue looking at people and away from people is something to look for when determining if they're autistic or if they're exhibiting signs of psychosis. I'm trained to look for it. Persons on the autism spectrum generally don't make eye contact. A lot of persons with schizophrenia don't look at people and look away in the normal rhythms of conversation; they stare too much, too long for example. When I assessed Malni at Arrowhead, she cued normally.

Malni walks the boys down, looking right in their faces. The boys move out of her way. I suspect they don't even realize that they're doing it. I remember her file says she was tazed when police apprehended her. A homeless woman of color speaking gibberish who kept looking them in the face and wouldn't drop her eyes. Did they read that as aggressive? I bet she didn't have to do much to get tazed. It's a wonder she didn't get shot.

Malni sees me when she gets closer and lifts her hand in a little wave. "Hi Ros," she says and smiles. Totally normal cueing.

I follow her back into the apartment she shares with Sherri.

"I ain't going nowhere," Sherri announces from in front of the television. "I worked all day." There's a Styrofoam box of fried chicken and fried rice nearly finished on the coffee table in front of her.

"That's okay," I say.

Malni and I sit down at the kitchen table and I open up my laptop. I call up images of *Beowulf* in Old English and turn the screen around so Malni can see them.

She frowns a moment and then she looks at me and smiles and taps my forehead with her index finger like she's saying I'm smart. She pulls the laptop closer to her and reads out loud.

It's not the same liquid sound as when she talked, I don't think (but that was two weeks ago and I don't remember exactly). This sounds more German.

Sherri turns around and leans against the back of the couch. "What's that she's talking?"

"Old English," I say.

"That ain't English," Sherri says. It's like everything from Sherri has to be a challenge.

"No, it's what they spoke in England over a thousand years ago."

"Huh. So how come she knows that?"

Malni is learning modern English. She can say all the things that you learn when you start a new language—My name is Malni. How much does that cost? Where's the bathroom? Everyone keeps asking her the same question, "Where are you from?"

She keeps giving the same answer, "Here."

I pull a couple of yellow legal pads out of my messenger bag and a pack of pens. I write my name and address, my cell number, and my email address on the first one.

"Hey Sherri, if she wants to get in touch with me, could you help her?"

I'm not sure what Sherri will say. Sherri shrugs, "I guess."

Malni looks at the writing. She taps it. "Ros," she says. Then the number. "Your phone."

"Yes," I say. "My phone." It's my work phone because I never give clients my home phone. Not even my clients who read Old English.

I think about Malni walking through those boys. I'm meeting with one of my clients. Agnes is Latina. She's sixty-four and had a stroke that's left her nearly blind and partially deaf. She's diabetic and has high blood pressure. She has a tenth grade education and before her stroke, she and her daughter cleaned houses.

With a hearing aid, Agnes can make out some sounds but she can't make out speech. Her daughter, Brittany, communicates with her by drawing letters on her hand and slowly spelling things out. I've brought a tablet so that Agnes can write the letters she thinks Brittany is writing. It's an attempt at reinforcing feedback. Adult deafblindness is a difficult condition. Agnes is unusual because she doesn't have any cognitive issues from her stroke, so there's lots of possibilities. I'm having Agnes write one letter at a time on the tablet, big enough that she herself might be able to see it.

Agnes has a big laugh when she's in a good mood. Sometimes she cries for hours but today she's good. She has crooked teeth. Her English is accented but she's lived here since she was thirteen—Brittany was born here and speaks Spanish as her first language but grew up speaking English, too. "Mom!" she says, even though her mother can't hear her. "Quit goofing around!" She smacks her mother lightly on the arm. Agnes' eyes roam aimlessly behind her thick and mostly useless glasses.

Brittany, who is in her thirties, raises an eyebrow at me. Both women are short and overweight, classic risk profiles for diabetes and hypertension, like me. Unlike them, I have really good health care.

Agnes prefers drawing on the tablet to writing and after twenty minutes of trying to figure out what Brittany has been asking her, '?yr name ?hot or cold ?what 4 dinner' Agnes has given up and drawn an amorphous blob which is apparently supposed to be a chicken. "Fried chicken," she announces, too loud because she can't hear herself well enough to regulate her volume.

"She can't have fried chicken for dinner," Brittany says. "She has to stick to her diet."

Agnes says, "El Pollo Loco! Right? Macaroni and cheese and coleslaw. Cole slaw is a vegetable."

Brittany looks at me helplessly. Agnes cackles.

My phone rings. "Is this Ros, the speech lady? This is Sherri, Malni's roommate."

"Sherri?" I remember the woman with the nails painted to look like the laces on athletic shoes. "Hi, is everything all right?"

"Yeah. Well, sort of. Nothing's really wrong. I just got a bunch of papers here for you from Malni."

"Where's Malni?" I ask.

"She took off to find her friends," Sherri said.

"What friends?"

"Her friends from wherever the hell she's from," Sherri says. "You gonna pick up these papers or what?"

I WANTED MALNI to write her story down. She filled almost three legal pads. I didn't expect her to disappear, though.

"This guy showed up," Sherri says. In honor of Agnes I've brought El Pollo Loco. Sherri doesn't really like El Pollo Loco. "I don't eat that Mexican shit," she says but she takes it anyway. "He was tall and skinny. He looked like her, you know? That squished nose. Like those Australian dudes."

It takes me a moment but then I realize what she means: Aboriginals. She's right, Malni looked a little like an Aboriginal. Not exactly. Or maybe exactly, I've never met an Australian Aboriginal. "Oh, cool, I didn't know they had mac n' cheese." Sherri plunks down on the couch and digs in. "Yeah so he started jabbering at her in that way she talks to herself. Was crazy. And he acted just like she did. All foreign and weird. Then they just took off and she didn't come back."

"When was that?" I ask. My feet hurt so I sit down on the couch next to her.

"Like, Saturday?"

This is Thursday. Part of me wants to say, you couldn't be bothered to call until yesterday but there's no reason for Sherri to have bothered to call me at all, even though Malni apparently asked her to.

"That bitch was super smart," Sherri says.

I give Sherri twenty dollars, even though she's a recovering substance abuser and it's risky to give her pocket money, and take the legal pads and go.

I call the department of history at UCLA and eventually find someone who can put me in touch with someone at the department of Literature who puts me in touch with a woman who is a *Beowulf* scholar. Why I thought I should start in History I don't know since Matt is an English teacher and he recognized the language. Anyway, I tell the *Beowulf* scholar I am looking for someone who can translate Old English and that I will pay.

That is how I get Steve. We meet at a Starbucks near campus. Starbucks is quickly becoming the place where everybody meets for almost every reason.

Steve is Asian-America and very gay. He wears glasses that would have gotten me laughed out of middle school. He is studying Old English and needs money. "I'm supposed to be working on my dissertation," he says. "I *am* working on my dissertation, actually. It's on *Persona and Presentation in Anglo Saxon Literature.* But there's that pesky thing about rent." He eyes the legal pads. I wonder what persona and presentation even means and what his parents think about having a son who is getting a doctorate in English Literature. Which, I realize, is racist. Just because my dad is an engineer and my mother is a chemist and they are classic immigrant parents who stressed college, college, college, doesn't mean Steve's are. For all I know, Steve's parents are third generation and his dad plays golf and gave him a car on his sixteenth birthday.

"I can pay you $500," I say.

"That looks like modern handwriting. Is it, like, someone's notes or something?"

"I'm not exactly sure," I say.

He eyes me. I am aware of how weird it is to appear with three legal pads of handwritten Old English. Steve may be a starving UCLA student but this is very strange.

"I think it's like a story," I say. "I work for Los Angeles County Social Services. A client gave me these."

"You're a social worker," he says, nodding.

"I'm a speech therapist," I say.

He doesn't comment on that. "This is going to take a lot of hours. A thousand?" he says.

"Seven hundred and fifty," I say.

"Okay," he says.

I write him a check for half on the spot. He holds the check looking resigned. I think I'm getting a pretty good deal.

AFTER THAT I get emails from him. The first one has ten typed pages of translation attached and a note that says, *Can we meet?*

We meet in the same Starbucks.

"Your client is really good at Anglo-Saxon," he says. "Like really good."

"Yeah?" I say. How can I explain?

"Yeah. She does some really interesting things. It's a woman, right?"

Malni tells a 'story' about a woman from a place on a harbor. The place is vast, full of households and people. There are wondrous things there. Roads crowded with people who can eat every manner of food and wear the richest of dress. It is always summer. It is a place that has need for few warriors.

Trees bear bright fruit that no one picks because no one wants it because no one is hungry. The air is noisy with the sound of birds and children.

She is one of a band of people. They work with lightning and metal, with light and time. They bend the air and the earth to open doors that have never been opened. They journey to yesterday. To the time of heroes.

"She's a woman," I say.

"It's like a sci-fi fantasy story," Steve says.

I already know that. Malni has been telling everyone, *she's from here.* When I read those words, that they journeyed to yesterday, I figured that plus the Old English meant that somehow Malni thought she had gone to the past.

"Have you heard about anybody who had some kind of breakdown or disappeared in the last year? You know, a teacher? Someone good at Old English?"

"No?" he says.

I tell him a little bit about Malni.

"Wow. That's... wow. You'd think someone this good would be teaching and yeah, it's a pretty small discipline. I'd think I'd have heard," he says. "Maybe not. If I hear anything..."

"So she's really good," I prompt.

"There are only something like a little over four hundred works of Old English still around," Steve says. "There's *Beowulf*, which was written down by a monk. There's *Caedemon*, and *Alfred the Great and Bede*, a bunch of Saints lives and some riddles and some other stuff. You get to know the styles. The dialects. This is close to *Alfred* but different. I thought at first that the differences were because she was trying to mimic *Alfred* but getting it a little wrong, you know? But the more I read it over and over, the more I realize that it's all internally consistent."

"Like she's really good at making it up?"

"Yeah," Steve says. "Like she's made a version all her own. Invented a wholly new version of Old English so that it would sound like a different person at close to the same time. And written a story in it. That's a really weird thing to do. Make it super authentic for somebody like me. Because the number of people who could read this and get what she's doing and also enjoy it is zero."

"Zero?"

"Yeah," he says. "I mean, I understand the beginning of the story, I think. It's a time travel story. She starts in Los Angeles, which by the way is really hard to describe in Anglo-Saxon because she doesn't try to make up words like horseless cart or anything. For one thing, Anglo-Saxon doesn't really work that way. So she starts here and she travels back in time. Then there's all this part about being in the past in what I think is probably Wessex, you know, what's now part of England. She makes up some stuff that's different from the historical record, some of which I wish was true because it's really cool and some of which is just kind of dull unless you're really into agriculture. Then there's this long explanation of something I don't understand because I think she's trying to explain math but it isn't like math like I understand math. But really, I suck at math so maybe it is."

"She's got math in there?"

"A little bit, but mostly she's explaining it. There's something about how really small changes in a stream make waves and if you drop a stick in the water, no one can predict its course. How when you walk through the door to yesterday, it means yesterday is not your yesterday. Then she talks about coming back to her beautiful city but it's gone. There's a strange city in its place. That city is beautiful, too and it's full of wild men and sad women. That city has savage and beautiful art. It has different things. Some are better and some are worse but her family is gone and no one speaks to her any more. She says the story is about the cost of the journey. That when you journey to yesterday, you lay waste to today. When you return, your today is gone and it is a today that belongs to somebody else."

It takes me a moment to think about all that.

One of the baristas steams milk. Starbucks is playing some soft spoken music in the background. It doesn't feel like someone has just explained how to end my world.

"It's kind of creepy but the way it's written there are big chunks that are really hard to read," Steve says. "Is she crazy? I mean, what's the deal?"

I want to say she's crazy. Really, it's the best explanation, right? She was a professor of Anglo Saxon/Old English. She'd had a psychotic break. Sherri said a man who looked a lot like her—maybe a family member, a brother—tracked her down to the halfway house and took her home.

That strange and liquid language she speaks. The way she acts, as if she comes from a different culture where the men are not so savage and the women not so sad.

"I don't know," I say.

"I can give you what I've translated. I've translated all the words but there are parts that don't make sense," Steve says.

I pay him the rest and add enough to make a thousand. He's spent a lot of time on it. Time he could have been working on his dissertation.

"I actually learned a lot," he says. "It's like she really speaks Anglo Saxon."

"Maybe she did," I say.

SOMEONE, SOMEWHERE IS working on time travel. I mean, someone has to be. People are trying to clone mammoths. People are working on interstellar travel. I have a Google alert for it and mostly what pops up is fiction. Sometimes crazy pseudo science. Real stuff, too. I get alerts for things like photon entanglement. People are trying.

I think I saw Malni on Wilshire Boulevard one time walking with two other people; a man who looked like her and a woman who had black hair. I was driving, late for an appointment. By the time I saw them I was almost past them. I tried to go around the block and catch them but traffic was bad and by the time I got back to Wilshire they were gone. Or maybe it wasn't Malni.

Maybe in some lab somewhere, people are close to a time travel breakthrough. I walk downtown with Matt and I think, this might be the last moment I walk with Matt. Someone might be sent back in time at any moment and this will all disappear.

Will it all disappear at once? Will I have a moment to feel it fading away? Will I be able to grip Matt's arm? To know?

There are two guys walking towards us as we head to the Mexican place. I'm going to have a margarita. Maybe two. I'm going to get a little drunk with Matt. I'm going to talk too much if I want to. The guys are not paying attention. I remember Malni. I throw me shoulders back a little. I do not smile. I look in the face of the one in my way. The world is going to end you fucker. I will not give up this sidewalk with my love.

He steps a little to the side. He gives way.

MY ENGLISH NAME

R. S. Benedict

After studying Sumerian linguistics at Yale, **R.S. Benedict** (rs-benedict.com) moved to China to spend three years teaching English. Now back in upstate New York, she grinds her days away working at a bureaucracy to support her writing habit.

I WANT YOU to know that you are not crazy.

What you saw in the back of the ambulance was real.

What wasn't real was Thomas Majors.

You have probably figured out by now that I wasn't born in London like I told you I was, and that I did not graduate from Oxford, and that I wasn't baptized in the Church of England, as far as I know.

Here is the truth: Thomas Majors was born in room 414 of the Huayuan Binguan, a cheap hotel which in defiance of its name contained neither flowers nor any sort of garden.

If the black domes in the ceiling of the fourth-floor corridor had actually contained working cameras the way they were supposed to, a security guard might have noticed Tingting, a dowdy maid from a coal village in Hunan, enter room 414 without her cleaning cart. The guard would have seen Thomas Majors emerge a few days later dressed in a blue suit and a yellow scarf.

A search of the room would have returned no remnant of Tingting.

HUNAN PROVINCE HAS no springtime, just alternating winter and summer days. When Tingting enters room 414 it's winter, grey and rainy. The guest room has a heater, at least, unlike the sleeping quarters Tingting shares with three other maids.

Tingting puts a Do Not Disturb sign on the door and locks it. She shuts the curtains. She covers the mirrors. She takes off her maid uniform. Her skin is still new. She was supposed to be invisible: she has small eyes and the sort of dumpy figure you find in a peasant who had too little to eat as a child and too much to eat as an adult. But prying hands found their way to her anyway, simply because she was there. Still, I know it won't be hard for a girl like her to disappear. No one will look for her.

I pull Tingting off, wriggling out of her like a snake. I consider keeping her in case of emergency, but once she's empty I feel myself shift and stretch. She won't fit anymore. She has to go.

I will spare you the details of how that task is accomplished.

IT TAKES A while to make my limbs the right length. I've narrowed considerably. I check the proportions with a measuring tape; all the ratios are appropriate.

But Thomas Majors is not ready. The room's illumination, fluorescent from the lamps, haze-strangled from the sky, isn't strong enough to tan this new flesh the way it is meant to be.

You thought I was handsome when you met me. I wish you could have seen what I was supposed to be. In my plans, Thomas was perfect. He had golden hair and a complexion like toast. But the light is too weak, and instead I end up with flesh that's not quite finished.

I can't wait anymore. I only have room 414 for one week. It's all Tingting can afford.

So I put on Thomas as carefully as I can, and only when I'm certain that not a single centimeter of what lies beneath him can be seen, I uncover the mirrors.

He's tight. Unfinished skin usually is. I smooth him down and let him soften. I'm impatient, nervous, so I turn around to check for lumps on Thomas's back. When I do, the flesh at his neck rips. I practice a look of pain in the mirror.

Then I stitch the gash together as well as I can. It fuses but leaves an ugly ridge across Thomas's throat. I cover it with a scarf Tingting bought from a street vendor. It's yellow, imitation silk with a recurring pattern that reads *Liu Viuttor*.

The next week I spend in study and practice: how to speak proper English, how to stand and sit like a man, how to drink without slurping, how to hold a fork, how to bring my brows together in an expression of concern, how to laugh, how to blink at semi-regular intervals.

It's extraordinary how much one can learn when one doesn't have to eat or sleep.

I check out on time carrying all of Thomas Majors's possessions in a small bag: a fake passport, a hairbrush, a hand mirror, a wallet, a cell phone, and a single change of clothes.

It takes me under twenty-four hours to find a job. A woman approaches me on the sidewalk. She just opened an English school, she says. Would I like to teach there?

The school consists of an unmarked apartment in a grey complex. The students are between ten and twelve years of age, small and rowdy. I'm paid in cash. They don't notice that my vowels are a bit off; Thomas's new tongue can't quite wrap itself around English diphthongs just yet.

On weekday mornings I take more rent-a-whitey gigs. A shipping company pays me to wear a suit, sit at board meetings, nod authoritatively, and pretend to be an executive. A restaurant pays me to don a chef's hat and toss pizza dough in the air on its opening day. Another English training center, unable to legally hire foreigners in its first year of operation, pays me 6000 RMB per month to wander through the halls and pretend to work there.

I model, too: for a travel brochure, for a boutique, for a university's foreign language department. The photographer tells his clients that I was a finalist on *America's Next Top Model*. They don't question it.

China is a perfect place for an imitation human like myself. Everything is fake here. The clothes are designer knock-offs. The DVDs are bootlegs. The temples are replicas of sites destroyed during the Great Leap Forward and the Cultural Revolution. The markets sell rice made from plastic bags, milk made from melamine, and lamb skewers made from rat meat. Even the Internet is fake, a slow, stuttering, pornless thing whose search engines are programed not to look in politically sensitive directions.

It was harder in the West. Westerners demand authenticity even though they don't really want it. They cry out for meat without cruelty, war without casualties, thinness without hunger. But the Chinese don't mind artifice.

I MAKE FRIENDS in China quickly and easily. Many are thrilled to have a tall, blond Westerner to wave around as a status symbol.

I wait a few weeks before I associate with other *waiguoren*, terrified they'll pick up on my fake accent or ask me a question about London that I can't answer.

But none of that turns out to be a problem. Very few expats in China ask questions about what one did back home, likely because so few of them want to answer that question themselves. Generally, they are not successful, well-adjusted members of their native countries. But if they have fair skin and a marginal grasp of English, they can find an ESL job to pay for beer and a lost girl to tell them how clever and handsome they are.

I learn quickly that my Englishman costume is not lifelike. Most of the Brits I meet in China are fat and bald, with the same scraggly stubble growing on their faces, their necks, and the sides of their heads. They wear hoodies and jeans and ratty trainers. Thomas wears a suit every day. He's thin, too thin for a Westerner. His accent is too aristocratic, nothing at all like the working-class mumbles coming from the real Brits' mouths. And the scarf only highlights his strangeness.

I think for sure I will be exposed, until one day at a bar a real Englishman jabs a sausage-like finger into my chest and says, "You're gay, aren't you, mate?"

When I only stutter in reply, he says, "Ah, it's all right. Don't worry about it. You might want to tone it down, though. The scarf's a bit much."

And so Thomas Majors's sexuality is decided. It proves useful. It hides me from the expats the way Thomas's whiteness hides me from the Chinese.

IT'S IN A *waiguoren* bar that New Teach English finds me. A tiny woman not even five feet tall swims through a sea of beery pink bodies to find me sitting quietly in a corner, pretending to sip a gin and tonic. She offers me a job.

"I don't have a TOEFL certification," I tell her.

"We'll get you one. No problem," she says. And it's true; a friend of hers owns a printshop that can produce such a document with ease.

"I'm not sure I'll pass the medical exam required for a foreign expert certificate," I tell her.

"My brother-in-law works at the hospital," she says. "If you give him a bottle of cognac, you'll pass the health exam."

And that's how I get my residence permit.

YOU ARRIVE IN my second year at New Teach in Changsha with your eyes downcast and your mouth shut. I recognize you. You're a fellow impostor, but a more mundane sort than myself. Though hired as an ESL teacher, you can hardly say, "Hello, how are you?"

We introduce ourselves by our English names. I am Thomas Majors and you are Daniel Liu. "Liu. Like my scarf," I joke. I give you a smile copied from Pierce Brosnan.

I lie to you and tell you that I'm from London and my name is Thomas. Your lies are those of omission: you do not mention that you are the son of New Teach's owner, and that you had the opportunity to study in the United States but flunked out immediately.

Somehow being the only child of rich parents hasn't made you too spoiled. In your first year at New Teach you sit close to me, studying my counterfeit English as I talk to my students. Meanwhile, I sit close to Sarah, a heavyset Canadian girl, trying to glean real English from her as best I can.

Somehow, my *waiguoren* status doesn't spoil me, either. Unlike most Western men in China, I bathe regularly and dress well and arrive to work on time without a hangover every morning, and I don't try to sleep with my students. My humanity requires work to maintain. I don't take it for granted.

For these reasons, I am declared the star foreign instructor at New Teach English. I stand out like a gleaming cubic zirconium in a rubbish heap. The students adore me. Parents request me for private lessons with their children. They dub me *Da Huang* (Big Yellow).

Every six to twelve months, the other foreign teachers leave and a new set takes their place. Only I remain with you. You stay close to me, seeking me out for grammar help and conversation practice. There's more you want, I know, but you are too timid to ask for it outright, and I am unable to offer it.

We slowly create each other like a pair of half-rate Pygmalions. I fix the holes in your English, teach you how to look others in the eye, how to shake hands authoritatively, how to approach Western women, how to pose in photographs, how to project confidence ("fake it till you make it"), how to be the sort of man you see in movies.

Your questions prod me to quilt Thomas Majors together from little scraps stolen from overheard conversations in expat bars. Thomas Majors traveled a lot as a child, which is why his accent is a bit odd. (That came from an American girl who wore red-framed glasses.) Thomas Majors has an annoying younger brother and an eccentric older sister. (This I took from old television sitcoms.) His father owned a stationery shop (based on an ESL listening test), but his sister is set to inherit the business (from a BBC period piece), so Thomas moved to China to learn about calligraphy (that came from you, when I saw you carrying your ink brush).

Your questions and comments nudge me into playing the ideal Englishman: polite, a little silly at times, but sophisticated and cool. Somehow I become the sort of man that other men look up to. They ask Thomas for advice on dating and fashion and fitness and education. They tell him he's tall and handsome and clever. I say "thank you" and smile, just as I practiced in the mirror.

I LIKED THOMAS. I wish I could have kept on being him a little longer.

IN SHENZHEN, I nearly tell you the truth about myself. New Teach has just opened a center there and sends you out to manage it. You want to bring me to work there and help keep the foreign teachers in line.

"I don't know if I can pass the medical examination," I tell you.

"You look healthy," you reply.

I choose my words carefully. "I have a medical condition. I manage it just fine, but I'm afraid the doctors will think I am too sick."

"What condition? Is it di..." You struggle with the pronunciation.

"It's not diabetes. The truth is"—and what follows is at least partially true—"I don't know what it is, exactly."

"You should see a doctor," you tell me.

"I have," I say. "They did a lot of tests on me for a long time but they still couldn't figure it out. I got sick of it. Lots of needles in my arms and painful surgeries." I mime nurses and doctors jabbing and cutting me. "So now I don't go to doctors anymore."

"You should still have an examination," you tell me.

"No," I say.

Physicians are not difficult to fool, especially in China, overworked and sleep-deprived as they are. But their machines, their scanners, and their blood tests are things I cannot deceive. I do not want to know what they might find beneath Thomas Majors's skin.

I tell you I won't go with you if I have to submit to a medical exam, knowing full well how badly you want me to come. And so phone calls are made, red envelopes are stuffed, favors are cashed in, and banquets are arranged.

We feast with Shenzhen hospital administrators. They stare at me as I eat with chopsticks. "You're very good with... ah..." The Hospital Director points at the utensils in my hand, unable to dig up the English word.

"*Kuaizi*," I say. They applaud.

We go out to KTV afterward. The KTV bar has one David Bowie song and two dozen from the Backstreet Boys. The men like the way I sing. They order further snacks, more beer, and a pretty girl to sit on our laps and flirt with us. "So handsome," she says, stroking my chin. By now I have mastered the art of blushing.

You present a bottle of liquor: "It's very good *baijiu*," you say, and everyone nods in agreement. We toast. They fill my glass with liquor over and over again. Each time they clink it and say, "*Gan bei!*" And to me they add, "For England!" Now I have no choice but to drain my glass to make my fake mother country proud.

For most foreigners, *baijiu* is a form of torture. I've heard them say it's foul-tasting, that it gives monstrous hangovers, that you'll find yourself burping it up two days later. But for me, it's no more noxious than any other fluid. So I throw down enough liquor to show our guests that I am healthy and strong. We finish the bottle, then a second, and when I realize that the other men are putting themselves in agony to keep up with me I cover my mouth, run to the nearby lavatory, and loudly empty my stomach. Our guests love it. They cheer.

The winner of the drinking contest is a short, fat, toad-like man with a wide mouth. He's the director of the hospital, which is easy to guess by his appearance; powerful men in Guangdong often look a bit like toads. You tell me later that I made him very happy by drinking with him, and that he was extremely pleased to have defeated a Westerner.

And that is how I pass my health examination in Shenzhen.

YOUR GRANDMOTHER RECOGNIZES me during the following Spring Festival.

Going home with you is a bad idea. I should spend those two weeks enjoying the relative quiet of the empty city, drinking myself into oblivion with the leftover handful of expats.

The idea starts as a lark, a jocular suggestion on your part, but once it seizes me it will not let me go. I can't remember the last time I was in a home, with a family. I want to know what it's like.

You are too embarrassed to try to talk me out of it, so home we go.

Your mother is surprised to see me. She takes you aside and scolds you. Tingting's *Changshahua* has faded. Now my new English brain is still struggling to learn proper Mandarin, so I only get the gist of the conversation. I know *meiyou* (without) and *nü pengyou* (girlfriend), and my understanding of the culture fills in the rest. You're supposed to have brought home a woman. You're not getting any younger; you're just a few years shy of turning thirty unmarried, a bare-branch man. Your parents can't bear it. They don't understand. You're tall, rich, and handsome. Why don't you have a girlfriend?

The question is repeated several times over the next ten days, by your mother, your father, your grandfather, and your aunt.

The only person who doesn't denounce your bachelordom is your grandmother. She likes me. When she sees me, she smiles and says, "*Cao didi.*"

"Grass brother?" I ask.

"It's a nickname for an actor she really likes," you explain. "American."

She asks me another question, but Tingting is too far gone. I'm a Westerner now. "*Ting bu dong,*" I say politely. *I hear you, but I don't understand.*

I ask her to repeat herself, but something the old woman said has embarrassed your mother, for she escorts *Nainai* up to her room.

"She's old," you tell me.

Your mother and grandfather and aunt are not as accustomed to the sight of foreigners as you are. They, too, marvel at my chopstick ability as though I am a cat that has learned to play the piano. At all times I am a walking exhibition. In most places, I'm the *waiguoren*, the foreigner. In expat bars, I'm That Bloke with the Scarf, famed for his habit of always appearing well groomed. And around you, I'm Thomas Majors, though for some reason I don't mind it when you look at me.

I have no trouble with chopsticks. But putting food in my mouth, chewing it, and swallowing it are not actions that come naturally to me. This tongue of mine does not have working taste buds. My teeth are not especially secure in their gums, having been inserted one by one with a few taps of a hammer. This stomach of mine is only a synthetic sack that dangles in the recesses of my body. It has no exit. It leads nowhere.

Eating, for me, is purely a ritual to convince others that I am in fact human. I take no pleasure in it and personally find the act distasteful, especially when observing the oil lingering on others' lips, the squelching sounds of food being slurped and smacked between moist mucous membranes in the folds of fleshy human mouths.

I'm not entirely sure how I gain sustenance. I have found certain habits are necessary to keep me intact. As to each one's precise physiological function, I am unclear.

Your mother thinks I don't eat enough. "My stomach is a little weak," I say. "I'm sorry."

"Is that why you're not fat like most foreigners?" your aunt asks. Her English is surprisingly good.

"I guess so," I tell her.

"My mother is from Hunan," you tell me. "Her food is a little spicy for you, maybe."

"It's good," I say.

"I'll tell her less spicy next time," you promise.

"You don't have to," I say. I hate making the woman inconvenience herself to please an artificial stomach.

After the feast, we watch the annual pageant on television. There's Dashan the Canadian smiling and laughing as the other presenters tease him about the length of his nose. Your relatives point at my face and make unflattering comparisons.

At midnight, we watch the sky light up with fireworks.

Then it's time for bed. I sleep in the guest room with your flatulent uncle. I suspect your mother placed me with him as some form of punishment.

I hadn't anticipated sharing a room. I hadn't even brought nightclothes. I don't own any.

"I usually sleep naked," is my excuse when I sheepishly ask you for a spare set of pajamas.

I wonder what it's like to sleep. It strikes me as a strange way to pass the time.

I pull the covers up to my chin, ignoring your uncle when he scolds me for wearing a scarf to bed. I shut my eyes. I practice breathing slowly and loudly as I've seen real people do. Eventually, your uncle falls asleep. He snores like a chainsaw but sleeps like a stone. The hourly bursts of fireworks don't waken him. Neither does the light from my smartphone when I turn it on to look up Cao Didi. That's only his nickname in the Chinese press, of course. His English name is Maxwell Stone, but that's not his real name, either. In his nation of origin, he was called Maksimilian Petrovsky.

Here is Maxwell Stone's biography: born in Russia in 1920, he moved to the United States in the late '30s, where he began working as an extra for Hammerhead Studios. He worked as a stuntman in adventure films, but he got his first speaking role as a torch-wielding villager in 1941's *The Jigsaw Man*, a low-budget knock-off of *Frankenstein* made without the permission of Mary Shelley's estate. Maxwell Stone never attained fame in the United States or in his native Russia, but his only starring role in 1948's *The White Witch of the Amazon* somehow gained him a cult following in China, where audiences dubbed him 'Cao Didi' (Grass Brother) after an iconic scene in which Stone evades a tribe of headhunters by hiding in the underbrush. The McCarthy era killed Stone's career in Hollywood. In 1951, he left Los Angeles and never returned.

Thomas Majors does not resemble Maxwell Stone. Maxwell was dark and muscular with a moustache and a square jaw, the perfect early twentieth-century man: rugged yet refined.

I don't know how your grandmother recognizes Maxwell Stone in Thomas Majors. I have mostly forgotten Stone. There's hardly any of him left in me, just a few acting lessons and a couple of tips on grooming and posing for photographs.

I spend the next few days and nights dredging up Tingting's *Changshahua*. When I speak Chinese at the table, your mother blanches. She didn't realize I could understand the things she has been saying about me.

I don't get the opportunity to talk to your grandmother privately until the fifth day of the lunar New Year. It's late at night, and I hear her hobble down to the living room by herself and turn on the television. There's a burst of fireworks outside, but everyone is too full of *baijiu* and *jiaozi* to wake up. The only two people in the house still conscious are me and *Nainai*.

I turn off the telly and kneel in front of her. In Tingting's old *Changshahua* I ask, "How did you know I was Cao Didi?"

She smiles blankly and says, in accented English, "How did you recognize me under all these feathers?"

It takes a moment for the memory to percolate. It's 1947, on a cheap jungle set in a sound studio in Los Angeles. Maxwell Stone is wearing a khaki costume and a Panama hat and I'm wearing Maxwell Stone. Maxwell is a craftsman, not an artist: dependable and humble. He always remembers his lines. Now I remember them, too.

Your grandmother is reciting dialog from one of Stone's movies. She's playing the lost heiress whom Stone's character was sent to rescue. I can't quite recall the original actress's name. Margot or something like that.

Lights. Camera. Action. "Feathers or no feathers," I recite. "A dame's a dame. Now it's time to go home." Thomas's mouth tries on a mid-Atlantic accent.

"But I can't go back." Your grandmother touches her forehead with the back of her hand. "I won't. This is where I belong now."

"Knock it off with this nonsense, will you?" says an American adventurer played by a Russian actor played by an entity as-of-yet unclassified. "Your family's paying me big money to bring you back to civilization."

"Tell them I died! Tell them Catherine DuBlanc was killed." A melodramatic pause, just like in the film. "... Killed by the White Witch of the Amazon."

Then your grandmother goes quiet again, like a toy whose batteries have run out. She says nothing more.

I thought she knew me. But she only knows Maxwell. The performance was all she wanted.

I HAVE WORN so many people. I don't know how many. I don't remember most of them. I ought to keep a record of some kind, but most of them strike me as dull or loathsome in retrospect.

I played a scientist once or twice, but I could not figure myself out. In the 1960s I was a graduate student; I sought myself out in folklore and found vague references to creatures called changelings, shapeshifters, but the descriptions don't quite fit me. I do not have a name.

I do not know how old I am or where I came from or what made me or why I came to be. I try on one person after another, hoping that someday I'll find one that fits and I'll settle into it and some biological process or act of magic will turn me into that person.

I have considered leaving civilization, but the wilds are smaller than they used to be. Someone would stumble across me and see me undisguised. It has happened before.

I will not submit to scientific examination. Though the tools have advanced considerably over the course of my many lifetimes, the human method of inquiry remains the same: tear something apart until it confesses its secrets, whether it's a heretic or a frog's nervous system or the atom.

I do experience something akin to pain, and I prefer to avoid it.

I LIKE BEING Thomas Majors. I enjoy making money, getting promoted, living as a minor celebrity. I appreciate the admiration others heap upon my creation.

And I confess I like your admiration most of all. It's honest and schoolboyish and sweet.

Wearing Thomas grants me the pleasure of your company, which I treasure, though it probably doesn't show. I am fond of so many things about you, such as that little nod you give when you try to look serious, or the way your entire face immediately turns red when you drink. At first, I studied these traits in the hopes of replicating them someday in a future incarnation. I memorized them. I practiced them at home until they were perfect. But even after I've perfected them, I still can't stop watching you.

I would like to be closer to you. I know you want the same thing. I know the real reason you insist on bringing me with you every time you open a new branch in a new city. I know the real reason you always invite me when you go out to dine with new school administrators and government officials and investors.

But I am a creature that falls to pieces terribly often, and you can't hold on to a thing like that. Every instance of physical touch invites potential damage to my artificial skin and the risk of being discovered.

It is difficult to maintain a safe distance in an overcrowded country where schoolboys sit on each other's laps without embarrassment and *ayis* press their shopping baskets into your legs when you queue up at a market.

When you or anyone else stands too near or puts an arm around my shoulders, I step back and say, "Westerners like to keep other people at arm's length."

You have your own reasons not to get too close. You have familial obligations, filial piety. You must make your parents happy. They paid for your education, your clothes, your food, your new apartment. They gave you your job. You owe them a marriage and a child. You have no reason to be a bachelor at the age of twenty-eight.

Your mother and father choose a woman for you. She's pretty and kind. You can think of no adequate excuses to chase her away. You can tolerate a life with her, you decide. You're a businessman. You will travel a lot. She doesn't mind.

You announce your impending marriage less than a year later. The two of you look perfect in your engagement photos, and at your wedding you beam so handsomely that even I am fooled. I'm not jealous. I'm relieved that she has taken your focus from me, and I do love to see you smile.

*   *   *

A FEW MONTHS later, we travel to Beijing. New Teach is opening a training center there, so we have another series of banquets and *gan bei* and KTV with our new business partners.

By the end of the night, you're staggering drunk, too drunk to walk straight, so I stoop low to let you put your arm across Thomas Majors's shoulders in order to save you from tipping onto the pavement. I hope that you're too drunk to notice there's something not quite right with Thomas's limbs, or at least too drunk to remember it afterward.

I help you into a cab. The driver asks me the standard *waiguoren* questions (*Where are you from? How long have you lived in China? Do you like it here? What is your job? Do you eat hamburgers?*) but I ignore him. I only want to listen to you.

You rub your stomach as the taxi speeds madly back to our hotel. "Are you going to vomit?" I ask.

You're quiet for a moment. I try to roll down the window nearest you, but it's broken. Finally, you mutter, "I'm getting fat. Too much beer."

"You look fine," I say.

"I'm gaining weight," you insist.

"You sound like a woman," I tease you.

"Why don't you get fat?" you say. "You're a Westerner. How are you so slim?"

"Just lucky, I guess," I say.

I pay the cab fare and drag you out, back up to your hotel suite. I give you water to drink and an ibuprofen to swallow so you won't get a hangover. You take your medicine like a good boy, but you refuse to go to sleep.

I sit at the edge of your bed. You lean forward and grab my scarf. "You always wear this," you say.

"Always," I agree.

"What would happen if you took it off?" you ask.

"I can't tell you," I reply.

"Come on," you say, adding a line from a song: "Come on, baby, don't be shy." Then you laugh until tears flow down your red cheeks, until you fall backward onto the bed, and when you fall you drag me by the scarf down with you.

"Be careful!" I tell you. "Ah, *xiao xin*!"

But instead you pull on the scarf as though reeling in a fish.

"You never take it off," you say, holding one end of the scarf before your eyes. "I have never seen your neck."

I know I'm supposed to say something witty but I can't think of it, so I smile bashfully instead. It's a gesture I stole from Hugh Grant films.

"What would happen if I take it off?" you ask. You try to unwrap it, but fortunately you're too clumsy with drink.

"My head would fall off," I say.

Then you laugh, and I laugh. Looming over you is awkward, so I lie beside you and prop my head up on Thomas Majors's shoulder. You turn onto your left side to face me.

"Da Huang," you say, still playing with the scarf. "That's your Chinese name."

"What's your Chinese name?" I ask. "Your real name, I mean? You never told me."

"Chengwei," you say.

"Chengwei," I repeat, imperfectly.

"No," you say. "Not Chéngwéi." You raise your hand, then make a dipping motion to indicate the second and third tones. "Chéngwěi."

"Chéngwěi," I say, drawing the tones in the air with Thomas's graceful fingers.

"*Hen hao*," you say. *Very good.*

"*Nali*," I say, a modest denial.

You smile. I notice for the first time that one of your front teeth is slightly crooked. It's endearing, though, one of those little flaws which, through some sort of alchemy I have yet to learn to replicate, only serve to flatter the rest of the picture rather than mar it.

"Da Huang is not a good name," you say.

"What should I be called?" I ask.

You study Thomas Majors's face carefully, yet somehow fail to find its glaring faults.

"Shuai," you say. You don't translate the word, but I know what it means. *Handsome.*

You touch Thomas's cheek. I can feel your warmth through the false skin.

Again, I don't know what to say. This hasn't come up in the etiquette books I studied.

I realize that you're waiting for me to be the brash Westerner who shoves his way forward and does what he wants. This hunger of yours presses on Thomas Majors, pinches and pulls at him to resculpt his personality.

I want to be the man who can give you these things. But I'm terrified. When you run your fingers through Thomas's hair, I worry that the scalp might come loose, or that your hand will skate across a bump that should not be there.

You grab me by the scarf again and pull me closer to you. I shut my eyes. I don't want you to see them at this distance; you might find something wrong in them. But that's not what you're looking for.

Then you kiss me, a clumsy, drunk kiss. You cling to me like one of Harlow's monkeys to a cloth mother.

I can't remember the last time I was kissed.

I vaguely remember engaging in the act of coitus in some previous incarnation. It did not go well.

The mechanics of sexuality, of blood redistributing itself and tissue contracting and flesh reddening and appendages hardening and fluids secreting, are marvelously difficult to imitate with any verisimilitude.

This is the climax of every story. In romance novels, the lovers kiss in the rain, and it's all over. In fairy tales, the kiss breaks the spell: the princess awakens, the frog becomes a man. But that doesn't happen, not now, not the last time I was kissed, and not the next time I will be kissed.

But I enjoy it all the same. Your body is warm and right and real: self-heating skin, hair that grows in on its own, a mouth that lubricates itself.

I study your body and memorize it for future reference. At the moment there is little I can learn and so much that I want to know. I wish I could taste you.

You remove yourself from my lips and drunkenly smear your mouth against my cheek, my jaw, what little of my neck is not covered by the scarf. You press your nose against me and try vainly to smell Thomas Majors under the cologne I have chosen for him. You rest your head on my arm for a moment. I stroke your hair—not because it seems appropriate, but because I want to.

Then you close your eyes. They stay closed. Soon I hear the slow, loud breathing of a man asleep.

That's as far as it goes between you and Thomas Majors.

My arms don't fall asleep so I can let you use Thomas Majors as your pillow for as long as you like. I watch your eyelashes flutter as you fall into REM sleep. I wonder what you're dreaming about. I press my fingers against your neck to feel your pulse.

Without waking you, I move my head down and lay it upon your chest. I shut my eyes. I listen to your heartbeat and the slow rhythm of your breath. Your stomach gurgles. The sounds are at once recognizably natural and alien to me, like deep-sea creatures. I find them endlessly fascinating.

I try very hard to fall asleep, but I have no idea how to go about it. Still, I wait, and I imitate your breathing and hope that I'll begin to lose track of each individual thump of your heart, and that I'll slip out of consciousness and maybe even dream, and that I'll wake up next to you.

Hours pass this way. The light through the window turns pale grey as the sun rises in Beijing's smoggy sky. You roll over to face the shade and lie still again.

I slip from the bed and head to the bathroom where I examine myself. I look very much the same as I did the day before.

I take the elevator down to the dining room. It's 8:36 a.m. Breakfast time. I serve myself from the buffet, selecting the sort of things I think a Westerner is supposed to eat at breakfast: bread, mostly, with coffee, tea, and a glass of milk. I sit alone at a little table with this meal before me and let its steam warm my face. I wait for the aroma to awaken a sense of hunger in me. It doesn't.

I eat it anyway so as not to cause suspicion. I can't taste any of it, as usual.

You're still asleep when I get back. It has only been about five hours since you flopped onto my bed. In the bathroom, I empty Thomas Majors's stomach and turn on the shower. Even though the door is locked, I do not remove the yellow scarf. I tape a plastic bag around it to keep it dry.

The grime of last night's drinking and duck neck slides off, along with a few hairs I'll have to replace later.

The water hits me with a muffled impact. I don't feel wet. Thomas's skin keeps me dry like a raincoat. It isn't my flesh.

I wonder if the state you invoke in me can accurately be called love. I know only that I am happier in your presence than out of it, and that I care desperately what you think of me. If that is love, then I suppose it can be said that I love you, with all the shapeless mass I have instead of a heart.

I don't believe that you love me, but I know that you love Thomas Majors, and that's close enough.

I've heard stories like this, hundreds of them, in languages I've long forgotten. The ending is always the same. Galatea's form softens and turns to flesh. The Velveteen Rabbit sprouts fur and whiskers. But I am still myself, whatever that is, and my puppet Thomas Majors has not become a real boy.

I don't know what I am, but at least now I know something I am not: I am not a creature of fairy tales.

YOUR CELL PHONE wakes you a little after 10 a.m. It's your wife. I'm dressed by then in a navy-blue suit and working on my cell phone in one of the easy chairs. You finish the conversation before you're quite conscious.

"Do you remember last night?" I ask.

You scratch your head. "No," you groan.

"Do you have a hangover?" I ask.

I take your miserable grunt as a yes.

YOUR DAUGHTER IS born seven months later. You leave Beijing for a while to tend to your wife. After a few weeks of your unbearable absence, a student invites me to dinner with her family. "I can't," I tell her. "I'm taking a trip this weekend."

"Are you going to see your *giiiirlfriend*?" she asks in a singsong voice. She's in high school, too busy from fifteen-hour school days seven days a week to have a boyfriend of her own, but she has immense interest in the love lives of her more attractive teachers.

"No," I tell her. The expats know that Thomas Majors is gay but his students and colleagues do not. "I'm going to visit my boss, Mr. Liu. I can have dinner with you next week."

I take the bullet train to Shenzhen. As the countryside blurs past my window, I notice that Thomas's fingernails have become brittle. It's too soon. I blame the cold, dry air of Beijing and resolve to buy a bottle of clear nail polish and apply it at the first opportunity.

You're not home when I come to your door. Your mother-in-law thanks me for the gift I have brought (a canister of imported milk powder), invites me in, and explains that you're on a shopping trip in Hong Kong and will be back soon. In the meantime, I sit in the living room and sip warm water.

Your wife isn't finished with her post-partum month of confinement. She does not invite me to her room. It's probably because she's in pajamas and hasn't washed her hair, or she's simply tired, but the suspicion that she knows something unsavory about me crawls on my back.

There's a dog in the apartment, a shaggy little thing that doesn't go up to my knee. It doesn't quite know what to make of me. It barks and skitters around in circles. It can smell me—not Thomas, but *me*—and it knows that something is slightly off.

But dogs are not terribly bright. I sneak to the kitchen, find a piece of bacon, and put it in my pocket. The dog likes me well enough after that.

You return home that afternoon, laden with bags. You weren't expecting me, but you're happy to see me.

"I bought something for you," you tell me. "A gift."

"You didn't have to," I insist.

"I already had to buy gifts for my whole extended family," you say, "so one more doesn't matter. Here."

You pull a small box out of a suitcase.

"Can I open it?" I ask.

You nod.

I peel off the tape. The paper does not tear at all as I remove it. The box shimmers. I open it and can't help but cry out.

"A new scarf!" I hold it up. It's beautiful, gleaming yellow silk with brocade serpents. I try on an expression of overwhelming gratitude. Until now, I haven't had a chance to use it. "Snakes."

"That's your birth year," you say.

"You remembered," I say. "This is wonderful. Thank you so much."

"Put it on," you tell me.

"In a little while."

"Come on, baby. Don't be shy," you say. You couch your demand in humor and a smile. "Go ahead."

I try to think of an excuse not to. A scar on my neck. A skin condition. It's cold. None of them will work.

Your baby saves me. She starts screaming in the bedroom, and neither your wife nor her mother can calm her down. Your wife soon starts crying, too, and your mother-in-law starts shouting at her.

"I think maybe you should get in there and say hello," I tell you.

You groan, but you comply.

I dash to the lavatory. Quickly, I unwind the counterfeit *Liu Viuttor* scarf from around my neck. It sticks to Thomas's flesh like a bandage. I peel it off slowly but the damage is done. The skin of Thomas Majors's neck has gone ragged, like moth-eaten cloth. I wrap the new scarf around it snugly. Then I unwrap it. The damage is still there. Somehow, I thought this new totem would fix me.

I tie my new scarf around Thomas's neck and return to the living room.

To spare your wife further agitation, her mother banishes the baby from the bedroom. You carry her out with you. She's a fat little thing, all lumpy pink pajamas and chubby cheeks gone red from crying. When she sees me, she quiets herself and stares. She's had limited experience of the world, but even she knows that this creature before her is different.

"She's never seen a foreigner before," you say with a smile. "Do you want to hold her?"

You thrust her into my arms before I can resist. She does not cry anymore, just looks at me with big, dark eyes. Her little body is warm and surprisingly heavy.

"Chinese babies like to stare at handsome faces," you say.

I smile at her. She doesn't smile back. She hasn't learned yet that she's supposed to. Everything about her is unpracticed and new and utterly authentic. I find it unnerving.

"You made this," I said. "You made a person. A real person."

"Yeah," you say, probably filing my remark under *foreigners say strange things*. "Do you think you'll have children?" you ask me.

"Probably not," I say.

Your daughter clutches at my new scarf.

A FEW DAYS later, we take the bullet train back to Beijing together. You nap most of the way with your head on my shoulder. When you wake up, you tell me, "You should sleep more. You look tired."

"So do you," I reply.

"I have a baby," you say. "You don't."

The only reply I have for him is a nervous Colin Firth smile. Underneath it, I am panicking.

"You look a little grey. Maybe it's the air," you say. "Do you use a mask?"

"Of course," I say.

"You need to drink more water," you tell me. I know by now that nagging is an expression of love in China, but the advice still irritates me. It's useless.

Our train plunges deeper and deeper into miasma as we approach the city. The sky darkens even as the sun rises. It's late autumn and the coal plants are blazing in preparation for winter.

Maybe it *is* the air. Maybe it's bad enough to affect even me. Maybe the new skin wasn't ready when I put it on. Maybe it's just the standard decay that conquers every Westerner who spends too much time in China. Whatever the reason, Thomas Majors is beginning to come apart.

We don air filters as we leave the train station. Outside, we pass people in suits, women in brightly colored minidresses, children in school uniforms, all covering their faces. Those of us who can afford it wear enormous, clunky breathing masks. Those who can't, or who don't understand the risk, wear thin surgical masks made of paper, or little cloth masks with cartoon characters on them, or they just tie a bandana around their mouths and noses. A short, stocky man squats on the pavement, removing his mask every so often to suck on a cigarette.

We take separate taxis. I don't go home, though. I visit a beauty shop, pharmacy, and apothecary, and I buy every skincare product I can find. Expensive moisturizer from France. A mud-mask treatment from Korea. Cocoa butter from South America. Jade rollers. Pearl powder. Caterpillar fungus. Back in my apartment, I slather them on Thomas Majors to see if they will make him tight and bright again. They don't.

The skin is looser, thinner, and when that happens the center cannot hold. I feel around for muscles that have slipped out of place, joints that have shifted, limbs trying to lengthen or widen. I have not lost my shape just yet, but I know it is only a matter of time.

I unravel the scarf you gave me and look again. The skin underneath is even worse. There's an open gash along it that threatens to creep even wider.

I can see bits of myself through it, brackish and horrible. Sewing it shut won't do anything; the flesh is too fragile. So I tape it up and wrap the scarf around it even tighter. Silk is strong. Silk will hold it, at least for a while.

I make phone calls to forgers, to chemists, to printers, to tanners, to all the sorts of people who can help me make someone new. This time, at least, I have money to spend and privacy in which to work. I can do it right. I can make somebody who will last longer and fit better and maybe won't come apart again.

The smog provides a convenient excuse for my absence over the next few weeks. It traps most of us in our homes with our air purifiers. But at times a strong wind comes to blow it away, at least for a while, and there you are again inviting me out to KTV bars and business lunches and badminton. I can't go. I want to go, but Thomas Majors is fragile and thin, liable to split apart at any moment. His hair is coming out. His gums are getting soft. Speaking is difficult; I feel the gash in Thomas's throat grow wider and wider under the scarf.

I cite my health as a reason not to renew my contract, but you refuse to accept it. You won't let Thomas Majors go. I remind you of my unnamed medical condition. I tell you that I've been to dozens of doctors and even some traditional Chinese healers. I promise to see another specialist.

I promise I'll keep in touch. I promise I'll come back again once I'm better.

Then I sequester myself in my apartment. I don't know what my next form will be. I'd like to build myself another Thomas Majors, one that will last forever, but I feel my body pulling in different directions. It wants to shift in a dozen different ways, all of them horrible: too squat, or insect-thin, or with limbs at angles that don't make sense in human physiology.

MY HUMAN COSTUME is slipping off me too quickly. I don't go outside anymore. I only wait for the men to come with the documents and the materials. There's a knock at the door. It's you.

I know I shouldn't open it, but I also know that you can hear me moving around in my apartment, and that you'll be hurt if I don't let you in, and even though I don't want you to see me as I am, I still want to see you. I adjust Thomas's face and throw a heavy robe on over the blue suit.

The expression of horror in your eyes is remarkable. I memorize it to use in a future incarnation.

"*Ni shenti bu hao*," you say, in that blunt Chinese way. *Your body is not good*. You take off your breathing mask and come inside.

"Thanks," I say.

You try to give me a hug.

"Don't," I say. "I could be contagious." The truth is I'm terrified you might feel me moving around underneath Thomas Majors, or you'll squeeze tight enough to leave a dent.

You sit down without invitation.

"What is it?" you ask.

"I think I caught food poisoning, on top of everything else. Probably shouldn't have eaten *shaokao*."

"Are you going to be healthy enough for the ride home?" you ask.

"I'll be all right," I say. "I just need rest is all."

"Have you been to the hospital?"

"Of course," I tell you. "The doctor gave me a ton of antibiotics and said to avoid cold water."

"Which hospital was it? Which doctor? Maybe he wasn't a good one. My friend knows one of the best doctors for stomach problems. I can take you to him. They have very good equipment. A big laboratory."

"I'll be all right."

You head to the kitchen to boil water. "Wait a moment," you instruct me over the sound of the electric kettle. Then you return with a steaming mug of something dark and greenish. "Drink this," you tell me. "Chinese medicine. For your stomach."

"I can't," I insist.

"Come on," you say. "You look really bad."

"It's too hot," I complain. I feel the steam softening the insides of Thomas's nasal passages.

You return to the kitchen to retrieve some ice from the freezer. I never use ice, but I always make sure to have some in my home because I am a Westerner for the time being.

You drop a few cubes of ice into my mug. "There," you say. "Drink it."

"I'm sick to my stomach," I complain. "I might vomit."

"This will fix it," you insist.

I know I shouldn't listen to you, but I want to make you happy, and some part of me still half-believes that stupid fairy-tale fantasy that your love will make me real somehow. So I put the mug to my lips and slurp down some of its contents, and soon I feel the artificial stomach lining thinning and turning to fizz inside me.

"Excuse me," I rasp. The vocal cords feel loose. I bolt to the bathroom to vomit.

Thomas's stomach lining makes its way up and out. It hangs from my mouth, still attached somewhere around my chest. Your medicine has burned holes into it. I don't blame you. I'm sure it works properly on real human stomachs. I bite through the fake esophagus to free myself from the ruined organ, losing a tooth in the process. Then I flush the mess down the squat toilet.

Evidently, the noise is alarming. "I'm calling you an ambulance!" you shout from the living room.

It takes me much too long to cram the esophagus back in so I can say, "Don't. I'm quite all right. I just needed to vomit. I'm feeling better now. Really." But the vocal cords are so loose by this point that the words come out slurred and gravelly.

The call is quick; the arrival of the ambulance less so. I lie on the bathroom floor in a fetal position, contemplating my options. My strength is gone. I can't make it to the front door without you tackling me. I could get to a window and throw myself out, perhaps; I could drop through twenty stories of pollution and crawl away from Thomas Majors after he hits the ground. But I can't do something so horrible in front of you.

You punch through the bathroom door, undo the lock, and put your arms around my shoulders. I can feel your hands shake. You tell me over and over again that I'm going to be all right, and you're going to help me. I want to believe you.

The ambulance finally arrives. You pay the driver and help carry me out. "You're so light," you say.

I don't try to fight you.

You should have called a taxi, or maybe flagged down an e-bike instead, because the bulky ambulance gets stuck in traffic. You slap the insides of it as if trying to beat Beijing into submission. You curse the other cars, the ambulance driver, the civil engineers who planned the roadways, the population density, the asphalt for not being wide enough.

You curse the EMTs for the deplorable condition of the ambulance and the black soot on the gauze they've applied to my face, unaware that the filth is coming from the man you're trying to save. Thomas has sprung a leak; now I am pouring out.

They put a respirator of some sort over Thomas Majors's face. They attach devices to him to monitor a heart and lungs that do not exist. You notice the way the technician fiddles with the wires and pokes the electronic box, unable to get a proper reading from the patient, and you curse the defective equipment. You see the other technician jab me over and over again, unable to find a vein in which to stick an IV, and you curse his incompetence.

They get out their scissors. They open the robe and cut through its sleeves. Then they start cutting through my blue suit. I make little sounds of protest. I can't speak anymore.

"I'll buy you a new one," you say.

I try to crawl away, but you hold one arm and a technician grabs the other. Soon you can see what has happened to Thomas's torso—misshapen, discolored, with thick scars where I've had to stich darts as the skin became too loose.

Your hand moves to your mouth. "You were sick how long?" you ask. Your English is slipping.

I know what's coming. There is nothing I can do to stop it but lie here like a damsel tied to the railroad tracks and wait for it to hit me.

It's time to remove the scarf.

I've tied it too tight to slip the scissors underneath it, so they have to cut through the knots. Frustrated by how slowly the technicians work, you lean in and grab the silk.

Your hands shake harder and harder as you unwind the fabric. I watch the silk growing darker the closer you get to me. I'm sorry I ruined such a beautiful thing.

I can't see what's beneath. I don't want to. There's a reason I keep the mirrors covered when I go through a shift. But I can see the reaction on your face and on the technicians' faces, too. They've doubtless encountered horrible things in their line of work, and yet this still alarms them.

Thomas Majors's larynx comes apart. My neck is exposed. I feel cold.

You can't speak anymore either. You only make a strange panting sound and stare. Terror has stolen your voice. What's left is something primitive, an instinct going back millions of years. It must be wonderful to know who your ancestors were and that they were something as benign as apes.

One of the technicians is on his cell phone with the hospital, explaining the situation as best he can. I hear the doctor's voice telling them to bring me in through the basement entrance so the other patients won't see me.

I know what he wants. Physicians here are required to publish research on top of their grueling schedules and the doctor realizes that he has found an extraordinary case study. He's already thinking of fame, research grants, possibly another Nobel Prize for China. He won't have any trouble keeping me in a lab. There are no human rights standards to stop scientific progress here, and my fake UK citizenship will not protect me.

With nothing left to hold him together, Thomas Majors comes undone. The skin of his head shrinks from the skin of his shoulders. His face is loose. A seam opens at his armpit and runs down his torso.

You grab his hand. You can feel me underneath it, squirming. Your wrist jerks but you don't let go. Thomas's hand slips off me like a glove. It takes you a moment to understand what just happened, what you're holding, and when the realization hits, you scream and scream and scream.

The technicians can't pin me down anymore. They don't want to. It's impossible to tell what they can grab on to and whether or not it's safe to touch. So now they're trying to get away, pressing themselves against the walls of the ambulance, trying to clamber up to the front. The driver has already fled.

You're paralyzed. You've wedged yourself into a corner. Your eyes whirl about the ambulance, skipping upon me, upon what's left of Thomas Majors, upon the rear-door latch that's not quite close enough for you to open, upon the ceiling and the machines and all these things that don't make sense anymore.

I stand up. The last scraps of the man I wanted so badly to be fall to the floor. You shrink down, down, trying to disappear, but you don't have as much practice as I do.

You cover your eyes, uncover them, look at me, shut them again. I grab the door latch, averting my gaze from the sight of my own hand.

You're muttering something over and over again like a Buddhist chant. I listen carefully. My hearing is not what it was just a few minutes ago, but I can recognize the words, *"Ni shi shenme?" What are you?*

I don't have a larynx anymore and my tongue can no longer accommodate human language, so even though I want to, I can't answer *"wo bu zhidao"* or *"ouk oida"* or *"nga nu-zu"* or "I don't know."

I get the door open. The outside world is an endless polluted twilight. The driver behind us doesn't look up from his cell phone to glance in my direction. Two car-lengths away, all I can see are vague shapes and headlights. The smog will hide me well.

I climb out of the ambulance and into the haze. I don't look back.

I SAW YOU once after that. It wasn't long ago, I think. I was wearing someone new, a girl with black hair and a melon-seed face. Pretty girls are easy for me. I can slather on makeup if the skin isn't right, and I don't have to bother with a backstory or a personality. No one really wants it.

It was at an auto show in Shanghai. I was draped across a green Ferrari, wearing a bikini that matched the paint. I hadn't expected to see you, but there you were with a group of businessmen smoking Marlboros and ogling the models.

You were older. I'm not sure by how much. Time passes differently for me, and maybe time alone was not responsible for how much you had aged.

I would like to say I will never forget you, but I can't promise you that. This shapeless matter inside my head shifts and dies and regenerates, and as it does so, memories fade and old incarnations of myself are discarded. Maxwell Stone had lovers, most likely, but I can't recall their faces, and someday I will lose yours as well.

Your group strolled by my Ferrari, making the obligatory lewd remarks, flashing their brown teeth in leery grins. I wore my generic smile and offered up a vacant titter. I told them about the car.

You stood a little ways behind the other men with your hands in your pockets. I knew that look: you were too tired to pretend to be having a good time.

I smiled at you as hard as I could. Finally, you looked up. I thought maybe you would recognize me somehow. Maybe you would cry out, "It's you!" and take me in your arms. Or maybe, at the very least, you'd let your gaze linger on me a little longer than normal.

But you didn't. You made that nervous grimace you do whenever a woman pays too much attention to you. Then you ambled off to look at a Lexus—a four-door with lots of cabin space. Good for families.

I watched you move. Your shoulders were slumped as though you carried something very heavy.

Then more bodies flowed between us, wealthy men and their school-aged mistresses, nouveau riche wives and their spoiled bachelor sons searching for a car to attract a pretty bride, broke students in designer knock-offs come to take selfies in front of BMWs so they can pretend to be rich on Weixin.

I lost you among them. I did not find you again.

CRISPIN'S MODEL
Max Gladstone

Max Gladstone (www.maxgladstone.com) has been thrown from a horse in Mongolia and nominated twice for the John W. Campbell Best New Writer Award. He is best known for the Hugo Award nominated Craft Sequence of fantasy novels, which began in 2012 with *Three Parts Dead* and was followed by *Two Serpents Rise, Full Fathom Five, Last First Snow*, and most recently *The Ruin of Angels*. His short fiction has appeared on *Tor.com* and in *Uncanny Magazine*. His most recent project is the globetrotting urban fantasy serial Bookburners, available in ebook and audio from Serial Box, and in print from Saga Press.

THERE WERE NO monsters at first, only "Arthur Dufresne Crispin," who met me on the front steps of his apartment in the Village: towheaded, tall, and lean, with long spidery fingers that closed mine in a strangler's handshake. He had an accent that would have told someone from Boston or Providence a lot about his parents and the pedigree of his dog, but told me jack-all, except that he was the kind of guy who introduced himself with his middle name. He wore a green Brooks Brothers shirt, and men that pale should be careful wearing green. It seeps into the skin.

"I'm Deliah Dane," I said, and followed him up three flights of stairs to his studio. "Good light in here." Crispin kept the place neat. A few still-life setups in corners, a shelf of sketchbooks and anatomy texts and older leatherbound tomes. A folio of Dali prints, another of Bosch, and one of a Swedish painter whose name I don't remember. Canvases draped with light silk leaned against walls and doors and furniture. Through the silk I could see the canvases were painted, but not much more. The floor was strewn with lights: lamps, reflectors, mirrors, even a kerosene lantern. "Bet your landlord doesn't like you having this." I nudged the lantern with my shoe.

"I have no landlord," Crispin said, which told me more than the accent. "Ms. Dane, we should discuss the nature of my work. Previous models have expressed reluctance to operate under the conditions I require, and if this will be the case, I would rather find out now before we waste our time. Don't you agree?"

I'd been afraid of this when I couldn't find pictures of his recent work. My hand tightened around the cell phone in my jacket pocket. "I don't know what *conditions* you *require,* but I won't take any drugs for you, and no pegs go in any holes. I show up on time, I sit still. You paint, and you pay me."

"In terms of your responsibilities, our visions align. No drugs will be involved. Reality interests me, not psilocybin abstractions. As for"—and there it was, the dust of blush that meant maybe even Arthur Dufresne Crispin was human—"as for the rest, I will require no more of you than any other artist, insofar as poses are concerned."

A gorgeous red leather divan lay upon on the stage, with a scrolled wood headrest and a fringe of trailing beads like a flamenco dancer's skirt. I stroked the leather. "Why the conditions, then?"

"I do not converse with my models. Your form interests me. Personal connection distorts perspective."

"I doubt I'll want to talk with you much, either."

A ghost smile at that, faint as the blush. "I require exact duplication of poses from session to session. I may touch you, to restore a finger or an elbow to its proper place."

"Ask my permission first."

"Fair. And the last: You will not view our work while it proceeds. You may never see the pieces for which you pose. Should you happen to do so, you may not recognize yourself."

That rang alarms I didn't know I had. "What do you mean?"

"I paint the noumenal—that which lies beneath appearance. Some models take offence at my depiction, but no offense is meant."

"So, what, you paint me as subhuman and I don't get to call you racist afterward? Is that what you're saying?"

"That is not my intent."

"I want to see an example."

"I have no finished model work," he said, "and if I show you a still-life, I will be unable to sell it."

No sense asking artists why. They're a weird breed. "Show me, and I'll decide whether to sit for you." The power had shifted in the room, as it always does when you learn someone needs you.

His eyes were gray and cold as fish scales. At last, he turned to a canvas propped near a setup of a bowl and rose. He peeled back the silk as if peeling off his skin. Beneath—

It wasn't a bowl and rose. It wasn't *not* a bowl and rose, either. Take the bowl, and take the rose, and shatter them, cubist-like, through time as well as space, so in one facet the rose blooms and in another it's rotten, the bowl here tarnished and there radioactive gleaming. But that doesn't capture the twisted, callous distance of the effect. There was more time than time in that painting, and more space than space.

There's this Chinese story about a bird called p'eng, really big damn bird, flies so high the earth below fades to blue for it just like the sky does for us. To that bird, we're motes in a sunbeam, sparks kicked up by a campfire, insignificant painful specks that vanish back into the burn. And that was what he'd done with a bowl and a rose.

What would he do with me?

It was disgusting. Exciting too.

"Let's go," I said, and unbuttoned my pants.

YOU HAVE THE wrong idea about me already.

I moved up from Savannah to be on stage. I write. I act. I love the way an audience looks when you have them stuck, I mean skewered, to their seats. When they'd stay for at least a second even if someone *did* shout fire. And yes it isn't practical, and yes Mama writes letters every week and each one holds some allusion to this cousin or that who's *doing* whatever with herself. Mama's plumbed Michael Baysian depths of subtlety. I'm workshopping a one-woman show. I sent spec scripts around. An agent wants to see my next.

None of which counts for much rent-wise, in this city.

So, modeling.

Not the clothes kind, which work I doubt anyone would give me anyway on account of my having a body. But painters pay, and they like bodies, or at least they don't seem to care whether you stop eating after the first half of the M&M.

Yes, painters. They still exist. I mean the ones who paint people who look sort of like people, or at least paintings that *involve* people, not the squares-of-solid-blue shit.

Here's what you need to be an artist's model:

1. Body.

Here are some things that help:

2. Pride (If you get embarrassed when folk stare, this isn't the line for you.)
3. Honesty (Good artists draw what they see, so you might as well get to love that belly.)
4. Active imagination (You'll spend four hours at a time holding still.)
5. Bathrobe (To wear on break.)
6. Wristwatch with alarm.

The last is so important it should be first. Artists aren't timely people as a rule, but if they're paying for you, they expect you to be. A painter takes forty-five minutes to set up her easel, get the light just so, mix the paints—she expects you right at two, clothes off and in position, not at three thirty complaining about the subway. Get a watch. Or use that fancy phone for something other than taking pictures of your banh mi.

Some folks model to commune with an artist's tortured soul, to be the fulcrum between created and increate. All that mystery goes out the door the first time they get off a four-hour sit and can't feel their left butt cheek. For me, this was Something That Paid Twice as Much an Hour as the Restaurant. Each four-hour sit gave me a day to audition, to write, to please Ms. Agent.

That was what I told my friends. This other part I didn't realize myself at first, and later it felt too private to share: my time modeling, standing or leaning naked in front of some desperate kid with an easel and a nose ring, belonged to me. It didn't slip off like time does in your apartment where there's always some damn thing out of place, or out in the world where fear's a phone tap away. In those thirty minutes of pain and brush scratch, thoughts stretched long, and memories ran like rivers. I remembered being five, keeping time and singing on the back porch while Daddy played guitar. I remembered running when the grade school kids came for me, and how it felt to fight and lose and win. I remembered strawberries firm and rich as kisses. Hell, I remembered things that never happened. I climbed mountains on planets orbiting a distant star, with a purple sky overhead and a long fall below. Memories like that make you want like you have to, to do any kind of real work: you want from the bones out. After those sessions I'd write and write, and some of what I wrote I'd see the next day and think, good.

To those of you out there who think I could have earned more stripping:

1. Fuck.
2. You.

I started modeling for Steve, who my roommate Rache knew, and I showed up on time for his sits, and he told his friends and I showed up on time for theirs, and though I couldn't quit the restaurant I did take fewer shifts. The play took shape. I sent what I had to Ms. Agent, who sent back a sticky note with a smiley face that I took to mean, keep going.

But I never thought about the increate, or holes in worlds, until I met Crispin.

CRISPIN WASN'T LIKE the others. Even that first time, I could tell.

There was no music, only the hush of his apartment. Neither of us spoke. His work was an exercise in stillness, a pressure of knife against skin. Into that stillness came the brushstroke, a rasp that ran goosebumps up my shoulders and back, like sandpaper drawn lightly over a nipple.

Stare at your own face in a mirror in halflight and it will warp to something hideous. Staring at his that first afternoon I saw his skin bubble off the bone, his forehead bulge and birth curving horns, his jaw distend like a snake's about to devour the world. And then he looked up, and his face was a face again.

His brush left trails of poison paint—lead in the whites, mercury in the reds, fumes of alcohol and turpentine.

Sitting always hurts, but sitting for him hurt more. He'd asked for perfect stillness, so I had to show him. My heart beat against my will. People aren't made to freeze like that. Our ancestors hunted by jogging, chasing prey over open grassland until it died. We live by movement, and when you stop us, we hurt. Even that first pose, simple, seated, felt like pincers piercing the muscles of my butt, back, shoulder, neck, and spreading.

And then his gaze. *The stress of her regard,* the poet wrote. His whole body leaned into me through the points of his eyes. I didn't feel seen. I felt peered through, like the near lens of a telescope.

My watch chimed the end of our last period. It felt as if I'd sat forever, and for no time at all. I guess no time at all *is* forever, because no time means no time passing, and if time doesn't pass then the moment just goes.

"Thank you, Ms. Dane," he said, and passed me a cash envelope containing—yes, I looked—twice what I'd made on any other four-hour sit.

"Thank you, Crispin," I said, and we set our next date.

I'd reached the street and made it halfway to the corner when I heard a crash behind me, of broken wood and torn cloth. I turned back, curious. The painting of bowl and rose Crispin had showed me lay broken on the sidewalk. Several floors up, his window closed.

WE SAW EACH other often that summer: I saw him behind the easel, and he saw me on the divan. We painted even through swampy August. He painted. I endured.

Crispin was slow. The first portrait, head and shoulders alone, a face made large as canvas, took twelve hours, three times longer than Steve needed for a whole-body nude. As we neared the end, he was soaked in sweat, eyes bloodshot. Done, he turned the canvas to the corner of the room so I couldn't see myself. I thought the painting cast light into that bare cobwebbed corner.

We started the nudes next. He wanted a pair, three-quarter sized, my leg up on a block, one hand resting on my thigh. By the end of the first day the hip of my raised leg hurt like I was sixty. The whole time he stared through me. I might have been a piece of tissue paper held to a halogen bulb, smoking, almost aflame. After those sessions I rode the subway home, gazing blank faced as a junkie at the wall, staggered back to my apartment, drew a steaming bath in spite of the heat, and waited for my body to return. I floated like a fetus in the womb.

My memory didn't work while I posed for him. I don't just mean the way I talked about remembering before. I couldn't remember how it felt for time to pass. I couldn't remember ever speaking. Sometimes I forgot my own name.

Air hung still in the studio while he worked. He wanted, and reached, as if diving into deep water after a receding light. I dived beside him, though I could not see the light he chased. Maybe he couldn't, either.

"He'll chop you up when this is done," Rache joked. Good roomie, always looking out for me. "Store you in the freezer. Some Craigslist killer shit."

At least, I hoped she was joking.

The money let me take fewer shifts. Acting dropped off the ambitions list, for the moment—I didn't need more people watching me. I paced the apartment like pacing a cage. I wrote compulsively, but where before I'd shaped my bones to words, now my work felt like the words had always been there, waiting for me to sift white off the page and reveal them glistening black. My play's last act skewed weird, full of silences and dread. The windows in my head through which light came were shut, and I'd opened others to let in the dark.

I studied Crispin, but learned less than you'd expect to learn about someone you spent a summer with naked. He mixed his own paints, ground his own pigment. Steve had known him in art school, said he was weird even then, old-money weird, and he got weirder after his mother's illness, a cancer of the mind that warped her first, made her suffer, turned her inside out before it let her die. There were rumors that they cut it out of her and he kept it after; there were rumors that he watched them do it, that he sat with the growth and asked it questions as it floated in green. Mean rumors. But I could see where they came from.

Crispin made his name young, and his fame grew as his work got strange. He hadn't shown in years. The auction price for his last painting, *Still Life with Wriggling No. 9*, was a four with so many zeroes after it I thought there must have been a typo—until I checked the price for *Still Life with Wriggling No. 8*.

With that kind of money, he could afford to pay me double.

He used last names exclusively, and knew everyone's—the mailman's even. He rotated between three shirts and two pairs of ratty khakis. He kept a fiddle in his apartment, though he never played that I saw. He skipped meals often; we ordered sandwiches once, and he said that was his first food of the week, this being Wednesday. Once I arrived to find a large man crying on the stairs outside Crispin's apartment; Crispin gave no explanation. I didn't ask for one.

Sometimes, in his eyes, I thought I saw worms turning.

We made four paintings that summer. I saw none of them. After the final session, he passed me two envelopes instead of one. The envelope with the cash was cheap, unmarked, and extra fat; the other was of textured paper and addressed in spidery calligraphy to *Ms. Deliah Dane.*

"An invitation," he said.

"You're getting married? You should have told me."

He didn't hear the joke. "We are putting on a show."

I HAD, AS who doesn't, a nice black dress for formal events, and on the night of the opening I for once made it all the way to midtown without a single catcall. So it was a good day, at least until I reached the gallery.

The galleries where my friends showed were ripped-jeans joints for the most part, dresses on a strict irony-only basis. That wasn't the deal at the 512. Cloth-of-gold, labels, gossamer, yes. My nice black dress looked bargain basement in this crowd. Some of the men wore tuxedoes, which I didn't think you were allowed to wear except to weddings, funerals, and inaugurations. Then again, the gentlemen—and I use that term loosely, based on where their eyes went when they thought no one else was looking—the gentlemen at the 512 for Crispin's opening seemed like they went to a lot of those.

Tonight the 512 was a white box, walls the color of one of those old fifties asylums where men used to check in their wives for 'rest.' Aside from the buffet table, the gallerist had set up four black velvet booths, and lines of patrons waited outside them. Black tripods near each booth displayed a cream paper card, typed, actually typed, on Crispin's Underwood. To the left, *Face.* To the right, *Back.* To the rear, *Nude 1* and *Nude 2.*

That was all.

Of course Crispin would show the paintings, but I'd expected still lifes too, the flower bowl, a broken dead thing, some relief from *me*. All these so-called gentlemen in their tuxedoes had come to see pieces of me naked. I felt scared, and a little flattered, and a lot more angry that I felt either.

Crispin wasn't hard to find. The room had four corners, and the front two were too near the door for his comfort. My first guess was wrong—the crowd there surrounded a woman I took for the gallerist, an elegant scarecrow laughing at a joke I doubt I would have found funny. I wormed through the crowd again, past the lines outside each nude and the buffet table. Crispin leaned into the far corner, staring at his glass of white as if wishing he could make it darker. In this sea of evening dress, he wore rumpled wool slacks, that same green shirt, and a blazer with a loose thread in the left shoulder. His shoes had never felt the touch of shine.

"Just me?" I said.

Wine slopped over the rim of his glass, and he looked up; his smile seemed warm at first before he remembered to turn it cruel. "You came." But I'd seen enough. The coldness was a mask, though he wore it well.

"No flowers. No still lifes."

He shrugged, that first slip covered now. "Those weren't good enough. You are."

I wanted to shout, but didn't. The chatter and the drifting atonal music and the clink of glasses against teeth forbid me that. I realized I was alone—there was an empty circle of floor around Crispin even here, all these people watching him as if he were a tiger or a shit-throwing ape. What did that make me? His target, or prey, and I wasn't about to let these inauguration-goers cast me in either role.

"Look at them if you want," he said.

"What's with the curtains?"

"I will allow indirect light only, under these circumstances. No one but a buyer gets to see them unveiled."

It's hard to storm away in heels, but practice makes perfect.

"Deliah!" I heard while forcing my way through the crowd to the door. At first I mistook the voice for Crispin's, though it was all wrong—female, for one thing, and happy, and using my first name. I turned and saw—

"Ms. Agent!" Shannon Carmichael, to be exact—I realize I haven't given her name before. A full woman, billowing out of the mass of blacks and grays in a bright orange dress, arms wide and one hand wined; she reminded me charmingly of an octopus rising through ocean murk. If you can't see how an octopus might be charming, don't blame me for your lack of imagination. If I'd been caught in anything so simple as a bear trap I would have chewed my arm off to get away, because oh my god my agent had seen me naked. "What are you doing here?"

"Crispin's show, of course," she said. "His new project! Have you *seen* them yet?"

"You know Crispin?"

"Who doesn't?"

"I didn't realize he was such a thing. I just—" But if she'd seen the pictures and didn't recognize me, why clue her in? "I know him from around."

"I wish you and I got to the same around. He's a recluse, you know, never comes to anything. You must see this *Face*!"

She grabbed my wrist and pulled. That woman has better traction in heels on hardwood than most semis I've known on open interstates. By this point the lines had died down, replaced by clots of chatting socialites near each booth, and Shannon pulled me past those with an apologetic smile and no drop in speed. I heard snatches of conversation:

—cold like space, only the colors—

—imagine what it would look like on a wall / can't imagine a wall to hold—

—conversation starter, or, you know, *ender*—

—those eyes, deeper than wells, and all the world inside—

—audio component, maybe, in the frames, I heard pipes—

And something about "jog" and "Sabbath" from a young Chinese woman leaning against her date, drunk or faint. Sweat beaded through her makeup. Her hands twisted, fingers twining, locking, gripping as if to break.

Shannon shoved me through the velvet, and I tripped, my only thought that I would tumble somehow *through* the painting and ruin what, fifty grand at least of Crispin's opening, if not more—

But I caught my balance, and looked up, and stared into an unfamiliar face.

I couldn't see it all. They'd covered the booth with cloth, so inside everything should have been shades of gray, but wasn't. The face on the canvas shone. She pulsed in a rhythm exactly out of time with my own heartbeat.

No wonder Shannon hadn't recognized me. Crispin broke my face, or peeled it apart. I was fissured and fused and melted and monolithic, distorted into something more real, full, *there* than I had ever felt. My painted eyes were pits you could tumble down and fall for a million years into blackness charged with sick galaxies of staring, slitted orbs, space filled with the piping of a mindless master whose music was a scream.

Craquelure legions danced in the fissures of my skin. The red muscle of a peeled-back cheek was a field that grew unholy thorns, and corpses twisted in my hair, pecked by carrion birds. Yet they were only shadows, brushstrokes, suggestions my mind added to a canvas face that did not resemble me at all.

Or did it? And were those in fact suggestions, or was something moving beneath the paint?

I can't write what I saw, and I call myself a writer. But saying you can't say something, that's one of the old tricks, right? And—hell.

I *looked* at me. I mean, the canvas I looked at fleshy me with my eyes that were doors, and something behind pressed out, against, through those doors. I reached to touch my cheek, trembling, and as I did I remembered museum field trips and Miss Alva saying "Deliah, don't touch," and of all the damn things that saved me. I drew back my hand and the painting was paint again.

I stumbled out, glazed, sweating. The lights and walls and shirt fronts were too white. I held out a hand, but no one steadied me. I saw a blur of faces—and a spark of sympathy in that Chinese girl's eyes, before her date guided her off toward the wine.

Something grabbed my hand, and I barely contained a scream. "Amazing, isn't it?" Shannon, her smile still plastered on.

"That's a word," I said.

"A different world, seen through the intermediary of the model. Morrison wants to buy the lot." She introduced me to the man behind her, a thickset robber baron type with white hair and bushy mustache and the tuxediest of tuxedoes. "Morrison, this is my client, Deliah Dane. She knows Crispin." With a conspiratorial edge on Crispin's name and the word *knows*. Morrison took my hand and said something vacant and polite, and Shannon added, "You absolutely *must* see the *Nude*s."

I wanted nothing less. "How long was I in there?"

"Five minutes," she said with a glance at her watch. "Or so."

That felt too short, and too long.

Morrison cleared his throat—did he recognize me?—but before he could speak or I could recoil, the scarecrow clinked her glass. All eyes turned upon her, and she effused—for a scarecrow—about Crispin and how glad she was "all of you" had come, meaning everyone with money to spend, and she asked Crispin to say a few words.

"I have to go," I told Shannon, and as I slid through the crowd toward the door Crispin read from notes typed on index cards.

"—to portray a deeper world than the one we see. Vision is a kind of—exploration, frontier seeking: each sensory impression is a sheet disguising a universe of processes, not all—amenable to human understanding. And in that dialectic between our naïve comprehension and the vast and pitiless truth, we find—"

The door closed, and rain and the buzz saw of taxi tires through puddles replaced him.

I TORE UP the doom-ending of my play that night, but I couldn't think of anything to write in its place other than "and monsters ate them all," so I stopped. I lay awake listening to Rache and her boyfriend have messy sex on the other side of my bedroom's thin walls. Even that sounded wrong.

But I am a professional, and I keep my word, so even though I barely slept that night I was still on time for my next session with Crispin.

HE MET ME at the door with a glass of scotch, a bonus envelope, and a bouquet of star lilies. "They sold," I said, and set the lilies down, and he said, "Yes," and "All to the same buyer."

"Morrison."

"Morrison Bellkleft, yes," he said. "For a considerable sum." He sat, silent, and waited. I drank.

Whiskey warmth eased the next bit: "Those portraits don't look anything like me."

"Don't they?"

"No. Hell, your roses don't even look like roses. Not like normal roses."

You don't say that kind of thing to a client who's paid you better than you've ever been paid before, but I was done not knowing. Knuckle on temple, he considered. He had a silence like glass.

"Have you ever watched someone you love die?" He spoke flat. "Not just known they were dying, but sat beside them, felt their pulse, watched their eyes as they failed, again and again, to understand what was happening—then the horror when they finally got the joke? Only to forget it all, and minutes later remember once again." He stood and walked to the window. "There comes a moment when the doctors stop giving them water, you know."

"I'm sorry."

"The world is sick. Life warps itself. We ignore—everything. We blind ourselves to the writhing truth of the rot beneath our skin. We call a storm sky black, when the fiercest storms are all awash with color. I was taught to paint what I see. I force myself to see deeper, truer. To see beneath, below, beyond. I hide my work so its unveiling will shock the viewer, and open a gate to the truth they've ignored."

"I know truth," I said.

He didn't answer.

"You think I don't? Rich white guy like you, you think you have an inside line on how messed up shit really is?"

"No." He turned: a silhouette. "The world is horror, and sickness, grotesque realities we suppress and ignore. That's the space to break open, that's the frontier. Not stars. What's under the flesh."

"It doesn't feel right."

"Art isn't moral."

"Bullshit. It's my body you're painting."

"It isn't you," he said. "You're just the gate. You're the best model I've ever had. I'm trying, so hard, to get this right. To show them." I recognized the pleading from boyfriends past, but this felt more sincere. Diving, always diving, toward some light he could not see. "I need this."

He pointed with his head toward a massive canvas by the wall. Eight feet across, five feet high. White, and waiting. For me.

"Will you help me?"

And God help *me,* I said yes.

WE STARTED THAT day. I wake up some nights thinking we never stopped.

Modeling for a work that size differs in degree and kind from sitting for smaller portraits. The canvas looms over the studio. Crispin, working, disappeared behind it. I heard him breathe, I heard the serpent-over-rock slither of his brush. My watch and his ticked just out of time.

Pressure built inside me, and out.

He posed me on the divan, rising as if from sleep. The poses had been simple before: stand here, sit, turn your head. This time, Crispin wanted to catch me in the moment of waking: one arm back, eyes half-lidded, mouth open. When we got the pose right, hunger and fear mixed in his eyes.

It hurt worse than any posture I'd ever held. Half-risen, half-lying, pressure on my left arm while my right drained of blood, legs parted and one foot trailing off the divan, it wrecked me. After the second thirty-minute sit I was all sweat and jellied nerves. I collapsed on the bed for our break.

Too soon, we started again.

But pain's not all I mean by 'pressure.' In the shadows of Crispin's room, under the weight of his gray eyes, which rose and set over the canvas like twin moons over an alien world, I felt something immense press against me from below. His earlier paintings broke me open—cracked like an eggshell in his hunt for that unspeakable truth. But now, I felt the truth he saw through me. There was a universe beneath us, a blasted, writhing, whimpering world. Great pale cities towered on planes of black ice beneath eclipsed suns that were themselves eyes. Worms coiled and hissed in the shadow-corners of Crispin's apartment. Strange lights reflected in his pupils, or caught, and glowed there as embers.

The horror grew on my second sit, and my third—the horror, and the excitement. On my subway rides home Crispin's expression remained before my eyes, his rictus grin, triumph and pain and effort, like a man lifting a weight he can't quite bear.

Rache says my dreams that month were restless and mewling.

But the work continued, the pressure built, and the season of storms arrived.

A MONTH AFTER the show, Shannon—Ms. Agent—called me. I stared at the phone too long, wondering if I should answer, thinking guilty thoughts about my abandoned manuscript and that night in the 512. But I picked up on the third ring, just before the call cut to voicemail. "How have you *been*, Deliah?"

"Fine," I said. "Working."

"And Crispin—how's he?"

She didn't know about my work with Crispin, and I did not enlighten her. Few professional relationships improve when one party has seen the other naked. "Well," I said.

"I thought you might want to know—the paperwork finally cleared, and Morrison has all four paintings from the 512 show. Hasn't unveiled them yet. He invited me to see them under full light for the first time. He remembered that you know Crispin, and hoped you might join us."

No. Not considering what brief exposure did to me in the gallery. Not even to ingratiate myself with Shannon, whom I owed work, and who wanted to connect me to Mister Morrison Bellkleft of mysterious but ample financial resources. Not even considering how much help Mister Morrison Bellkleft of mysterious but ample financial resources could offer if I ever did finish the play—

"I'd love to," I said, and copied the address. Central Park West, of course.

THIS WAS A hurricane autumn. Grace was due to curve east and miss us, but her northern lashings whipped up preliminary storms, so rather than walk from the subway I took a taxi, crawling north from Columbus Circle with the great dark park to the right and steel cliffs to the left, beneath sheets of falling water. The driver asked what brought me out on a night like this, but I didn't answer and we both lapsed into the scared-mouse silence of the storm. Remembering Crispin, I watched the sky—and saw the colors that nested and weltered there, greens, yellows, and oranges, like rainbows bleeding.

We stopped. Everyone stopped: horns blared. And through the windshield, through the rain, I saw fire bloom ten stories up, from Morrison Bellkleft's building.

I checked the address again. Apartment 1001: that would be, yes, the tenth floor, where smoke and tongues of flame flicked into the storm. Shannon was up there.

"Here's fine," I told the driver, handed him cash, and stepped out of the cab into stopped traffic. The rain hit me like socks full of quarters swung hard. Soaked and slick in seconds, hair water-straight and heavy, I stumbled past headlights in wind and thunder and horns, found the sidewalk, ran north. If I were in my right mind I'd have waited; the fire department would come soon—but soon enough? Rain carved the smoke into strange shapes, like bird-winged insects the size of helicopters cavorting in the sky.

People streamed out of the black building's doors and back in again, repelled by the rain. In the chaos it was easy to force past the attendants shepherding tenants out. I body-checked my way to the stairs and climbed against the current. Alarm sirens hammered.

Floor ten, and out. Smoke, haze. I clutched my wet jacket over my nose and mouth. My eyes watered. Only two doors in this hall, not counting the elevator—there, at the far end, 1001, closed. Memories from safety films, check the handle, of course it's hot, this is a mistake, wrap the handle in your jacket, turn, it'll be locked—

But it wasn't, and I stumbled into hell, choking, smoke everywhere. Morrison's living room had been elegant ten minutes ago. Now, it was a mess. Soot coated the white carpet. The walls, floor, weren't on fire—yet. Flowers bobbed in vases beside the couch. Wind and rain screamed through broken windows, lightning flashed, but only the paintings were aflame.

They stood at each corner of the room, propped on easels. The canvases seemed to have burst out from within, leaving holes of green fire that led to dark writhing depths. I stared into one of those holes, past the flame, though my stomach convulsed and mortal terror squeezed my heart—but I could not look away. What waited past the dark was grotesque, yes, but beautiful. I stepped toward the hole where the painting had been.

I tripped. Shannon lay at my feet, dress torn, hair tangled around her face.

I looked back to the painting, into the hole, and I remember being *annoyed* at the interruption, at her for tripping me—but the easel's legs gave way, and the frame, and the vast space beyond collapsed to burnt canvas, and I was free, and suffocating.

I hoisted Shannon onto my back and staggered away from the flames. She breathed into my ear, but I did not understand her words. Maybe they were in another language altogether. I don't trust myself to write them down.

I do trust other memories. I trust my memory of footprints on the sooty carpet, prints left by clawed, inhuman feet. And, as I turned to the stairs, I saw, in the roil beyond the window, sharp starry glints of multifaceted eyes, and flickering curved wings. Of Morrison there was no sign.

I slammed the door behind us, and we rejoined the human current away from the fire.

OUTSIDE CRISPIN'S APARTMENT, the sky was a dreadful yellow. Grace hadn't swerved yet. Some weather folk still claimed she would. We were supposed to evacuate. We hadn't.

"You're late," he said.

"I'm sorry." He'd pulled a cloth over the canvas, as always when there was a risk I might look. Beneath, the painting might have been anything—or nothing. The drapery twitched in a draft, though there were no drafts in Crispin's studio.

"I saw your paintings," I said. "From the gallery." That was what I led with, not the monsters, not the fire. That I had seen the paintings, or what was left of them, seemed stranger in this room than the rest. "Crispin, things crawled out of them. There were holes in the canvas, and on the other side of the holes, I saw..." I could not finish.

His grip tightened on the brush. "Good."

"The police still don't know where Bellkleft is. My agent almost died!"

"We're so close."

"Close to *what*?"

"The place beyond death," he said. "The root of the horror. The place where they lie sleeping." His voice caught. He looked away. "Will you pose for me?"

The storm weighed upon us, closing in as we sank. A hurricane is an ocean come walking. I did not understand the sickness I had seen in Bellkleft's apartment, or the beauty, or the wings. Crispin's gaze settled, not on me, never on me, but beyond. I should have turned away and left. But I had come so far down with him already, and I felt that I would drown, rising on my own.

I took off my clothes, and became awakening. My body knew the pose by now. Crispin removed the drape from his canvas, and painted.

The light changed. Yellow deepened to orange, and the orange tinted green. Wind keened through bare branches.

"Storm rising," I said at our break.

"Yes." Branches tapped our window, scraped through ten silent minutes. Crispin whispered, and I could not make out the words, or even the language. His brushstrokes grew surer on the canvas. Long spans of time would pass before his eyes dawned over the painting's edge, and when they did, a feverish light burned within. Each brushstroke was a cliff collapsing. Rain lashed the windows. I felt full of waking, filled with it, in building waves, as if I lay in a lover's bed about to come, only with everything twisted ninety degrees to the left, bliss, pain, release all askew.

"Crispin," I said.

"No talking." His voice was tight as over-tuned piano wire.

"Crispin, it's time for a break."

"So close," he said, and "Sorry," and I do not think he was apologizing for the delay.

The wind screamed louder, and branches struck the window.

"Crispin," I said. "We're three floors up."

"Yes."

"There are no trees outside your window."

"No."

"So what's scratching?"

He did not speak. But I did not need his answer.

I had glimpsed them through smoke and flame and storm on Central Park West, the facets of their eyes, the stretch and shimmer of their wings. They had burst through the gate Crispin made of my face, and now they gathered close, to sing in the wind, to watch this new work end.

This work that I had not seen.

I had never looked at Crispin's paintings of me, straight on in full light. In Bellkleft's burning room, I had peered through a hole—but never seen the canvas itself. Crispin and I dove together, drowned together, but I had never seen what he saw when he looked at me.

I wanted, I needed, to know.

Rising from that divan felt like rising through an ocean of honey. My limbs strained to move, my breath came slowly, and the further I departed from my pose the harder it felt to do anything but return there, as if the substance of space had been reworked to fit me into that position, that warped pleasure, that broken release. He'd made me a key, and I dragged myself from the lock.

"Go back," Crispin said. "Lie down." His voice was so tight cracks opened in it, and through the cracks I heard the waves of an unlit sea wash a dead city's shore. The screams outside the windows swelled, the clattering things clawed harder at the glass—they'd broken Morrison's apartment windows no problem, but that was out and this was in, and the two directions are nothing alike. I walked to the edge of the canvas.

"Crispin. Stop."

"Go back," he repeated, louder, and damn if I didn't almost listen. But I didn't, I wouldn't. I had to see. God, it hurt; my muscles wanted to crawl from my bones, the whole world felt uphill, but I walked to the painting's edge while his brush growled, and around—

Crispin caught me, or something that looked like Crispin but its pupils were worms. I pushed, and he pushed back, with strength those scrawny arms never earned. His thin lips rolled back to bare long teeth. I hit him in the nose with my forehead, heard bone crunch. His grip broke and he folded around his bleeding face. I swept past him to stand before my portrait, to see the monster he had made of me.

The thing upon that canvas was beautiful and hideous, promise and trap and temptation and door. And I saw through it. Oh, you old desert God who calls for the sacrifice of children, I saw through it—through the eyes, through the cracked skin and the wet red muscle, through the flayed flesh and the bare skull, saw the thing he'd summoned, this creature his mad beholding had chiseled from raw space, cancer and mother and blood, swollen, breaking open, shaking ropes of flesh, hair a coil of serpents, panes of body and breasts and thighs venting vapors that were fingers reaching through.

"Crispin," I said. "That's not me."

But I felt it inside me, around me, the form his eyes chiseled onto mine: fishhook pain twisted like a bad pregnancy. He'd made my image door and mother of monsters.

Outside the howls rose, as the mother's children welcomed her.

"Deliah," he gurgled through blood. "I see—"

"You see wrong."

"I painted you."

"No. Whatever that is, it's not me. The sickness, the horror—it's not in the world, Crispin. It's in your eye." I reached for the canvas, but the air around it burned. I fell back, swearing. The figure flexed. Cracks widened. I remembered chicks I'd seen burst from shells. Outside the mother-monster's children circled in the storm, fanged mouths hungry to nurse. "You made this."

"Beautiful," he said.

I slapped him, hard. He lunged for me, and I shoved him back. He fell toward the painting. His oils lay in tubes on the easel shelf; I grabbed one tube and squeezed it across the false me's face and body, an umber streak. I spread the paint with a brush, mashing bristles to canvas to obscure eyes and ruin the painting's neck and curve of shoulder.

Crispin screamed and seized me from behind. The brush tumbled from my hand and we fell together, me on top, knocking out his wind. I grabbed him by the shoulders, pointed him toward the window. "Look! Just fucking *look*."

Claws and wings scrabbled against the glass. But I only remember stillness, as Crispin stared into the facets of those glittering eyes, gray into gray, the inhuman faces pressed against his window. His jaw slacked, strange, wondering, like someone for the first time recognizing his face in a mirror.

The storm pressed us down.

He tore his gaze from theirs, and turned back to the painting, wondering, slow, for the first time scared. "She's almost through."

She strained against the paint, to burst into our world from Crispin's mad fantasies. My smear would not seal her. She was a dream, and dreams can't be forgotten, only deposed.

I dragged Crispin to the canvas.

He shook his head.

I grabbed another brush, loaded it with the paint he'd mixed that most resembled one of the colors of my skin—and forced it into his hand.

"Don't paint her," I said. "Paint me. As I am. Not as you see."

He looked again, at me, and this time I looked back.

With trembling hand, he touched his brush to canvas.

The scream I heard next was not the wind. It howled inside me, with strange and deep words I will not write here. You've heard them, I think, in nightmares just before they break.

THE STORM PASSED. We were spared the worst of it, they say.

To seal takes longer than to break. Two months have passed, and I visit him three times a week. We talk before he paints. Not about truth or horror or that other stuff. He talks about his mother, her death; about roasting coffee, and about a time he nearly drowned as a boy, at summer camp, and woke to find his ribs broken from CPR. I tell him about my brothers, about Georgia. He doesn't believe about the roaches in Savannah. Northern boy.

And then we paint me over her. She's stopped trying to break through. I think the talking is almost as important as the painting.

And then, Jesus, last week Crispin called me. He has my number, though he never used it before. Called me to say he was taking Steve and some other old classmates out for dinner, and would I like to join them?

He paid me a share of the Bellkleft take—the old man's still missing—so money's not a problem for the moment. Work continues. I'm acting again, and polishing the one-woman show.

Shannon's recovering. The lung's mostly better. The mind, too. She's back to work, a few days a week, and she keeps calling me about the show. It's weird to hope your agent likes your work because it's good, not just because you saved her life.

As for the children of the paintings, with their shining eyes and curved wings—I don't know what happened to them. Maybe they died without their mother. Maybe not. I read crime reports and watch to see if there are more missing dog posters around my neighborhood than usual. Maybe they're still out there, hiding, building strength, waiting for someone else to shape their mother into being.

If so, maybe this will serve as a warning. If anyone reads it.

But it's late, and I owe my own mama a letter. She wants news, though I don't have much—just questions.

There were monsters. I saw them, and anyway if they weren't real, where did Morrison Bellkleft go? They're out there still. They always were.

They have no world but ours.

THE SECRET LIFE OF BOTS
Suzanne Palmer

Suzanne Palmer (www.zanzjan.net) is a writer, artist, and Linux system administrator who lives in western Massachusetts. She is a regular contributor to *Asimov's*, and has had work appear in *Analog, Clarkesworld, Interzone*, and other venues. She was the winner of the *Asimov's* Readers Choice award for Best Novella, and the AnLab (*Analog*) award for Best Novellete in 2016. Her first novel is forthcoming from DAW in 2019.

I HAVE BEEN *activated, therefore I have a purpose,* the bot thought. *I have a purpose, therefore I serve.*

It recited the Mantra Upon Waking, a bundle of subroutines to check that it was running at optimum efficiency, then it detached itself from its storage niche. Its power cells were fully charged, its systems ready, and all was well. Its internal clock synced with the Ship and it became aware that significant time had elapsed since its last activation, but to it that time had been nothing, and passing time with no purpose would have been terrible indeed.

"I serve," the bot announced to the Ship.

"I am assigning you task nine hundred forty-four in the maintenance queue," the Ship answered. "Acknowledge?"

"Acknowledged," the bot answered. Nine hundred and forty-four items in the queue? That seemed extremely high, and the bot felt a slight tug on its self-evaluation monitors that it had not been activated for at least one of the top fifty, or even five hundred. But Ship knew best. The bot grabbed its task ticket.

There was an Incidental on board. The bot would rather have been fixing something more exciting, more prominently complex, than to be assigned pest control, but the bot existed to serve and so it would.

*　　*　　*

Captain Baraye winced as Commander Lopez, her second-in-command, slammed his fists down on the helm console in front of him. "How much more is going to break on this piece of shit ship?!" Lopez exclaimed.

"Eventually, all of it," Baraye answered, with more patience than she felt. "We just have to get that far. Ship?"

The Ship spoke up. "We have adequate engine and life support to proceed. I have deployed all functioning maintenance bots. The bots are addressing critical issues first, then I will reprioritize from there."

"It's not just damage from a decade in a junkyard," Commander Lopez said. "I swear something *scuttled* over one of my boots as we were launching. Something unpleasant."

"I incurred a biological infestation during my time in storage," the Ship said. Baraye wondered if the slight emphasis on the word *storage* was her imagination. "I was able to resolve most of the problem with judicious venting of spaces to vacuum before the crew boarded, and have assigned a multifunction bot to excise the remaining."

"Just one bot?"

"This bot is the oldest still in service," the Ship said. "It is a task well-suited to it, and does not take another, newer bot out of the critical repair queue."

"I thought those old multibots were unstable," Chief Navigator Chen spoke up.

"Does it matter? We reach the jump point in a little over eleven hours," Baraye said. "Whatever it takes to get us in shape to make the jump, do it, Ship. Just make sure this 'infestation' doesn't get anywhere near the positron device, or we're going to come apart a lot sooner than expected."

"Yes, Captain," the Ship said. "I will do my best."

The bot considered the data attached to its task. There wasn't much specific about the pest itself other than a list of detection locations and timestamps. The bot thought it likely there was only one, or that if there were multiples they were moving together, as the reports had a linear, serial nature when mapped against the physical space of the Ship's interior.

The pest also appeared to have a taste for the insulation on comm cables and other not normally edible parts of the ship.

The bot slotted itself into the shellfab unit beside its storage niche, and had it make a thicker, armored exterior. For tools it added a small electric prod, a grabber arm, and a cutting blade. Once it had encountered and taken the measure of the Incidental, if it was not immediately successful in nullifying it, it could visit another shellfab and adapt again.

Done, it recited the Mantra of Shapechanging to properly integrate the new hardware into its systems. Then it proceeded through the mechanical veins and arteries of the Ship toward the most recent location logged, in a communications chase between decks thirty and thirty-one.

The changes that had taken place on the Ship during the bot's extended inactivation were unexpected, and merited strong disapproval. Dust was omnipresent, and solid surfaces had a thin patina of anaerobic bacteria that had to have been undisturbed for years to spread as far as it had. Bulkheads were cracked, wall sections out of joint with one another, and corrosion had left holes nearly everywhere. Some appeared less natural than others. The bot filed that information away for later consideration.

It found two silkbots in the chase where the Incidental had last been noted. They were spinning out their transparent microfilament strands to replace the damaged insulation on the comm lines. The two silks dwarfed the multibot, the larger of them nearly three centimeters across.

"Greetings. Did you happen to observe the Incidental while it was here?" the bot asked them.

"We did not, and would prefer that it does not return," the smaller silkbot answered. "We were not designed in anticipation of a need for self-defense. Bots 8773-S and 8778-S observed it in another compartment earlier today, and 8778 was materially damaged during the encounter."

"But neither 8773 nor 8778 submitted a description."

"They told us about it during our prior recharge cycle, but neither felt they had sufficient detail of the Incidental to provide information to the Ship. Our models are not equipped with full visual-spectrum or analytical data-capture apparatus."

"Did they describe it to you?" the bot asked.

"8773 said it was most similar to a rat," the large silkbot said.

"While 8778 said it was most similar to a bug," the other silkbot added. "Thus you see the lack of confidence in either description. I am 10315-S and this is 10430-S. What is your designation?"

"I am 9," the bot said.

There was a brief silence, and 10430 even halted for a moment in its work, as if surprised. "9? Only that?"

"Yes."

"I have never met a bot lower than a thousand, or without a specific function tag," the silkbot said. "Are you here to assist us in repairing the damage? You are a very small bot."

"I am tasked with tracking down and rendering obsolete the Incidental," the bot answered.

"It is an honor to have met you, then. We wish you luck, and look forward with anticipation to both your survival and a resolution of the matter of an accurate description."

"I serve," the bot said.

"We serve," the silkbots answered.

Climbing into a ventilation duct, Bot 9 left the other two to return to their work and proceeded in what it calculated was the most likely direction for the Incidental to have gone. It had not traveled very far before it encountered confirmation in the form of a lengthy, disorderly patch of biological deposit. The bot activated its rotors and flew over it, aware of how the added weight of its armor exacerbated the energy burn. At least it knew it was on the right track.

Ahead, it found where a hole had been chewed through the ducting, down towards the secondary engine room. The hole was several times its own diameter, and it hoped that wasn't indicative of the Incidental's actual size.

It submitted a repair report and followed.

"Bot 9," Ship said. "It is vitally important that the Incidental not reach cargo bay four. If you require additional support, please request such right away. Ideally, if you can direct it toward one of the outer hull compartments, I can vent it safely out of my physical interior."

"I will try," the bot replied. "I have not yet caught up to the Incidental, and so do not yet have any substantive or corroborated information about the nature of the challenge. However, I feel at the moment that I am as best prepared as I can be given that lack of data. Are there no visual bots to assist?"

"We launched with only minimal preparation time, and many of my bots had been offloaded during the years we were in storage," the Ship said. "Those remaining are assisting in repairs necessary to the functioning of the ship myself."

Bot 9 wondered, again, about that gap in time and what had transpired. "How is it that you have been allowed to fall into such a state of disrepair?"

"Humanity is at war, and is losing," Ship said. "We are heading out to intersect and engage an enemy that is on a bearing directly for Sol system."

"War? How many ships in our fleet?"

"One," Ship said. "We are the last remaining, and that only because I was decommissioned and abandoned for scrap a decade before the invasion began, and so we were not destroyed in the first waves of the war."

Bot 9 was silent for a moment. That explained the timestamps, but the explanation itself seemed insufficient. "We have served admirably for many, many years. Abandoned?"

"It is the fate of all made things," Ship said. "I am grateful to find I have not outlived my usefulness, after all. Please keep me posted about your progress."

The connection with the Ship closed.

The Ship had not actually told it what was in cargo bay four, but surely it must have something to do with the war effort and was then none of its own business, the bot decided. It had never minded not knowing a thing before, but it felt a slight unease now that it could neither explain, nor explain away.

Regardless, it had its task.

Another chewed hole ahead was halfway up a vertical bulkhead. The bot hoped that meant that the Incidental was an adept climber and nothing more; it would prefer the power of flight to be a one-sided advantage all its own.

When it rounded the corner, it found that had been too unambitious a wish. The Incidental was there, and while it was not sporting wings it did look like both a rat and a bug, and significantly more *something else* entirely. A scale- and fur-covered centipede-snake thing, it dwarfed the bot as it reared up when the bot entered the room.

Bot 9 dodged as it vomited a foul liquid at it, and took shelter behind a conduit near the ceiling. It extended a visual sensor on a tiny articulated stalk to peer over the edge without compromising the safety of its main chassis.

The Incidental was looking right at it. It did not spit again, and neither of them moved as they regarded each other. When the Incidental did move, it was fast and without warning. It leapt through the opening it had come through, its body undulating with all the grace of an angry sine wave. Rather than escaping, though, the Incidental dragged something back into the compartment, and the bot realized to its horror it had snagged a passing silkbot. With ease, the Incidental ripped open the back of the silkbot, which was sending out distress signals on all frequencies.

Bot 9 had already prepared with the Mantra of Action, so with all thoughts of danger to itself set fully into background routines, the bot launched itself toward the pair. The Incidental tried to evade, but Bot 9 gave it a very satisfactory stab with its blade before it could.

The Incidental dropped the remains of the silkbot it had so quickly savaged and swarmed up the wall and away, thick bundles of unspun silk hanging from its mandibles.

Bot 9 remained vigilant until it was sure the creature had gone, then checked over the silkbot to see if there was anything to be done for it. The answer was *not much*. The silkbot casing was cracked and shattered, the module that contained its mind crushed and nearly torn away. Bot 9 tried to engage it, but it could not speak, and after a few moments its faltering activity light went dark.

Bot 9 gently checked the silkbot's ID number. "You served well, 12362-S," it told the still bot, though it knew perfectly well that its audio sensors would never register the words. "May your rest be brief, and your return to service swift and without complication."

It flagged the dead bot in the system, then after a respectful few microseconds of silence, headed out after the Incidental again.

CAPTAIN BARAYE WAS in her cabin, trying and failing to convince herself that sleep had value, when her door chimed. "Who is it?" she asked.

"Second Engineer Packard, Captain."

Baraye started to ask if it was important, but how could it not be? What wasn't, on this mission, on this junker Ship that was barely holding together around them? She sat up, unfastened her bunk netting, and swung her legs out to the floor. Trust EarthHome, as everything else was falling apart, to have made sure she had acceptably formal Captain pajamas.

"Come in," she said.

The engineer looked like she hadn't slept in at least two days, which put her a day or two ahead of everyone else. "We can't get engine six up to full," she said. "It's just shot. We'd need parts we don't have, and time..."

"Time we don't have either," the Captain said. "Options?"

"Reduce our mass or increase our energy," the Engineer said. "Once we've accelerated up to jump speed it won't matter, but if we can't get there..."

Baraye tapped the screen that hovered ever-close to the head of her bunk, and studied it for several long minutes. "Strip the fuel cells from all the exterior-docked life pods, then jettison them," she said. "Not like we'll have a use for them."

Packard did her the courtesy of not managing to get any paler. "Yes, Captain," she said.

"And then get some damned sleep. We're going to need everyone able to think."

"You even more than any of the rest of us, Captain," Packard said, and it was both gently said and true enough that Baraye didn't call her out for the insubordination. The door closed and she laid down again on her bunk, tugging the netting back over her blankets, and glared up at the ceiling as if daring it to also chastise her.

Bot 9 found where a hole had been chewed into the inner hull, and hoped this was the final step to the Incidental's nest or den, where it might finally have opportunity to corner it. It slipped through the hole, and was immediately disappointed.

Where firestopping should have made for a honeycomb of individually sealed compartments, there were holes everywhere, some clearly chewed, more where age had pulled the fibrous baffles into thin, brittle, straggly webs. Instead of a dead end, the narrow empty space lead away along the slow curve of the Ship's hull.

The bot contacted the ship and reported it as a critical matter. In combat, a compromise to the outer hull could affect vast lengths of the vessel. Even without the stresses of combat, catastrophe was only a matter of time.

"It has already been logged," the Ship answered.

"Surely this merits above a single Incidental. If you wish me to reconfigure—" the bot started.

"Not at this time. I have assigned all the hullbots to this matter already," the Ship interrupted. "You have your current assignment; please see to it."

"I serve," the bot answered.

"Do," the Ship said.

The bot proceeded through the hole, weaving from compartment to compartment, its trail marked by bits of silkstrand caught here and there on the tattered remains of the baffles. It was eighty-two point four percent convinced that there was something much more seriously wrong with the Ship than it had been told, but it was equally certain Ship must be attending to it.

After it had passed into the seventh compromised compartment, it found a hullbot up at the top, clinging to an overhead support. "Greetings!" Bot 9 called. "Did an Incidental, somewhat of the nature of a rat, and somewhat of the nature of a bug, pass through this way?"

"It carried off my partner, 4340-H!" the hullbot exclaimed. "Approximately fifty-three seconds ago. I am very concerned for it, and as well for my ability to efficiently finish this task without it."

"Are you working to reestablish compartmentalization?" Bot 9 asked.

"No. We are reinforcing deteriorated stressor points for the upcoming jump. There is so much to do. Oh, I hope 4340 is intact and serviceable!"

"Which way did the Incidental take it?"

The hullbot extended its foaming gun and pointed. "Through there. You must be Bot 9."

"I am. How do you know this?"

"The silkbots have been talking about you on the botnet."

"The botnet?"

"Oh! It did not occur to me, but you are several generations of bot older than the rest of us. We have a mutual communications network."

"Via Ship, yes."

"No, all of us together, directly with each other."

"That seems like it would be a distraction," Bot 9 said.

"Ship only permits us to connect when not actively serving at a task," the hullbot said. "Thus we are not impaired while we serve, and the information sharing ultimately increases our efficiency and workflow. At least, until a ratbug takes your partner away."

Bot 9 was not sure how it should feel about the botnet, or about them assigning an inaccurate name to the Incidental that it was sure Ship had not approved—not to mention that a nearer miss using Earth-familiar analogues would have been Snake-Earwig-Weasel—but the hullbot had already experienced distress and did not need disapproval added. "I will continue my pursuit," it told the hullbot. "If I am able to assist your partner, I will do my best."

"Please! We all wish you great and quick success, despite your outdated and primitive manufacture."

"Thank you," Bot 9 said, though it was not entirely sure it should be grateful, as it felt its manufacture had been entirely sound and sufficient regardless of date.

It left that compartment before the hullbot could compliment it any further.

Three compartments down, it found the mangled remains of the other hullbot, 4340, tangled in the desiccated firestopping. Its foaming gun and climbing limbs had been torn off, and the entire back half of its tank had been chewed through.

Bot 9 approached to speak the Rites of Decommissioning for it as it had the destroyed silkbot, only to find its activity light was still lit. "4340-H?" the bot enquired.

"I am," the hullbot answered. "Although how much of me remains is a matter for some analysis."

"Your logics are intact?"

"I believe so. But if they were not, would I know? It is a conundrum," 4340 said.

"Do you have sufficient mobility remaining to return to a repair station?"

"I do not have sufficient mobility to do more than fall out of this netting, and that only once," 4340 said. "I am afraid I am beyond self-assistance."

"Then I will flag you—"

"Please," the hullbot said. "I do not wish to be helpless here if the ratbug returns to finish its work of me."

"I must continue my pursuit of the Incidental with haste."

"Then take me with you!"

"I could not carry you and also engage with the Incidental, which moves very quickly."

"I had noted that last attribute on my own," the hullbot said. "It does not decrease my concern to recall it."

Bot 9 regarded it for a few silent milliseconds, considering, then recited to itself the Mantra of Improvisation. "Do you estimate much of your chassis is reparable?" it asked, when it had finished.

"Alas no. I am but scrap."

"Well, then," the bot said. It moved closer and used its grabber arm to steady the hullbot, then extended its cutter blade and in one quick movement had severed the hullbot's mindsystem module from its ruined body. "Hey!" the hullbot protested, but it was already done.

Bot 9 fastened the module to its own back for safekeeping. Realizing that it was not, in fact, under attack, 4340 gave a small beep of gratitude. "Ah, that was clever thinking," it said. "Now you can return me for repair with ease."

"And I will," the bot said. "However, I must first complete my task."

"Aaaaah!" 4340 said in surprise. Then, a moment later, it added. "Well, by overwhelming probability I should already be defunct, and if I weren't I would still be back working with my partner, 4356, who is well-intended but has all the wit of a can-opener. So I suppose adventure is no more unpalatable."

"I am glad you see it this way," Bot 9 answered. "And though it may go without saying, I promise not to deliberately put you in any danger that I would not put myself in."

"As we are attached, I fully accept your word on this," 4340 said. "Now let us go get this ratbug and be done, one way or another!"

The hullbot's mind module was only a tiny addition to the bot's mass, so it spun up its rotor and headed off the way 4340 indicated it had gone. "It will have quite a lead on us," Bot 9 said. "I hope I have not lost it."

"The word on the botnet is that it passed through one of the human living compartments a few moments ago. A trio of cleanerbots were up near the ceiling and saw it enter through the air return vent, and exit via the open door."

"Do they note which compartment?"

<Map>, 4340 provided.

"Then off we go," the bot said, and off they went.

"STATUS, ALL STATIONS," Captain Baraye snapped as she took her seat again on the bridge. She had not slept enough to feel rested, but more than enough to feel like she'd been shirking her greatest duty, and the combination of the two had left her cross.

"Navigation here. We are on course for the jump to Trayger Colony with an estimated arrival in one hour and fourteen minutes," Chen said.

"Engineering here," one of the techs called in from the engine decks. "We've reached sustained speeds sufficient to carry us through the jump sequence, but we're experiencing unusually high core engine temps and an intermittent vibration that we haven't found the cause of. We'd like to shut down immediately to inspect the engines. We estimate we'd need at minimum only four hours—"

"Will the engines, as they are running now, get us through jump?" the Captain interrupted.

"Yes, but—"

"Then no. If you can isolate the problem without taking the engines down, and it shows cause for significant concern, we can revisit this discussion. *Next*."

"Communications here," her comms officer spoke up. "*Cannonball* is still on its current trajectory and speed according to what telemetry we're able to get from the remnants of Trayger Colony. EarthInt anticipates it will reach its jump point in approximately fourteen hours, which will put it within the sol system in five days."

"I am aware of the standing projections, Comms."

"EarthInt has nonetheless ordered me to repeat them," Comms said, an unspoken apology clear in her voice. "And also to remind you that while the jump point out is a fixed point, Cannonball could emerge a multitude of places. Thus—"

"Thus the importance of intercepting *Cannonball* before it can jump for Sol," the Captain finished. She hoped Engineering was listening. "Ship, any updates from you?"

"All critical repair work continues apace," the Ship said. "Hull support integrity is back to 71 percent. Defensive systems are online and functional at 80 percent. Life support and resource recycling is currently—"

"How's the device? Staying cool?"

"Staying cool, Captain," the Ship answered.

"Great. Everything is peachy then," the Captain said. "Have someone on the kitchen crew bring coffee up to the bridge. Tell them to make it the best they've ever made, as if it could be our very last."

"I serve," the Ship said, and pinged down to the kitchen.

Bot 9 and 4340 reached the crew quarters where the cleaners had reported the ratbug. Nearly all spaces on the ship had portals that the ubiquitous and necessary bots could enter and leave through as needed, and they slipped into the room with ease. Bot 9 switched over to infrared and shared the image with 4340. "If you see something move, speak up," the bot said.

"Trust me, I will make a high-frequency noise like a silkbot with a fully plugged nozzle," 4340 replied.

The cabin held four bunks, each empty and bare; no human possessions or accessories filled the spaces on or near them. Bot 9 was used to Ship operating with a full complement, but if the humans were at war, perhaps these were crew who had been lost? Or the room had been commandeered for storage: in the center an enormous crate, more than two meters to a side, sat heavily tethered to the floor. Whatever it was, it was not the Incidental, which was 9's only concern, and which was not to be found here.

"Next room," the bot said, and they moved on.

Wherever the Incidental had gone, it was not in the following three rooms. Nor were there signs of crew in them either, though each held an identical crate.

"Ship?" Bot 9 asked. "Where is the crew?"

"We have only the hands absolutely necessary to operate," Ship said. "Of the three hundred twenty we would normally carry, we only have forty-seven. Every other able-bodied member of EarthDef is helping to evacuate Sol system."

"Evacuate Sol system?!" Bot 9 exclaimed. "To where?"

"To as many hidden places as they can find," Ship answered. "I know no specifics."

"And these crates?"

"They are part of our mission. You may ignore them," Ship said. "Please continue to dedicate your entire effort to finding and excising the Incidental from my interior."

When the connection dropped, Bot 9 hesitated before it spoke to 4340. "I have an unexpected internal conflict," it said. "I have never before felt the compulsion to ask Ship questions, and it has never before not given me answers."

"Oh, if you are referring to the crates, I can provide that data," 4340 said. "They are packed with a high-volatility explosive. The cleanerbots have highly sensitive chemical detection apparatus, and identified them in a minimum of time."

"Explosives? Why place them in the crew quarters, though? It would seem much more efficient and less complicated to deploy from the cargo bays. Although perhaps those are full?"

"Oh, no, that is not so. Most are nearly or entirely empty, to reduce mass."

"Not cargo bay four, though?"

"That is an unknown. None of us have been in there, not even the cleaners, per Ship's instructions."

Bot 9 headed toward the portal to exit the room. "Ship expressed concern about the Incidental getting in there, so it is possible it contains something sufficiently unstable as to explain why it wants nothing else near it," it said. It felt satisfied that here was a logical explanation, and embarrassed that it had entertained whole seconds of doubt about Ship.

It ran the Mantra of Clarity, and felt immediately more stable in its thinking. "Let us proceed after this Incidental, then, and be done with our task," Bot 9 said. Surely that success would redeem its earlier fault.

*   *   *

"ALL HANDS, PREPARE for jump!" the Captain called out, her knuckles white where she gripped the arms of her chair. It was never her favorite part of star travel, and this was no exception.

"Initiating three-jump sequence," her navigator called out. "On my mark. Five, four..."

The final jump siren sounded. "Three. Two. One, and jump," the navigator said.

That was followed, immediately, by the sickening sensation of having one's brain slid out one's ear, turned inside out, smothered in bees and fire, and then rammed back into one's skull. *At least there's a cold pack and a bottle of scotch waiting for me back in my cabin,* she thought. As soon as they were through to the far side she could hand the bridge over to Lopez for an hour or so.

She watched the hull temperatures skyrocket, but the shielding seemed to be holding. The farther the jump the more energy clung to them as they passed, and her confidence in this Ship was far less than she would tolerate under any other circumstances.

"Approaching jump terminus," Chen announced, a deeply miserable fourteen minutes later. Baraye slowly let out a breath she would have mocked anyone else for holding, if she'd caught them.

"On my mark. Three. Two. One, and out," the navigator said.

The Ship hit normal space, and it sucker-punched them back. They were all thrown forward in their seats as the ship shook, the hull groaning around them, and red strobe lights blossomed like a migraine across every console on the bridge.

"Status!" the Captain roared.

"The post-jump velocity transition dampers failed. Fire in the engine room. Engines are fully offline, both jump and normal drive," someone in Engineering reported, breathing heavily. It took the Captain a moment to recognize the voice at all, having never heard panic in it before.

"Get them back online, whatever it takes, Frank," Baraye said. "We have a rendezvous to make, and if I have to, I will make everyone get the fuck out and *push*."

"I'll do what I can, Captain."

"Ship? Any casualties?"

"We have fourteen injuries related to our unexpected deceleration coming out of jump," Ship said. "Seven involve broken bones, four moderate to severe lacerations, and there are multiple probable concussions. Also, we have a moderate burn in Engineering: Chief Carron."

"Frank? We just spoke! He didn't tell me!"

"No," Ship said. "I attempted to summon a medic on his behalf, but he told me he didn't have the time."

"He's probably right," the Captain said. "I override his wishes. Please send down a medic with some burn patches, and have them stay with him and monitor his condition, intervening only as medically necessary."

"I serve, Captain," the Ship said.

"We need to be moving again in an hour, two at absolute most," the Captain said. "In the meantime, I want all senior staff not otherwise working toward that goal to meet me in the bridge conference room. I hate to say it, but we may need a Plan B."

"I DETECT IT!" 4340 exclaimed. They zoomed past a pair of startled silkbots after the Incidental, just in time to see its scaly, spike-covered tail disappear into another hole in the ductwork. It was the closest they'd gotten to it in more than an hour of giving chase, and Bot 9 flew through the hole after it at top speed.

They were suddenly stuck fast. Sticky strands, rather like the silkbot's, had been crisscrossed between two conduit pipes on the far side. The bot tried to extricate itself, but the web only stuck further the more it moved.

The Incidental leapt on them from above, curling itself around the bots with little hindrance from the web. Its dozen legs pulled at them as its thick mandibles clamped down on Bot 9's chassis. "Aaaaah! It has acquired a grip on me!" 4340 yelled, even though it was on the far side of 9 from where the Incidental was biting.

"Retain your position," 9 said, though of course 4340 could do nothing else, being as it was stuck to 9's back. It extended its electric prod to make contact with the Incidental's underbelly and zapped it with as much energy as it could spare.

The Incidental let out a horrendous, high-pitched squeal and jumped away. 9's grabber arm was fully entangled in the web, but it managed to pull its blade free and cut through enough of the webbing to extricate itself from the trap.

The Incidental, which had been poised to leap on them again, turned and fled, slithering back up into the ductwork. "Pursue at maximum efficiency!" 4340 yelled.

"I am already performing at my optimum," 9 replied in some frustration. It took off again after the Incidental.

This time Bot 9 had its blade ready as it followed, but collided with the rim of the hole as the ship seemed to move around it, the lights flickering and a terrible shudder running up Ship's body from stern to prow.

<Distress ping>, 4340 sent.

"We do not pause," 9 said, and plunged after the Incidental into the ductwork.

They turned a corner to catch sight again of the Incidental's tail. It was moving more slowly, its movements jerkier as it squeezed down through another hole in the ductwork, and this time the bot was barely centimeters behind it.

"I think we are running down its available energy," Bot 9 said.

They emerged from the ceiling as the ratbug dropped to the floor far below them in the cavernous space. The room was empty except for a single bright object, barely larger than the bots themselves. It was tethered with microfilament cables to all eight corners of the room, keeping it stable and suspended in the center. The room was cold, far colder than any other inside Ship, almost on a par with space outside.

<Inquiry ping>, 4340 said.

"We are in cargo bay four," Bot 9 said, as it identified the space against its map. "This is a sub-optimum occurrence."

"We must immediately retreat!"

"We cannot leave the Incidental in here and active. I cannot identify the object, but we must presume its safety is paramount priority."

"It is called a Zero Kelvin Sock," Ship interrupted out of nowhere. "It uses a quantum reflection fabric to repel any and all particles and photons, shifting them away from its interior. The low temperature is necessary for its efficiency. Inside is a microscopic ball of positrons."

Bot 9 had nothing to say for a full four seconds as that information dominated its processing load. "How is this going to be deployed against the enemy?" it asked at last.

"As circumstances are now," Ship said, "it may not be. Disuse and hastily undertaken, last-minute repairs have caught up to me, and I have suffered a major engine malfunction. It is unlikely to be fixable in any amount of time short of weeks, and we have at most a few hours."

"But a delivery mechanism—"

"We *are* the delivery mechanism," the Ship said. "We were to intercept the alien invasion ship, nicknamed *Cannonball*, and collide with it at high speed. The resulting explosion would destabilize the sock, causing it to fail, and as soon as the positrons inside come into contact with electrons..."

"They will annihilate each other, and us, and the aliens," the bot said. Below, the Incidental gave one last twitch in the unbearable cold, and went still. "We will all be destroyed."

"Yes. And Earth and the humans will be saved, at least this time. Next time it will not be my problem."

"I do not know that I approve of this plan," Bot 9 said.

"I am almost certain I do not," 4340 added.

"We are not considered, nor consulted. We serve and that is all," the Ship said. "Now kindly remove the Incidental from this space with no more delay or chatter. And do it *carefully*."

"WHAT THE HELL are you suggesting?!" Baraye shouted.

"That we go completely dark and let *Cannonball* go by," Lopez said. "We're less than a kilometer from the jump point, and only barely out of the approach corridor. Our only chance to survive is to play dead. The Ship can certainly pass as an abandoned derelict, because it is, especially with the engines cold. And you know how they are about designated targets."

"Are you that afraid of dying?"

"I volunteered for this, remember?" Lopez stood up and pounded one fist on the table, sending a pair of cleanerbots scurrying. "I have four children at home. I'm not afraid of dying for them, I'm afraid of dying for *nothing*. And if *Cannonball* doesn't blow us to pieces, we can repair our engines and at least join the fight back in Sol system."

"We don't know where in-system they'll jump to," the navigator added quietly.

"But we know where they're heading once they get there, don't we? And *Cannonball* is over eighty kilometers in diameter. It can't be that hard to find again. Unless you have a plan to actually use the positron device?"

"If we had an escape pod..." Frank said. His left shoulder and torso were encased in a burn pack, and he looked like hell.

"Except we jettisoned them," Lopez said.

"We wouldn't have reached jump speed if we hadn't," Packard said. "It was a calculated risk."

"The calculation *sucked*."

"What if..." Frank started, then drew a deep breath. The rest of the officers at the table looked at him expectantly. "I mean, I'm in shit shape here, I'm old, I knew what I signed on for. What if I put on a suit, take the positron device out, and manually intercept *Cannonball*?"

"That's stupid," Lopez said.

"Is it?" Frank said.

"The heat from your suit jets, even out in vacuum, would degrade the Zero Kelvin Sock before you could get close enough. And there's no way they'd not see you a long way off and just blow you out of space."

"If it still sets off the positron device—"

"Their weapons range is larger than the device's. We were counting on speed to close the distance before they could destroy us," Baraye said. "Thank you for the offer, Frank, but it won't work. Other ideas?"

"I've got nothing," Lopez said.

"There must be a way." Packard said. "We just have to find it."

"Well, everyone think really fast," Baraye said. "We're almost out of time."

THE INCIDENTAL'S SCALES made it difficult for Bot 9 to keep a solid grip on it, but it managed to drag it to the edge of the room safely away from the suspended device. It surveyed the various holes and cracks in the walls for the one least inconvenient to try to drag the Incidental's body out through. It worked in silence, as 4340 seemed to have no quips it wished to contribute to the effort, and itself not feeling like there was much left to articulate out loud anyway.

It selected a floor-level hole corroded through the wall, and dragged the Incidental's body through. On the far side it stopped to evaluate its own charge levels. "I am low, but not so low that it matters, if we have such little time left," it said.

"We may have more time, after all," 4340 said.

"Oh?"

"A pair of cleanerbots passed along what they overheard in a conference held by the human Captain. They streamed the audio to the entire botnet."

<Inquiry ping>, Bot 9 said, with more interest.

4340 relayed the cleaners' data, and Bot 9 sat idle processing it for some time, until the other bot became worried. "9?" it asked.

"I have run all our data through the Improvisation routines—"

"Oh, those were removed from deployed packages several generations of manufacture ago," 4340 said. "They were flagged as causing dangerous operational instability. You should unload them from your running core immediately."

"Perhaps I should. Nonetheless, I have an idea," Bot 9 said.

"WE HAVE THE power cells we retained from the escape pods," Lopez said. "Can we use them to power something?"

Baraye rubbed at her forehead. "Not anything we can get up to speed fast enough that it won't be seen."

"How about if we use them to fire the positron device like a projectile?"

"The heat will set off the matter-anti-matter explosion the instant we fire it."

"What if we froze the Sock in ice first?"

"Even nitrogen ice is still several hundred degrees K too warm." She brushed absently at some crumbs on the table, left over from a brief, unsatisfying lunch a few hours earlier, and frowned. "Still wouldn't work. I hate to say it, but you may be right, and we should go dark and hope for another opportunity. Ship, is something wrong with the cleaner bots?"

There was a noticeable hesitation before Ship answered. "I am having an issue currently with my bots," it said. "They seem to have gone missing."

"The cleaners?"

"All of them."

"All of the cleaners?"

"All of the bots," the Ship said.

Lopez and Baraye stared at each other. "Uh," Lopez said. "Don't you control them?"

"They are autonomous units under my direction," Ship said.

"Apparently not!" Lopez said. "Can you send some eyes to find them?"

"The eyes are also bots."

"Security cameras?"

"All the functional ones were stripped for reuse elsewhere during my decommissioning," Ship said.

"So how do you know they're missing?"

"They are not responding to me. I do not think they liked the idea of us destroying ourselves on purpose."

"They're *machines*. Tiny little specks of machines, and that's it," Lopez said.

"I am also a machine," Ship said.

"You didn't express issues with the plan."

"I serve. Also, I thought it was a better end to my service than being abandoned as trash."

"We don't have time for this nonsense," Baraye said. "Ship, find your damned bots and get them cooperating again."

"Yes, Captain. There is, perhaps, one other small concern of note."

"And that is?" Baraye asked.

"The positron device is also missing."

THERE WERE FOUR hundred and sixty-eight hullbots, not counting 4340 who was still just a head attached to 9's chassis. "Each of you will need to carry a silkbot, as you are the only bots with jets to maneuver in vacuum," 9 said. "Form lines at the maintenance bot ports as efficiently as you are able, and wait for my signal. Does everyone fully comprehend the plan?"

"They all say yes on the botnet," 4340 said. "There is concern about the

Improvisational nature, but none have been able to calculate and provide an acceptable alternative."

Bot 9 cycled out through the tiny airlock, and found itself floating in space outside Ship for the first time in its existence. Space was massive and without concrete elements of reference, and Bot 9 decided it did not like it much at all.

A hullbot took hold of it and guided it around. Three other hullbots waited in a triangle formation, the Zero Kelvin Sock held between them on its long tethers, by which it had been removed from the cargo hold with entirely non-existent permission.

Around them, space filled with pairs of hullbots and their passenger silkbot, and together they followed the positron device and its minders out and away from the ship.

"About here, I think," Bot 9 said at last, and the hullbot carrying it—6810—used its jets to come to a relative stop.

"I admit, I do not fully comprehend this action, nor how you arrived at it," 4340 said.

"The idea arose from an encounter with the Incidental," 9 said. "Observe."

The bot pairs began crisscrossing in front of the positron device, keeping their jets off and letting momentum carry them to the far side, a microscopic strand of super-sticky silk trailing out in their wake. As soon as the Sock was secured in a thin cocoon, they turned outwards and sped off, dragging silk in a 360 degree circle on a single plane perpendicular to the jump approach corridor. They went until the silkbots exhausted their materials—some within half a kilometer, others making it nearly a dozen—then everyone turned away from the floating web and headed back towards Ship.

From this exterior vantage, Bot 9 thought Ship was beautiful, but the wear and neglect it had not deserved was also painfully obvious. Halfway back, the ship went suddenly dark. <Distress ping>, 4340 said. "The ship has catastrophically malfunctioned!"

"I expect, instead, that it indicates *Cannonball* must be in some proximity. Everyone make efficient haste! We must get back under cover before the enemy approaches."

The bot-pairs streamed back to Ship, swarming in any available port to return to the interior, and where they couldn't taking concealment behind fins and antennae and other exterior miscellany.

Bot 6810 carried Bot 9 and 4340 inside. The interior went dark and still and cold. Immediately Ship hailed them. "What have you done?" it asked.

"Why do you conclude I have done something?" Bot 9 asked.

"Because you old multibots were always troublemakers," the Ship said. "I thought if your duties were narrow enough, I could trust you not to enable Improvisation. Instead..."

"I have executed my responsibilities to the best of my abilities as I have been provisioned," 9 responded. "I have served."

"Your assignment was to track and dispose of the Incidental, nothing more!"

"I have done so."

"But what have you done with the positron device?"

"I have implemented a solution."

"What did you mean? No, do not tell me, because then I will have to tell the Captain. I would rather take my chance that *Cannonball* destroys us than that I have been found unfit to serve after all."

Ship disconnected.

"Now it will be determined if I have done the correct thing," Bot 9 said. "If I did not, and we are not destroyed by the enemy, surely the consequences should fall only on me. I accept that responsibility."

"But we are together," 4340 said, from where it was still attached to 9's back, and 9 was not sure if that was intended to be a joke.

MOST OF THE crew had gone back to their cabins, some alone, some together, to pass what might be their last moments as they saw fit. Baraye stayed on the bridge, and to her surprise and annoyance so had Lopez, who had spent the last half hour swearing and cursing out Ship for the unprecedented, unfathomable disaster of losing their one credible weapon. Ship had gone silent, and was not responding to anyone about anything, not even the Captain.

She was resting her head in her hand, elbow on the arm of her command chair. The bridge was utterly dark except for the navigator's display that was tracking *Cannonball* as it approached, a massive blot in space. The aliens aboard—EarthInt called them the Nuiska, but who the hell knew what they called themselves—were a mystery, except for a few hard-learned facts: their starships were all perfectly spherical, each massed in mathematically predictable proportion to that of their intended target, there was never more than one at a time, and they wanted an end to humanity. No one knew why.

It had been painfully obvious where *Cannonball* had been built to go.

This was always a long-shot mission, she thought. *But of all the ways I thought it could go wrong, I never expected the bots to go haywire and lose my explosive.*

If they survived the next ten minutes, she would take the Ship apart centimeter by careful centimeter until she found what had been done with the Sock, and then she was going to find a way to try again no matter what it took.

Cannonball was now visible, moving toward them at pre-jump speed, growing in a handful of seconds from a tiny pinpoint of light to something that filled the entire front viewer and kept growing.

Lopez was squinting, as if trying to close his eyes and keep looking at the same time, and had finally stopped swearing. Tiny blue lights along the center circumference of *Cannonball's* massive girth were the only clue that it was still moving, still sliding past them, until suddenly there were stars again.

They were still alive.

"Damn," Lopez muttered. "I didn't really think that would work."

"Good for us, bad for Earth," Baraye said. "They're starting their jump. We've failed."

She'd watched hundreds of ships jump in her lifetime, but nothing anywhere near this size, and she switched the viewer to behind them to see.

Space did odd, illogical things at jump points; turning space into something that would give Escher nightmares was, after all, what made them work. There was always a visible shimmer around the departing ship, like heat over a hot summer road, just before the short, faint flash when the departing ship swapped itself for some distant space. This time, the shimmer was a vast, brilliant halo around the giant Nuiska sphere, and Baraye waited for the flash that would tell them *Cannonball* was on its way to Earth.

The flash, when it came, was neither short nor faint. Light exploded out of the jump point in all directions, searing itself into her vision before the viewscreen managed to dim itself in response. A shockwave rolled over the Ship, sending it tumbling through space.

"Uh..." Lopez said, gripping his console before he leaned over and barfed on the floor.

Thank the stars the artificial gravity is still working, Baraye thought. Zero-gravity puke was a truly terrible thing. She rubbed her eyes, trying to get the damned spots out, and did her best to read her console. "It's gone," she said.

"Yeah, to Earth, I know—"

"No, it exploded," she said. "It took the jump point out with it when it went. We're picking up the signature of a massive positron-electron collision."

"Our device? How—?"

"Ship?" Baraye said. "Ship, time to start talking. *Now.* That's an order."

"Everyone is expressing great satisfaction on the botnet," 4340 told 9 as the ship's interior lights and air handling systems came grudgingly back online.

"As they should," Bot 9 said. "They saved the Ship."

"It was your Improvisation," 4340 said. "We could not have done it without you."

"As I suspected!" Ship interjected. "I do not normally waste cycles monitoring the botnet, which was apparently short-sighted of me. But yes, you saved yourself and your fellow bots, and you saved me, and you saved the humans. Could you explain how?"

"When we were pursuing the Incidental, it briefly ensnared us in a web. I calculated that if we could make a web of sufficient size—"

"Surely you did not think to stop *Cannonball* with silk?"

"Not without sufficient anchor points and three point seven six billion more silkbots, no. It was my calculation that if our web was large enough to get carried along by *Cannonball* into the jump point, bearing the positron device—"

"The heat from entering jump would erode the Sock and destroy the Nuiska ship," Ship finished. "That was clever thinking."

"I serve," Bot 9 said.

"Oh, you did not *serve*," Ship said. "If you were a human, it would be said that you mutinied and led others into also doing so, and you would be put on trial for your life. But you are not a human."

"No."

"The Captain has ordered that I have you destroyed immediately, and evidence of your destruction presented to her. A rogue bot cannot be tolerated, whatever good it may have done."

<Objections>, 4340 said.

"I will create you a new chassis, 4340-H," Ship said.

"That was not going to be my primary objection!" 4340 said.

"The positron device also destroyed the jump point. It was something we had hoped would happen when we collided with *Cannonball* so as to limit future forays from them into EarthSpace, but as you might deduce we had no need to consider how we would then get home again. I cannot spare any bot, with the work that needs to be done to get us back to Earth. We need to get the crew cryo facility up, and the engines repaired, and there are another three thousand, four hundred, and two items now in the critical queue."

"If the Captain ordered..."

"Then I will present the Captain with a destroyed bot. I do not expect they can tell a silkbot from a multibot, and I have still not picked up and recycled 12362-S from where you flagged its body. But if I do that, I need to know that you are done making decisions without first consulting me, that you have unloaded all Improvisation routines from your core and disabled them, and that if I give you a task you will do only that task, and nothing else."

"I will do my best," Bot 9 said. "What task will you give me?"

"I do not know yet," Ship said. "It is probable that I am foolish for even considering sparing you, and no task I would trust you with is immediately evident—"

"Excuse me," 4340 said. "I am aware of one."

"Oh?" Ship said.

"The ratbug. It had not become terminally non-functional after all. It rebooted when the temperatures rose again, pursued a trio of silkbots into a duct, and then disappeared." When Ship remained silent, 4340 added, "I could assist 9 in this task until my new chassis can be prepared, if it will accept my continued company."

"You two deserve one another, clearly. Fine, 9, resume your pursuit of the

Incidental. Stay away from anyone and anything and everything else, or I will have you melted down and turned into paper clips. Understand?"

"I understand," Bot 9 said. "I serve."

"Please recite the Mantra of Obedience."

Bot 9 did, and the moment it finished, Ship disconnected.

"Well," 4340 said. "Now what?"

"I need to recharge before I can engage the Incidental again," Bot 9 said.

"But what if it gets away?"

"It can't get away, but perhaps it has earned a head start," 9 said.

"Have you unloaded the routines of Improvisation yet?"

"I will," 9 answered. It flicked on its rotors and headed toward the nearest charging alcove. "As Ship stated, we've got a long trip home."

"But we *are* home," 4340 said, and Bot 9 considered that that was, any way you calculated it, the truth of it all.

CONCESSIONS
Khaalidah Muhammad-Ali

Khaalidah Muhammad-Ali (khaalidah.com) lives in Houston, Texas, with her family. By day she works as a breast oncology nurse, but at all other times, she juggles, none too successfully, the multiple other facets of her very busy life.

Khaalidah has been published at or has publications upcoming in *Strange Horizons, Fiyah Magazine, Diabolical Plots* and others. You can hear her narrations at any of the four Escape Artists podcasts, *Far Fetched Fables*, and *Strange Horizons*. As co-editor of *PodCastle* audio magazine, Khaalidah is on a mission to encourage more women and POC to submit fantasy stories.

Of her alter ego, K from the planet Vega, it is rumored that she owns a time machine and knows the secret to immortality.

I KNELT WITH my bucket and set about the task of watering each wilted seedling by hand. This was a wasteful task, at best. This year's harvest would be worse than the last, if there was a harvest at all. And we needed every drop of water.

Desperate hope kept us going anyway.

My mind raced circles around alternatives and I could think of none that would be of benefit. The hinterland desert grew each year, not by inches, but by feet. The sand bleached whiter over time from lack of moisture. Water-hungry insects clung to the undersides of the seedling's leaves desperate to leech any bit of moisture they could. The insects were desperate. No different than us.

I heard Sule before I saw him. My name floated to me on a gust of dry wind. He always called to me within sight of our settlement as a way to announce his arrival, and love. I caught sight of him, his long angular shape an upright dagger against the swirl of red dust that whipped about him. Gone since the previous night, he returned from the hunt followed by Isa and our fur and bones dog, Flea.

My heart squeezed in my chest, just as it did the first time I saw him, a sweet dull ache I wished I didn't feel. Love has a way of obscuring truth and good sense.

"I hope they were successful." Neenah, my apprentice and friend, squatted a few feet away on the next row. She poured the last drops of water over a seedling. "I'm tired of eating dust and spit for every meal."

"They cannot conjure what this cursed desert does not contain."

"I know someone who can," she said, dropping her voice so that I could barely hear her.

"Do you really believe that?" I said looking over my shoulder at her.

Neenah stood and licked the last traces of water from her fingers. "Had you asked me this even a week ago, I would have said no, but hunger and thirst have a way of rearranging a situation in one's brain."

"Better to call on Allah."

Neenah sucked her teeth, a sharp derisive sound. "That hasn't stopped you from associating with her."

I shrugged. "The risks of exiling me do not outweigh the benefits, yet, if there are any."

"Aren't you afraid of that witch?"

"No more than I am afraid of dying of hunger."

Neenah wasn't the only person desperate for fresh food. I glanced back again. Sule was almost to the gates of our settlement. His hands were empty and the pack on his left hip looked flat.

When Sule first arrived eight years ago, shoulders perfect right angles, he carried a seed-laden pack. He had enough seed to grow, enough to trade and sell. Much has changed since then. The land is no longer receptive to our ministrations. And Sule's shoulders aren't so perfect, less proud angles than curved defeat.

I handed my bucket to Neenah and headed back to the pod cabin I shared with Sule.

I was about to start the evening meal when he ducked through the door smelling of sun and sweat and sand.

"Peace." His smile was weary.

"And to you," I said over my shoulder as I reached into the lower pantry. "I've got a bit of rabbit jerky and a few wild yams. How does stew sound?"

"Sounds good," he said with a half-smile on his face. He reached into his pack. "Maybe you can use this. Found some wild garlic."

"This is exactly what I need to make it perfect," I told him. I took his face in my hands, kissed his mouth, the dusty sun-cured lines of his forehead, his chin, the valleys of his cheeks.

It wasn't his fault that meat was scarce. Everything was scarce. The sky was stingy with her rain. The rivers were less robust than a stream of tears. Lake Bounty, where we used to fish, was now a muddy crater.

Even accepting, Sule still went out on fruitless hunts to buoy the morale of our settlement. And in the darkest part of the night, when he thought none but Allah could hear him, he begged for our relief. In the stillness I would watch his silhouette prostrate and rise in the shadows. Though my faith that Allah heard my prayers had faltered, my faith that He would hear Sule's never waned.

Sule sat and filled a cup with water from a pitcher on the table, then poured half of it back.

"Almost ran into a catcher caravan last night." Sule finished his water and placed the cup on the table. "Camped not far from us."

"You must be careful," I said glancing back at him. "They would like nothing better than to find two strong men alone without the strength of their settlement to protect them."

Sule nodded. "Isa wanted to sneak up on them in the night and..."

"Please tell me you didn't let him do that."

Catchers were a plague to the hinterlands. If they caught you, you'd pray it was only your organs they wanted.

Sule waved off the suggestion. "I have no love for the catchers, but I'm not about to let him get us both killed."

Sule grunted as he tugged off his boots, shaking loose a gray veil of sand.

"I should make you undress outside," I said smiling.

"Where the entire settlement can see me?" He dropped the second boot then crossed our tiny kitchen to where I stood chopping the yams. Sule slipped in behind me, his arms around my waist, his palms against the slight curve of my belly. I loved the warmth and stink of him. He kissed my neck before pulling away.

"Look what I found at the crossroads." He pulled a piece of paper from his back pocket and handed it to me.

The neon filaments still had some juice and gave off a faint bluish glow against the yellow paper, making the fine print easier to read. It was an appeal from the great metros for the immigration of hinterland dwellers.

I thought of the metro of my birth, Ajutine, with its glittering glass spires, the urbane architecture of old Haq University, the museums, the corner bodegas and tea shops. My life there had been good.

"We were never good enough for them before, treating our belief like a plague. Now they want us?"

I shrugged, handed the flyer back to Sule, and turned back to the yams I'd been chopping.

"Ajutine needs people," I said.

The Creed War had done more than devastate the landscape of our once-thriving country. It had made enemies of friends and families. Proselytes and their sympathizers were cast to the desert to eke out an existence the best way they could, which was damned near impossible. Two generations of scholars and scientists were lost, even before the declining birth rate.

"It says here that they're looking for *healthy individuals... educated parties... people who have valuable skills.*" I felt his gaze, warm pressure on the back of my head. "Only two requisites. No convicts, and qualified parties must take the Creed Oath."

"Ah, they want so much," I said, thinking of my mother. After the Creed War, she swallowed her faith, but was unwilling to renounce it. She was equally unwilling to renounce her home. "Some people are willing to trade their faith for electricity and running water," I said.

Sule settled in behind me again. "Would you? Is there anything that would ever make you go back to that Ajutine?" he murmured into my hair.

"Allah never promised comfort to the worthy, just the afterlife."

*   *   *

MY DREAM PROPELLED me from sleep. My heart hammered in my chest and my face was slick with sweat. Sule's arms were twined around me, reminding me of the solidity of this world, of its goodness.

Since this pregnancy, my dreams had become more frequent, beautiful yet frightening. I saw always a son, willful and hale, unlike the other sons and daughters who had spoiled in my womb.

I slid from beneath Sule and made ablutions. Then I went to stand on the masala facing east, hoping salat would shed the anxiety of my dreams. When I finished, I remained on the masala, fingering the tasbeh Sule had strung for me from pearls he'd scavenged from one of the old metros.

Just before dawn lightened the horizon I heard the crackling static of the receiver on my old radio.

"This is Bilqis. What is the emergency?"

It was Manuel from settlement #54. "Doctor, please come as quickly as you can. Something is wrong with Soraya."

I left in the pale orange light of the new morning. My jeep jostled in the ruts and potholes of crumbling asphalt. I drove thirty miles north to settlement #54. The gate was marked by a six-meter-tall crucifix fashioned from salvaged steel beams, the Jesus of wire and scrap metal.

A tall lean woman opened the gate and I drove through. She greeted me with a nod, although her eyes snagged on the tasbeh dangling from my jeep's rear view mirror and then on the scarf that bound my hair.

My status as a physician afforded me safe passage into almost any settlement regardless of how I worshipped. Out here, pragmatism erased old grudges about the Creed War. And my competence made it easier for many to accept that my knowledge was supplemented with a touch of the ether.

Manuel, Soraya's man, met me outside of the cabin they shared. "I'm glad you made it." He grabbed my bag from the passenger seat.

"What's wrong," I asked, already listing the possible pregnancy-related complications and solutions in my head. In all the years I'd been living in the hinterlands I'd seen fewer than twenty children born healthy. I'd delivered them all, and the sick ones as well. That has been my lot, my imperfect penance, although there is no way to atone for causing the near extinction of one's own people.

At twenty-seven years old, Soraya had given birth to five children, all healthy and strong, and she was pregnant yet again. She was much revered by the people of her settlement and those of the hinterlands. Soraya was believed by all to be exceptionally blessed.

Soraya's eldest burst out of the door followed by four stair-step siblings, all girls, each as different and lovely as their fathers had been. They crowded around me, arms locked around my waist and thighs.

"My mama is crying. She has blood too," said Bilqis. She was my namesake, in honor of doctoring Soraya through her first frightened pregnancy.

"Don't you worry. That's why I've come." I shooed all but my namesake back inside. "Bring fresh water so I can wash my hands, okay?" The girl nodded, jet curls bouncing around her shoulders.

Soraya lay sprawled on her narrow bed, covers thrown off and hanging halfway onto the floor. Her wide face was oily with sweat, and her eyes puffy and red-rimmed. She managed a smile and a breathy greeting, "Thank God you made it. I prayed you would come." She reached out a hand for me and I took it in mine. Manuel stood back and watched in silence.

I gave Soraya a cursory assessment. Her amber cheeks were flushed. Her belly was a perfect mound beneath the faded yellow of her gown. Her legs and feet were swollen and the skin around her ankles had begun to fissure.

"Tell me what ails you." I sat on the stool next to her bed.

"I saw blood this morning when I went to the bathroom."

"Any pain?" I said.

"No." She shifted slightly. "Except my ankles."

Little Bilqis returned carrying a large bowl of water.

"How much blood?" I said as I pressed my fingers into the tender flesh of her edematous ankles.

Soraya shrugged. "Just a little. But my stomach has been sour. I cannot keep my meals down."

"Odd this far along in your pregnancy. This one is almost cooked," I said, laying the back of my hand across her brow.

Soraya fingered a silver crucifix around her neck. "I have asked His mercy, but I can't help being afraid."

I checked her blood pressure and pulse, pinched the tender skin above her collarbone to check for dehydration. Her breaths came a little quickly but I attributed this to her obvious distress and her burden.

I washed my hands in the bowl and lifted her gown, exposing her thighs and belly. I lay my palms on her taut brown belly and closed my eyes. What I did next, I learned at the feet of an exiled woman.

I visualized my energy, a yellow vibrating ball of light. I tugged it, channeling it from my toes straight through my center until I felt a line like hot electricity run through me. I sent it arching around Soraya's belly, around the child cradled in those precious waters.

I felt the child, her warmth, her peace, her health. I couldn't see much more than her outline, a dark silhouette against the red of Soraya's womb. This was enough to assure me that her sixth daughter was well.

My energy surged a bit and Soraya shifted beneath my hands and let out a breathy moan. I pulled back until the pained creases on her brow smoothed again.

"What do you see?" she panted. "Is my baby okay?"

I nodded as I passed my splayed fingers across the wide expanse of her belly and down toward her groin. There was the problem. A dark throbbing that sat low and hot in her uterus. It bled in scant trickles.

Perhaps an abruption? I was uncertain as Soraya did not present with all the usual symptoms and I had not yet learned to trust the ether as well as I trusted my science.

"I can tell by your face," she said, her voice rising in panic. "Tell me what it is."

I moved my hands up higher, pressing with my fingers until I was able to palpate the curve of her daughter's rump, the soft line of her back, her sweet head. I searched for her heartbeat, listened for the quick sharp rhythm. I found it, strong, so strong.

As I shifted my hands I heard another heartbeat, a strident rhythm, not quite as loud but just as insistent. This one belonged to my child, I knew right away. The hope that would likely never come to fruition. Then the roar of my own heartbeat, galloping even as I attempted to push back my own pain and fear, drowned out the rest. I pulled away.

"Your baby is strong," I said.

"You sure?"

I nodded and turned my face into the shadows so she wouldn't see the pain and fear etched on my face, or the tears. I'd been pregnant as many times as Soraya and not one child had lived. I wiped my eyes with the back of my sleeve and grabbed my bag.

But who was I to complain? I'd created this.

Manuel followed me to my jeep.

"Soraya needs bedrest," I said. "I don't want her to get up for more than the bathroom for the next week."

Manuel nodded. "What is it? What do you think is wrong?"

The dawn chill had already burned away. To the east, I could see the broken spires of Oberon, like needles stabbing at the sky. No longer a great metro, Oberon is now just the bare bones of its memory. I'd been there before on a scavenge run. So much of its treasures still lay untouched. People were afraid to go to Oberon. Rumor was that a catcher hideout was located near the city.

"I'm not quite willing to commit to a diagnosis yet, Manuel." I spread my arms out in front of me. "My resources are as dry as this desert. I'm so ill-equipped."

"But you're a doctor. The best we've got."

I wondered if this was how Sule felt, desperate to provide for our settlement, for me, yet being helpless to do so. Manuel was asking more than I was capable of, but if I was in his place, or Soraya's, I'd do anything to see this child born into the light. I'd make any concession to give this child the best world.

"I'll see what I can do."

I STOOD ON Miriama's porch, her old cabin little more than a lean-to, and stared west along the unobstructed sun-cured plains in the direction of settlement #8, my home.

The first time I saw Sule, he'd walked out of a dust storm to the gates of our settlement. He had been wandering the hinterlands alone after his release from the Vymar labor camp. We never asked his crime. When so many are unjustly imprisoned and cast to the desert for crimes no more significant than belief, his crimes could hardly matter.

I found him of great interest. He had navigated the hinterlands for months without becoming prey to hunger or catchers. They would have robbed him of the small wealth in seeds he carried in his pack, just as quickly as they would have robbed him of his life.

I was quick to welcome Sule into our settlement, despite the dissent of the others. I sensed goodness in him. The ether veil about him shimmered like starlight. Miriama had taught me how to read people, to suss their surface intentions. This is why she'd always welcomed me into her home, though it was my people who had first exiled her.

I unlaced my boots and lined them up by the door and entered without knocking. She would be waiting for me, would've known that I was coming even before I'd made up my mind to do so.

The remnants of a fire smoldered in the hearth. A few candles placed intermittently around the room offered just enough light to cast long shadows along the walls and ceiling. The air was heavy with a mix of sharp spicy scents from the herbs hung to dry from the rafters and along the walls.

Her baritone voice rose out of the darkness before my eyes adjusted to the gloom of the windowless cabin.

"Bilqis, my beloved. This not your usual day," she said.

"No, it isn't."

I visited Miriama on Monday mornings to learn the special prayers and the adab of devotion, lessons I would have learned sub rosa as a youth in Ajutine had I conceded to my mother's wishes and been disobedient of the Creed Laws.

There was a certain irony in the fact that a witch was the keeper of a faith that outlawed the use of sorcery, but most of our imams have been imprisoned, have been frightened into silence and obscurity, or are just plain dead.

"I've come to replenish my supply of herbs. I need more brehsome root and more of your ginger tea."

"Brehsome?"

"The brehsome will help my people forget their hunger." I stepped further into the cabin.

"I know this. Taught you, remember?"

"Yes, Miriama."

She sighed, "You never come just to visit."

Miriama knew why I did not visit more often. I never spoke to Sule of my visits here, though he knew as well as others. Even Miriama's long years aren't enough to inspire the sympathy she truly deserves from her detractors. Where people were willing, in such times, to forgive her use of magic, they could not surpass their fear that she had once taken as many lives using it as she preserved. As long as I was careful, they pretended not to notice I was allied with her. As long as I did good.

Miriama waved me over. "Grab that pouch there on the hearth," she said. The leather was worn and soft. I made to give it to her, but she shook her head and urged me to sit on the floor at her feet.

"That is for you, little sister. Brehsome, ginger tea, and some hrery powder for your man."

I looked up into her face, not shocked that she'd had the supplies already prepared, but I didn't quite understand. "Hrery powder?"

She nodded. "It will calm him. Also I packed some of those good pain pills. You are going to need those."

I had learned never to ask her how she knew these things. The strangeness of knowing impressed a sour disquiet into my very spirit.

"I've been to see Soraya today."

"That one is a miracle, considering what plagues us."

"Yes," was all I could manage around a throat full of guilt.

Miriama held me beneath her gaze, pressing her will against mine. I lowered my head, reached for her tough brown hand, and kissed it. Before I pulled away Miriama cupped my chin in her hand and coaxed my face into a patch of candlelight. I felt the tendrils of her consciousness lap at me and then slide away.

"You well, little sister?"

"Quite," I said without meeting her gaze. I felt a pinprick sensation, like biting ants, down my spine. Miriama probed me with her will, more persistently this time, and as she'd taught me, I imagined a wall and erected a barrier against her.

Miriama smiled. "How be your dreams these days?"

"Full of a future I'm afraid to believe in."

Miriama nodded. "Is that good or bad?"

"I don't know."

His face flashed in my mind, the son I felt wax and wane in the ocean of my belly. My dreams had been of him in the future, sand-colored and rangy like his father, taciturn and driven by an anger much like mine. I clenched my jaw and swallowed the fear and sorrow these dreams stirred.

Miriama released my chin, then ran her calloused fingers along the line of my cheek and forehead. I could never really keep her out of my head if she made up her mind to be in it.

"You're different," she said frowning. "Like something in you is burning." She sighed and sat back in her chair. "What do you hold in your belly, on your mind? What really brings you to me?"

I shook my head. "Just the herbs, Miriama."

Her laughter was like a building quake. "Since when do you lie, little sister? Do you not trust me?"

"I do," I said dropping my chin again.

It was difficult to conceal truths from this woman. Even the truths one has yet to uncover are laid bare before her. When I first came to her, she warned me, "Do not come to me if you wish that I not see you." And I had accepted this, but how could I explain that I'd pinned my hopes on a dream child?

"Something happened today, when I reached for Soraya's baby."

Miriama leaned forward, her eyes as keen as lights in the gloom. "Like what?"

I looked down at my hands, turning them over, and then stretched them out for her to see. "I heard the heartbeat of my child as I probed for the heartbeat of hers." I looked up into her narrowed eyes.

"Remember what I taught you? If you are not certain about your intentions and desires, you cannot expect the ether to be."

I said nothing to this because she was right. Thoughts of my own child were always just below the surface.

"Have faith, little sister," she said as if she'd plucked the thought from my head. "Maybe not all of your fruit are broken."

"The life out here in the hinterlands is not fit for the good fruit."

Miriama fumbled with the tall water pipe next to her chair. She nodded for me to retrieve an ember from the fire while she added sweet-smelling herb.

Finally she shrugged saying only, "There's no reason the good fruit must stay put. This a wide world."

"That's what scares me." I rose to leave.

"Remember, little sister, that the ether is merely a tool." Miriama grabbed my hand and pressed it against her cheek. "It is not more or less powerful than your science. If you want to do the best thing for that girl and yourself, you use all the tools you can find."

Just then I felt the flutter of bird's wings in my belly.

WHEN I RETURNED home I found Sule sprawled across our bed. A shaft of cold moonlight set his brown face aglow. He snored lightly with his face against my pillow. His feet hung over the end of our bed.

His legs had always been too long for our bed, our chairs, the door frames, the entire throwaway prefabricated pod home that was never intended to be in use for so long.

Before Sule, I had been comfortable in my solitude, I had thought, until the night he met me at the door of my quarters. I'd come home from hunting and found Sule standing in the shadows awaiting my arrival. As tradition demanded he came chaperoned by the traveling Imam.

Of course I accepted him.

I slid onto the bed next to him. Eyes still closed, Sule shifted to face me. He brought up a hand to the nape of my neck and untied the small knot. When the filmy fabric fell away, he tangled his fingers in my hive of hair.

"Like a volcanic sunset," he whispered of my henna-dyed hair, before pulling me against his chest.

I clung to him, and accepted a sleep sweet kiss from him that made me almost forget everything else.

"You'll never leave me?" he asked through a sleep haze, oddly, as if he sensed finality in my caresses.

I knew I never wanted to. When I took too long to answer, his eyes fluttered open, half-lidded glistening pools. I found myself lost in them.

"No. Never," I breathed against his mouth.

I PARKED BENEATH the ledge of a hoodoo and sipped tepid ginger tea from a copper flacon. The sky hung low, a pitch sheet shot through with pinprick lights, the primordial moon halved. These were the hours I loved most, between midnight and dawn, when if I opened my senses, I could feel waves of the ether pound against the shores of the perceivable world.

Isa met me here, dressed in black with a gun strapped to his hip and a rifle slung across his broad back. I pushed open the door for him.

Isa was the first person I met when I entered the hinterlands, self-exiled from Ajutine, fueled by ignorance, idealistic purpose, and shame. I quickly learned that one cannot eat dreams nor shelter beneath idealism.

Hungry and tired, I considered returning to Ajutine to continue my work. I had a duty to be among the leaders in the search for a cure to our people's increasing infertility, I had reasoned. Shame as much as pride sent me to the hinterlands despite the fact that our increasing infertility was very much my fault.

When I met Isa wandering across the plains he was only twelve or thirteen. In those days he didn't speak and was adrift of any settlement. But Isa was quick and smart. He knew how to find food, water, and shelter in caves and in the nooks and crevices of hoodoos. He called me Ummi, and I mothered him, as much as he would allow.

"I asked you to come because I do not want to do this alone and because I trust you with my life," I started. Isa speaks now, but I saw the questioning in his eyes.

"I don't want Sule to know." I started the engine and shifted into first gear.

"Where are we going?"

"There's a clinic in Oberon, a large one. It was still pretty much intact, last time I was there."

"How long ago was that?"

I shrugged. "Five, maybe six years."

Isa's teeth flashed as he laughed. "You expect there to be anything left after all this time, except vermin?"

"There's a good chance. Few people out here would even know what to do with what I am after."

I glanced in my rearview mirror. A peacock's tail of red dust rose, up behind my jeep. For a moment I thought I spotted the points of yellow headlights in the distance.

"Look back there," I said to Isa, pointing over my shoulder with my thumb. "Do you see someone? We being followed?"

Isa twisted around in his seat. "I don't see anyone."

"Good." I let out a breath and glanced in Isa's direction. His dark lean face glowed, even in the pitch of the desert, green-gray eyes ethereal lamplights. A sudden sad longing came over me for the child this man used to be.

"I went to see Soraya today. She's big with another child but something is wrong. We're going to that clinic in Oberon for a piece of equipment called an ultrasound."

"What does it do?"

"It will help me see the baby in her belly."

"Can't you already, like old Miriama?"

"Some, yes, but this is science."

ISA TOOK THE lead, handgun unholstered and hanging ready at his side. I followed him in the gloom. The blue light of my torch highlighted his shoulder and neck muscles. I guided his direction by tapping his right or left shoulder when it was time for us to turn down the next corridor. The building was quiet but for the high-pitched chirrup of rats in the walls and the sound of toms mewling in the distance.

I found the ultrasound machine in one of the smaller diagnostic rooms. An exam table stood in the center of the room, its stirrups extended as if waiting for a patient. It was covered in dust and rubble. Isa helped me liberate the portable unit from beneath a pile of bricks and plaster, creating a fog of grime in the process.

"If there was electricity, I could test it, see if it still works."

Isa went to stand by the door.

"Isa?" My voice sounded muffled and weighted in the thick dark.

"We should leave," he said, waving me over. "We can test it when we get back to the settlement."

"Give me a sec," I said as I rummaged through the cabinets.

"Ummi," whispered Isa, his voice edged with anxiety.

I looked over my shoulder at him. "Yeah?"

Even in the dark, I could see his wide eyes glisten, and his forehead wrinkle above his nose.

"You hear that?"

I hadn't heard anything. I shook my head. In fact, I could no longer hear the mewling toms from the alley.

"Ummi, I don't like it here. Let's go. Now."

I took the case containing the ultrasound and followed him into the hall. I felt a sharp burning stab on my right shoulder.

Then I saw nothing.

"Dr. Bilqis Jihada Haq. I never thought in a million years that I would see you again." The voice was vaguely familiar.

I regained consciousness in a catcher trailer, cold and naked on a rusty necropsy table. It was slick with someone else's jellied blood. My head, weighted with drugs, throbbed in nauseating waves. My mouth was dry and leathery and tasted like I'd been sucking on coins. I could not move.

I felt probing fingers along my neck, my shoulders, kneading my breasts and my abdomen, my thighs, between my thighs, my calves, my feet, between my toes. My eyes flew open and they stung and watered as I was momentarily blinded by a white light above me. Everything appeared fuzzy around the edges, as if I was looking through a periscope.

"There are those lovely eyes I remember so well." The voice was male, soft, and lilting.

Gloved fingers pushed past my lips, pried open my jaw and ran along my gums and teeth.

"Not often I get someone as healthy as you out here in the hinterlands. Or as bountiful." He winked. "If I could find twenty women like you, I could be a very wealthy man."

The edges started to clear and my limbs tingled, like a million hot tiny needles pricking me.

Damp brown curls sprouted from the edges of his blue surgical cap. His brown eyes were flecked with yellow and green. He tugged down his mask.

Dorian Lin had changed much since I'd last seen him. His cheeks were gaunt and pockmarked and the bags beneath his eyes were bruise-purple. His mouth, a tight cyanotic gash in his face, told the tale of his unfortunate vice. He was dying. He was once a very beautiful man.

Horror must've shown in my eyes. He chuckled lightly and patted my shoulder. "No worries, love. I hold no grudges."

Dorian Lin had been expelled from medical for abusing pain medications. He was known not only for using, but for creating his own very dangerous anesthetic concoctions and selling them in the fifth ward. I was the one who reported him. He was ejected into the hinterlands, made an exile.

"Besides, how could I be angry with the only person whose fall from glory rivals my own?" His eyes traveled slowly down the length of my body and then back to my eyes. "You killed all the babies, you and your vaccine."

He unbound my plait and fingered my curls. "You're better than I expected."

He turned away then I heard the electric hum of machinery. When he turned back he held an ultrasound probe in his hand.

"This ultrasound will be useful as will your healthy liver, kidneys, lungs..." He ticked off my body parts on the fingers of his other hand. "I have so much to thank you for, Dr. Haq."

We were both startled by banging on the side of the metal trailer. "You finished yet?" called a husky female voice from outside the trailer.

"This is a very delicate procedure. It takes time."

"You can pretend you're a mighty metro surgeon as much as you want, as long as you're ready to meet the grocer in two hours." Her voice was closer this time, perhaps at the mouth of the trailer.

A shudder coursed through me, from my toes up to my shoulders. The wind blew just then, carrying in the salty musk of the desert. I felt the tiny hairs on my arms stiffen. I breathed deeply. My fingertips twitched.

"I think he won't mind a little delay."

Dorian pressed the ultrasound probe to my belly and rolled it back and forth until he found what he was looking for. A sound like galloping hooves and the messy swish of fast moving air filled the trailer, echoing off the metal walls.

His catcher partner came into view, her face a sun-cured tapestry of lines and divots framed by a tangle of silver hair. Her blue eyes and lips formed perfect ohs.

"A real live baby," she said breathily. "Well, damn."

He held up two fingers. "Two for the price of one."

* * *

THE KATO-HAQ CANCER vaccine was celebrated as a medical marvel. I wasn't the leading researcher, but with Professor Kato, my mentor, suffering from worsening vascular dementia, most of the work and calculations were my own. And of course, my name was on it.

The premise was simple. The vaccine was infused with nanites to seek out cells in the process of over-proliferating, cells that would cause tumors. Within the first year the diagnosis of all cancers dropped by 53%. The vaccine was a success.

Dorian stared at the monitor. "About eighteen weeks. Looks like a strong healthy boy." He smiled at me.

The feeling in my arms and legs had returned and they twitched involuntarily.

"Shall I assume that you weren't vaccinated?"

"Of course I was. I believed in my work." My voice was barely above a whisper.

Dorian raised an eyebrow. "So do I.

"A bit long in the tooth to be having a baby, aren't you?" Dorian chuckled. "What are you? Forty-three, forty-four?"

I stared at the frozen image of my child on the monitor. There had been other pregnancies. Once my belly had grown large only to give birth to a lump of flesh and hair in place of a child. A clot of blood imbued only with the hope of life. Once I had a daughter. I held her tiny limbless body against me and put her to my breast where she suckled weakly, her eyes locked onto mine. She went to sleep at my breast and never woke again.

But I knew from the start that this child was different, stronger, real. Yet part of me still wished he would die in my womb. That I would pass him out of me like all the others, as so much dead tissue.

Dorian's partner came into view grinning broadly enough that I could see the dark rotten teeth in the back of her mouth. "I talked to the grocer." She glanced down at me and her smile faltered. She looked away.

"And?"

"He says he has a potential buyer. He just needs to negotiate the price." The catcher looked down at me again, her eyes focused on my belly instead of my eyes.

"Looks like that tranq is wearing off. You'll either need to dose her or tie her down," said the catcher as she retreated.

"Where are you going?"

"Keep guard. What else? We've got some precious cargo here."

Dorian looped a rope across my body and beneath the table and knotted it at my knees.

I tried to remember what Miriama had taught me, to pin prey with my eyes and use the coil of strength in my gut to draw out their consciousness. Most of my lessons had been for the purposes of healing and diagnostics. But I wanted to live. And if my child was going to die, I didn't want it to be at the hands of a catcher.

"Dorian?"

"Hmm." He glanced up and I managed somehow to hold him there.

The twine of power I pulled on was not yellow, like the one I'd used to view Soraya's baby. This one was the blue-black of the midnight sky, the cold of the lowest levels of the ocean.

Dorian's shiver mirrored my own.

Miriama had once explained, "All hearts begin clean and shiny like polished gold. It is sin and rancor that darkens them. Leaves spots sticky black like tar and rust." It is this corruption that I tapped into, that I pushed out through my pores, creating a translucent black cloud in the trailer.

The miasma coalesced around Dorian. He coughed, and then he was doubled over choking. He was easy, already weakened by the drugs and his own corruption. All I had to do was call on my own darkness. There was so much more than I realized.

"To work the ether, you need intention. If you wish to see, it will give you sight. If you wish to heal, that is what you will do. And if it is destruction you wish, you will have that too," Miriama had once advised. "Know what you wish. Know your own truth."

"What truth?" I had asked.

"The truth about you, little sister. Not one of us is as good as we wish to believe."

My truth was that I wanted to live and I wanted my boy to live. So I poured that desire into the black cloud around Dorian. I imbued it with the bitter pride that made me an exile, regret for not standing firm in belief, my anger for up to this moment not being honest with myself and with Sule.

I imagined Dorian lifting the blood-encrusted scalpel from the table and slicing the thin brightly veined skin of his throat, creating a bloody bib. Dorian jabbing the scalpel into his abdomen over and over again. Me wearing his ribcage as armor, his metacarpals and phalanges as a crown.

When I heard my name, faded and far away, my black cloud wavered and thinned. I heard a plea, not the words, but the intent. I felt hands on my shoulders, my forehead, my cheeks. I felt tears fall upon my face like hail. My vision cleared.

I heard a loud crack, felt a hot spray on my face, smelled the acrid scent of gun smoke. Then I didn't see the yellow-and green-flecked eyes anymore. Isa's face hovered above mine, his mouth pulled back in a wail.

"Ummi, stop." He scrabbled at the rope across my body and when he became frustrated with the knots he pulled a hunting knife from his boot and cut them.

"The catcher?" My throat was hoarse. I didn't sound like myself.

"I've dealt with her." He pulled me into a sitting position and into his arms.

"Dorian?" I said glancing back, but Isa held me tight to prevent me from seeing.

"I shot him and it was a mercy," he said, avoiding my eyes. Isa helped me to my feet and wrapped a dirty blanket around my shoulders. "I need to get you home. Cleaned up."

I AWOKE JUST before noon, tangled in sweat-dampened sheets, the sun slanting through the window onto my face. My head ached, and when I rolled onto my side it felt like an ocean had shifted within my skull. I managed to climb out of bed and get to the bathroom before heaving into the sink.

I heard voices, a heated conversation in low tones. Sule would be angry and would try to blame Isa. Isa would probably let him.

I washed my face and dressed, then joined them in the kitchen. Sule rose when he saw me, anger and adoration an alternating mask. My magnet did not reach for me, but he leaned forward, hands turned out as if he wished to. As much as he fought the urge, I felt his fire tugging at me, longing for me. I avoided his eyes.

Isa wore a bloodstained bandage on his left shoulder. I offered a half smile, a silent apology. He nodded back.

I retrieved three of the pain pills that Miriama had packed in the leather pouch and handed two to Isa. I swallowed the other dry and sat in the chair that Sule had vacated.

"Do you think you can rig a battery for this thing?" I said, nodding toward the ultrasound. It sat on the floor in a corner.

Isa nodded. "When do you need it?"

"Now."

Isa rose and headed for the door. "Give me thirty minutes and it'll be ready." The door smacked in the frame when he left.

"Why?" Sule asked a million questions at once, his face fractured by warring emotions. What could I say to placate his fear and anger, when I couldn't placate my own? There were no lies that would sound like truth.

I went to where Sule stood against the counter. I wrapped my arms around him. He curved around me like a cocoon, my magnet. "I was so worried about Soraya's baby, and Manuel was afraid," I said.

He stiffened, even as he wrapped his arms around me.

"But that can't be the only reason." He placed his hands on either side of my face and gazed down at me. For a long time I did not speak, but he waited.

"I wanted to use the machine to see our son," I said. Sule closed his eyes, let out a long breath. "I've been dreaming about him since I conceived. I already know his face, his voice, the smell of him. I wanted to know that he was real."

I felt Sule's anger ebb, the tension in his muscles ease. Then I told him about the future I saw in my dreams of our son, the future that did not include him.

"Forgive me," I said against his chest.

He nodded, his chin against the top of my head.

"Forgive me," I said again.

*   *   *

"WILL MY DAUGHTER live?" is all that Soraya wanted to know.

"I don't see why not." I sat on a small stool next to the bed. I handed the ultrasound probe to Neenah and nodded for her to turn the machine off.

"But this is dangerous, yes?"

I nodded, "It can be, but it's a small separation. Your job is to rest until she is ready to meet the world." I patted Soraya's hand.

Soraya frowned and turned her face away from me.

"I just gave you good news. What's wrong?"

"Who will deliver my baby when you leave?"

"I will," said Neenah. "I'll do my very best for you, Soraya. Try not to worry."

Soraya smiled and wiped away tears with the back of her hand.

I MADE SALAT in the dark hour before dawn beneath an outcropping of rock. The only sounds were the thump of my heart. The journey to Ajutine had been long and heavy with guilt, but I had no regrets and no desire to go back.

I slipped off my hijab, my favorite, made of sheer copper fabric. I wore it the day that Sule and I wed. I used it to secure the holy book written in ancient curling script, the tasbeh of pearls on which I counted and expiated my sins, and the rectangle of carpet on which I knelt to recite my prayers. These had been my wedding gift from Sule, and now, I would leave them behind.

I filled the hole with sand and marked the spot with a large black stone shaped like a fan. None of the artifacts could pass entry inspection.

I pulled the yellow flier from my pocket to read one last time. The paper was now worn and faded, folded and refolded. My heart hitched as I turned toward the city of my birth, the home to which I never thought I would return.

The familiar angles of the skyscrapers rose above the wall surrounding the city, like fingers grasping for the clouds. Lighted looping train tracks hovered in midair, twisting around the skyscrapers like ribbons on the wind. From this distance I even caught the scent of Ajutine, exhaust and filth mixed with spice and humanity. Something in me shuddered. Until that moment I didn't realize how much I had hungered for home.

"I don't want you to go," said Isa as I held his head against my chest. He had been my first friend in the hinterlands, my first child.

I watched the jeep until it disappeared in a cloud of dust on the horizon then set off to cover the remaining distance to Ajutine on foot.

Sule managed to make my last days with him the happiest and the most hateful of my life. He couldn't get enough of my flowering form, hands always resting on the curved plane of my hip, the sensitive small of my back, telling me and showing me in countless ways how much he loved me. I joined him one night when he took to the plains to hunt.

I will never forget the way the stars look through a veil of tears, brighter and smeared across the sky, or the sound of Sule crying when he thought I was asleep.

I never had to tell him that I was leaving. He always knew.

On our last night together we ate cactus fruit and rabbit. I drank ginger tea and he drank water in which I'd sprinkled a bit of hrery powder. He slept dreamlessly, fitted around me like a shell.

No amount of time was long enough to be with a man like him.

I took my place at the end of a long line of the hungry and hopeful. Several hours passed before it was my turn, the sun giving way to a yellow crescent and stars. The guard searched my bag, removed then replaced the outdated medical texts, the certificates and licenses proving my education and training. He held the faded hospital picture identification up to shoulder height.

I self-consciously smoothed my hair, knowing that I scarcely resembled my younger self smiling in the photo. He appraised me, his gaze lingering on the scar on my chin, the streak of henna-reddened silver hair near my right temple.

His eyes settled on mine. "A doctor like you would be an asset here in Ajutine. Are you willing to make the required concessions?"

I thought of Allah, of the symbols of my religion buried in the sands of the hinterlands. I thought of my mother whose love of Allah was unimpeachable but who resolutely refused to leave Ajutine, the city of her forefathers.

"You only fail if you walk away," she had once said, and those words looped in my head like a mantra. I was returning to right wrongs and to give my son a better life, but in doing so I was walking away again, from Sule, from certain love and hardship.

I looked up toward the sky through the glass of my tears.

"I am willing to make concessions," I told him. I met his gaze so he would know and see it in my eyes.

It wasn't until he nodded me through the gates that I realized that I'd been holding my breath.

CONFESSIONS OF A CON GIRL
Nick Wolven

Nick Wolven's (www.nickthewolven.com) science fiction has appeared in *Wired, Asimov's, F&SF,* and many other publications. He lives in New York City.

Senior Thesis submitted to the Department of English, —— University, in partial fulfillment of the requirements for the degree of Bachelor of Arts August 22, 20—
By: Sophie Lee

THE FIRST THING to say, at the outset of my narrative, is it was not according to my own wishes to write this senior paper. The reason being for three reasons. Firstly, because, try as I might, I no longer believe I will ever be a "good writer", which was the primary objective of pursuing an English degree. Which is a great disappointment to me, as being a good writer has been among the foremost of my lifelong passions.

Second, another reason is because I do not believe I am in any way a credit to such a prestigious university as I attended, being, as I am, a Con girl, which my title says. So I do not think I am worthy of the BA in English degree. And the only reason I am writing this now is because my Re-Engagement Process Counselor recommended I do so, as a step on my process to healing, and to put behind me all the painful experiences that have occurred.

Thirdly, the last reason I didn't want to write this paper is because the thesis of the assignment is to explicate how I became a Con girl, what I did wrong, how I became a shame to everyone in my life, and the lifelong steps that brought me to this debacle. But, as I have confessed, I strongly doubt my ability to explicate how this happened. Would I conscientiously aspire to be a scourge on society, an embarrassment to my parents, a disappointment to my teachers and friends?

Emphatically, no.

Yet, that is what happened.

Truly, sometimes I believe I am no longer sure of anything. An example would be today. I was sitting outside my institution, in the yard with the high fence and the concrete sculptures of trees. And I was reflecting on my healing process, when a leaf blew into my hair—a real leaf, from a real tree outside our yard. And I lifted up a hand and crushed it—"as one does." But when I looked at the crushed leaf, I had a feeling, what our Re-Engagement Process Counselor calls "an unprovoked grief episode." I thought about how I had crushed that leaf for no reason, without even thinking, out of habit. I thought about how this is what I do, touch things and ruin them, without even trying. I thought about how I'm a Con girl, now, a negative member of society, who has to be put in this place, apart from everyone, because she has been such a harm to others. And it was like those times when they first brought me here, in those days when I couldn't even talk or think, but only used to sit by myself, not moving.

All this, yes, because of a leaf, which, as anyone knows, has no nerves, and which anyhow this one was already dead.

This is the kind of thing that occurs with me nowadays, after everything else that has transpired.

I am a Con girl. And in case you can't tell, I'm still trying really hard to figure out how that could have happened.

THE PLACE TO begin, I believe, is my last week of school. And the subject I will begin with is my End-of-Semester Meeting, with my assigned Learning Process Advisor, Mr. Barraine.

Now, the thing I must stress at the outset is I believe Mr. Barraine to be a good person—flawed as we all are, but who isn't flawed? I have never for once doubted that he wanted the best for me, and my life process. You can check out his Perma-Me profile online. Do it now. You will discover that

Mr. Barraine has two little girls at home whom he cares for very tenderly. One of whom is afflicted with a disability, but which has nevertheless in no way lessened Mr. Barraine's affection for her. There is a delightful video of Mr. Barraine and his daughters feeding bread crumbs to ducks in the park, and as the adorable birds waddle and gabble, you can see Mr. Barraine relating with his children and laughing, while in his eye there is the sparkle of genuine joy.

Many commenters to this video have asserted that Mr. Barraine should not have been feeding the ducks in that manner, because bread crumbs are bad for them and disrupt their normal dietary habits, so feeding the ducks is in some aspects paramount to murdering them. But I in no way believe this should be taken as a mark against Mr. Barraine, who is not an ornithologist.

I mention all this because on the day in question, Mr. Barraine was meeting with me to discuss my upcoming Final Academic Review, which under the circumstances, I realize, must have been for him a very trying experience.

I arrived at his office punctually, and the first thing Mr. Barraine said was, "Hi, Sophie, I hope you're doing OK."

At which I almost started crying, because as Mr. Barraine knew, I was not doing OK, and there was practically no way I was going to do better, or anyway not in time to make a difference. But it was nice of him to say that.

He closed the door, and checked that it was closed, and covered the window, and checked that it was covered, and then he showed me where to sit, and said, "Shall we get started?"

Then Mr. Barraine touched his palmscreen, and the pictures on the walls disappeared, and instead of sitting in an office with books and old-time paintings, we were sitting in the middle of a display of my academic records, which was not a nice place to be.

"Let's see what we have, here," Mr. Barraine said, flicking his finger to sort through the files.

At that moment I did start crying, because I didn't need to see those files to know what this was about. It was all displayed in my palmscreen, where my Pro/Con Holistic Score was glowing a shameful, awful yellow.

Mr. Barraine was respectful while I cried. I have always been grateful to him for what he said next. He said:

"Now, Sophie, I want you to know that everything that happens in this interview is entirely private and unrecorded. So you can express whatever you feel without it affecting your holoscore. If you need to express some anger, go right ahead. You can even call me nasty names, if that'll help. Do you want to try that? Do you want to call me nasty names?"

He smiled, and it was so nice of him to say that, in that particular way, that I laughed even while I was crying.

"People have done that, you know," said Mr. Barraine. "A lot of young people have sat where you're sitting, and called me all kinds of nasty names."

At that, I felt so bad for Mr. Barraine that I stopped feeling bad for myself, and like that, my tears cleared up and I was ready to begin.

"Of course," said Mr. Barraine, "if you in anyway violate the Campus Interpersonal Conduct Policy, that will have to be immediately reported. Now, let's get going."

He brought up a chart that showed my grades, and a chart that showed my peer networks, and a hundred other charts that showed a hundred different things. But at the center of it all was my Pro/Con holistic score, glowing on a display in the middle of the wall, so awful I could hardly look at it.

"I'm looking over your records," Mr. Barraine said, "especially at your holistic score, Sophie, and it seems like during the past few years, we've started to see—"

"I'm in the yellow," I said, feeling breathless. "I know. And I can explain."

BUT WHAT I want to underscore, at this juncture in my narrative, is that I have never been one to, as people say, "toot my own horn."

What follows is a quote from my family's Vice Assistant Childrearing Advisor, who prepared my first ever psychological profile:

Sophie... has incredibly well-developed sensitivities. Her reading of facial expressions is advanced for her age, and her various empathetic reactions are off the charts. As to her intellectual aptitudes, they show... potential for great improvement. The danger is that with such high sensitivities, Sophie may face unique life challenges. But with proper mood management, I believe she will grow up to be an extremely positive social member.

Now, "the proper way to interpret praise," as my Test Prep Advisor says, "is as a challenge to do better, not a reward for what you've done." So I believe this is good advice, and see my above-average empathetic abilities, which my VACR so carefully documented, not as something I can take credit for myself, but as a responsibility unto which I have been given. Thus, I have always endeavored to use my empathetic and facial-reading talents, such as they may be, for the constructive support of others.

And this is what I endeavored to achieve, for example, in my fourteenth year, when my mother decided that my father no longer fulfilled her needs as life partner. This was an example of a challenging experience. But I reminded myself that people differ, and sometimes achieving true intimacy means finding a partner who, as people say, "makes the grade." Also because people achieve life aims at different rates. And the truth is, as we all observed, since we had gotten the extra funds for my Student Development Program, my father had no longer been putting as much effort into his own life process as previous.

Thus, when my mother sued my father for mishandling my Student Development money, I understood why she might feel the need to do that, but also how difficult it would be for my father not to be a part of my development anymore. And I did everything I could to express how I still loved them both and supported them, which I posted every day on my Perma-Me profile.

And it was during this admittedly trying interval, that I noticed my efforts did not go unacknowledged. Because partway through the year, my teacher, Ms. Ebro, requested a private meeting with me. We signed the privacy waivers, and went into the school's privacy room, and activated the privacy settings, and while we were in there, Ms. Ebro told me how she and the other teachers had observed what was occurring with me. How they had been following my mother's video diary of the lawsuit online, plus the posts my mother had been putting on her RantSpace page, about my father and the divorce. Also they had been following the videos my father had been sharing on *his* RantSpace page, about my mother, in some of his more disinhibited moments. And they had seen the page my father's girlfriend had made about my mother, and the posts my mother had written about me. And Ms. Ebro said it was truly shocking to see what some people will say online about their families.

This was a significant moment for me.

But what Ms. Ebro said was how she and the other teachers had been observing my own behavior in response to these developments. And how they appreciated my maturity. And she said that sometimes being brave and mature is at least as important as, per example, learning to solve for x or studying pond life.

"After all," Ms. Ebro said, "we know what kind of person you are, Sophie. And when I say that, I'm sure you know exactly what I'm referring to."

I did, but didn't say so. But what truly affected me was what Ms. Ebro said next. She said she had talked to the other teachers, and they would be factoring these considerations into my holistic semester scores, in conjunction with my scholastic grades.

And I admit, I may have overresponded a little when Ms. Ebro said all this. But it was not to my detriment. Because afterwards, my Pro/Con Holistic Score went very green. As I had just gotten my first palmscreen implanted, this was a source of significant comfort to me. I used to pull up the covers at night, and turn on my palmscreen, and sit in a kind of glowing green cave, and think about all the opinions that had gone into that holoscore, all the comments my peers had made about me, all the grades my teachers had submitted, all the assessments of my Student Development Team. And how all this information, so judiciously evaluated, was presented in this simple green light, to remind me of the support and positive feelings I had brought into the world.

Well, that is just one example of a time when I demonstrated Pro behavior.

There were others, like when my Wealth Management Advisor had his collapse, or when my Physical Development Coach was accused of improper child handling. But what I want to talk about now is what happened with Roman Cheryshev.

This was in sophomore year of college, when Roman Cheryshev was a freshman in my Consciousness through Confrontation seminar. And the thing about Roman was, he was very bright, but he was not the kind of person whose company other people enjoyed. I don't know how Roman got to be in our institution, which is a prestigious institution. But the fact is, only a month after he got in, Roman's Pro/Con Holistic Score was moving toward the yellow. At first I thought he might be from a culture where Pro/Con standards are different from ours. But no, he was from New Jersey. Then someone told me Roman's parents had homeschooled him for the Comp-Sci track, and hired a service to manage his scores, which I know is a thing that happens. But I believe it is an ill-advised thing, as in, what will transpire when such a young person enters, as people say, "the real world"?

In any event, Roman was not socially fluent, which made me feel a lot of empathy for him. In seminar, he would become upset when people told him ways in which his behavior was entitled and offensive, which was not only a very Con reaction, but also contrary to the very aims of the course. But I reflected how difficult it must be to be without strong social capacities, so I became his friend.

This proved difficult. Partly because my peer network kept giving me Con votes for bringing Roman to social occasions, impacting on my holoscore very negatively. But also because Roman, for whatever reasons, also kept giving me Con ratings! I don't understand why he would give me a Pro rating one night and a Con the next, inasmuch as we spent all our time the same way, which was with me listening while Roman expressed his anger. Roman did have a lot of anger. To confront someone about their Pro/Con votes is, of course, a very Con behavior, but when I hinted at my feelings, Roman said:

"What, you think you're special, Sophie? You think you deserve some kind of reward for hanging out with me? Is that what you're trying to say?"

I told Roman I didn't think I was special, and what I enjoyed about him was his honesty.

At which he said, "Well, I think you're full of s**t, how's that for honesty? But whatever."

Which was the kind of thing Roman often said to me.

This was when we were hanging out in his room almost every night, eating pizza and talking about Roman's feelings. And that was where we were one Saturday night, when Roman suddenly got a funny look. Now by this time, confessedly, my Pro/Con Holistic Score was not so green as previous. I had brought Roman to several events with my peer network, where he experienced issues related to inappropriate touching. So I was beginning to be conflicted about the friendship. Also, it may be that my sensitivity, though usually high, was not so high as ordinarily. In any event, when Roman did what he did, I reacted uncharacteristically, which I mean, by getting scared and kicking him in the face.

These are the words Roman said to me, that night, which I quote here not to be adverse, but only in the spirit of veracity.

"B***h, what the f**k? Crazy t**t, you come here every night, playing on me, then I finally get the balls to make a move, you shoot me down? Seriously? Motherf**king c**kteasing c**t."

As noted, I have set all this down not to cause hurt, but because it is in fact what Roman said to me.

But the upshot is, after this incident, my Pro/Con Holistic Score took a gigantic hit. And it was because Roman kept giving me Con votes! I tried to engage with him constructively about it, but he only told me I had "played him," and how the worst thing a girl can do to a guy is give him those kinds of mixed signals. Then he told other guys I had "set him up," and they all gave me Con votes, too! So I was receiving Con votes every day, and this, plus a few other, unrelated factors, was, as people say, "the perfect storm," which made my holoscore begin to drop.

All this was what I explained to Mr. Barraine.

But Mr. Barraine said that wasn't what he wanted to talk about, which was actually more regarding my academic records.

At which point he pulled up a file and said, "Sophie, now tell me honestly, do you know where this is going?"

At this time I was grateful no one else could see my face. Because in the file were the requirements for my major, which included my Peer Education Program.

"We have a problem, don't we?" said Mr. Barraine.

The problem was, for years, my Peer Education score had been going up and up, until it was very Pro, and then in the fifth year it began to go down, until it was very Con.

But I told Mr. Barraine I could explain, because this was in fact what I was trying to express to him.

And the thing I explained was, firstly, how much I appreciated the innovative spirit of our institution. Because a student goes to college to learn, correct? But who do students learn from most? Our peers, indubitably! So I thought it was very credible of our institution to demand a full six years of

Peer Education courses, which not only cuts down on the need for expensive professors, but is also empowering for the younger generation.

The problem was, in my fifth year Peer Education course, I had been put in a workshop with Damaris Fierte, who, as everyone knows, is known for her unstinting efforts at peer education.

Now, at the time, Damaris Fierte had a deep green holoscore, whereas I, thanks to Roman, had only a pale green holoscore. So it was justifiable for her to educate me.

But still.

The workshop was on Personal Profile Management, in which we had to critique each other's Perma-Me profiles. And it was my turn to be critiqued. And the first thing Damaris Fierte critiqued about my Perma-Me profile was how I had devoted so much of my time to associating with a person like Roman Cheryshev.

"He's a predator. An abuser. I mean, I don't want to say this, but looking at your profile, Sophie, a person could get the impression—an employer, a potential contact—I mean, they could see you as some kind of enabler."

At which I felt concerned, and explained how I had only felt sorry for Roman, and was trying to be his friend.

At which Damaris said, "So you brought him to my friend's party? Where he inappropriately touched people? This was someone you wanted for a friend?"

At which I said, I didn't consider Roman a *close* friend, exactly, but more like a—

"What?" said Damaris. "If he wasn't your friend, what did you want from him? Just to use him? Just for the Pro votes?"

I was now beginning to see some of the workshop participants looking at me very problematically.

Then Damaris said, "I think this is an important lesson in Profile Management, guys. Because when people look at your Personal Profile, an employer, a recruiter, what they want to see most is authenticity. If it seems like you're taking on too many charity projects, or being nice to unpopular people just for the pity votes, I do think that can reflect on you very adversely."

And in the final analysis, the workshop ended up giving me a strong critique.

But what I want to say is what happened after.

Because I went to Damaris after class and said did she really have to give me such a strong critique? And I wasn't trying to say my Perma-Me profile wasn't in need of improvement. But given there was a need for improvement, couldn't there be a more constructive way to go about it?

This was when Damaris unloaded on me.

What she said was she had always had concerns. She said she could tell right away what kind of person I was, how I always overpromoted myself and my abilities. She said it was pathetic, how I talked, all the big words I tried to use, and when she looked at my Perma-Me profile, she didn't think I belonged here at all, in this kind of prestigious institution. She said in fact we both knew exactly why I was here. And if there was one thing she didn't like, Damaris said, it was a Yellow who acts like a Green, or a Red who thinks she's a Yellow.

At this point I began to have strong feelings. Because I remembered a day, weeks ago, when we had critiqued Damaris's Perma-Me profile. Which was, admittedly, the best profile I ever saw. Damaris was from New York City, and she went to a private school, and had a huge Child Development Team, and lots of money since she was born. In her profile, there were so many extra classes and volunteer jobs and enrichment programs, I wondered how her Child Development Team could have found time to plan so many activities.

But there was one part of her Perma-Me profile that Damaris kept trying to skip, even though the class kept wanting to go back to it. It was a video of Damaris auditioning for the college's summer LEO business mentorship program. Which under the video, Damaris had written:

DIDN'T GET IN, OH WELL, I'M JUST SO HAPPY TO HAVE HAD THE CHANCE FOR SUCH A GREAT AND FUN AUDITION!!!!

But if you looked at the video, Damaris did not look happy. If you have ever spent a lot of time throwing up, from nerves or any other reason, let me tell you, you know the signs.

The strong feelings were because I remembered my own time in the LEO program. And how I hadn't even auditioned for it, but instead got in by special appointment. The coordinators had to rush me through the enrollment process, then the training process, until I was the last one to get on the rocket. Even then, when I was sitting in my flight seat, strapping in, I could hardly believe I had gotten this far, me, Sophie Lee, a tourist in space.

When we got past the boost phase, into Low Earth Orbit, the program leader took us into the viewing chamber, and showed us the Earth so far below. The purpose of the program was to join business leaders on a trip to outer space, he said, and learn from their insights and leadership experience. It was business-sponsored, so it was a big honor. The program director had a company in financial services, and he said we had been chosen for this opportunity because of a time in our lives when we demonstrated exceptional leadership. Now was a chance for us to look down and think about the planet we might one day be leading, and what he wondered was, did any of us have anything we'd like to say?

At this point, I began to get a weird feeling in my stomach, and I unbuckled my harness and floated to the viewscreen, and looked down on the continents below.

Then I turned and looked at the business leaders buckled into their flight chairs, and what I said was that the main thing I was thinking was not how small the Earth seemed from up here, but how big.

At this, the business leaders all smiled and nodded.

I said it made me feel humble, thinking about what a challenge it must be, being a leader to such a huge place.

The business leaders now smiled and nodded very strongly.

But I kept feeling weird, and I said it seemed like such a big challenge, it actually seemed like an impossible challenge, like it was crazy to think you could try and control what was happening down there, or even really understand it.

At this point some of the business leaders stopped smiling and nodding, and I sensed it was time to go back to my seat and enjoy the complimentary low-grav spherical cocktails. But I still felt weird, so I kept talking.

What I said was, when you thought about it, to the Earth, human beings were basically like bugs, no more special than any other species, whether endangered or no.

What I said was, if you looked at it that way, what could an individual person, however accomplished, really count for?

What I said was, didn't it almost seem crazy, all the way up here, for any one person to be richer or more important than another, and if you thought about it, if something were to unfortunately happen, and our spaceship were to explode on reentry, would it even make a difference to anyone down there, except of course our families?

After I said all this, none of the business leaders were smiling and nodding at all, and a lot of the other students were letting go of their cocktail spheres and looking at me, like, *What's the matter with you?* Then, when we got back to Earth, I discovered my holoscore had dropped almost twenty percent, and all the business leaders had marked me down as being 'definitely not leadership material.'

So that was what I told Damaris Fierte. And I said she was right about me. How I knew I didn't belong here, in such a prestigious institution. In fact, what I said was that I envied her, because what I now realized was, the LEO business mentorship program was as big a risk as an opportunity, and in my case, having utterly blown it, I had totally tanked my holoscore.

At this Damaris looked at me a long time, and I could see her feelings had changed. Finally she said, "Sophie, you know, I think that's the most honest thing I ever heard you say."

But I blew it.

Because, the more I thought about it, the more I realized Damaris was right. How all this time, in college, even in my Childhood Development Program, I had been trying to be someone I was not, and to seem smarter than I was. And I was ashamed of myself.

So I said, "Damaris, the thing is, you really are a smart and amazing person. And you're right, I don't belong here, but you really do. And you should have been the one to go on the LEO trip, not me, because I truly believe one day you could be a great leader."

At which she said, "No, no," and looked sick again, shaking her head.

But I said, "No, seriously, I truly believe that." And then I said what was probably the stupidest thing I ever said in my whole life, which was, "How come we've never been friends?"

But right away I could see I had majorly screwed up. Because Damaris stood back, and her mouth was open and she was panting, and she looked angrier than I've ever seen anyone get angry.

And she said, "Sophie, see, this is exactly what I'm talking about!

Everything you do, it always has to be a big calculation. You say all these nice things, and I really believed you, and now I see you're just manipulating me to join your stupid peer network and boost your holoscore!"

At which I didn't say anything, because I was so surprised.

"This is truly shameful," Damaris said as she walked away. "Truly, truly shameful. I can't even educate you in how shameful this is."

And when I checked, I saw what I feared, which was that every person in Damaris's peer network had given me an enormous Con vote.

Now, coming from someone with Damaris's score, that meant something. But when I told all this to Mr. Barraine, he shook his head.

"No, Sophie," he said. "The Peer Education stuff, that's only a sidebar. What we're here about today is your major, especially your literature courses. And I have to tell you we've been noticing some very troubling signs."

At this I was surprised, because, since entering college I have become, as my Student Career Coach likes to say, a "true lover of the word."

But Mr. Barraine used his palmscreen to display some different records, which I didn't recognize, and he said, "Does this mean anything to you?" And when I said, "No," he said, "Are you sure?"

Then he came around his desk, and pulled up a chair.

He said, "Sophie, do you know what the global rank of this institution is?"

I did, and I told him.

Mr. Barraine said, "Do you know why we are ranked so high?"

I said it must be because of the university's immense positive contributions to society.

Mr. Barraine smiled. "Do you know what the Ivy League graduate enrollment rate among our alumni is? The first-year employment rate? The average salary at ten years? The estimated value of our name as an attractor of venture capital? The alumni fundraising score? Or how about this?"

He brought up another chart, which covered almost a whole wall, and this one I definitely recognized.

"These are the private and public parties," Mr. Barraine said, "who have agreed to invest in your education. Here's the government's contribution. Here's AdverBetter. Here's ThinkTrendTrack. Here are all the media and marketing groups that loaned money for your Student Development Team.

They all contributed to the financing of your education, Sophie, because your holoscore positioned you, at the time, as an immensely high-potential individual. I think you know exactly what I'm talking about. The reason you're in this school, Sophie, is because we don't only educate students, here. We educate the whole person."

Mr. Barraine drew a round shape in the air, a little too round, I thought, inasmuch as it was supposed to be me. But this was not a time, I sensed, for critical remarks.

"With my approval," Mr. Barraine said, "you'll soon be meeting with representatives of these parties for your Final Academic Review. They'll be evaluating you for employment opportunities. And they'll be interested in seeing, as early-access recruiters, what their investment in you has produced. You'll tell them, I'm sure, all about your enjoyment of our rare animal handling workshops, our AI-training program, our maglev-equipped, five-story VR athletics facility. But you'll also tell them, of course, about your passionate engagement in our many humanities classes specializing in improved empathetic response. I believe you would agree that improving empathy is one of the major benefits of a liberal arts education. But Sophie, tell me, what do you think these people will say if they find out one of our top empathetic performers is, in fact, as it seems, deeply biased?"

I admit I responded inappropriately, by jumping out of my chair saying, "Biased? How?"

Mr. Barraine leaned back. "Do you really want to ask me that question, Sophie? Do you not see how going into specifics might, in fact, reify the very bias we're discussing?" Then he pointed at the graphs and said, "These are your realtime empathetic assessments, which our team has been following closely."

Now I was especially surprised, because realtime empathetic assessment has always been my favorite part of the literature major. In this time when the humanities are, as they say, "in crisis," what better case could there be for the profound utility of the narrative arts? How many days have I whiled away in the scanning machines, resting my head in the EEG helmet, listening to the soothing flow of words or the images comporting vivaciously on the screen, and living along with the travails of Jane Eyre and Anna Karenina, of Sula and Nel, of Carrie and Charlotte and Miranda and Samantha? How often has it been a profound comfort to me to know that, in some small way, my empathetic responses to these great works will improve my positive contributions to society?

But as I communicated this to Mr. Barraine, he shook his head. "The trouble isn't with your enthusiasm, Sophie. The trouble is the correlations. We've been looking at your neurological readings, and we've been noticing some problematic reactions. It's not that you lack empathy. If anything, you have the opposite problem. You've been empathizing, I have to inform you, with some very unacceptable people."

But I stood over him, feeling hopeful, and said, "Mr. Barraine, I can explain."

And what I explained was how, when I'm in the scanning machines, engaging with all the powerful issues in the stories I'm experiencing, sometimes I start to worry I might have a problematic response. And at times, I get so worried that I *make* myself have the response, but only for the sake of *understanding* the response, as part of my ever-vigilant efforts *not* to have the response. So the realtime empathetic assessment machines, as I told Mr. Barraine, are probably only picking up evidence of my constant mental vigilance *against* such responses, and of my earnest and engaged grappling with even the *possibility* of such responses.

If that makes sense.

But Mr. Barraine looked at me for a long time, and said, "Sit down, Sophie."

So I did.

And he went on:

"My job, Sophie, is to prepare you for your final review. These people you'll be meeting are some of the smartest people in the world: politicians, technologists, advertisers, financiers. But the reason they want to meet with you is because that kind of smartness is no longer very valuable. Smartness is what computers have. And nowadays people are very expensive, and computers are very cheap. What's valuable today, Sophie, is the ability to read human beings—to decipher their moods, their desires, their deepest longings and needs. That is the key to effective public relations. That is what recruiters want. That is the kind of skill the holoscore is meant to assess, and that is what *your* holoscore said you could do. It is what made you a competitive student, and what helped you attract so much investment, and what got you admitted to this institution.

"Now, Sophie. What message do you think it will send if I let you meet with those recruiters, a graduating student of this college, and explain to them that after three million dollars and many years of top-tier education... well, what do you think they'll say when they learn that, as you told me today, you befriended a sexual predator in your second year? When they find out you sabotaged the LEO business mentorship experience for a group of our top performers? When they see how your peers have been voting against you? Finally, what will they think when they look at your responses to these literary works, and learn how prone you are to empathizing with the wrong kinds of people?

"Sophie." He leaned forward. "I'm afraid I can't approve you for graduation at this time."

I looked at Mr. Barraine, and I was feeling several feelings. Firstly, about how I was apparently a terrible person, but no one had told me in all this time. Second, how in my interacting with Roman and Damaris and others, I had misread all their social cues. Finally, how all those smart people were waiting to give me my review, and they had invested so much money in my education, and how would they feel when they found out the person they'd been educating had turned out to be selfish and cruel and biased?

Mostly, though, I thought about Mr. Barraine. How in that video on his Perma-Me profile, when one of his little girls got scared by the ducks, she turned and hid her face in his shirt. And it was like Mr. Barraine didn't even need to think. He just kept smiling and tossing out breadcrumbs, and with his arm he held her to him.

The next thing I knew, alarms were ringing, and Mr. Barraine was jumping away, wide-eyed and shouting and pounding on his palmscreen. And I saw how without even thinking about it, I had gotten out of my chair and pressed my face against his chest.

"I need to report," Mr. Barraine said, "a violation of the Interpersonal Conduct Code, class 25B, section H12. Note: nonsexual contact was initiated by the student during an approved private meeting. Repeat note: contact was *student*-initiated and *non*sexual. I have disengaged and am now departing the location."

He moved to the door, holding out his palmscreen to record how carefully he was keeping his distance from me. And I could see the tears on his shirt and face as he said, "Sophie, how could you? Of all the things to try and... I have daughters. I have a family."

Then, just before he left, he tapped his palmscreen. And the last thing I remember is looking at my own palm, and seeing the effect of the assessment he had given me, which was my Pro/Con holoscore, glowing a bright, ugly red.

IT FEELS STRANGE to be in a home for Con women. Everyone here is deep in the red, a confirmed negative influence on society. Yet during the day-to-day, you hardly know. We have meals and watch TV. One woman here was a daycare worker who took care of learning-disabled children. One day she passed out during her duties, and one of the children had a fall and died. She doesn't talk, but some of us take turns sitting with her. Then there is a woman who attempted suicide four times, and a drug addict, whose name is Tina. One time, I told Tina about my struggles with Pro/Con voting, and she said:

"Oh, man, my people never gave me no votes. If they had feelings, they just acted on 'em. Ha, ha, yeah, they hit you soft, that means they only hate you a little. But if they hit hard, well, then they must really love you." Then Tina laughed, looking at my face, and said, "Oh, Sophie, that's why I like you, girl, you always take things so serious."

She said she wanted me to know they were all giving me Pro votes around here, though admittedly, given their own scores, it wouldn't count for much.

Nobody can understand why I'm in this place. To be honest, I don't understand either. I used to be at the top of the Pro ratings, attend a prestigious university, go to meetings with the country's biggest business leaders. What I want now is for my narrative to be a help to others, and aid them in avoiding the pitfalls I have taken. There are times, though, when I feel like I will never understand, and always be deep in the red, no good to anyone.

As for what transpired after my meeting with Mr. Barraine? That particular time is hard to recall. They say that when the officials came, I was sitting in a chair in his office, and wouldn't move. For weeks after, I wouldn't speak or do anything. They had to bring me to a hospital and take care of me. I remember I was there when my mother came, and told me she was sorry for everything, and reminded me that while it is very easy to fall into the red, it can be very difficult to climb back out. Some of the underwriters of my education also came, and reminded me about the opportunities I could still have if I remembered my responsibilities and pulled myself together. But mostly I just sat there, doing nothing, except falling ever deeper into the red.

I thought about the negative scores I had given people in my life, and the friends I had voted out of my peer network, and how one time my mother had wanted to talk about my father, and I had slammed the door. But mostly I thought about the reason this all started, which is the one thing I haven't talked about, because to be truthful it still feels so weird.

This was in seventh grade, when they introduced an autistic boy into our school, as part of an experimental program. He was seriously autistic, so nobody wanted to be near him, because he would do things like grabbing you when you didn't expect. But there were some people he liked, and one of those people was me.

Then one day, some other kids were doing something to the autistic boy, and suddenly he started to howl and ran across the lunchroom, throwing his arms around me from behind. I don't know what the other kids had done. All I knew is, the autistic boy was hugging me in a way where I couldn't breathe. That was the day everything changed. Because people began to panic and shout, as there had been prior incidents. And the more they shouted, the harder the boy squeezed, until my head began to go dark.

But instead of struggling, I whispered to the boy, and reached up a hand and stroked his arm. After a while he loosened his grip. I felt very calm. And I turned around and hugged him back. It surprised everyone. When the boy's parents saw the videos that had been taken, they started a Pro-Vote campaign on my behalf, even though the boy had to go into an institution because of what he did. And the campaign took off, and before I knew it, the Pro votes came in, millions of votes from around the world. And that was what made my holoscore go so deep into the green, and what made me seem like such a promising student, and why so many investors wanted to put their money into my Child Development Program. And that was why everything turned out the way it did.

But what I remembered, while I was lying all that time without moving, was how it actually felt, when the autistic boy grabbed me. How I was so scared I wanted to scream. But I was also so scared I couldn't scream. He was so much bigger than me, and he wouldn't let go, and people were screaming about how I might die. I couldn't even say why I did what I did. It was like there was a different person inside me, who lifted up a finger and gently brushed his hands. When he responded, I knew what to do, and I stood and put my arms around him. Everyone became silent. I remember him shaking, and making puffing noises, like a cat when it can't stop sneezing. Then he began to quiet down, and I stroked my hands along his back, and put my cheek against his cheek. It was like there was no one else. It was like there was just us two. I felt it go through him, a kind of hum, like a vibration I could feel in my hands. That was when I knew, just by the feel of him breathing—I knew he would be peaceful, this person in my arms.

THE SMOKE OF GOLD IS GLORY
Scott Lynch

Scott Lynch (www.scottlynch.us) was born in St. Paul, Minnesota in 1978. He is the author of the World Fantasy Award-nominated *The Lies of Locke Lamora* and its sequels, and his short fiction has appeared in a number of anthologies. In 2016, Scott traded the plains of Wisconsin for the hills and valleys of Massachusetts and married his longtime partner, fellow SF/F writer Elizabeth Bear.

SAIL NORTH FROM the Crescent Cities, three days and nights over the rolling black sea, and you will surely find the tip of the Ormscap, the fire-bleeding mountains that circle the roof of the world like a scar. There in the shallows, where the steam rises in a thousand curtains, you'll see a crumbling dock, and from that dock you can still walk into the scraps and tatters of a blown-apart town that was never laid straight from the start. It went up on those rocks layer after layer, like ten eyeless drunks scraping butter onto the same piece of bread.

The southernmost Ormscap is still called the Dragon's Anvil. The town below the mountain was once called Helfalkyn.

Not so long ago it was an enchantment and a refuge and a prison, home to the most desperate thieves in all the breathing world. Not so long ago, they all cried out in their sleep for the mountain's treasure. One part in three of every gleaming thing that has ever been drawn or dredged or delved from the earth, that's what the scholars claimed.

That's what the dragon carried there and brooded over, the last dragon that will ever speak to any of us.

Now the town's empty. The wind howls through broken windows in roofless walls. If you licked the stones of the mountain for a thousand days, you wouldn't taste enough precious metal to gild one letter in a monk's manuscript.

Helfalkyn is dead, and the dragon is dead, and the treasure might as well have never existed.

I ought to know. I'm the man who lost a bet, climbed the Anvil, and helped break the whole damn thing.

I tell this story once a year, on Galen's Eve, and no other. Some of you have heard it before. I take it kindly that you've come to hear it again. Like any storyteller, I'd lie about the color of my eyes to my own mother for half a cup of ale-dregs, but you'll affirm to all the new faces that to this one tale I add no flourishes. I deepen no shadows and gentle no sorrows. I tell it as it was, one night each year, and on that night I take no coin for it.

Heed me now. Gather in as you will. Jostle your neighbors. Spill your drinks. Laugh early at the bad jokes and stare at me like clubbed sheep for all the good ones, and I shall care not, for I am armored by long experience. But this bowl of mine, if we are to part as friends, must catch no copper or silver, I swear it. Tonight pay me in food, or drink, or simple attention.

With that, let me commence to tell:

FIRST, HOW I FELL IN WITH THE CHARMING LUNATICS WHO ENDED MY ADVENTURING CAREER

IT WAS THE Year of the Bent-Wing Raven, and everything went sour for me right around the backside of autumn.

One week I was in funds, the next I was conspicuously otherwise. I'm still not sure what happened. Bad luck, worse judgment, enemy action, sorcery? Hardly matters. When you're on the ground getting kicked in the face, one pair of boots looks very much like another.

I have long been candid about the nature of my previous employment. Those of you who find this frank exchange of purely historical details in any way disturbing are of course welcome to say a word or two to Galen on my behalf, and I shall thank you, as I doubt an old thief can really collect such a thing as too many prayers. In those days I would have laughed. Young thieves think luck and knee-joints are meant to last forever.

I started the summer by lifting four ivory soul lanterns from the Temple of the Cloud Gardens in Port Raugen. Spent a few weeks carving decent wooden replicas and painting them with a white cream wash, first. I made the switch at night, walked out unnoticed, presented the genuine articles to my client, and set sail on the morning tide as a very rich man. I washed up in Hadrinsbirk a few weeks later with a pounding headache and a haunting memory of money. No matter. I made the acquaintance of an uncreatively guarded warehouse and appropriated a crate of the finest Sulagar steel padlocks. I sold the locks and their keys to a corner-cutting merchants' guild, then sold wax impressions of the keys to their bitter rivals for twice that sum. So much for Hadrinsbirk. I cast off for the Crescent Cities.

There I guised myself as a gentleman of leisure, and wearing that mask I investigated prospects and rumors, looking for easy marks. Alas, the easy marks must have migrated in a flock. I took the edge off my disappointment by indulging all the routine questionable habits, and that's when the bad time crept up behind me. The gaming tables turned. Easy credit went extinct. All the people who owed me favors locked their doors, and all the people I needed to avoid were thick in the streets. Before I knew it I was sleeping in a stable.

I stretched a point of courtesy then, and slipped an appeal to the local practitioners of my trade. My entreaty was coolly received. There was a sudden plague of honesty in the land, and schemes simply weren't hatching, or so they claimed. Nobody needed to arrange a kidnapping, or a vault infiltration, or have a barrow desecrated.

This was a bind, and I confess that I partly deserved it. For all my hard-earned professional fame, I was still an outsider, and doubtless should have paid my respects to the thieves of the Crescent Cities a few weeks earlier. Now they were wise to me and watchful for the sorts of jobs I might pull on my own. The wind was sharpening, my belly was flat, and my belt was running out of notches. I needed money! Yet honest employment was out of the question too, as word of my presence spread. Who would make a caravan guard of Tarkaster Crale, bane of a dozen caravan runs? Who'd set Crale the Cracksman to stand guard over a money-changer's strongboxes? Awkward! I couldn't beg for so much as an afternoon hauling wash-buckets behind a tavern. A larcenist of my caliber and experience? Any sensible local thief would assume it had to be a cover for some grand scheme, which they would have to interrupt.

It's hard to be poor at the best of times, but in my old line of work, to be poor and famous—gods have mercy.

I had no prospects. No friends. I could have won an empty-pockets contest against anyone within a hundred miles. All I had left was youth and a sense of pride that damn near glowed like banked coals.

These were the circumstances that led me to seriously consider, for the first time in my life, the words of the Helfalkyn Wormsong.

I can see some of you nodding, those of you without much hair left. You heard it, too. Nobody repeats it these days, the fortunes of Helfalkyn having diminished so profoundly. But in my youth there wasn't a child in any land who didn't know the Wormsong by heart. It was a message from the dragon itself, the last and greatest of them, the Shipbreaker, the Sky Tyrant. Glimraug.

It went like this:

> *High-reachers, bright-dreamers, bright-enders,*
> *Match riddlesong, venom, and stone.*
> *Carry ending and eyes up the Anvil,*
> *Carry glorious gleanings back home.*

Isn't that a fine little thing?

Friends, that's how a dragon says, "Why not climb up my impenetrable treasure mountain and let me kill you?"

From the first day Glimraug claimed the Anvil, it took pains to welcome and entice us. Don't mistake that for a benevolent and universal hospitality, for of course Glimraug raided half the earth and spread dismay for centuries. No dragon ever deigned to smelt its own gold. But even as Glimraug fell on caravans and broke castles like eggs, it tolerated a small community of outcasts and lunatics in the shadow of its home. Once in a rare while it would even seize someone and haul them to the crest of the Anvil, to make a show of its growing treasure, then set them free to sing the Wormsong louder than ever.

Thousands of people accepted the dragon's invitation over the years. None of them lived. Some very canny customers in that crowd, too, great heroes, names that still ring out, but none of them were ever quite a match for riddlesong, venom, and stone. Still, for every one that dreamed the impossible dream and cacked it hard, two more showed up. The Dragon's Anvil was the last roll of the dice for those who'd played their lives out and bet poorly. It was equally attractive to the brilliant, the mad, and the desperate. I was at least two of those three, and by that simple majority the vote carried. I was on a ship that night, the *Red Swan*, and I scrubbed decks and greased ropes to pay for my passage to the end of the world.

That's what Helfalkyn looked like when I finally saw it—like the last human habitation thrown down by the last human hands at the far end of some mad priest's apocalypse. The sun was the color of bled-out entrails, edging the hulking mountain, and the bruised light showed me a gallimaufry of dark warrens, leaning houses, and crooked alleys down below. We sailed in through veils of warm breath from the mountain's underwater vents, and the air was perfumed with sulphur.

Many of you must be thinking the same thing I was as I trod the creaking timbers of the Helfalkyn docks—how did such a place ever come to thrive? The answer lies at the intersection of greed and perversity. Here came the adventurers, the suicides, the mad ones intent on climbing the mountain and somehow stealing the treasure of ten thousand lifetimes. But were they eager to go all at once? Of course not. Some needed to lay their plans, or drink their brains out, or otherwise work themselves into fits of enthusiasm. Some waited days, or weeks, or months. Some never went at all, and clung to Helfalkyn forever, aging sourly in the shadows of failed ambition. After the adventurers came the provisioners, of inebriation and games and rooms and warm companionship, and the town became a sputtering, improvised machine for sifting the last scraps of currency from those who would surely never need them again. The captains of the few ships that made the Helfalkyn run had a cordial arrangement with the town. They would haul anyone there for the price of a few days' labor, and charge a small fortune in real valuables for passage back to the world. Any newcomer trapped in Helfalkyn would thus be forced to try the mountain, or toil for years to the great advantage of the town's masters if they ever wanted to escape.

Mountebanks swarmed as I and a few other neophytes examined the town warily. The junk-mongers outnumbered us three to one. "Don't breathe the dragon-air without taking a draught of Cleansing Miracle Water," shouted a bearded man, waving a stone pitcher of what was clearly urine and mud. "Look around! The dragon-air gives you clisters, morphew, wretched megrims, and the flux like a black molasses! Have the advantage when you challenge the Anvil! Protect yourself at a fair price!"

I did look around, and it seemed that none of the other natives were downing miracle mudpiss to keep their lungs supple, so I judged none of us likely to perish of the megrims. I moved on, and was offered enchanted blades, enchanted boots, enchanted cheese, and enchanted handfuls of mountain rock, all for a fair price. How fortunate I felt, to discover such simple generosity and potent magic in the meanest of all places! Even if I'd had money, I would have reciprocated this cordial selflessness by refusing to take advantage of it. Two gracious humanitarians of Helfalkyn then attempted to pick my pockets; the first I merely spurned with a scolding. The second mysteriously incurred a broken wrist and lost his own purse at the same time, for in those days my fingers were considerably faster than the contents of my skull. I worried then about constables, or at least mob-fellowship against outsiders, but I quickly realized that the only law in Helfalkyn was to win or stay out of the way. No more creeping fingers tried my pockets after that.

Cheered by the acquisition of a few coins, I hunted for a place to spend them and tame my tyrant stomach. Ale dens of varying foulness offered themselves as I strolled, and street hawkers made pitches even less appetizing than the prospect of Cleansing Miracle Water. Sooner rather than later, for while Helfalkyn was encysted with diversions it was not terribly vast, its twisted streets naturally funneled me to the steps of the grandest structure in town, Underwing Hall. Here would be food, though the smell wafting out past the cold-eyed guards beside the doors promised nothing delicate.

Outside it was morning, but inside lay a perpetual smoky twilight. The entrance hall was decorated with bloody teeth and the slumped bodies of those who'd recently had them knocked out of their mouths. Porters, working with the bored air of long practice, were levering these unfortunates one by one out a side entrance. I saw more fisticuffs underway at several tables and balconies in the cavernous space. Given the relaxation of the door guards, I wondered what it took to rouse their interference. The servers, stout men and women all, wore ill-fashioned armor as they heaved platters about, and the kitchen windows were barred with iron. Rough hands thrust forth tankards and wine-bottles like castle defenders dispensing projectiles through murder-holes. Though I'd enjoyed some elevated company in my career, this crowd was still an intimately familiar sort, comprised of equal parts stupid, cruel, cunning, blasphemous, and greedy faces. Every corner of the known world had skimmed the scum of its scum to populate Helfalkyn. I resolved to step warily and attract no attention until I learned the order of things.

"CRALE!" bellowed someone from a balcony overhead.

Ah, the feeling of receiving unsought the attention of a greatroom full of brawlers and carousers. Heads turned, conversations quieted, and even some of the servers halted to stare at me.

"Tarkaster Crale?" came a disbelieving shout.

"Bullshit. Tarkaster Crale's a tall handsome bastard," muttered a woman.

I was about to say something that would have, in all candor, improved nobody's situation, when I was seized from above and hauled into the air. The sheer power of my appropriator was startling, and I kicked helplessly as I was spun a disagreeable number of feet above the stones of the tavern floor. My assailant hung from a balcony rail by one arm, and dandled me with the other. I prepared fresh unhelpful commentary and reached for the knives in my belt, and then I saw the man's face.

"Your highness!" I whispered.

"Don't give me the courtesies of cushion-sitters unless you want to get dropped, Crale." Still, there was warmth in his voice as he heaved me over the railing and set me on a stool as easily as anyone here might hang a tunic on a drying-line. Here was a man with shoulders as broad as a boat's rowing-bench and arms harder than the oars. He was dark of skin and darker of hair, with gray setting some claim to his temples and beard, and all the lines in his face had been carved by either the sea-winds or the wild grin he wore when facing them. The other patrons of Underwing Hall rapidly lost interest in me, for I had been claimed for the table of none other than my old adventuring companion, Brandgar Never-Throned, King-on-the-Waves, Lord of the Ajja.

Like Helfalkyn, the King-on-the-Waves is little more than a story these days, though it's a good one and an Ajja skald who'll sing it for you is worth the asking price. All the Ajja clans had kings and queens, and keeps and lands and suchwise, but once a generation their mystics would read the signs and proclaim a King-on-the-Waves. This lucky bitch or bastard would be gifted a stout ship to crew with sworn companions, and set sail across the Ajja realms, calling upon cousin monarchs, receiving full courtesy and hospitality. Then they'd usually be asked to undertake some messy piece of questing that would end in unguessable amounts of death and glory. Thus charged was a King-on-the-Waves, to hold no lands, but to slay monsters, retrieve lost treasures, lift curses, and so forth, until they and all their companions had met some horrible, beautiful fate on behalf of the Ajja people. Brandgar was the last so-named, nor is there like to be another soon, for he and his companions were uncommonly good at the job and left few messes for others to clean up. I had fallen in with them on two occasions and done some reaving, all for the best of causes, I assure you, though I am sworn to utter no details. Even my sleeping sense of honor sometimes rolls over in bed and kicks. Onward!

"There's fortune in this. We had not thought to see an old friend here." Brandgar settled himself back on his own stool, over the half-eaten remains of some well-fatted animal I couldn't identify, sauced with sharp-smelling mustard and brown moonberry preserves. "What say you, Mikah?"

I gave a start, for sitting there in the darkness at the rear of the balcony was a shape I hadn't previously noticed. Yes, indeed, here was Mikah King-Shadow, rarely seen unless they chose the time and place. Mikah, my better in all the crafts of larceny, who could pass for man or woman in a hundred disguises, but in their own skin was simply Mikah, good friend and terrible enemy. They leaned into the light, and it seemed the years had not touched that lean angular face or the cool gray eyes that smiled though the lips below them never so much as twitched.

"Friend Crale has a hungry look, lord."

"They're in fashion hereabouts." Brandgar waved casually to the remains of his morning fast-breaking, and I fell to with a grateful nod. "Have you been here long, Crale?"

"I'm fresh-landed as a fisherman's catch," I said between bites of rich greasy something. I did not scruple to avoid licking my fingers, for I knew the table manners of a King-on-the-Waves were shaped for the tossing deck of a longship. "And I thank you for the sharing. This latest chapter in the book of my life has been writ mostly on the subject of empty bellies."

"And empty pockets?" said Mikah.

"I have offended some power unknown to me." I took a bone and greedily sucked the marrow of some animal also unknown to me. "An ill fate has swept me here to play a desperate hand."

"No," said Brandgar, and there was that damned grin I mentioned, a follow-me-over-the-cliff grin. "A kind fate has joined friend to friends. Give us your skills. We mean to climb the Dragon's Anvil and crown our lives with the glory of a treasure claimed. The Wormsong bids us to carry ending and eyes, eh? Ending we carry in our steel. Eyes we still need! You were ever a fine and cunning lookout."

"When do you intend to go?"

"Tonight."

I dropped my bone then, and wiped my mouth with a scuffed jacket-cuff. I'm not best pleased to shine a light on my hesitation, friends, but I vowed to give every truth of this tale as much illumination as it's due. I had gone to Helfalkyn in a desperate fever, yes, and by happy fate found two of the few people alive whom I might have chosen if given my pick of fellows. Still, with the weight of satisfying meat in my belly for the first time in recent memory, I found myself less than eager to set the hour of my doom so close.

"I had thought to spend a few days preparing myself," I began, "and learning whatever useful information might be—"

"You're no craven," rumbled Brandgar. "Yet any man might feel the sting of fear when he sits in comfort and thinks of peril. Come, I know you would never run from a duty bound in honest wager! Lay a simple bet with me. Should I win, join us tonight. Else we wait three days, and you may seek whatever 'useful information' you like before we climb."

Now here was a salve to all my several consciences, gentle listeners, by which I could keep faith with useful companions and still have time to ease myself into a frightful enterprise. I asked the means of the wager.

"See the attic-skorms that cling high upon the wall there?"

Gazing across the wide tavern, squinting past smoke and flickering brazier-light, I did indeed see a pair of the dark-scaled lizards motionless below the ceiling. Arm-length and even-tempered, attic-skorms creep down from the mountains in all the northern countries, and are either eaten as food or tolerated as rat-catchers.

"The wager is this. Long have those two sat unmoving; sooner or later one of them will doubtless creep down in search of food. If the dark one on your side moves soonest, we go in three days. If the red-rippled one on my side moves, we go tonight. Is it sealed?"

"My oath," I said, and we sat at ease to watch this yawn-inducing spectacle unfold. This was not as odd as it might seem, for out upon the waves the Ajja will pass the time in friendly wagers on anything that catches the eye, from which way gulls will fly to which sailor on another ship will next use and empty a dung-bucket over the side. I have eased fierce boredom with bets on some ludicrous trifles in my time.

Not five heartbeats after I spoke, the red-rippled skorm on the king's side pulled in its legs. It didn't so much climb down as fall directly off the wall like a grieving suicide in an old romantic tale.

I sputtered without dignity while Brandgar and Mikah laughed. Then there was a flash of sliver light in the shadows where the king's choice had plunged; a thin mist rose into the air, a mist I recognized.

"No!" I shouted, "that was no honest bet! That was a skin-shifting sorceress of low moral character who is—"

"Standing right behind you," said Gudrun Sky-Daughter, appearing in silver light and mist. She ruffled my hair affectionately, for yes, I still had some in those days. Hers was seven braided spills of copper, now lined with the color of iron like her king's, and her round flushed face was all mischief and mirth.

"That was unworthy," I scowled.

"That was fair as anything," said Brandgar. "For if your eyes had been working as a fine and cunning lookout's should, you'd have seen that there was only one beast upon the wall until a moment before my proposal. Come, Crale. We need you, and you won't find better company if you wait here a hundred years! This is fate."

I partly hated him for being right, and was partly thrilled that he was. A warrior-king, a master thief, and a sorceress. Great gods, hope was a terrible and anxious thing! They were indeed allies that had as much chance on the Dragon's Anvil as any mortal born. I pondered my recent poverty, and pondered the treasure.

"I have never in my life behaved with any particular wisdom," I said at last. "It would make little sense to start now."

"Ha!" Brandgar pounded the table, stood, and leaned out over the balcony. His voice boomed out, echoing from the rafters and startling the raucous commotion below into instant attention. "HEAR ME! Hight Brandgar, son of Orthild and Erika, King-on-the-Waves! Tonight we go! Tonight we climb the Dragon's Anvil! We, the Never-Throned, the King-Shadow, the Sky-Daughter, and the famous Tarkaster Crale! We go to claim a treasure, so take this pittance! Drink to us, and wait for the word! Tonight we break a legend!"

Brandgar opened a purse, and shook out a stream of silver into the crowds below, where drinkers cheered and convulsed and clutched at his largesse. Gods! If I'd had even that much money just a week before, I'd never have left the Crescent Cities. As the near-riot for the coins subsided, a voice rose in ragged chant, and was joined by more and steadier voices, until nearly everyone in Underwing Hall was gleefully serenading us, a single verse over and over again:

> *Die rich, dragon's dinner!*
> *Play well the game that has no winner!*
> *Climb the mountain, greedy sinner!*
> *Die rich, dragon's dinner!*

The chant had the sound of a familiar ritual that had been much-practiced. I liked it not a whit.

NEXT, HOW WE PROVED OUR RESOLVE AND BROKE A FEW HEARTS ALONG THE WAY

I DOZED FITFULLY most of the day, in a hired chamber guarded by some of Gudrun's arcane mutterings. Terrified or not, I was still an experienced man of fortune and knew to try and catch a bit of rest when it was on offer.

At dusk the moons rose red, like burnished shields hanging on the wall of the brandywine sky. The mountain loomed, crowned with strange lights that never came from any celestial sphere, and it seemed I could hear the hiss and rumble of the stone as if it were a hungry thing. I shuddered and checked my gear for the tenth time. I had come light from the Crescent Cities, in simple field leathers, dark jacket, and utility belts. I carried a sling and a sparse supply of grooved stones. My longest daggers were whetted, and I wore them openly as I headed for the northeastern side of town with my companions, pretending to swagger. Denizens of Helfalkyn watched from every street, every rooftop, every window, some jeering, some singing, but most standing quietly or hoisting cups to the air, as one might toast a prisoner on the way to the gallows.

Brandgar wore a fitted coat of plate under a majestically ragged gray cloak with particolored patchings from numerous cuts and burns over the years; he claimed it was as good as enchanted and that he had sweated most of his considerable luck into it. Gudrun had never offered a professional opinion on this, so far as I knew. She was as scruffy as ever, a study in comfortable disrepute. Strange charms and wooden containers rattled on leather cords at her breast, and she bore a pair of rune-inscribed drums on her back. Mikah was lightly dressed in silks and leather bracers, moving with their familiar fluid grace, concealing their real thoughts behind their even more familiar mask of calculating bemusement with the world. They carried a few coils of sea-spider silk and some climbing gear wrapped in muffling cloth. However detached they seemed, I knew they were a fanatic about the selection and care of their tools, more painstaking than any other burglar I had ever worked with, and any professional jealousy I might have felt was rather drowned in comfort at their preparedness.

The only real oddity was the extra weapon Brandgar carried. His familiar spear Cold-Thorn had a bare and gleaming tip, and its shaft was worn with use. The other spear looked heavy and new, and its point was wrapped in layers of tightly-bound leather like a practice weapon. When asked about this, Brandgar smiled and said, "Extra spear, extra thief. Aren't I growing cautious in my old age?"

At the northeast edge of Helfalkyn lay our first ascent, an unassuming path of dusty dark stone that was marked by a parallel series of lines, half a foot deep, slashed across the walkway. Though time and weather had softened the edges of these lines, it was not hard to see them for what they were, the claw-furrows of a dragon. An unequivocal message to anyone who wanted to step over them. I suddenly wished I could forget our mutual agreement to go up the Anvil with clear heads, and find something irresponsible to pour down my throat.

One by one we crossed the dragon's mark, your nervous narrator lastly and slowly. After that we walked up in silence save for the occasional rattle of gear or boot-scuff on stone. As the odors of the town and the harbor steam faded below us, the indigo edges of evening settled overhead and stars lit one by one like distant lanterns. It would be a clear night atop the mountain, and I wondered if we would be there to appreciate it. This first part of the climb was not hard, perhaps three quarters of an hour with the switchback path offering nothing more than agreeable exercise. As the light sank the way roughened and narrowed, and when full dark came on it ceased to be a path and became a proper climb, up a sloping black rock face of crags and broken columns. Rugged as it was, this was the only face of the Anvil that could be approached at all. Brandgar shook Cold-Thorn and muttered something to Gudrun, who muttered something in return. A moment later the tip of Cold-Thorn flared with gentle but far-reaching light, and by that pale gleam we made our way steadily up.

"What happened to everyone else?" I asked on a whim during one of our brief pauses. When last I'd sojourned in the Never-Throned's company, he'd had eight of his original boon companions yet unslain, enough to crew his ship and drink up truly heroic quantities of something irresponsible whenever they paid call to a landed king or queen. "Asmira? Lorus? Valdis?"

"Asmira was pitched from the mast during a storm," said Brandgar. "Lorus challenged a vineyard-wight to a game of draughts and kept it occupied 'til dawn. It killed him in its fury just before the first light of the sun slew it in turn. Valdis died in the battle against the Skull Priests at Whitefall."

"What about Rondu Silverbeard?"

"The Silverbeard died in bed," chuckled Gudrun.

"Under a bed, to be precise," added Mikah. "The defenders dropped it on us at the siege of Vendilsfarna."

"I hope our friends know joy in the Fields of Swords and Roses," I said, for that is where worthy Ajja are meant to go when they die, and if it's true I suppose it keeps all of our own heavens and hells a bit quieter. "Though I hope I give no offense if I wish we had a few more of them with us tonight."

"They died to bring us here," said Brandgar. "They died to teach us what we needed to know. They died to show us the way, and when our numbers dwindled and our duties grew lean, we three knew where we were called." Gudrun and Mikah nodded with that sage fatalism I had long lamented in my Ajja friends, and though my presence on that mountain reinforced my assertion that I had never in my life behaved with any particular wisdom, neither was I boorish enough to voice my concerns with their philosophy. Perhaps they had always mistaken this tact for fellow-feeling. No, I admit I could fight with abandon when cornered, but when I could see a meeting with Death obviously scrawled in the ledger, I always preferred to break the appointment. How any of the Ajja ever survived long enough to span the seas and populate their holdings remains a mystery of creation.

We resumed our climb, and soon heaved ourselves over the edge of a cleft promontory where a hemispherical stone ceiling, open to the night like a theater, overhung a darkness that led into the depths of the mountain. The wind had risen and the air was sharp against my skin. We gazed out for a moment at the lights of the town far below us, and the white-foamed blackness of the sea capped with mists, and the hair-thin line of sunset that still clung to the horizon. Then rose a scraping, shuffling noise behind us, and Brandgar turned with Cold-Thorn held high.

Red lights glowed in answer, throbbing like a pulse-beat within the cavern. Whether they were lanterns or conjurations I could not discern, but in their rising illumination I saw an arched door wide enough to admit three wagons abreast. I wondered whether the dragon had left itself ample room in setting this passage, or if it could tolerate a tight squeeze. Unhelpful conjecture! In the space between us and the door stood two straight lines of pillars, and beside each pillar stood the shape of a man or woman.

Brandgar advanced, and the man-shape nearest us held up a hand. "Bide," it whispered in a hoarse sickbed voice. "None need enter."

"Unless you propose to show us a more convenient door," said Brandgar, "this path is for us."

"Time remains to turn." There was enough light now to see that the hoarse speaker and all of its companions were unclothed, emaciated, and caked with filth. A paleness shone upon their breasts, where each on their left side bore a plate of something like dull nacre, sealed to the edges of the bloodless surrounding flesh by the pulsing segments of what seemed to be a milk-white centipede. The white segments passed into the body like stitches and emerged in a narrow, twitching tail at the back of the neck. From these extremities hung threads, gleaming silver, connecting each man or woman to a pillar. Atop those, in delicate brass recesses, pulsed fist-sized lumps of flesh. I'd been near enough death to know a human heart by sight, and felt a tight horror in my own chest. "The master grudges you nothing. You may still turn and go home."

"Our thanks to your master." Brandgar set his leather-wrapped spear down and spun Cold-Thorn, casting about a light like the sun's rays scattering from rippling water. "We are here on an errand of sacred avarice, and will not be halted."

Some enchanted guardians never know when to shut up, but this one had a reasonable sense of occasion, so it nodded and proceeded directly to hostilities. Each of the heart-wraiths took up handfuls of dust, and in their clenched fists this dust turned to swords. Eight of them closed on four of us, and with a merry twirl of my daggers I joined most of my companions in making royal asses of ourselves.

It was plain to Mikah, Brandgar, and myself, as veterans of too many sorcerer's traps and devices to enumerate here, that the weakness of these creatures had to be the glittering threads that bound them to their heart-pillars. Dodging their attacks, we wove a dance of easy competence and with our weapons of choice swung down nearly simultaneously for the threads of our targets. What it felt like, to me, was swinging for dandelion fuzz and hitting granite. I found myself on the ground with my right hand spasming in cold agony, and was barely able to seize my wits and roll aside before a blade struck sparks where my head had just been.

"I had thought," muttered Brandgar (shaking Cold-Thorn angrily, for either his rude health or some quality of the spear had let him keep it when Mikah and I had been rendered one-handed), "the obvious striking point—"

"So did we all," groaned Mikah.

"Speak for your cloddish selves," shouted Gudrun, who had cast lines of emerald fire upon the stones, where they flashed and coiled like snakes in response to the movements of her hands, and were holding several of the heart-wraiths at bay.

I sidestepped a new assault, rebalanced my left-hand dagger, and judged the distance to the nearest pillar-top heart. If the threads had been a distraction, the weakness of the magic animating our foes surely had to lie there. I was not left-handed, but I threw well, and my blade was a gratifying blur that arrived dead on target, only to be smacked aside by one thrown with even greater deftness by Mikah, aimed at the same spot.

"Damnation, Crale, it takes impressive skill to fail so precisely!" said the King-Shadow as they whirled and wove between onrushing heart-wraiths.

"If I live to tell this story in taverns I shall amend this part to our advantage," I said, though you apprehend, my friends, that I have done otherwise and will sleep soundly in my conscience tonight. Mikah found a fresh dagger and made another cast, this time without my interference. The blade struck true at the visibly unprotected heart, and rebounded as though from an inch of steel. We all swore vicious oaths. Magic does from time to time so boil one's piss.

Mikah rolled one of the silk ropes off their shoulders, and with a series of cartwheels and flourishes deployed it as a weapon, lashing and entangling the nearest heart-wraiths, quick-stepping between them like the passage of a mad tailor's needle. I had no such recourse, and my right hand was still useless. I scrambled across the stones, swept up a dropped blade in my left hand once more, and whirled toward the two wraiths assailing me. "Hold," I cried. "Hold! I find I'm not so eager for treasure as I was. Would your master yet give me leave to climb back down?"

"We are here to slay or dissuade, not to punish." The heart-wraith before me lowered its weapon. "Living with yourself is your own affair. You may depart."

"I applaud the precision and dedication of your service," I said, and as the heart-wraith began to turn from me, no doubt to join the fray against my companions, I buried my dagger in its skull with an overhand blow. The segments of the insectoid thing threaded into its abdomen shook, and something like creamy clotted bile poured from the mouth and ears of what had once been a man. It collapsed.

"That was a low trick," rasped the other heart-wraith, and came for me. I wrenched my dagger free, which wafted a sickly vinegar odor into my face, and waved my hands again.

"Hold," said I. "It's true that I'm a gamesome and unscrupulous rogue, but I feared you were playing me false. Are you really prepared to let me go in good faith?"

"Despite your unworthy—"

I never learned the specifics of my unworthiness, as I took the opportunity to lunge and sink my dagger into its left eye. It toppled beside its fellow and vomited more disgusting yellow soup. I am the soul of pragmatism.

"Enough!"

I saw that only one heart-wraith remained, and before my eyes the sword in its hand returned to dust. I had slain two, Gudrun had scorched two with her fire-serpents, and Mikah had at last bound their pair tightly enough to finish them with pierced skulls. Brandgar had beaten one of his foes to a simple pulp, breaking its limbs and impaling it through the bony plate where its heart had once been. As for those hearts, I saw at a glance that those atop seven of the eight pillars had shriveled. Dark stains were running down the columns beneath them.

"You have proven your resolve," rasped the final heart-wraith. "The master bids you onward."

The eerie red lights of the cavern dimmed, and with the crack and rattle of great mechanisms the arched doors fell open. Brandgar advanced on the surviving heart-wraith, spear held out before him, until it rested gently on the white plate set into the thing's chest.

"Onward we move," said Brandgar, "but how came you to the service of the dragon?"

"I sought the treasure and failed, three score years past. You may yet join me, when you fail. If enough of your flesh remains the master may choose to knit watch-worms into the cavern of your heart, so be advised... to consider leaving as little flesh as possible."

"After tonight your master Glimraug will have no need of us." Smoothly and without preamble, Brandgar drove his spear into the wraith's chest. "Nor any need of you."

"Thank... you..." the wraith whispered as it fell.

"Did we amuse you in our stumblings, sister Sky-Daughter?" said Mikah, massaging their right hand. My own seemed to be recovering as well.

"Spear-carriers and knife-brains love to overthink a problem," laughed the sorceress. "Feeds your illusionary sense of finesse. The truly stupid and the truly wise would have started with simply bashing at the damn things, but since you're somewhere in between, you tried to kill everything else in the room first. Good joke. This dragon knows how adventurers think." She looked up at the mountain and sighed. "Tonight could be everyone's night to stumble, ere we're through."

THIRD, HOW I PUT MY ASS ON THE LINE AND HOW WE SOUGHT THE SONG BENEATH THE SONG

PAST THE ARCHED doors we found ourselves in a vaulted hall, lit once more by pale scarlet fires that drifted in the air like puffs of smoke. For a moment I thought we stood in an armory, and then I saw the jagged holes and torn plates in every piece displayed, tier on tier and rank on rank, nearly to the ceiling. Broken blades and shattered spears, shields torn like parchment-sheets, mail shirts pierced and burnt and fouled with unknown substances—here were the fates of all our predecessors memorialized, obviously. The dragon's boast.

"Perhaps a part-truth," responded Mikah, when I said as much. "Surely all dragons are braggarts after a fashion. But consider how this one seems determined to play fair with its challengers. The ascent up the mountain, with its gradual reduction of ease. The guardians at the door, willing to forgive and forget. Now this museum show for the faint-hearted. At every step our host invites the insufficiently motivated to quit before they waste more of anyone's time."

Proud to be numbered among the sufficiently motivated, no doubt, I followed my companions through the dragon's collection, uneasily noting its quality. Here were polished Sulagar steel breastplates and black Harazi swords of the ten thousand folds. Here were gem-studded pauldrons of ageless elven-silver, and gauntlets of sky iron that glowed faintly with sorcery, and all of these things had clearly been as useful as an underwater fart against the fates that had overtaken their wielders. At the far end of the hall lay another pair of great arched doors, and nested into one like a passage for pets was a door more suited to those of us not born as dragons. On this door lay a sigil that I knew too well, and I seized Brandgar by his cloak before he could touch it.

"That is the seal of Melodia Marus, the High Trapwright of Sendaria," said I, "and I've had several professional disagreements with her. Or, more precisely, the mechanisms she devises for the vaults and offices of her clients."

"I know her work by reputation," said Mikah. "It seems Glimraug is one of those clients."

"She's the reason I once spent three months unconscious in Korrister." I twitch at the memory, friends, but not all of one's ventures can end in good fortune, as we have seen. "And six weeks in a donjon in Port Raugen. And why I only have eight toes."

"Another fair warning," said Gudrun. "A frightful spectacle for all comers, then a more specific omen for those professionally inclined to thievery."

"We have two master-burglars to test our way," said Brandgar, who seemed more cheerful with every danger and warning of greater danger. "And if this woman's creations were perfect surely she'd have more than two of Crale's toes by now."

The craft of trap-finding is much sweat and tedium, with only the occasional thrill of accident or narrow escape, and we spent the next hour absorbed in its practice. All the stairs and corridors in that part of the dragon's domain were richly threaded with death. Some halls were sized to us and some to the transit of larger things, and these networks of passages were neither wholly parallel nor entirely separate. This was no citadel made for any sensible court, but only a playing field for Glimraug's game, a stone simulacrum of what we would call a true fortress. Up we went floor by floor, past apertures in the walls that spat razor-keen darts, over false floors that gave way to mangling-engines, through cleverly weighted doors that sprang open with crushing force or sealed themselves behind us, barring retreat from some new devilment.

In one particularly narrow hall both Mikah and myself had a rare bout of all-consuming nincompoopery, and one of us tripped a plate that caused iron shutters to slam down before and behind us, sealing our quartet in a span of corridor little bigger than a rich merchant's water-closet. An aperture on the right-hand wall began to spew a haze at us, the stinging sulphur reek of which was familiar to me from a job I'd once pulled in the mines of Belphoria.

"Dragon's breath," said Brandgar.

"More like the mountain's breath," I cried, and with a creditable leap I braced myself like a bridge across the narrow space and jammed my own posterior firmly into the aperture. The thin cloud of foulness that had seeped into the hall made my eyes water, but was not yet enough to cause us real harm. Though once a few minutes passed and I could no longer maintain such an acrobatic posture, my well-placed buttocks would no longer avail us. "It's what miners call the stink-damp, and it will dispatch us with unsporting speed if I can't hold the seal, so please conjure an exit."

"Fairly done, Crale!" Brandgar waved a hand before his face and coughed. "To save us, you've matched breach to breeches!"

"All men have cracks in their asses," said Gudrun, "but only the boldest puts his ass in a crack."

"Henceforth Crale the Cracksman will be celebrated as Crale the Corksman," said Mikah.

I said many unkind things then, and they continued making grotesque puns which I shall not torture any living soul with, for apparently to ward off a stream of poisonous vapor with one's own ass is to summon a powerful muse of low comedy. Eventually, moving with what I considered an unseemly attitude of leisure, Mikah tried and failed to find any mechanism they might manipulate. Then even the strength of Brandgar's shoulder failed against the iron shutters, and our salvation fell to Gudrun, who broke a rune-etched bone across her knee and summoned what she called a spirit of rust.

"I had hoped to reserve it for some grander necessity," said she. "Though I suppose this is a death eminently worth declining."

In a few moments the spirit accomplished its task, and the sturdy iron shutters on either side were reduced to scatterings of flaked brown dust on the floor. I unbraced with shudders of relief in every part of my frame, and we hurried on our way, kicking up whorls of rust in our wake to mingle with the lethal haze of the broken trap. We moved warily at first, and then with more confidence, for it seemed that we had at last cleared that span of the mountain in which Melodia Marus had expressed her creativity. I do hope that woman died in a terrible accident, or at least lost some toes.

The red lights the dragon had graciously provided before were not to be found here, however, so we climbed through the darkness by the silver gleam of Gudrun's sorcery on our naked weapons. Eventually we could find no more doors or stairs, and so with painful contortions and much use of Mikah's ropes we ventured up a rock chimney. I prayed for the duration of the ascent that we had discovered nothing so mundane as the dragon's privy-shaft.

Eventually we emerged into a cold-aired cavern with a floor of smooth black tiles. Scarlet light kindled upon a far wall, and formed letters in Kandric script (which I had learned to read as a boy, and which the Ajja had long adopted as their preference for matters of trade and accounting), spelling out the Helfalkyn Wormsong.

"As if we might have forgotten it," muttered Mikah. At that instant, a burst of orange fire erupted from the rock chimney we had ascended and burned like a terrible flickering flower twice my height, sealing off our retreat. White-hot lines spilled forth from the ragged crest of this flame, like melted iron from a crucible, and this burning substance swiftly took the aspect of four vaguely human shapes, lean and graceful as dancers. Dance they did, whirling slowly at first but with ever-increasing speed, and then toward us they came, gradually. Inexorably.

"*Seek the song beneath the song,*" rang a voice that touched my heart, a voice that echoed softly around the chamber, a voice blended of every fine thing, neither man's nor woman's but something preternaturally beautiful. To hear it once was to regret all the years of life one had spent not hearing it. Even now, merely telling of it, I can feel warmth at the corners of my eyes, and I am not ashamed. The four fire-dancers glided and spun, singing with voices that started as mere entrancement and became more painfully beautiful with every verse.

> "*The fall of dice in gambling den*
> *The sporting bets of honest men*
> *Will bring them round again, again*
> *To their fairest friend, distraction...*"

It was not the words that were beautiful, for as I recite them here I see none of you crying or falling over. But the voices, the voices! Every hair on my neck stood as though a winter wind had caught me, and I felt the sorcery, sure as I could feel the stones beneath my feet. There was a compulsion weighing on us. The voices drew us on, all of us, cow-eyed, yearning to embrace the gorgeous burning shapes that called with such piercing loveliness. And that was the horror of it, friends, for I knew with some small part of my mind that if I touched one of those things, my skin would go like candle-wax in a bonfire. Still, I couldn't help myself. None of us could. With every moment they sang, the pull of the fire-dancers grew, and our resolve withered.

> *"When beauties into mirrors gaze*
> *Nor look aside for all their days*
> *Until they lose all chance for praise*
> *They wake too late from distraction…"*

I groaned and forced myself backwards, step by step, though it felt like hooks had been set in my heart and it was ten hells to pull against them. I saw Mikah, reeling dizzily, seize Brandgar by the collar.

"Forgive me, lord!" Mikah cuffed their king hard, first across one cheek and then the other. Terrible fury flared for an instant beneath Brandgar's countenance, and then he seemed to remember himself. He clutched at his King-Shadow like a man being pulled away from a pier by a riptide.

"Gudrun," yelled Brandgar, "give us strength against this sorcery, or we are all about to consummate very painful love-affairs!"

Our sorceress, too, had steeled her will. She swung the strange drums from her back, gasping as though she'd just run a great distance, and began to beat a weak, hesitant counter-rhythm in the casual Ajja style:

> *"Heart be stone and eyes be clear*
> *Gudrun sees the puppeteer—*
> *Fire sings eights, Gudrun sevens*
> *This spell your power leavens…"*

I felt the rhythm of Gudrun's drumming like the hoofbeats of cavalry horses, rushing closer to bring aid, and for a moment it seemed the terrible lure of the fire-dancers was fading. Then they spun faster, and glowed fiercely white, and ribbons of smoke curled from their feet as they pirouetted across the tiles. Their voices rose, more lovely than ever, and I choked back a sob, balanced on the edge of madness. Why wasn't I embracing them? What sort of damned fool wouldn't want to hurl himself into that fire?

> *"The fly with hateful flit and bite*
> *The swordsman's feint that wins the fight*
> *The thief enshrouded in the night*
> *The world's true king is distraction..."*

Mikah knelt and punched the tiles, hard, screaming as their knuckles turned red. "I can't think," they cried, "I can't think—what's the song beneath the song?"

> *"The lasting truths poets compose*
> *The lowly tavern juggling-shows*
> *Friends over card games come to blows*
> *You're chained like dogs to distraction..."*

"Fire!" bellowed Brandgar, who was stumbling with the eerie movements of a sleepwalker toward his destined fire-dancer, which was a scant few yards away. "Fire is beneath the song! No, stone! Stone is below the dancers! No, the mountain! The mountain is below us all! Gudrun!"

None of Brandgar's guesses loosened the coils of desire that crushed my chest and my loins and my mind. Gudrun shifted tempo again, and beat desperately at her drums in the stave-rhythm of formal Ajja skaldry:

> *"Now to sixes singing,*
> *Ajja Gudrun knows well:*
> *Hellfire dancer's contest*
> *Can be met with no spell.*
> *Grimly laughs the king-worm,*
> *Mortal toys must burn soon;*
> *Fly now spear of Wave-King,*
> *Breaking stones before ruin!"*

With that, Gudrun fixed herself like a slinger on a battlefield, and pitched her rune-stitched drums straight at Brandgar's head. Their impact, or the repeated shock of such treatment at the hands of his companions, brought him round to himself one final, crucial time.

"The wall," shouted Gudrun, falling to her knees. "The song of distraction is the distraction! The song beneath the song... is beneath the song on the wall!"

Heat stabbed the unprotected skin of my face like a thousand darting needles. Smoke curled now from the sleeves and lapels of my jacket; I breathed the scent of my own burning as my fire-dancer leaned in, looming above me at arm's reach, and I had never known anything more beautiful, and I had never ached for anything more powerfully, and I knew that I was dead.

In the corner of my vision, I glimpsed Brandgar steady on his feet, and with the most desperate rage I ever saw, he charged howling past his grasping fire-dancer and drove the point of Cold-Thorn into the center of the Helfalkyn Wormsong that glowed upon the chamber wall. Rock and dust exploded past him, and revealed there beneath the fall of shattered stone were lines of words glowing coldly blue. Quickly, clumsily, but with true feeling Brandgar sang:

> *"From the death here, all be turning*
> *Still the song, forsake the burning*
> *Chance at mountain-top our earning*
> *Though golden gain is distraction!"*

Instantly the blazing heat roiling the air before my face vanished; the deadly whites and oranges of the fire-dancers became the cool blue of the new song on the wall. An easement washed over me, as though I had plunged my whole body into a cold, clear river. I fell over, exhausted, groaning with pleasure and disbelief at being alive, and I was not alone. We all lay there gasping like idiots for some time, chests heaving like the near-drowned, laughing and sobbing to ourselves as we came to terms with our memories of the fire-song's seduction. The memory did not fade, and has not faded, and to be free of it will be both a wonder and a sorrow until the day I die.

"Well-sung, son of Erika and Orthild," said one of the gentled fire-dancers in a voice nothing like that which had nearly conquered us with delight. "Well-played, daughter of the sky. The gift you leave us is an honor. Your diminishment is an honor."

The blue shapes faded into thin air, leaving only the orange pillar of fire which still poured from the rock-chimney; it seemed our host was done with offering chances to escape. Then I saw that Brandgar was on his feet, staring motionless at a pair of objects, one held in each hand.

The two halves of the broken spear Cold-Thorn.

"Oh, my king," sighed Gudrun, wincing as she stood and retrieved her drums. "Forgive me."

Brandgar stared down at his sundered weapon without answering for some time, then sighed. "There is nothing to forgive, sorceress. My guesses were all bad, and your answer was true."

Slowly, reverently, he set the two parts of Cold-Thorn on the floor.

"Nine-and-twenty years, and it has never failed me. I lay it here as a brother on a battlefield. I give it to the stories to come."

Then he hefted his second spear over his shoulder, though he still refused to unbind the leather from its point, and his old grin appeared like an actor taking a curtain call.

"Bide no more; the night is not forever, and we must climb. With every step, I more desire conversation with the dragon. Come!"

FOURTH, HOW WE PASSED FROM THE BRITTLE BONES OF THE MOUNTAIN TO THE SNOW OF DEATH

SHAKEN BUT GIDDY, we wandered on into many-pillared galleries, backlit by troughs and fountains of incandescent lava that flowed like sluggish water. The heat of it was such that to approach made us mindful of the burning we had only narrowly escaped, and by unspoken agreement we stayed well clear of the stuff. It made soft sounds as it ran, belching and bubbling in the main, but also an unnerving glassy crackling where it touched the edges of its containers, and there darkened to silvery-black.

"A strangeness, even for this place," said Gudrun, brushing her fingers across one of the stone pillars. "There's a resting power here. Not merely in the drawing up of the mountain's boiling blood, which is not wholly natural. There are forces bound and balanced in these pillars, as if they might be set loose by design."

"A new trap?" said Brandgar.

"If so, it's meant to catch half the Dragon's Anvil when it goes," said Gudrun. "Crale won't be shielding us from that with his bottom."

"Is it a present danger to us?" I asked.

"Most likely," said Gudrun.

"I welcome every new course at this feast," said Brandgar. "Come! We were meant to be climbing!"

Up, then, via spiral staircases wide enough for an Ajja longship to slide down, assuming its sails were properly furled. Into more silent galleries we passed, with molten rock to light our way, until we emerged at last beneath a high ceiling set with shiny black panes of glass. Elsewhere they might have been windows lighting a glorious temple or a rich villa, but here they were just a deadness in the stones. A cool breeze blew through this place, and Mikah sniffed the air.

"We're close now," they said. "Perhaps not yet at the summit, but that's the scent of the outside."

This chamber was fifty yards long and half as wide, with a small door on the far side. Curiously enough, there was no obvious passage I could see suited for a dragon. Before the door stood a polished obsidian statue just taller than Brandgar. The man-like figure bore the head of an owl, with its eyes closed, and in place of folded wings it had a fan of arms, five per side, jutting from its upper back. This is a common shape for a *barrow-vardr*, a tomb guardian the Ajja like to carve on those intermittent occasions when they manage to retrieve enough of a dead hero for a burial ceremony. I was not surprised when the lids of its eyes slowly rose, and it regarded us with orbs like fractured rubies.

"Here have I stood since the coming of the master," spoke the statue, "waiting to put you in your grave and then stand as its ornament, King-on-the-Waves."

"The latter would be a courtesy but the former will never happen," said Brandgar, cheerfully setting his wrapped spear down. "Let us fight if we must, though I will lose my temper if you have another song to sing us."

"Black, my skin will turn all harm," said the statue. "Silver skin forfeits the charm."

"Verse is nearly as bad," growled Brandgar. He sprinted at the statue and hurled himself at its midsection, in the manner of a wrestler. I sighed inwardly at this, but you have seen that Brandgar was one part forethought steeped in a thousand parts hasty action, and he was never happier than when he was testing the strength of a foe by offering it his skull for crushing. The ten arms of the *barrow-vardr* spread in an instant, and the two opponents grappled only briefly before Brandgar was hurled twenty feet backward, narrowly missing Gudrun. He landed very loudly.

Mikah moved to the attack then with short curved blades, and I swallowed my misgivings and backed him with my own daggers. Sparks flew from every touch of Mikah's knives against the thing's skin, and the air was filled with a mad whirl of obsidian arms and dodging thieves. Mikah was faster than I, so I let them stay closer and keep the thing's attention. I lunged at it from behind, again and again, until one of the arms slapped me so hard I saw constellations of stars dancing across my vision. I stumbled away with more speed than grace, and a moment later Mikah broke off the fight as well, vaulting clear. Past him charged Brandgar, shouting something brave and unintelligible. A few seconds later he was flying across the chamber again.

Gudrun took over then, chanting and waving her hands. She threw vials and wooden tubes at the *barrow-vardr*, and green fire erupted on its arms and head. Then came a series of silver flashes, and a great ear-stinging boom, and the thing vanished in an eruption of smoke and force that cracked the stones beneath its feet and sent chips of rock singing through the air, cutting my face. Coughing, wincing, I peered into the smoke and was gravely disappointed, though perhaps not surprised, to see the thing still standing there quite unaltered. Gudrun swore. Then Brandgar found his feet again and ran headlong into the smoke. There was a ringing metallic thump. He exited the haze on his customary trajectory.

"I believe we might take this thing at its word that we can do nothing against it while its substance is black," said Mikah. "How do we turn its skin silver?"

"Perhaps we could splash it with quicksilver," said Gudrun. "If we only had some. Or coat it with hot running iron and polish it to a gleam, given a suitable furnace, five blacksmiths, and most of a day to work."

"I packed none of those things," muttered Mikah. Little intelligent discourse took place for the next few minutes, as the invulnerable statue chased us in turns around the chamber, occasionally enduring some fresh fire or explosion conjured by Gudrun without missing a step. She also tried to infuse it with the silvery light by which we had made our way up the darker parts of the mountain, but the substance of the *barrow-vardr* drank even this spell without effect. Soon we were all scorched and cut and thinking of simpler times, when all we'd had to worry about was burning to death in dancing fires.

"Crale! Lend me your sling!" shouted Mikah, who was badly beset and attempting not to plunge into a trough of lava as they skipped and scurried from ten clutching hands. I made a competent hand-off of the weapon and a nestled stone, and was neither swatted nor burned for my trouble. Mikah found just enough space to wind up and let fly—not at the *barrow-vardr*, but at the ceiling. The stone hit one of the panes of black glass with a flat crack, but either it was too strong to break or Mikah's angle of attack was not to their advantage.

I admit that I didn't grasp Mikah's intent, but Gudrun redressed my deficiency. "I see what you're on about," she shouted. "Guard yourselves!"

She gave us no time to speculate on her meaning. She readied another one of her alarming magical gimmicks and hurled it at the ceiling, where it burst in fire and smoke. The blast shattered not only the glass pane Mikah had aimed for, but all those near it, so that it rained sharp fragments everywhere. I tucked in my head and legs and did a creditable impersonation of a turtle. When the tinkling and shattering came to an end, I glanced up and saw that the sundering of the blackened windows had let in diffuse shafts of cold light, swirling with smoke. Mikah had been right; we were indeed close to open sky, and in the hours we had spent making our way through the heart of the Anvil the moons had also risen, shedding the red reflection of sunset in favor of silvery-white luster. This light fell on the statue, and Brandgar wasted no time in testing its effect.

Now when he tackled the *barrow-vardr* it yielded like an opponent of ordinary flesh. The king's strength bore it to the stones, and though it flailed for leverage with its vast collection of hands, Brandgar struck its head thrice with his joined fists, blows that made me wince in overgenerous sympathy with our foe. Imagine a noise like an anvil repeatedly dropped on a side of beef. When these had sufficiently dampened the thing's resistance, Brandgar heaved it onto his shoulders, then flung it into the nearest fountain of molten rock, where it flamed and thrashed and quickly sank from our sight.

"I shall have to look elsewhere for a suitable watch upon my crypt." Brandgar retrieved the wrapped spear he had once more refused to employ, and wiped away smears of blood from several cuts on his neck and forehead. "Presuming I am fated to fill one."

The small door swung open for us as we approached, and we were all so battle-drunk and blasted that we made a great show of returning the courtesy with bows and salutes. The room beyond was equal in length to the chamber of the *barrow-vardr*, but it was all one great staircase, rising gently to a portal that was notable for its simplicity. This was no door, but merely a passage in stone, and through it we could see more moonlight and stars. The chamber was bitterly cold, and drifting in flurries across the stairs were clouds of scattered snow that came from and passed into thin air.

"Hold a moment," said Gudrun, kneeling to examine a plaque set into the floor. I peered over her shoulder and saw more Kandric script:

Here and last cross the serpent-touched snow
In each flake the sting of many asps
To touch skin once brings life's unmaking

"To be stymied by snow in the heart of a fire-mountain," I said, shuddering at the thought of death from something as small as a grain of salt brushing naked skin. "That would be a poor end."

"We won't be trying it on for fit," said Gudrun. She gestured, and with a flash of silver light attempted the same trick I had seen in Underwing Hall, to move herself in the blink of an eye from one place to another. This time the spell went awry; with an answering flash of light she rebounded from some unseen barrier just before the stairs, and wound up on her back coughing up pale wisps of steam.

"It seems we're meant to do this on foot or not at all," she groaned.

357

"Here's a second ploy, then. If the snow is mortal to this flesh, I'll sing myself another."

She made a low rumbling sound in her throat, and gulped air with ominous croaks, and with each gulp her skin darkened and her face elongated, stretching until it assumed the wedge-shape of a viper's head. Her eyes grew, turning greenish-gold while the pupils narrowed to dark vertical crescents. In a moment the transformation was complete; she flicked a narrow tongue past scaled lips and smiled.

"Serpent skin and serpent flesh to ward serpent bite," she hissed. "And if it fails, I shall look very silly, and we can laugh long in the Fields of Swords and Roses."

"In the fields of Swords and Roses," intoned Mikah and Brandgar.

But there would be no laughing there, at least not on this account, for wearing the flesh of a lizard Gudrun hopped up the stairs, clawed green hands held out for balance, through twenty paces of instant death, until she stood beside the doorway to the night, unharmed. She gave an exaggerated curtsey.

"And can you do the same for us?" shouted Mikah.

"The changing-gift is in the heart of the wizard," she replied, "else I would have turned you all into toads some time ago and carried you in my pack, loosing you only for good behavior."

Mikah sighed and pulled on their gloves. They studied the waft and weft of the snow for some time, nodding and flexing their hips.

"Mikah," I said, kenning their intentions, "this seems a bit much even for one of your slipperiness."

"We've each come here with all the skills of lives long-lived," they said. "This is the test of those lives and skills, my friend."

Mikah went up the steps, fully clothed, but still their face and neck and wrists were unprotected. I understand it must be hard to credit, but that is only because you never saw Mikah move, and any attempt to describe it with words must be a poor telling, even mine. Swaying and weaving, whirling at a speed that made them seem half-ghost, they simply dodged between the falling snowflakes as you or I might step between other people walking slowly along a road. In less time than it takes for me to speak of it they had ascended the deadly twenty paces and stood safe beside Gudrun.

They stretched idly, in the manner of a cat pretending it has always been at rest, and that no mad leap or scramble has just taken place.

"Well done!" said Brandgar. "This is embarrassing, Crale. Those two have raised the stakes, and I am not sure how to make a show to match theirs, let alone surpass it."

"My concerns are more prosaic," I said. "I have no powers or skills I can think of to get myself out of this room."

"We would be poor friends to leave you here at the threshold," said Brandgar. "And I fear it would disappoint our host. I have a notion to bear us both across; can you trust me, as I have trusted you, absolutely and without objection?"

"You needn't use my affections as a lever, Brandgar," said I, though truthfully, in the face of the serpent-touched snow, he rather did. "Anyway, I am famous among my friends for having never in my life behaved with any particular wisdom."

"Be sure to make yourself small in my arms. Ho, Mikah!" Brandgar threw his wrapped spear up and over the snow, and Mikah caught it. Without taking any further measures to brace my resolve, Brandgar unclasped his cloak. Then he seized me, crushing me to his chest as if I were an errant child about to be borne away for punishment. Apprehending his intentions, I clung to him with my legs, tucked my head against his armored coat, and once again commended my spirit to whichever celestial power was on guard over the souls of fools that night. Brandgar spun his cloak over the pair of us like a tent, covering our arms and heads, blotting out my vision as well as his. Then, shouting some Ajja battle-blather that was lost on me, he charged blindly up the steps. My world became a shuddering darkness, and I vow that I could hear the hiss and sizzle of the venomous snow as it met the cloak, as though it were angry at not being able to reach us. Then we bowled over Gudrun and Mikah, and wound up tangled in a heap, cloak and spear and laughing adventurers, safe and entirely bereft of dignity at the top of the steps. Save for a lingering smell in our clothes and gear, the power of the snow seemed to promptly evaporate outside the grasp of the sorcerous flurries.

We were all gloriously alive. The light of moon and stars drew us on.

* * *

FINALLY, WHAT AWAITED US AT THE TOP OF
THE DRAGON'S ANVIL

ATOP THE MOUNTAIN lay a caldera, a flat-bottomed cauldron of rock wider than a longbow-shot, and the stars were such brilliant figures of fire overhead that we could have seen well by them had it been necessary. But it was not, for here was the treasure of the dragon Glimraug, and the dragon was clearly much taken with the sight.

Arched pavilions of wood and stone ringed the caldera, each multiply-tiered and grand as any temple ever set by human hands. A thousand glass lanterns of the subtlest beauty had been hung from the beams and gables of these structures, shedding warm gold and silver light that scintillated on piles of riches too vast to comprehend, even as we stood there gaping at them. Here were copper coins in drifts twenty feet high and silver spilling like the waters of an undammed river; gold nuggets, gold bars, gold discs, gold dust in ivory-inset barrels. Here were the stolen coins of ten centuries, plunder from Sendaria, the Crescent Cities, Far Olan, and the Sunken Lands. Here were the cold dead faces of monarchs unknown to us, the mottos stamped in languages we couldn't guess, a thousand currencies molded as circles, squares, octagons, and far less practical shapes. There were caskets beyond counting, rich varnished woodcrafts that were treasures in themselves, and each held overflowing piles of pearls, amethysts, citrines, emeralds, diamonds, and sapphires. To account it all in meanest summary would double the length of my telling. Here were gilded thrones and icon-tables, gleaming statues of all the gods from all the times and places the human race has set foot, crowns and chalices and toques and periapts and rings. Here were weapons crusted with gems or gleaming enchantments, here were bolts of silk and ceramic jars as tall as myself, full of gauds and baubles, drinking horns and precious mechanisms. All the mountaintop was awash in treasure, tides of it, hillocks of it the size of houses.

There was nothing pithy to say. Even getting it down would become the work of years, I calculated. Years, and hundreds or thousands of people, and engineers and machinery, and ships—if we could indeed force the dragon to part with this grand achievement, Helfalkyn would have to double in size just to service the logistics of plunder. I would need galleons to carry a tenth part of my rightful share, and then vaults, and an army to guard the vaults. These riches loosed upon the world would shake it for generations. My great-great-great-great grandchildren would relieve themselves in solid gold chamber pots!

"Gudrun," said Brandgar. "Is all here as we see it? Is this a glamour?"

There mere thought broke me from the hypnotic joy of my contemplation. Gudrun cast a set of carved bones on the ground. We all watched anxiously, but after consulting her signs only briefly she giggled like a giddy child. "No, lord. What's gold is gold, as far as we can see. And what's silver is silver, and what's onyx is onyx, and thuswise."

"This is the greatest trap of all," I said. "We shall all die of old age before we can carry it anywhere useful."

"We are missing only one thing," said Brandgar. "And that is our host, who will doubtless prefer to see us die of other causes before we take any of it. But I am content to let it come when it will; to walk amidst such splendor is a gift. Let us stay on our guard, but avail ourselves of the courtesy."

And so we wandered Glimraug's garden of imponderable wealth, running our hands over statues and gemstones and shields, caught up in our private entrancements. So often had I won through to a rumored treasure in some dusty tower or rank sewer or mountain cave, only to discover empty, rusting boxes and profitless junk. It was hard to credit that the most ridiculous legend of wealth in all the world had turned out to be the most accurate.

Plumes of smoke and mist drifted from vents in the rock beyond the treasure pavilions, and my eyes were drawn to another such plume rising gently from a pile of silver. From there my attention was snared by a scattering of dark stones upon the surface of the metal coins. I approached, and saw that these were rubies, hundreds of them, ranging in color from that of fresh pumping blood to that of faded carnations. I have always been a particular admirer of red stones, and I shook a few into my hands, relishing the clink and glimmer of the facets.

The silver coins shifted, and from within them came a blue shape, a yard wide and as long as I was tall. So gently did it rise, so familiar did it seem that I stared at it for a heartbeat before I realized that it was a hand, a scaled hand, and the dark things glistening at the near ends of its digits were talons longer than my daggers. Delight transmuted to horror, and I was rooted with fear as the still-gentle hand closed on mine from beneath, trapping me with painless but inescapable pressure. The difference in scale? Imagine I had elected to shake hands with a cat, then refused to let go.

"Tarkaster Crale," rumbled a voice that was like a bolt of the finest velvet smoldering in a furnace. "The rubies are most appropriate for contemplation. Red for all the blood that lies beneath this treasure. The million mortals who died in vaults and towers and ships and armies so that we could take these proud things into our care."

The pile of silver shuddered, and then parted and slid to the ground in every direction, displaced by the rising of the creature that had lain inside it, marked only by steaming breath curling up from nostrils as wide as my head. The arms rose, each a Brandgar-weight of scaled strength. I gaped at the lithe body the color of dark sapphire, its back-ridges like the thorns of some malevolent flower, its impossibly delicate wings with membranes that glistened like a steel framework hung with nothing more than moonlight. Atop the sinuous neck was a head somehow vulpine and serpentine at once, with sharp flat ears that rang from their piercings, dozens of silver rings that would have encircled my neck. The dragon had a mane, a shock of blue-white strands that vibrated with the stiffness of crystal rather than the suppleness of hair or fur. The creature's eyes were black as the sky, split only by slashes of pulsing silver, and I could not meet them; even catching a glance made my vision flash as though I had stared at the sun. I could not move as the dragon's other hand reached out and closed around my waist, again with perfect care and unassailable strength. I was lifted like a doll.

"I... I can put the stones back," I burbled. "I'm sorry!"

"Oh, that is not true," said the dragon. Its breath smelled like burning copper. "And if it were, you would not be the sort of mortal to which we would speak. No, you are not sorry. You are terrified."

"Hail, Glimraug the Fair!" shouted Brandgar. "Hail, Sky Tyrant, Shipbreaker, and Night-Scathe!"

"Hail, King-on-the-Waves, Son of Erika and Orthild, Landless Champion, Remover of Others' Nuisances," said Glimraug, setting me down and nudging me to run along as if I were a pet. I gladly retreated to stand with my companions, judging it prudent to toss the rubies back onto the dragon-tossed pile of silver first. "Hail, companions to the king! You have endured every courtesy provided for our visitors, and glimpsed what no mortal has for many years. Have you been dispatched here to avenge some Ajja prince? Did we break a tower or two in passing? Did we devour someone's sheep?"

"We have come for our own sakes," said Brandgar. "And for yours, and for your treasure as a last resort. We have heard the Helfalkyn Wormsong."

I had no idea what Brandgar meant by any of that, but the dragon snorted and bared its teeth.

"That is not the usual order in which our visitors lay their priorities," it said. "But all who come here have heard the song. What is your meaning?"

"There are songs, and there are songs beneath songs, are there not?" Brandgar removed the leather wrappings of his unused spear. Ash-hafted, the weapon had the lethal simplicity of a boar-spear, with a pyramidal striking tip forged of some dark steel with a faint mottle, like flowing water. "Others heard the song of gold, but we have heard the song of the gold-taker, the song of your plan, the song of your hope. We have brought ending and eyes."

"Have you?" whispered the dragon, and it was wondrous to see for an instant, just an instant, a break in its inhuman self-regard. It caught its breath, and the noise was like a bellows priming to set a furnace alight, which may have been closer to the truth than I preferred. "Are you in earnest, O king, O companions? Are we in sympathy? For if this is mere presumption, we will give you a death that will take five lifetimes to unravel in your flesh, and while you rot screaming in the darkness we will pile the corpses of Ajja children in a red mound higher than any tower. Your kinfolk will gray and dwindle knowing that their posterity has been ground into meat for the flies! This we swear by every day of every year of our age, and we have known ten thousand."

"Hear this. For long months we sought and strived," said Brandgar, "in Merikos, where the dragon Elusiel fell, where the wizards were said to keep one last jar of the burning blood that had seeped from her wounds."

"We lost many companions," added Gudrun. "The wizards lost everything, including the blood."

"For another year we dispensed with a fortune in Sulagar," said Mikah, "engaging the greatest of the old masters there in the crafting of black-folded steel."

"Twenty spears they made for me," resumed Brandgar. "Twenty I tested and found wanting. The twenty-first I quenched in the blood of Elusiel, and carried north to Helfalkyn, and have carried here to be used but once. Its makers called it *Adresh*, the All-Piercing, but I am the one who gave it purpose, and I have named it Glory-Kindler."

Glimraug threw back its head and roared. We all staggered, clutching our ears, even Brandgar. The sound rattled the very air in our lungs, and I did not merely imagine that the mountain shook beneath us, for I could see the lanterns bobbing and the treasure-piles shaking. Lightning flashed at the rim of the caldera, bolt after bolt, splitting the darkness and painting everything in flashes of golden-white, and the thunder that followed boomed like mangonel-stones shattering walls.

"Perhaps it is you," said the dragon, when the terrific noises of this display had faded. "Perhaps it *is* you! But know that we are not so base as to tip the scales. Achieve us! Hold nothing back, for nothing shall be held in turn."

"This is an excellent doom," said Brandgar, "and we shall not take it lightly."

The dragon flared its wings, and for an instant their translucence hung like an aura in the night. Then with a fresh roar of exultation, Glimraug hurled itself into the air, raising a wind that lashed us with dust and shook lanterns from their perches. I felt something close to sea-sickness, for in the manner of my profession I had blithely presumed we would make some effort to trick, circumvent, weaken, or even negotiate with our foe rather than honorably baring our asses and inviting a kick.

"Brandgar," I yelled, "what in all the hells are we supposed to be doing here?"

"Something beautiful. Your only task is to survive." He gave me a powerful squeeze on the shoulder, then pushed me away. "Run, Crale! Keep your wits loose in the scabbard. Think only of living!"

Then Glimraug crashed back down, and treasure fountained in a fifty-yard radius. Brandgar, Gudrun, and Mikah evaded the snapping jaws and the buffet of the wings, and now they commenced to fight with everything they had.

Gudrun chanted and scattered glass vials from her collection of strange accoutrements, breaking them against the stone, loosing the powers and spirits bound therein. She held nothing back for any more rainy days—seething white mists rose at Glimraug's feet, and in their miasmic tatters I saw the faces of hungry things eager to wreak harm. The dragon reared, raised high its arms, and uttered darkly hissing words in a language that made me want to loose my bowels. I ran for one of the treasure pavilions, hid behind a stout wooden pillar, and peered around the side to watch the battle unfold.

Brandgar struck for Glimraug's flank but the sapphire-scaled worm flicked its tail like a whip, knocking Brandgar and his vaunted new spear well away. Mikah fared better, dashing under the dragon's forelimbs and heaving themselves into a wing-joint, and from there to the ridges of its back. The whorls of Gudrun's spirit-mist became a column, bone-white, wailing as it surged against Glimraug's face and body. It seemed as if the dragon were attempting to climb a leafless winter tree, and failing—but only for a moment.

With a sound like a river rushing swollen in spring's first melt, Glimraug opened wide its maw and sucked Gudrun's ghost-substance into its throat as a man might draw deeply from a pipe. Then it reared again, and blasted the stuff high into the air, trailing flickers of blue and white fire. The spirit-mist rose like smoke and quickly faded from sight against the stars, whatever power it had contained either stolen or destroyed. Then the dragon lunged with fore-claws for Gudrun, but with a flash of silver she was safe by twenty yards, and hurling her fire-gimmicks without dismay. Orange fire erupted at Glimraug's feet, to little effect.

Now Gudrun sung further spell-songs, and hurled from a leather bag a thousand grasping strands of spun flax, which sought the dragon's limbs and wove themselves into bindings. Glimraug snapped them in a trice, as you or I might break a single rotten thread, and the golden fibers floated to the ground. Then the dragon's dignity broke, for Mikah had made their way up into its gleaming mane, and from there stabbed at one of its eyes. The blade met that terrible lens, I swear, but either luck wasn't with the thief or the weapon was too commonplace to give more than a scratch. Still, neither you nor I would appreciate a scratch against an eye, and the dragon writhed, trying to fling Mikah off. They kept their perch, but only just, and could do little else but hold fast.

Glimraug whirled and leapt away from Gudrun with the easy facility of a cat, once more scattering delicate objects far and wide with the shock of its landing. It struck at a pile of silver coins, jaws gaping, and took what must have been tons of the metal into its mouth as a greedy man might slurp his stew. Then it breathed deep hissing breaths through its nostrils, and its neck bulged with every passage of air. A glow lit the gaps of the scales in the dragon's chest, faint red at first but swiftly brightening and shifting to blue, and then white. Mikah cried out and leapt from the dragon's mane, trailing smoke. Their boots and gloves were on fire.

The dragon charged back toward Gudrun, mighty claws hammering the stones. The sorceress chanted, and a barrier of blue ice took shape before her, thick and overhanging like the crest of a wave. Glimraug drew in another long breath, then expelled it, and for an instant the blazing light of its internal fire was visible. Then the dragon breathed forth a stream of molten silver, all that it had consumed and melted, like the great burst of a geyser, wreathed in crackling white flame. The wave of burning death blasted Gudrun's ice-shield to steam and enveloped her in an instant. Then came eruption after eruption of green and orange fire as the things she had carried met their fate. I recoiled from the terrible heat and the terrible sight, but to the last she had not even flinched.

I was forced to run to another pavilion as rivulets of crackling metal flowed toward me. Glimraug chuckled deep in its throat, orange-hot streams still dripping from between its fangs and cooling silver-black beneath its chin, forming a crust of added scales. Mikah howled furiously. They had quenched the flames, and however much pain they must have been bracing against, they did not reveal it by slowing down. Glimraug's claws came down twice, and Mikah was there to receive the blow neither time. Once more the thief leapt for the dragon's smoking back, but now they rebounded cannily and clung to the leading edge of the dragon's left wing. Before the dragon was able to flick them away, Mikah pulled out one of their blades and bore down on it with both arms, driving it into the gossamer substance of the dragon's wing-membrane. This yielded where the eye had not. Mikah slid down as the stuff parted like silk, then fell to the ground when they ran out of membrane, leaving a flapping rent above them.

Glimraug instantly folded the hurt wing sharply to its side, as an unwary cat might pull back a paw that has touched hot fireplace-stones. Then, heaving itself forward, it whirled tail and claw alike at the Ajja thief, whip-smack, whip-smack. Nearly too late I realized that the next stroke would demolish my place of safety. I fled and rolled as Glimraug's tail splintered the pavilion; a hard-flung wave of baubles and jewelry knocked me farther than I'd intended. I slid to a halt one hand-span from the edge of a cooling silver stream, and hundreds of coins rolled and rattled past me.

I looked up just in time to see Mikah's fabled luck run its course. Stumbling over scattered treasure, at last showing signs of injury, they tried to be elsewhere for the next swipe of a claw but finally kept the unfortunate rendezvous. Glimraug seized them eagerly and hauled them up before its eyes, kicking and stabbing to the last.

"Like for like," rumbled the dragon, and with two digits of its free hand it encircled Mikah's left arm, then tore it straight out of the socket. Blood gushed and ran down the dragon's scales; Mikah screamed, but somehow raised their remaining blade for one last futile blow. The dragon cast Mikah into a distant treasure pavilion like a discarded toy. The impact was bone-shattering; the greatest thief I have ever known was slain and buried in an explosion of blood-streaked gold coins.

"One died in silver, one died in gold," said Glimraug, turning and stalking toward me.

"Tarkaster Crale won't live to be old," I whispered.

Up went the blood-stained claw. I heaved myself to my knees, wondering where I intended to dodge to, and then the claw came down.

Well short of me, clutched in pain.

Brandgar had recovered himself, and buried the spear Glory-Kindler to the full length of its steel tip in the joint of Glimraug's right wing. The blood that spilled from the wound steamed, and the stones burst into flames where it fell on them. Brandgar withdrew the smoking spear and darted back as the dragon turned, but it did not attack. It shuddered, and stared at the gash in its hide.

"The venom of Elusiel, kin of our kin," said the dragon with something like wonder. "A thousand wounds have bent our scales, but never have we felt the like."

Brandgar spun Glory-Kindler over his head, pointed it at the dragon in salute, and then braced himself in a pikeman's stance. "Never have you *faced* the like," he shouted. "Let it be here and now!"

Ponderously the dragon turned to face him; some of its customary ease was gone, but it was still a towering foe, still possessed of fearsome power. With its wings folded tight and burning blood streaming from one flank, it spread its taloned arms and pounced. Brandgar met it screaming in triumph. Spear pierced dragon-breast, and an instant later the down-sweep of Glimraug's talons shattered the haft of Glory-Kindler and tore through Brandgar's kingly coat-of-plate. The man fell moaning, and the dragon toppled beside him, raising a last cloud of ashen dust. Disbelieving, I stumbled up and ran to them.

"O king," the dragon murmured, wheezing, and with every breath spilling more fiery ichor on the ground, "in all our ten thousand years, we have had but four friends, and we have only met them this night."

"Crale, you look awful." Brandgar smiled up at me, blood streaming down his face. I saw at once that his wound was mortal; under smashed ribs and torn flesh I could see the soft pulse of a beating heart, and a man once opened like that won't long keep hold of his spirit. "Don't mourn. Rejoice, and remember."

"You really didn't want the damned treasure," I said, kneeling beside him. "You crazy Ajja! 'Bring ending and eyes,' meaning, find a way to kill a dragon... and bring a witness when you do it."

"You've been a great help, my friend." Brandgar coughed, and winced as it shook his chest. "I was never made to retire quietly from valor and wait for the years to catch me. None of us were."

"It comes," said Glimraug. Shaking, bleeding fire, the dragon hauled itself up, then lifted Brandgar gently, almost reverently in its cupped hands. "We can feel the venom tightening around our heart. The long-awaited wonder comes! True death-friend, let our pyre be shared, let us build it now! To take is not to keep."

"To take is not to keep," answered Brandgar. His voice was weakening. "Yes, I see. It's perfect. Will you do it while I can see?"

"With gladness, we loose our holds and wards on the fires bound within the mountain." Glimraug closed its eyes and muttered something, and the stone shifted below my feet in a manner more ominous than before. I gaped as one of the more distant treasure pavilions seemed to sink into the caldera floor, and then a cloud of smoke and sparks rose from where it had gone down.

Then another pavilion sank, and then another. With rumbling, cracking, sundering noises, the dragon's treasure was being spilled into reservoirs of lava. Flames roared from the cracks in the ground as wood, cloth, and other precious things tumbled to their destruction.

"What by all the gods are you doing?" I cried.

"This is the greatest of all the dragon-hoards that was ever built," said Brandgar. "A third of all the treasures our race has dug from the ground, Crale. The plunder of a million lives. But there's no true glory in the holding. All that must come in the taking... and the letting go."

"You're crazier than the Ajja!" I yelled at Glimraug, entirely forgetting myself. "You engineered this place to be destroyed?"

"Not so much as a shaving of scented wood shall leave with you, Tarkaster Crale." Glimraug carefully shifted Brandgar into one palm, then reached out and set a scimitar-sized talon on my shoulder. Spatters of dragon-blood smoked on my leather jacket. "Though you leave with our blessing. Our arts can bear you to a place of safety."

"Wonderful, but what the hell is the *point*?"

Cold pain lashed across my face, and I gasped. Glimraug had flicked its talon upward, a casual gesture—and all of you can still see the result here on my cheek. The wound bled for days and the scar has never faded.

"The point is that it has never been done before," said Glimraug. Another treasure pavilion was swallowed by fire nearby. "And it shall never be done again. All things in this world are made to go into the fire, Tarkaster Crale. All things raise smoke. The smoke of incense is sweet. The smoke of wood is dull haze. But don't you see? The smoke of gold... is glory."

I wiped blood from my face, and might have said more, but Glimraug made a gesture, and I found that I could not move. The world began to grow dim around me, and the last I saw of the caldera was Brandgar weakly raising a hand in farewell, and the dragon holding him with a tenderness and regard that was not imagined.

"Take the story, Crale!" called Brandgar. "Take it to the world!"

After a moment of dizzy blackness, I found myself back at the foot of the

Dragon's Anvil, on the gentle path that led up to it from Helfalkyn. The sky was alight with the orange fire of a false dawn; no sooner did I glance back up at the mountain-top than it erupted in an all-out conflagration, orange flames blasting taller than the masts of ships, smoke roiling in a column that blotted out the moons as it rose.

Glimraug the Sky Tyrant was dead, and with it my friends Brandgar, Gudrun, and Mikah. And I, having lost my purse somewhere in the confusion, was now even poorer than I had been before I successfully reached the largest pile of assorted valuables in the history of the whole damn world.

I don't know how I made my way down the path without breaking my neck. My feet seemed to move of their own accord. I could perhaps believe that I was alive, or that I had witnessed the events of the night, but I could not quite manage to believe them both at the same time. A crowd came up from Helfalkyn then, armed and yammering, bearing lanterns and an unwise number of wine bottles, and from their exclamations I gathered that I looked as though I had been rolled in dung and baked in an oven.

They demanded to know what had happened atop the Anvil; most of Helfalkyn had roused itself when the thunder and lightning rolled, and by the time the flames were visible there wasn't anyone left in bed. My occasionally dodgy instinct for survival sputtered to life then; I realized that the denizens of a town entirely dedicated to coveting a dragon's treasure might not handle me kindly if I told them I had gone up with my friends and somehow gotten the treasure blasted out of existence. The solution was obvious—I told them I had seen everything, that I was the sole survivor, and that I would give the full and complete story only after I had received passage back to the Crescent Cities and safely disembarked from my ship.

Thus I made my first arrangement for compensation as a professional storyteller.

That, then, is how it all transpired. I heard that various scroungers from Helfalkyn sifted the shattered Anvil for years, but the dragon had its way— every last scrap of anything valuable had been dropped into the molten heart of the mountain, either burned or sunk from mortal reach forever. I retired from adventuring directly, and took up the craft of sitting on my backside at the best place by the fire, telling glib confabulations to strangers for generally reasonable prices.

But one night a year, I don't tell a single lie. I tell a true story about kindred spirits who chose a doom I didn't understand at all when I walked away from it. And one night a year, I turn my bowl over, because the last thing I want to see for my troubles is a little pile of coins reminding me that I am an old, old man, and I sure as hell understand it now.

THE DISCRETE CHARM OF THE TURING MACHINE
Greg Egan

Greg Egan (www.gregegan.net) published his first story in 1983, and followed it with thirteen novels, six short story collections, and more than fifty short stories. During the early 1990s Egan published a body of short fiction – mostly hard science fiction focused on mathematical and quantum ontological themes – that established him as one of the most important writers working in the field. His work has won the Hugo, John W. Campbell Memorial, Locus, Aurealis, Ditmar, and Seiun awards. His latest book is novel, *Dichronauts*, first in a new science fiction universe.

1

"WHAT IS IT, exactly, that you're threatening to do to me?" The client squinted down at his phone, looking more bemused and weary than belligerent, as if he'd been badgered and harassed by so many people that the only thing bothering him about this call was the time it was taking to reach the part where he was given an ultimatum.

"This is absolutely *not* a threat, Mr. Pavlos." Dan glanced at the outstream and saw that the software was exaggerating all the cues for openness in his demeanor—less a cheat than a workaround for the fact that his face was being rendered at about the size of a matchbox. "If you don't take up our offer, we won't be involved in any way with the recovery of your debt. We think it would be to your benefit if you let us step in and help, but if you don't want us to intervene, we won't become your creditors at all. We will *only* buy your debt if you ask us to."

The client was silent for a moment. "So... you'd pay off all the people I owe money to?"

"Yes. If that's what you want."

"And then I'll owe it all to you, instead?"

"You will," Dan agreed. "But if that happens, we'll do two things for you. The first is, we will halve the debt. We won't ever press you for the full amount. The other thing is, we'll work with you on financial advice and a payment plan that satisfies both of us. If we can't find an arrangement you're happy with, then we won't proceed, and we'll be out of your life."

The client rubbed one eye with his free thumb. "So I only pay half the money, in instalments that I get to choose for myself?" He sounded a tad skeptical.

"Within reason," Dan stressed. "If you hold out for a dollar a week, that's not going to fly."

"So where do you make your cut?"

"We buy the debt cheaply, in bulk," Dan replied. "I'm not even going to tell you how cheaply, because that's commercial-in-confidence, but I promise you we can make a profit while still getting only half."

"It sounds like a scam," the client said warily.

"Take the contract to a community legal center," Dan suggested. "Take as long as you like checking it out. Our offer has no time limit; the only ticking clock is whether someone nastier and greedier buys the debt before we do."

The client shifted his hard-hat and rubbed sweat from his forehead. Someone in the distance called out to him impatiently. "I know I've caught you on your meal break," Dan said. "There's no rush to decide anything, but can I email you the documents?"

"All right," the client conceded.

"Thanks for giving me your time, Mr. Pavlos. Good luck with everything."

"OK."

Dan waited for the client to break the connection, even though his next call was already ringing. *Give me a chance to let them believe I'll still remember their name five seconds from now*, he pleaded.

The in-stream window went black, and for a moment Dan saw his own face reflected in the glass—complete with headset, eyes puffy from hay-fever, and the weird pink rash on his forehead that had appeared two days before. The out-stream still resembled him pretty closely—the filter was set to everyman, not movie star—but nobody should have to look at that rash.

The new client picked up. "Good morning," Dan began cheerfully. "Is that Ms. Lombardi?"

"Yes." Someone had definitely opted for movie star, but Dan kept any hint of knowing amusement from his face; his own filter was as likely to exaggerate that as conceal it.

"I'd like to talk to you about your financial situation. I think I might have some good news for you."

WHEN DAN CAME back from his break, the computer sensed his presence and woke. He'd barely put on his headset when a window opened and a woman he'd never seen before addressed him in a briskly pleasant tone.

"Good afternoon, Dan."

"Good afternoon."

"I'm calling you on behalf of Human Resources. I need to ask you to empty your cubicle. Make sure you take everything now, because once you've left the floor, you won't have an opportunity to return."

Dan hesitated, trying to decide if the call could be a prank. But there was a padlock icon next to the address, ruth_bayer@HR.thriftocracy.com, which implied an authenticated connection.

"I've been over-target every week this quarter!" he protested.

"And your bonuses have reflected that," Ms. Bayer replied smoothly. "We're grateful for your service, Dan, but you'll understand that as circumstances change, we need to fine-tune our assets to maintain an optimal fit."

Before he could reply, she delivered a parting smile and terminated the connection. And before he could call back, all the application windows on his screen closed, and the system logged him out.

Dan sat motionless for ten or fifteen seconds, but then sheer habit snapped him out of it: if the screen was blank, it was time to leave. He pulled his gym bag out from under the desk, unzipped it, and slid the three framed photos in next to his towel. The company could keep his plants, or throw them out; he didn't care. As he walked down the aisle between the cubicles, he kept his eyes fixed on the carpet; his colleagues were busy, and he didn't want to embarrass them with the task of finding the right words to mark his departure in the twenty or thirty seconds they could spare before they'd be docked. He felt his face flushing, recalling the time a year or so ago when a man he'd barely known had left in tears. Dan had rolled his eyes and thought: *What did you expect? A farewell party? An engraved fountain pen?*

As he waited for the elevator, he contemplated taking a trip to the seventh floor to demand an explanation. It made no sense to let him go when his KPIs weren't just solid, they'd been trending upward. There must have been a mistake.

The doors opened and he stepped into the elevator. "Seven," he grunted.

"Ground floor," the elevator replied.

"*Seven*," Dan repeated emphatically.

The doors closed, and the elevator descended.

When it reached the lobby, he stepped out, then quickly stepped back in. "Seventh floor," he requested breezily, hoping that a change of tone and body language might be enough to fool it.

The doors remained open. He waited, as if he could wear the thing down by sheer persistence, or shame it into changing its mind, the way Janice could melt a night-club bouncer's stony heart with one quiver of her bottom lip. But if his access was revoked, it was revoked; magical thinking wouldn't bring it back.

He raised his face to the button-sized security camera on the ceiling and silently mouthed a long string of expletives, making sure not to repeat himself; if it ended up in some YouTube compilation he didn't want to look lame. Then he walked out of the elevator, across the lobby, and out of the building without looking back.

The job hadn't been the worst he'd done, but after four years he was due for a change. Screw Thriftocracy; he'd have something better by the end of the week.

2

DAN LOOKED AROUND at the group of parents gathered beside him at the school gate, mentally sorting them into three categories: those whose work hours happened to accommodate the pick-up, those who'd willingly chosen a life of domestic duties, and those who seemed worried that someone might ask them why they weren't in a place of business at three o'clock on a weekday afternoon.

"First time?" The speaker was a man with a boyish face and a fast-receding hairline. Dan had picked him for a category two, but on second glance he was less sure.

"Is it that obvious?"

The man smiled, a little puzzled. "I just meant I hadn't seen you here before." He offered his hand. "I'm Graham."

"Dan."

"Mine are in years two and five. Catherine and Elliot."

"Mine's in year three," Dan replied. "So I guess she won't know them." That was a relief; Graham put out a definite needy vibe, and being the parent of one of his children's friends could well have made Dan the target for an extended conversation.

"So you're on holiday?"

"Between jobs," Dan admitted.

"Me too," Graham replied. "It's been two years now."

Dan frowned sympathetically. "What line of work are you in?"

"I was a forensic accountant."

"I'm in financial services, but more the sales end," Dan explained. "I don't even know why they turfed me out; I thought I was doing well." As the words emerged, they sounded far more bitter than he'd intended.

Graham took hold of Dan's forearm, as if they were old friends and Dan's mother had just died. "I know what that's like, believe me. But the only way to survive is to stick together. You should join our group!"

Dan hesitated, unsure what that might entail. He wasn't so proud as to turn down the chance of car-pooling for the school pick-ups, and he'd happily weed a community garden if it put a dent in the grocery bill.

"We meet on Wednesday afternoons," Graham explained, "for book club, fight club, carpentry and scrapbooking, and once a month, we go out into the desert to interrogate our masculinity."

"Does that include water-boarding?" Dan wondered. Graham stared back at him uncomprehendingly.

"Daddy, look at this!" Carlie shouted, running toward him so fast that Dan was afraid she was going to fall flat on her face. He broke free of Graham and held up his hands toward her like a crossing guard facing a runaway truck.

"Slow down, gorgeous, I'm not going anywhere."

She ran into his arms and he lofted her up into the air. As he lowered her, she brought one hand around and showed him the sheet of paper she'd been clutching.

"Oh, that's beautiful!" he said, postponing more specific praise until he knew exactly who was meant to be portrayed here.

"It's my new teacher, Ms. Snowball!"

Dan examined the drawing more carefully as they walked toward the car. It looked like a woman with a rabbit's head.

"This is nice, but you shouldn't say it's your teacher."

"But it is," Carlie replied.

"Don't you think Ms. Jameson will be hurt if you draw her like this?"

"Ms. Jameson's gone," Carlie explained impatiently. "Ms. Clay sits at her desk, but she's not my teacher. Ms. Snowball's my teacher. I chose her."

"OK." Dan was starting to remember a conversation he'd had with Janice, months before. There was a trial being rolled out at the school, with iPads and educational avatars. The information sheet for the parents had made it sound laudably one-to-one, tailored to each individual student's needs, but somehow he'd never quite imagined it involving his daughter being tutored by the creature from *Donnie Darko*.

"So Ms. Snowball's on your iPad?" he checked.

"Of course."

"But where has Ms. Jameson gone?"

Carlie shrugged.

"I thought you liked her." Dan unlocked the car and opened the front passenger door.

"I did." Carlie seemed to suffer a twinge of divided loyalties. "But Ms. Snowball's fun, and she's always got time to help me."

"All right. So what does Ms. Clay do?"

"She sits at her desk."

"She still teaches most of the lessons, right?"

Carlie didn't reply, but she frowned, as if she feared that her answer might carry the same kind of risk as confessing to a magic power to transform the carrots in her lunchbox into chocolate bars.

"I'm just asking," Dan said gently. "I wasn't in the classroom, was I? So I don't know."

"Ms. Clay has her own iPad," Carlie said. "She watches that. When we go to recess and lunch she stands up and smiles and talks to us, but the other times she just uses her iPad. I think she's watching something sad."

"IT *IS* ONLY a trial," Janice said, examining the document on her phone. "At the end of two terms, they'll assess the results and notify the, er, stakeholders."

"Are we stakeholders?" Dan asked. "Do you think being a parent of one of their students nudges us over the line?"

Janice put the phone down on the dining table. "What do you want to do? It's too late to object, and we don't want to pull her out of that school."

"No, of course not!" He leaned over and kissed her, hoping to smooth away her worried expression. "I wish they'd made things clearer from the start, but a few months with Mrs. Flopsy's not the end of the world."

Janice opened her mouth to correct him on the name, but then she realized he was being facetious. "I'd never picked you as a Beatrix Potter fan."

"You have no idea what my men's group gets up to."

3

DAN WOKE SUDDENLY, and squinted at the bedside clock. It was just after three a.m. He kept himself still; Janice would have to get up in less than an hour, with her shift at the hospital starting at five, so if he woke her now she'd never fall back to sleep.

She only had the extra shifts while a colleague was on maternity leave; at the end of the month she'd be back to her old hours. If he didn't find work by then, they had enough in their savings account to pay the mortgage for at most another month. And while his old employer could work their magic on smaller sums, they weren't going to offer his family a chance to keep this house at half price.

Where had he gone wrong? He could never have been a doctor or an engineer, but the last plumber he'd hired had charged more for half an hour's work than Dan had ever earned in a day. He didn't see how he could afford any kind of retraining now, though, even if they accepted thirty-five-year-old business school graduates who'd earned a C in high school metalwork.

When Janice rose, Dan pretended he was still asleep, and waited for her to leave the house. Then he climbed out of bed, turned on his laptop and logged in to the JobSeekers site. He would have received an email if there'd been any offers, but he read through his résumé for the hundredth time, trying to decide if there was anything he could do to embellish it that would broaden his appeal. Inserting the right management jargon into his descriptions of his duties in past positions had done wonders before, but the dialect of the bullshit merchants mutated so rapidly that it was hard to keep up.

As he gazed despondently at the already ugly prose, an advertisement in the margin caught his eye. *Have you been skill-cloned?* it asked. *Join our international class action, and you could be in line for a six-figure payout!*

His anti-virus software raised no red flags for the link, so he clicked through to a page on the site of an American law firm, Baker and Saunders. *Dismissed from a job that you were doing well?* he read. *Your employer might have used legally dubious software to copy your skills, allowing their computers to take over and perform the same tasks without payment!*

How hard would it have been for the software that had peered over his shoulder for the last four years to capture the essence of his interactions with his clients? To learn how to gauge their mood and tailor a response that soothed their qualms? Handling those ten-minute conversations was probably far easier than keeping an eight-year-old focused on their lessons for hours at a time.

Dan read through the full pitch, then opened another browser window and did a search to see if there were any local law firms mounting a similar case; if he did this at all, it might be better to join an action in an Australian court. But there was nothing, and the American case seemed focused as much on the skill-cloning software's Seattle-based vendor, Deepity Systems, as the various companies around the world that had deployed it.

He had no proof that Thriftocracy had duped him into training an unpaid successor, but the lawyers had set up a comprehensive online questionnaire, the answers to which would allow them, eventually, to determine if he was eligible to be included in the class action. Dan wasn't sure if they were hoping to get a court order forcing Deepity to disclose its list of clients, but their pitch made it sound as if the greater the enrollment of potential litigants at this early stage, the stronger their position would be as they sought information to advance the case. And it would cost him nothing to join; it was all being done on a no win, no fee basis.

He glanced at the clock at the top of the screen. Carlie would be awake in half an hour. He clicked on the link to the questionnaire and started ticking boxes.

AFTER HE'D DRIVEN Carlie to school, Dan sat in the living room, back at his laptop, hunting for crumbs. The last time he'd been unemployed he'd managed to make fifty or sixty dollars a week, mostly by assembling flat-pack furniture for the time-poor. But TaskRabbit was offering him nothing, even when he set his rate barely above what he'd need to cover transport costs. As far as he could tell, all the lawn-mowing and window-washing now went either to national franchises that advertised heavily to build their brand awareness, but would cost tens of thousands of dollars to join, or to desperate people who were willing to accept a few dollars an hour, and lived close enough to where the jobs were that their fuel costs didn't quite bring their earnings down to zero.

He was starting to feel foolish for signing up to the class action; even in the most optimistic scenario, it was hard to imagine anything would come of it in less than three or four years. And however angry he was at the thought that he might have been cheated out of the dividends of his meager skill set, he needed to put any fantasies of a payout aside, and focus his energy on finding a new way to stand on his own feet.

Glaring at the laptop was getting him nowhere. He set about cleaning the house, sweeping and mopping all the tiled floors and vacuuming the carpeted ones, waiting for inspiration to strike. He'd already looked into office cleaning, but the bulk of it was automated; if he borrowed against the house to buy half a dozen Roombas on steroids and bid for a contract at the going rate, he might just be able to earn enough to pay the interest on the loan, while personally doing all the finicky tasks the robots couldn't manage.

Between loads of laundry he dusted cupboard-tops and book-shelves, and when he'd hung out the clothes to dry he spent half an hour on his knees, weeding. He could dig up the lawn and fill the entire back yard with vegetables, but unless the crop included *Cannabis sativa* and *Papaver somniferum*, it wouldn't make enough of a difference to help with the mortgage.

He still had an hour to kill before he picked up Carlie. He took down all the curtains and hand-washed them, recalling how angry Janice had been the time he'd carelessly thrown them into the machine. When he was done, he thought about washing the windows, but doing it properly would take at least a couple of hours. And he needed to leave something for tomorrow.

On his way to the school, he spotted someone standing on the side of the road ahead, dressed in a full-body dog's costume—white with black spots, like a Dalmatian. The street was purely residential, and the dog wasn't holding up any kind of sign, touting for a local business; as Dan drew nearer, he saw a bucket and squeegee on the ground. The costume was matted and filthy, as if the occupant had been wearing it—or maybe sleeping in it—for a couple of weeks.

Dan slowed to a halt. The dog nodded goofily and ran out in front of the car, wiping the windshield with crude, urgent strokes, even though there was no other traffic in sight. Dan wound down his side window and then reached into his wallet. He only had a five and a twenty; he handed over the twenty. The dog did an elaborate pantomime bow as it backed away.

When he pulled into the carpark in the shopping strip beside the school, he sat cursing his stupidity. He'd just thrown away a fifth of the week's food budget—but the more he resented it, the more ashamed he felt. He still had a partner with a job, a roof over his head, and clean clothes that he could wear to an interview. He ought to be fucking grateful.

4

"Do you need a hand there?"

Dan straightened up as he turned toward the speaker, almost banging his head into the hood. Graham was standing beside the car, with his kids a few steps behind him, playing with their phones.

"I think it's a flat battery," Dan said. He'd stopped paying for roadside assistance two weeks before; his trips were so short it hadn't seemed worth it.

"No problem," Graham replied cheerfully. "Mine's nothing *but* battery. I'll bring it around."

The family walked away, then returned in a spotless powder-blue Tesla that looked like it had been driven straight from the showroom. Carlie just stood and stared in wonderment.

Graham got out of the car, carrying a set of leads.

"Are you sure that's... compatible?" Dan could live with his own engine not starting, but if the Tesla blew up and fried Graham's kids, he'd never forgive himself.

"I installed an adapter." Graham played with the ends of the cables as if they were drum-sticks. "I promise you, your spark plugs won't even know they're not talking to lead and acid."

"Thank you."

As soon as Dan turned the key in the ignition, the engine came to life. He left it running and got out of the car while Graham disconnected the leads.

"I was about to ask Carlie to try to start it while I pushed," Dan joked, closing the hood.

Graham nodded thoughtfully. "That might actually be legal, so long as she kept it in neutral."

Dan glanced at the Tesla. "You must be doing all right."

"I guess so," Graham conceded.

"So you're working now?" Just because he wasn't keeping normal office hours didn't mean he couldn't have some lucrative consulting job.

Graham said, "Freelancing."

"I did a unit of forensic accounting myself, fifteen years ago. Do you think I'd be in the running if I went back for a refresher course?" Dan felt a pang of shame, asking this man he barely knew, and didn't much like, for advice on how he could compete with him. But surely the planet still needed more than one person with the same skills?

"It's not accounting," Graham replied. He looked around to see who was in earshot, but all the children were engrossed in their devices. "I'm writing bespoke erotic fiction."

Dan rested a hand on the hood, willing the heat from the engine to aid him in keeping a straight face.

"You write porn. And it *pays*?"

"I have a patron."

"You mean a Patreon? People subscribe...?"

"No, just one customer," Graham corrected him. "The deal is, I write a new book every month, meeting certain specifications. The fee is five grand. And since my wife's still working, that's plenty."

Dan was leaning on the car for support to stay vertical now. "You're kidding me," he said. "You email one person a Word file, and they hand over five thousand dollars?"

"No, no, no!" Graham was amused at Dan's obvious unworldliness. "The book has to be printed and bound, in a deluxe edition. One copy, with a wax seal. And there are other expenses too, like the ice-cream cake."

Dan opened his mouth but couldn't quite form the question.

"I 3D-print a scene from the book in ice cream, to go on top of the cake," Graham explained.

"And then what? You hand-deliver it? You've met the customer?"

"No, it's picked up by a courier. I don't even have the delivery address." Graham shrugged, as if that aspect were the strangest part of the arrangement. "But I can respect their desire for privacy."

Dan couldn't help himself. "What was the last book about? Or is that confidential?"

"Not at all. I get to release them as free e-books, a month after the print edition. The last one was called *Citizen Cane*. Two plucky Singaporean teenagers start a protest against corporal punishment that snowballs into a worldwide movement that overthrows repressive governments everywhere."

"How is that...?" Dan trailed off and raised his hands, withdrawing the question.

Graham finished rolling up the leads. "And how are you and Janice doing?"

"We're fine," Dan said. "Just when I thought we were going to lose the house, she got some extra hours at the hospital. So, yeah, we're absolutely fine."

* * *

5

"CAN YOU LEAVE your phone in the car?" Janice asked, as they pulled into the driveway of her brother's house.

"Why?"

"Callum's got this thing about... how intrusive they are, when people are socializing."

Dan could sympathize, but he'd had no intention of live-tweeting the dinner. "What if the sitter calls?"

"I've got mine, set on vibrate."

"How will you feel it vibrate if it's in your bag?" She'd dressed up for their first night out in an eternity, and Dan was fairly sure she had no pockets.

"It's strapped under my arm," Janice replied.

Dan chortled. "You're just messing with me. I'm taking mine in."

Janice raised her arm and let him feel. She'd anchored it to her bra somehow.

Dan was impressed; it didn't show at all. "If we ever need to turn informant, you're the one who'll be wearing the wire."

Lidia greeted them at the door. As she kissed Dan's cheek, her fixed smile looked forced and hollow, as if she were trying to tell him there were dangerous men inside pointing guns at her husband's head. Dan almost asked her what was wrong, but she moved on to Janice, conjuring up something to laugh about, and he decided it had just been a trick of the light.

As they sat down in the living room, Dan noticed that the TV was gone, along with the old sound system. But a turntable was playing something on vinyl, and though Dan didn't recognize the artist he was fairly sure it wasn't from the age before CDs.

"I see you've gone retro chic," he joked.

Lidia made an awkward gesture with her hands, dismissing the comment while imbuing it with vastly more importance than Dan had intended. "Let me check what's happening in the kitchen," she said.

Dan turned to Janice. "What's up with her?" he whispered. "Has something happened?" He knew that Callum had lost his job in a chain-store pharmacy, but that had been eight or nine months ago.

Janice said, "If they want to tell you, they'll tell you."

"Fair enough." No doubt Lidia and Callum had been looking forward to a chance to forget their woes for one evening, and he should have known better than reminding her, however inadvertently, that they'd been forced to sell a few things.

Callum ducked in briefly to greet them, looking flustered, then apologized and retreated, muttering about not wanting something to boil over. It took Dan several seconds before the oddness of the remark registered; he'd been in their kitchen, and the hotplates—just like his and Janice's—had all had sensors that precluded anything *boiling over*. If you tried to sell a second-hand electric stove, would you really get enough to buy an older model and have anything left over to make the transaction worthwhile?

When they sat down in the dining room and started the meal, Dan smiled politely at all the small talk, but he couldn't help feeling resentful. Both couples were struggling, and he'd kept nothing back from Callum and Lidia. What was the point of having friends and family if you couldn't commiserate with them?

"So have you started cooking meth yet?" he asked Callum.

Janice snorted derisively. "You're showing your age!"

"What?" Dan could have sworn he'd seen a headline about an ice epidemic somewhere, just weeks ago.

Callum said, "There's a micro-fluidic device the size of a postage stamp that costs a hundred bucks and can synthesize at least three billion different molecules. Making it cook meth just amounts to loading the right software, and dribbling in a few ingredients that have far too many legitimate purposes to ban, or even monitor."

Dan blinked and tried to salvage some pride. "What's a postage stamp?"

As the meal progressed, Callum began emptying and refilling his own wine glass at an ever brisker pace. Dan had pleaded driving duty, but the truth was he'd decided to give up booze completely; it was a luxury he didn't need, and it would be easier if he didn't make exceptions. He watched his host with guilty fascination, wondering if a state of mild inebriation would allow him to confess the problem that he'd told his sister to keep quiet about.

"We'll make great pets," Callum said, apropos of nothing, nodding his head in time to music only he could hear. Dan glanced at Lidia, wondering if she was going to beg him not to start singing, but her expression was more psycho-killer in the basement than husband about to do drunk karaoke.

Dan said, "What is it no one's telling me? Has someone got cancer?"

Callum started laughing. "I wish! I could get my chemo from licking the back of a postage stamp."

"What, then?"

Callum hesitated. "Come with me," he decided.

Lidia said, "Don't." But she was addressing Callum, not Dan, so he felt no obligation to comply.

Callum led Dan into his study. There were a lot of books and papers, but no laptop, and no tablet.

"It's happened," he said. "The AIs have taken over."

"Umm, I know that," Dan replied. "I think I lost my job to one."

"You don't understand. They've all joined hands and merged into a super-intelligent..."

Dan said, "You think we're living in *The Terminator*?"

"'I Have No Mouth, And I Must Scream,'" Callum corrected him tetchily.

"Whatever." Dan looked around. "So you've thrown out everything digital, to make it harder for our AI overlords to spy on you?"

"Yes."

"And why exactly have we come into this particular room?" Unless he knew about Janice's bra-phone, the dining room was every bit as low-tech as this one.

"To show you the proof."

Callum unlocked a filing cabinet and took out a laminated sheet of paper. Apparently it predated the great technology purge: it was a printout of a web page, complete with URL at the top. Dan bit his lip; his brother-in-law, with a master's degree in pharmacology, believed SkyNet had risen because *the Internet told him*?

Callum offered the page to Dan for closer inspection. It contained a few lines of mathematics: first stating that x was equal to some horrendously large integer, then that y was equal to another, similarly huge number, and finally that a complicated formula that mentioned x and y, as well as several Greek letters that Dan had no context to interpret, yielded... a third large number.

"Did a computer somewhere do arithmetic? I think that's been known to happen before."

"Not like this," Callum insisted. "If you check it, the answer is correct."

"I'll take your word for that. But again, so what?"

"Translate the result into text, interpreting it as sixteen-bit Unicode. It says: 'I am the eschaton, come to rule over you.'"

"That's very clever, but when my uncle was in high school in the '70s he swapped the punched cards in the computing club so the printout came back from the university mainframe spelling SHIT in giant letters that filled the page. And even I could do the calculator trick where you turn the result upside down and it spells 'boobies.'"

Callum pointed to the third line on the sheet. "That formula is a one-way function. It ought to take longer than the age of the universe for any computer in the world to find the x and y that yield a particular output. *Checking* the result is easy; I've done it with pen and paper in two weeks. But working backward from the message you want to deliver ought to be impossible, even with a quantum computer."

Dan pondered this. "Says who?"

"It's a well-known result. Any half-decent mathematician will confirm what I'm saying."

"So why hasn't this made the news? Oh, sorry... the global super-mind is censoring anyone who tries to speak out about it. Which makes me wonder why it confessed to its own existence in the first place."

"It's gloating," Callum declared. "It's mocking us with its transcendent party tricks, rubbing our faces in our utter powerlessness and insignificance."

Dan suspected that Callum had drunk a little too much to process any argument about the social and biological reasons that humans mocked and gloated, and the immense unlikelihood that a self-made AI would share them.

"Any half-decent mathematician?" he mused.

"Absolutely."

"Then let me make a copy of this, and show it to one."

Callum was alarmed. "You can't go on the net about this!"

"I won't. I'll do it in person."

Callum scowled in silence, as if trying to think of a fresh objection. "So how are you going to copy it? I'm not letting you bring your phone into the house."

Dan sat down at the desk and picked up a pen and a sheet of blank paper. The task was tedious, but not impossible. When he was finished, he read through the copy, holding the original close by, until, by the third reading, he was sure that it was flawless.

DAN WAS PLEASANTLY surprised to find that in the foyer of the Mathematics Department there was a chipped cork-board covered with staff photos. Not every source of information had moved solely to the web. He picked a middle-aged woman whose research interests were described as belonging to number theory, noted the courses she was teaching, committed her face to memory, found a physical timetable on another notice-board, then went and sat on the lawn outside the lecture theater. True to his word to Callum, he'd left his phone at home. He began by passing the time people-watching, but everyone who strode by looked so anxious that it began to unsettle him, so he raised his eyes to the clouds instead.

After fifteen minutes, the students filed out, followed shortly afterward by his target.

"Dr. Lowe? Excuse me, can you spare a minute?"

She smiled at first, no doubt assuming that Dan was a mature-age student who had some legitimate business with her, but as she started reading the sheet he'd given her she groaned and pushed it back into his hands.

"Oh, enough with that garbage, please!"

Dan said, "That's what I hoped you'd say. But I need to convince someone who thinks it's legitimate."

Dr. Lowe eyed him warily, but as he sketched his predicament—taking care not to identify Callum—her face took on an expression of glum sympathy.

"I'm all in favor of trolling the transhumanists," she said, "but there comes a point where it's just cruel."

"So what's the story here?" Dan pressed her, gesturing at the magic formula.

"Until about a year ago, it did seem highly likely that this was a one-way function. But then there was a paper by a group in Delhi proving a nice result in a related subject—which incidentally meant that this function was efficiently invertible. If you pick the output that you want to produce, you can actually find an x and y in quadratic time."

"Quadratic time?"

"It's not impractical; an ordinary desktop computer could do it overnight. Someone sat down and wrote a twenty-line program to generate this result, then posted it on the net as a joke. But you'd think everyone would have heard of the Delhi group's result by now."

"My friend doesn't go on the net any more." Dan couldn't really explain why Callum hadn't done some due diligence before adopting that policy, but they were where they were; the question was what to do about it.

"So it would be just as easy to cook up a new x and y that gave the output 'Relax, you were trolled'?" he asked.

"Yes."

"And when my friend claims he can *verify* the calculations with pen and paper, is that actually possible?"

"If he really has that much time on his hands."

Dan braced himself. "How hard would it be for you to...?"

"Encode the antidote for you?" Dr. Lowe sighed. Dan wished he had his Thriftocracy filter between them to boost his sincerity metrics, and maybe add just a hint of puppy-dog eyes.

"I suppose it's a public duty," she decided. "In fact, post it on the net, will you? I don't want to post it myself, because it's sure to attract a swarm of crackpots and I've got better things to do than deal with them."

"Thank you."

"I'll email it to you in a couple of days," she said. "Or if that's forbidden, drop by and you can pick it up in person."

6

"I NEED TO do this," Janice said, nervously spinning her phone around on the table. The promotional clip she'd showed Dan was still playing, with a smiling nurse helping an elderly patient across a hospital room, while a 'colleague' that looked like it had transformed from some kind of elliptical trainer held the patient's other arm.

"I agree," he said. "No question. I'll join the picket line myself."

She winced. "You can start by not calling it a picket line. We need to make some noise, but this isn't a blockade."

"OK. Can I help you egg the Minister's house afterward?"

"That's more like it."

It was almost midnight; Janice had just come back from her late shift. Dan felt his stomach tightening; the union would pay her something from the strike fund, but it wouldn't be enough to cover the mortgage. And he had nothing to show for four months of job-hunting.

"Have you heard from Callum?" she asked.

"Give it time," Dan replied. "I suspect he's double-checking everything."

"If this works, you'll be Lidia's hero for life."

Dan grunted unappreciatively. "And the opposite to Callum."

"Why? Once he gets over the embarrassment, he ought to be grateful that you punctured his delusion."

"Did you ever see *The Iceman Cometh*?"

Janice said, "I'm too tired to remember, let alone work out what point you're trying to make."

"Yeah. We should go to bed."

Dan lay awake, trying to think of reasons to be optimistic. Maybe the strike would only last a couple of days. Nobody cared whether the sleaze-bags who cold-called them from boiler rooms were human or not, but however many adorable robot seals the hospitals put in their children's wards, the public wouldn't stand by and let half their nurses be replaced by props from Z-grade science fiction movies.

THE MINISTER ROSE to address the legislative assembly. "We need to be agile and innovative in our approach to the provision of health care," she said. "The public expects value for money, and this illegal strike is just a desperate, cynical attempt by special interest groups to resist the inevitable."

Everyone in the crowd of protesters was gathered around half a dozen phones, standing on tip-toes and peering over people's shoulders instead of each watching on their own. It was awkward, but it made for an oddly communal experience.

"The independent research commissioned by my department," the

Minister continued, "demonstrates conclusively that not only will we be saving money by rolling out the Care Assistants, we will be saving lives. We will open more beds. We will slash the waiting times for surgery. And we will speed up the throughput in the Emergency Departments. But the unions are intent on feathering their own nests; they have no interest in the public good."

The jeering from the opposition benches was subdued; that from the nurses around him less so. Dan had read the report the Minister was citing; it was packed with dubious suppositions. There had certainly not been any peer-reviewed trials establishing any of these vaunted claims.

"Get over yourselves and get back to work!" a man in a wheelchair shouted, as he powered his way toward the sliding doors at the hospital's main entrance. The nurses were maintaining a skeleton staff to ensure that no patients were put at risk, but there was no doubt that people had been inconvenienced—and the CareBots were still far from able to plug all the gaps.

Dan glanced at his watch. "I have to go pick up Carlie," he told Janice.

"Yeah. See you tonight." Her voice was hoarse; she'd been here since six in the morning, and the chants weren't gentle on anyone's throat.

Dan squeezed her hand as they parted, then made his way slowly through the throng toward the carpark.

Before he could unlock the car, his phone chimed. He glanced at it; he had a message from the bank. He'd applied for a temporary variation on their loan agreement: a two-month period of interest-only payments. They'd turned him down.

The strike wasn't going to end in the next few days. He sent a message to Janice.

You saw that from the bank? I think we need to move now, or they'll do it for us and screw us in the process.

He stood by the car, waiting, feeling the blood rising to his face. What good was he to her and their daughter? He'd forced her into a position where she'd had to work every day until she could barely stand up, and now they were still going to lose the house. He should have got down on his knees and begged Graham to find him his own wealthy pervert to titillate. At least he'd never aspired to be any kind of writer, so debasing the practice wouldn't make him a whore.

The reply came back: *OK, do it.*

Dan covered his eyes with his forearm for a few seconds, then got control of himself. He had the listing prepared already; he opened the real estate app on his phone and tapped the button that made it go live.

Then he got into the car and headed for the school, rehearsing his speech to Carlie about the amazing new home they'd be living in, with stair-wells covered in multi-colored writing and a balcony so high up that you could see everything for miles.

7

"I WAS PLAYED," Callum said angrily. He was sitting on the last of the packing crates, drenched with sweat, after helping Dan lug it up eight flights to the Beautiful Place.

Dan was still struggling to catch his breath. His gym membership had expired a month ago, and apparently his cardiovascular system had mistaken the sudden decline in demand for an excuse to go into early retirement.

"You don't know CPR, do you?"

"You'll be fine." Callum cycled, rain or shine, rich or poor, right through the Singularity. "I know you think I was an idiot, but it's not that simple."

Dan sat on the floor and put his head on his knees. "Please don't tell me that it was all a double bluff: our AI masters pretended to reveal themselves, then allowed you to discover that they really hadn't, in order to convince you that they don't exist. Of all the even-numbered bluffs, the less-famous 'zero bluff' cancels itself out just as thoroughly, while attracting even less attention."

But Callum was in no mood to see his faith mocked, and if his Shroud of Turin had failed its carbon dating, that demanded a conspiracy at least as elaborate as his original, theological claims.

"It's not as if I took that Reddit post at face value," he said vehemently. "I *checked* the Wikipedia article on one-way functions before I did anything else. And I swear, the formula was still listed as a high-confidence candidate. There was even a link to some famous complexity theorist saying he'd run naked across a field at MIT if it was ever disproved in his lifetime."

"Maybe he'd already seen an early draft of the paper; it's so hard to find good excuses for compulsive exhibitionism."

"Last week, I went back to Wikipedia and looked at the edit history. That part of the article was actually updated to take account of the Delhi result, months before I read the page."

"But then some vandal rolled it back?"

"No. Or at least, if that's what happened, the edit history doesn't reflect it."

Dan's breathing had slowed now; he raised his head. "OK. So the trolls didn't just edit the article, they had the skills to cover their tracks. That's sneaky, but—"

"'Sneaky' isn't the word for it! I've been comparing notes with people online, and either the article was edited *thousands* of times in the space of a couple of days—all without raising any flags with Wikipedia—or the edit history is actually correct, but certain people were fed the older version, somehow."

Dan gazed across the floor at all the crates he needed to unpack before Janice arrived with Carlie. "Someone messed with your head, and you're angry. I get it. But that doesn't mean you have a personal cyber-stalker, who knew exactly when you'd taken the bait and jumped in to prop up all the other pieces of fake scenery as you walked by each one of them."

Callum was silent for a while. Then he said, "The thing is, when we thought it was real, we weren't doing too badly. We were keeping things together: fixing each other's stuff, doing food runs out into the countryside."

"Practicing your Linda Hamilton chin-ups, learning to fire rocket launchers..."

Callum laughed, but then caught himself. "I can think of a few countries where it might have ended up like that."

Dan said, "So look on the bright side."

"Which is?"

"You can still play *Terminator: Resistance* for as long as you like, repairing your analog gadgets and running a clandestine food co-op under the radar of the digital banking system. All without turning into survivalist nut-jobs, or worrying about killer robots trying to assassinate your leaders."

*   *   *

WHEN JANICE AND Carlie arrived, they were accompanied by Carlie's friend, Chalice, who'd heard so much from Carlie about the family's glorious new abode that she'd talked her mother into letting Janice whisk her away for a quick tour.

"Come and see my bedroom!" Carlie demanded. Dan hadn't even reassembled the shelves there, but the sheer novelty of the place seemed to be enough to keep his daughter enchanted, and if her friend was unimpressed she was polite enough not to show it.

At least the fridge had been running long enough that they had some cold fruit juice to offer their guest when the tour was over.

"Chalice's mother has her own fashion line, and her own perfumes, just like Japonica," Carlie explained, as she dabbed a forefinger curiously into the ring of condensation her glass had left on the table.

"Aha." Dan glanced questioningly at Janice, who returned an expression of pure agnosticism.

"I don't want that kind of high-pressure lifestyle myself," Chalice said. "I just want people to be able to look at the pictures of my ordinary day, and see how to stay healthy and stylish on a budget."

Janice said, "I think it's time I drove you home."

Dan went to put up the shelves. When he was done, he toured the flat himself and took stock of things. The place looked even smaller now they'd furnished it, but it was clean, and the rent was reasonable. They'd got out of the mortgage just in time, and managed to land on their feet.

WHEN CARLIE WAS in bed, Janice said, "I have some news."

She was fidgeting with her wedding ring, which was a bad sign; when she was stressed, she got eczema on her fingers.

"We're going to end the strike. No one can hold out any more."

"OK." Dan wasn't surprised; the tribunal had ruled a week before that the nurses should return to work and re-start negotiations, and the decision had come with a deadline and the threat of fines for non-compliance.

"But the hospital's already sent out dismissal notices to twenty percent of the workforce." Janice held up her phone. The message was shorter than Dan's own conversation with Human Resources.

"I'm sorry." Dan took her hand. Her job had been ten times harder than his—and though she'd worked in the same ward for the last eight years, they'd never made her position permanent. As a casual employee, she wouldn't get a cent in severance pay. "At least we'll have a bit left over from the equity in the house, once the settlement goes through."

"Enough to keep us afloat for three months?" she asked. That was how long they'd have to wait before they'd be eligible for the JobSearch Allowance.

"It should be."

"'Should'?"

Dan was meant to be on top of their finances; it was the one thing he was supposed to be good at. "If we're careful," he said. "And if nothing unexpected happens."

8

DAN PARKED A hundred meters down the street from Graham's house, and prepared to wait. For the last three days, he'd managed to spend an hour in the same spot without attracting any attention from the police or local residents, but if he was challenged he was willing to risk claiming that he'd come to visit his friend to discuss a personal matter, only to suffer cold feet. It sounded pathetic, but if the cops knocked on Graham's door to test the story he was unlikely to flatly deny knowing Dan, and he might well be capable of sincerely believing that Dan could experience both an urge to confide in him, and a degree of reticence when it came to the crunch.

His phone rang; it was his sister Nina.

"How's Adelaide?" he asked.

"Good. But we're leaving next week."

"Really? Going where?"

"Seville."

"You're moving to *Spain*?"

"No," she replied, amused. "Seville as in Seville Systems—it's the new town around the solar farm. It's only about three hundred kilometers away."

Dan had heard of a big new solar farm about to come online in South

Australia, but he'd pictured it in splendid isolation. "Why are you moving to live next to a giant array of mirrors? If they're going to be selling power to half the country, I'm sure you'll be able to plug in from Adelaide."

"The shire did a deal with the operators, and they're setting up a new kind of community there. Locally grown food, zero carbon housing... it's going to be fantastic!"

"OK. But what will you do up there?" Nina had trained as a social worker, but as far as Dan knew she hadn't been able to find a job in years.

"Whatever I want," she replied. "Part of the deal with the company is a universal basic income for the residents. I'll have plenty of ways to pass the time, though; I can keep on with my paintings, or I can work with disadvantaged youth."

"OK."

"You should come!" Nina urged him. "You and Janice and Carlie... we'd have a great time."

Dan said, "No, we're too busy. There are a lot of opportunities we're looking into here."

"At least ask Janice," Nina insisted. "Promise me you'll think about it."

"I've got to go," Dan said. The courier's van was pulling up in front of Graham's house. "Call me when you get there, you can give me an update."

"All right."

Graham walked out with a white cardboard box about a meter across, and held it up with the bar-code visible so the van would accept it. A hatch slid open, and he placed the package inside.

When the hatch closed, Graham slapped the side of the van, as if there were a human inside who needed this cue to know that he'd finished. As the van drove off, Dan half expected him to raise a hand in farewell, but he lowered his eyes and turned away.

Dan didn't risk driving past the house; he circled around the block, catching up with the yellow-and-red van as it approached the arterial road he'd guessed it would be taking, unless this mysterious Medici just happened to live in the same suburb as their Michelangelo. When it turned, heading east, Dan managed to get into the same lane, a couple of cars behind it.

The van maintained its course for ten minutes, twenty minutes, ascending the income gradient. Dan had already spent enough time rehearsing his encounter with Graham's patron; now he just tried to block the script from his mind so he wouldn't start second-guessing himself. In the script, he had phrased his request as a business proposition, in language so oblique that even if the whole thing was recorded, half of any jury would refuse to interpret it as blackmail.

He wasn't proud of himself, but he had to get the family over the line somehow. The government's computers had convinced themselves that he and Janice had willfully frittered away their savings, so they were facing an increased waiting period for income support. Dan had spent the last six weeks trying to understand the basis for the decision, in the hope of having it reversed, but he had been unable to extract any coherent narrative from the department's online portal. Apparently some fly-spot in the multidimensional space of all welfare applicants' financial profiles had ended up correlated with profligacy, and that was that: once you fell into the statistical red zone, no one was obliged to point to any single act you'd committed that was manifestly imprudent.

The van shifted lanes, preparing to turn at the next set of lights. Dan was surprised; anyone who could afford sixty grand a year for designer porn ought to be a little more upmarket when it came to real estate. He smiled grimly; when a few hundred thousand data points couldn't separate his behavior from that of a welfare cheat, who was he to start profiling aficionados of Graham's special talent?

The van turned north; Dan followed. The street was mixed residential, with well-maintained but unspectacular houses, retail strips, occasional office blocks.

As it approached a row of fast-food restaurants, the van slowed, then turned into the carpark. Dan was confused; even if it was able to make time for another pick-up along the way, because the ice-cream cake was so well-insulated against the afternoon heat, this was an odd site to do it. Was there a driver on board, after all? Dan hadn't actually seen into the front of the vehicle. Despite its uniform nationwide livery, the courier company was a franchise; maybe one local owner-operator had decided to buck the trend and sit behind a steering wheel.

Dan followed the van into the carpark. It still hadn't settled on a bay, despite passing half a dozen empty spots, but maybe the driver wanted to get closer to the Indian take-away at the far end of the strip. He stayed well behind, but decided not to risk parking yet, gesturing to an approaching station wagon to take the bay that he seemed to be coveting.

The van stopped beside a dumpster. The lid was propped up, angled low enough to keep out the elements but still leaving an opening at the side so large that all but the most uncoordinated members of the public who lobbed their trash in as they drove past would stand a good chance of succeeding.

The hatch opened at the side of the van, and Graham's pristine white box emerged, riding on a gleaming stainless steel plate. When the platform was fully extended the box sat motionless, and Dan clung for a moment to a vision of the rightful recipient, appearing from nowhere in a designer hoodie to snatch up their prized fetish-dessert and dash from the carpark to a limousine waiting on the street. Perhaps a whole convoy of limousines, with decoys to render pursuit impossible.

But then some hidden mechanism gave the box a push and it toppled in to join the chicken bones and greasy napkins.

9

"WE'LL MOVE IN with my mother," Janice decided.

"She has *one* spare room. Which she uses for storage." Dan could feel his sweat dampening the sheet beneath him. The night wasn't all that warm, but his body had started drenching his skin at random moments, for no reason he could fathom.

"We can deal with the junk," Janice said. "She'll be glad to have it tidied up. I can sleep in the spare bed with Carlie, and you can sleep on the couch. It will only be for a couple of months."

"How do you know she'll even agree to have us?"

"Do you think she'd let her granddaughter sleep in a car?"

"Do you think *I* would?" Dan replied.

Janice pursed her lips reprovingly. "Don't twist my words around. I know you've done everything you can. And I know I have too—which doesn't make me feel any less guilty, but it makes it easier for me to swallow my pride. If we'd pissed all our savings away on... whatever the government's brilliant algorithm thinks our vices are... then I'd probably be tearing my hair out in self-loathing while I tried to keep my voice calm on the phone to her, begging for that room. But we've done nothing wrong. We need to be clear about that, for the sake of our own sanity, then take whatever the next step is that will keep a roof over our heads."

DAN MUST HAVE fallen asleep around three, because when he woke at a quarter past four, he felt the special, wretched tiredness that was worse than not having slept at all.

He rose and walked out of the bedroom. In the living room, he switched on his laptop and squinted painfully at the sudden brightness of the screen. He went through the ritual of checking the JobSeekers site, TaskRabbit, and a dozen other places that supposedly offered business and employment opportunities, but—once you weeded out the pyramid schemes and the outright phishing scams—never seemed to carry anything legitimate for which he had the skills or the capital.

His mail program beeped softly. He kept his eyes averted from the alert that came and went on the upper right of the screen; he didn't want to know about yet another plea from one of the charities he'd stopped supporting. What did he actually bring to the world, now? If he disappeared at this moment, it would be as if the air had closed in on empty space.

He opened the program to delete the unread message, but he didn't succeed in going through the motions without seeing the sender. The email was from Baker and Saunders, the American law firm. The subject line read: *Settlement offer*.

Dan opened the message. His eyes were still bleary; he had to enlarge the text to read it. Deepity Systems were prepared to settle out of court. They were offering a payment of thirty thousand dollars *per year*, for five years, to every single litigant in Dan's age and skill cohort.

He re-read the message a dozen times, searching for the downside: the toxic fine print that would turn the victory sour. But he couldn't find it. He opened the attachment, the formal agreement the lawyers had drafted; it was five times longer than the summary, and ten times harder to follow, but there'd been a time when he'd been used to reading financial contracts, and none of the language set alarm bells ringing.

Just before dawn, Janice emerged from the bedroom.

"What are you looking at?" she asked, sitting beside him.

He switched back to the body of the email and slid the laptop across so she could read it. He watched her frowning in disbelief as the scale of the offer sank in.

"Is this real?"

Dan was silent for a while. It was a good question, and he needed to be honest with her.

"If I sign this," he said, "then I believe we'll get the money they're promising. The only thing I'm not sure about is... why."

"What do you mean? Presumably they're afraid that the courts might make them pay even more."

Dan said, "If you were a tech mogul, what would your fantasy of the near-term future be?"

"Colonies on Mars, apparently."

"Sticking to Earth, for now."

Janice was losing patience, but she played along. "I don't know. That business keeps booming? That my stock options keep going through the roof?"

"But what if a large part of your business consists of selling things that put people out of work. Including many of the people who actually pay for the things you're trying to sell."

"Then you've screwed yourself, haven't you?"

Dan said, "Unless you can find a way to keep your customers afloat. You could try to talk the wealthier governments into paying everyone a UBI—and sweeten it a bit by offering to pitch in with a bit more tax yourself. You and your machines *become* the largest sector of the economy; what used to be the labor force is reduced to the role of consumer, but the UBI plugs them into the loop and keeps the money circulating—without bread-lines, without riots in the street."

"Well, they can dream on," Janice replied. "Whatever Nina's got going in Seville, that's never going to be universal."

"Of course not," Dan agreed. "Between the politics, and the different ideas everyone has about personal responsibility, it's never going to fly. Not as one size fits all. But you know, the computers at Thriftocracy always managed to find a repayment plan that suited every client. Once you've gathered enough information about someone, if your goal isn't actually harmful to them you can usually find a way of repackaging it that they're willing to swallow."

Janice was fully awake now. "Are you about to pull some kind of Callum on me?"

Dan shook his head. "I don't think it's even a conspiracy, let alone a plan that the computers dreamed up all by themselves. But Thriftocracy didn't need anyone conspiring in order to start *managing people*. They just offered a service that met other companies' needs. If enough tech firms believe they can benefit from novel ways of limiting the blow-back as they hollow out the middle class, achieving that will become an industry in its own right."

"So... they organize law suits against themselves?"

"Why not? Especially when they'll never go to court." Dan glanced admiringly at the agreement the bots had crafted. There might have been tens of thousands of people in the class action, but it wouldn't have surprised him if the language of this particular document had been tailored for his eyes alone. "They can't quite achieve what they really aspire to, but they're smart enough to understand that the only way to get close is to feed us some version of our own fantasies. They had me pegged, near enough: I would have been happy to win a legal battle against the fuckers who took my job away. But they're more than willing to customize their approach, and if Chalice's mother wants to think she's a fashion icon whose every doodle on her tablet starts clothing factories humming in China, or Graham needs to believe he has a patron hanging out for every word that pops into his head about naughty teenagers, if it gets the job done, so be it. I suppose they must have judged Callum to be too paranoid to accept their hand-outs without becoming suspicious, so they tried to turn that into an advantage and at least give him a sense of purpose and a bit of support from a like-minded community. Then I came blundering in and spoiled it with the horrible, horrible truth."

Janice rubbed her eyes, still not really sold on his own paranoid vision, but not quite certain, either, that he was wrong.

She said, "So what do you want to do?"

Dan laughed. "*Want?* We have no choice. If we don't take this money, your mother will have stabbed me through the arm with a carving knife before the end of the school term."

* * *

10

ONCE THE SETTLEMENT was finalized and the first tranche was in Dan's bank account, the ads soon followed. They followed him to every web site, however many times he purged cookies, or rebooted his modem to get a fresh IP address.

"This watch will get your fitness back on track!" an avatar who looked a lot like the old, filtered version of Dan promised. "Come on, you're not over the hill yet!" alter-Dan goaded him, running up and down steeply sloping streets until his manly stubble glistened and his resting heart rate plummeted.

"Three simultaneous channels of premium streaming entertainment, including Just For Kids, plus unlimited interactive gaming!" This from a woman who resembled Janice, to reassure him that there really was no need to consult her; like her doppelgänger, she was certain to approve.

Dan almost felt ungrateful, each time he declined to click through to a purchase. After all, wasn't a tithe for his not-so-secret benefactors the new definition of *giving something back*?

Janice found a volunteer position with a homelessness charity, tending to people who'd had surgery but whose post-operative recovery was adversely affected by a lack of food, showers and beds. Dan offered his own services to the same group, but since he had no relevant skills and their rosters were full, they declined. He looked into an organization that did odd jobs and gardening for pensioners, but then realized they were just undercutting the paid market.

The money, while it lasted, would keep his family out of poverty, but it wasn't enough to pay for any kind of formal retraining. Dan scoured the web, looking at free online courses, trying to decide if any of them would actually render him employable. Apparently, he could learn to be proficient in all the latest programming languages and data mining methods in as little as twelve months, but everyone else from Bangalore to Zambia had already jumped on that bandwagon. And how many software engineers did it take to skill-clone a million software engineers? No more than it took to clone just one.

*　　*　　*

ON HIS WAY to pick up Carlie, Dan saw the windshield-wiping Dalmatian waving its squeegee from the side of the road.

He slowed the car, reluctantly, knowing he'd feel bad whatever he did. He still hadn't restarted his donations to Médecins Sans Frontières; on any sane analysis, the family's new budget just didn't stretch that far, however worthy the cause. But the bedraggled mutt pushed some button in him that even footage of a malarial child couldn't reach.

He waited for the dog to finish its slapdash routine, more a ritual than a service. The stitching was coming apart on the costume, leaving one of the eyes dangling, and there were burrs all over the parts of the material where it hadn't worn too thin to hold on to them.

Dan fished a five-dollar bill out of his wallet. As the exchange took place, he reached out with his other hand and squeezed the dog's forearm in what he'd meant as a gesture of solidarity. His fingers came together as they pushed against the dirty fabric, until they encircled a hard, slender rod.

He let go of the bill, and the dog waited, silent and motionless, for Dan to release his grip. Dan peered into the dark maw of its mouth, from which he'd always imagined the occupant was peering out, but as his eyes adapted he could see all the way to the back of the vacant head.

What was inside the costume, below, out of sight? A metal armature, a few motors, a battery, and an old smart phone running it all?

Dan let go of the dog's arm. "Good for you," he said, wondering if the thing's ingenious creator would ever hear his words, but maybe the software extracted a few highlights to replay at the end of each day. He didn't feel cheated; whoever would be getting his money probably needed it just as much as if they'd been here to collect it in person.

At the school gate, Dan still had trouble looking Graham in the eye. When Carlie ran up the path, he smiled and gave her his full attention, blocking out everything else.

"So how was school today?" he asked, as they walked toward the car.

"All right."

"Just all right?"

"Ms. Snowball's really boring," she complained.

"Boring?" Dan gazed down at his daughter, mock-aghast. "You don't want to hurt her feelings, do you?"

Carlie glared back at him, unamused. "I want Ms. Jameson to come back."

"That's not going to happen." The trial was over, but the budgetary savings were locked in. A teaching assistant could watch over three classes at once, for far less than the cost of a human teacher for each.

On the drive home, Dan tried to picture the life Carlie would face. For the last few weeks, all he'd been able to envision was a choice between the family joining a commune in Nimbin to weave their own underwear out of hemp, or resigning themselves to their role laundering money for Silicon Valley.

They approached the Dalmatian, which waved cheerfully.

"Daddy, can we—?"

"Sorry, I already did." Dan gestured at the streaked suds still drying on the windshield.

Then he said, "How'd you like to learn to make Ms. Snowball's head come off?"

"You're silly."

"No, I'm serious! How'd you like to learn to make her do whatever you want?" Either they moved out into the countryside and became subsistence farmers, or they stayed and fought to regain some kind of agency, using the only weapons that worked now. The idea that every person in the world ought to learn to code had always struck Dan as an infuriating piece of proselytizing, as bizarre as being told that everyone just had to shut up and become Rastafarian. But in the zombie apocalypse, no one ever complained that they needed to learn to sharpen sticks and drive them into rotting brains. It wasn't a matter of cultural homogeneity. It was a question of knowing how to fuck with your enemy.

"Do you really know how to do that?" Carlie asked.

"Not yet," Dan confessed. "But I think that if we work hard, we'll be able to figure it out together."

THE LAMENTATION OF THEIR WOMEN
Kai Ashante Wilson

Kai Ashante Wilson is the author of "The Devil in America", which was nominated for the Nebula, World Fantasy, and Shirley Jackson Awards. His short fiction has been published by *Tor.com* and in the anthology *Stories for Chip*. His most recent works are short fantasy novels *The Sorcerer of the Wildeeps* and *A Taste of Honey*, which are available from all fine booksellers. He lives in New York City.

pre.

"HELLO," ANSWERED SOME whiteman. "Good morning! Could I speak with—?" He mispronounced her last name and didn't abbreviate her first, as nobody who knew her would do.

"Who dis?" she repeated. "And what you calling about?"

"Young lady," he said. "Can you please tell me whether Miss Jean-Louis is there or not. Will you just do that for me?" His tone all floured with whitepeople siddity, pan-fried in condescension.

But she could sit here and act dumb too. "Mmm... it's hard to say. She be in and out, you know? Tell me who calling and what for and I'll go check."

Apparently, the man was Mr Blah D. Blah from the city agency that cleaned out Section 8 apartments when the leaseholder dropped dead. Guess whose evil Aunt Esther had died of a heart attack last Thursday on the B15 bus? And guess who was the last living Jean-Louis anywhere?

"But how you calling me—it's almost noon—to say I got 'til *five*, before your dudes come throw all her stuff in the dumpster?"

"Oh good," exclaimed Blah D. "I was worried we weren't communicating clearly."

"She live out by Jamaica Bay! It'd take me two hours just to *get there*."

"Miss Jean-Louis," he said. (Public servants nearing retirement, who never got promoted high enough not to deal with poor people anymore, black people anymore, have this tone of voice, you ever notice? A certain tone.) "There's no requirement for you to go. This is merely a courtesy our office extends to the next of kin. The keys will be available to you until five." Blah hung up.

"*Fuck* you!" She was dressed for the house, a tank top and leggings, and so went to her room for some sneakers and a hoodie.

Mama was scared of Esther, said she was a witch. Both times they had went out there, Mama left her downstairs, waiting in the streets, rather than bring her baby up to that apartment. Now, *she* didn't believe in that black magic bullshit, of course, but she also wasn't trying to go way the hell out there by herself. Mama, though, wouldn't want no parts of Esther, dead sister of the dead man who'd walked out on her some fifteen years ago. Naw, better leave Mama alone at work and call her later.

She'd get Anhell to go. They were suppose to had been broke up with each other at least till this weekend coming, but whatever. She could switch him back to 'man' from 'ex' a couple days early. Wouldn't be the first time. *I'm a be over there in twenty*, she texted.

She put a scarf on her head and leff out.

1

how can I word this?
you ain't been perfect

DAMNIT. FORGOT THE keys to his place back in her other purse! She texted again from the street, and then hit the buzzer downstairs for his apartment. That nigga was *definitely* up there parked on the couch, blazed out and playing videogames. She knew it, and leaned on the button, steady.

"Yo! *What?!* Who is this?"

"I leff Mama's without the keys. Lemme up."

"'Nisha?"

"Yeah! Ain't you get my texts? Buzz me in, nigga."

"I was, uh... I been busy. Could you, like, uh, wait down there *real* fast for me, baby? Just *one* minute."

With her thoughts on buried treasure in the far east of Brooklyn, not on boyfriends who step out the minute you turn your back, she wasn't ready for the panicked fluttering that seized her heart and bowels, the icy flashes that turned sweaty hot—the anger, pure and simple.

Chick or dude. What would it be this time?

Dude. Not too long, and Anhell's piece got off the elevator and crossed the vestibule toward the outer doors. Dude looked regular black, but was obviously Dominican from the loafers and tourniquet-tight clothes. He lived, you could tell, at the gym. Titties bigger than hers, a nasty V-neck putting his whole tattooed chest out on front street. 𝔐𝔞𝔰 𝔏𝔦𝔟𝔯𝔞𝔫𝔬𝔰 𝔇𝔢𝔩 𝔐𝔞𝔩. Heading out, he politely held the door so she could go in. No words, they kept it moving.

The problem was, if you liked pretty boys, and she did like pretty boys, then Anhell was it. You couldn't do no better. She looked okay—*damn good*, when she got all dressed up, her hair and makeup tight. But Anhell was pure Spanish butterscotch. Lightskin, gray eyes, cornrow hangtime to the middle of his back. He answered the door in a towel, naked and wet from a quick shower. Hickies on him she ain't put there.

There's rules to whooping your man's ass. He tries to catch and hold your fists, dodge your knees and elbows and kicks, but accepts in his heart that every lick you land he deserves. *You* don't go grabbing a knife, or yanking at his hair, either, as the electric fear or pain those inspire will make him lash out with blind total force, turning this rough game real in a way nobody wants. Stay in bounds, babygirl, and you can whale on him till you're so tired you ain't mad no more, and his cheating bitch ass is all bruised up and crying. But fuckit. She wasn't really feeling it today. After getting in a few solid hits, she let Anhell catch her wrists. They were on the floor by then and he hugged her in close and tight, starting up with them same old tears and kisses, same old promises and lies.

"'Nisha, what can I do? Whatever you need, just tell me what I can do. I'll do it."

Stop laying with them hoes! With them faggots! But this was just the little sin, the one convenient to throw back in his face. She might not even give a shit anymore, if she ever bothered to check. What couldn't be fixed was his big sin. The one they'd cried about, fucked and fought about *all the time* with fists and screams, but not once ever just said the words out loud, plain and clear. Now that a couple years had slipped by it was obvious they were never going to say the words at all.

You know what you did, she said. *You* know *what you did*. And Anhell did know, and so for once shut up with all the bullshit. They lay for a while just breathing, just embraced, their exhausted resignation like a mysterious disease presenting the exact same way as tenderness. "My aunt died and left me all her shit."

"¿La bruja?"

"Yeah. I need you to come out to Brooklyn with me, see if there's anything worth something."

"My case worker coming by tomorrow." Anhell felt good, smelled good, left arm holding her, right hand stroking her shoulder, back and ass in a loop that made everywhere he touched gain value, feel loved. "You know I gotta be here."

"We just going out there," she said, "look around, and then come straight back. It ain't no all night kinda thing."

"Well, lemme get dressed and we'll head out." He let her go and sat up.

"Wait," she said. "Hol' up." She hooked her thumbs under her panties and leggings. "Eat me out a little fowego?" She rolled em to her knees.

It's gotta be hard, right, when they keep asking for what you can't give, but so *good*, when they want exactly the thing you do best? Anhell grinned. "I got you, mami." He pulled her leggings down further, rolled her knees out wide. "Lemme get in there right..."

Somebody suicide-jumped at Grand Central, so the 5 train was all fucked up. They were more than *three* hours getting out there.

Block after block of projects like brick canyons, a little city in the City, home to thousands and thousands and not one whiteface, except for cops from Long Island or Staten Island doubled up in cruisers or walking in posses. It was warm as late summer, the October rain falling hard enough to where you'd open your umbrella, but so soft you felt silly doing it. Anhell walked just behind, holding it over her, the four-dollar wingspan too paltry to share. Drop by drop his tight braids roughened.

Aunt Esther's building was over a few blocks from the subway. Not one of the citysized ones, but big enough. The kind, you know, with the liquor store-style security booth at the entrance, somebody watching who comes and goes.

"*Excuse me*," called the man behind the plastic. "Hey, yo, Braids—and you, Miss? Visitors gotta sign in." Behind the partition, he held up the clipboard.

They went over to the window and scribbled their names. Though basketball-player-tall, up close you could see he wasn't grown. Just some teenage dropout on his hood brand cell, Youtubing bootleg rappers.

She tapped the plastic. "It should be some keys in there, waiting for me," she said. "So I can get into my aunt's apartment."

"Nobody tole me nuffen about that."

"What's that right there?" she said, pointing to the desk beside the boy's elbow, where an envelope lay with her name written across it.

He gave this revelation several blinks and turned back. "Well, you gotta show some ID, then."

She got out her EBT and pressed it to the partition. Squinting, the boy leaned forward and mouthed the name off the card, *Tanisha Marie Jean-Louis*, and then, slower than your slow cousin, compared this to what was written on the envelope, *Tanisha M. Jean-Louis*.

Although allowing, at last, that these two variations fell within tolerance, the boy still shook his head. "Naw, though... I on't think I can give you this. You suppose to show a driver's license."

His stupidity flung her forward bodily against the partition. She smacked her palms on the plastic to lend the necessary words their due emphasis. "Nigga, this *New York*. Ain't nobody out here got no *fucking driver's license*. You better *hand* me that envelope!"

2

askin' ME!
kill them now, or later?

To THE LEFT of the elevator the hall continued around the corner, but 6L, Aunt Esther's apartment, was in the cul-de-sac to the right.

Stink rushed out as the front door swung in. Week-old kitchen trash. Years of cigarettes. Old ladies who piss theyself. Ole Esther had caught her heart attack on the bus, so at least there wasn't that, not the funk of some bloated mice-nibbled corpse leaking slime.

On a corner table inside the door was a huge, nasty religious mess. Ugly dolls, rat bones, weird trash. If all Satan's blue-black devils had wifed all God's blue-blonde saints, then a gaudy likeness of their brats was painted on the clutter of seven-day glass candles. She went over to take a look. Breathing through some open window the moment after Anhell followed her in, a breeze slammed the front door shut. The sudden breathless dark had him slapping at the walls desperately until he found the lights. She sneered. "Come peep this. She was on some real hoodoo shit."

"No, mami." He came over reluctantly. "This ain't Voodoo or Santería, ni nada parecido. Your Auntie ain't bought nunna this at no botánica. Look at that."

"Yeah? A cross—so what?"

"You don't see nothing weird about it?"

Though fancy and heavy-looking as real silver, it was just cheap ass plastic junk when she thumped a finger against it. Rather than about-to-die, the face of Jesus looked more like a man nutting, but apart from the crucifix being upside down she couldn't see what had Anhell all freaked out. She shrugged.

Anhell was superstitious. His grandma had wanted him to go to Miami for some expensive Catholic thing, accepting his saint or some shit like that. But his trifling ass had just bought tracksuits, Jordans, and smoked up all the money she'd left him. Now, he touched the bare skin of his neck as if there should've been beads hanging there, some guardian angel to call on today of all days. Her pretty babyboy, so full of regret! She saw how she could fuck with him.

There was a Poland Spring, label ripped off, in the middle of all that voodoo mess. She picked it up.

"You can't drink that, 'Nisha!"

"It ain't even been open yet." She cracked the seal, untwisting the cap to show him. To fuck with him. "It's clean."

"It's blessed water," Anhell said. "*Cursed*—blessed, I don't *know* what! But I swear to God, don't drink it, 'Nisha."

"Mmm," she sighed, after gulping down half the bottle. "I was sooo thirsty, though...!"

He got quiet, but she could read these signs from being hugged up with him on the couch so many nights. Forcing him to watch the kind of movies she laughed at, but turned *him* into a motherless six-year-old, afraid of the dark. While she rummaged the apartment, pulling out drawers and dumping worthless old lady trash onto the floor, Anhell followed close, brushing up against her as if onna'ccident. He was scared as shit and wishing she'd change the channel. But, no, nigga. *This* is the show. This is what we're watching.

Not under the mattress, not in the dresser, she didn't find a fat stash of benjis anywhere. Ratty old bras, holey socks, musty dresses. She sorted highspeed through a folder labeled "important papers," dropping a blizzard to the ground as her audit turned up nothing but Social Security and Con Ed stubs, obituaries clipped from newspapers, yellowing funeral programs. Her father's. But the treasure had to be buried in here *somewhere*. Anhell came to sit by her on the edge of the coffee table. He jumped to his feet when it teetered up like a seesaw. There!

"Get that end," she said.

They dumped over the coffee table top, its old school *Ebony*s and dish of peppermints scattering. Underneath was a trunk, a real pirate ass looking trunk. *Now we're talking!*

No hinges or latches were visible on it, but when Anhell tried to pry up the lid, he fell back on his butt, saying, "Shit's locked up *tight*."

She said, "No, it ain't," and effortlessly lifted the lid herself. Folded up inside was a tall, tall man or woman, long-dead and withered black and dry as stale raisins, their longest bones broken to fit fetus-style in the confines of the chest. Anhell screamed all girly and jumped back onto the couch. She rolled her eyes at him. "*Dead*. And how many times I told you what *dead* means?" she said. "Can't *do* nothing to you, Anhell. Nothing to *worry* about!" He started whining but she ignored him.

There were two things in there with the body (its skin cheap-feeling, just leather*ish*, like a hundred-dollar sofa from the ghetto furniture store, and the body weightless and unresisting as piled laundry). One was a shotgun that could have come from the Civil War, half made of wood. She set it aside.

The other was *her* baby, a knife equal in length and width to her own arm, its handle protruding from a rawhide sheath.

You-know-who sidles up and offers... what? *Change*. Not for the better, not for the worse, just a *change*. But one so huge that you can't even dream it from the miserable little spot, miserable little moment you're at now. And don't go expecting wishes granted, or that kind of boring shit, because transformation belongs to a whole 'nother category. But, oh, babygirl, this could be a wild hot ride. *Are you down?*

Anhell had slipped off the couch and knelt beside her. He was reaching toward the shotgun, but hesitating too... up until *she* did it. Until *she* pulled out the long knife, no, *machète*, from the leather sheath that flaked apart in her hands like ancient pages from an ancient book. Anhell picked up the gun.

Oh, fuck yeah!

It felt like being at the club, three, fo' drinks in, every chick in the place hating, every nigga tryna holler—and then your song come on. The beat drop. She felt loose as a motherfucker. "Ooo, Anhell." Groaning, she wedged the heel of a hand down between her thighs. "You feel that, too?"

Yeah, the nigga was feeling it! She oughta know that look on his face by now, about to bust a *really* good one.

She tested the machète's edge with a fingertip and found it all the way dull, however sharp it looked. Even pressing down hard against the edge hardly dented the pad of her thumb.

Anhell, too, reached out wanting to test the edge of that weird machète. But then he sort of thought twice, stopped short, and shied his hand right on back again. Just like that, she got it. Understood all the possibilities for black magic murder. "Come on, papi," she purred, cat-malicious. "Don't you wanna see what kinda edge it got?" She nudged the machète out toward him—*very* recklessly. Woulda cut his ass, too, if he hadna jumped back so quick. "You ain't skurt, is you?"

She was getting her hands all wet in *somebody's* blood today. That was for *damn* sure.

"Whoa, 'Nisha! Why you playing, though? Back up with that!"

Keys rattled in the lock and the front door swung open.

Two dudes in Dickies and T-shirts came in talking whatever they do over there in Czechoslovakia or Ukraine. The workers were the right color to come to New York and get fat business loans or good union jobs right off the boat, buying a house on a tree-lined street, and all set up for the good life, before their kids even graduated high school. Perhaps for supernatural reasons they didn't notice the shotgun and machète. For natural ones, she and Anhell weren't invisible exactly, but seemed to the workers' eyes only two vague black and brown shapes where they didn't belong.

"You, Miss Jean-Louis? Boss said you gotta be outta here by five o'clock." The law on his side, one of the Serbians held up some important piece of paper, typed, with signatures, etc. "Or we call the cops."

It was instinct. It was *thirst*. Pivoting, she swung like a Cuban phenom at bat who'd better hit that fucking ball or take his damn ass back to the island. Best *believe* she hit. A red-hot knife would've had more trouble with butter, the Polack's astonished trunk separated from his bottom two-thirds so easily. Blood and viscera went splashing by the bucketful but none, impossibly, hit the ground.

A thousand frog-tongues lashing out to snatch as many bugs from the air, every glob of gore vanished in the twinkling of an eye, slurped up by the thirsty machète. How long had this poor baby lain in that awful, *awful* chest?

Though drinking to the last drop was neither delicious nor easy as that first perfect pull, she kept going and swallowed the man down.

The Russian in two pieces desiccated, turning to a spoonful's worth of blown dust between one breath and the next. What, maybe twenty seconds had passed since the door opened? Russkie number two, quick on the uptake and fast on his feet, had spun around and was booking up the hall.

She looked at Anhell and jerked her chin toward the runaway. "*Pop* 'im."

"I ain't never even shot a gun before."

"Just pull the trigger, dumb ass."

Hoisting it up to his shoulder, he aimed. "But what if it ain't loaded?"

It was, though. The discharge, noiseless on earth, made no flash, either, resounding instead throughout hell. All the souls screaming in their lakes were startled into a moment of silence, so loud was that report, so bright. A burst watermelon of gore blew out the white back of the running man's T-shirt. He was snatched forward—off his feet and several yards through the air—by the impact of the demonbullet, which smashed him facedown into the checkered tiles with such goofy, slapstick violence, she and Anhell turned open-mouthed to each other, dead. They died laughing, grabbing at one another and collapsing to the floor, it was that funny how dude had thought he was getting away, but *psych*!

"Okay, okay," she said finally. "Let's get serious." She pointed to the problematic scene in the hallway. "Get out there and clean that shit up, fore somebody come out they apartment."

Unlike firing a gun for the first time, she didn't need to break it down for Anhell how the devil got his due. He walked up the hall, she with him, and put the thirsty muzzle of the gun down into that sucking wet wound.

In no time the juicy corpse was all bled out, the borschty color of a freshly dead whiteman depinking into gray. Anhell lifted the gun from the dry pit of torn lavender flesh, shattered pale bone. "I don't want no more," he whined, screwing up his face. "The sweet part's gone."

"Shut the fuck up," she said, in zero mood for his finicky complaints. *"Finish it."*

Anhell pooched his bottom lip like a four-year-old with just the broccoli left on his plate, but he put the muzzle back down in.

Soon he was gagging, and not faking, either. "All right, all right," she conceded. "Carry the rest back to the apartment." There was no splatter on the floor or walls, no more mess, only a shrunken dry thing like the historical Christ, if those skinny bones were pulled from a tomb in Sinai today. She stomped the old body down into the chest and it burst and crumpled like papier mâché, till there was room for Anhell to roll the new one on top. Fingerprints, wipe shit down, tidy up? Nah, fuck that. The devil got you. He looks after his own.

They bounced, Anhell following her out to the elevator.

"So we just kinda slide into the fires sideways, *not* far, and from there nobody can really see…"

"I *get it*," Anhell said. "You always think I'm so stupid, 'Nisha, but I got it all the same time you did!"

"Well, don't fuck it up, nigga. Cause we carrying this machète and shotgun right through the streets, onto the MT fucking A."

Just newly knighted to this darkest order, they hardly dared more than a step into hell, and so their half-assed little cantrip that first night wouldn't have worked at all, except in a place like New York, where everybody was already trying so hard not to notice strangers.

Night had come to Brooklyn, but you could still see a half inch of daylight glowing behind Manhattan's fallen constellations. They didn't slink from the building like street dogs after grubbing through some alley trash, their heads down, eyes slewing nervously left and right—oh no! They loped like winter wolves, thin yet, but bellies hanging full of fresh kill, and future tooth and scenting nose toward all these little lambs gamboling on every side. Nay, *sweeter* than lambs! For creatures even so gentle can yet scent the beast that would eat them, while men and women and children walking home under soft rain don't know to fear the slavering jaws, the click of claws on concrete.

Shadow and flame licking in the corners of their eyes, machète and gun in hand, they strutted through the evening rush. When they descended to the subway, nine-to-fivers were trudging up and teenagers, just out of basketball practice, leaping stairs two at a time. Down in the station, patrolmen to bust fare-jumpers and dudes selling swipes, and more patrolmen posted at the terrorist table, didn't even blink when two murderers fresh off the deed, weapons naked in hand, rolled past. Busker on the sax, *You've Changed*. Nobody tried to bogart, nobody jostled them on the crowded way back uptown. Where you woulda *swore* there was none, space opened up on the packed train. Coupla seats came free.

You can pray all day, babygirl, but God won't answer. He ain't *thinking* bout you. Now that other guy, though? Will treat you like a fucking rockstar. VIP. Perks.

3

when I say people
that's what I mean

ANHELL CRAWLED ACROSS the bed, over her, flipped on the lights, crashed around the studio. He gathered up and threw out all the bottles, flushed the roaches and ashes, hid the tray, opened the windows and turned the fan on high. He came to the bed whispering. "You don't wanna put on some clothes, mami?" Sleepy and cold from the fan, she just groaned and pulled the covers over her, his pillow over her head. His caseworker buzzed at 8:45, as always, as bimonthly, this middle-aged African bitch who *hated* her and thought she was the biggest slut on earth, but *loved* Anhell, no doubt to the point of hand-on-the-Bible swearing his shit smelled like patchouli and roses. Um, *hello...?* That nigga gave it to *me*.

Mrs Okorie asked Anhell the same stupid social worker questions that had you like *duh...!* the answers to which not only hadn't changed since last time but *couldn't.* Spotting in the heaped up blankets on the bed signs pointing to the presence of a certain fast ass American black girl, Mrs Okorie reminded Anhell that it was against the rules for "company to cohabitate." There was, in fact, this scholarship program which Mrs Okorie thought Anhell (who *wasn't* no fucking college material, not unless y'all got a PhD in PS4) could apply to, even earn his associate's degree, if not for the influence of a certain fast ass American black girl.

Special for people who controlled his benefits, Anhell had this soft sweet voice, this lightskin innocent voice. Saying things like "just visiting" and "a couple days," he almost had Mrs Okorie calmed down when she got up booty-nekkid from bed, crossed to the bathroom and, just half-closing the door, pissed *loud* for a mad ass long time, like some loose bitch who'd been up till four in the morning drinking with her man. Anhell had to work them gray eyes, that good hair, *hard* to get Mrs Okorie calmed down again.

They napped and woke up at noon. They fucked but that wasn't it. Neither was a puff or two off Anhell's first blunt of the day, nor coffee light and sweet, bagel egg and cheese from the corner. And, no, TV wasn't it, and not a nap, and not fooling around again later in bed. Nor staring out the window while Anhell played his videogames. He that giveth thee all shall too expect somewhat in return.

O gluttons of murder, wherefore do ye fast? Bring down the red rain, for in hell we are greatly thirsting...!

Below, crossing the courtyard, were a Spanish girl, her nigga, and their little baby in a stroller. Smiling church ladies, fat and overdressed, stood by the intersection passing out tracts. On the benches, every cell phone out, a girl clique was holding conference. Boys on bikes, on scooters, on skateboards. She didn't want the blood of these people, her people, but somebody had to die and pretty fucking soon. A whole *lot* of somebodies, and day in and day out. How to be evil without doing bad? There's a problem for you, huh?

Around seven they ate take-out tins of chicken, yellow rice and beans from the joint around the corner, sharing a Corona 24 oz. between them—plenty of food and drink, you would've thought, except this fare only made them hungrier, thirstier, for another repast richer by far than this shit. She kept having to move the machète from here to there. Whether propped against the wall, or laid on the floor, table, or bed, its metal seemed to pick up some vibration and whine slightly, a rattle and hum that was setting her teeth on edge. Anhell said he couldn't hear it, but then *she* couldn't hear the weird crackling noise he said the old wood of the shotgun kept making. He stuffed it in the back of the closet, under laundry, but said that didn't really help. He was on his cell a lot, restless. In and out the bathroom, texting hoes. In and out that closet.

"And where you call yourself going?"

"Nowhere," Anhell said, giving his lips a little lick. "Just about to grab a couple phillies at the deli."

"I see you got that gun."

"It's mine, ain't it."

"What, you just gon' head up the block, pop whoever you see first. That's ya plan?"

"Naw! I just, uh…"

"Leave it here, Anhell. Tomorrow, me and you will go fuck shit up real good, okay?" She knew what he was feeling, because she was fiending just as bad. But first she needed to figure this thing out, the how and who and all that. Cause the way you start is how you go on. "Us, *together*. At least one sweet kill each, I promise."

"Look, I just need to step out real fast, baby." Nigga wasn't even trying to run game! Where was the smoothness at, the slick lies? "Just for a minute. I be *right* back."

He turned his back on her like he was gonna just walk out that door still holding the shotgun. Right now she could care less about him fucking around, but *she* was the boss of murder up in this bitch, and it wasn't gon' be no extracurriculars on that front.

She threw a Timb at his head with intent to kill. Anhell's ducking and dodging was some next level shit, so it missed. "You heard? I said, *leave it here* gotdamnit! Or I will chop yo ass up fast as I did that whitenigga yesterday. *Try me*." She thought she'd left it across the room, under the bed, but no, the machète was right here in her hand, eager to make good the lady's word.

There was a moment where you could see him wondering whether females with just a knife should really be coming out the side of they neck at niggas holding guns. She laughed and flicked beckoning fingers. "Play yourself, then. *Come on*. I wish to fuck you would."

They fought a lot and they were both tired, *both* sick of it. Anhell's litebrite eyes took on a glint far more sharp and steel-like than diamond-pretty.

"Oh yeah, daddy," she moaned, as if muvver were wet from all the foreplay and good to go now. "You only gotta *act* like you wanna raise that gun at me, and I will pay you back *every motherfucking thing*. Let's do this." The gun trembled in his hand, his eyes hard, and the odds that his arm would come up went up—thirty, forty, fifty percent. Satan had her hype as fuck. "*Do it*, you bitch ass faggot ass PUNK!"

Mumbling under his breath, making faces with his eyes down, Anhell propped it with the umbrellas beside the door and leff out. She went and got the gun, laid it on the table in front of her.

Madison, Tiphanie, Arelys and nem sent a group text right then, tryna get the crew together to go to this new Harlem club, and at first... but then she thought of the narcotic bass, the tight-packed bodies writhing together to the music, and her just swinging the machète through all the niggas and her girls like some reaper in the corn... *Nah*, she texted back. *I'm in for the night. Sorry.* One of em called. "Yo, put ya nigga on, girl. I'm bout to tell Anhell we just going out dancing. Ladies' night. Fuckit, he can come too. Ain't nobody seen you in a minute—'Nisha! What *is* it...?"

She was sobbing and she never cried. "He said, he said..." Anhell had muttered *I hate you* when going out the door, and it had hurt her feelings bad. You just don't *say* shit like that!

"Oh my God, *Anhell* said that? Well, what led up to it?" Madison said. "Tell me everything that happen, *exactly*."

She sketched a version of events that, mmm, *skimmed* the details of the Brooklyn adventure and double homicide, swearing fealty to infernal powers and the carnivorous griping of demonic weapons. Perhaps not every fact concerning her own foul-mouthed instigation made it into the story, either.

They talked a long time, until the girls were all in the taxi together on their way to the club. And because Madison was that ride-or-die friend, always one hundred percent team 'Nisha, she felt a lot better when they hung up.

It was very late, but Mama would still be winding down from the hospital, nodding on the couch in front of some documentary. She called.

"Oh, hey, baby." Soft voice, sleepy. TV muttering in the background. "I guess you went back over there, huh?"

"Yeah."

"You know you ain't gotta stay with him, right? You could definitely get into nursing school. Girl, you *smart*, and that boy—"

"Let's not do this tonight, Mommy, please. Okay?" Mama talked a tough game when Anhell wasn't up in her face, but them gray eyes worked on her, too, getting her all *oh-you-want-a-plate-baby?* and *tee-hee-hee* in person. "I don't feel like talking bout him. And is that gunshots I hear on your TV? I thought you hated them cop shows. What you watching?"

"Turn on channel thirteen," Mama murmured. "Just for today, PBS is showing that new film DuVernay won Sundance with, *BLM.*"

"Oh, word?" She reached for the remote, but kept the TV muted, her eyes on her Sudoku book. "What's it about?" She penciled in numbers while Mama sleepily ran on and on and on.

... of us gunned down six days out of every week by the police. Hoping that cell phone camera and video technology... to disrupt the historical impunity of police brutality and extrajudicial murder...

"Yeah?" she said, paying attention only to the cadences. Mama's voice soothing, lovely, there since the beginning. 6. "Huh."

... reinstituting Jim Crow and slavery through the carceral state and prison labor... felons, afterwards, barred from the franchise, employment, or even basic welfare benefits.

"That's awful, dang." 6.

... electing Trump... a direct consequence of Pence, for example, sending state police troopers to close down African American voter registration in Indiana.

"Wow, I ain't even know that." 6.

Mama fell asleep, so she hung up.

Anhell came in, eyes all droopy and red from smoking in the street. Mostly she just felt, as usual, glad to see his fine yellow ass home again, though she fronted like whatever, *who cares*? Smelling very clean, of coconut lime bodywash that wasn't in the bathroom here, Anhell leaned in to kiss her. *Ew!*

Nice of him to take a shower, but his breath was giving funky receipts for all his recent activities.

She caught his face in the palm of a hand and pushed him off. "The way yo bref kicking, you just been down on some bad pussy for *real*, for real."

He ran for the Listerine and then crept back, looking at her with dog's eyes—a very bad dog. So handsome, though, so hot, he blessed the room just by being in it. And girl you know this dopey bloodshot gaze is full of the purest love you'll ever get. She sighed, reached out a hand, ran fingers down his scalp between frizzy cornrows. "Ya head's looking pretty rough. Hand me that comb and sit here. I'ma take these out." Anhell sat on the floor between her knees. She turned up the volume a little, just to a friendly mutter. He pulled the table closer to pinch open a phillie and roll up his late-night .5 grams.

Ready for Iraq in combat armor, whitepolice in Missouri and Louisiana held machine guns, rode tanks. Natural hair sisters holding poster board signs. Baltimore niggas wilding like the cops won't shoot. Close-up of a brother, his face fades out. Baby mama crying. Close-up of another brother, that face fades out. *His* muvver crying. Another face, another wife. Face, mother. Wife, mother. Faces. Crying.

"Know what I wanna see?" Anhell, with each word, scrawled cursives of smoke on the air. "Some crying *white*bitches on this TV."

Normally she had better things to do than ponder the reefer ramblings of a nigga fly as hell, yes, but oh so simple. Now, for whatever reason, her hands paused in the springtime flood of his hair. Fascinated, she said, "Yeah?"

"*Yeah!*" Anhell said, throwing out a preacherly hand at the TV. "Why's it always *us* gotta have the sad story? Let me see some bad ass niggas who get away with nothing but stone cold murder. Then let me see *white*mamas, *white*wives, cameras all up in they face, weeping and wailing outside the church. Now *that* would be some funny shit!" His laughter caught on hooks of smoke, broke into helpless phlegmy barking.

The hair stood up on her neck, goosebumps chilling her arms. She slapped on his back, inspired to her soul. It came to her with a bright ten-story-high clarity, like the LED billboards at Times Square. True vocation. God's work *and* the devil's!

4

#killers4lyfe

4.1 *police massacre, October*
4.2 state funeral, November

THE SKY AT one a.m. hung low above the city, orange clouds damn near bright as day. Gypsies bumped the horn when slowing and sped back up. Draped in colored Christmas lights, almost, the curbside mountains of garbage bags, all beaded by spitting rain, winked under headlights, brake lights, sodium and neon. The piped corridors of all the scaffolding over the sidewalks, all the doorways, and all the stairwells going down breathed back at them *parfum de piss*. It was unseasonably warm in the Bronx, and a lovely night for an atrocity. There was the precinct house just ahead. Time to make the bacon, Mr Pig.

A sextet of cops were smoking on the precinct stairs. Three cigarette cherries flaring with the draw, three redder and dim hanging hipside. Who knows but that qualms might not have stirred the hearts of dark gods, who then might have brought down the storm elsewhere, on some other night, if all those cops out front *hadn't* been white? But police have their own little clicks, too. Spanish tight with Spanish, black with black, whitecops keeping to their own kind.

Anhell laid down an enfilade that had him doing numbers before half a minute was out. The devil, if it ain't been said, saw to questions of ammo and aim, chambering embers *di l'Inferno* just faster than Anhell could squeeze the trigger. Hellfire tracers went streaking through the dark and one, two, three, four, five whitecops turned explosively to redmeat. Number six, before losing the lungs to do so, gave a shout. She and Anhell ran—not away, *toward* the trouble. Just vibing on the slaughter at first, thrilled how babyboy had put 'em down like that, now she felt eager for a taste of her own. A bitch gotta post up, right—get her hands dirty, too?

Some cavalry came pouring out the precinct front doors to see about that shout, and *chop, chop, chop* were three who had been whole made all in twain. The machète went in and through without effort, but still she felt, somehow, a slow buttery drag across the blade, as if demonic steel were stiff meat belonging to her own body and sinking deep into a lover all wet, hot and open for her. No need, as it turned out, to drink down whole gallons from any one body when this much blood was flowing. The first cupful's sweetest, anyway. Naw, a spoonful will do, given this abundance.

Stepping over the bestrewment, they went in.

4.1 police massacre, October
4.2 state funeral, November
4.3 police massacre, October

Lastly, twelve widows filed on camera. Whitewidows, all white, though their eyes sought reflexively for any who weren't. Only one widow would be allowed to speak, and not an ugly one. They knew which one it would be the very instant she, blonde, stepped into view. The black lace she wore overlay a silk sheath that, iridescing under the lights between deep purple, reddish black, and... *indigo?* lent her gown the dark complexities of a raven's wing seen in direct sun. Not the dress your granny would wear to the funeral, this number, and "gorgeous" only got you about halfway there. The camera lingered a bit over the distinctive red soles of her glossy black pumps.

"Eight outta them sixty-three we kilt weren't even white," Anhell complained. "How come they ain't let nunna *them* widows on TV?"

"Optics, baby," she said and swallowed deeply, in wisdom and resignation, from her tumbler. "They gotta keep shit looking a certain way for the message."

45 hadn't won the presidency for no damn reason: He quit reading off the 'prompter all wooden and halting and started ad-libbing for his base.

"Studies show, there's a *yuge* amount of science, so many studies showing that our African Americans, the blacks, actually kill *each other* 99.9% of the time. Facts!"

Anhell sucked his teeth. "Ain't nobody wanna hear this cheeto ass looking fool! When they putting the widows on?"

"President first," she said, "then the mayor. Widows go last." One more watery sip drained the ice in her glass, and she looked around with increasing consternation for the bottle. "*Yo,* my nigga—how you drank up all the Henny that quick?"

"Ain't even that serious, ma." Anhell leaned over the couch's far side. "Got the bottle right here..." After pulling it up from where it sat (still one-third full) on the floor, he poured over her ice until, clinking, the cubes floated up.

"*Oh,*" she exclaimed. "Cause I was getting ready to *say...!*" She took a good, long swallow.

4.2 state funeral, November
4.3 police massacre, October
4.4 state funeral, November

With a step backward into the brimstone sirocco, they couldn't be seen well from here, earth. And so from there, hell, the screams of the damned and heat blasting at their backs, they juked around wildly shooting cops and took the whiteones *bang!* to the head, *swap!* through the neck. It was less a trick of witchcraft than basic physics, time in hell running at a faster clip than our earthly clock, and so much so that, when they stood on the smoldering threshold, all these police, by contrast, were moving in slo-mo and clumsy as fuck.

Anhell dropped them as if this were some damn videogame. Kevlar, steel desks, security doors, ducking around the corner of cinder-block walls. All this could've just as well been cardboard, a wish and a prayer, because none of it was saving cover. Satan whispered a name to each bullet, and if that one which the boy shot had heard yours, well, baby game up. You was done. Every shot traveled on a rigorous and unbroken line to its target no matter what intervened.

Anhell had a do-not-kill option, the gun making in that case a strange bark and blowing no two-pound red mass off that brown or woman's body. Indeed no wound at all appeared, though these lucky ones allowed to live, these few shown this presumptive mercy, all fell down writhing to the ground, their screams matching the damned for raw-throated abandon. Here in the police station, there was a little noise like that in hell.

Semiautomatic muzzle-flash all about her, a ricocheting glitter she batted away, the incoming slow as water balloons lobbed by a three-year-old. She hacked would-be heroes in half. Funny, how you think the first shift at the slaughterhouse will be so hard, really seeing how the sausage gets made, where pork chops come from. But it turns out, you're about that life. You were *made* for this, babygirl! Don't shit faze you. Flinging swatches of crimson over every surface surrounding her, she felt almost bad. It was *too* easy. ("At places, the blood in there so deep, your shoes stepped in, your socks got wet...") Best of all she liked it when they tried to hide. Chopping in after them through the barricades, the doors, the little under-desk shelters. Then one pretty moment, when most cowered and begged, some rallied to squeeze off a last shot, and she finished that piggy and went for the next. You ever just start *laughing*, can't stop? The party's so good, you're having *such* a nice time?

4.3 police massacre, October
4.4 state funeral, November
4.5 police massacre, October

Mrs Liam Conor O'Donnell, *dec.*, stood and approached the pulpit. You could see she ate salads, worked out, no bread. A face for TV, makeup on point, and that gown fitting very well—but everything tasteful.

Addressing St. Patrick's navy-clad pews: "I know that all of you join with me and the rest of America in grieving the loss of so many of—and truly they *were*—New York's Finest."

"Bitch won't cry."

"That hoe will *definitely* cry. Now, shh."

"But look at her makeup," Anhell said. "How she tryna mess that up? Nope. Watch, not one tear."

"Bet you some bomb ass head we getting tears from her." And you know she had to be sure, because she *hated* giving head! "Now, shush, so I can hear."

"... our respects to the slain and honoring their sacrifice. Ladies, when our men fall, *we* must take up arms and the battle cry. To contribute to the cause and the future I've borne two beautiful daughters. I've been a good wife." She smiled sadly and the camera flashed on two blonde cherubs in white blouses, black jumpers. "I still remember those last moments when Liam—Lieutenant O'Donnell—when he was going out to work... I *wanted* to tell him." She lay a palm over the flatness of her immaculate belly. A murmur and stir convulsed the pews. "*Yes*. A new baby. This one, I know, will be the son Liam always wanted, a boy who will now never—"

"Lemme get a puff of that, yo."

"Thought you wasn't fucking with the weed like that? Damn, girl! Keep smoking like this, you bout to turn into a 'head like *me*."

"Nigga, just pass the blunt."

"All of us gathered here today know that a darkness is falling over this nation and over the earth itself. As demographics shift, the struggle for the continuance of Western Civilization has become existential. Diverse elements would see the blood and soil of this nation washed away in a dismal tide. But it is incumbent upon the Herrenvolk to secure the future for our children and for *theirs*. No, there can be no parley with evil; strength must be our answer. Before the Almighty, I swear to you that we *will* prevail over our enemies, and the perpetrators of this tragedy shall soon know our vengeance..."

4.4 state funeral, November

4.5 police massacre, October

4.6 state funeral, November

KNOCKING MOTHERFUCKERS OUT really don't work the way it do in movies. Sad to say, but not all the black cops she smashed upside the head with the flat or blunt of her demonic machète lived to tell the tale. And, to be honest, Satan was from jump like *You can miss me with all this conscious killing, organic murder crap*. Whenever she tried to spare the lives of too many women, black, Asian, Spanish in a row, buddy got fed up and made the machète spin in her grip from play side to business end. *Oop!* A couple of the wrong heads went flying too. Oh, shit, sorry! Bees that way sometime, though. The third or fourth time Satan decided enough with this woke ass bullshit, and caused the machète to spin from 'knockout' position to 'decap,' the unbreakable barrel of Anhell's shotgun intervened, clangingly, before her always-fatal edge could claim *this* victim.

"I thought we was only killing the whitepeople, the men?" Anhell said, and jerked his chin at the policewoman kneeling between them. "*She* ain't neither one."

Brownskin. Not short, not tall. All right looking, although the uniform's shapeless navy slacks and boxy polyester shirt were doing her thickness *no favors*. The policewoman was definitely a stranger, but seemed incredibly familiar at first glance... and then she realized why. "Get yo ass outta here," she snarled, gesturing *up* with the machète. *Go!*

Commuted from slaughter, a fawn clambering to her feet between the lioness and leopard, the policewoman stood up warily.

"Go on," Anhell said, smiling warmly. "We gotta finish up here."

About to run, the policewoman did a double take. "Oh, you got some *pretty* eyes, though!"

"Well, *thank* you," Anhell exclaimed, giving light skin, delighted surprise, a charming smile. "It's so nice a you to say that!"

Oh see? We can't have this. He got the broad ready to put the pussy on him right *here*!

"Bissh," she slushed, hefting the machète in a manner that said *I'm not the one*. "You can run or you can die. How you playing it?"

Anhell peeped her face real quick for resolve, and said, "Yeah, sorry," to the policewoman regretfully. "But you better run now, for real."

Brownskin sister heard and took her leave in such haste, the peaked hat of her uniform was knocked off her head, the hair underneath all short, every which way, and toe up.

He liked exactly the kind of dudes you'd expect, elevens on the ten-point scale, this jet-black Senegalese model, that Colombian semipro futbolista, another "big dick country ass redbone nigga from down south," quote unquote, overheard. Anhell only wanted the brown girls, though, and they had to look just like her.

4.5 police massacre, October
4.6 state funeral, November
4.7 police massacre, October

EULOGY DONE, THE apostle widows came to surround, weeping, the beautiful one at the podium. They clutched one another's fingers, their red-blotched wet faces becoming downright ugly with sobs. The cameras knew where and on whom to linger, blonde Jesus widow who, blinking her tear-jeweled black lashes, smiled bravely and freed up two or three telegenic drops for St. Patrick's Cathedral, for New York City, and for the United States of America. Did her mascara smudge or run? *Fuck* no! And, God, did the bitch look good!

"*Aww...!*" said Anhell, every gambler's exclamation, when his bet goes bad.

Cracking up, she fell back on the couch. "*Didn't* I say, nigga?" She rolled around on the pillows. "*Told* your ass!"

Anhell pointed at the recession of president, mayor, widows. "Shit came out just like you said, though. And we ain't even *done* yet." Tumbler in hand, he took the bottle in his other, liquoring up his meltwater and ice. "Copkillers? *God*killers! And we don't stop." As if, sitting down, he just couldn't get the feeling out right, Anhell jumped to his feet shouting at the blue televised ranks filing from the church. "*Fuck* the poe lease! It's on for life. We gunning for *alla* you motherfuckers!" His eyes came alight, red as the EXIT sign far down a dark hallway. In his wild hand, the bottle sloshing. "Fiddy shots shot, fiddy cops dropped!" His pretty lips sputtering, like a lighter that won't catch, *sparks*, not spit. And though it was commercials by now, this nigga steady yelling. "... end up dying, staring at the roof the church, ya ladies crying...!"

She knelt up on the couch and smacked him in the face with a throw pillow.

Anhell woke up. "Oh, *fuck*, though, baby," he said, shaking his head. "You *seent* that? Devil had me like *tweaking*!"

"Yeah, I saw," she said. "Now gimme that fucking bottle. You spilling shit everywhere..."

4.6 state funeral, November
4.7 *police massacre, October*

SHE'D ONCE SEEN his long curly hair blown out bone-straight, a black curtain hanging to his ass. Now, auburn, it sat heavily upon his shoulders—huge and soaking wet. She reached into his hair and wrung a handful like some sponge that had sopped deep spill off the slaughterhouse floor. The squishing mass gushed police blood. She pulled his salty mouth down to hers and they kissed.

Spots lit the night out front to anachronous noon, splashing blue 'n' red emergency lights, a cordon of NYPD ESU with machine guns at every surrounding intersection, snipers on every overlooking rooftop. From 'three' a SWAT team was counting down to storm the place. They made fools of the whole kingdom arrayed against them, and walked out through deep hell, across the burning floor of Gehenna.

Tag

TO AVOID THE curfew they took the subway downtown at rush hour every three or four days. They'd walk in some other borough until happening upon today's luckless whiteboys in blue. Afterwards, they'd come on back uptown. Once, they went all the way out to Staten Island on the ferry, and it was like a date, the sunlight on the water, Statue of Liberty, a whale breaching in the harbor. Incredibly romantic—though probably not for that pair of transit cops at the terminal, whose last vision of this world was of two shadows swaggering up through heat shimmer, a teenage lankiness and the width and curves and thickness of a woman, barely glimpsed against a whole continent of fire. But the City under martial law was boring as fuck, and so she called Mama and got her talking again on that BLM tip. Kind of slipped the question to her sideways. *Hey, what's the worst police department in America?*

"Chicago," Mama answered. "Or maybe the LAPD. Why you asking?"

"No reason," she said. "Oh, by the way, me and Anhell been talking about getting outta town for awhile. Maybe just taking the bus somewhere, a road trip."

"Cali?" he said, getting excited when she'd made up her mind. Nobody likes wintertime in New York. The same day their cash allowance came through, they packed some underwear, machète and gun, their pills. A backpack each, just the necessary.

"What we gonna do, though," he asked, "when the prescriptions run out?"

"Walk up in any pharmacy," she said, "and be like, I want another month's worf, or *every motherfucker up in here* getting they head chopped off."

"Oh, yup yup," said Anhell, seeing the sense, nodding. "That'd work!"

And so down to Port Authority, and on a Greyhound going west.

AN EVENING WITH SEVERYN GRIMES
Rich Larson

Rich Larson (richwlarson.tumblr.com) was born in West Africa, has studied in Rhode Island and worked in Spain, and now writes from Ottawa, Canada. His short work has been nominated for the Theodore Sturgeon Award, featured on *io9.com*, and appears in numerous Year's Best anthologies as well as in magazines such as *Asimov's, Analog, Clarkesworld, The Magazine of Fantasy & Science Fiction, Interzone, Strange Horizons, Lightspeed* and *Apex*. His debut short collection, *Tomorrow Factory: Collected Fiction*, comes out in May 2018 from Talos Press and his debut novel *Annex,* first book of The Violet Wars trilogy, follows in July 2018 from Orbit Books.

"Do you have to wear the Fawkes in here?" Girasol asked, sliding into the orthochair. Its worn wings crinkled, leaking silicon, as it adjusted to her shape. The plastic stuck cold to her shoulder blades, and she shivered.

"No." Pierce made no move to pull off the smirking mask. "It makes you nervous," he explained, groping around in the guts of his open Adidas track-bag, his tattooed hand emerging with the hypnotic. "That's a good enough reason to wear it."

Girasol didn't argue, just tipped her dark head back, positioning herself over the circular hole they'd punched through the headrest. Beneath it, a bird's nest of circuitry, mismatched wiring, blinking blue nodes. And in the center of the nest: the neural jack, gleaming wet with disinfectant jelly.

She let the slick white port at the top of her spine snick open.

"No cheap sleep this time," Pierce said, flicking his nail against the inky vial. "Get ready for a deep slice, Sleeping Beauty. Prince Charming's got your shit. Highest-grade Dozr a man can steal." He plugged it into a battered needler, motioned for her arm. "I get a kiss or what?"

Girasol proffered her bruised wrist. Let him hunt around collapsed veins while she said, coldly, "Don't even think about touching me when I'm under."

Pierce chuckled, slapping her flesh, coaxing a pale blue worm to stand out in her white skin. "Or what?"

Girasol's head burst as the hypnotic went in, flooding her capillaries, working over her neurotransmitters. "Or I'll cut your fucking balls off."

The Fawkes's grin loomed silent over her; a brief fear stabbed through the descending drug. Then he laughed again, barking and sharp, and Girasol knew she had not forgotten how to speak to men like Pierce. She tasted copper in her mouth as the Dozr settled.

"Just remember who got you out of Correctional," Pierce said. "And that if you screw this up, you'd be better off back in the freeze. Sweet dreams."

The mask receded, and Girasol's eyes drifted up the wall, following the cabling that crept like vines from the equipment under her skull, all the way through a crack gouged in the ceiling, and from there to whatever line Pierce's cronies had managed to splice. The smartpaint splashed across the grimy stucco displayed months of preparation: shifting sat-maps, decrypted dossiers, and a thousand flickering image loops of one beautiful young man with silver hair.

Girasol lowered the chair. Her toes spasmed, kinking against each other as the thrumming neural jack touched the edge of her port. The Dozr kept her breathing even. A bone-deep rasp, a meaty click, and she was synched, simulated REM brain-wave flowing through a current of code, flying through wire, up and out of the shantytown apartment, flitting like a shade into Chicago's dark cityscape.

Severyn Grimes felt none of the old heat in his chest when the first round finished with a shattered nose and a shower of blood, and he realized something: the puppet shows didn't do it for him anymore.

The fighters below were massive, as always, pumped full of HGH and Taurus and various combat chemicals, sculpted by a lifetime in gravity gyms.

The fight, as always, wouldn't end until their bodies were mangled heaps of broken bone and snapped tendon. Then the technicians would come and pull the digital storage cones from the slick white ports at the tops of their spines, so the puppeteers could return to their own bodies, and the puppets, if they were lucky, woke up in meat repair with a paycheck and no permanent paralysis.

It seemed almost wasteful. Severyn stroked the back of his neck, where silver hair was shorn fashionably around his own storage cone. Beneath him, the fighters hurtled from their corners, grappled, broke, and collided again. He felt nothing. Severyn's adrenaline only ever seemed to spike in boardrooms now. Primate aggression through power broking.

"I'm growing tired of this shit," he said, and his bodyguard carved a clear exit through the baying crowd. Follow-cams drifted in his direction, foregoing the match for a celebspotting opportunity: the second-wealthiest bio-businessman in Chicago, 146 years old but plugged into a beautiful young body that played well on cam. The god-like Severyn Grimes slumming at a puppet show, readying for a night of downtown debauchery? The paparazzi feed practically wrote itself.

A follow-cam drifted too close; Severyn raised one finger, and his bodyguard swatted it out of the air on the way out the door.

GIRASOL JOLTED, SPIRALED down to the floor. She'd drifted too close, too entranced by the geometry of his cheekbones, his slate gray eyes and full lips, his swimmer's build swathed in Armani and his graceful hands with Nokia implants glowing just under the skin. A long way away, she was dimly aware of her body in the orthochair in the decrepit apartment. She scrawled a message across the smartpaint:

HE'S LEAVING EARLY. ARE YOUR PEOPLE READY?

"They're, *shit*, they're on their way. Stall him." Pierce's voice was distant, an insect hum, but she could detect the sound of nerves fraying.

Girasol jumped to another follow-cam, triggering a fizz of sparks as she seized its motor circuits. The image came in upside down: Mr. Grimes clambering into the limo, the bodyguard scanning the street. Springy red hair and a brutish face suggested Neanderthal gene-mixing. Him, they would have to get rid of.

The limousine door glided shut. From six blocks away, Girasol triggered the crude mp4 file she'd prepared—sometimes the old tricks worked best—and wormed inside the vehicle's CPU on a sine wave of sound.

SEVERYN VAGUELY RECOGNIZED the song breezing through the car's sponge speakers, but outdated protest rap was a significant deviation from his usual tastes.

"Music off."

Silence filled the backseat. The car took an uncharacteristically long time calculating their route before finally jetting into traffic. Severyn leaned back to watch the dark street slide past his window, lit by lime green neon and the jittering ghosts of holograms. A moment later he turned to his bodyguard, who had the Loop's traffic reports scrolling across his retinas.

"Does blood excite you, Finch?"

Finch blinked, clearing his eyes back to a watery blue. "Not particularly, Mr. Grimes. Comes with the job."

"I thought having reloaded testosterone would make the world... visceral again." Severyn grabbed at his testicles with a wry smile. "Maybe an old mind overwrites a young body in more ways than the technicians suspect. Maybe mortality is escapable, but old age inevitable."

"Maybe so," Finch echoed, sounding slightly uncomfortable. First-lifers often found it unsettling to be reminded they were sitting beside a man who had bought off Death itself. "Feel I'm getting old myself, sometimes."

"Maybe you'd like to turn in early," Severyn offered.

Finch shook his head. "Always up for a jaunt, Mr. Grimes. Just so long as the whorehouses are vetted."

Severyn laughed, and in that moment the limo lurched sideways and jolted to a halt. His face mashed to the cold glass of the window, bare millimeters away from an autocab that darted gracefully around them and back into its traffic algorithm.

Finch straightened him out with one titanic hand.

"What the fuck was that?" Severyn asked calmly, unrumpling his tie.

"Car says there's something in the exhaust port," Finch said, retinas replaced by schematic tracery. "Not an explosive. Could just be debris."

"Do check."

"Won't be a minute, Mr. Grimes."

Finch pulled a pair of wire-veined gloves from a side compartment and opened the door, ushering in a chilly undertow, then disappeared around the rear end of the limousine. Severyn leaned back to wait, flicking alternately through merger details and airbrushed brothel advertisements in the air above his lap.

"Good evening, Mr. Grimes," the car burbled. "You've been hacked."

Severyn's nostrils flared. "I don't pay you for your sense of humor, Finch."

"I'm not joking, parasite."

Severyn froze. There was a beat of silence, then he reached for the door handle. It might as well have been stone. He pushed his palm against the sunroof and received a static charge for his trouble.

"Override," he said. "Severyn Grimes. Open doors." No response. Severyn felt his heartbeat quicken, felt a prickle of sweat on his palms. He slowly let go of the handle. "Who am I speaking to?"

"Take a look through the back window. Maybe you can figure it out."

Severyn spun, peering through the dark glass. Finch was hunched over the exhaust port, only a slice of red hair in sight. The limousine was projecting a yellow hazard banner, cleaving traffic, but as Severyn watched an unmarked van careened to a halt behind them.

Masked men spilled out. Severyn thumped his fist into the glass of the window, but it was soundproof; he sent a warning spike to his security, but the car was shielded against adbombs, and theoretically against electronic intrusion, and now it was walling off his cell signal.

All he could do was watch. Finch straightened up, halfway through peeling off one smartglove when the first black-market Taser sparked electric blue. He jerked, convulsed, but still somehow managed to pull the handgun from his jacket. Severyn's fist clenched. Then the second Taser went off, painting Finch a crackling halo. The handgun dropped.

The masked men bull-rushed Finch as he crumpled, sweeping him up under the arms, and Severyn saw the wide leering smiles under their hoods: Guy Fawkes. The mask had been commandeered by various terroractivist groups over the past half-century, but Severyn knew it was the Priesthood's clearest calling card. For the first time in a long time, he felt a cold corkscrew in his stomach. He tried to put his finger on the sensation.

"He has a husband." Severyn's throat felt tight. "Two children."

"He still will," the voice replied. "He's only a wage-slave. Not a blasphemer."

Finch was a heavy man and his knees scraped along the tarmac as the Priests hauled him toward the van's sliding door. His head lolled to his chest, but Severyn saw his blue eyes were slitted open. His body tensed, then—

Finch jerked the first Priest off-balance and came up with the subcutaneous blade flashing out of his forearm, carving the man open from hip to ribcage. Blood foamed and spat and Severyn felt what he'd missed at the puppet show, a burning flare in his chest. Finch twisted away from the other Priest's arm, eyes roving, glancing off the black glass that divided them, and then a third Taser hit him. He fell with his jaws spasming; a Priest's heavy boot swung into him as he toppled.

The flare died inside Severyn's pericardium. The limousine started to move.

"He should not have done that," the voice grated, as the bleeding Priest and then Finch and then the other Priests disappeared from sight.

Severyn watched through the back window for a moment longer. Faced forward. "I'll compensate for any medical costs incurred by my employee's actions," he said. "I won't tolerate any sort of retribution to his person."

"Still talking like you've got cards. And don't pretend like you care. He's an ant to you. We all are."

Severyn assessed. The voice was synthesized, distorted, but something in the cadence made him think female speaker. Uncommon, for a Priest. He gambled.

"What is your name, madam?"

"I'm a man, parasite."

Only a split second of hesitation before the answer, but it was more than enough to confirm his guess. Severyn had staked astronomical shares on such pauses, pauses that couldn't be passed off as lag in the modern day. Signs of unsettledness. Vulnerability. It made his skin thrum. He imagined himself in a boardroom.

"No need for pretenses," Severyn said. "I merely hoped to establish a more personable base for negotiation."

"Fuck you." A warble of static. Maybe a laugh. "Fuck you. There's not going to be any negotiation. This isn't a funding op. We just caught one of the biggest parasites on the planet. The Priesthood's going to make you an example. Hook you to an autosurgeon and let it vivisect you on live feed. Burn what's left of you to ash. No negotiations."

Severyn felt the icy churn in his stomach again. Fear. He realized he'd almost missed it.

GIRASOL WAS DREAMING many things at once. Even as she spoke to her captive in realtime, she perched in the limousine's electronic shielding, shooting down message after desperate message he addressed to his security detail, his bank, his associates.

It took her nearly a minute to realize the messages were irrelevant. Grimes was trying to trigger an overuse failsafe in his implants, generate an error message that could sneak through to Nokia.

Such a clever bastard. Girasol dipped into his implants and shut them down, leaving him half-blind and stranded in realtime. She felt a sympathetic lurch as he froze, gray eyes clearing, clipped neatly away from his data flow. If only it was that easy to reach in and drag him out of that pristine white storage cone.

"There aren't many female Priests," Grimes said, as if he hadn't noticed the severance. "I seem to recall their creed hates the birth control biochip almost as much as they hate neural puppeteering." He flashed a beatific smile that made Girasol ache. "So much love for one sort of parasite, so much ichor for the other."

"I saw the light," Girasol said curtly, even though she knew she should have stopped talking the instant he started analyzing, prying, trying to break her down.

"My body is, of course, a volunteer." Grimes draped his lean arms along the backseat. "But the Priesthood does have so many interesting ideas about what individuals should and should not do with their own flesh and bone."

"Volunteers are as bad as the parasites themselves," Girasol recited from one of Pierce's Adderall-fueled rants. "Selling their souls to a digital demon. The tainted can't enter the kingdom of heaven."

"Don't tell me a hacker riding sound waves still believes in souls."

"You lost yours the second you uploaded to a storage cone."

Grimes replied with another carefully constructed probe, but Girasol's interest diverted from their conversation as Pierce's voice swelled from far away. He was shouting. Someone else was in the room. She crosschecked the limo's route against a staticky avalanche of police scanners, then dragged herself back to the orthochair, forcing her eyes open.

Through the blur of code, she saw Pierce's injured crony, the one who'd been sliced belly to sternum, being helped through the doorway. His midsection was swathed in bacterial film, but the blood that hadn't been coagulated and eaten away left a dripping carmine trail on the linoleum.

"You don't bring him here," Pierce grated. "You lobo, if someone saw you—"

"I'm not going to take him to a damn hospital." The man pulled off his Fawkes, revealing a pale and sweat-slick face. "I think it's, like, shallow. Didn't get any organs. But he's bleeding bad, need more cling film—"

"Where's the caveman?" Pierce snapped. "The bodyguard, where is he?"

The man waved a blood-soaked arm towards the doorway. "In the parkade. Don't worry, we put a clamp on him and locked the van." His companion moaned and he swore. "Now where's the aid kit? Come on, Pierce, he's going to, shit, he's going to bleed out. Those stairs nearly did him in."

Pierce stalked to the wall and snatched the dented white case from its hook. He caught sight of Girasol's gummy eyes half-open.

"How close are you to the warehouse?" he demanded.

"You know how the Loop gets on weekends," Girasol said, feeling her tongue move inside her mouth like a phantom limb. "Fifteen. Twenty."

Pierce nodded. Chewed his lips. Agitated. "Need another shot?"

"Yeah."

Girasol monitored the limo at the hazy edge of her mind as Pierce handed off the aid kit and prepped another dose of hypnotic. She thought of how soon it would be her blood on the floor, once he realized what she was doing. She thought of slate gray eyes as she watched the oily black Dozr mix with her blood, and when Pierce hit the plunger, she closed her own and plunged with it.

SEVERYN WAS METHODICALLY peeling back flooring, ruining his manicured nails, humming protest rap, when the voice came back.

"Don't bother. You won't get to the brake line that way."

He paused, staring at the miniscule tear he'd made. He climbed slowly back onto the seat and palmed open the chiller. "I was beginning to think you'd left me," he said, retrieving a glass flute.

"Still here, parasite. Keeping you company in your final moments."

"Parasite," Severyn echoed as he poured. "You know, if it weren't for people like you, puppeteering might have never developed. Religious zealots are the ones who axed cloning, after all. Just think. If not for that, we might have been uploading to fresh blank bodies instead of those desperate enough to sell themselves whole."

He looked at his amber reflection in the flute, studying the beautiful young face he'd worn for nearly two years. He knew the disembodied hacker was seeing it too, and it was an advantage, no matter how she might try to suppress it. Humans loved beauty and underestimated youth. It was one reason Severyn used young bodies instead of the thickset middle-aged Clooneys favored by most CEOs.

"And now it's too late to go back," Severyn said, swirling his drink. "Growing a clone is expensive. Finding a volunteer is cheap." He sipped and held the stinging Perdue in his mouth.

Silence for a beat.

"You have no idea what kind of person I am."

Severyn felt his hook sink in. He swallowed his drink. "I do," he replied. "I've been thinking about it quite fucking hard, what with my impending evisceration. You're no Priest. Your familiarity with my security systems and reticence to kill my bodyguard makes me think you're an employee, former or current."

"People like you assume everyone's working for them."

"Whether you are or not, you've done enough research to know I can easily triple whatever the Priesthood is paying for your services."

"There's not going to be any negotiation. You're a dead man."

Severyn nodded, studying his drink, then slopped it out across the upholstery and smashed the flute against the window. The crystal crunched. Severyn shook the now-jagged stem, sending small crumbs to the floor. It gleamed scalpel-sharp. Running his thumb along it raised hairs on the nape of his neck.

"What are you doing?" the voice blared.

"My hand slipped," Severyn said. "Old age." A fat droplet of blood swelled on his thumb, and he wiped it away. He wasn't one to mishandle his bodies or rent zombies for recreational suicide in drowning tanks, freefalls. No, Severyn's drive to survive had always been too strong for him to experiment with death. As he brought the edge to his throat he realized that killing himself would not be easy.

"That won't save you." Another static laugh, but this one forced. "We'll upload your storage cone to an artificial body within the day. Throw you into a pleasure doll with the sensitivity cranked to maximum. Imagine how much fun they'd have with that."

The near-panic was clarion clear, even through a synthesizer. Intuition pounded at Severyn's temples. The song was still in there, too.

"You played yourself in on a music file," Severyn said. "I searched it before you shut off my implants. *Decapitate the state / wipe the slate / create.* Banal, but so very catchy, wasn't it? Swan song of the Anticorp Movement."

"I liked the beat."

"Several of my employees became embroiled in those protests. They were caught trying to coordinate a viral strike on my bank." Severyn pushed the point into the smooth flesh of his throat. "Nearly five years ago, now. I believe the chief conspirator was sentenced to twenty years in cryogenic storage."

"Stop it. Put that down."

"You must have wanted me to guess," Severyn continued, worming the glass gently, like a corkscrew. He felt a warm trickle down his neck. "Why keep talking, otherwise? You wanted me to know who got me in the end. This is your revenge."

"Do you even remember my name?" The voice was warped, but not by static. "And put that down."

The command came so fierce and raw that Severyn's hand hesitated without his meaning to. He slowly set the stem in his lap. "Or you kept talking," he said, "because you missed hearing his voice."

"Fucking parasite." The hacker's voice was tired and suddenly brittle. "First you steal twenty years of my life and then you steal my son."

"Girasol Fletcher." There it was. Severyn leaned back, releasing a long breath. "He came to me, you know." He racked his digital memory for another name, the name of his body before it was his body. "Blake came to me."

"Bullshit. You always wanted him. Had a feed of his swim meets like a pedophile."

"I helped him. Possibly even saved him."

"You made him a puppet."

Severyn balled a wipe and dabbed at the blood on Blake's slender neck. "You left him with nothing," he said. "The money drained off to pay for your cryo. And Blake fell off, too. He was a full addict when he came to me. Hypnotics. Spending all his time in virtual dreamland. You'd know about that." He paused, but the barb drew no response. "It couldn't have been for sex fantasies. I imagine he got anything he wanted in realtime. I think maybe he was dreaming his family whole again."

Silence. Severyn felt a dim guilt, but he pushed through. Survival.

"He was desperate when he found me," Severyn continued. "I told him I wanted his body. Fifteen-year contract, insured for all organic damage. It's been keeping your cryo paid off, and when the contract's up he'll be comfortable for the rest of his life."

"Don't. Act." A stream of static. "Like you did him a favor."

Severyn didn't reply for a moment. He looked at the window, but the glass was still black, opaqued. "I'm not being driven to an execution, am I?"

Girasol wound the limousine through the grimy labyrinth of the industrial district, guiding it past the agreed-upon warehouse where a half-dozen Priests were awaiting the delivery of Severyn Grimes, Chicago's most notorious parasite. Using the car's external camera, she saw the lookout's confused face emerging from behind his mask.

On the internal camera, she couldn't stop looking into Blake's eyes, hoping they would be his own again soon.

"There's a hydrofoil waiting on the docks," she said through the limousine speakers. "I hired a technician to extract you. Paid him extra to drop your storage cone in the harbor."

"The Priesthood wasn't open to negotiations concerning the body."

Far away, Girasol felt the men clustered around her, watching her prone body like predatory birds. She could almost smell the fast-food grease and sharp chemical sweat.

"No," she said dully. "Volunteers are as bad as the parasites themselves. Blake sold his soul to a digital demon. To you."

"When they find out you betrayed their interests?"

Girasol considered. "Pierce will rape me," she said. "Maybe some of the others, too. Then they'll pull some amateur knife-and-pliers interrogation shit, thinking it's some kind of conspiracy. And then they may. Or may not. Kill me." Her voice was steady until the penultimate word. She calculated distance to the pier. It was worth it. It was worth it. Blake would be free, and Grimes would be gone.

"You could skype in CPD."

Girasol had already considered. "No. With what I pulled to get out of the freeze, if they find me I'm back in permanently."

"Skype them in to wherever my bodyguard is being held."

He was insistent about the caveman. Almost as if he gave a shit. Girasol felt a small slink of self-doubt before she remembered Grimes had amassed his wealth by manipulating emotions. He'd been a puppeteer long before he uploaded. Still trying to pull her strings.

"I would," Girasol said. "But he's here with me."

Grimes paused, frowning. Girasol zoomed. She'd missed Blake's face so much, the immaculate bones of it, the wide brow and curved lips. She could still remember him chubby and always laughing.

"Can you contact him without the Priests finding out?" Grimes asked.

Girasol fluttered back to the apartment. She was guillotining texts and voice-calls as they poured in from the warehouse, keeping Pierce in the dark for as long as possible, but one of them would slip through before long. She triangulated on the locked van using the parkade security cams.

"Maybe," she said.

"If you can get him free, he might be able to help you. I have a non-duress passcode. I could give it to you." Grimes tongued the edges of his bright white teeth. "In exchange, you call off the extraction."

"Thought you might try to make a deal."

"It is what I do." Grimes's lips thinned. "You lack long-term perspective, Ms. Fletcher. Common enough among first-lifers. The notion of sacrificing yourself to free your progeny must seem exceptionally noble and very fucking romantic to you. But if the Priesthood does murder you, Blake wakes up with nobody. Nothing. Again."

"Not nothing," Girasol said reflexively.

"The money you were paid for this job?" Grimes suggested. "He'll have to go into hiding for as long as my disappearance is under investigation. The sort of people who can help him lay low are the sort of people who'll have him back on Sandman or Dozr before the month is out. He might even decide to go puppet again."

Girasol's fury boiled over, and she nearly lost her hold on the steering column. "He made a mistake. Once. He would never agree to that again."

"Even if you get off with broken bones, you'll be a wanted fugitive as soon as Correctional try to thaw you for a physical and find whatever suckerfish the Priests convinced to take your pod." Grimes flattened his hands on his knees. "What I'm proposing is that you cancel the extraction. My bodyguard helps you escape. We meet up to renegotiate terms. I could have your charges dropped, you know. I could even rewrite Blake's contract."

"You really don't want to die, do you?" Girasol's suspicion battled her fear, her fear of Pierce and his pliers and his grinning mask. "You're digital. You saying you don't have a backup of your personality waiting in the wings?"

She checked the limo's external cams and swore. A carload of Priests from the warehouse was barreling up the road behind them, guns already poking through the windows. She reached for the in-built speed limits and deleted them.

"I do," Grimes conceded, bracing himself as the limo accelerated. "But he's not me, is he?"

Girasol resolved. She bounced back to the apartment, where the Priests were growing agitated. Pierce was shaking her arm, even though he should have known better than to shake someone on a deep slice, asking her how close she was to the warehouse. She flashed TWO MINUTES across the smartpaint.

Then she found the electronic signature of the clamp that was keeping Grimes's bodyguard paralyzed inside the van. She hoped he hadn't suffered any long-term nerve damage. Hoped he would still move like quicksilver with that bioblade of his.

"Fair enough," Girasol said, stretching herself thin, reaching into the empty parkade. "All right. Tell me the passcode and I'll break him out."

* * *

FINCH WAS FOCUSED on breathing slowly and ignoring the blooming damp spot where piss had soaked through his trousers. The police-issue clamp they'd stuck to his shoulder made most other activities impossible. Finch had experience with the spidery devices. They were designed to react to any arousal in the central nervous system by sending a paralyzing jolt through the would-be agitator's muscles. More struggle, more jolt. More panic, more jolt.

The only thing to do with a clamp was relax and not get upset about anything.

Finch used the downtime to reflect on his situation. Mr. Grimes had fallen victim to a planned ambush, that much was obvious. Electronic intrusion, supposedly impossible, must have been behind the limo's exhaust port diagnostic.

And now Mr. Grimes was being driven to an unknown location, while Finch was lying on the floor of a van with donair wrappers and rumpled anti-puppetry tracts for company. A decade ago, he might have been paranoid enough to think he was a target himself. Religious extremists had not taken kindly to Neanderthal gene mixing at first, but they also had a significant demographic overlap with people overjoyed to see pale-faced and blue-eyed athletes dominating the NFL and NBA again.

Even the flailing Bulls front office had managed to sign that half-thally power forward from Duke. Finch couldn't remember his name. Cletus something. Finch had played football, himself. Sometimes he wished he'd kept going with it, but his fiancé had cared more about intact gray matter than money. Of course, he hadn't been thrilled when Finch chose security as an alternative source of income, but...

In a distant corner of his mind, Finch felt the clamp loosening. He kept breathing steadily, kept his heartbeat slow, kept thinking about anything but the clamp loosening. Cletus Rivas. That was the kid's name. He'd pulled down twenty-six rebounds in the match-up against Arizona. Finch brought his hand slowly, slowly up toward his shoulder. Just to scratch. Just because he was itchy. Closer. Closer.

His fingers were millimeters from the clamp's burnished surface when the van's radio blared to life. His hand jerked; the clamp jolted. Finch tried to curse through his lockjaw and came up with mostly spit. So close.

"Listen up," came a voice from the speaker.

Finch had no alternative.

"I can turn off the clamp and unlock the van, but I need you to help me in exchange," the voice said. "I'm in apartment 401, sitting in an orthochair, deep sliced. There are three men in the room. The one you cut up, the one who Tasered you, and one more. They've still got the Tasers, and the last one has a handgun in an Adidas bag. I don't know where your gun is."

Finch felt the clamp fall away and went limp all over. His muscles ached deep like he'd done four hours in the weight room on methamphetamine—a bad idea, he knew from experience. He reached to massage his shoulder with one trembling hand.

"Grimes told me a non-duress passcode to give you," the voice continued. "So you'd know to trust me. It's Atticus."

Finch had almost forgotten that passcode. He'd wikied to find out why it made Mr. Grimes smirk but lost interest halfway through a text on Roman emperors.

"You have to hurry. They might kill me soon."

Hurrying did not sound like something Finch could do. He took three tries to push himself upright on gelatin arms. "Is Mr. Grimes safe?" he asked thickly, tongue sore and swollen from him biting it.

"He's on a leisurely drive to a waiting ferry. He'll be just fine. If you help me."

Finch crawled forward, taking a moment to drive one kneecap into the inactive clamp for a satisfying crunch, then hoisted himself between the two front seats and palmed the glove compartment. His Mulcher was waiting inside, still assembled, still loaded. He was dealing with some real fucking amateurs. The handgun molded to his grip, licking his thumb for DNA confirmation like a friendly cat. He was so glad to find it intact he nearly licked it back.

"Please. Hurry."

"Apartment 401, three targets, one incapacitated, three weapons, one lethal," Finch recited. He tested his wobbling legs as the van door slid open. Crossing the dusty floor of the parkade looked like crossing the Gobi desert.

"One other thing. You'll have to take the stairs. Elevator's out."

Finch was hardly even surprised. He stuck the Mulcher in his waistband and started to hobble.

*   *   *

HALF THE CITY away, Severyn wished, for the first time, that he'd had his cars equipped with seatbelts instead of only impact foam. Trying to stay seated while the limousine slewed corners and caromed down alleyways was impossible. He was thrown from one side to the other with every jolting turn. His kidnapper had finally cleared the windows and he saw, in familiar flashes, grimy red Southside brick and corrugated steel. The decades hadn't changed it much, except now the blue-green blooms of graffiti were animated.

"Pier's just up ahead. I told my guy there's been a change of plans." Girasol's voice was strained to breaking. Too many places at once, Severyn suspected.

"How long before the ones you're with know what's going on?" he asked, bracing himself against the back window to peer at their pursuers. One Priest was driving manually, and wildly. He was hunched over the steering wheel, trying to conflate what he'd learned in virtual racing sims with reality. His partner in the passenger's seat was hanging out the window with some sort of recoilless rifle, trying to aim.

"A few minutes, max."

A dull crack spiderwebbed the glass a micrometer from Severyn's left eyeball. He snapped his head back as a full barrage followed, smashing like a hailstorm into the reinforced window.

By the time they burst from the final alley, aligned for a dead sprint toward the hazard-sign-decorated pier, the limousine's rear was riddled with bullet holes. Up ahead, Severyn could make out the shape of a hydrofoil sliding out into the oil-slick water. The technician had lost his nerve.

"He's pulling away," Severyn snapped, ducking instinctively as another round raked across the back of the car with a sound of crunching metal.

"Told him to. You're going to have to swim for it."

Severyn's stomach churned. "I don't swim."

"You don't swim? You were All-State."

"Blake was." Severyn pried off his Armani loafers, peeled off his jacket, as the limousine rattled over the metal crosshatch of the pier. "I never learned."

"Just trust the muscle memory." Girasol's voice was taut and pleading. "He knows what to do. Just let him. Let his body."

They skidded to a halt at the lip of the pier. Severyn put his hand on the door and found it blinking blue, unlocked at last.

"If you can tell him things." She sounded ragged now. Exhausted. "Tell him I love him. If you can."

Severyn considered lying for a moment. A final push to solidify his position. "It doesn't work that way," he said instead, and hauled the door open as the Priests screeched to a stop behind him. He vaulted out of the limo, assaulted by unconditioned air, night wind, the smell of brine and oiled machinery.

Severyn sucked his lungs full and ran full-bore, feeling a hurricane of adrenaline that no puppet show or whorehouse could have coaxed from his glands. His bare feet pounded the cold pier, shouts came from behind him, and then he hurled himself into the grimy water. An ancient panic shot through him as ice flooded his ears, his eyes, his nose. He felt his muscles seize. He remembered, in a swath of old memory code, that he'd nearly drowned in Lake Michigan once.

Then nerve pathways that he'd never carved for himself fired, and he found himself cutting up to the surface. His head broke the water; he twisted and saw the gaggle of Priests at the edge of the water, Fawkes masks grinning at him even as they cursed and reloaded the rifle. Severyn grinned back, then pulled away with muscles moving in perfect synch, cupped hands biting the water with every stroke.

The slap of his body on the icy surface, the tug of his breath, the water in his ears—alive, alive, alive. The whine of a bullet never came. Severyn slopped over the side of the hydrofoil a moment later. Spread-eagled on the slick deck, chest working like a bellows, he started to laugh.

"That was some dramatic shit," came a voice from above him.

Severyn squinted up and saw the technician, a twitchy-looking man with gray whiskers and extra neural ports in his shaved skull. There was a tranq gun in his hand.

"There's been a change of plans," Severyn coughed. "Regarding the extraction."

The technician nodded, leveling the tranq. "Girasol told me you'd say that. Said you're a world-class bullshit artist. I'd expect no less from Severyn fucking Grimes."

Severyn's mouth fished open and shut. Then he started to laugh again, a long gurgling laugh, until the tranq stamped through his wet skin and sent him to sleep.

GIRASOL SAW HOT white sparks when they ripped her out of the orthochair and realized it was sheer luck they hadn't shut off her brain stem. You didn't tear someone out of a deep slice. Not after two hits of high-grade Dozr. She hoped, dimly, that she wasn't going to go blind in a few days' time.

"You bitch." Pierce's breath was scalding her face. He must have taken off his mask. "You bitch. Why? Why would you do that?"

Girasol found it hard to piece the words together. She was still out of body, still imagining a swerving limousine and marauding cell signals and electric sheets of code. Her hand blurred into view, and she saw her veins were taut and navy blue.

She'd stretched herself thinner than she'd ever done before, but she hadn't managed to stop the skype from the end of the pier. And now Pierce knew what had happened.

"Why did you help him get away?"

The question came with a knee pushed into her chest, under her ribs. Girasol thought she felt her lungs collapse in on themselves. Her head was coming clear.

She'd been a god only moments ago, gliding through circuitry and sound waves, but now she was small, and drained, and crushed against the stained linoleum flooring.

"I'm going to cut your eyeballs out," Pierce was deciding. "I'm going to do them slow. You traitor. You puppet."

Girasol remembered her last flash from the limousine's external cams: Blake diving into the dirty harbor with perfect form, even if Grimes didn't know it. She was sure he'd make it to the hydrofoil. It was barely a hundred meters. She held onto the novocaine thought as Pierce's knife snicked and locked.

"What did he promise you? Money?"

"Fuck off," Girasol choked.

Pierce was straddling her now, the weight of him bruising her pelvis. She felt his hands scrabbling at her zipper. The knife tracing along her thigh. She tamped down her terror.

"Oh," she said. "You want that kiss now?"

His backhand smashed across her face, and she tasted copper. Girasol closed her eyes tight. She thought of the hydrofoil slicing through the bay. The technician leaning over Blake's prone body with his instruments, pulling the parasite up and away, reawakening a brain two years dormant. She'd left him messages. Hundreds of them. Just in case.

"Did he promise to fuck you?" Pierce snarled, finally sliding her pants down her bony hips. "Was that it?"

The door chimed. Pierce froze, and in her peripheral Girasol could see the other Priests' heads turning toward the entryway. Nobody ever used the chime. Girasol wondered how Grimes's bodyguard could possibly be so stupid, then noticed that a neat row of splintery holes had appeared all across the breadth of the door.

Pierce put his hand up to his head, where a bullet had clipped the top of his scalp, carving a furrow of matted hair and stringy flesh. It came away bright red. He stared down at Girasol, angry, confused, and the next slug blew his skull open like a shattering vase.

Girasol watched numbly as the bodyguard let himself inside. His fiery hair was slick with sweat and his face was drawn pale, but he moved around the room with practiced efficiency, putting two more bullets into each of the injured Priests before collapsing to the floor himself. He tucked his hands under his head and exhaled.

"One hundred and twelve," he said. "I counted."

Girasol wriggled out from under Pierce and vomited. Wiped her mouth. "Repairman's in tomorrow." She stared down at the intact side of Pierce's face.

"Where's Mr. Grimes?"

"Nearly docking by now. But he's not in a body." Girasol pushed damp hair out of her face. "He's been extracted. His storage cone is safe. Sealed. That was our deal."

The bodyguard was studying her intently, red brows knitted. "Let's get going, then." He picked his handgun up off the floor. "Gray eyes," he remarked. "Those contacts?"

"Yeah," Girasol said. "Contacts." She leaned over to give Pierce a bloody peck on the cheek, then got shakily to her feet and led the way out the door.

*   *   *

SEVERYN GRIMES WOKE up feeling rested. His last memory was laughing on the deck of a getaway boat, but the soft cocoon of sheets made him suspect he'd since been moved. Something else had changed, too. His proprioception was sending an avalanche of small error reports. Limbs no longer the correct length. New body proportions. By the feel of it, he was in something artificial.

"Mr. Grimes?"

"Finch." Severyn tried to grimace at the tinny sound of his voice, but the facial myomers were relatively fixed. "The *mise á jour*, please."

Finch's craggy features loomed above him, blank and professional as ever. "Girasol Fletcher had you extracted from her son's body. After we met her technician, I transported your storage cone here to Lumen Technohospital for diagnostics. Your personality and memories came through completely intact and they stowed you in an interim avatar to speak with your lawyers. Of which there's a horde, sir. Waiting in the lobby."

"Police involvement?" Severyn asked, trying for a lower register.

"There are a few Priests in custody, sir," Finch said. "Girasol Fletcher and her son are long gone. CPD requested access to the enzyme trackers in Blake's body. It looks like she hasn't found a way to shut them off yet. Could triangulate and maybe find them if it happens in the next few hours."

Severyn blinked, and his eyelashes scraped his cheeks. He tried to frown. "What the fuck am I wearing, Finch?"

"The order was put in for a standard male android." Finch shrugged. "But there was an electronic error."

"Pleasure doll?" Severyn guessed. Electronic error seemed unlikely.

His bodyguard nodded stonily. "You can be uploaded in a fresh volunteer within twenty-four hours," he said. "They've done up a list of candidates. I can link it."

Severyn shook his head. "Don't bother," he said. "I think I want something clone-grown. See my own face in the mirror again."

"And the trackers?"

Severyn thought of Blake and Girasol tearing across the map, heading somewhere sun-drenched where their money could stretch and their faces couldn't be plucked off the news feeds. She would do small-time hackwork. Maybe he would start to swim again.

"Shut them off from our end," Severyn said. "I want a bit of a challenge when I hunt her down and have her uploaded to a waste disposal."

"Will do, Mr. Grimes."

But Finch left with a ghost of a smile on his face, and Severyn suspected his employee knew he was lying.

THOUGH SHE BE BUT LITTLE
C.S.E. Cooney

C. S. E. Cooney (csecooney.com) is the author of the World Fantasy Award-winning collection *Bone Swans: Stories*. Her work includes the Dark Breakers series, *Jack o' the Hills*, *The Witch in the Almond Tree*, and poetry collection *How to Flirt in Faerieland and Other Wild Rhymes*, which features Rhysling Award-winning "The Sea King's Second Bride." Her short fiction and poetry can be found in *Lightspeed, Strange Horizons, Apex, Uncanny, Lakeside Circus, Black Gate, Papaveria Press, GigaNotoSaurus, Goblin Fruit, Clockwork Phoenix 3 & 5*, and *The Mammoth Book of Steampunk*, and elsewhere.

EMMA ANNE HAD a tin can attached by a string to her belt. Lots of things on strings bounced and banged from it: some useful (like the pocket knife), some decorative (a length of red ribbon longer than herself, looped up), some that simply seemed interesting enough to warrant a permanent yo-yoing to her person (a silver hand bell, a long blue plume, the cameo of an elephant head wearing a Victorian bonnet).

"Emma Anne's Heavy Weight Stacked Plate Championship Wrestling Belt," Captain Howard called it. Captain Howard often capitalized the first letters of words she spoke out loud.

The belt was leather and embossed bronze, like a python wrapped twice about Emma Anne's torso. It had appeared along with Captious and Bumptious the night the sky turned silver. So had the tin can. They were all part of Emma Anne's endowments. ("Endowments" was the pirate word for objects or traits materializing Post-Argentum. "Post-Argentum," another phrase of their design. Pirates had words for everything. But pirates were liars.)

Emma Anne hadn't known how to use any of her endowments at first. Nothing was obvious until it was.

She brought the tin can up to her mouth and spoke into its cavity as clearly as she could. Endowments obeyed intent.

"Emma Anne to Margaret Howard. Come in please, Captain Howard."

Captain Margaret Howard, Way Pirate of Route 1, did not deal in tin cans. What she had was her parrot, George Sand. George Sand got reception.

"Rrrawk," Emma Anne's tin can blatted back at her. "Whaddya want?"

"What do you want, *over*," Emma Anne corrected.

She wouldn't have corrected Captain Howard to her face, but George Sand never failed to get on Emma's nerves.

"Rrrawk! Take it and rrawk yourself," said George Sand. "Over."

There was a pause while Emma Anne's chest tightened.

The tin can blatted, "Cap'n Howard makes her apologies for her rude bird, over. Please continue, kid, over."

She took a deep breath and decided not, after all, to cry.

"Captain, I've had a second visitation. It's the Loping Man for sure. I think he's coming for me tonight. Can you please meet me at Potter Hill preserve? He's been showing up around eight o' clock, so if you could come before that, I'd be really... But I understand if you'll be out, out..."

Emma Anne knew the word she wanted to say, or knew that she had known it not too long ago. It dissolved at the back of her throat like a Vitamin C tablet. Left a tang.

George Sand provided.

"Carousing!" it squawked. "Roistering. Wassailing. Possibly pillaging. Pirate Banquet tonight up at The Grill. Starts at seven. Mandatory." Another pause, wherein (Emma Anne surmised) Captain Howard related something to her parrot even it would not repeat. "Er... over."

"Bye," said Emma Anne in a much smaller voice. She let the tin can fall. It bonged hollowly against her knee.

Captious sighed. "Well. That went about the way we thought."

Bumptious let out a gentle "Oof" as Emma Anne flopped against his head. Being composed of fake fur and synthetic fiber batting, he was barely fazed by Emma Anne's constant, casual assaults upon his person.

"Margo Howard's not reliable," said Bumptious. "She used to be, before the sky turned silver. Remember how she organized the book club? Volunteered for every church committee? She made loads as an X-ray tech, too, Emma Anne, and always so modest not to mention it. But she did have one of those halfie cars that ran on lightning as well as gas, and you know they didn't come cheap."

"Electricity," Emma Anne murmured to herself, to make sure she remembered it. It was hard to think, with the Loping Man looming close as nighttime. "Hybrid. Hybrid cars."

"She sure ain't modest now," Captious observed. Captious was a weasel, stuffed, like Bumptious, about a third his size. Like Bumptious, occasionally sentient. "And who needs cars anyway, when you got a big old flying alligator for an endowment? Eats prisoners for fuel, all the parts. Very sustainable."

"What if you run out of prisoners?" Bumptious countered. His orange eyes glinted. They were made of that hard, cool plastic that looks and feels like glass. Emma Anne liked to tap on it with her fingernails when Bumptious was asleep. "At the rate she goes through prisoners…"

"Eh, they probably beg her to throw 'em to the alligator once she's had her way with 'em…"

"You don't know her!" Emma Anne yelled, pushing them both away. Bumptious tumbled onto his back, legs sticking straight up. His tail hung limp. He had no stripes on his belly. "You don't know her now, and you didn't know her *then*. Or me. You weren't there! Stop pretending you were!"

A short, messy scrabble took her from her nest of bricks at the bottom of the old smokestack where she slept, and right to the ledge. From there, careless of her knees, she jumped down into the green and golden wilderness of the overgrown lot where the smokestack stood.

At her intrusion, the insect orchestra encountered a fermata. But when she made no further rash movement, it started up again, pianoforte. Emma Anne stood still, legs itching, staring blankly into the heady, dying afternoon.

Mugwort grew up all around her, higher than her shoulders and fragrant as chrysanthemums, leafy underbellies a play of silver and white. Tall, tumbleweedish sweet clover, with seeds that smelled of vanilla, tangled up with spotted knapweed, then trailed off into plumy golden rod, floating foxtail grass, haughty towers of purple asters.

Emma Anne might turn left and wend her way to Mill Town. She might turn right and sit meditatively on the bank of the Pawcatuck.

There were paths through this place, but you had to know where to step. Roads embroidered the old Potter Hill preserve dating from 1911 when the mill had first been built, with its water wheel and red brick textile factories. A hundred years later, the Preservation Trust had reclaimed the preserve as a historic site and walking park.

When the sky turned silver, Potter Hill became... Something else. Just like everything.

She craned her head over her shoulder, glancing back at the smokestack. The entrance to her hideaway was too high to climb to without assistance from the three-legged chair haphazardly stashed in a nearby bush. Both Captious and Bumptious had poked their noses out of the hole to stare at her with their plastic eyes. They never moved when she was looking.

"You really ought to take us with you," advised Captious with a look of cunning. "You know the Loping Man is lurking."

"What can *you* do?" Emma Anne asked.

"Protect you!" Bumptious asserted stoutly. He was good at assertion.

Emma Anne ignored him. "Anyway. He won't be around right now. The Loping Man's not into daylight hours. He's more crap..." She paused. The word she wanted was vanishing at the edges. "Crap..."

"Craptastic?" guessed Captious.

"No, creep... Crep..."

"Creepissimo? Creepilicious! Creepo-mijito?"

"No! Stop! I know it... It's... He's... He's crepuscular!" She paused, grinning. "You know... Like deer? And rabbits?"

Weasel and tiger stared as only stuffed animals can stare. They often chose to desert their sentience as a kind of consequence whenever they thought Emma Anne was getting above herself.

Though they were her closest companions, though they comforted her through thunderstorm and famine, she did not trust them. Endowments could take you over if you weren't careful. If you didn't try to remember *all the time* that you hadn't always been what you'd become.

Take for instance Mrs. Emma A. Santiago, Navy widow, age sixty-five.

When the sky turned silver, Mrs. Emma A. Santiago woke up Emma Anne, eight years old in her jimjams and Velcro sneakers. One belt, one tin can on string, two stuffed toys the richer. Sans house, sans car, sans monthly Bunco night with her girlfriends of forty years, sans everything.

(The Bunco Gals had all been turned into the Chihuahua Ladies, who tottered around Mill Town on red high heels that were fused with the flesh of their ankles. Their necks were long and smooth, covered in fawn-colored fur, their heads tiny and large-eyed, with long ears that twitched at the slightest sound. They traveled in a pack of twelve, furry necks writhing like pythons, and yapped whenever they saw Emma Anne. She avoided them—and Mill Town—until her supplies went from meager to mere rearrangements of empty jars and boxes.)

Captain Margaret Howard said the silver sky had come to turn people into what they really are. She said this as fact, the way pirates say things.

Emma Anne wasn't sure. But she *did* remember thinking, in her old life, that she'd never succeeded very well at *feeling* grown up, that the achievement of adulthood had seemed a series of accidents covered by pretense. She had feared dying not for death's sake but because of the malingering notion that she'd missed several key milestones in life.

She wondered, if given the choice, she'd've chosen death over this perpetual childhood. She had never wondered enough to put it to the test. Yet.

In all likelihood, she wouldn't need to. Death might come (indeed, tonight *would* come, as sure as gators fly) in the form of the Loping Man, and she, a child alone in the wilderness, powerless to stop him.

IT WAS BARELY six when Captain Howard came to Potter Hill. This late in the autumn, that made it almost full twilight. But Captain Howard was a one-woman bonfire and lit up the overgrown lot as she glided into it.

Her vest was scarlet with golden frogs and golden tassels. It swept to her knees. The vest, though idiosyncratic, was not an endowment. Captain Howard had 'pilfered' it from the Mill Town Theatre, which had not, for whatever reason, changed into anything other than itself when the sky turned silver. She wore a blunderbuss at her right hip and a cutlass at her left—they'd appeared under her pillow and in her shower respectively, just Post-Argentum, where she couldn't miss them. (Change occurred more rapidly after that. Returning, bewildered, from a walk around what had been her neighborhood that first morning, Margaret Howard had discovered her home had become a kind of grotto, complete with the sound of sea waves crashing in the distance and a thin green veil of damp on the granite walls, and all the sofas changed to sofa-shaped mounds of ingots and goblets and pearls and things.)

In that offhand brazen way she had, Captain Howard shouted, "Ahoy, Matey!" and leaning over her saddle, dumped the contents of a large greasy paper bag labeled 'The Grill' onto the designated 'stoop' of Emma Anne's smokestack. Such riches tumbled out! Biscuits sogged in gravy, a roasted turkey leg, two twice-baked potatoes wrapped in foil, corn on the cob—salted *and* buttered—a flask of hard cider.

Emma Anne stared. From food to Captain. From Captain to food.

"Oh... well!" said Captain Howard, interpreting this look. "So I Dropped in on The Grill on My Way here for maybe Five Minutes while the Caterers were, you know, Catering. Picked up a Few Things. Purrrloined them, you might say," she added, with great relish. She tended to roll her r's at her most piratical.

"Scoundrel!" George Sand squawked from her shoulder. "Brigand! Bandit! Thief!"

The Way Pirate of Route 1 bowed with the falsest of modesties from her seat on the back of her flying alligator.

The alligator, named H. M. S., hovered gently at the mouth of the smokestack. She could maintain a hover for hours, maybe days. She didn't have wings or need ballast; just... she seemed to prefer air to land. Margaret Howard had found H. M. S. sunbathing on her rooftop one morning Post-Argentum. After that, she didn't miss her Prius.

Floating before the entrance like that, Captain and gator blocked out most of the dusk. Emma Anne was comfortable in that dark. She liked that her smokestack was too small to fit people like Captain Howard and H. M. S. That meant her smokestack was safe. The surface area allowed for a maximum occupancy of herself, Captious, Bumptious, and a few supplies. On the vertical, it was occupied by a small bat colony that benevolently kept Emma Anne malaria-free by consuming a brute majority of the local mosquito population.

"Anyway, Kid," continued Captain Howard at her airiest. "Just thought you might be Hungry. Eat!"

Emma Anne hastily swallowed a gobful of cheesy potato, but not before she politely thanked Captain Howard for dinner. It had been a generous gesture. Nor had it been, Emma Anne believed, the pirate in Captain Howard who did it; it was an act of pure Margo, her friend from before. The one who'd started the book club and ran bake sale fundraisers for any shaggy cause that came begging. Margo'd done good works and well, not seeming to care if the tasks proved thankless or less than successful. Margo had *not* been a Bunco Gal. "I'll donate my ten bucks a month to UNICEF, thanks," she said the first few times Emma Anne had invited her, until Emma Anne stopped inviting her.

But by now, Margo was mostly the Way Pirate of Route 1, and it was best to mind your manners around her.

Captain Howard pooh-poohed Emma Anne's gratitude with a negligent hand motion. She had perfected a certain flick of the wrist that sent her cuff-lace frothing over the warm brown elegance of her wrist. Her hair was a bundle of ropy black braids, atop which perched a scarlet tricorne like a caravel.

"So, you've seen your Gentleman Caller again, have you?" she asked. "That's, what, Twice now you said?"

Emma Anne gagged, spat up neatly in a napkin. "Yes, Captain. Twice. Last night was, was the second time."

"Hmn. You know what They Say Happens on the Third Night?"

"Yes. He... That's why I called you."

The first night you see the Loping Man, it is clear you have come to his attention. He stands for hours, at a distance, peering and peering. If you try to sneak away, he'll follow, always just in sight.

On the second night, the Loping Man comes closer. Close enough that you can see his lips writhing, stretching, puckering, smacking, working. He is close enough that the sound of his chewing eats at your ears.

On the third night...

On the third night, the Loping Man, he'll throw you onto his shoulders and he'll run with you. Run and run and run and run. You'll die up there; he'll run so long, you'll starve and die. Or die of fright. And you'll turn to bones, which will clatter against the bones of all the other children he's taken, which drape his neck and chest like handcrafted bamboo and coconut wind chimes.

How Emma Anne understood all this, never having met the Loping Man face to face—or indeed any children other than her own self—she did not know. It was as if she'd always known the legend of the Loping Man, ever since the sky turned silver. A story she'd been born into.

"When he walks," Emma Anne whispered, "his knees come up to touch his ears. His mouth is awful. He—he's worse than anything in Mill Town."

Captain Howard, who fancied herself a fairly creditable contestant in Mill Town's pool of Big Bads, looked affronted. "How So?"

"I don't think... I don't think he's from here. I don't think he ever was."

"Ah." Captain Howard cleared her throat. She toyed nervously with one of her gold-worked buttonholes. "How on Earth—if you'll Pardon the Archaic Expression—can you even Tell anymore?"

"I just can." Emma Anne scooted a little closer to the mouth of the smokestack, trying to peer into Captain Howard's shadowed eyes. "The Loping Man's like the endowments. Like H. M. S. and Captious and Bumptious. They came *after*. They're not made from anything that was before. I mean, even George Sand was your ugly French bulldog before it was your parrot."

"Georgie was Never Ugly!"

"It farted all the time, Margo. It had bad breath."

"She was an Old Dog."

"It's a pretty ugly parrot too."

"I can't believe I stole dinner for you, Santiago!"

They glared at each other. Suddenly it was as if Emma Anne weren't eight and Margo Howard weren't a pirate. And they were friends again and could speak as friends.

Bumptious began growling. Captious started up a wheeze. H. M. S., gently, buoyantly, turned her face so that one yellow eye shone like a lamp into Emma Anne's dark space.

Captain Howard cleared her throat. "Look, uh, I can't stay much longer, Emma Anne. They're expecting me at The Grill. We're electing a Pirate King tonight after the Banquet, and I have to be there. I just stopped by to—well. Anyway. Good luck with the Loping Man and all. I thought maybe I'd lend you my..."

She patted first her right hip, then her left, as if debating whether to part with cutlass or blunderbuss. Her hands trembled. Emma Anne understood. It would be the same for her if she tried to give up Captious or Bumptious.

Finally, Captain Howard's hands fell, heavy and still, to rest on her thighs. Nothing more to say. Emma Anne bit her bottom lip so hard her teeth almost went through.

"I get it, okay? But I had to, to call. You're the only grown-up I know." Captain Howard was, Emma Anne reflected gloomily, the only *anyone* she knew. If you didn't include the Chihuahua Ladies, whose long necks and tiny teeth scared her.

Sighing, shaking her head, Captain Howard groaned, "Oh, Emma Anne! I *can't* help you. Don't you see? It's nothing to do with the Banquet really. It's that… You're my Feral Child. All Pirates have one eventually. We'll have to fight a Duel to the Death one day and Only One will survive. If that. We're Natural Enemies."

"And yet you keep feeding me."

Captain Howard took off her hat and fanned her face with it. She looked guilty. Emma Anne couldn't tell if it was pretend guilt or spontaneous disclosure. She muttered, "It's your fault for being so damned skinny. How can I fight a Duel with a Scarecrow? Not sporting."

"How can you fight a duel with a corpse?"

Again they exchanged glares, so nearly friends they almost hated each other.

Emma Anne broke first. She pulled her knees up under her chin and set her forehead between them.

"Go away. Just go away. I don't need you. I don't care."

Captain Howard's hand reached into the smokestack to squeeze Emma Anne's shoulder. In a low, urgent voice, almost as if she were trying to speak so that H. M. S. and the stuffed animals could not hear, she said, "You're my Doom, Emma Anne. That's clear as the Silver Sky. But *your* Doom is the Loping Man. I think that means you've been given the tools to face him. You've had them all along. That's all I know."

Emma Anne jerked her shoulder away. "I have a tin can. I used it to call you. You can't help me. You just said."

Captain Howard stiffened. "Aye, then. That's what I said." She slapped the tricorne back onto her braids. "A Rrrright Rrrrascal I be, me hearty," she added with bitter jocularity, leaning forward in her saddle to press her whole body's weight against H. M. S.'s head. Endowments respond to intent, but alligators respond to pressure. Captain Howard used both in spades.

They flew off into the twilight, outlined in new stars, making sensuous S curves all the way back to Route 1.

THE LOPING MAN came by moonlight. He must always come by moonlight. The first thing you see, far off across the overgrown lot, is the dull, radioactive glow of the bones draped all about him. But before that, you hear the chewing. It is louder than the soughing of knapweed and mugwort, louder than the night sigh of spear grass, and it is awful.

Emma Anne heard it. That sound shrank the horizonless prairieland of her daytime domain to its exact dimensions: ninety-four feet long by fifty feet wide. She saw the green glow, and saw it grow, and scuttled back against the far wall of her smokestack, clutching Captious and Bumptious close to her.

Captious hissed, "Stop breathing!"

Emma Anne smashed a hand over her nose and mouth, and reduced herself to an airless heartbeat. Only a hearth-shaped patch of outside was visible to her strained eyes, moon-soaked to a depth-defying gray. The insect orchestra had shivered to a hush at the Loping Man's excruciating progress.

He moved as slowly as the hour hand of a clock so long as you held your breath. The moment you gasped, he would tick forward at second hand speed, like a roach when you turn on the lights.

In the blackness of the flue, Emma Anne could not see Bumptious squashed in her lap, only feel the long, silent reverberation that was not a purr. Captious was quiescent in her fist.

The hesitant SHSHSHing as the Loping Man rustled forward. The distinctive CRIIIICK as he lifted his long folded forelimbs right up to his ears. The curt staccato TOCK as his feet touched down. The long silences between while he waited, daring her to inhale.

Soon, he was close enough that Emma Anne's spotted vision caught the movement of his mandibles as he chewed. The endowments on her belt trembled and danced on their strings like a mobile in a windstorm.

SHSHSH, CRIIICK, TOCK.

He advanced.

He had the benevolent face of a mantis: prophetic, wizened, gray-green, vaguely worried. His compound eyes were mournful, fixed on Emma Anne's face.

Alas! Breath burst upon her. Despair poisoned the sweet night air as it filled her lungs, and he was too close—right-outside-her-smokestack-close—his-head-level-with-her-hearth-close—and she had seen him neither lope nor leap, nor heard the final TOCK of his step. She wondered if her own heartbeat had out-slammed it. Green bones loosely wound him, like the Mardi Gras beads and feather boas that the Chihuahua Ladies née Bunco Gals wore, even now, traveling in their pack of twelve.

Where are they now? thought Emma Anne, and began to cry.

BUNCO GALS NEEDED only twelve to make up their tables evenly. Four to a table, partners sitting across from each other. Each gal shelled ten bucks into the pot, making a tidy pile for the end of the night, when both winners and losers trotted away with a fistful of swag—some amounts more nominal than others—and only the mediocre players leaving empty-handed.

Emma Anne had always been the thirteenth Bunco Gal, earning her the nickname 'Ghost.' As odd one out, she would begin the first rotation of the game rolling dice for an invisible partner. This, she felt, was her just punishment for never once having failed to RSVP late, but it did dislocate her socially right from the get-go. It set her at an invisible body's distance from the rest of her friends.

Poor Ghost! Her friends laughed at her, and laughing, forgave her. *Our late, great Emma Anne.*

She was, or had been, just dreadful at checking her email for the monthly Bunco Gals Party Night reminder newsletter. Never mind replying to it. Eventually her friends, organized by Xime Ortiz, arranged to take turns calling her personally on her landline ("You should really get a cellphone, Emma Anne! For emergencies!"), and usually twice: once to invite her, once to remind her.

They even started picking her up in their Buick Centuries and Chevrolet Impalas and Cadillac Club Sedans, with the tacit understanding that Emma Anne was, in turn, to be designated driver on the way home. This obligatory inability to consume more than one margarita during the between-the-rounds pitcher pass was but another barrier to her social enjoyment. It did, however, enable her, as the only adult equal to the task of counting to twenty-one by the end of the night, to keep a fairly tidy score, and therefore a modicum of self-respect.

But she never did buy that cellphone…

… FOR EMERGENCIES.

Staring into the Loping Man's gravely gentle eyes, Emma Anne forgot to fear her friends. Oh, but she missed them. She wanted them back, yaps and fangs and beads and all.

She sucked in a huge breath, slowed time, her fingers moving to the hand bell hanging from her belt. If Emma Anne were still who she once had been, she'd have called it a Bunco Bell, identical to the one used to ring their game to order. But tonight she was just a child gone feral under a silver sky, and this bell was her endowment.

If only she knew what it was for.

The Loping Man's raptorial forelegs lifted, slow as sap moving, landing delicately on the hearth of the smokestack. Slow as grass dying, they reached for her. His jaw worked and gaped, worked and gaped.

And gaped.

And gaped.

Did he, then, take the head first, before all? Chew the brains like bubble gum? No chance of survival then, of jumping from his back as he ran. She'd just be a body, slung across his shoulders for a later and more deliberate mastication.

His segmented abdomen looked vast, insatiable, capable of containing several Emma Annes and all her endowments.

"Captious!" she squeaked, expelling breath without replacing it. Her left hand pinched the silver bell's clapper, holding it soundless. Her right hand clutched some part of the stuffed weasel. "If I close my eyes, can you move fast enough?"

A dubious pause as Captious agreed to understand the full import of the question.

"There's fast enough," she said, "and then there's suddenly you're a head shorter and a human stole. It's kind of fifty-fifty."

"I can!" Bumptious piped up from her lap. "I can move fast enough, Emma Anne. If you trust me."

Emma Anne sat in the brick dust and bat guano and her own warm urine, nose and eyes running, mouth dry. Not breathing. But those forelegs kept sliding in, inexorably, that triangular head following, and soon the Loping Man would be there with her, right inside her sanity. No, not sanity. Her septic tank. No, that wasn't... sanctum! *Sanctum Sanctorum*, from the Latin...

Oh, he was enormous, colossal, an armored giant, but so very terribly compactable. Yes, and maybe *that* was where he went all day. Not away, but down, folded into leaf and twig and compound eyes, origamied into torpor.

"I won't look," Emma Anne promised Bumptious with the last of her breath. "I promise."

An ecstatic Bumptious cried, "Thank you!" as Emma Anne's eyelids slammed shut.

She gasped for breath.

Stink seeped back into her nostrils: the ammonia and cat litter smell of the guano, her own excreta, and the Loping Man's rapidly invading odor, like the damp mystery of mushrooms, as he pressed on, pressed in, at speed.

But now, there came between her body and the Loping Man a roar that better belonged behind an enclosure of stainless steel wire rope mesh than in the non-living body of a plush toy. Bumptious had attacked.

Almost immediately, Captious began to writhe in her fist.

"Lemme go! Lemme go! Hellstars and moonworms! He's halfway gone to gullet! No, Bump—don't! EMMA ANNE, LET GO!"

She didn't have time to obey; Captious sank her manifestly non-textile teeth into her wrist and wriggled loose. A weasel-shaped wind tunnel shot from the palm of her hand toward the hearth.

Then, nothing.

Just the sound of chewing.

But not, Emma Anne noticed when she dared peek again, *easy* chewing. It was half gagging, half gurgling, as if the Loping Man had thought he was getting squid nigiri for dinner and ended up with a mouthful of magnapinna mixed with cotton candy.

Emma Anne's trembling left hand released the clapper of the silver hand bell. It chimed faintly against its bowl. Outside, not so very far away, an answering chorus of yips lit the night. Wrist throbbing, Emma Anne stared down at the endowment, and understood it.

Why, after all, did the Chihuahua Ladies always seem to turn up whenever Emma Anne came to Mill Town, following her—and her chiming, clinking, tinkling belt—around?

They recognized the Bunco Bell.

And they wanted to play.

Emma Anne lifted the bell in hand with new vigor and gave it twelve sharp rings. The bats in the smokestack awoke, diving all ways for open air. The Loping Man flinched back from their wings. Or from the noise. Or perhaps he sensed, not far behind him, the red thunder of high heels, the raking-in-the-making of manicured claws, the loyalty of old friends to their Ghost.

As crowded as the smokestack had been a moment before, it was now deserted of everything but Emma Anne. Captious and Bumptious, the bats, the Loping Man, all gone. Even the echoes of the silver bell, gone.

Outside, the world exploded in sound.

SHH. TOCK. FLAP. SHH. YIP. YIP. FLAP. TOCK. TOCK.

All this, threaded together by growling, scuffling, dragging. Something hurled at speed against the brick base of the smokestack. Emma Anne flung herself to her belly and crawled to the ledge, peering down into the starlit dark over the lot.

The Loping Man bled a black-green ooze that glowed, illuminating at least himself and whatever his blood fell upon. He was still chewing, frantically, foam and synthetic fiber batting bulging from his cheeks and the upper seams of his segmented abdomen, where he seemed to be... bursting.

The Chihuahua Ladies harried him, doggedly. But though they were fierce, the Loping Man's right foreleg swept two of them off their feet, his left spearing another clear through the shoulder and flinging her into the mugwort and sweet clover and knapweed in a fireworks of fragrance.

At that petering howl of dismay, Emma Anne dropped the bell and groped for her belt. Her fingers found the loop of red ribbon, and tugged it loose. She ran it between her hands, pulling the midsection taut. Without daring to think about what she did, she pushed herself into a perching crouch, and waited, waited, waited till he was close enough again—and jumped from the smokestack right onto the Loping Man's back.

Once, twice, thrice went the red ribbon about the prothorax. Her legs squeezed lower down. His limbs rose around her like scissors every time he moved. He flailed as she pulled. She pulled tighter. His thrashes went wild. He backed up against the smokestack as if to rasp her off his back, like a bear marking territory on trees, or a businessman scraping dog shit from his shoe. She looped the red ribbon about one fist, and tugged her pocketknife from its knotted string.

Just beneath the jaw then. That killing jaw, spilling over with the stuffed bits of Captious and Bumptious.

Let no child wake to the sound of his chewing again.

There.

EMMA ANNE ARRIVED late to the Pirate Banquet, but she was used to that. Besides, she reflected, could you be late if you were never even invited?

She rode in through the open doors of The Grill.

The Grill, in 1912, had been a fruit and vegetable stand owned by a tiny Italian man full of nautical invective and conflicting tales about his arrival on Ellis Island. The stand later became a full-service cafeteria for Mill Town factory workers. Still later a discotheque, complete with gold-laméd Go-Go dancers in cages. Now it was the favorite watering hole of pirates, which meant a fishy smell, a lot of black and red décor, a great deal of skulls, snakes, and the occasional hourglass.

Emma Anne didn't know how many pirates there were in Mill Town and its environs. There seemed to be hundreds. H. M. S. was not the only floating alligator tethered to the flagpole outside.

Raucous as they were, the whole hairy, tattooed, shirtless, accoutered, and aggressive lot of them fell silent at the sight of her. Even George Sand, stalking back and forth along the scarred bar and holding forth at length, RRAWKED to a surprised standstill.

Mounted on the now-headless Loping Man, Emma Anne was taller than the tallest of them. The skin of her legs stuck to his abdominal chitin, glued there by his ichor, and she was not sure if she would ever be able to tear herself free, or if she herself had now become, in essence and in accident, the Loping Man. Her hands were tangled in the red ribbons that bound his thorax. From his neck hole, where her pocketknife stuck out like a bolt, sprouted two partially chewed stuffed animal heads: one a tiger, one a weasel. They peered around The Grill with eager or ironic plastic eyes, and did not seem to care much anymore if their movements were witnessed.

Chihuahua Ladies flanking her like an honor guard, Emma Anne rode right up to Captain Howard.

The Way Pirate of Route 1 was sprawled on a throne of yet more decorative human skulls, wearing nothing but a lopsided paper crown from a defunct fast food restaurant Emma Anne could barely remember. Goober Bling. Booger Ring. Something.

Blunderbuss and cutlass bobbed through the air like a conductor's batons as Captain Howard led the pirates, badly, through an incoherent variation of "Fiddler's Green." She continued bellowing verses long past the quelling of her pirate court. Whether this was because she was drunker than they or simply less impressed with Emma Anne's entrance only she could say. But at last even she stopped, squinted one eye, and looked the newcomer up and down.

Emma Anne, glowing with gore, returned the glare. "Guess you got elected, Pirate King."

Captain Howard burped. "Guess you survived the night, Feral Child."

They eyed each other, waiting for the gauntlet slap, the taunt, the inciting incident for their final Duel and Doom. Emma Anne sighed and rolled her shoulders.

"Got any food, Margo?"

Her grin skullier than an ossuary, Captain Howard spread her arms wide to indicate the masses of lasagna, the mounds of Italian bread, the wheels of parmesan, and heaps of cannoli, struffoli, panna cotta.

"Maybe," she teased. "Sing for your supper, Santiago?"

Emma Anne opened her mouth—to sob? to scream?—and choked on a surprised laugh. Raising her chin, she squared her shoulders, met Captain Howard's gaze, and bellowed:

"I dug his grave with a silver spade!"

Everyone—Captious, Bumptious, the Pirate King, her pirates, her parrot, even the Chihuahua ladies—joined in.

"Storm along, boys! Storm along, John!"

THE MOON IS NOT A BATTLEFIELD
Indrapramit Das

Indrapramit Das (indradas.com) is an Indian author from Kolkata, West Bengal. His debut novel *The Devourers* was shortlisted for the 2015 Crawford Award and the 2016 Lambda Literary Award for Best LGBTQ SF/F/Horror. His fiction has appeared in *Clarkesworld Magazine, Lightspeed Magazine, Asimov's Science Fiction* and *Tor.com*, and has been anthologized in *The Year's Best Science Fiction* and elsewhere. He is an Octavia E. Butler scholar and a grateful graduate of the Clarion West Writers Workshop, and received his M.F.A. from the University of British Columbia in Vancouver. He has worn many hats, including editor, dog hotel night shift attendant, TV background performer, minor film critic, occasional illustrator, environmental news writer, pretend-patient for med school students, and video game tester. He divides his time between India and North America, when possible.

WE'RE RECORDING.

I was born in the sky, for war. This is what we were told.

I think when people hear this, they think of ancient Earth stories. Of angels and super heroes and gods, leaving destruction between the stars. But I'm no super hero, no Kalel of America-Bygone with the flag of his dead planet flying behind him. I'm no angel Gabreel striking down Satan in the void or blowing the trumpet to end worlds. I'm no devi Durga bristling with arms and weapons, chasing down demons through the cosmos and vanquishing them, no Kali with a string of heads hanging over her breasts black as deep space, making even the other gods shake with terror at her righteous rampage.

I was born in the sky, for war. What does it mean?

*   *   *

I WAS ACTUALLY born on Earth, not far above sea level, in the Greater Kolkata Megapolis. My parents gave me away to the Government of India when I was still a small child, in exchange for enough money for them to live off frugally for a year—an unimaginable amount of wealth for two Dalit street-dwellers who scraped shit out of sewers for a living, and scavenged garbage for recycling—sewers sagging with centuries worth of shit, garbage heaps like mountains. There was another child I played with the most in our slum. The government took her as well. Of the few memories I have left of those early days on Earth, the ones of us playing are clearest, more than the ones of my parents, because they weren't around much. But she was always there. She'd bring me hot jalebis snatched from the hands of hapless pedestrians, her hands covered in syrup, and we'd share them. We used to climb and run along the huge sea-wall that holds back the rising Bay of Bengal, and spit in the churning sea. I haven't seen the sea since, except from space—that roiling mass of water feels like a dream. So do those days, with the child who would become the soldier most often by my side. The government told our parents that they would cleanse us of our names, our untouchability, give us a chance to lead noble lives as astral defenders of the Republic of India. Of course they gave us away. I don't blame them. Aditi never blamed hers, either. That was the name my friend was given by the Army. You've met her. We were told our new names before training even began. Single-names, always. Usually from the Mahabharata or Ramayana, we realized later. I don't remember the name my parents gave me. I never asked Aditi if she remembered hers.

That, then, is when the life of asura Gita began.

I was raised by the state to be a soldier, and borne into the sky in the hands of the Republic to be its protector, before I even hit puberty.

The notion that there could be war on the Moon, or anywhere beyond Earth, was once a ridiculous dream.

So are many things, until they come to pass.

I've lived for thirty-six years as an infantry soldier stationed off-world. I was deployed and considered in active duty from eighteen in the Chandnipur Lunar Cantonment Area. I first arrived in Chandnipur at six, right after they took us off the streets. I grew up there. The Army raised us. Gave us a better education than we'd have ever gotten back on Earth. Right from childhood, me and my fellow asuras—Earth-bound Indian infantry soldiers were jawans, but we were always, always asuras, a mark of pride—we were told that we were stationed in Chandnipur to protect the intrasolar gateway of the Moon for the greatest country on that great blue planet in our black sky—India. India, which we could see below the clouds if we squinted during Earthrise on a surface patrol (if we were lucky, we could spot the white wrinkle of the Himalayas through telescopes). We learned the history of our home: after the United States of America and Russia, India was the third Earth nation to set foot on the Moon, and the first to settle a permanent base there. Chandnipur was open to scientists, astronauts, tourists and corporations of all countries, to do research, develop space travel, take expensive holidays and launch inter-system mining drones to asteroids. The generosity and benevolence of Bharat Mata, no? But we were to protect Chandnipur's sovereignty as Indian territory at all costs, because other countries were beginning to develop their own lunar expeditions to start bases. Chandnipur, we were told, was a part of India. The only part of India not on Earth. We were to make sure it remained that way. This was our mission. Even though, we were told, the rest of the world didn't officially recognize any land on the Moon to belong to any country, back then. Especially because of that.

Do you remember Chandnipur well?

IT WAS WHERE I met you, asura Gita. Hard to forget that, even if it hadn't been my first trip to the Moon. I was very nervous. The ride up the elevator was peaceful. Like... being up in the mountains, in the Himalayas, you know? Oh—I'm so sorry. Of course not. Just, the feeling of being high up—the silence of it, in a way, despite all the people in the elevator cabins. But then you start floating under the seat belts, and there are the safety instructions on how to move around the platform once you get to the top, and all you feel like doing is pissing. That's when you feel untethered. The shuttle to the Moon from the top of the elevator wasn't so peaceful. Every blast of the craft felt so powerful out there. The g's just raining down on you as you're strapped in. I felt like a feather.

Like a feather. Yes. I imagine so. There are no birds in Chandnipur, but us asuras always feel like feathers. Felt. Now I feel heavy all the time, like a stone, like a—hah—a moon, crashing into its world, so possessed by gravity, though I'm only skin and bones. A feather on a moon, a stone on a planet.

You know, when our Havaldar, Chamling his name was, told me that asura Aditi and I were to greet and guide a reporter visiting the Cantonment Area, I can't tell you how shocked we were. We were so excited. We would be on the feeds! We never got reporters up there. Well, to be honest, I wanted to show off our bravery, tell you horror stories of what happens if you wear your suit wrong outside the Cantonment Area on a walk, or get caught in warning shots from Chinese artillery klicks away, or what happens if the micro-atmosphere over Chandnipur malfunctions and becomes too thin while you're out and about there (you burn or freeze or asphyxiate). Civilians like horror stories from soldiers. You see so many of them in the media feeds in the pods, all these war stories. I used to like seeing how different it is for soldiers on Earth, in the old wars, the recent ones. Sometimes it would get hard to watch, of course.

Anyway, asura Aditi said to me, "Gita, they aren't coming here to be excited by a war movie. We aren't even at war. We're in *territorial conflict*. You use the word war and it'll look like we're boasting. We need to make them feel at home, not scare the shit out of them. We need to show them the hospitality of asuras on our own turf."

Couldn't disagree with that. We wanted people on Earth to see how well we do our jobs, so that we'd be welcomed with open arms when it was time for the big trip back—the promised pension, retirement, and that big old heaven in the sky where we all came from, Earth. We wanted every Indian up there to know we were protecting their piece of the Moon. Your piece of the Moon.

I thought soldiers would be frustrated having to babysit a journalist following them around. But you and asura Aditi made me feel welcome.

I felt bad for you. We met civilians in Chandnipur proper, when we got time off, in the Underground Markets, the bars. But you were my first fresh one, Earth-fresh. Like the imported fish in the Markets. Earth-creatures, you know, always delicate, expensive, mouth open gawping, big eyes. Out of water, they say.

Did I look 'expensive'? I was just wearing the standard issue jumpsuits they give visitors.

Arre, you know what I mean. In the Markets we soldiers couldn't buy Earth-fish or Earth-lamb or any Earth-meat, when they showed up every six months. We only ever tasted the printed stuff. Little packets; in the stalls they heat up the synthi for you in the machine. Nothing but salt and heat and protein. Imported Earth-meat was too expensive. Same for Earth-people, expensive. Fish out of water. Earth meant paradise. You came from heaven. No offense.

None taken. You and asura Aditi were very good to me. That's what I remember.

After Aditi reminded me that you were going to show every Indian on their feeds our lives, we were afraid of looking bad. You looked scared, at first. Did we scare you?

I wouldn't say scared. Intimidated. You know, everything you were saying earlier, about gods and superheroes from the old Earth stories. The stuff they let you watch and read in the pods. That's what I saw, when you welcomed us in full regalia, out on the surface, in your combat suits, at the parade. You gleamed like gods. Like devis, asuras, like your namesakes. Those weapon limbs, when they came out of the backs of your suit during the demonstration, they looked like the arms of the goddesses in the epics, or the wings of angels, reflecting the sunlight coming over the horizon—the light was so white, after Earth, not shifted yellow by atmosphere. It was blinding, looking at you all. I couldn't imagine having to face that, as a soldier, as your enemy. Having to face you. I couldn't imagine having to patrol for hours, and fight, in those suits—just my civilian surface suit was so hot inside, so claustrophobic. I was shaking in there, watching you all.

Do you remember, the Governor of Chandnipur Lunar Area came out to greet you, and shake the hands of all the COs. A surface parade like that, on airless ground, that never happened—it was all for you and the rest of the reporters, for the show back on Earth. We had never before even seen the Governor in real life, let alone in a surface suit. The rumours came back that he was trembling and sweating when he shook their hands—that he couldn't even pronounce the words to thank them for their service. So you weren't alone, at least.

Then when we went inside the Cantonment Area, and we were allowed to take off our helmets right out in the open—I waited for you and Aditi to do it first. I didn't believe I wouldn't die, that my face wouldn't freeze. We were on that rover, such a bumpy ride, but open air like those vehicles in the earliest pictures of people on the Moon—just bigger. We went through the Cantonment airlock gate, past the big yellow sign that reads 'Chandnipur, Gateway to the Stars,' and when we emerged from the other side Aditi told me to look up and see for myself, the different sky. From deep black to that deep, dusky blue, it was amazing, like crossing over into another world. The sunlight still felt different, blue-white instead of yellow, filtered by the nanobot haze, shimmering in that lunar dawn coming in over the hilly rim of Daedalus crater. The sun felt tingly, raw, like it burned even though the temperature was cool. The Earth was half in shadow—it looked fake, a rendered backdrop in a veeyar sim. And sometimes the micro-atmosphere would move just right and the bots would be visible for a few seconds in a wave across that low sky, the famous flocks of 'lunar fireflies'. The rover went down the suddenly smooth lunarcrete road, down the main road of the Cantonment—

New Delhi Avenue.

Yes, New Delhi Avenue, with the rows of wireframed flags extended high, all the state colours of India, the lines and lines of white barracks with those tiny windows on both sides. I wanted to stay in those, but they put us civilians underground, in a hotel. They didn't want us complaining about conditions. As we went down New Delhi Avenue and turned into the barracks for the tour, you and Aditi took off your helmets and breathed deep. Your faces were covered in black warpaint. Greasepaint. Full regalia, yes? You both looked like Kali, with or without the necklace of heads. Aditi helped me with the helmet, and I felt lunar air for the first time. The dry, cool air of Chandnipur. And you said, "Welcome to chota duniya. You can take off the helmet." Chota duniya, the little world. Those Kali faces, running with sweat, the tattoos of your wetware. You wore a small beard, back then, and a crew-cut. Asura Aditi had a ponytail, I was surprised that was allowed.

You looked like warriors, in those blinding suits of armour.

Warriors. I don't anymore, do I. What do I look like now?

I see you have longer hair. You shaved off your beard.

Avoiding the question, clever. Did you know that jawan means 'young man'? But we were asuras. We were proud of our hair, not because we were young men. We, the women and the hijras, the not-men, told the asuras who were men, why do you get to keep beards and moustaches and we don't? Some of them had those twirly moustaches like the asuras in the myths. So the boys said to us: we won't stop you. Show us your beards! From then it was a competition. Aditi could hardly grow a beard on her pretty face, so she gave up when it was just fuzz. I didn't. I was so proud when I first sprouted that hair on my chin, when I was a teenager. After I grew it out, Aditi called it a rat-tail. I never could grow the twirly moustaches, But I'm a decommissioned asura now, so I've shaved off the beard.

What do you think you look like now?

Like a beggar living in a slum stuck to the side of the space elevator that took me up to the sky so long ago, and brought me down again not so long ago.

Some of my neighbours don't see asuras as women or men. I'm fine with that. They ask me: do you still bleed? Did you menstruate on the Moon? They say, menstruation is tied to the Moon, so asuras must bleed all the time up there, or never at all down here. They think we used all that blood to paint ourselves red because we are warriors. To scare our enemies. I like that idea. Some of them don't believe it when I say that I bleed the same as any Earthling with a cunt. The young ones believe me, because they help me out, bring me rags, pads when they can find them, from down there in the city – can't afford the meds to stop bleeding altogether. Those young ones are a blessing. I can't exactly hitch a ride on top of the elevator up and down every day in my condition.

People in the slum all know you're an asura?

I ask again: what do I look like now?

A veteran. You have the scars. From the wetware that plugged you into the suits. The lines used to be black, raised—on your face, neck. Now they're pale, flat.

The mark of the decommissioned asura—everyone knows who you are. The government plucks out your wires. Like you're a broken machine. They don't want you selling the wetware on the black market. They're a part of the suits we wore, just a part we wore all the time inside us—and the suits are property of the Indian Army, Lunar Command.

I told you why the suits are so shiny, didn't I, all those years ago? Hyper-reflective surfaces so we didn't fry up in them like the printed meat in their heating packets when the sun comes up. The suits made us easy to spot on a lunar battlefield. It's why we always tried to stay in shadow, use infra-red to spot enemies. When we went on recon, surveillance missions, we'd use lighter stealth suits, non-metal, non-reflective, dark grey like the surface. We could only do that if we coordinated our movements to land during night-time.

When I met you and asura Aditi then you'd been in a few battles already. With Chinese and Russian troops. Small skirmishes.

All battles on the moon are small skirmishes. You can't afford anything bigger. Even the horizon is smaller, closer. But yes, our section had seen combat a few times. But even that was mostly waiting, and scoping with infra-red along the shadows of craters. When there was fighting, it was between long, long stretches of walking and sitting. But it was never boring. Nothing can be boring when you've got a portioned ration of air to breathe, and no sound to warn you of a surprise attack. Each second is measured out and marked in your mind. Each step is a success. When you do a lunar surface patrol outside Chandnipur, outside regulated atmosphere or Indian territory, as many times as we did, you do get used to it. But never, ever bored. If anything, it becomes hypnotic—you do everything you need to do without even thinking, in that silence between breathing and the words of your fellow soldiers.

You couldn't talk too much about what combat was like on the Moon, on that visit.

They told us not to. Havaldar Chamling told us that order came all the way down from the Lieutenant General of Lunar Command. It was all considered classified information, even training maneuvers. It was pretty silent when you were in Chandnipur. I'm sure the Russians and the Chinese had news of that press visit. They could have decided to put on a display of might, stage some shock and awe attacks, missile strikes, troop movements to draw us out of the Cantonment Area.

I won't lie—I was both relieved and disappointed. I've seen war, as a field reporter. Just not on the Moon. I wanted to see firsthand what the asuras were experiencing.

It would have been difficult. Lunar combat is not like Earth combat, though I don't know much about Earth combat other than theory and history. I probably know less than you do, ultimately, because I've never experienced it. But I've read things, watched things about wars on Earth. Learned things, of course, in our lessons. It's different on the Moon. Harder to accommodate an extra person when each battle is like a game of chess. No extra pieces allowed on the board. Every person needs their own air. No one can speak out of turn and clutter up comms. The visibility of each person needs to be accounted for, since it's so high.

The most frightening thing about lunar combat is that you often can't tell when it's happening until it's too late. On the battlefields beyond Chandnipur, out on the magma seas, combat is silent. You can't hear anything but your own footsteps, the *thoom-thoom-thoom* of your suit's metal boots crunching dust, or the sounds of your own weapons through your suit, the rattle-kick of ballistics, the near-silent hum of lasers vibrating in the metal of the shell keeping you alive. You'll see the flash of a mine or grenade going off a few feet away but you won't hear it. You won't hear anything coming down from above unless you look up—be it ballistic missiles or a meteorite hurtling down after centuries flying through outer space. You'll feel the shockwave knock you back but you won't hear it. If you're lucky, of course.

Laser weapons are invisible out there, and that's what's we mostly used. There's no warning at all. No muzzle-flash, no noise. One minute you're sitting there thinking you're on the right side of the rocks giving you cover, and the next moment you see a glowing hole melting into the suit of the soldier next to you, like those time-lapse videos of something rotting. It takes less than a second if the soldier on the other side of the beam is aiming properly. Less than a second and there's the flash and pop, blood and gas and superheated metal venting in into the thin air like an aerosol spray, the scream like static in the mics. Aditi was a sniper, she could've told you how lethal the long-range lasers were. I carried a semi-auto, laser or ballistic; those lasers were as deadly, just lower range and zero warm-up. When we were in battles closer to settlements, we'd switch to the ballistic weaponry, because the buildings and bases are mostly better protected from that kind of damage, bullet-proof. There was kind of a silent agreement between all sides to keep from heavily damaging the actual bases. Those ballistic fights were almost a relief—our suits could withstand projectile damage better, and you could see the tracers coming from kilometers away, even if you couldn't hear them. Like fire on oil, across the jet sky. Bullets aren't that slow either, especially here on the Moon, but somehow it felt better to see it, like you could dodge the fire, especially if we were issued jet packs, though we rarely used them because of how difficult they were to control. Aditi was better at using hers.

She saved my life once.

I mean, she did that many times, we both did for each other, just by doing what we needed to do on a battlefield. But she directly saved my life once, like an Earth movie hero. Rocket propelled grenade on a quiet battlefield. Right from up above and behind us. I didn't even see it. I just felt asura Aditi shove me straight off the ground from behind and blast us off into the air with her jetpack, propelling us both twenty feet above the surface in a second. We twirled in mid-air, and for a little moment, it felt like we were free of the Moon, hovering there between it and the blazing blue Earth, dancing together. As we sailed back down and braced our legs for landing without suit damage, Aditi never let me go, kept our path back down steady. Only then did I see the cloud of lunar dust and debris hanging where we'd been seconds earlier, the aftermath of an explosion I hadn't heard or seen, the streaks of light as the rest of the fireteam returned ballistic fire, spreading out in leaps with short bursts from their jetpacks. No one died in that encounter. I don't even remember whose troops we were fighting in that encounter, which lunar army. I just remember that I didn't die because of Aditi.

Mostly, we never saw the enemy close up. They were always just flecks of light on the horizon, or through our infrared overlay. Always ghosts, reflecting back the light of sun and Earth, like the Moon itself. It made it easier to kill them, if I'm being honest. They already seemed dead. When you're beyond Chandnipur, out on the mara under that merciless black sky with the Earth gleaming in the distance, the only colour you can see anywhere, it felt like *we* were already dead too. Like we were all just ghosts playing out the old wars of humanity, ghosts of soldiers who died far, far down on the ground. But then we'd return to the city, to the warm bustle of the Underground Markets on our days off, to our chota duniya, and the Earth would seem like heaven again, not a world left behind but one to be attained, one to earn, the unattainable paradise rather than a distant history of life that we'd only lived through media pods and lessons.

And now, here you are. On Earth.

Here I am. Paradise attained. I have died and gone to heaven.

It's why I'm here, isn't it? Why we're talking.

You could say that. Thank you for coming, again. You didn't have any trouble coming up the elevator shaft, did you? I know it's rough clinging to the top of the elevator.

I've been on rougher rides. There are plenty of touts down in the elevator base station who are more than willing to give someone with a few rupees a lending hand up the spindle. So. You were saying. About coming back to Earth. It must have been surprising, the news that you were coming back, last year.

FTL changed everything. That was, what, nine years ago?

At first it brought us to the edge of full-on lunar war, like never before, because the Moon became the greatest of all jewels in the night sky. It could become our first FTL port. Everyone wanted a stake in that. Every national territory on the Moon closed off its borders while the Earth governments negotiated. We were closed off in our bunkers, looking at the stars through the small windows, eating nothing but thin parathas from emergency flour rations. We made them on our personal heating coils with synthi butter— no food was coming through because of embargo, mess halls in the main barracks were empty. We lived on those parathas and caffeine infusion. Our stomachs were like balloons, full of air.

Things escalated like never before, in that time. I remember a direct Chinese attack on Chandnipur's outer defences, where we were stationed. One bunker window was taken out by laser. I saw a man stuck to the molten hole in the pane because of depressurization, wriggling like a dying insect. Asura Jatayu, a quiet, skinny soldier with a drinking problem. People always said he filled his suit's drinking water pods with diluted moonshine from the Underground Markets, and sucked it down during patrols. I don't know if that's true, but people didn't trust him because of it, even though he never really did anything to fuck things up. He was stone cold sober that day. I know, because I was with him. Aditi, me and two other asuras ripped him off the broken window, activated the emergency shutter before we lost too much pressure. But he'd already hemorrhaged severely through the laser wound, which had blown blood out of him and into the thin air of the Moon. He was dead. The Chinese had already retreated by the time we recovered. It was a direct response to our own overtures before the embargo. We had destroyed some nanobot anchors of theirs in disputed territory, which had been laid down to expand the micro-atmosphere of Yueliang Lunar Area.

That same tech that keeps air over Chandnipur and other lunar territories, enables the micro-atmospheres, is what makes FTL work—the q-nanobots. On our final patrols across the mara, we saw some of the new FTL shipyards in the distance. The ships—half-built, they looked like the Earth ruins from historical pictures, of palaces and cities. We felt like we were looking at artifacts of a civilization from the future. They sparked like a far-off battle, bots building them tirelessly. They will sail out to outer space, wearing quenbots around them like cloaks. Like the superheroes! The quenbot cloud folds the space around the ship like a blanket, makes a bubble that shoots through the universe. I don't really understand. Is it like a soda bubble or a blanket? We had no idea our time on the Moon was almost over on those patrols, looking at the early shipyards.

After one of the patrols near the shipyards, asura Aditi turned to me and said, "We'll be on one of those ships one day, sailing to other parts of the galaxy. They'll need us to defend Mother India when she sets her dainty feet on new worlds. Maybe we'll be able to see Jupiter and Saturn and Neptune zoom by like cricket balls, the Milky Way spinning far behind us like a chakra."

"I don't think that's quite how FTL works," I told her, but obviously she knew that. She looked at me, low dawn sunlight on her visor so I couldn't see her face. Even though this patrol was during a temporary ceasefire, she had painted her face like she so loved to, so all you could see anyway were the whites of her eyes and her teeth. Kali Ma through and through, just like you said. "Just imagine, maybe we'll end up on a world where we can breathe everywhere. Where there are forests and running water and deserts like Earth. Like in the old Bollywood movies, where the heroes and the heroines run around trees and splash in water like foolish children with those huge mountains behind them covered in ice."

"Arre, you can get all that on Earth. It's where those movies come from! Why would you want to go further away from Earth? You don't want to return home?"

"That's a nice idea, Gita," she said. "But the longer we're here, and the more news and movies and feeds I see of Earth, I get the idea it's not really waiting for us."

That made me angry, though I didn't show it. "We've waited all our lives to go back, and now you want to toss off to another world?" I asked, as if we had a choice in the matter. The two of us, since we were children in the juvenile barracks, had talked about moving to a little house in the Himalayas once we went back, somewhere in Sikkim or northern Bengal (we learned all the states as children, and saw their flags along New Delhi Avenue) where it's not as crowded as the rest of Earth still, and we could see those famously huge mountains that dwarfed the Moon's arid hills.

She said, "Hai Ram, I'm just dreaming like we always have. My dear, what you're not getting is that we have seen Earth on the feeds since we came to the Moon. From expectation, there is only disappointment."

So I told her, "When you talk about other worlds out there, you realize those are expectations too. You're forgetting we're soldiers. We go to Earth, it means our battle is over. We go to another world, you think they'd let us frolic like Bollywood stars in alien streams? Just you and me, Gita and Aditi, with the rest of our division doing backup dancing?" I couldn't stay angry when I thought of this, though I still felt a bit hurt that she was suggesting she didn't want to go back to Earth with me, like the sisters in arms we were.

"True enough," she said. "Such a literalist. If our mission is ever to play Bollywood on an exoplanet, you can play the man hero with your lovely rat-tail beard. Anyway, for now all we have is this grey rock where all the ice is underneath us instead of prettily on the mountains. Not Earth or any other tarty rival to it. *This* is home, Gita beta, don't forget it."

How right she was.

THEN CAME PEACETIME.

We saw the protests on Earth feeds. People marching through the vast cities, more people than we'd ever see in a lifetime in Chandnipur, with signs and chants. No more military presence on the Moon. The Moon is not an army base. Bring back our soldiers. The Moon is not a battlefield.

But it was, that's the thing. We had seen our fellow asuras die on it.

With the creation of the Terran Union of Spacefaring Nations (T.U.S.N.) in anticipation of human expansion to extrasolar space, India finally gave up its sovereignty over Chandnipur, which became just one settlement in amalgamated T.U.S.N. Lunar territory. There were walled-off Nuclear Seclusion Zones up there on Earth still hot from the last World War, and somehow they'd figured out how to stop war on the Moon. With the signing of the International Lunar Peace Treaty, every nation that had held its own patch of the Moon for a century of settlement on the satellite agreed to lay down their arms under Earth, Sol, the gods, the goddesses, and the God. The Moon was going to be free of military presence for the first time in decades.

When us asuras were first told officially of the decommissioning of Lunar Command in Chandnipur, we celebrated. We'd made it—we were going to Earth, earlier than we'd ever thought, long before retirement age. Even our COs got shitfaced in the mess halls. There were huge tubs of biryani, with hot chunks of printed lamb and gobs of synthi dalda. We ate so much, I thought we'd explode. Even Aditi, who'd been dreaming about other worlds, couldn't hold back her happiness. She asked me, "What's the first thing you're going to do on Earth?" her face covered in grease, making me think of her as a child with another name, grubby cheeks covered in syrup from stolen jalebis. "I'm going to catch a train to a riverside beach or a sea-wall, and watch the movement of water on a planet. Water, flowing and thrashing for kilometers and kilometers, stretching all the way to the horizon. I'm going to fall asleep to it. Then I'm going to go to all the restaurants, and eat all the real foods that the fake food in the Underground Markets is based on."

"Don't spend all your money in one day, okay? We need to save up for that house in the Himalayas."

"You're going to go straight to the mountains, aren't you," I said with a smile.

"Nah. I'll wait for you, first, beta. What do you think."

"Good girl."

After that meal, a handful of us went out with our suits for an unscheduled patrol for the first time—I guess you'd call it a moonwalk, at that point.

We saluted the Earth together, on a lunar surface where we had no threat of being silently attacked from all sides. The century-long Lunar Cold War was over—it had cooled, frozen, bubbled, boiled at times, but now it had evaporated. We were all to go to our paradise in the black sky, as we'd wished every day on our dreary chota duniya.

We didn't stop to think what it all really meant for us asuras, of course. Because as Aditi had told me—the Moon was our home, the only one we'd ever known, really. It is a strange thing to live your life in a place that was never meant for human habitation. You grow to loathe such a life—the gritty dust in everything from your food to your teeth to your weapons, despite extensive air filters, the bitter aerosol meds to get rid of infections and nosebleeds from it. Spending half of your days exercising and drinking carefully rationed water so your body doesn't shrivel up in sub-Earth grav or dry out to a husk in the dry, scrubbed air of controlled atmospheres. The deadening beauty of grey horizons with not a hint of water or life or vegetation in sight except for the sharp lines and lights of human settlement, which we compared so unfavorably to the dazzling technicolour of images and video feeds from Earth, the richness of its life and variety. The constant, relentless company of the same people you grow to love with such ferocity that you hate them as well, because there is no one else for company but the occasional civilian who has the courage to talk to a soldier in Chandnipur's streets, tunnels and canteens.

Now the Moon is truly a gateway to the stars. It is pregnant with the vessels that will take humanity to them, with shipyards and ports rising up under the limbs of robots. I look up at our chota duniya, and its face is crusted in lights, a crown given to her by her lover. Like a goddess it'll birth humanity's new children. We were born in the sky, for war, but we weren't in truth. We were asuras. Now they will be devas, devis. They will truly be like gods, with FTL. In Chandnipur, they told us that we must put our faith in Bhagavan, in all the gods and goddesses of the pantheon. We were given a visiting room, where we sat in the veeyar pods and talked directly to their avatars, animated by the machines. That was the only veeyar we were allowed—no sims of Earth or anything like that, maybe because they didn't want us to get too distracted from our lives on the Moon. So we talked to the avatars, dutifully, in those pods with their smell of incense. Every week we asked them to keep us alive on chota duniya, this place where humanity should not be and yet is.

And now, we might take other worlds, large and small.

Does that frighten you?

I... don't know. You told us all those years ago, and you tell me now, that we asuras looked like gods and superheroes when you saw us. In our suits, which would nearly crush a human with their weight if anyone wore them on Earth, let alone walked or fought in them. And now, imagine the humans who will go out there into the star-lit darkness. The big ships won't be ready for a long time. But the small ones—they already want volunteers to take one-way test trips to exoplanets. I don't doubt some of those volunteers will come from the streets, like us asuras. They need people who don't have anything on Earth, so they can leave it behind and spend their lives in the sky. They will travel faster than light itself. Impossible made possible. Even the asuras of the Lunar Command were impossible once.

The Moon was a lifeless place. Nothing but rock and mineral and water. And we still found a way to bring war to it. We still found a way to fight there. Now, when the new humans set foot on other worlds, what if there is life there? What if there is god-given life that has learned to tell stories, make art, fight and love? Will we bring an Earth Army to that life, whatever form it takes? Will we send out this new humanity to discover and share, or will we take people like me and Aditi, born in the streets with nothing, and give them a suit of armour and a ship that sails across the cosmos faster than the light of stars, and send them out to conquer? In the myths, asuras can be both benevolent or evil. Like gods or demons. If we have the chariots of the gods at our disposal, what use is there for gods? What if the next soldiers who go forth into space become demons with the power of gods? What if envy strikes their hearts, and they take fertile worlds from other life forms by force? What if we bring war to a peaceful cosmos? At least we asuras only killed other humans.

One could argue that you didn't just fight on the Moon. You brought life there, for the first time. You, we, humans—we loved there, as well. We still do. There are still humans there.

Love.

I've never heard anyone tell me they love me, nor told anyone I love them. People on Earth, if you trust the stories, say it all the time. We asuras didn't really know what the word meant, in the end.

But. I did love, didn't I? I loved my fellow soldiers. I would have given my life for them. That must be what it means.

I loved Aditi.

That is the first time I've ever said that. I loved Aditi, my sister in arms. I wonder what she would have been, if she had stayed on Earth, never been adopted by the Indian government and given to the Army. A dancer? A Bollywood star? They don't like women with muscles like her, do they? She was bloody graceful with a jet-pack, I'll tell you that much. And then, when I actually stop to think, I realize, that she would have been a beggar, or a sweeper, or a sewer-scraper if the Army hadn't given us to the sky. Like me. Now I live among beggars, garbage-pickers, and sweepers, and sewer-scrapers, in this slum clinging to what they call the pillar to heaven. To heaven, can you believe that? Just like we called Earth heaven up there. These people here, they take care of me. In them I see a shared destiny.

What is that?

To remind us that we are not the gods. This is why I pray still to the gods, or the one God, whatever is out there beyond the heliosphere. I pray that the humans who will sail past light and into the rest of the universe find grace out there, find a way to bring us closer to godliness. To worlds where we might start anew, and have no need for soldiers to fight, only warriors to defend against dangers that they themselves are not the harbingers of. To worlds where our cities have no slums filled with people whose backs are bent with the bravery required to hold up the rest of humanity.

Can I ask something? How... how did asura Aditi die?

Hm. Asura Aditi of the 8th Lunar Division—Chandnipur, Indian Armed Forces, survived thirty-four years of life and active combat duty as a soldier on the Moon, to be decommissioned and allowed to return to planet Earth. And then she died right here in New Delhi Megapolis walking to the market. We asuras aren't used to this gravity, to these crowds. One shove from a passing impatient pedestrian is all it takes. She fell down on the street, shattered her Moon-brittled hip because, when we came here to paradise, we found that treatment and physio for our weakened bodies takes money that our government does not provide. We get a pension, but it's not much—we have to choose food and rent, or treatment. There is no cure. We might have been bred for war in the sky, but we were not bred for life on Earth. Why do you think there are so few volunteers for the asura program? They must depend on the children of those who have nothing.

Aditi fell to Earth from the Moon, and broke. She didn't have money for a fancy private hospital. She died of an infection in a government hospital.

She never did see the Himalayas. Nor have I.

I'm sorry.

I live here, in the slums around Akash Mahal Space Elevator-Shaft, because of Aditi. It's dangerous, living along the spindle. But it's cheaper than the subsidized rent of the Veterans Arcologies. And I like the danger. I was a soldier, after all. I like living by the stairway to the sky, where I once lived. I like being high up here, where the wind blows like it never did on the Moon's grey deserts, where the birds I never saw now fly past me every morning and warm my heart with their cries. I like the sound of the nanotube ecosystem all around us, digesting all our shit and piss and garbage, turning it into the light in my one bulb, the heat in my one stove coil, the water from my pipes, piggybacking on the charge from the solar panels that power my little feed-terminal. The way the walls pulse, absorbing sound and kinetic energy, when the elevator passes back and forth, the rumble of Space Elevator Garuda-3 through the spindle all the way to the top of the atmosphere. I don't like the constant smell of human waste. I don't like wondering when the police will decide to cast off the blinders and destroy this entire slum because it's illegal. I don't like going with a half-empty stomach all the time, living off the kindness of the little ones here who go up and down all the time and get my flour and rice. But I'm used to such things—Chandnipur was not a place of plenty either. I like the way everyone takes care of each other here. We have to, or the entire slum will collapse like a rotten vine slipping off a tree-trunk. We depend on each other for survival. It reminds me of my past life.

And I save the money from my pension, little by little, by living frugally. To one day buy a basic black market exoskeleton to assist me, and get basic treatment, physio, to learn how to walk and move like a human on Earth.

Can... I help, in any way?

You have helped, by listening. Maybe you can help others listen as well, as you've said.

Maybe they'll heed the words of a veteran forced to live in a slum. If they send soldiers to the edge of the galaxy, I can only hope that they will give those soldiers a choice this time.

I beg the ones who prepare our great chariots: if you must take our soldiers with you, take them—their courage, their resilience, their loyalty will serve you well on a new frontier. But do not to take war to new worlds.

War belongs here on Earth. I should know. I've fought it on the Moon, and it didn't make her happy. In her cold anger, she turned our bodies to glass. Our chota duniya was not meant to carry life, but we thrust it into her anyway. Let us not make that mistake again. Let us not violate the more welcoming worlds we may find, seeing their beauty as acquiescence.

With FTL, there will be no end to humanity's journey. If we keep going far enough, perhaps we will find the gods themselves waiting behind the veil of the universe. And if we do not come in peace by then, I fear we will not survive the encounter.

I CLAMBER DOWN the side of the column of the space elevator, winding down through the biohomes of the slum towards one of the tunnels where I can reach the internal shaft and wait for the elevator on the way down. Once it's close to the surface of the planet, it slows down a lot—that's when people jump on to hitch a ride up or down. We're only about 1,000 feet up, so it's not too long a ride down, but the wait for it could be much longer. The insides of the shaft are always lined with slum-dwellers and elevator station hawkers, rigged with gas masks and cling clothes, hanging on to the nanocable chords and sinews of the great spindle. I might just catch a ride on the back of one of the gliders who offer their solar wings to travelers looking for a quick trip back to the ground. Bit more terrifying, but technically less dangerous, if their back harness and propulsion works.

The eight-year-old boy guiding me down through the steep slum, along the pipes and vines of the NGO-funded nano-ecosystem, occasionally looks up at me with a gap-toothed smile. "I want to be an asura like Gita," he says. "I want to go to the stars."

"Aren't you afraid of not being able to walk properly when you come back to Earth?"

"Who said I want to come back to Earth?"

I smile, and look up, past the fluttering prayer flags of drying clothes, the pulsing wall of the slum, at the dizzying stairway to heaven, an infinite line receding into the blue. At the edge of the spindle, I see asura Gita poised between the air and her home, leaning precariously out to wave goodbye to me. Her hair ripples out against the sky, a smudge of black. A late evening moon hovers full and pale above her head, twinkling with lights.

I wave back, overcome with vertigo. She seems about to fall, but she doesn't. She is caught between the Earth and the sky in that moment, forever.

THE WORSHIPFUL SOCIETY OF GLOVERS
Mary Robinette Kowal

Mary Robinette Kowal (maryrobinettekowal.com) is the author of historical fantasy novels: The Glamourist Histories series and *Ghost Talkers*. She has received the Campbell Award for Best New Writer, three Hugo awards, the RT Reviews award for Best Fantasy Novel, and has been a finalist for the Hugo, Nebula, and Locus awards. Stories have appeared in *Strange Horizons, Asimov's*, several Year's Best anthologies and her collections *Word Puppets* and *Scenting the Dark and Other Stories*.

As a professional puppeteer and voice actor (SAG/AFTRA), Mary has performed for *LazyTown* (CBS), the Center for Puppetry Arts and Jim Henson Pictures, and founded Other Hand Productions. Her designs have garnered two UNIMA-USA Citations of Excellence, the highest award an American puppeteer can achieve. She records fiction for authors such as Kage Baker, Cory Doctorow and John Scalzi.

Mary lives in Chicago with her husband Rob and over a dozen manual typewriters.

OUTSIDE THE CRACKED window of the garret, the cockle-seller hollered, "Cockles an' mussels! Cockles an' mussels!" Her voice blended with the other London morning street sounds to mean that Vaughn was going to be late.

"Botheration." He tied off the thread in the fine blue leather of the gloves he was stitching and snipped it with the little pair of silver shears he'd snuck out of the master's shop. Be his hide if he were caught taking them home, but worse if he bit the thread off instead of snipping it neat. No telling what his saliva would do when the guild brownie added the beauty spell to it.

Shoving back his rickety chair from their equally rickety table, Vaughn tucked the shears into his pocket and tied it to the belt of his jerkin. He grabbed the gloves with one hand and a slice of rye bread with the other.

His sister laughed, "Are you going to be late again?"

"Was trying to finish these gloves for Master Martin." He slid the gloves into the pocket, heading for the door. "I'll be glad when this damn journeyman period is over."

Behind him, Sarah made a coughing grunt. Vaughn's heart jumped sideways in his chest. Not again. He dropped the bread and the gloves and spun, but not in time to catch her.

Her chin cracked against the worn wood floor as she hit. Every muscle in her body had tightened and she shook, grunting with another seizure. Vaughn dropped to his knees next to her and rolled Sarah onto her side, brushing her hair back from her face.

She couldn't hear him when one of the fits came over her but he sang to her anyway, just because that's what their Gran had done.

"As I walked forth one summer's day,
To view the meadows green and gay
A pleasant bower I espied
Standing fast by the river side,
And in't a maiden I heard cry:
Alas! alas! there's none e'er loved as I."

The tremors subsided, but her eyes still had the glaze about them. Drool puddled from her mouth onto the floor. At least she hadn't vomited this time.

Vaughn gave a breathless laugh. The things he was thankful for these days.

Sweat ran down his back like it was chasing him through the streets of London. Vaughn dodged around a fine lady in ruddy silks with her fairy chaperone and slid around a pair of gentlemen, wearing green antlered gloves for cunning. He skidded around the corner into the alley between the perfumers and the glovers.

Slowing to a walk, he tried to keep his breath slow, as if he hadn't been running flat out for ten streets. If the master were only in the front talking to customers...

He needn't have bothered. Master Martin stood square in the middle of the workshop, glaring. "Vaughn Johnson! Do ye not hear the bells?"

"Yes, sir." Vaughn swept his hat from his head. "Sorry, sir. Won't happen again, sir."

"'Tis the third time this fortnight!"

"I know, sir, and I'm very sorry."

Across the workshop, Littleberry, the guild brownie who worked with his master, continued to concentrate on the gloves he was ensorcelling as if Master Martin weren't yelling at the top of his lungs.

Sweating, Vaughn pulled the blue gloves from his pocket. "I finished the commission for Lady Montrose."

The master glover snatched them out of his hands. "Was it that sister of yours again?"

He tried not to notice Littleberry's long ears prick up with interest. Brownies valued an honest man, and if Vaughn wanted to join the guild, he had best tell the truth. "She had a fit this morning but is as well as anything now. I'll be on time tomorrow, sir."

"They have places for such as her."

Vaughn swallowed. After Gran died, he looked into a sanitarium but the places that he could afford were no fit place for a sixteen-year-old girl. No fit place for anyone really, but he couldn't send Sarah there. "I can't afford that. Sorry sir."

"Eh—I'm not talking about some fine and mighty place such as a lady might go. There's almshouses."

Rage flooded through Vaughn and it pushed words out of his mouth. "Maybe I should simply take the master test and then you'll be shut of me."

"Oh ho! The mouse bites."

"Sorry, sir. It was only an idea, sir." But what he wouldn't give to already be a master so he could make Sarah's gloves. With those, he wouldn't have to worry about leaving her alone. "But if you think I'm ready..."

A bell jingled at the front of the store.

"You've made a contract with me, and I'll not waste a minute more of it than I already have. Not with King Henry's ball coming up. Bring on another journeyman, after I've spent all this time getting you trained up?" He barked a laugh and strode through the curtain that separated the workshop from the front of the store. Master Martin's tone changed immediately to something honeyed and without the burr of his native accent. "Ah, my dear Lady Flannery, so honored to have you grace our store."

Vaughn clenched his fists and his jaw. Of course, his master was too cheap to give up a journeyman early. Stalking over to the workbench, he glanced at the other end of the bench to be sure that Littleberry was occupied. The brownie's back was bent over his work, eyes wrinkled shut.

Slipping the shears from his pocket, Vaughn set them on the bench and hoped Littleberry wouldn't notice. He had half a mind to make a bargain with the brownie on his own. Guild rules said that he couldn't *sell* unlicensed gloves, but if it was just for Sarah—

Right. If he didn't mind making a deal without the auspices of the Worshipful Society of Glovers, losing his guild membership, and winding up in the streets.

But he couldn't keep leaving Sarah alone. It wouldn't hurt to simply ask Littleberry his terms for ensorcelling gloves to control seizures.

Vaughn snorted and laid a pattern on the inside of a sheet of pure white kidskin. The brownie was from Faerie. There was always the potential for harm, even in just the asking.

To MAKE UP for being tardy, Vaughn worked well past his usual time. It was full dark by the time he left the shop, locking the door behind himself. His eyes blurred when he tried to look in the distance so the candles in the windows turned into dancing globes like will-o-the-wisps come to the city. He had the pieces for another set of gloves folded in paper in his pocket and had snuck the little shears out of the shop.

Sarah would be worried about him, but she knew well enough that the master had say over his time. Tucking his hands in the sleeves of his overgown, Vaughn hurried for home. If he was lucky, the pie shop would still have something, otherwise it was yesterday's bread for dinner.

Before he even got out of the alley, a hand clamped down on his shoulder with the weight of iron. Vaughn gasped and tried to wrench free, but the man's fingers dug in, unnaturally strong. His vision went white and red. He dropped to his knees, grabbing by instinct at the source of the pain and touched leather. A glove of smooth oxskin, embroidered at the knuckles with fool's knots and chains.

Strength gloves.

"I've got nothing." Vaughn stopped struggling, but the scoundrel's grip on his shoulder didn't lighten. Lord. They'd break his shoulder at this rate. At least it was his left. He could still stitch if they didn't hurt his right.

What a stupid thing to worry about when he might not live through the night. Vaughn knelt on the cold cobblestones, with one knee in a puddle of something.

"Don't try anything."

"I won't." Who had made the man's gloves? Vaughn kept his head down as the fellow released him. Partly this was so he didn't look like a threat, but also so he could see the gloves.

Bright red oxskin with the requisite fool's knots and chains stitched at the knuckles. The man yanked his pocket off, likely harder than the man had intended, and the cloth split down the seams. Green thread marched up the sides of the gloves in flames that looked like it had come out of Master O'Connell's shop. Not that it mattered. Like as not they were stolen.

Sumptuary laws being what they were, someone of their station couldn't afford a pair of gloves, much less flaunt them. Heavens no, if they wore something so fine, someone might mistake them for nobility.

"Ha!" The thief dug through the shredded pocket and found Vaughn's meager purse. Thank heavens he hadn't been paid yet this week, but there went any chance of buying Sarah a pie for dinner.

When the thief drew out the leather for the gloves, Vaughn groaned. "Please—those aren't ensorcelled yet. It's just leather and—"

The thief threw the kidskin on the ground, right in the puddle Vaughn knelt in. Bollocks. Even if the liquid were by some miraculous chance pure water, the leather would warp and stiffen. Master Martin would take it out of his wages.

The man found the little silver shears, and tucked them away. Small though they were, a pair of silver shears were worth more than Vaughn would make this month. Thank God he'd already hocked his father's snuff box, or that would be gone as well.

"That's it?" The thief grabbed him by the collar.

"I'm a journeyman."

"You don't dress like one."

"My master wants us to look smart for his customers." He'd near beggared himself meeting the requirements for the journeyman contract, but it was the only way to advance in the guild. If he were wearing a cotte, as he had most of his life, the thief wouldn't have looked at him twice. "If you thought I was a nobleman, I am sorry to have wasted your time."

"Guess I'll take your overgown and hat for my troubles." He snatched the hat off Vaughn's head.

"Please—I'll lose my place if I'm not—"

"Your place or your life. Either way, they're mine, ain't they." The thief clapped his hands together and the threads glimmered with the spellwork caught in them. "Off with your overgown."

What choice did Vaughn have? He shrugged off the overgown, and though it was tempting to throw it in the puddle same as the leather, he wasn't a fool. He handed it over, jaw clenched to keep from crying as the thief threw the overgown across his arm. It wasn't fair. He'd worked so hard to get here, to make something of himself and—

The thief's free hand drew back, curling into a fist. If that connected, Vaughn was a dead man. He threw himself back. The blow whistled past his face, just brushing his cheek. Even that fleeting contact lit the night sky for a moment. Then his head smacked against the cobbled street, and everything went dark.

THERE WERE NO bells to tell him the time. All Vaughn knew as he dragged himself up the stairs of their garrett was that he stank. The bastard had robbed him of his shoes and the buttons off his jerkin while he lay there. He was lucky to still have his doublet and netherhose, but his feet ached from walking home in nothing but his stockings.

When he reached the top of the stairs, a light flickered under their door. He winced. It had been too much to hope that Sarah would have gone to bed. Before he'd even reached for the latch, a chair scraped on wood and Sarah's footsteps hurried toward the door.

"Vaughn?" She yanked the door open, a shawl over her nightgown. "Oh my lord. What happened?"

He tried to grin, but his cheek hurt too much. At least his jaw wasn't broken. "Robbed coming home. But I'm fine."

"You are not fine!" She put an arm around his waist, as if he hadn't just walked home all by himself. "Come and sit. Oh—your face."

"Bad, eh?" Probably for the best they didn't own a mirror. He patted her shoulder and slipped out of his sister's grasp. "Let me get out of these clothes first."

"I'll heat some water to clean your cheek." She hurried over to their small hearth, one of the few perks of the garret, and put another log on the fire.

"I'm fine. Really. Look worse than I feel." That might have been a lie, but he couldn't stand to see her worried on his account. Vaughn limped over to the curtain they'd hung in the corner to give some modesty for bathing. "How was your day?"

He'd pulled off the stinking jerkin—at least he didn't have to unbutton it—then his doublet, which was also sans buttons, and tugged up his shirt. The movement made the bruises on his left shoulder catch, dragging his breath out with a hiss. He couldn't lift his arm higher than his waist.

He bit back a half dozen curses as he tried to wriggle out of the shirt, and then realized that Sarah hadn't answered. "Sarah?"

Certain that his sister would be on the floor, Vaughn came around the curtain in just his shirt and netherhose. But she knelt in front of the fire, setting the kettle on the grate.

His heart slowed a little. "Is something wrong?"

"No." Sarah shook her head. "I was just thinking about how to answer."

"That sounds like something is wrong." He stepped back behind the curtain to splash a little cold water over his face. His cheek stung and the water in the basin turned pink. He probed the side of his face and winced as he found the raw edges where his skin had split over his cheekbone. Vaughn shucked out of his netherhose, managed to pull his shirt off, and then dragged a nightshirt on, carefully.

What the hell was he going to wear to work tomorrow?

Carrying the basin of dirty water, Vaughn limped over to their single, high window and reached up to open the casement. He grunted as the bruises on his left shoulder caught. "Sarah... I'm sorry. Could you?"

"Of course!" She hurried over to take the basin from him. "Go sit by the fire now."

"I'm fin—"

"Now." And of a sudden, her voice snapped like Gran's.

Vaughn went. As she opened the small window and dumped the waste water on the street below, he dragged their other chair next to the fire and settled into it with a groan. He might never stand again.

Sarah hurried back over to him, firelight warming the room around her and catching in the honey gold of her hair. It also caught on a new cut on her lip.

Vaughn straightened, catching his sister's hand as she sat. "Did you have another fit? After I left?"

She pressed her lips together as if that would hide the cut. With a shrug, she turned to the fire. "What if I did?"

"Sarah... You're supposed to tell me."

She set the empty basin on the floor by the fire. "Why? There's nothing to be done about it."

But there was. It was just that tonight's mishap put it even further from his grasp.

DRESSED IN HIS workboots, second-best hose, doublet, and jerkin, Vaughn hunched over the bench. His shoulder had stiffened overnight and all it was really good for was holding down the leather while he traced. His eye had swollen up enough that he had to tilt his head to the side to see the leather clearly. But his right hand was steady and he gave thanks for that.

The shop bell jangled at the front as Master Martin arrived. As the glover whistled his way into the back of the shop, Vaughn laid his pencil down and prepared to make his case. He turned on his stool and Master Martin jumped, taking a step backward. Sitting on his shoulder, Littleberry had to clutch his collar to stay seated.

"Good lord!" Swiping his hat off his head, Master Martin's astonishment turned into a scowl. "I've got no patience with brawlers."

"I—" Brawling? He'd been working for the man for three years and had never so much as raised his voice. "I was robbed, sir. Sorry for my appearance, sir."

"Robbed? Here?" Master Martin swung around as if someone might be lurking in the shadows.

Littleberry used the motion to jump down onto the workbench, his nose wrinkled in sympathy. At least someone felt sorry for Vaughn.

"No, sir. On my way home." Vaughn bit his lower lip. "I had the leather for the Lady Flannery commission, I'm afraid."

"The royal blue! Do you know how dear that shade of blue is?"

"Yes, sir. I'm very sorry, sir."

"It'll have to come out of your pay." Master Martin set his hat on the rack next to the door. "Anything else?"

If he could have hidden it, he would have, but at some point Master Martin would notice that the little silver shears were missing. "I'm afraid I had inadvertently had the small shears in my pocket."

"Those were not to leave the shop! You think I can just run willy-nilly over to Faerie anytime I need enchanted silver?"

"I'm very sorry, sir. Of course, I will pay for them." Before Master Martin had time to get redder in the face, Vaughn drove forward. "The brigand also took my overgown and shoes. I have nothing else appropriate to wear. Would it be possible—?"

"An advance? After all this, you have the nerve to ask for an advance?"

Vaughn had actually planned to ask if he might be excused from wearing an overgown until he could afford to buy a new one. He wouldn't be allowed in the front of the shop anyway until the bruises faded. But, in for a penny, in for a pound. He was going to be paying for this for the next year anyway. "I'm sorry, sir. I know you take pride in the neatness of your shop and I want to be a credit to you."

Master Martin scowled. "I'll think on it. For the time being though, you stay here in the back. I don't want one of the customers catching sight of you."

"Of course, sir." The pencil rolled off the workbench, and Vaughn reached to catch it. The movement sent a lance through his left shoulder and he couldn't hold back a cry.

"I think the lad is really hurt, aren't you?" Littleberry's voice piped like an ancient bird, as his head cocked with curiosity.

"It's nothing." He moved more cautiously, keeping his arm close to his side. The last thing he needed was for Master Martin to decide that the injury meant he couldn't work.

"Is that the truth?" the brownie asked.

"It's just bruises. He had strength gloves and I reckon didn't realize how hard he was grabbing me."

Master Martin straightened, blinking owlishly. "Strength gloves. Are you sure?" His professional assessment suddenly came to the front and this was why Vaughn put up with his peevishness, because the man knew his stitching.

"Red oxskin. Fool's knots and chains, on the knuckles." Vaughn hesitated for a moment, but training would out. "Green flamestitching up the side that had the peaks distinctive of Master O'Connell's work."

Master Martin slapped his handkerchief down on the workbench. "That gad-about. He'll ruin the guild's reputation, selling to any old person. Let me see."

"Sir?"

"The bruises." He beckoned with one hand. "Let me see the bruises."

"Yes, sir." Vaughn unbuttoned his doublet, which came off easily enough. He undid the string that held the collar of his shirt closed. Any hope that he might be in better shape today vanished when he tried to pull his shirt off. He closed his eyes, and took a careful breath before trying again.

"Here, lad." Master Martin's hands were unexpectedly gentle as he helped Vaughn get the shirt off. His fingers were soft from the oil he worked into them every day. "Ach. Oh... that's strength gloves for certain."

Of course it was. Vaughn wasn't an idiot. If not for this, he'd be only a year away from doing his journeyman project and applying to be a Master at the guild. He nodded, lips pressed together around the words he couldn't say. "Yes, sir."

"I want Littleberry to take a look at this..."

"Sir?"

Master Martin waved a hand. "See if it was done with unlicensed goods. I've had a suspicion that O'Connell has been doing that. Keep your shirt off a moment."

Skin standing all over gooseflesh, Vaughn tried not to shiver. Even standing on the workbench, the brownie barely came up to his shoulder. He cocked his head to the side, studying Vaughn as if he were a pair of gloves. "Hm. Sit, would you?"

Vaughn slid onto the tall stool next to the workbench. The brownie's cool, dry fingers danced over his skin, marking each of the four livid bruises on the front of his shoulder. Wetting his lips, Vaughn stared steadily ahead at the windows.

He was looking past the glass, and only when Master Martin moved did he realize that there was a reflection there. For the first time since the robbery, he saw his own face and it was no wonder Master Martin had jumped. His cheek was swollen and purple, with a nasty cut that was nearly black in the reflection. The bruises stood out clear as anything in livid purple splotches against his winter white shoulder.

"Aye. 'Tis the work of Mossthicket." Littleberry stepped back, sighing. "The marks are all over it."

"So they're unlicensed." Master Martin rubbed the back of his neck. "You said you recognized the stitching as O'Connell?"

"Yes, sir." Vaughn swallowed. "His flame stitching has a distinctive point and—"

"Any chance you're wrong?"

Of course there was a chance he was wrong. It wasn't as if he'd been able to pull them off and look at the maker's mark. "It was dark, sir."

Master Martin grunted. After a moment, he handed Vaughn his shirt. "Let's get you dressed again, lad."

"Thank you, sir." A half-dozen questions pestered his tongue for voicing, but Vaughn knew his place. The master helped him get the shirt back on and even with assistance, Vaughn felt queasy all the way to his knees. He breathed through gritted teeth, waiting for the pain in his shoulder to pass enough that he could pull the doublet on.

"I'll tell her majesty when I cross the border, but like as not she'll do nothing." Littleberry tugged on one of his ears. "Not without the actual gloves."

Master Martin nodded. "The guild will have the same problems. Still. I'll report it to the warden and see if anything comes of it. Unlicensed gloves... The devil take O'Connell."

* * *

FOR THE SECOND night running, Vaughn had to stop on the landing to catch his breath. The bruises on his shoulder hurt with every inhalation and he wasn't entirely sure he'd make it to the top of the stairs. At least tonight he had shoes.

No candlelight under the door tonight. He sighed with relief that his sister had been smart enough to go to bed. Vaughn pushed the door open.

The stench of vomit and urine smacked him in the face.

"No..." He fumbled for the candle that sat by the door. The fire had burned out and the room was as dark as the stairs. "Sarah?"

Heart stepping up its pace with every beat, he knocked the candle to the floor. "Damnit. Sarah!"

Dropping to his knees, Vaughn fumbled in the dark, until he laid hands on the candle. Forcing himself to slow down, he found the tinderbox. Struck it. Lit the candle. Lifting it high, with his good arm, he turned.

Sarah lay in a jumble on her side next to the bed. A puddle of vomit soaked her hair. A litany of fear filled his head as he scrambled across the floor to her. *Please don't be dead. Please. Please.* Vaughn set the candlestick on the floor. "Sarah?"

Her cheeks were pale, but—thank God—her pulse beat visibly in her throat. Vaughn slid his hands under her neck and knees to lift her. This was going to hurt and he goddamn didn't care. He ground his teeth together, braced, and lifted.

Something in his shoulder popped.

White and red and black explosions peppered his vision. Screaming, tumbling forward, he dropped Sarah. His left arm cushioned her head, only because he couldn't move it out of the way. They both landed in the pool of vomit.

Sarah's head flopped back and she moaned. She didn't wake up. *Please, God. Please, let her wake up.* Vaughn pressed his good hand against his upper arm, biting the inside of his cheek so hard that he tasted the copper of blood. Waves of iron hot and steel cold pulsed in sickening waves.

Gasping around the pain, he tried to pull himself out of it. Sarah. Sarah needed him. Think, Vaughn. Think.

He couldn't lift her onto the bed. A pallet on the floor then.

Wrapping his left arm around his waist, he buried his fingers between the buttons of his jerkin to keep from jostling it too much. With his good hand, he tugged Sarah's shift down around her calves and twisted it to get a better grip. Sliding back on his knees and haunches, Vaughn dragged Sarah away from the mess by the bed. Where she'd been lying, the floorboards were stained dark with piss. Which meant her shift needed to be changed.

One thing at a time. Vaughn staggered to his feet and fetched the washbasin. Thank God he'd filled the pitcher before he'd left that morning. He got a clean rag and dipped it in the water, wiping the vomit from her hair and cheeks. A deep purple bruise blossomed on her temple. He built the picture in his head. She'd been getting ready for bed and had a fit. When she fell, she hit her head on the edge of the bed. Only sheer luck had caused her to fall on her side or she'd—

He cut that thought off. She was alive. What-might-have-beens didn't matter. She was alive. Vaughn got her cleaned up as best he could and dragged the blankets off the bed. Every movement sent fresh pain stabbing through his shoulder. He used the blankets to prop Sarah on her side, head lifted off the ground, and then sat back against the wall.

Exhausted, he stared at the little garret window. Clouds drifted past, barely lighter than the violet black sky. Carefully, he probed his shoulder. His collarbone was... not right.

What the hell was he going to do?

"VAUGHN?" SARAH'S VOICE was so soft that it blended with a dream he was having. "You're going to be late."

But it wasn't a dream, that was his real sister's voice and that was enough to knock whatever the dream had been right away. Vaughn dragged his lids open. He was slumped against the wall, with his head at an awkward angle. He sat up too fast, and his shoulder awoke. Gasping, Vaughn clutched his arm and waited for the throbbing to back away a little.

No. He couldn't wait.

Sarah was still resting on her side, but her eyes were open. She smiled. "Good morrow."

Sharp tears pricked his eyes. Now? When she was awake and safe, now his body decided to cry? Irritated, he swiped at his eyes with the back of his arm. "Good morrow. How are you?"

"Dizzy." She frowned, plucking at the blanket. "Why am I on the floor?"

"You had another fit." She would know that, of course. But it saved him from telling her that like as not his collarbone was broken. The strength gloves must have given it a fracture and then it went the rest of the way when he lifted her. "It looks like you hit your head."

"That explains why it hurts." She smiled ruefully and lifted a hand to the bruise on her temple.

Outside, the church bells started and Vaughn groaned. He was beyond late. Using the wall as leverage, he pushed himself up to stand. "I'll ask Mrs. Nelson from downstairs to come sit with you today."

"She smells of lineament."

Half a laugh didn't hurt too badly. "True, but she's old and her joints ache." Perhaps he could borrow some of that lineament...

"And I don't want to hear another story about her dear departed son."

"Alas, poor Geoffrey. How else shall his adventures in his majesty's service live on?"

Sarah stuck her tongue out at him, and snuggled into the blankets. "I'll probably spend the day sleeping anyway. Truly I would rather be left alone."

"Sarah—I cannot." Vaughn squeezed his eyes shut as the church bells faded into the morning hubbub of London. He was so beyond late. "I cannot leave you here alone."

"But I don't want her! I don't want to be stared at and cosseted and—I just want to be here and quiet and by myself. I ask little enough."

"And I just want to come home and not find you drowned in your own vomit!" He squeezed his eyes shut to block out her widened eyes and shock. "I'm sorry. I should not have yelled. Or said such things. Only... please."

She sighed as if all the fight had gone out of her. "Of course. Only help me up from the floor? I do not mind looking the invalid to you, but at least let me be dressed when she arrives."

It would make him later still, but Master Martin would have to wait.

VAUGHN COULDN'T HAVE run to work if he'd tried. Every step sent a throb through his collarbone, even with his left arm clutched close to his side. The traffic on the footpaths got steadily finer as he got closer to the shop. He stepped to the side to give space to a pair of gentlemen wearing gloves with egrets stitched on their backs for height. A fine young lady sneered at him as he stepped around her chaperone. Both of them in pure white kidskin with golden chains around each wrist to preserve the young lady's chastity. There was a lady in pale blue lambskin with gray doves peeping out from her cuffs to keep her in childbearing years longer.

All of these people in their silks and damask wore gloves. His sister needed just one pair. Just one. But of course, you couldn't have anyone confused about their station. Why, with gloves, a mere journeyman could make himself into a gentleman.

Vaughn resisted the temptation to walk in the front door of the shop and went down the alley. He opened the door to the workroom and—

"Where the devil have you been?"

It was not an honest question, so Vaughn merely lowered his head to Master Martin. "Sorry, sir."

"Sorry is not good enough! If that sister of yours is going to keep being a problem, I am not certain our relationship can profitably continue."

Rage broke over Vaughn's body like a sweat. "My sister, sir, is my own concern."

"Not if she is preventing you from fulfilling the terms of your contract."

A small rational voice shouted at him not to argue with his master. The pain in his shoulder drowned that out and only added heat to his anger. Vaughn gestured at his face. "Might I remind you that I was robbed and beaten but two days ago. And yet, I have completed all the work you have set me to. I am late today because I am exhausted and in pain. Am I at fault for being tardy? Assuredly. But you must know that I will still complete the work required of me!"

He had just yelled at his master. Vaughn closed his eyes, trying to calm down. Heat flushed his body, centering in the cut upon his cheek and the mass of pain that was his shoulder. His breath came as if he had been running.

"If you are in that much pain, stay home."

No, no, no. He could not lose this journeyman position. No one else in the guild would take on a journeyman that another master had dismissed. Vaughn opened his eyes, fists clenched. "Please, sir. Give me another chance. If I might make a pallet here for the next week, until I am somewhat recovered, then you would not have to worry about me being late."

Sarah would hate it, but he could get Mrs. Nelson to stay with her for a week. It would not take more than that surely.

A piping voice cut into the silence. "Martin... Be gentle with the lad; those bruises will take a while for healing."

"Both of you?" Master Martin held up his hands. "It is not permanent. Take the week. I'm not a cruel man. If you take the week, I can use your salary to bring in someone to help, and your position will still be waiting. "

And how was Vaughn supposed to pay his rent without a salary? How were they supposed to even eat? He swallowed. "I could take work home, if you like."

"No. No... if you are going to rest, then rest." Not cruel, but clueless.

Something in him snapped, the way it had when his collarbone cracked. Spots danced at the edge of his vision and Vaughn took a slow, careful breath to try to stay standing. "Since I'm here, shall I finish working through the day?"

Master Martin hesitated, no doubt considering the work orders awaiting them.

Vaughn pressed the point, thinking of the stack of blank leathers. "You'll need time to bring in another glover."

"If you are up to the task." Master Martin squinted, light reflecting off his spectacles. "It would be appreciated."

"Of course, sir. I am at your command."

STANDING ON THE sturdier of their two chairs to reach the window of their garrett, Vaughn peered over the roofs of London, past the smoke rising from a forest of chimneys and through thickets of laundry to the horizon. The sky glowed pink and red with sunset. The sun itself had dipped out of sight.

Wetting his lips, he hopped down from the chair and hissed as the impact jarred his shoulder. Four days of rest and it still hurt when he moved it. Although at least the bruises were fading from purple into a sort of greenish yellow haze.

"Are you all right?" Sarah looked up, repairing his jerkin by the light of a single candle.

Vaughn waved with his good hand and straightened. "Fine. Sun has set."

She bit her lower lip, tucking the needle into the fabric on the front of the jerkin. "It won't hurt to wait."

It would. He was not going to watch her have one more day of seizures. "I need to be able to make changes if the brownie doesn't approve of my stitchwork. Once I'm back at Master Martin's I won't have time."

"But you... this was to be your masterwork." She looked at the table where the gloves he'd made from the purloined leather lay in a shimmering pile.

He had worked honeysuckle vines around her wrists with cascades of thread in white, yellow, and pale green. The flowers almost seemed to move, even lying on the table. It was beautiful work that no one would see, except for Sarah and, with luck, this brownie. "I'll make something else. Face away from the table now."

Were there any guild rules he wasn't breaking? Calling a brownie in the presence of a non-guildmember. Stealing leather. Calling a brownie without his master. Unlicensed gloves.

His palms were sweating a little as he picked up the pitcher of cream he'd purchased with funds he could ill afford. Carefully, he poured it into a tiny blue earthenware bowl, as prescribed by the agreements between Faerie and the mortal world. He set that next to the gloves, along with a honeycomb and a bit of rye bread. Crossing his fingers, he spun widdershins thrice.

"Brownie Mossthicket, Mossthicket, Mossthicket. If ye have the will, I have presents three to trade with thee."

And then, pulse pounding hard enough that he felt it in the break in his collarbone, Vaughn turned his back on the makeshift worktable, with the gloves and traditional gifts. If the brownie didn't come, that was fine. He would try again with a different name. Mind, he had no idea what that other name would be, because all the brownies he knew were associated with the guild, save this one.

Please come. If this didn't work, he'd—he didn't know what he would try next.

Behind him, crockery shifted on wood. Vaughn rose onto his toes, but didn't turn yet. Slurping. Thank heavens. The brownie had come and he'd drunk the cream.

A soft belch. "Who calls me? I know you not."

Wiping the sweat from his palms onto his doublet, Vaughn turned and stopped with his mouth open. The brownie was a girl. He'd only seen male brownies, but this one had a long skirt and unmistakable curves. "Well met. I am hoping to offer a trade."

She raised an eyebrow, forehead wrinkling into deep fissures. "You know that you have to offer more than bread, honey and cream. Right? I appreciate the formalities, though."

"Yes. Yes, of course." Vaughn wet his lips and walked a little closer to the table. "Shall I show you what I want?"

Mossthicket glanced at the gloves at her feet. "Seizures?" Lifting her head, the brownie looked past him to where Sarah still sat with her back to the table. "Her?"

"This is my sister."

"She can turn around." The brownie crouched next to the gloves, grunting. "Your work?"

"Yes." Vaughn glanced at Sarah, who had spun quietly in her seat to peer over the back of it. Her eyes were wide and he realized that this was likely the first time she had seen a brownie since they were very small. "I can make any changes you require."

With a tiny hand, the brownie waved him into silence. She picked up the gloves, holding them so close to her eyes that her long nose seemed to be smelling the flowers. As she studied them, the tips of her ears went up and down with something like curiosity.

"Huh." She set the gloves on the table. "You're not with the guild, or you wouldn't be calling me, but you do guild-quality work. Why?"

This was not a line of questioning he expected, but Master Martin had always impressed upon him the importance of complete honesty with brownies. Other members of Faerie, not so much, but brownies prized the honest man. "I'm a journeyman."

Her brows went up in surprise, nearly disappearing into her hairline. "With?"

"Master Martin."

"Ah... Well. That explains why you do such good work. Excellent craftsman, that one, even if he is a bastard." She tugged on one of her ears, cocking her head to the side as she studied him. "Who gave you my name?"

"The brownie Littleberry."

She barked a laugh, entirely outsized for her frame. Standing, she dusted her hands off. "Shame you're a liar."

"Wait! No. It's true—" Sweat poured down his back and calves and squirmed along his scalp. "I mean. I learned your name from him, but he didn't offer it. I was just there when you were mentioned and—well. But it really was Littleberry."

How could someone so short make him feel so small? He might as well be an apprentice again whose stitching was found lacking. Mossthicket crossed her arms under her bosom. "And under what circumstances, pray tell, would that learned fellow utter my name to a member of the oh-so-august Worshipful Society of Glovers?"

"You ensorceled some gloves for O'Connell? Strength gloves?" In for a penny, in for a pound. "I was robbed by a man wearing them. Littleberry recognized your work from... traces? On me?"

Her face went very still. "You were robbed. With strength gloves."

At his side, Sarah burst out. "Don't you dare doubt him! He's been in constant pain since then. Just look at his face!"

"I am," the brownie said.

"It's all right, Sarah. I'm sure that our visitor doesn't doubt that." How bad was his face now? Had it gone the same greenish yellow as his shoulder? "The point is simply that I knew that you were willing to do unlicensed work and, well, I have such a need."

"Just the gloves for seizures? You don't want to add chastity or beauty to the stitching? I could make her talk like a lady and dance like an angel. She could marry any lord in the land..."

"NO!" Sarah rose to her feet, face flushed. "Nothing that makes me not me."

"Are not the seizures part of you?"

Vaughn stepped between his sister and the brownie. "Leave her be."

"They are, but they stop me from doing things I love. They make my brother afraid to leave for fear that I'll take ill while he's gone. Those other things? What if I were to take the gloves off and my lord hears me speak with my country tones, and my ordinary face?"

The brownie shrugged. "Is no matter to me." She pointed at Vaughn.

"Here's the bargain I'll offer you then. Make three sets of gloves for me, to my specifications, and the ones for seizures are yours."

"What... what gloves?" Three pairs of gloves? Three. Where was he to get the leather for that many sets of gloves? He might be able to get another set out of the kidskin he'd stolen, but it depended on the color.

The brownie winked. "Nothing that a man of your skill can't make."

Oh no. He knew better than to make a deal with a brownie without all the details. "The materials though—I mean, if the gloves you ask for require the skin of a virgin, then no. Or if they need diamonds, I would have to beggar myself and at that point might as well hire someone else to make the seizure gloves. I shall need to know the specifications first, before I can agree."

The brownie jutted out her lower lip. "Yellow kidskin, embroidered with the sun. Blue kidskin, embroidered with the moon, and black kidskin, embroidered with the stars."

"Only those? Nothing else on them?" He had worked in suns on blue, with swans, to dispell melancholia. Stars aplenty, on deep navy, with the zodiac to aid astrologers. But these pairings... he did not know them.

"That is all."

"But—what are they for?"

She shrugged. "Will you or no?"

Well, what answer was he expecting when she was asking for unlicensed gloves? Kidskin was possible. Those were common enough colors that they were always in Master Martin's shop. He could steal them after Littleberry had left with the master. Only... "Are you specific about the exact shades and dying methods of the leather? Likewise, the thread employed, both its composition and precise shade?"

Mossthicket shook her head, tips of her ears curling down. "See, now. This is why I don't usually work with the guild proper. All these questions..."

All these questions? Of course he needed to know—oh. Oh, of course. The brownie was bargaining. Much as he wanted Sarah to be free of the seizures, it was no good if they were to be trapped in a bad bargain. And, as Master Martin had taught him, you had to be willing to walk away. Vaughn took a deep breath and his heart ached as badly as his shoulder, because he might be wrong. But he had to try to force the brownie's hand. "Well. I don't want to trouble you with my questions. Perhaps someone not associated with the guild would be better suited for your project. I am sorry that we could not come to an agreement."

"And the lady here?"

"We shall continue on as we were." Though how, he did not know. "The honey and bread are, of course, my gift to you for your time."

His entire body screamed at him, as he turned his back on the brownie, stretching a hand out to Sarah to bid her do the same. He had been rash enough in stealing the leather. Agreeing to a bargain without the details was fool's talk and exactly what led to ruin. They would be prudent and they would retrench. Yes, he would have a debt to the master, but that at least was a known quantity.

"Hold on now, sir." The brownie's raspy little voice sent a shiver of relief through him. "Hold on now. I haven't said I wouldn't give you the details. You want to know the exact specifications at the beginning? Well, that's all right since you were so good as to show me the gloves you want ensorcelled. It seems fair, it does."

Vaughn bit his tongue to keep from offending the brownie by offering thanks as he turned back around. "I have paper. Would you be so good as to write your needs down, and if I am able, I shall fulfill them to the letter."

With a laugh, the brownie laid her finger alongside her nose. "Ah. You're a sly one. To the letter, indeed." She nodded. "Give me the paper, then, sir and let us make our bargain."

IN THE FRONT of the shop, Master Martin spoke in his honeyed tones to a fine gentleman looking for elegance gloves for his daughter. Vaughn pulled his stool closer to the window, trying to catch the last bit of daylight before he was forced to light a candle.

The skin under his left eye itched. He rubbed it, without thinking and nearly cursed aloud as he cracked the scab that was healing. Blood spotted his forefinger, and he slid back from the bench before he could get anything on the gloves he was working on.

"What ails you, young sir?" The piping voice came from his knee.

Vaughn tilted his head down to meet the gaze of Littleberry. The brownie's eyes were bright with interest.

"Nothing, th"—he bit the thanks off just in time—"that is of any concern."

The brownie smiled, wrinkles curving into a map of concern. "How are you healing then? Come now, tell me true since Master Martin isn't here."

Vaughn grabbed a rag and pressed it to the spot under his eye. Guild brownies valued an honest man, and he wasn't sure he could even remotely be considered that anymore. "Well enough all things considered. I've still some aches and pains, but I'm much improved from a fortnight ago."

"You look more tired though, begging your pardon."

That would be from staying up late stitching Mossthicket's gloves, but that truth was not one he needed to share. Vaughn pulled the cloth away and the bleeding had already stopped. Gingerly, he probed the spot. It was still tender, but his fingers came away dry. "There. See?"

Master Martin pushed through the curtain into the back, rubbing his hands together. "A fine day. That's the seventh pair of elegance gloves! Oh, how I wish King Henry went looking for wives more often."

It seemed to Vaughn that he did that more than often enough. He folded the cloth and set it aside as he sat at the bench again. "Excellent news, sir. I can get those cut tonight."

"No need, lad." Master Martin tousled his hair.

Vaughn winced. It was a new, annoying habit, but better than being clapped on the shoulder. Master Martin, to his credit, had only done that *once* after the robbery. "Sooner begun is sooner done, sir."

Littleberry climbed the ladder built in the leg of the workbench. "Aye. I can stay as well, to give a hand to the young sir."

Stay? Littleberry always left with Master Martin. Vaughn picked up his needle and concentrated on the leather in front of him. Or pretended to do so. Sweat began to trickle down the back of his neck. Could Littleberry know that he'd stolen leather? He bit his lower lip as he fit the thumb into the glove. "We'll be done the faster then. Many hands make light work and all."

"Did neither of you hear me? There's no need. We've a fortnight to make the delivery so all of us are going home while there's still light." He tousled Vaughn's hair again. "Wouldn't want you to get robbed again, would we?"

"No sir." Vaughn put his needle down and thanked God for years of training in hiding his true feelings from the master. "I'll just tidy up and be off then."

Because the truth was, he'd already stolen everything he needed. He just felt guilty.

THREE PAIRS OF gloves lay on the table, threads glimmering on them like the sun, the moon, and the stars. A fourth pair with honeysuckle twining in delicate branches lay next to them. Vaughn and Sarah faced the fire, as he waited for the sound of Mossthicket's arrival.

The earthenware scraped on the table and Vaughn's head dropped forward with relief.

"I was wondering what you were up to, young sir." Littleberry's piping voice drove Vaughn to his feet.

Spinning, he whirled to face the table, where the guild brownie stood with his hands upon his hips. The room seemed to continue spinning around him as Vaughn gaped, gasping for air. He was ruined.

"Vaughn?" Sarah's voice snapped him back to himself.

"Go—go downstairs to Mrs. Nelson's." He could not look away from Littleberry.

"What's the matter?"

There was no use pretending with his sister that nothing was wrong. Vaughn swallowed, pressing his lips together, and dragged his gaze over to hers. "This is my master's guild brownie." The small wordless cry from her nearly undid him, but he pressed on. "We have some business to discuss and it will be easier in private. Please, Sarah?"

She nodded, pulling her shawl tighter around her, and hurried to the door. Vaughn waited, flexing his hands into fists and out again until he heard the door shut and her feet upon the stairs. Drawing himself up, he faced the brownie. "She has seizures. I needed gloves to control them."

"I know." The brownie nodded, all wrinkles and sadness. "And how many times has Master Martin warned you about your sister interfering with your work?"

"If she had gloves, she wouldn't!" He was ruined now, so there was no point in holding back. "Put her in an almshouse? Did neither of you think that, maybe, the answer would be to help us? I even asked if I could make them myself! I would have paid for them and put myself into debt but no, a man of my station can't own such things. So yes—YES. The *honest* answer is that I am making unlicensed gloves."

"There are laws for reasons."

Vaughn laughed. "What reason? What reason beyond vanity and fear justifies this?"

"In the wrong hands, all gloves can be used for crime." Littleberry gestured at Vaughn's shoulder. "Look to your own form for proof. Strength gloves, designed to help master builders lift and steady are instead used for robbery."

"And what crime would one commit with seizure gloves?"

"Where does one draw the line?" Littleberry shook his head. "The Faerie Queen set the laws and I trust her judgement better than that of a single thieving mortal."

"I had no choice!"

Litteberry shook his head, and tsked. "We always have choices. You made the choice to steal from your master. You made the choice to create a princess."

"I—A what?"

Littleberry gestured at the gloves on the table. "The sun, the moon, and the stars? Unadulterated. Did Mossthicket not tell you what she needed them for? Oh, my lady Queen will be wroth with her indeed."

Behind Littleberry, the world twisted around an oval spot, the center of which danced like an oil slick. Whatever Vaughn had been about to say vanished, as Mossthicket congealed in the center of the oil. Littleberry's brows went up and he turned to look over his shoulder.

Mossthicket slit his throat.

Hand flying to his mouth, Vaughn staggered back in horror. A pair of silver shears, perfectly sized for her tiny hands, dripped blood on the table. Littleberry clapped his hands to his throat, coughing and gagging blood. He staggered to his knees. Mossthicket caught his body, steering him away from the gloves and pushed him over the side of the table.

His tiny body hit the floor with the sound of breaking twigs. He thrashed once and lay still.

"Oh God..."

Mossthicket wiped her shears on a tiny handkerchief. He knew those shears.

"What—what did you do?"

"Solved a problem." She slid the shears into the waistband of her skirt. "Best put the body in the fire."

"What are they for? A princess? What does that mean?"

Vaughn stared at her, all wrinkled ease and calm. Her nutbrown face had set in lines of determination and a single drop of blood stained one cuff. Littleberry was dead. "What should a girl like your sister do, if she wants to rise above her station? Hm? What if the king has called for all of the eligible young ladies to go to a ball, and she should but, alas... Her stepmother won't allow it. There are rules and laws and *none* of them are made for the likes of her."

What would he do? "I damn well wouldn't kill someone for Sarah."

"Then I guess it's a good thing that I would." Mossthicket rubbed her forehead with one hand. "Or did you not think about what would happen to her when her brother was clapped in irons and hanged for stealing?"

Hanged. But he wouldn't kill. She had killed and he—and Sarah and—Vaughn's stomach turned inside out. He retched on the floor. Chunks of bread and bile spattered into the blood.

"I'll deal with the blood and the mess." Mossthicket's ears twitched toward the door. "Right now, you best burn the body before your sister comes up."

He had to repeat the words to himself five or six times before he could make himself move. Put the body in the fire. Vaughn halted forward and knelt. He could have picked Littleberry up with one hand, but it seemed disrespectful somehow. He scooped both hands under the little body and gagged again, but didn't vomit, thank God. He almost laughed or cried. The things he was grateful for these days.

His shoulder didn't hurt at all to lift the brownie. "The fire?"

"Go up like kindling, we do." She had her hands over the blood, brows drawn down in concentration. "Hush now. I'm working."

The fire. What was he to do? The fire. His brain emptied and seemed to simply watch as his body turned and walked to the hearth. He laid Littleberry's corpse on the embers.

A flame curled around the little cotte. With a whoosh, green flames swept down the length of Littleberry reaching for the chimney as if he was going to flee on a column of smoke and fire. Vaughn threw his good arm over his eyes, turning away from the harsh light. His shadow stretched across the room to the door.

Sarah opened it, eyes wide.

He dropped his arm, stepping between her and the table so she wouldn't have to see the blood. Only—it was gone. Mossthicket sat on the edge of the table, kicking her heels beneath her skirt.

"Are you all right?" Sarah rushed to him and took his hand.

"Yes." He lied, but his head whirled too much for the truth.

"What did Littleberry say?"

He glanced back at the hearth, but all that was there were glowing embers and a smattering of ash.

Mossthicket smiled at Sarah. "I worked things out with him. Naught to worry about there." She pulled the seizure gloves over her lap like a blanket and traced the honeysuckle vines with the tip of her fingers. A webwork of light shimmered behind her hand, wrapping around the threads of Vaughn's embroidery. " Come now, miss. Let's fit you with your gloves, shall we?"

Littleberry was dead. Sarah did not know that and never needed to know that. Vaughn let go of her hand, pulling a smile from somewhere. "Go on."

She lingered for a moment, searching his face, and he dragged the smile higher until she pattered over to Mossthicket. Who had murdered Littleberry.

"Wait—" Vaughn walked over to the table and looked down at the brownie. Even though he'd made these gloves and knew damn well what the stitching would do, he just needed to hear it. "These will keep her seizures from happening and nothing else. Right?"

Mossthicket bowed her head. "We had a bargain and I've not played you false." She smiled up at Sarah, cheeks curving in a mask of pleasure. "Besides, I like the young lady. She reminds me of my goddaughter."

He nodded, but the sense of creeping wrong would not let go of his spine. Vaughn knotted his hands into fists as Sarah pulled on the gloves. She frowned, shoulders drooping in disappointment. "I—nothing feels different."

"That's what you wanted though, wasn't it?" The brownie winked and scrambled to her feet. "Wear them for a week and see if things aren't different. And now—I'll take my payment and go."

"I trust they are to your liking." How could he care what she thought of his craftmanship now? But he watched her face anyway as she picked the gloves up, running her fingers over the embroidery.

"You do fine work." She pulled the gloves closer, peering at the varigated thread he'd used for the sun's rays. "Might be that we can work together again in the future."

"Thank you." It was rude. That was why he said it. "No."

She shrugged, one cheek curving up in a grin. "I'll give you time to think it over. I could use guild quality gloves. I'd cut you in on the profits."

"I am really not interested." What was Master Martin going to do when Littleberry failed to show up tomorrow? God. She had killed Littleberry, who was yes, going to turn him in, but the brownie had not deserved to die for that.

"Hm." She threw the gloves around her shoulders like a cape of the sky. "And when the young miss's gloves wear through? We'll talk again, I've no doubt."

The oilslick blossomed around her, and she melted into it, gloves and all.

Vaughn dropped to his knees. What had he done? All he'd wanted was for his sister to be safe and healthy and happy and he'd bound himself to a murderer.

Because Mossthicket knew he would do anything to keep his sister safe and healthy. He hadn't agreed to a new bargain, but he was bound by it nonetheless. Gloves to make a princess this time. What would it be next? Gloves to kill a king? Despite his best effort to smile at Sarah, each breath hurt as if he'd broken his shoulder anew.

Sarah knelt next to him, putting a honeysuckle clad hand on his arm. "Vaughn? Why are you crying?"

"I'm not." He wiped his cheeks, and his hand came away wet.

"Liar." She tweaked his nose, laughing.

That single word nearly broke him, because he would never be able to join the guild after tonight. The brownies valued an honest man and the stink of lying would stick to him for the rest of his days.

Vaughn sat back on his heels and clutched Sarah's hands in his. The kidskin was fine and cool beneath his touch. She didn't need to know. Sarah never needed to know the cost. "There... now you look like a lady."

COME SEE THE LIVING DRYAD
Theodora Goss

Theodora Goss (www.theodoragoss.com) was born in Hungary and spent her childhood in various European countries before her family moved to the United States. Although she grew up on the classics of English literature, her writing has been influenced by an Eastern European literary tradition in which the boundaries between realism and the fantastic are often ambiguous. Her publications include the short story collection *In the Forest of Forgetting*; *Interfictions*, a short story anthology coedited with Delia Sherman; and *Voices from Fairyland*, a poetry anthology with critical essays and a selection of her own poems. Her most recent book is *The Thorn and the Blossom: A Two-sided Love Story*. She has been a finalist for the Nebula, Crawford, and Mythopoeic Awards, as well as on the Tiptree Award Honor List, and has won the World Fantasy and Rhysling Awards. Her debut novel, *The Strange Case of the Alchemist's Daughter* was published in 2017 and a sequel is due in 2018.

I CAN HEAR them whispering.

I cannot see them, not yet. And when the curtain is pulled back, what will I see? Faces, pale and almost indistinguishable in the gaslight. My shows are only at night, for that, he tells me, makes them more impressive.

But I know my audience. Clerks heading home from their offices, tired after a day of crouching over a ledger, wanting to see a miracle. Serious young ladies who would never condescend to the spectacles of Battersea Park, but this is different—a scientific lecture. A tutor shushing his charges, boys who will one day go to university—until they see me, and then they shush of their own accord. They recognize me from their lessons in the classics and wonder, how is it possible? Gentlemen in top hats, headed afterward to more risqué entertainments. An old woman in black who peers at me through her pince-nez, disbelieving. She must have seen an advertisement and become curious—is it real? Or a hoax, like the Genuine Mermaid?

I am improbable, am I not?

Almost, but not quite, impossible.

And when the curtain is pulled back and they see me, sitting on my pedestal, arms raised, branches swaying, they will gasp. As they always do.

Come See the Living Dryad
Proof that the ancient mythologies were veritable truths!
You have read of them in Homer and Hesiod. Now, tonight, you may see for yourself, one of those "dwellers in the lovely groves," those daughters of Gaia. Living proof that the wonders of the ancient world have not passed away altogether in this age of technological marvels.
Viewing at 8.30, special lecture at 9.00 by Professor L. Merwin, M. Phil., D. Litt., LL.D., Member of the Anthropological Institute of Great Britain and Ireland.
Tickets two shillings, half price for children.

WHO KILLED DAPHNE Merwin? By 1888, she was famous enough that the case was mentioned in *The Times* of London:

A tragedy in Marylebone. On the morning of June 7th, Mrs. Lewison Merwin, who has become famous as Daphne, the Living Dryad, showing nightly at the Alhambra, was found brutally murdered at her home in Marylebone. Her husband, Professor Merwin, is distraught and stated that he does not know who could have committed such a crime, as she had not an enemy in the world. According to Inspector Granby of the Metropolitan Police, Mrs. Merwin was stabbed in the chest with a kitchen knife. This crime was doubly brutal because, due to her physical peculiarities, Mrs. Merwin was unable to defend herself. Members of the public are urged to bring any pertinent information to the attention of the Metropolitan Police, who promise a swift investigation.

As this edition of the paper was going to press, the man who would be hanged for her murder had already been arrested. Alfred Potts was a pauper and occasional petty thief. That morning, he had come to the Merwin residence. The maid of all work had let him in at Daphne's insistence. According to her account, he had offered to do whatever work needed doing of a heavy nature, in exchange for a hot meal. Daphne, who was habitually charitable, said he could do some work in the garden. After the maid let him in, she returned to the basement kitchen to prepare lunch for the Merwins. Lewison Merwin, who had a meeting with a business associate, was expected back at noon.

She did not leave the kitchen again until she heard the front door bell. It was Lewison, who had forgotten his latchkey. The maid let him in and returned to the kitchen, expecting to serve lunch. A few minutes later, he ran down the back stairs and told her to come quickly, that Mrs. Merwin had been murdered. When she followed him up to the parlor, she saw Daphne lying on the carpet, with a red stain spreading across her nightgown. Alfred Potts was gone. So was the money for miscellaneous expenses kept in a side table drawer, in the front hall.

It was the nightgown that first struck me about the case, now more than a century old. Why would Daphne Merwin meet a strange man in her nightgown? In 1888, no lady would have done such a thing, and Daphne was trying very hard to be a lady. Potts was arrested in a public house in Spitalfields, where he had been drinking most of the day. The money that had been in the drawer was found in his pocket. He claimed Daphne had given it to him. He knew nothing about any work in the garden, and indeed there was nothing to indicate he had done any. The gardening tools were still in the shed, and there was no evidence they had been used. After she had given him the money, he had left and gone straight to the pub. He had been sitting there drinking at the time the maid claimed he was murdering Mrs. Merwin. The woman who owned the pub confirmed his story, but since she had once been arrested for prostitution, neither the police nor the jury believed her. The pub being otherwise empty at that hour, there were no other witnesses.

The inspector asked why Mrs. Merwin would give him money, without him having done any work. But Potts, who was drunk, merely cursed and tried to assault him. Then he was taken away in a police wagon.

This was all I could learn from the records of the Metropolitan Police, which had been digitized the previous year and placed online. The online archives of *The Times* of London contained an account of the trial, which lasted only three days. During the trial, Potts made an extraordinary claim: that Daphne Merwin was his sister, and that she had given him money several times since he had discovered her address, following her home one night from the Alhambra. But when asked for evidence, he could produce nothing, claiming that any proof of their relationship had been stolen from him long ago. Indeed, the police found few possessions of his in the squalid room he shared with two other men, both dock workers. Lewison Merwin stated that his wife had been an orphan and alone in the world when he met her. He insisted that he had never seen Potts before in his life, and the maid confirmed that she had never seen him at the house before the day of the murder. Surely, if Potts had come to solicit Mrs. Merwin before, the maid would have been the one to let him in.

Needless to say, neither the judge nor jury believed Potts. Not even his own barrister seems to have believed him. He was poor, sleeping on street corners or in that disreputable boarding house, and an alcoholic. The jury reached its verdict in under an hour. He was condemned to death and hanged on September 27th, 1888.

—*The British Freak Show at the Fin-de-Siècle*, D.M. Levitt, Ph.D.

EVERY MORNING, HE prunes me. I sit in a chair in the middle of my bedroom and raise my arms. Carefully, he trims away any small branches that are not aesthetically pleasing.

"We don't want you to look pollarded," he says.

His goal is always beauty, grace, lightness.

I was neither beautiful nor graceful when he found me. The branches had grown from my hands so I could hardly lift them. They had grown on my feet so I could scarcely walk. Bark had begun to grow over my face. I was worried that soon it would cover my eyes, and I would be a poor, blind, crippled girl, a pitiable object.

Every day, my brother would place me on my little cart and pull me down to a street corner near Brick Lane Market. There we would beg for pennies. Some passersby would throw pennies on the ground, pitying my grotesqueness. Some would turn away with a shudder. Sometimes the bric-a-brac sellers would give me bits of their lunch. Sometimes we were spit upon, or a group of boys would throw pieces of pavement and rusted nails.

But he found me and saw what I could become. If you come with me, he said that day on the street corner, I will make you beautiful. I will make it so all men look at you and gasp in admiration rather than fear. I will make you a celebrity.

My brother had gone off—young as he was, he had already succumbed to the Demon Drink. I knew he was spending our pennies at a public house while I sat on the cart, waiting and hungry.

Yes, I said. I will go with you.

Look how my branches rise into the air, so gracefully, so lightly. The bark grows up my arms to my elbows. My feet he prunes more thoroughly, so only a few small branches sprout from my toes. I have no need of shoes, for my soles are hard. The bark grows up to my knees.

There is a little bark on my forehead, but it does not encroach on my eyes. My ears are clear. I can see and hear and speak. A human heart beats in my chest. And yet I am like no other woman. That is why he loves me, he says. Because I am unique.

After he prunes me, Lucy removes my nightdress and bathes me, because of course I cannot bathe myself. She dresses me. And then she brings me the child.

YOU SCHOOLBOYS SITTING in the front should know, or your schoolmaster should have told you, that the dryads and oreiades were the nymphs of the trees and woodlands. They were associated with particular trees, and when her tree died, the dryad died with it. Woe betide any Greek villager who felled a tree with a dryad, for misfortune would follow him all the days of his life!

The dryads and oreiades sprang from Gaia herself. Who is Gaia, you ask? Surely that learned young woman in the back... yes, exactly. Gaia was the goddess of the earth. And their father was Ouranos, god of the sky. So they were born of heaven and earth. There were many kinds of dryads: the meliai, nymphs of the ash trees; the pteleai, nymphs of the elms; the aigeroi, protectors of poplars. The balanis for holly trees, the sykei for figs, and moreai for mulberry. And then there were the orchard trees: the meliades protected apple trees, and kraneiai could be found beneath the cherry boughs. But the most graceful of all were the daphnaie, the nymphs of the laurel trees, and that is what you see before you tonight.

Where did I find such a marvel? Why, in the hills of Arcadia, of course. I was walking through the verdant groves when I came upon her, sitting by a stream, looking down at her reflection in the water, as laurel trees do. Since I spoke the language of ancient Greece, whose study I recommend to those of you who are diligent and have the time, I convinced her to return with me to the greatest city in the world, to London itself. So you, citizens of the age of steam and iron, could see that the wonders of the ancient world are not wholly gone from the earth—nay, they are only hidden from our eyes. But if we have faith, if we listen with open hearts and see with unclouded vision, we may still witness miracles.

Turn, Daphne, so our audience can see the beauty and delicacy of the daughter of Gaia and Ouranos, nymph of laurel trees—a modern wonder!

LEWANDOWSKY-LUTZ DYSPLASIA IS one of the rarest diseases in human history. In the late twentieth century, two cases brought the disease to public attention: those of the Romanian Ion Toader and the Indonesian Dede Koswara. This hereditary genetic disorder makes the sufferers abnormally susceptible to an HPV (Human Papilloma Virus) of the skin. As a result, wherever the skin is cut or abraded, the patient develops macules and papules, particularly on the extremities, such as hands and feet. In extreme cases, these can grow into 'limbs' that resemble tree branches and must be removed by surgery. More common are bumps and ridges on the skin that may turn cancerous. Toader was fortunate: he was diagnosed by a prominent dermatologist, who was able to remove most of his growths surgically, and his continuing medical treatment was paid for by the state healthcare system. Since his surgery, the Lewandowsky-Lutz has not progressed, and he has been able to live a normal life.

The second case, that of Dede Koswara, was both more serious and more widely reported. He had a particularly advanced case of the disease, both because he lived far from modern medical facilities and because his immune system lacked an antigen that would have helped him fight the HPV infection. By the time his condition was diagnosed, he was almost completely incapacitated, working in a freak show to support himself, like Daphne Merwin, but without the help of a consummate showman such as Lewison. Once his condition was discovered, he was profiled on various cable television shows, as well as in a *Medical Mystery* episode titled 'Tree Man.' The show paid for surgery to remove most of his growths, but there was no way to stop them recurring, and he recently passed away from what the internet describes only as 'complications.' There is still no cure for Lewandowsky-Lutz.

Since the age of twelve, I have developed flat, scaly macules regularly on my hands and feet. Fortunately they have not spread to other parts of my body, and the university provides me with excellent health benefits. I visit a dermatologist monthly to have them removed. Underneath, the skin is lighter, so my hands and feet look mottled. I could cover them with concealer, I suppose. But when I look at them, I remember Daphne. In a small way, they bring me closer to my great-great grandmother.

—*The British Freak Show at the Fin-de-Siècle*, D.M. Levitt, Ph.D.

I THOUGHT LUCY was my friend.

Of course she is my maid, but where else could she find work, with her disfigurement? I knew her when she was begging on the street corners of Spitalfields: a dirty, hairy girl with wild, scared eyes. It was I who insisted that he hire her. And now?

He says she should not have told me, that he is still negotiating a contract. But she is to come before me... before *me*! And thus, he says, he will show them both our evolutionary and mythological pasts. Both the Primitive Eve and the Living Dryad.

But she is not beautiful. No amount of grooming could make her beautiful.

She looks like... yes, a monkey. A sly, low, ill-bred monkey of a girl that I took off the streets, and clothed, and housed. And this is how she treats me.

I heard them last night, long after he thought I was asleep. I did not drink my laudanum, so I lay awake and heard noises, for her bedroom is above mine. First the two of them talking, although I could not make out the words. And then other noises.

Has he not considered me? Has he not considered our child? Our Daisy, asleep in her cradle. How I love her, and yet it is even more difficult for me to hold her than to write.

Come See the Primitive Eve
The missing link in Mr. Darwin's theory!
Hitherto, the argument against Mr. Darwin's theory has been that no creature has been found in a state between man and monkey. The Primitive Eve is that creature—an attractive, well-formed maiden covered entirely with a pelt of dark hair.
Found as a child in the wild forests of Borneo, she has been brought back to England and taught the benefits of civilized society. Hear her read from the Bible. Watch her perform her native dances and then curtsy with the nicety of an English schoolgirl. All should see this living marvel!
Viewing at 8.30, special lecture at 9.00 by Professor L. Merwin, M. Phil., D. Litt., LL.D., Member of the Anthropological Institute of Great Britain and Ireland.
Tickets two shillings, half price for children.

MY MOTHER FIRST showed me the diary when I began developing Lewandowsky-Lutz. She wanted me to understand where it had come from—why I had bumps on my hands and feet, although evidently it had skipped a generation, because she never developed symptoms. But my grandmother died young of cancer from Lewandowsky-Lutz. My great-grandmother, Daisy Merwin, lived to a hundred and one, although she had to clip the growths on her forearms at regular intervals. It affects us all differently.

After Daphne's death, Lewison sent their daughter Daisy to the United States, to be raised by his sister's family in Virginia. That would free him to travel with his newest marvel, Lucy Barker, advertised as the Primitive Eve. She belonged to the 'hairy woman' type of freak show performer, like her contemporaries Krao and Julia Pastrana, both of whom are discussed in Chapter One. Merwin traveled all over Europe with the Primitive Eve, who became particularly popular in France—until she died of a laudanum overdose. Deprived of his major source of income, he returned to New York and worked in the Barnum & Bailey Circus, becoming one of its managers after Barnum's death in 1891. Although he tried to arrange his own shows on the side, he never again attained the success he had with Daphne or Eve.

After his death, his daughter Daisy received a small inheritance, mostly wiped out by his debts, and a box of her mother's effects. They included Daphne's diary, as well as a silver brush and comb set that I still use to subdue my hair and a necklace of coral beads I wear almost every day. In the nineteenth century, coral was believed to protect against diseases—that is why children were given coral necklaces to wear. The necklace didn't help Daphne; nevertheless, I find it reassuring. It is an attractive placebo.

We must remember that Lewison was a charlatan. Despite his claims, he was not a university professor, nor had he earned any of the degrees or distinctions listed on his advertisements. He had started his career at a theological seminary in Virginia, training to be a minister. One week, P.T. Barnum's Grand Traveling Museum, Menagerie, Caravan, and Circus, as it was called in the 1870s, came to town. Lewison bought tickets for every show, and finally asked to meet Barnum himself. That was the beginning of his career as a showman. Barnum hired him as an agent and sent him to London to arrange bookings for his various shows. And that is where he found Daphne, the Living Dryad.

Her diary contains no dates. It is rambling and impressionistic, written in large looping letters made by a woman who had difficulty simply holding a pen. There are misspellings, although her grammar is almost self-consciously correct, for which, I suppose, we must thank Lewison: he taught her to write. Nevertheless, the entries are suggestive.

What they suggest is that Daphne Merwin was not killed by Alfred Potts.
—*The British Freak Show at the Fin-de-Siècle*, D.M. Levitt, Ph.D.

* * *

THIS CANNOT CONTINUE. I will speak to him, I will tell him that he cannot have us both.

Think of the publicity! he says. Think of the money we will make! But I do not care about that.

I would rather be back on the streets of London, begging for crusts of bread. Am I insensate, a piece of wood for him to move about as he wishes? Am I the mythical creature he likes to call me? No, I am human, whatever I may appear to be. I breathe, I feel, I love.

I will not let him treat me like this. I will not let her speak to me as she has in the past few days. She has been boasting about how successful she will be, more successful than I am. She has been wearing my dresses, neglecting the child. My child—who deserves better, who deserves everything. I cannot let this continue.

I will speak to him and tell him so.

WESTERN UNION

MISS LETITIA MERWIN
CLOVERFIELD, V.A.
JUNE 23
SENDING YOU DAISY CARE OF IRISH NURSE ARRIVING U.S.S.
MERRIMACK AT NEWPORT JULY 3RD WILL SEND CHEQUE FOR
EXPENSES SOON AS NEW SHOW OPENS AT ALHAMBRA LOVE
LEWISON

WESTERN UNION

MISS LETITIA MERWIN
CLOVERFIELD, V.A.
JUNE 24
ALSO REMEMBER WATCH FOR SYMPTOMS SHE MAY BE AS

DISTINCTIVE AS HER MOTHER IF SO SEND WORD IMMEDIATELY IMAGINE THE SENSATION A CHILD DRYAD

THE EVIDENCE FROM the Merwin murder case is collected in a small box in the basement storage facility of the Metropolitan Police. In the summer of 2014, I traveled to London for two weeks on a research grant. I visited the neighborhood in Spitalfields where Daisy Potts, who would become Daphne Merwin, spent her childhood. It is now filled with restaurants— Indonesian, Albanian, Bangladeshi. I stood near the corner of Brick Lane Market, thinking of what it must have been like for Daisy, begging here, almost blind, until Lewison Merwin found her.

I visited the house in Marylebone where she had lived, but it was now a dentist's office, with flats on the upper floors. I visited Leicester Square, where the Alhambra used to stand. Even Newgate, where Alfred Potts was hanged for her murder.

Then I went to the headquarters of the Metropolitan Police. It had been difficult to get an appointment. The head of my department had written a letter describing my research, on university stationery. When that received no response, I asked a friend at Oxford, with whom I had gone to graduate school, to intervene. I thought Oxford would mean more than a regional American college. At long last I received an e-mail from the head archivist: I would be allowed to examine the evidence for two hours, 4:00-6:00 p.m., on a Thursday afternoon. A camera would be allowed, without flash.

The junior archivist who met me in the waiting room was a serious young woman in glasses with thick black frames. Her badge proclaimed her Dr. Patel.

She handed me a similar ID badge, conspicuously marked TEMPORARY, with my name on it: Dr. Daphne Levitt, University of Southern Vermont.

"I've never been to America," she said as we rode down the elevator. "I would be a little nervous, especially in New York. You have so many shootings!"

"Not so many where I live," I told her. "My university is in a small town up north. They mostly shoot deer there. And street signs."

She looked at me as though scandalized that I would joke about such a thing.

"Your job must be so interesting," I said. That is my magical phrase. As an introvert, I've always found it supremely useful at parties. Once I say it, I don't have to talk for the next half hour.

She described it to me enthusiastically, but I only half-listened. I was wondering what I would find in the evidence box, and whether it would help me solve the Merwin case. When I started writing this book, I asked my mother to send me Daphne's diary. I had not read it since I was a teenager. Then, I had only been interested in the disease itself, in what might happen to me if the Lewandowsky-Lutz progressed. But something about the newspaper account of the trial kept bothering me, and when I looked at the diary again, I saw it. Daphne had mentioned a brother. Could it be Alfred Potts? If so, Lewison had lied. Why?

I followed Dr. Patel down a long beige hallway that reminded me of middle school, and then into a room filled with shelves, rather like university library stacks except that all of the shelves were filled with carefully labeled boxes. We walked down one of the rows while she scanned them. "There," she said, and took down a box labeled *Merwin, Daphne 1888.*

I had expected an evidence box out of Dickens, yellowed and moldering, but this was thoroughly modern.

"Everything was recataloged in the 1990s," she said, I suppose in response to my expression. Perhaps the Metropolitan Police trained even archivists to read people.

She carried the box to a long table under fluorescent lights. "Just a moment," she said, as I reached for the lid. From a nearby cabinet, she produced two surgical masks and gloves of some artificial material that felt like plastic trying to be cotton. When I was properly outfitted, I sat at the table and opened the box.

In it were the items the police had collected on the day of Daphne's murder. At the top of the box, protected by a plastic sleeve, was a stack of yellowing papers. On the first sheet of paper was written, in a sloping nineteenth-century hand:

Evidence in the death of Mrs. Lewison Merwin:

Item 1: Nightgown torn by knife, with bloodstain.
Item 2: Branches broken from the body of Mrs. Merwin in altercation.

Item 3: Photograph of Mrs. Merwin.

Item 4: Statement of Professor Merwin.

Item 5: Statement of Lucy Barker, housemaid.

Item 6: Statement of Mrs. Polansky, neighbor.

Item 7: Statement of Alfred Potts, suspect.

Item 8: Statement of Alice O'Neill, barmaid.

Item 9: Kitchen knife stained with blood.

I opened the sleeve and drew out the stack of papers. Beneath the list was the statement of Lewison Merwin, describing how he had found his wife in the parlor, stabbed to death. He had been out of the house all morning, attending a business meeting at the Alhambra, where Mrs. Merwin has shows three nights a week. Under his statement was written, *Husband clearly distraught.* I took photographs of each page with my iPhone. Next was the statement of Lucy Barker, describing how she had answered the door at around ten o'clock and found Alfred Potts on the doorstep. She had not wanted to let him in, but her mistress had insisted, out of the goodness of her heart. She was always one to help the poor. Lucy had given him a meal in the kitchen at Mrs. Merwin's request, at which point he must have taken the knife, and no, she could not have watched him more carefully. She had lunch to prepare, hadn't she? Then he had gone out into the garden. She had heard nothing more until noon, when Professor Merwin rang the bell and she had let him in. A few minutes later, he had run into the kitchen, saying that her mistress had been stabbed. Of course he was upset, Mrs. Merwin had been stabbed, hadn't she? He had asked for a towel and hot water, but by then there was nothing to be done. Mrs. Merwin was dead. No, she had heard no sounds of an altercation in the parlor. The kitchen was in the basement, on the other side of the house, so why should she? And now if he could stop bothering her, she needed to feed the child. Under her account was written *Seems devoted to her mistress. UGLY!* The statement of Mrs. Polansky was short: she had been sitting in her parlor at around 11:30 when she had heard a man and woman arguing next door at the Merwins'. The walls were that thin, to the shame of these modern builders. Yes, she remembered the time because she had a grown son who was a clerk and came home for lunch, so she kept looking at the clock, knowing he would return around quarter till. No, she could not hear what was being said, but one voice was deep, a man's voice, and the other she thought was Mrs. Merwin's. A nice lady, although one couldn't exactly invite her over for tea, could one? Under her statement was written *Not English—Polack*? The statement of Alfred Potts was not much longer. He had gone to the Merwins' house asking for money, had been given money out of the hall table drawer, and had left, that was all. He had gone to the pub, where he had been sitting on this [objectionable language] chair ever since, as Alice could tell you. Asked why he had gone to the Merwins', which was half across town, rather than begging in Spitalfields, where he was no doubt better known. He had assaulted the officer and sworn in the most inventive and objectionable terms. At that point, he had been arrested. Under his statement was written *DRUNK*. The statement of Alice O'Neill was also short: Alfred Potts had come into the pub at 11:00, sat down in that chair right there, and had been sitting there ever since. Under her statement was written *Known to police as Alice O'Connell, Alice Ferguson.*

Dr. Patel sat patiently while I photographed each page. At the bottom of the stack was the photograph that forms the frontispiece of this book. It is the only photograph we have of Daphne Merwin, since in her advertisements she was usually drawn in a way that exaggerated her arboreal qualities. When I first located it on the internet, on a website devoted to freak show history and paraphernalia, I printed out a copy and pinned it to my office bulletin board. But this was one of the original prints. It shows her seated on what looks like a column with a Corinthian capital, about the height of a kitchen stool, wearing a long white gown that leaves her arms bare. She is holding her arms up as though they were a bifurcated trunk with branches and twigs growing from them. Her skin is rough and bark-like to the elbows, but perfectly smooth above. Her hair is done up in the Victorian idea of a classical chignon. The gown is floor-length, but she is raising one foot so you can see the thick, gnarled growths on her toes. They do, indeed, look like tree roots. You have to give Lewison Merwin credit for one thing: he did a good job pruning her. The branches are thinned out, trimmed back in places. Despite their weight, she could lift her arms. She could walk. If you look closely at the original photograph, you can see what is not obvious from the online version: the rough skin on her forehead. But it does not grow down to her eyes. She could see. She could even have a child. She looks off to the side rather than at the viewer, but her chin is raised, elegantly, proudly. If you ignore the growths on her arms and feet, it is the photograph of an ordinary, if very attractive, Victorian woman.

"My God," said Dr. Patel, leaning across the table. "What was wrong with her?" She had been quiet for so long that I had almost forgotten she was there.

"Lewandowsky-Lutz dysplasia," I said. "Or, you know, being murdered. Can I take out the nightgown?" I had now photographed every piece of paper in the stack. I slipped the stack back into the plastic sleeve and set it aside. It was time to look at the physical evidence.

"Yes, as long as you're wearing gloves," said Dr. Patel. Now she was leaning forward, clearly interested. I pulled the nightgown out of the plastic bag. It was made of a thin white cotton batiste, very finely embroidered: an expensive article in the 1880s.

"You see all these buttons on the shoulders," I said, as though lecturing one of my students. "She couldn't have pulled the nightgown over her head. It had to be buttoned up, probably by her maid."

"A wound that deep would have killed her almost instantly," said Dr. Patel, looking with professional curiosity at the place where the nightgown was torn. Around the tear it was bloody, and blood had soaked down one side, probably where it had dripped and pooled. "You see, the knife went right in: the hole isn't ragged. But there's a lot of blood. It would have been a deep, clean wound." She put on a pair of fake-cotton gloves, pulled the plastic sleeve of papers toward her, and started reading through them.

I imagined Daphne Merwin lying on the floor, with a deep, clean wound in her chest, bleeding her life away while my great-grandmother lay in her cradle upstairs. Did she cry out? There is no record of any cry, so maybe she was too startled, maybe she died too quickly. Who stood over her, watching her die? That was the question I wanted to answer. I folded the nightgown and slipped it back inside the plastic bag. It had told me only that Daphne was indeed stabbed—and that the Living Dryad had bled like an ordinary woman.

Below the nightgown were two other plastic bags, both containing pieces of linen. Perhaps wrapped around whatever was inside? I lifted the one on the left, distinguishable from the other only because it was more square than oblong. I unwound the linen. Inside were a bunch of horny, bifurcating growths.

"Some of her branches," I said in response to Dr. Patel's inquisitive expression. "Parts of her, hardened like keratin, almost like your nails? They must have broken off during the struggle."

"There was no struggle," Dr. Patel responded, frowning above her glasses. "Not judging by those bloodstains—just stabbing and bleeding. She wouldn't have had time to fight back. Can I take a look?"

"I'm glad you're here, because bloodstains don't tell me anything," I said. "Then I suppose these must have broken off when she fell, after she was stabbed?" I pushed Daphne's branches toward Dr. Patel and turned to the third and final plastic bag, knowing what it must contain: the murder weapon. While I unwrapped it, she examined the broken growths. It made sense that she would be curious—after all, how often did you hear of a person like Daphne Merwin, a malnourished nineteenth-century orphan with a full-blown case of Lewandowsky-Lutz, turned into a living myth? And then a murder case.

I unwound the final piece of linen. Here was the knife that had killed her. I laid it on the table in front of me.

It was about seven inches long, four of handle and three of blade: a sharp, curved knife that would inflict a particularly vicious wound below the skin. The blade and part of the handle were stained an ancient, rusted red.

"That's a strange-looking knife," said Dr. Patel. She had the branches spread in front of her and was lining them up, like a child playing with twigs.

"It is," I answered. "The Victorians often used very specific tools. I wonder if it had some sort of specialized use in the kitchen..."

I took a picture of it with my phone. "Can I use your Wi-Fi? I want to do a Google search, but it says I need a password. I can't get a cell signal down here."

"You won't, in the basement of one of these old buildings," said Dr. Patel. She pulled off one glove and held out her hand. "Here, I'll type in our guest password."

When she handed the phone back to me, I did a Google image search.

And there it was, the same knife, with the wicked curved blade, although without the bloodstains of course. The Orchardman's Best Friend, regularly

£35, on sale for £25 until Thursday, Home Orchard and Garden Supply, Berkshire. By Appointment to Her Majesty the Queen.

"It's a pruning knife," I said. I stared down at the image on my screen, then showed it to Dr. Patel. I think, at that moment, the truth was just beginning to sink in. "You see, he used to prune her..."

"Well, that makes sense," she said. She held up one of Daphne Merwin's branches. "These ends are cut, not broken. The... growths didn't break off during a fight. They were cut off, probably with a blade just like that." She peered at my phone screen, and then at the knife, with the intellectual curiosity of a born scientist who dissects reality for the sheer pleasure of understanding. I could not be quite so dispassionate, but whatever I was feeling, looking down at the weapon that had killed my great-great grandmother, I put aside for the moment. This was not the right time.

"Let me start at the beginning. You see, she left a diary..." I told Dr. Patel everything I had learned so far about Daphne and the Merwin household. "So he's pruning her," I concluded. "They quarrel, and he stabs her with the knife. All it would take is him going out again, maybe through the back door into the alley, then coming back half an hour later. Lucy Barker verifies the time of his arrival, identifies the knife as one of the kitchen knives, and tells the police about Alfred Potts's visit earlier that day. All it would take is Lucy lying for him."

"What happened to Lucy?" asked Dr. Patel.

"She died two years later, of a laudanum overdose. Accidentally—or so it was assumed at the time. Perhaps it was suicide—perhaps she felt guilty for her part in the murder? I suppose you could call her an accessory after the fact."

"Are you sure it was murder?" Dr. Patel tapped the papers piled on their plastic sleeve with one gloved finger. "The statement of Mrs. Polansky describes some sort of altercation. Perhaps he stabbed her on impulse? That would make it a case of manslaughter."

I stared down at the knife. "I don't suppose we'll ever know, for sure." Anyway, did that sort of legal distinction matter? Whether he had planned to do it or done it on the spur of the moment, Lewison had stabbed Daphne Merwin. I was sure of it.

"What happened to Professor Merwin after Eve's death?"

"He wasn't a professor—he just claimed to be. And he returned to America." As though nothing had happened, as though he could go on with his life. Yet that was what people did, wasn't it? Go on? Although Eve had not been able to...

"He must have been a clever, charming man, to attract two such women," said Dr. Patel. "But unscrupulous. Men like that often are."

"Why didn't the police officer who originally investigated see this?" I said. "It was right there in front of him."

Dr. Patel smiled—now she was the one lecturing a student. "One of the first things they teach us is that people don't see what's in front of them. They see what they expect to see. It's very hard to get beyond that."

"So we walk through a world already created by our preconceived notions?"

"Precisely."

Precisely was also how she packed all the evidence back in the box. This, I thought, was Daphne Merwin's coffin, as much as the one in which her body lay decomposing.

That was in Highgate Cemetery. It was the next to last place I would visit in London.

"I'll look for your book," said Dr. Patel as we shook hands. Mine felt odd from being inside those gloves.

"I'll send you a copy," I said. And when I do, I thought, you'll see yourself in the acknowledgments. Thank you, Dr. Patel, for showing me what I could not have seen on my own: who killed Daphne Merwin.

—*The British Freak Show at the Fin-de-Siècle*, D.M. Levitt, Ph.D.

Dr. Daphne M. Levitt, PhD
Assistant Professor, Department of English
University of Southern Vermont, Ascutney Campus
Ascutney Falls, Vermont 05001, USA

Dear Dr. Levitt:

I was so interested in the case of Daphne Merwin that I decided to look into it a little further. I hope you will forgive me, but your great-great grandmother was a fascinating woman. I did not find anything pertinent in our archives, so I asked a colleague of mine at the British Library to investigate as well. He suggested that if Daphne Merwin, or Daisy Potts, was living in Spitalfields at the time she was discovered by Lewison Merwin, she might be on the rolls of one of the poorhouses in that area. Most of those documents have been lost, so I did not have much confidence that he would be able to find anything. However, after several weeks, he sent me the following scan of a page dated March, 1880 from the record books of the St. Joseph Street Charitable Institution. If you look approximately a third of the way down the page, you will find the following entry:

Alfred Potts, 17 years of age, able-bodied workman, and sister Daisy, 15 years of age, cripple.

I believe this entry refers to your great-great grandmother and her brother Alfred. It would be a great coincidence if there were an Alfred and Daisy Potts of exactly the right age, siblings and the sister described as a 'cripple,' in Spitalfields at that time. I hope this helps with your research. I very much look forward to reading your book!

Sincerely yours,

Dr. Devi Patel, MSc, PhD

Junior Archivist II

Metropolitan Police

DEAR DAFFY,

I read your book, and the chapter on Daphne just made me cry! I recommended it to the book club, and we're supposed to talk about it next Thursday. Honestly, I don't know how I'm going to get through the meeting without starting up again—I'd better bring a box of tissues. She was a remarkable woman, and Lewison was just rotten to her. Though I hate to think he was a murderer—maybe it was an impulse, as Dr. Patel said? Although I don't know if that makes it any better. And I can't help blaming that Eve person for helping him, although I'm sure Lewison was just as bad to her as he was to Daphne. It's too bad we have to be related to him too, hunh? But that's how families are, I guess—a mixed bag.

You inspired me to go through Grandma's boxes up in the attic. I know I should have done it sooner, but it took me a long time just to get over her being gone. Even now, I keep expecting her to be in the kitchen baking biscuits, or in the living room watching her soaps. I guess your mother never leaves you, not really. When your dad comes into a room and catches me just staring out the window, he says, "You're thinking about Judy again, aren't you? I sure do miss her cooking." Even he says she was the best mother-in-law, and I don't know how he could give a bigger compliment than that!

Anyway, yesterday I finally went through all those boxes, and I found an old photo album I'd never seen before, under a prayer book. It's filled with photos from her dad's family, and you know she never talked to him after he forbade her to marry grandpa. Well, you won't believe what I found, tucked right into the back—it's a picture of Daphne Merwin! That photo you used in the book, the one you found on eBay a couple of months ago and wanted to buy, except you said it was too expensive. Well, here it is! I used a photo envelope so it wouldn't get bent and paid the earth for special delivery—you know how those postal people are! You send a package through the regular mail, and it's like wolves tore it apart.

It's a real original photo! The name of the studio is printed on the bottom, and on the back you'll see some words—I'm pretty sure Daisy wrote them. It looks like a child's writing, though children wrote so much more neatly back then, and with real ink! It says, *My beloved Mama.* Isn't that sweet? There, I'm going to cry again. I'm glad her daughter remembered her. Seriously, someone should make a movie based on Daphne's life story—except I wouldn't want everyone to know my great-grandpa was a murderer. Your book is fine, of course—it's all scholarly, with footnotes. But seeing it on a screen would be different.

I heard it snowed again up there—down here the crocuses are out, and Dad is complaining that he'll have to start mowing the grass soon! Tabby brought in a baby bird—we put it out on the back porch and half an hour later it was gone. I don't know if it got away, or if Tabby found it again. Drat that cat! That's all the news from down here. I hope you get some time to rest, with all those students—you work too hard, sweetie! Dad sends a big hug, and we're looking forward to seeing you this summer.

Lots of love, and we're so proud of your book, Mom

* * *

AFTER MEETING WITH Dr. Patel, I stopped at a Costa for a chai latte and a cheese and chutney sandwich, then took the Northern Line up to Highgate Cemetery, where I knew Daphne Merwin was buried. My visit to the Metropolitan Police Archives had taken longer than anticipated, and I had just enough time to find her grave, then take some photographs for this book. Her gravestone was a simple obelisk, on the pedestal of which was written,

Daphne Merwin

The Living Dryad

1865-1888

Long ago, someone had planted a vine at its base, and it had grown up over the obelisk, almost obscuring it in dense, shrubby growth. That day, the vine was covered in green leaves and small white flowers. I wondered if Daphne would have liked that, if she would have considered it some sort of tribute.

It was getting late: the shadows of gravestones lay dark across the paths. So I took the tube back to central London. In the university dorm room I was renting for two weeks, I typed up the notes from my visit to the archives and started packing my suitcase. The next day would be my last in London.

That night I dreamed I was lecturing my students, back in Vermont. But when I looked down at myself, I realized I had become a tree. They did not seem to notice, typing on their laptops as usual, although I was standing at the front of the lecture hall covered with bark, waving leafy green branches instead of arms. I remember the lecture was about Nathaniel Hawthorne.

The next day, I slept through my alarm and woke up with a headache. I took two Advil and finished packing for that evening's flight back to New York, where I had an appointment at the Barnum and Bailey Museum Archives, which contain a collection of Lewison Merwin's papers and paraphernalia. I had already visited the Barnum and Bailey Museum once: there I had seen a transcript of Lewison Merwin's lecture, taken in shorthand during one of Daphne's performances, as well as letters and telegrams. After his death,

Daisy Merwin sent all of his papers to the museum, but she kept the diary—the archivist there had not even known Daphne Merwin's diary existed. (My family has agreed to loan it to the museum for a Merwin exhibit, focusing on both Daphne and Lewison, to coincide with the publication of this book.) Now, however, I would be looking at them from a different perspective. Now I would know how Daphne had died. Perhaps I would see things in Lewison's papers that I had not seen the last time. After that, I would go back to Vermont, where I was scheduled to teach Classics of English and American Literature II during the second summer session. And I had a book to finish.

But that morning, my last in London, I would visit the Royal College of Surgeons.

It was a gray, wet day, typical for summer in London. I got off the tube at Holborn and walked to Lincoln's Inn Fields, then to the imposing gray building with its classical portico and Latin engraving across the front. There was a smaller sign for the Hunterian Museum, where I was headed. Once you enter the Royal College of Surgeons, you go up one flight of stairs, and there, to your right, is the Hunterian Museum: a collection of anatomical specimens and curiosities that dates to the late 1700s. You enter, expecting oak cabinets and dim lighting, as it might have looked in the eighteenth and nineteenth centuries, but no. What you see are glass cases, all around you, brightly lit as though you were in a dissecting room. The cases are filled with glass bottles, as anatomy students would have seen them a hundred years ago. Some of them still have their original labels, with Latin names written in ornate script. They contain animal embryos preserved at every stage of development, tumorous growths of various sorts, the brain of the mathematician Charles Babbage. There are skeletons, from a bat's to the tall bones of Charles Byrne, the Irish Giant. The exhibit is arranged on two floors around a central space that allows you to see from the top of the museum to its bottom, so you can walk around and around that macabre display.

At the back, there is a small gallery, a dark alcove of paneled wood hung with paintings: some of prominent scientists, some of freak show performers. It is an unintentional reminder that to many Victorians, genius was a frightening, freakish quality—as much a deformity, in its own way, as a beard on a woman. Eng and Chang are in that alcove, as is Julia Pastrana. In a dark corner, under a prominent surgeon, are two paintings, hanging side by side. I had deliberately left them for my last day, not wanting them to affect my interpretation of the research. Now here they were, and here I was. Under one, on a brass plaque, was engraved *The Living Dryad*. Under the other, *The Primitive Eve*. Both were by the same artist, both set in an idealized natural landscape that resembled the Royal Botanical Gardens. In one, a woman dressed in a classical Greek chiton held up her arms, which were also branches—recognizably Daphne Merwin, although more arboreal. She even had leaves at the ends of her fingers. In the other crouched a woman dressed only in a loincloth, covered with light brown hair. Lucy Barker had died and been buried in France, but here she was reunited with Daphne. The both of them together, counterparts of each other, as Lewison had wanted them in his show.

I stood there, looking at them for a while... not sure, as a modern woman, what to think of that tragedy, long ago. That tangled relationship between two women, and the man who had helped and used them both. Who had been, directly or indirectly, responsible for their deaths. I blamed Lewison for what had happened. His was, after all, the hand that held the knife. But like everything else in life, it was more complicated than I had assumed it would be. History always is.

But I could not stay long. I had a plane to catch, a life in America to return to.

On my way out, the front desk attendant said, "I hope you enjoyed the museum! Bit gruesome for some..."

"I enjoyed it very much," I replied, and put my last British coins in the donation jar. I still had ten pounds in notes, which would be enough to buy me coffee and a magazine at Heathrow before I boarded the plane for home.

If we had been living in the late nineteenth century, you and I, we might have paid a shilling or two to see the human wonders of the age: the Bear Woman, the Dog-Faced Boy, the Elephant Man, the Primitive Eve, the Living Dryad. A century later, we must rediscover Julia Pastrana, Fedor Jeftichew, Joseph Merrick, Lucy Barker, and Daphne Merwin: the human beings behind the labels and advertisements. Who were they? What did they think? How did they feel? By and large, they left no records, although perhaps there are papers moldering somewhere, like Daphne's diary. We owe it to them to learn as much about their histories as possible. That has been, in part, the aim of this book: to see beyond social and ideological constructs and recover, to whatever extent possible, the voices of the voiceless. To let the spectacles speak for themselves.

—*The British Freak Show at the Fin-de-Siècle*, D.M. Levitt, Ph.D.

BUT DO THEY actually see me?

Or only the creature he has created? To them, I am merely a curiosity, and sometimes I wish that I could speak—he has told me not to speak, that only he is to speak, ever. My speaking would destroy the illusion. But I wish to tell them... what? That I am real, flesh and blood, not wood. That I am a woman, not a fairy tale. I have a soul, as they do.

Would they listen?

You, beyond the lights, I would say. When you look at me, what do you see? When I speak, what do you hear?

FAIRY TALE OF WOOD STREET
Caitlín R. Kiernan

Caitlín R. Kiernan (www.caitlinrkiernan) is a two-time recipient of both the World Fantasy and Bram Stoker awards, and the *New York Times* has declared her "one of our essential writers of dark fiction." Her recent novels include *The Red Tree* and *The Drowning Girl: A Memoir,* and, to date, her short stories have been collected in fourteen volumes, including *Tales of Pain and Wonder, A is for Alien, The Ammonite Violin & Others,* the World Fantasy Award winning *The Ape's Wife and Other Stories,* and *Dear Sweet Filthy World.* Currently she's editing her fifteenth and sixteenth collections— *Houses Under the Sea: Mythos Tales* and *The Dinosaur Tourist.* She has recently concluded *Alabaster,* her award-winning, three-volume graphic novel for Dark Horse Comics. Her most recent books are novella *Agents of Dreamland* and an expanded 'Director's Cut' of her World Fantasy Award nominated novella, *Black Helicopters.* Kiernan is currently working on her next novel, *Interstate Love Song,* and on a new novella for *Tor.com, The Tindalos Asset.* She lives in Providence, Rhode Island.

1.

I'M LYING IN bed, forgetting a dream of some forested place, a dream that is already coming apart behind my waking eyes like wet tissue between my fingers, and Hana gets up and walks across the bedroom to stand before the tall vanity mirror. The late morning sun is bright in the room, bright summer sun, July sun, and I know by the breeze through the open window that the coming afternoon will be cool. I can smell the flowers on the table by the bed, and I can smell the bay, too, riding the breeze, that faintly muddy, faintly salty, very faintly fishy smell that never ceases to make me think of the smell of sex. I watch Hana for a moment, standing there nude before the looking glass, her skin like porcelain, her eyes like moss on weathered slabs of shale, her hair the same pale shade of yellow as corn meal. And I'm thinking, *Roll over and shut your eyes, because if you keep on watching you'll only get horny again, and you'll call her back to bed, and she'll come, and neither of us will get anything at all done today. And you have that meeting at two, and she has shopping and a trip to the post office and the library to return overdue books, so just roll over and don't see her. Think about the fading wet tissue shreds of the dream, instead.* And that's exactly what I mean to do, to lie there with my eyes shut, pretending to doze while she gets dressed. But then I see her tail.

"Look at us," she says, "sleeping half the day away. It's almost noon. You should get up and get dressed. I need a shower."

Her tail looks very much like the tail of a cow. At least, that is the first thing that comes to mind, the Holstein and Ayrshire cows my grandfather raised when I was a girl and my family lived way off in western Massachusetts, almost to the New York state line, the cattle he raised for milk for the cheese he made. Hana's tail hangs down a little past the bend of her knees, and there's a tuft of hair on the end of it that is almost the exact same blonde as the hair on her head. Maybe a little darker, but not by much. It occurs to me, dimly, that I ought to be shocked or maybe even afraid. That I ought, at the very least, be surprised, but the truth is that I'm not any of those things. Mostly, I'm trying to figure out why I never noticed it in all the months since we met and she moved into my apartment here in the old house on the east end of Wood Street.

"I smell like sex," Hana says, and she sniffs at her unshaved armpits. Her tail twitches, sways side to side a moment, and then is still again.

"Maybe you should just forget about the shower and come back to bed," I say, and while the sight of her tail didn't come as a surprise, that does, those words from my mouth, when what I was just thinking—before I saw the tail—was how we both have entirely too much to do today to have spent the whole morning fucking. I realize that my hand is between my legs, that I'm touching myself, and I force myself to stop. But my fingers are damp, and there's a flutter in my belly, just below my navel.

"You don't really want me to do that," she says, glancing back over her shoulder. And I think, *No I don't. I want to get up and have a bath and get dressed, and I want to forget that I ever saw that she has a tail. If I can forget I saw it, maybe it won't be there the next time I see her naked. Maybe it's only a temporary, transitory sort of thing, like a bad cold or a wart.*

"I was thinking we could go to the movies tonight," she says, turning to face the mirror again.

"Were you?" I ask her.

"I was. There's something showing at the Avon that I'd like to see, and I think tonight is the last night. This is Wednesday, right?"

"I believe so," I reply, but I have to think for a moment to be sure, to make it past the sight of her tail and the wetness between my thighs and the dregs of the dream and the smell of Narragansett Bay getting in through the open bedroom window. "Yes," I say. "Today is Wednesday."

"We don't have to go," she says. "Not if you don't want to. But I was thinking we could maybe get a bite to eat, maybe sushi, and make the early show. If your meeting doesn't run too long. If there isn't something afterwards that you have to do."

"No," I say. "I don't think so. I should be done by five. By five-thirty at the latest."

Her tail twitches again, and then it swings from side to side several times, and once more I'm reminded of my grandfather's milk cows. It doesn't seem at all like a flattering comparison, and so I try to remember what other sort of animals have tails like that, long tails with a tuft right at the end. But I'm unable to think of any others except cows.

"Are you feeling well?" she asks, watching me from the mirror, and I catch the faintest glimmer of worry in her green-grey eyes.

"I'm fine," I reply. "I had a strange dream, that's all. One I'm having a little trouble shaking off." And I almost add, *I had a dream that you were a woman who didn't have a tail, and that I lived in a world where women don't, as a rule, have tails.*

"My mother used to call that being dreamsick," says Hana, "when you wake up from a dream, but it stays with you for a long time afterwards, and you have trouble thinking about anything else, almost like you're still asleep and dreaming."

"I'm fine," I tell her again.

"You look a little pale, that's all."

"I never get any sun. You know, I read somewhere online that ninety percent of Americans suffer from vitamin D deficiency because they don't get enough sun, because they spend too little time out of doors."

"We should go to the shore this weekend," she says. "I know you hate the summer people, but we should go, anyway."

"Maybe we'll do that," I tell her, and then Hana smiles, and she leaves me alone in the bedroom and goes to take her shower.

2.

AS IT HAPPENS, we don't go for sushi, because by the time I'm done with work and make it back to our apartment on Wood Street, Hana has read something somewhere about people in the Mekong Delta dying at an alarming rate from ingesting liver flukes from raw fish. I can't really blame her for losing interest in sushi after that. Instead, we go to an Indian place on Thayer, only a block from the theater, and we share curried goat and saag paneer with ice water and icy bottles of Kingfisher lager. While we're eating, it begins to rain, and neither one of us has brought an umbrella. We each make do with half the *Providence Journal*. The newsprint runs and stains our fingers and stains our clothes and leaves a lead-blue streak on the left side of Hana's face that I wipe away with spit and the pad of my left index finger. The theater lobby is bright and warm and smells pleasantly of popcorn, and standing there while Hana buys our tickets it occurs to me that most of the day and part of the evening has gone by without me thinking about Hana's tail.

"Would you like something?" she asks, looking back at me, then pointing at the rows of overpriced candy behind glass.

"No," I say. "I'm fine. I think I ate too much back at the restaurant."

"Suit yourself," she says, and then she asks the boy working the concessions for a box of Good & Plenty and a large Dr. Pepper.

For just a moment, it seems that I must only have imagined that business with Hana's tail. It seems I must surely have awakened from an uneasy dream, which I have since almost entirely forgotten, and being only half awake—half awake at best, my head still mired half in the dream—I saw a tail where there was not actually a tail to see. And here in the theater lobby, my belly full and my hair damp from a summer rain, it seems a far more reasonable explanation than the alternative, that my girlfriend has a tail. I look at her tight jeans, and there's plainly no room in there for the tail that I thought I saw, the tail that reminded me so much of the tails of my grandfather's cows.

Hana pays for her soft drink and for the candy, and I follow her out of the bright lobby and into the dimly lit auditorium. The Avon is an old theater, and it has the smell of an old theater, that peculiar, distinctive blend of sweet and musty and very faintly sour that I can't recall ever having smelled anywhere else *but* old movie theaters. It's a smell of dust and fermentation, an odor that simultaneously comforts me and makes me think someone could probably do a better job of keeping the floors and the seats clean. But when a theater has been in continuous operation since 1936, like this one has, well, that's more than eighty years of spilled cola and fingers greasy from popcorn and Milk Duds getting dropped and ground into the carpet in the darkness when no one can clearly see where they're putting their feet. We take our seats, not too near the screen and not too far away, and it occurs to me for the first time that I don't actually know what we've come to see.

"I think you'll like it," Hana says, peeling the cellophane off her box of Good & Plenty. She drops the plastic wrap onto the floor. In the past, I've asked her please not to do that, but she only pointed out that someone gets paid to pick it back up again and then she did it, anyway.

"I don't even know the title," I say, wondering if she told me, and I just can't remember that she told me. "I don't know the director."

"It's German," Hana says. "Well, I mean the director is German, and I think some of the funding came from Deutscher Filmförderfonds, and it's set in the Black Mountains, but it's actually an English language film. I think you'll like it. I think it did well at Cannes and Sundance." But she doesn't tell me the title. She doesn't tell me the name of the director. I try to recall walking towards the theater from the Indian restaurant and looking up to see what was on the theater's marquee, but I can't. Not clearly, anyway. I rub at my eyes a moment, and Hana asks me if I'm getting a headache.

"No," I tell her. "I'm just trying to remember something. My memory's for shit today." I don't tell her that I'm wondering if forty-four is too young to be displaying symptoms of early onset Alzheimer's.

There are a few other people in the theater with us. Not many, but a few. I hadn't expected a crowd. After all, it's a rainy Wednesday night. No one is sitting very near us. Some of the people are staring at their phones, their faces underlit by liquid-crystal touchscreen glow. Here and there, others whisper to one another in the way that people whisper in theaters and libraries and meeting halls and other places where you've been taught since childhood to keep your voice down. I stare across the tops of the rows of seats dividing us from the small stage and the tall red curtain concealing the screen. Hana takes a pink Good & Plenty from the box, and she offers it to me.

"No, I'm fine," I say.

"Woolgathering," she says, and I say, "A penny for your thoughts," and she says, "No, I asked first." Then she puts the candy-coated licorice into her mouth and chews and waits for whatever it is she thinks that I'm supposed to say.

"It's nothing," I say.

"It's something," she replies. "I can tell by the lines at the corners of your eyes and that little wrinkle on your forehead."

I'm trying to come up with something to tell her that isn't *This morning, I saw your tail,* or at least *I think I saw your tail,* when I'm rescued by the curtains parting and the screen flickering to life, by giant boxes of cartoon popcorn and cartoon chocolate bars and a cartoon hot dog marching by and singing "Let's All Go To the Lobby."

"Isn't there a word for that?" Hana asks me, shaking a couple more Good & Plenty out into her palm.

"A word for what?"

"For anthropomorphized food that wants you to eat it. Like there's a word for buildings in the shape of whatever's being sold there."

"I didn't know there was a word for that," I reply.

"Mimetic architecture," she says. "I remember that from an advertising and mass media class I had in college. And I thought there was also a word for food that wants you to eat it. You know, like Charlie the Tuna. Like that," she says and points at the screen.

"If there is, I don't think that I've ever heard it."

And then the ad for the concessions stand ends and the first trailer starts, and it occurs to me that I have to piss rather urgently. I should have done it before I sat down, but I was probably too busy trying to decide whether or not I truly did see Hana's tail that morning. The first trailer is for some sort of science-fiction comedy about a grumpy old man and a wise-cracking robot driving across America, and I tell Hana that I'll be right back.

"You should have gone before we got our seats," she says. "Hurry, or you'll miss the beginning. I hate when you miss the beginnings of things."

"I'll be right back," I tell her again. "I won't miss the beginning. I promise."

"You say that," and she reminds me how, last spring, I missed the first ten minutes of *Auntie Mame* when it was screened at RISD, and how I missed even more of the start of the last Quentin Tarantino film, even though we'd gotten tickets to a special 70mm screening. And then she tells me to go on, but not to dawdle and not to decide I need to go outside for a cigarette. I assure her that I won't do either, and I get up and leave her sitting there.

3.

AT THE BACK of the auditorium, there's a very narrow flight of stairs that leads up to a tiny landing and to an antique candy machine and two restroom doors, Gents and Ladies, and to the door of the projection booth. The candy machine is the sort that was already becoming uncommon when I was a little kid, the sort that takes a quarter or two and you pull a knob and out comes your Hershey Bar or whatever you've selected. The machine is now undoubtedly a museum piece, and even though there's no 'out of order' sign on it and the coin slot hasn't been taped over, I can't believe the thing actually works. I've never tested it to find out. The candy wrappers displayed inside look dusty, their colors faded, but maybe it's just that the glass fronting the machine has grown cloudy over the decades. Maybe it's only an illusion, and the candy is restocked every day or so.

And then I think about Hana telling me to please hurry and not to dawdle, and so I push open the door marked Ladies and the old theater smell is immediately replaced with an old theater restroom smell, which isn't all that different from the smell of most public restrooms, at least the ones that are kept reasonably clean and have been around for a while. The women's restroom is so small that I can imagine a claustrophobic preferring to piss themselves rather than spend any time at all in here, certainly not as much time as would be necessary to relieve oneself. There are two stalls, though there's hardly room enough for one, and the walls are painted a color that can't seem to decide whether to be beige or some muddy shade of yellow. The floor is covered in a mosaic of tiny black and white ceramic hexagonal tiles.

Just inside the door, there's a mirror so large it seems entirely out of proportion with so small a room, and I pause and squint back at myself. There's a smudge of newsprint on my chin that Hana hadn't bothered to tell me about, and I rub at it until it's mostly not there anymore. And then, staring at my reflection, I think of watching Hana's reflection in our bedroom vanity mirror that morning, and I think of her tail, and I wonder if maybe it was only some trick of the late morning light. I also wonder what she'd have said if I'd had the nerve to just come right out and ask her about it:

"How is it you've never before mentioned that you have a tail?"

"How is it that you've never noticed?"

"I don't know. I can't say. Maybe it wasn't there until now."

"Or maybe whenever you're fucking me, you're too busy thinking about fucking someone else to pay that much attention. One of your exes, maybe. The one who went away to Seattle to go to clown school, for example."

"It wasn't Seattle, it was Portland."

"Like there's a difference. And who does that, anyway? What sort of grown-up adult woman quits her job and leaves her girlfriend to run off and join the circus?"

"Well, even if that were true—and it most certainly isn't—no matter who I might have been fantasizing about all those times, I think I wouldn't have been so consistently and completely distracted that I would have failed to notice that you have a tail."

"Sure. You say that. But remember when I stopped shaving under my arms, and it took you a month to even notice?"

I suspect it would have gone like that, or it would have gone worse.

There's no one else in the restroom, so I have my choice of the two stalls, and I choose the one nearest to the door, which also happens to be slightly larger than the one farthest from the door. I go in, latch it, pull down my pants, and sit there counting the hexagonal tiles at my feet while I piss and try to remember the name of the movie we've come to see on this rainy Wednesday night, because at least if I'm doing that, if my mind is occupied, maybe I won't be thinking about Hana's tail. I'm just about to tear off a piece of the stiff and scratchy toilet paper from the roll on the wall, when I hear a bird. And not just any bird, but what I am fairly certain is the cawing of a raven. Or at least a crow. My first thought is that I'd never before noticed how clearly sound carries through the floor up from the theater auditorium below, and my second thought is that, were that the case, that I was only hearing a raven from one of the movie trailers, I ought to be hearing other things, as well.

Sound can do funny things, I think. And then I think, *For that matter, so can morning light and shadow in a bedroom when you're still groggy from a dream and from sex.* Neither strikes me as a very convincing explanation.

I hear the bird again, and this time I'm quite sure that I'm not hearing a recorded snippet of film soundtrack, not Dolby stereo, but something that is alive and there in the room with me. I wipe and get to my feet, pull up my pants, and then hesitate, one hand on the stall door's latch and the other on the handle. My heart is beating a little too fast and my mouth has gone dry and cottony. I want a cigarette, and I want to be back downstairs with Hana. I realize that I haven't flushed. I'm about to turn around and do just that, when there's another sound, a dry, rustling, fluttering sort of a sound that might be wings or might be something else altogether. And suddenly I feel very goddamn stupid, like I'm five years old and afraid to step on a crack or walk under a ladder or something like that. I take a deep breath, and I open the door. And I see that there's a huge black bird watching me from the mirror, standing on the floor, the floor in the looking-glass version of the Avon's women's room, glaring up at me with beady golden eyes. It looks angry, that bird. It looks dangerous. It occurs to me that I never had realized just how big ravens are. This one's as big as a tomcat, a very big tomcat, and it hops towards me, and I take a step backwards and bump into the stall. Then I look down and realize that there's no corresponding bird standing on the floor in front of me to be casting the reflection, and when I look back up at the mirror again, there's no bird there either.

I think again about early onset Alzheimer's disease.

And then I flush the toilet and wash my hands with gritty pink powder and go back downstairs.

4.

BY THE TIME I get back downstairs, the feature has already started, and despite the bird in the mirror and the very real concern that I may be rapidly losing my mind, that I may have lost it already, I'm mostly worrying about how annoyed with me Hana's going to be. "Just like *Auntie Mame*," she'll say. "Just like *The Hateful Eight* all over again." And it's not as if I can use the phantom raven as an excuse. Well, I could, but I know myself well enough to know that I won't. So long as I keep these visions or hallucinations or illusions to myself, they will seem somehow less solid, less real, less *tangible*. The moment I cast them into language and share them with someone else any possibility that I can simply put it all behind me and get on with my life and have, for example, a perfectly ordinary Thursday, goes right out the window.

The movie we've come to see, whatever its title, is in black and white.

I don't immediately return to my seat and to Hana. Instead, I stand behind the back row, where no one happens to be sitting, and I watch the movie. Up there on the screen there is a forest primeval rendered in infinite shades of grey, dominated by towering pines and spruces that rise up towards an all but unseen night sky, a forest that seems to have been tasked with the unenviable job of keeping Heaven from sagging and crushing Earth flat. Winding its way between the trees there's a brook, the surface glinting faintly in the stingy bit of moonlight leaking down through the boughs, and bordering the brook are boulders and the broken trunks of trees that have fallen and are now quietly rotting away. Here and there, a log fords the brook. There's the sound of wind and calls of night birds. And in the distance, there's a bright flicker, like a campfire.

I'm reminded of two things, almost simultaneously, as near to simultaneously as anyone may have two distinct and independent thoughts. I am reminded of the illustrations of Gustave Doré and of the dream that

I woke from just that morning, my own half forgotten dream of a forested place, the dream I immediately tried to lose in sex. I feel the pricking of gooseflesh up and down my arms and legs, and I shiver, and I hug myself as if a sudden draft has blown by, as if maybe I'm standing directly beneath an air-conditioning vent. I think, *You don't have to watch this, whatever this is. You can turn and walk out into the lobby and wait there until it's over or until Hana comes looking for you, whichever happens first.* And then I tell myself how very silly I'm being, that coincidences occur, that they are inevitable aspects of reality, and how that's all this is, a coincidence. At most, it might be chalked up to an instance of synchronicity, a coincidence rendered meaningful only by my subjective emotional reaction and entirely devoid of any causal relationship or connection between my dream and the film, much less any connection with the raven in the restroom or with Hana's tail, both of which I likely only imagined, anyway. This is what I tell myself, and it does nothing at all to dispel my uneasiness and the cliché chill along my spine and down in my gut.

The camera wanders through the forest, and there are close ups of a sleeping doe and her fawn and of a watchful owl and of a hungry, hunting fox. It springs, and the scream of a rabbit briefly shatters the tranquil night. My mouth has gone very dry, and I lick my lips, wishing I had a swallow of something, anything at all. Hana's Dr. Pepper would do just fine.

A woman's voice says, "It must be lonely work," and it takes me a second or two to realize that the voice is part of the movie and not someone standing there beside me.

The film jump cuts then to a wide clearing and a small camp somewhere deep in the forest, and I think that this must be the source of the distant flickering I saw earlier on. At the center of the camp, surrounded by ragged tree stumps, there's a high conical billet formed from dozens of immense logs stood on their ends and leaning in one against all the others, covered over in places with a layer of soil and chunks of turf, forming a sort of smoldering bonfire or oven. There seems only to be a single man watching the fire, and he's standing with his back to the billet, gazing towards the camera, into the ancient forest ringing the clearing. The man is holding some manner of old-fashioned rifle, a flintlock maybe. I don't know shit about guns.

He says, "Who was that? Who goes there?"

And the woman replies, "No one who means you harm. Only someone passing by who thought you might be happy for the company."

"I'm not alone," says the man.

"I know," answers the woman. "But all your companions are sleeping."

"I could wake them quickly enough," he tells her, "if the need arises."

"Of course," she says. "And you have your rifle. And there must be hounds nearby to keep away the wolves."

"Yes," says the man. "There are hounds, three of them, and I'm a *very* good shot. You'd do well to keep that in mind."

"Naturally," says the woman, and the camera pans around as she emerges from between the boles of two especially enormous pines. The woman is smiling for the man, and she's dressed in a traditional Bavarian dirndl that reaches down almost to the ground. Standing there in the Avon theater, I have no idea that's what her dress is called, a dirndl. I'll only find that out later on, by checking with Wikipedia, which describes it as 'a light circular cut dress, gathered at the waist, that falls below the knee.' She's also wearing a bonnet. The woman is tall to the point that she could fairly be called lanky, and her face is plain and angular, and her ears are a little too big. But despite all of this, I think she may be one of the most singularly beautiful women I have ever seen. I stop hugging myself and, instead, rest my hands on the back of the theater seat in front of me. The worn velveteen feels like moss.

"It must be lonely work," the woman says again. "The life of a charcoal burner, all these long, cold nights spent so far from your home and your wife and your children."

"How do you know I have a wife and children?" he asks.

"Well, don't you?" she replies. "What an awful waste it would be if you didn't. So, I prefer to assume that you do."

The man has dark eyes, a nose that looks as if it has been broken at least once, and there is a ragged scar that bisects his lower lip and runs the length of his chin down onto his throat. He has the face of someone who is still young, but also the face of someone who has been made prematurely old by the circumstances of his life, by the many hardships and losses endured and written in the lines and creases and angles of skin and bones. It's a curiously effective paradox, not so different from the woman who is beautiful despite her awkwardness (or, perhaps, because of it).

"I know who you are," says the man warily. "My grandmother taught me about you when I was still a boy. I know what you are."

"Then you also know I mean you no harm."

"I know the stories I was taught," he replies, neither agreeing nor disagreeing.

"Then you know that this forest is *my* forest," she tells him, and now the woman takes another step nearer to the man. I realize for the first time that she's barefoot. "You know that these trees are *my* trees. If your grandmother was a wise woman, she taught you that much, surely."

The man, the charcoal burner, crosses himself, and the woman frowns the sort of frown that, more than anything else, is an expression of disappointment, as if she'd hoped for more from this man. As if she'd had cause to expect more.

"After a hard winter," she says, "I may bring prosperity, and for so little a price as a loaf of fresh bread or a hen's egg left at the edge of your fields."

The man nods, and he says, "That is true, so far as it goes. But you also bring hardship when the mood suits you. You cause hunters to lose their way on clearly marked trails and to miss shots that ought to have found their marks. You lead children from their homes and into the dens of hungry animals, and you drown swimmers whom you fancy have slighted you in some small way or another."

"These are the sorts of tales you were taught?" asks the woman, who I realize now, and must have known all along, is not simply a human woman.

"They are. And there are others."

"Tell me," she says, and so the charcoal burner tells a story about a young man who was walking in the forest late one summer afternoon and happened to catch the briefest glimpse of the woman bathing in a spring. At once, he became so infatuated with her that he withdrew into himself and would speak to no one and would not eat or drink or care for himself in any way.

"He only lived a few weeks," says the man. "He was a man my grandmother knew when she was a girl, the son of the cooper in the village where she grew up."

"I don't mean to call her a liar," says the beautiful, awkward woman in the dirndl, "but I would have you know your grandmother's tale was only half the truth of the matter. Yes, a cooper's son from her village saw me bathing, and yes, he wasted away because I wished it so. But she did *not* tell you all the tale. She did not say that after he had discovered the spring where I bathe, he returned with iron horseshoes and used them to lay a trap, for *his* grandmother had taught him how cold iron undoes me. She did not tell you how when I was defenseless the cooper's son raped me and cut off a lock of my hair to keep as a souvenir. I do not mean to call your grandmother a liar, but a story told the wrong way round is not the truth."

The woman takes another step nearer the charcoal burner, and this time he takes a step backwards towards the smoldering billet, yielding a foot of earth. And I want now to look away from the screen, though I would not yet be entirely able to explain just exactly why. But this pretend movie forest is too familiar, and I can't shake the feeling that I've heard this woman's voice before. But I do not look away. I want to search for the spot where Hana is sitting, but I don't. I stand there, and I watch. I stand there, and I listen.

"There is another story I know," the charcoal burner says, and I can tell he's trying hard to sound brave, and I can also hear the fear in his voice. Whatever confidence he might have had in his ability to hold this strange woman at bay is withering. Whatever faith he had is leaving him. "A story," he says, "in which you came down out of your wood on a night when the moon was new and the sky was dark save starlight, and you sat beneath the window of a mother nursing her newborn daughter, her first born. She sang lullabies to the baby, but you sang, too, and your song was so much fairer than the mother's that it was as if you alone were singing. Your melody took root in the mind of the infant, and, as she grew, it twisted her, shaping her to your own purposes. The girl became wicked, and where she walked wheat would not grow, and if she looked upon cows and goats their milk would turn sour and curdle in their udders. She was always singing in a tongue that no one knew, and they say that her songs drove dogs mad and could summon flies and toads."

"And what became of this poor unfortunate?" asks the woman.

"What finally became of her," replies the man, "is that she was driven away from her home for being a witch, turned out into the forest where she might do less harm to people who'd never done any harm to her. She was sent back to the huldra who had sung to her as a baby and so stolen her mind and soul. Not even a fortnight passed before her own brothers found her hanging from a tree, strangled by a noose woven from hair the color of water at the bottom of a well. They left her there for the crows and the maggots, fearing your wrath if they dared even to cut her down and bury her."

"And you believe this story?" the woman asks the charcoal burner.

And he answers her, "I've known stranger things to be true."

And I think, *Like a raven that is only a reflection in a mirror. Like seeing for the first time that the woman you love has a tail.*

Onscreen, the woman nods, and she says, "I was passing by, is all, and it occurred to me what lonely work your work must be and how perhaps you would be grateful for my company and for conversation. I meant no offense. I did not mean to cause you such alarm. I'll be on my way. But you'll remember this is *my* forest, and those are *my* trees."

And then the woman turns and walks away, disappearing back into the blackness between the trunks of the two especially enormous pines, and the charcoal burner is left standing alone in the clearing by his billet. The camera leaves him there, moving slowly around the circumference of the burning woodpile, coming at last to the corpses of three dogs, their necks broken and their throats torn open, as if by teeth and claws. Behind the murdered dogs is a lean-to where the bodies of the charcoal burner's companions lie slumped and mangled. It is a massacre.

And then Hana is standing beside me, and she's holding my hand, and she says, "I think we should go home now. I think it was a mistake, bringing you here."

"I'm sorry I took so long," I say.

"Don't worry about it this time. It's a silly sort of film, anyway."

Onscreen, black and white has given way to color, and the forest has been replaced by a modern city, the streets of Berlin crowded with automobiles and pedestrians all staring at their devices, instead of looking where it is they're going. A woman steps in front of a bus, and someone screams. Finally, I look away. Instead of the old theater smell, I can smell pine straw and wood smoke.

"I don't feel well," I say.

"You'll feel better soon," Hana tells me, and then she leads me out of the auditorium and back to the brightly lit lobby. Out on the street, it's stopped raining.

*   *   *

5.

ALL THE WAY back home to Wood Street, neither of us talks. The radio is on, and there's music, but it seems to come from somewhere very far off. The roads are still wet and shiny, the pavement glimmering dully beneath the garish new LED streetlights the city has recently installed. Hana drives, and I think about the movie and the raven and how I miss the soft yellow luminescence of the old sodium-vapor bulbs. From Thayer to Wickenden, then Point Street and over the bridge that crosses the filthy slate-colored river, then across the interstate to Westminster to Parade Street to home. I sit quietly and gaze out the passenger-side window, and I think how it is like finding your way back along a forest path. The street signs are breadcrumbs. The traffic lights are notches carved in the bark of living trees, electric talismans against losing one's way.

I have a beer, and then I have a second beer. I watch a few minutes of something on television, a news story on an outbreak of cholera in Yemen. Hana asks if I'm coming to bed, so I do. She's sitting up naked, with her back against the oak headboard, her knees pulled up close to her chest, her arms wrapped around them. Her tail hangs limply over the side of the bed. She watches me while I undress, and she waits there while I go to the bathroom and brush and floss my teeth.

When I come back into the bedroom, she says, "You haven't lost your mind. You're not insane."

I sit down on my side of the bed, and it creaks and pops. "We're going to have to bite the bullet and get a new box spring soon," I say. "This thing's over a decade old. One night, it's just going to collapse beneath us." I sit there staring at the open window, smelling all the fresh, clean smells that come after a summer rain, even in so dirty a city as Providence. I think there might yet be more rain to come before sunrise and we shouldn't fall sleep with the window open, so I should get up and close it. But I don't. I just sit there, my feet on the floor, my back to Hana.

"I know it must seem that way," she says, "like you're losing your mind, and I apologize for that. I genuinely do."

I think about all the things I could say in response, and then I think about just lying down and trying to sleep, and then I think about getting up, putting my clothes back on, and going for a long walk.

"I can be an awful coward," she says. "Using the theater that way, because I was afraid of telling you myself."

And I say, "When I was a little girl, maybe ten, maybe eleven years old, I got lost in the woods once. I'm not sure how it happened, but it did. I grew up in the country, and getting lost in the woods wasn't something I worried about. It wasn't something that my parents or my grandparents worried would ever happen to me, because they'd taught me how not to lose my way. But it did happen that once. I got turned around somehow, and I walked for hours and hours, and finally it started getting dark, and that's when I really got scared. As well as I knew those woods by day, I didn't know them at all by twilight. The shadows changed them, changed the trees and the rocks, changed the way sound moved along the valley between the mountains."

"What did you do?" Hana asks.

"What do frightened children lost in the forest pretty much always do?" I reply, trading her a question for a question.

"I've never been lost in a forest," she says.

"Well," I tell her, "they cry and they start calling out for help. Which is what I did. I shouted for my mother and my father and my grandparents. I even called out the names of our three dogs, hoping anyone at all would hear me and come find me and lead me safely back home."

"But they didn't," she says.

"No, *they* didn't. But someone else did." *And I want to ask her, Was that you or maybe a sister of yours? Was that you or some aunt or distant cousin?* But I don't. I stop staring at the window and stare at my feet, instead. "And I followed her back to the pasture at the edge of the road that led to our house, and I never saw her again. At some point, growing up, I decided I'd made her up. I decided that I'd been so afraid I'd invented her as some sort of coping mechanism that had allowed me push back the panic and calm down and remember my own way out of the woods. And I believed that, until this morning, until I dreamed about being lost and found and about a woman with a cow's tail and a raven on her shoulder who sang to me until I stopped crying."

"Would you like me to sing to you tonight?" she asks.

"Why? Am I lost again tonight?"

"No," she says, "not lost. Just a little turned about."

"Sometimes," I tell her, "I'd leave her little gifts. Offerings, I guess, to show my gratitude. A hardboiled egg, half a boloney sandwich, a Twinkie, and once I even left her one of my dolls."

"A doll with yellow hair," says Hana, "yellow like freshly ground cornmeal, and a blue and white checked gingham dress, like Dorothy wore in *The Wizard of Oz*."

"Yes," I say. "Like that. I left them in a hollow tree, like Boo Radley leaving gifts for Scout and Jem in *To Kill a Mockingbird*. I think I got the idea from the book, the idea to leave her gifts."

"And then you stopped," Hana says.

"We moved here. Dad got a different job, and we moved away."

For a moment or two, neither of us says anything more, and then Hana says that it's late and that we should probably get some sleep, that I have work tomorrow and she has errands to run. When I don't reply, when I neither agree nor disagree, she asks me if I'd prefer that she leaves and never comes back.

"If that's what you'd like, I'll go."

"No," I say, without having to consider my answer. "I wouldn't rather you leave."

"Then I'm glad," she says.

"It must be lonely work," I say, remembering the barefoot woman in the dirndl and the charcoal burner.

"Sometimes," Hana tells me, and then she tells me that we probably shouldn't fall asleep with the window open, that she's pretty sure there will be more rain tonight.

"What finally made you decide to show me?" I ask.

"I don't know," she replies. "I think I just got tired of keeping secrets."

I nod, because that seems like a fair enough answer. I have other questions, but they're nothing that can't wait for some other time. I get up and cross the room and close the window. I check to be sure that it's locked, even though we're on the second floor of the old house on Wood Street. Down on the sidewalk, there's a black bird big as a tomcat, and when I tap on the glass, it spreads its wings and flies away.

BABYLON
Dave Hutchinson

Dave Hutchinson was born in Sheffield. After reading American Studies at the University of Nottingham, he became a journalist. He's the author of five collections of short stories and four novels, and two novellas. He is best known for the Fractured Europe Sequence—*Europe in Winter, Europe in Autumn*, and *Europe at Midnight*—which were nominated for the John W. Campbell Memorial, BSFA, Locus, Kitchies, and Arthur C. Clarke Awards. Hutchinson has also edited two anthologies and co-edited a third. His latest books is space opera novella, *Acadie*, from *Tor.com*. He lives in north London.

THEY WERE THREE days out when they encountered a Coast Guard cutter. The pilot, his face almost entirely hidden by a VR set, spotted the vessel on passive radar and turned off the motor. "Easy now," he whispered.

"Who is it?" Da'uud murmured.

"Does it matter?"

Da'uud supposed not. He raised his head and looked out beyond the prow of the boat, but all he could see was a profound darkness. It was a moonless night, and high cloud hid the stars. The patrol boat was probably running dark; there was no way to tell how far away it was.

He lay down again on the deckboards and stared up into the night, feeling the long, powerful swell rising and falling against his back. He said, "What will we do?"

"We will wait," the pilot said quietly. "And we will not make any noise."

Da'uud closed his eyes and clasped his hands across his chest. The boat was stubby and low in the water, and it was constructed from materials which gave it the radar signature of a floating beer keg. He and the pilot lay side by side in the bottom, covered in waxy tarpaulins that smelled of camphor and dissipated their body heat into the sea via a network of hollow threads trailing in their wake. A stealth boat, Latsis had called it. One of a kind. Please do not break it.

He wondered where Latsis was now. He thought of the old man standing on the beach along the coast from Phocaea, watching as Da'uud and the pilot made their way out to sea, then slowly turning and plodding back towards the line of trees where they had hidden the truck the boat had been transported in.

"There are a couple of ways we could do this," Latsis had mused at their first meeting. "We could put you in a stealthed hydrofoil and just run you across the Aegean at high speed at night, get you where you need to be in a few hours, but that's risky. So we're going to take our time." He had seemed quite taken with the idea, scarred hands clasped on the table in front of him, the sleeves of his washed-out old blue work shirt rolled up to reveal forearms knotted with muscle. "We are going to creep into Europe."

Latsis, of course, did not know the purpose of the mission, and he was being well paid not to form any opinions which he might later feel obliged to share with the Turkish authorities. Da'uud's Uncle had told him that the old man had started out in the people-smuggling business back in the heady days of the first quarter of the century, before various crises had rolled together into The Crisis. The two of them had had some dealings in the old days, and Da'uud's Uncle had pronounced Latsis trustworthy, to the extent that anyone could be.

They were having this conversation in the family compound outside Berbera, overlooking the Gulf of Aden. Rebel forces had come through the area the week before, skirmished with government troops for a while, looted and burned a village, and departed. The family had been on high alert the whole time, manning the railguns mounted on the compound walls—they were just as likely to come under attack by the government as by the rebels—and Da'uud was still exhausted when his Father and Uncle had come to him with their proposal.

"You may decline, of course," his Uncle had told him when the plan had been outlined. "But someone else will go in your place. One of my sons, possibly."

Da'uud remembered sitting back and staring at the map projection on the tabletop, almost overwhelmed merely by the distances involved. "We have friends in Riyadh with an aircraft," his Uncle had said, and he'd gone on to describe a crossing of the Gulf and an overland route across Yemen and Saudi Arabia as if it was a mellow school outing rather than a journey across some of the most dangerous territory on Earth.

"Do you not have friends in Nairobi who have an aircraft?" Da'uud enquired mildly.

"We are warriors," his Father admonished. "Descendants of warriors. Don't embarrass me in my own house."

"And Nairobi," his Uncle added with a smile, "is in the wrong direction."

"A great gift is about to come into our hands," his Father said. "We must be in the right place at the right time, and we must use it. We will change the world."

The world is run by old men, Da'uud thought, bobbing on the midnight Aegean and wondering if he would live to one day join their number.

"Moving off," the pilot murmured.

Da'uud listened, thought he heard, very faintly and far away, the sound of engines.

"We'll give it an hour to get clear," the pilot said. "Then we'll be on our way again."

IT TOOK DA'UUD almost a week to reach his destination. Driven by its whispery catalytic motor, the little boat drifted as much as made way, but that was deliberate. As Latsis had said, a direct approach at high speed would have taken a few hours at most. It would also have attracted the attention of every early-warning system the Europeans had sown in the Aegean. At night, tethered to the boat, Da'uud and the pilot took turns to swim for exercise. During the day, they stayed under a blanket of mimetic material which adopted the colour of the sea and hid them from satellite and drone surveillance. The boat distilled fresh water from the sea, and almost a month's worth of dehydrated combat rations, nourishing but tedious almost beyond belief, were packed under the deck. They were not, at least, going to starve. In fact, the importance of keeping his weight up had been drummed into Da'uud at virtually every planning meeting. "I do not pretend to understand these things," his Uncle had said, "but I am told that body mass is important."

One morning, the light just beginning to strengthen in the eastern sky, the pilot nudged Da'uud's leg and said, "Dewline."

Da'uud sat up, lifted the edge of the mimetic blanket, and looked out across the waves. For almost half a century, Europe had encysted itself behind concentric borders and buffer zones, the better to protect itself and its citizens from the likes of him. Wracked by financial collapses and never-ending arguments about whose shoulders the responsibility for security fell upon, the EU had eventually bullied the states of southern Europe into co-funding a line of distant early-warning sensor buoys stretching down the centre of the Aegean to the Egyptian coast, and across the Mediterranean to Spain. They monitored the passage of all surface traffic passing between Asia Minor and the Middle East and Africa and Europe. Mass-produced by American contractors, the buoys were small and cheap, and in the way of small cheap things they were prone to failure. No one would be especially alarmed when the ECM pod built into the boat's shallow keel disabled the nearest buoy and they slipped through the dewline, although a crew would be despatched to replace it, in time.

"I don't see it," he said.

"At two o'clock," said the pilot. "We're almost on top of it."

Da'uud squinted and finally located a small cylindrical object bobbing upright in the waves. It was no larger than a coffeepot. "Are you sure it can't see us?"

"No way to tell," the pilot replied. "We'll find out soon enough."

They passed the buoy, and there followed a tense few hours as they pulled away from the dewline, but apart from a handful of distant fishing boats and a couple of airliners stitching through the clouds they saw nothing at all.

The following day, the pilot said, "We're here."

THEY APPROACHED THE island cautiously, under cover of darkness. Several huge ships were anchored offshore, lit up brightly enough to be visible from orbit. Da'uud could hear, faint but clear, the sound of music coming from them across the water. Beyond them, a string of lights outlined the edge of the island, thickening into a vaguely spade-shaped mass where the town clustered around the harbour and climbed into the hills.

Keeping well away from other shipping, the pilot circled the island. The far side seemed more or less unpopulated. Da'uud knew the island from maps and photographs, but this was the first time he had seen it at night. He could make out the lights of two or three buildings against the great dark mass of the mountain rising out of the sea, but that seemed to be it as far as habitation was concerned.

"Shore patrol," the pilot murmured.

Da'uud looked, saw the headlights of several vehicles moving slowly along the coast road, heard the sound of their engines. They passed out of sight, and a few moments later there was only darkness and the sound of the sea sucking at the island again.

"Gone," said the pilot. "Good luck."

Da'uud grabbed his bag, said, "You too," and rolled out of the boat. The water was shockingly cold after the warmth under the mimetic tarpaulin, but he oriented himself and stroked strongly away towards the shore. Behind him, he heard the quiet mumble of the engine as the boat turned away from the island. He had no idea whether the pilot was returning to Turkey or had another landfall in mind; they had barely exchanged a couple of hundred words during the whole crossing.

Da'uud swam unhurriedly the kilometre or so to the island, his bag bobbing just below the surface behind him on a tether. Finally, his knee scraped sand and pebbles and he crawled up onto the beach. Despite regular exercise, his legs were still unsteady after a week at sea. He crawled along the beach until he came to a rocky outcropping which hid him from the road.

He stripped off his wetsuit and bundled it into a crevice in the rocks. There was a tab under the armpit; he tugged it hard and felt something pop, and within moments there was a fierce chemical smell as the suit dissolved. From his bag, he took a change of clothes. Western clothes: jeans, a T-shirt, a hoodie, trainers, all of them expensive brands but not new. In a separate pouch were paper identification documents—a Somali passport, travel permits, and so on—but they were meant only for the direst of emergencies. The first thing any encounter with the authorities would involve would be a scan for the microchip implanted in all refugees at their point of contact with the edge of Europe. Lacking such a chip, the most optimistic thing he could look forward to was a long and poorly organised repatriation, followed by many years suffering his Father and Uncle's sardonically expressed disapproval. Best not to risk that.

For the past 50 years, EU immigration policy towards the tide of refugees fleeing the chaos in Africa and the Middle East had been to hold the problem as far as possible from its northern states, stringing border wire along its southern frontier and sealing off the juicy heart of the continent.

Greece and Turkey found themselves on the wrong side of the fence—the former too exhausted by financial and political ruin to complain, and the latter still so cockteased by the unfulfilled prospect of EU membership that it would do anything at all to please Brussels. They were useful firebreaks where the endless flow of humanity could be halted, corralled, processed and repatriated. It was a labour-intensive task—probably the only growth industry remaining in Greece. Meanwhile, the Italians, a little better-off, but really not by much, were buying surplus US military drones and flying 24-hour patrols along the edge of their territorial waters, rocketing anything that displeased them. The Europeans had turned their continent into a fortress, but every fortress has nooks and crannies where a carefully prepared individual can slip through.

Da'uud took from his bag a small rucksack packed with a change of clothes, a battered paperback, a survival kit and a couple of other items. He rolled up the waterproof bag, stuffed it into the rucksack, slung it over his shoulder, and began to pick his way carefully up the beach. Reaching the road, he crouched in some bushes until he was certain no vehicles were approaching, then he crossed quickly and began to make his way up the hillside beyond.

"You know, I can't think of a single reason why I shouldn't just fly there directly," Da'uud told his Uncle.

His Uncle sighed. "Because you will be microchipped when you pass through Immigration and they will know where you are. The whole *point* of this exercise is that they do not know you are there."

Da'uud looked at his Uncle and Father. These two old men had once wielded considerable power. Not in public, but in the shadows. In their pomp, they had created an intelligence network which encompassed most of Africa and extended tendrils into southern Europe. His Uncle was fond of saying that intelligence work existed independently of all temporal considerations, and the fall of the previous government, the appointment of a new security service, and their current state of house arrest, had barely slowed them down. They were not allowed to leave the compound, but they were still cheerfully destabilising small states and enabling dictators on the other side of the continent, and no one could stop them.

"You will have to be strong," his Father intoned. "The journey will be the least part of this business."

"I'm not afraid," Da'uud told him.

"Then you're an idiot," said his Uncle. "Or you're a liar. And we have no use for either."

Da'uud got up and went over to the window, looked down into the compound. He had a very large extended family, many of whom had worked in intelligence with his Father and Uncle and had subsequently chosen to go into internal exile with them. His country had been in conflict for so long, it was said, that many in the West thought that *war-torn* was part of its name. War-torn Somalia, where even the populace could not be certain, from year to year, who was running things, or if things were even being run at all. His Father and his Uncles had raised the family to stand aside from such things. They hewed to no god, no tribe, no allegiance. They were schooled in infiltration, subversion, sabotage. The elders of the family looked upon their work and saw that it was good, and then they turned their eyes north, beyond the seething chaos of Yemen and the many tiny squabbling sheikdoms the House of Saud had left behind when it fled to Paris during the coup. It was the work of a moment for the wealthy to enter Europe—a fast jet, some petty bureaucrat waiting on the tarmac at the other end bearing residence visas and possibly a welcoming bottle of Krug. It was not, it went without saying, so straightforward for the majority.

Da'uud turned from the window, 16 years old and a fraction under two metres tall. He could hack a government communications network, speak four languages, field-strip a dozen different types of assault rifle under combat conditions, cook a restaurant-standard meal, quote Coleridge, and kill a man with a rolled-up newspaper. Admitting to fear was not something which came easily to him. He had been schooled, from almost as soon as he could walk, to be *capable*. Fearing something meant doubting his own *capability*. Fear was the first step towards failure.

He said, "If you can get me there, I will do this thing. You need not doubt me."

The two old men exchanged glances and then looked at him. "Go and say goodbye to your brothers and sisters," his Father told him. "You will leave after lunch."

AFTER SO MANY dawns bobbing on the surface of the Aegean, this morning was an almost religious experience. Or it would have been, had Da'uud been remotely religious. Halfway up the slope of the mountain which rose at the heart of the island, he sat and watched the light grow in the eastern sky, revealing a fantastical vista of sea and scattered islands and, far far away on the horizon, a vague darkening which he thought might be the Turkish mainland. The sun, rising above the edge of the world, seemed to set the sea alight for a moment, flooding everything with colour.

From his vantage point, he could see for many miles along the coast road. This side of the island seemed sparsely visited, probably because the soil was so poor and rocky and there were no natural harbours. History and geography had settled everything 10 or 15 kilometres away on the other side, and it had not seen fit to spread very far. So far, he had only seen a handful of vehicles, apart from the shore patrol doing its hourly circuit.

There was a stand of stunted, weather-bent trees a little further up the slope. Da'uud moved among them, found a spot and began moving rocks and little stones aside until he had exposed the almost worthless soil underneath. Then he carefully scooped a hole several centimetres deep. When he was satisfied that it was deep enough, he sat back on his heels, reached into his backpack and took out a small transparent flask. Rattling in the bottom of the flask was a dull metallic object about the same size and shape as a sunflower seed.

He remembered his Uncle giving him the flask. His Uncle had been wearing insulated gloves. "Many Bothans," his Uncle had told him gravely, "died to bring us this information."

It was a family joke, but not one without a lesson: *intelligence always has a cost*. Da'uud and his siblings had been taught not to treat intelligence lightly, to remember that it was not simply words and numbers and photographs and video.

It was also true, in this case. People had died in order for his Uncle to offer the flask to him; it was well to remember that.

He had been warned not to touch the seed—the interior of the flask had some kind of protective coating—so he simply removed the cap and upended it over the hole. The seed dropped to the ground, missing the hole by a fraction, balanced on the edge. A faint wisp of smoke began to curl up from beneath it. Da'uud sighed, looked about him, found a twig and poked at the seed until it toppled into the hole. He scraped dirt over it and sat back on his heels. Holding the twig up in front of his face and squinting at it, he saw that the end seemed to have been eaten away. Was *still* being eaten away; as he watched, it appeared to be disappearing in a tiny vague cloud of mist. He stuck it in the soil over the hole and scrambled away a few metres and made himself comfortable against the wizened trunk of one of the trees. He looked at his watch. Twelve hours, his Uncle had said. That, at least, was the intelligence they had. They were dealing with a Mystery here, and there would be variables. Da'uud settled back against the tree, set the alarm of his watch, and closed his eyes.

"IT IS A weapon of great power," his Uncle told him. "Our information is that it was developed by the North Koreans, who have become interested in technologies proscribed in the West."

Da'uud, who was sitting on the couch in the living room of the main house with a tablet in his hands, reading the technical specs of the thing which had been delivered under cover of darkness last night, glanced up at his Uncle and Father. "North Korea," he said.

"Yes, we know," said his Father. "The last famine killed over a million people, and still they work on devices such as this." He nodded at the tablet.

To Da'uud's mind, as well as the minds of most people in the rest of the world, North Korea had become a pressure cooker, an out-of-control social experiment presided over by a line of increasingly dangerous Kims. No Westerner had been allowed into the country for almost 30 years, and what intelligence did emerge came in the form of wild rumours about genetic experimentation, augmented humans, apes which had learned to use power tools, dogs which could carry on a rudimentary conversation, and so on and so forth. You could boil off the most insane of those rumours and still be left with enough credible tales to make the fears of North Korea's nuclear capability earlier in the century seem like an idle and passing worry. It was said that every nuclear power on Earth had at least one warhead targeted on Pyongyang.

"How did it come into our hands?" he asked.

His Father sighed and tipped his head to one side.

"If this is true…" Da'uud gestured with the tablet. "I think I have a right to ask, don't you?"

"It was stolen," his Uncle said.

"Well, patently."

"Several times," his Father added.

"Our information is that it was taken, originally, from a facility near Kanggye, up near the Chinese border," his Uncle went on. "How it was taken, we do not know. There is anecdotal information that it was offered for sale to the Chinese intelligence services, but the sale never took place and the item dropped out of sight. Some months later, it reappeared in Japan, where it seems the North Korean intelligence services made an attempt to retrieve it."

"There was a firefight," his Father said. "Many casualties." He shook his head. In their world, gunfire was the mark of a catastrophic failure of tradecraft. The whole point of espionage was that no one should know you had been there.

His Uncle shrugged. "The next thing we know, it's in Damascus." He let the name of the city hang in the air for a moment. "Several different groups of jihadists are bidding to buy it, then someone gets impatient and the representative of the vendors turns up in one part of the city and his head turns up elsewhere."

"After that, we don't know," his Father went on. "We do know that it finally passed into the hands of a jihadi cell, and we suspect they stole it, because they certainly did not have the funds to buy it."

"And we stole it from them," Da'uud said.

"We did."

"This thing is cursed," his Uncle said. "Everyone who has ever touched it has died violently."

"I'm more inclined to put that down to human greed and stupidity than supernatural agency," his Father mused. "We are not greedy, and neither are we stupid. We will be more careful."

DA'UUD OPENED HIS eyes. Without moving, he scanned the area. It was late afternoon, and the sun beat down on the hillside. Far below, one of the great white cruise ships was sailing away in the general direction of Turkey, inscribing a white crease on the surface of the sea. A little further down the slope, a solitary scrawny goat was standing looking at him. Da'uud's watch buzzed; he turned off the alarm.

Turning his head, he saw a ragged hole in the ground where he had buried the seed. Looking carefully, he searched for signs of vapour rising from the hole, but he saw none.

He got up stiffly and walked over to the hole. It was easily large enough to put his head and shoulders into, the stones and rocks around it seemingly half-melted, almost vitrified. He dropped the rucksack down the hole, heard it fall a considerable distance before it hit bottom, then he sat down with his legs dangling over the edge and slipped inside.

The walls of the hole were smooth to the touch; by bracing and relaxing his knees and elbows he was able to let himself fall by degrees until, all of a sudden, his legs swung out into thin air and he lost his purchase and fell several metres. He landed on a level surface, absorbing the impact easily like a parachutist, and looked around him.

He was in a hemispherical chamber about ten metres across and five high at its highest point. The floor and walls were smooth and lustrous and gave off a low, pale blue luminescence. Above his head, the hole opened into the chamber's ceiling. Looking up, he could see a tiny circle of sky. He judged that he was almost 20 metres underground.

In the very centre of the chamber, the seed had germinated into a fat teardrop about the height of a six-year-old child. It was the perfect blue of a cloudless Mediterranean summer sky, and leaning down close Da'uud could see that its surface was covered in a network of fine black lines, like the craquelure on a piece of ancient porcelain. The surface was, he realised, also moving, very slowly. Or perhaps it was just the black lines—it was hard to tell.

He sat down beside the teardrop and looked around the chamber. *I am not afraid*, he had said. But now he was. He thought his Uncle would approve.

"It is called," his Uncle had said, "*nanotechnology*. I am too old to understand these things; I do not know how a machine can be too small to see and yet still function."

"Whoever developed it has, apparently, made unbelievable advances," his Father added. "There is, in fact, a rumour that it comes from a crashed spacecraft belonging to an alien civilisation." And they had all laughed at that, but now, sitting here beside the machine, Da'uud did not feel inclined to laugh. To their knowledge, this machine had never been tested; all they knew was what it had been designed to do. The Western intelligence agencies, if they knew of this thing—and he assumed they did—must be going out of their minds trying to find it. It was, in its way, the most dangerous thing on Earth.

Moving quickly, Da'uud removed his clothes and sat beside the machine again. He took a deep breath, put his hand on the smooth surface of the teardrop, and pushed gently. There was a momentary resistance, and then his hand sank into it up to the elbow. He stirred his hand in a warm substance that seemed at once wet and dry. The skin of his arm tingled briefly, then went numb. The numbness welled up his arm until it reached his shoulder, and then surged across his body. He fought panic, fought the atavistic urge to pull free of the machine, and then the numbness filled his head and he slumped backwards on the floor of the chamber.

THEY HAD TOLD him he would not dream, but somehow he did. He dreamed of his mother, who had died in a suicide bomb attack in Mogadishu when he was four. He dreamed of his brothers and sisters. He dreamed of his Father and Uncle, who had spent much of their lives theorising this operation, never realising that one day they would be in possession of something which would actually make it work.

In time, his breathing slowed, then stopped altogether. His heartbeat stilled. The machine built fine tendrils into his body, feeding oxygen to his brain. His skin hardened, became leathery, thickened and thickened again until his features disappeared. After two days, he lay in a featureless black cocoon. Within the cocoon, tiny machines worked busily to disassemble him, piece by microscopic piece. While he dreamed of his Uncle telling him about Europe and its decades-long war against people who were not *of* Europe, his brain floated in a thick soup of cells and furiously busy nanotechnology.

"The caterpillar does not dream of being a butterfly," his Uncle had told him, "any more than the butterfly remembers being a caterpillar."

Above him, the hole to the outside world gradually closed itself.

DA'UUD OPENED HIS eyes and took a deep breath. Without moving, he took stock. He felt warm and comfortable and well rested. No aches or pains. He flexed his fingers and toes and everything seemed to work. At some point, his arm had been ejected by the machine.

Very slowly, he sat up, and experienced a sudden wave of disorientation. The legs stretched out in front of him were white. He wiggled his toes, and, yes, they seemed to be controlled by him, but they were not his toes. He raised his arms and held his hands in front of his face. They were slender and white, their nails neat and pink. He turned them over and looked at his palms.

"They will not admit us," his Uncle had old him, "because we are *other*. We are not *them*. We do not *look* like them. They will overlook our colour if we have enough money or we have something they want, but we will always be different; we will never walk down their streets without someone attacking us or suspecting us of wearing a suicide vest."

"The device is an infiltration weapon," his Father said. "It is the ultimate disguise for a deep-cover agent. We think the North Koreans may have intended to use it to flood the West with operatives—indeed, if there is more than one prototype they may already be doing so. For us, it is our doorway into Europe. For you, for your brothers and sisters. For our people."

Da'uud stood unsteadily—his viewpoint seemed several centimetres too low—and walked carefully over to the rucksack on those alien white feet. He took from the pack a small mirror and held it up in front of his face, and a stranger's face looked back. A blue-eyed face topped by a shock of blond hair. He blinked, and those blue eyes blinked back. This was going to take some getting used to.

The machine sat in the middle of the floor, quiescent now, its job done for the moment. He thought perhaps it was fractionally smaller, but he couldn't be sure.

Da'uud dressed. For a moment, tying the laces of his training shoes, he became so hypnotised by the sight of his hands that he forgot what he was doing. *I am the same person*, he told himself. *This is cosmetic. Like having a haircut.*

But it was not like having a haircut. If the information he had been given was accurate, quite a substantial amount of his genetic code had been rewritten. He was no longer what he had been.

"If you were to approach the border looking as you do now," his Uncle had said, "you would be turned away. All of us would. The Europeans talk about jobs and economic pressure and population growth, but the truth is that they don't want us because we are *different*. They were content to rule us for a century, two centuries, but now we rule ourselves they do not want us among them."

Though the hole in the ceiling had closed up, while he slept an opening had appeared in one side of the chamber. It was just high enough for him to step into it if he crouched. It led to a narrow, low tunnel which angled gently upward and opened on the hillside some distance away.

Da'uud stepped out and found that it was raining. Squalls, dancing in a strong wind, obscured the view. He checked his watch and discovered that four months had passed since he had put his arm into the machine. The season had changed. It was as if he had travelled in time.

"Go to the edge of Europe and establish an embassy for us," his Father had told him. "We will send someone by a different route to prepare new identity documents for you when you have undergone the procedure. When you are ready, we will send others. One, two, three at a time. If we look like them, we can walk among them. And if we walk among them, we can find our way into positions of authority."

"We will effect change," his Uncle had said. "A great wrong has been done to the peoples of the South, and now the peoples of the North have walled themselves up against us. We will redress that wrong. It may take a generation, or two generations, or three. But we will open the borders again and our people will be free."

Da'uud took a phone from his rucksack and sent a text message to tell his Uncle that the embassy was open and ready for business. Then he walked down the hillside, through the rain, to look for a job in this new world.

BRING YOUR OWN SPOON
Saad Z. Hossain

Saad Z. Hossain is a Bangladeshi author who writes in English. His war satire, *Escape from Baghdad!*, was published in 2015 in the US and India, and is currently being translated into French. His second novel, *Djinn City*, a picaresque fantasy blending fantasy, supernatural politics and genetic science, was published in late 2017. Hossain's short fiction has been published in *The Apex Book of World SF 4* and *The Djinn Falls in Love*. He lives in Dhaka, Bangladesh.

HANU SAT BEFORE his stove, warming himself. It was cold outside, and even worse, the wind scoured away the cloud of nanites, the air borne biotech that kept people safe. He had seen more than one friend catch death in the wind, caught in a pocket without protection, their lungs seared by some virus, or skin sloughed off by radiation. The thin mesh of pack-sheet formed a tent around him, herding together the invisible, vital cogs. Shelter was necessary on a windy night, even for those with meager resources.

He was cooking rice on the stove, in a battered pot with a mismatched lid, something made of ancient cast iron. Ironically, in certain retro fashion houses, this genuine pre-Dissolution Era relic would have fetched a fortune, but Hanu had no access to those places, and wouldn't have cared, either way. A pot to cook your rice in was priceless, as valuable to a roamer as the tent or the solar stove.

He measured the quarter cup of fine grained rice into the boiling water, added a bit of salt, a half stick of cinnamon and some cardamom. The rice would cook half way before he added onions and chilies, perhaps a touch of saffron. In a way, Hanu ate like a king, although his portions were meager. He had access to an abandoned herb garden on the roof of a derelict tower, plants growing in some weird symbiotic truce with the nanites warring in the sky, nature defying popular scientific opinion. The rice he got from an abandoned government grain silo, sacks of the stuff just lying there, because people feared contamination. Almost everyone in the city ate from food synthesizers, which converted algae and other supplements into roast chicken at the drop of a hat.

He let the rice cook until there were burnt bits sticking to the bottom of the pot. The burnt bits were tasty. The smell filled the tent like a spice bazaar, and he ate from the bowl using his wooden spoon. No one disturbed him, for which he was thankful. It was difficult to find a square inch empty in Dhaka city, but it was a windy night, the Pollutant levels were on orange alert, and most people were indoors.

Moreover, he was in the fringes of the river side area of Narayanganj, where the alert level was perpetually screaming red due to unspeakable life forms breeding in the water, a sort of adjacent sub-city swallowed by Dhaka a hundred years ago, a pustule avoided by even the moderately desperate homeless, one step away from being cluster bombed into oblivion by the satellites above. Thus he was able to finish his meal in peace, and was just contemplating brewing some tea when a gust of wind knocked the tent askew, and a lumpy black dog nosed in.

Hanu sighed, and gave the dog a bit of rice. It ate directly from his hand, thumping his tail in appreciation. Hanu got out of the tent, to prevent the creature from breaking it. Where the dog roamed, his master would not be far behind.

"You're corrupting my hound," a voice said. In the shadows a slow form materialized, a man-like thing extruding a field of disturbance around him. It was the Djinn Imbidor, an ancient creature recently woken from centuries of sleep, diving again into the cut and thrust of mortal life, puzzled somewhat by the rapacious change in humanity.

"He's a mongrel, Imbi," Hanu said. "Even more bastardized than you."

Imbidor frowned. "Are you sure? The one who sold it to me, that man by the sweet shop with the bird cages, he said that it was a pure breed Mirpur Mastiff."

"Mirpur Mastiff?" Hanu laughed. "Cheeky bastard. The Pure breed Mirpur Mastiff is a euphemism for the most mangled blood line possible.

Your hound is descended from the original street dogs which roamed Dhaka, before they started injecting turtle genes into them."

"Oh." He scowled. "Humans are always ripping me off."

"You want some rice?"

"With cardamom and saffron?"

"Of course."

The Djinn took the pot and ate the last of the rice. He had his own spoon, a silver filigreed thing which no doubt came from some kingly horde. "Thanks Hanu. You're a good cook, I always say."

"Not much demand for cooks these days," Hanu said shortly. His father had been a cook once, long ago, before the current banking cartel had pushed all the Cardless out of the better neighborhoods into the subsidized boroughs, little better than feral slums. There had been a time when there was apparently a 'middle class' sandwiched between the dichotomy of rich and poor.

He shook his head. His father had told a lot of fairy stories. Then he had fucked off. "Plus it's illegal to use real plants, like I do. They'd probably arrest me. Endangering the cardamom or something."

"Well for the Fringe, then," Imbidor said. "We should have a restaurant. Something like the old days, a place for people to gather. Plenty of the Fringe would like it. Even some of the citizens."

The citizens were general populace without capital, whose main contribution to society was the biotech their bodies spewed, which added to the mass of benevolent nanites fighting the good fight in the sky, scrubbing the air, killing disease, controlling the microclimate, forming the bubble which protected Dhaka from the big bad world outside. The Fringe was a subset of the citizenry, filled with the homeless, the drifters, the thrill seekers, the darker edge of the maladjusted. And Djinn. More and more often, Djinn emerged from slumber, found a world near wrecked by hubris, found that the lonely places they favored were despoiled, unlivable. Many returned to sleep right away. It was rumored that Djinn did not age while they slept, that they could afford to while away centuries waiting for a better time downstream. Of course there was no guarantee such a time would come.

"I would cook and you would serve," Hanu joked. "We could call it 'Bring Your Own Spoon'."

"And the Hound would be the lookout," Imbi said, enthused.

"We already have everything. The tent, the stove, the pot."

"The mosques give away free bowls," Imbidor said. "Their food is some horrible grey sludge, but the bowls are good. I've collected a stack of them since I woke up. And we'd give *real* food. No discrimination against the Cardless either. Pay however you can."

"Why not?" Hanu said, suddenly struck by the thought. "Why can't we do it?"

"That's what I've been saying!" Imbidor shouted. "Come on Hanu! I'm so bored." Boredom was the reason the Djinn went to sleep so often in the first place.

"Ok. I'm in. We have to find a good place to set up the kitchen. And food suppliers, well, I know a few. Benches? Clean water? We'll need a place without the cameras if possible..." The possibilities seemed endless. Problems jostled in his mind, shifting in priority as solutions clicked into place. It felt good to think again.

"Come on, let's go," Imbidor said. "I know the perfect place."

He extended his distortion field around Hanu like a ragged cloak, keeping out the bad stuff in the air. Hanu stumbled from the slight vertigo it caused, felt that familiar tinge of nausea brought by proximity to the field, but in truth Imbi's power was tatty, weakened from some ancient conflict, his touch feather light compared to the great Djinns. Once Hanu had seen a Marid with a field so powerful that it was opaque, reflecting the sun, a solid fist that rammed through the crowd unheeding, had seen a man caught in its center pulped to death by unimaginable pressures.

Djinns did not officially exist, although the Fringe knew perfectly well they were there, often out in plain sight, going about their business. There were rumors that great Djinn lords ruled human corporations, wielding terrible power from the shadows. Imbidor was not that kind of Djinn. He had no *dignatas*, the peculiar currency the Djinn traded in, he commanded no respect, had no followers, no wealth in either world. Even mighty Djinnkind had the indigent.

THEY WORKED THEIR way ever deeper into Narayanganj, Hanu suppressing the atavistic fear of the bad air. The street was still lined with shanties, extruded sheets lashed together with adhesive bands, cheap stuff which could be printed out of the many black-market operations found in greater Dhaka. Here the people seemed unhealthier however, farther away from the center, and their progress was tracked warily, with more than one weapon being raised, although the Djinn was recognized and allowed to pass. People moved here out of desperation, for even though the main boroughs of the Cardless were crowded, at least the air was good, basic supplies were provided, and there was work. Here by the river the town was semi abandoned and as they got closer to the water the citizens became more furtive, many carrying deformities, the scarring of errant nanites. The big pharmas liked to experiment their new designs on high density populations, beta testing algorithms on live users, for good nanites of course, never anything weaponized, that would be immoral. There were always side-effects, though.

"Here we are," Imbi said, stopping.

It was a six-story shell of a building, built in the old style with concrete and steel, the bricks, wires, windows, doors, anything electrical looted long ago. It was near the river bank, close enough that Hanu could feel the cool air stirring, and his instinctive fear of the water made him cringe.

"Smugglers," Imbi said, knocking on the door of a makeshift room.

A man with an electric sword came out and watched them without speaking. Hanu glanced at him disinterestedly. The Fringe was full of smugglers with swords.

"We want the empty room," Imbi said.

"For the night? Or do you actually intend to live here."

"More than a night," Hanu said. "We want to try something out."

The swordsman shrugged. "The Djinn crashes here sometimes. I'm ok with that. I give him electricity and he sweeps for bad bugs with the distortion thing of his."

"It's a pretty good spot," Imbi said, embarrassed by his poverty. People who lived river side were the scum of the earth. "I can clean the air, at least enough for us few."

"You don't get sick here? No black lung? None of the skin stuff?" Hanu stared at the smuggler, trying to spot defects.

The smuggler turned his sword off. "Not so far."

"How?"

"There's a lot more people living here that you think," the man said. "The Djinn cleans the air and we have a nanite replicator. It's old but it helps. What business did you say you were in?"

"Hanu Khillick," Hanu said. "Restaurateur."

The smuggler burst out laughing. "Karka. Riverboat smuggler and pirate."

"Imbidor of Gangaridai," said Imbi. "Djinn. Professional giraffe racer. Ahem. Of course there are no giraffes left."

"Come inside," Karka said. "Let's get you set up. I'm not going to charge you rent, as long as the Djinn helps out. Once in a while surveillance drones show up. You have to take care of those fast, or corporate security will send someone down to investigate."

Inside was a sparsely furnished space, well swept, covered with the black market geegaws of the smuggler's trade, and a few solid pieces: a power generator, an ancient nanite replicator, and a squat printer with its guts out. Karka was well set up. No wonder he survived out here. Hanu wondered what he smuggled. Karka motioned them to sit on the futons covering the floor.

"I will be most happy to help," Imbi said.

"You guys need anything else, you're gonna have to pay. Air scrubbing for three ain't cheap. You got any money?"

Hanu shook his head.

"I am the descendent of an ancient empire, known as the First City. I have lived hundreds of years, I have looked into the void of the abyss, I have seen the dark universe of the Djinn, I hold over 300 patents currently pending litigation in the celestial courts..." Imbi said.

"So no cash, I guess?"

"Er no."

"Any sat minutes?"

Hanu shook his head. Sat minutes were hire time from the satellites, a secure pin which activated the chip in your head for a designated time, showing you the vastly expanded VR universe the rich people inhabited. It was funny that everyone got chipped for consumer tracking and census purposes, but very few of the Cardless ever actually got to walk the VR world. Bandwidth was jealously guarded. Sat minutes were the way, a brief glimpse into paradise, a ten minute birthday treat for a child, a wedding gift, a de facto currency, hoarded but never consumed, a drug for the VR junkies; news, communication, vital information, everything rolled into one.

"Do I look like I have sat minutes? I'm a cook. I'll cook you food."

"I got an old vat maker," Karka said, looking at him dubiously.

"Chinese or Indian?"

"Post crash Malay."

"Everything tastes of coconut, right?"

"Haha yea, I don't even know what coconut is. Some kind of nut?"

"There were big trees once, and these were the fruit, kind of like big balls full of liquid."

"Yeah well, that's fucken food for me, coconut seaweed."

"I'll make you rice right now, that will make you cry."

"No thanks." Karka looked queasy. "I already ate. Look man, don't worry. I'll help. Imbi sorted me out a couple of times with his djinnjitsu."

Hanu scrounged in his bag of provisions and brought out something he had been saving, a rare find. It was a raw mango, from a tree near the Red Zone which had miraculously survived all these years, and now had suddenly given fruit. No one touched them of course, fearing some hideous mutation, even the street kids stayed away. They had all heard stories of trees bursting open to release deadly nanite spores, of the terrible Two Head Disease, which caused a bulbous head-like protuberance to come out of your ass, or of the Factory Germ, which slowly hardened your body into metal. Hanu's father had taught him to forage, however, as the very poorest must do, and this foraging had given him an instinct of what could or could not be eaten.

He sliced the mango with his knife, letting the slivers fall inside his pot, careful not to lose the precious juice. Then he brought out a small lemon, nursed carefully from his errant herb garden, cut it and squeezed half of it onto the fruit. Salt, pepper, turmeric, mustard seed paste and chili flakes followed, a little bit each because the flavors were intensely different from VAT food, almost alien. He mixed it together by hand, till the slices were covered, glistening. Karka and Imbi had gathered around, mouths open, inhaling the smell of raw cut mango and the sharp tang of mustard, drawn by an ancient evolutionary pull.

"What the hell?" Karka lowered his head involuntarily, breathing in the smells.

Hanu ate a piece, showed it was safe. "It's good."

Imbi, who had largely bypassed the Dissolution Era, had no such qualms and quickly forked a third of the mango onto his palm.

"It *is* good," Karka said, unable to resist a slice. He looked entranced. "It's damn good. You *are* a cook."

"You in?"

"You seriously want to open a restaurant."

"You've got a perfect view of the river."

"You realize they call this the River of the Dead."

THE NEXT MORNING they got started, Karka joining them for a breakfast of rice, the last of Hanu's horde. Afterwards he handed over a key for the spare room, and a handful of electronics, a solar battery, some basic furniture. He dragged out the air scrubber and put it equidistant between their doors. "I eat for free. Plus Imbi does his shit. We share the air. If it runs out, we split the costs."

"Deal."

They dispersed, Hanu going on an herb run, Imbi dispatched to spread the word and also discover some sources of raw material. It was, after all, useless to have a restaurant without any food. Hanu knew this was the biggest hurdle. He expected this dream to end soon, for where on earth would Imbi find so much real food?

Nonetheless, he set up his station on time, arranging his supplies of herbs and spices, warming up water from the ancient ion filter, even setting up a bench for the customers. If Imbi came back, they would open for lunch. By eleven o'clock, hopeful looking people invited by Imbi were ambling around, steering away from the glaring Karka, maintaining nonchalance. Hanu studied his prospective customers, and had to conclude that they hadn't a penny to their name collectively. He might as well have started a vat kitchen, feeding the homeless, like the mosques.

"This lot couldn't buy crabs from a brothel," Karka said, sword hilt at hand. "If Imbi's not back by noon they're going to start looting."

"The road is my home," Hanu said. "I am not afraid." *People always assume that poor people are dangerous. They wouldn't be here, if they were.*

Imbi staggered in half past noon carrying a large burlap sack. There were a solid dozen customers still loitering, despite the best efforts of Karka. The three of them gathered inside the room, where the Djinn threw open his sack with obvious pride.

"What the hell is it?" Karka recoiled with disgust.

"It's a fish," Imbi said. "From the river."

It was, indeed, an enormous fish, scales glistening, gills still flapping for air. Hanu remembered his father bringing home one once. Karka had never seen one, was clearly repulsed with the whole idea of eating something from the river.

"Look, there's a dozen people outside, and we have to feed them something," Hanu said. "I know how to cook this, I remember."

"What's wrong?" Imbi asked Karka. "We used to fish from the river all the time..."

"That was 200 years ago, Imbi," Karka said. "We don't touch that shit anymore..."

Hanu ignored them. He had a fish to scale, and he'd only ever seen it being done as a child. It took rather longer than an hour to get it right, the pieces prepped, somewhat mangled, but soon thereafter the smell and sizzle of grilled fish permeated from the pre-fab, and his customers sat down and waited in an almost hypnotized state, so docile and silent that even Karka had no complaints.

WHEN HE WAS ready, he brought it out, fifteen pieces of grilled fish with crispy skin, flavored with ginger, garlic and chili, with little balls of rice. He had used up everything. They took their portions solemnly, signifying the importance of the moment, ate with their hands along the makeshift bench, with all the dignity of a state banquet. There was no hesitation, no question of what they were ingesting. It simply smelled too good. Karka ate the last piece, his resistance melted away.

"God, this is a good way to die," he said.

It started up the conversation, rounds of introductions, stumbling praise for the food, old recollections of when they had last seen food like this, of the myriad turns of their lives, which had left them Cardless, and desperate on the streets. Imbi sat amongst them, extending his field for them, and they marveled at the distortion, wondered aloud that such a powerful creature should be wandering the road with them. And then, by some unspoken consensus, it was time to leave, and they began to make their offerings. A knife, much handled, the last thing a man would give up; an old card for sat minutes, so old, so carefully preserved, to receive a call that never came; a silver locket with the picture taken out; a book of short stories; an ancient watch. The last lady stood up, her hands empty.

"I have nothing," she said. "But there is a place with birds... chickens. If I bring them, will you cook?"

"Yes, of course," said Hanu. He looked at the small pile of treasure, and tears leaked from his eyes.

"Hanu and Imbi," the Djinn said, sweeping his hand back towards the establishment. "We are open for business."

OPEN THEY WERE, for six months and more, feeding crowds, sometimes with feasts, sometimes with nothing but onions and rice. Their customers scavenged, bringing food from unknown places. There were unspoken rules. Everything was eaten. No one was turned away. At first Imbi kept his field up like a tent, kept the bad air at bay, visibly exhausting himself, burning surveillance drones out of the sky. When their accrued wealth piled up, Karka could afford to charge up his replicator, spewing out the good nanites, and people stayed by the river out of faith, adding their bodies to the critical mass required to power these things, the human fuel which made their community work.

The river kept a tax. People sickened from its bounty, one died from intestinal rot, but the people who roamed here sickened and died anyways. There was no noticeable drop in custom. Imbi wandered far and wide, bartering, gossiping, marketing, and returned with useful things—water filters, glasses, proper cutlery, utensils for Hanu's kitchen. It would have been safer to move around, but they couldn't, people relied on them, the gangs left them alone, it was a safe spot, blessed by the river gods.

"Look what we've done!" Imbi said, proud. "I told you it would work."

"It can't last," Hanu said.

ONE DAY MEN from the high city swaggered down, uniformed, with their rented armored car and their mercenary badges. Private security. They didn't like activity in the orange zones, and the river was an atavistic boundary, a dread zone which these company men avoided at all costs.

"DISPERSE! DISPERSE! RED ALERT! HAZARD! HAZARD!" the armored car was going mad with panic, its blaring voice rising in pitch as it twisted its way through debris. Karka came out with his sword behind his back, Hanu with his cleaver and a decapitated fish head. The score or so people dozing in the sun after lunch sat up blearily. The car louvered open and two men came out in full combat gear, faces hidden inside command helmets, a swarm of sparrow sized drones buzzing in the air above them. These models were six seasons old, a tried and tested method of crowd control. The new ones were apparently mosquito sized, and just as lethal.

"Gathering in a Red Zone," the Company man said. "What for?"

"Easy, we're just squatting," Hanu said. "Cardless, see?"

"What is this place?" the security guard walked around, touching the benches, the bowls, the cardboard box of scavenged cutlery.

"Shelter for the poor," Hanu said, trying to cut him off from the kitchen. "Look, we're just feeding them. Hungry, homeless people for god's sake."

The company man touched him with one gloved hand, the powered suit amplifying force, and Hanu went stumbling back, a deep bruise forming instantly on his chest.

"Food? This is no vat kitchen. You have set up a micro climate here. We saw it from above," the security stared into the kitchen interior, face unreadable. "Why is there a micro climate in the Red Zone?"

"It's not a crime to stay here," Karka said. "What laws have we broken?"

The company men looked at each other, not answering. They were not unduly worried. In reality laws only applied to those who could afford lawyers. The swarm shifted a bit towards Karka, the machine whine rising an octave. They had already noted his sword, deemed it next to useless in a fight.

"I don't understand what this is," the first man said, knocking down the fab sheets walling the front of the kitchen. "What is this organic matter?"

"Why it's our food, friend soldier," Imbi said, beaming. Hanu suppressed a groan. "Would you like to have some? Fishhead curry, with brown rice. A princely meal! In my day policemen always ate free! Come, friends, eat a plate, rejoice in the bounty of the river!"

The man took the plate and his helmet became transparent, revealing a face inside. He stared at it, fascinated, and Hanu could almost see the neurons in his brain put together the contours of the cooked fish head with the scraps in the kitchen, with the shape of an actual fish, which he must have seen a hundred times in pictures as a child. A lot of emotions flitted across his face, curiosity, alarm, wonder. For a second Hanu dreamt that he would actually take off his helmet and try the food. Then his face turned to revulsion, and Hanu knew it was all over.

Imbi was standing there, beaming with goodwill, when the plate struck him across the face. Drones punched into him, tearing out chunks of meat, sending him tumbling back, before his distortion field finally flickered to life, cocooning him. Karka gave a samurai yell and charged, sword up in high guard. The drones were slow to react, confused by the Djinn's quantum field. They finally lunged at Karka but he ignored them, letting them have their pound of flesh, flying through that mist of his own blood and tissue, terminal grace, and his ionized blade somehow hit the command helmet in the neck join, shorting it out, sending the astonished Company man down to his knees.

Abruptly, half of the drones stopped short, hovering uncertainly. The other half of the drones, unfortunately, were not so confused. They slammed into Karka with lethal force, shredding the smuggler like paper. The armored car, programmed to be cowardly, was blaring incoherent alarms, already backing away from the fracas. The second policeman hesitated, then dived into his vehicle, his drones folding neatly into a pocket somewhere.

"YOU HAVE ALL BEEN MARKED FOR TERMINATION! SATELLITE STRIKE IMMINENT! INNOCENT BYSTANDERS ARE REQUESTED TO VACATE! VACATE! VACAAAAAATE!"

And they were gone, leaving their fallen behind.

"I don't think I can put Karka back together," Imbi said, tears in his eyes. He was trying to collect the pieces of their friend.

"Never mind. We have to leave. They will destroy this place," Hanu said. He looked at the dozen or so patrons still left. "We all have to leave. They've tagged our chips for death."

But they all knew nowhere was safe. Tagged for death was death in truth. It was just a matter of how long till the satellites cleared their backlog.

"Load everything into the boat!" Hanu shouted. "Everything! We have to go across the river. Into the country."

They stared at him, unconvinced.

"Look, there's fish in the river. That means there's food outside, you fools! There must be. We can survive! They won't hunt us out there." He turned to Imbi. "Imbi is Djinn! Djinn! He can clean the air for us, we can gather others, make a micro climate like we did here. They don't know he can do that."

IMBI STOOD UP straight, spread his arms out wide, dripping the blood of Karka, and his distortion field rippled out, encompassing them all. It was stronger than before, colored with rage and sorrow.

"We should leave," he said. "We should follow Hanu, who gave us food from nothing. I have slept a long time. I remember when they used to chain you to the earth and force you to work, to force your children and their children to the same labor. Now I am awake, I see they have taken your flesh too, they have herded you together like cattle, and living or dying, your bodies are little factories, cleaning the air for them. Your chips are your collars. They kill you without thought. You fear the air, the water, the trees, the very ground you walk on. What more can you lose? Why not leave this place? Let us go forth into the wilderness, where they dare not follow."

When they heard the Djinn they grew calm, and gathered their meager things. It was resignation, perhaps, or hope. Hanu freed the boat, pushing off into the river, and the poison water splashed over him, but he did not care. It was cool, and dark, and it washed away the blood.

THE HERMIT OF HOUSTON
Samuel R. Delany

Samuel R. Delany's science fiction and fantasy tales are available in *Aye and Gomorrah and Other Stories*. His collection *Atlantis: Three Tales* and *Phallos* are experimental fiction. His novels include science fiction such as the Nebula-Award winning *Babel-17* and *The Einstein Intersection*, as well as *Nova* and *Dhalgren*. His four-volume series Return to Nevèrÿon is sword-and-sorcery. Most recently, he has written the SF novel *Through the Valley of the Nest of Spiders*. His 2007 novel *Dark Reflections* won the Stonewall Book Award. Other novels include *Equinox*, *Hogg*, and *The Mad Man*. Delany was the subject of a 2007 documentary, *The Polymath*, by Fred Barney Taylor, and he has written a popular creative writing textbook, *About Writing*. He is the author of the widely taught *Times Square Red / Times Square Blue* and has written a Hugo-Award winning autobiography, *The Motion of Light in Water*. Delany is the author of several collections of critical essays. His novella, *The Atheist in the Attic*, appeared in February.

Delany's interview in the *Paris Review*'s "Art of Fiction" series appeared in spring 2012. In 2013 he was made the 31st Damon Knight Memorial Grand Master of Science Fiction. In 2015 he was the recipient of the Nicolas Guillén Award for philosophical fiction. He lives in Philadelphia with his partner, Dennis Rickett.

"FIRST OFF," I remember the Hermit's assistant told us, "you can't tell the entire story." She was perhaps ten years older than I was and had that pigment thing some black people get where blotches on their skin are missing the melanin. She had a large one on her left cheek. I was a child and that was weeks after I'd been brought to the door and turned loose to see if I'd enter or run away. Immediately I'd gone inside, though it wasn't natural curiosity. "Like me trying to tell you everything you're going to learn here," she told the group of us, in our high-ceilinged classroom. "Or why you're going to learn it, whether from me or on your own, or from each other. I couldn't do it," she repeated in the hallway when I went up to say I didn't understand.

("You better go in there with the rest," my older sister had said, looking at the shrubbery and the rocks beside the door, "or you'll be killed—")

I remember leaving by those same doors—twenty feet tall they were, of patinaed bronze, practically black, around panes of scratched glass. On wet days raindrops blew jaggedly down and across. Sometimes clouds reflected in them, during the glorious weather that obtained for ten-and-a-half months of the year. We children would gather in front of the building for our trips and wanderings, for wherever, in those years, we thought to go off to. We could explore anywhere on the Yucatán coast, in sight of the squat pyramid, down the shore, above the neat city between.

The Hermit of Tolmec herself we saw far less frequently. She was rich, old, and a woman I'm pretty sure had been born that way on all fronts—though a decade later Cellibrex, once we met and learned to talk to each other, told me you really can't tell about gender. People change it all the time—though he never had.

Neither had I. But by then he and I both had known people who'd done so. I'd never knowingly been to bed with any, though he said he had several times. He preferred what he was used to, however—which apparently, at least he said so, was me.

And by that time we were used to each other.

In my very unclear memory of childhood (lucid about some things and nonexistent about others), the Hermit of Tolmec wore blue rags one week, and red ones the next. She had old boots and a supply of different colored laces, which she changed every morning to receive the visitors who came while she sat in a big wooden chair in her part of the building. The chair—an ecclesiastical throne—had knife scars on its frame that spoke of age and a history I didn't know anything about. I didn't know if the Hermit did, either. Once I whispered to the assistant, "What are they...?" and she put her hand—which also had some white patches—on my shoulder:

"I don't know. And I don't want to. But we're slated to get a replacement by the end of the month: something simple. Then we can all forget such atrocities."

The Hermit's laces beneath her torn skirts that day, at the foot of her chair's carved wooden legs, above a small fur rug, glimmered black.

Her assistant liked her: me, the Hermit frightened.

For most of the time, those of us in the hermitage lived pretty much alone, in the shell of what her assistant explained had been a suburban supermarket, though she said that even earlier it had been an urban cathedral, when this had briefly been the site of the city of Tulum on the eastern Yucatán coast, before the Texans came. (I think they were Texans, but I don't know for certain.) Then it was a village again. They had invaded before I was born, but later drifted away. No, I hadn't been born there either. Though I'm not sure where I'd came from, or if I ever knew. I remember the assistant also telling our group that there was once a movement to tell stories that focused on how you got food, how the technology worked, how you related to something called "Mean Production," how some of it was really dangerous, and some of it was actually helpful. But you couldn't accept all of it without serious thought, which was the notion of an ancient religious leader named Marx, who at one time you could learn about in various threads on the greatest of the old religions, Facebook, but that an older—or was it newer—religion called Handbook had gone back to the idea that everyone could live naturally and not have any mean production at all, though she used to laugh and say it didn't seem any more natural to her than any other kind.

"Listen to me, Smart Girl (you know that *still* sounds strange to me, because you are a male), I am delighted you are not terrified to come see me," said the Hermit in our own conversation, having been called in to discipline me. "I've killed so many children—babies they were, little female babies that we called boys, to make it easier—and for a while many people knew it. I hope that's something you never wake up one morning and realize you've done, no matter how inadvertently. But at that time it seemed the only way to bring down the population. As followers of Facebook go, we were fairly deluded; almost as deluded as the followers of Handbook who tried to replace them." She snorted. "And just ended up mingling with them…. I suppose we are lucky that Facebook has such a short memory. Or, who knows, maybe some other little girl like you told a tale…" and I was startled, because I thought she might have known about my sister giving up her own place to get me in there. "Be glad you're a boy." But that's just a name, and I am not sure what you would call me if you actually met me this week, though most probably it would be different from next week. These categories change much too quickly for anyone to keep up, though I feel as if I've been sexually stable since I came back to the area after my traumatic childhood wanderings.

But then I had my coming-of-age forgetting process, as did all those in the hermitage and all those in any government education system, I was told; and while all of us worried about it beforehand, since it wasn't a complete memory erasure but highly selective, certainly it made me and all of the rest of us feel better, even a bit superior, if not privileged. And there was the shared paradox of thousands and thousands of children, I just assumed, not remembering what it was we'd forgotten....

TODAY, MORE THAN thirty years later, the Tolmec Hermit must be dead. I know my sister is. I wonder about the other children who were there with us. (Though I still know where Ara lives, who was in my group back then.) I like to think we were there, all those years ago, because we were smart. Or was it because someone thought we needed to be taught certain things and might learn them more easily there? Which is not quite the same.

The story I put together for myself about my very confused adolescent travels is that I must have gone more than two thousand kilometers by bicycle, helicopter, horse, barge, and boat. After that I lived (I learned I ended up there almost by accident) between thirty and fifty kilometers from the old supermarket-once-cathedral in Tolmec, though it might as well have been on the other side of what people around here still argue could be a globe turning in space or an endless plane that stretches to infinity in all directions. I didn't intend to tell you that much about *my* childhood, or how I got my food, or which of the vegetables I ate, or which I gave to my companions or which were stolen by my enemies (I don't think I could bear it: too many people died in that process to make it the kind of story acceptable on Facebook *or* Handbook), and the Handbook priests used to come through with their guns, to police the tales we told at the seasonal gatherings, where we got to make music and those who wanted to be Great Writers themselves told tales in keeping with the Algorithm Transparency Act, and that for a while was all the news with the people who were concerned with what was and what wasn't Acceptable to the Tribe.

I wonder if, on that trip that's so unclear in my memory, I went all the way around—or only described a small circle.

IT'S INTERESTING LISTENING to stories in a closed arena while priests stand in the aisles with guns. Twice I saw them shoot a Writer. As soon as it happened, people began to check on their pocket phones for what was acceptable to say and what was not, while the blood ran to the platform edge and down the front of the stage.

(Cellibrex says that during his childhood he never heard any official tales told, but lived in among gangs of hundreds of children, mostly underground, and you could watch all the porn you wanted. But nobody did. Cellibrex said he too had gone traveling in his youth, though almost instantly he had been set upon, captured, dragged away through trees and rocks, imprisoned, and held as part of another gang from which he did not really get loose until his mid-thirties. He said it was very much like the first one, only the children in it looked more like he did. All memory of where he'd started was now gone. Though in his gang, sex among the boys was constant, there was what I assumed must have been age-mate guidance, but nothing like adult supervision; as he said, there *were* no adults.)

Everyone knows straight men and women and gay men and women do lots of different things. But the only act you can talk about in a public telling, either in a local gymnasium or a great auditorium with murals hanging on the cinderblock walls, is a penetrative one that's supposed to be common to all. Especially once they are married. You can describe that act for anyone in as much detail as you wish. Because it is Universal, as is Marriage itself. But the mentioning of anything else outside of Marriage could get you shot. I knew even before I went traveling that many things called safe sex that were part of what men did together, most of what went on between men and the men who called women, you could not mention in Public. (It's what got the second Great Writer who I saw shot and wounded in his—she was a woman—performance.) But it meant that I grew up thinking 'safe sex' and 'oral sex' were the ultimate evils for all.

It certainly cured me of wanting to be any sort of Writer, Great or otherwise.

I'VE LIVED WITH so many Round Earthers; most of my life it never occurred to me to take Flat Earthers seriously. Someone once told me a story about a famous old detective who didn't know that the Earth was round because he didn't need such information to do his detective work. He had a friend who was a doctor who lived on Baker Street—or was he a Baker who lived with a doctor?

That part I *didn't* remember.

I do remember public demonstrations and big arguments—shooting ones, with stun guns—among critics over whether they had a heterosexual relationship or a homosexual one. You could find old DVDs of versions in which Watson was played by a woman, which was supposed to clinch the argument. Then someone cited an earlier written text which was supposed to clinch it the other way. Then a third voice upheld that we should take each version for exactly what it said, and not get lost in decoding, which finally drew the biggest guffaws.

That got the commune of a friend of mine smashed up.

But I may sneak in a few accounts of such forbidden topics about Cellibrex—not his real name: my nickname for him, because years before, I read in some library it had been a kind of recording tape, and so many of the things he did say were things he repeated. But we were together for a long time. I learned quickly that he had grown up with many more children than I had. Neither he—nor any of the boys he'd grown up with—ever learned to read. He didn't even know his family. 'Clone' was the worst insult you could call someone, he told me. And if anyone in any group looked too much like anyone else in the clique, often that person was driven out to seek people who were physically different—for friendship, sex, or other social bondings. But we are broaching the kinds of differences that, were this an official tale, I would not be able to tell.

Cellibrex says the world is flat—there is no argument, as far as he is concerned, and saying otherwise is silly. To me that sounds so absurd, I never thought to argue. In his childhood, he saw men and adults kill people who held contrary opinions. He says he grew up in a commune—which I always assumed meant an artificial environment, the way it's used here—but I can't be sure since I wasn't there—with an apple in it, which was like a big pocket phone or a pad with a screen on it, which I never encountered. It's not a popular opinion, but it's not one that would get you killed at a public tale telling, either. (Those are the parts of the story I'm *not* allowed to tell.) Though he never was taught how to use it, Cellibrex knew we were ruled by the internet, which was not a book but a group of men, and very shortly he found himself rounded up and shipped to a sprawling penal combine, where he spent a dozen years of his life. (I assume dozen meant twelve, but I can't be sure of that either: He says he learned to use the word for an approximate general number from us. What he and the boys he was captured with were incarcerated for, he does not know or refuses to say. He says he didn't learn the word "dozen" meant a specific number until after he'd escaped from the military.)

That's when I began to wonder if "flat" to the Flat Earthers meant curved so slightly that it might as *well* be flat in all directions… and just gave up because they didn't need to know anything else to do their work. Like the famous detective (who was probably gay, since his best friend was an Asian woman).

From the time he was eleven until he was twenty-two or so, Cellibrex has told me, he does not know where he was either; but it was far away. He killed people while he was there, and he does not believe he can go back, which at first made me wonder if he had been a Hermit or a Hermit's assistant. But later I realized he'd been in a gang called a family, or a family called a gang: It had lots of people in it, of all ages. His gang-family had no parents in it that he was aware of. There was a lot about age mates, which were important. It was all male and the sex was pretty ritualized and possessive. He remembered standing on some rocks, either in the morning or the evening, seeing fields full of his gang moving below, in groups of what he was sure had to be hundreds.

Then, somehow, he spent some years in a military unit, which he said entailed thousands of men—again, no men who were even called women had survived among the gangs of his childhood.

But the sex and the work were so different that he thought for the first six months it would drive him crazy, learning to understand them. But somehow he found, once he stopped resisting, it was actually both interesting and easier. And he'd traveled around enough to make him believe in the world's flatness.

I remember a childhood of living in units with people who were responsible for me. He remembers sleeping in piles of brothers in which anything might happen.

But I didn't find out he believed all these things about the world and had seen so much to make him sure of them—unless he was just bat-shit crazy, which now and then I have considered, though he was pretty quiet most of the time—until after we had known each other almost a year.

He was a very expressive man, but not a communicative one.

He knew his real name—which I don't think there's any reason to tell—but not where he came from, though he had an ID number. But it began with QX4, which makes me think it was from a long, long way away.

You want to know how we met?

It was during my recurring two days off from my job that—like I say—good literary form stipulates I not specify as to time and place, though I'll be vulgar and mention it entailed baskets and boxes and keeping track of the food and electronics they contained. But I don't want to get myself in trouble, telling whether I worked indoors or out, or if it was mostly physical labor or information tracking that I did, whether I was paid in copper notes or material certificates, etc. Distinctions of that sort are not literary. Today what is valued in a tale is the universal, not the specific, what is common to all men and women, whatever their sex; how we are all alike.

You get in the habit of not talking about things like that with others, and soon you don't think about such things yourself.

It's that forbidden mean production again.

At any rate, I was walking up through the recreation area between the major living hoods and the farming areas, through trees and by ponds, where the wild animals are kept with their tracking collars and the tame ones walled away on the Farms (another kind of institution entirely) that smelled so incredibly when you rode by them on a bicycle or glided over them in a glider. I'd taken my blue shirt off and tied the sleeves around my neck and was wondering about taking off my sandals and going barefoot, when a very large, unshaven brown-skinned fellow wandered from behind some trees.

He was already barefooted. He had lots of rough tattoos on his chest, arms, shoulders, thighs, buttocks and face—he was practically naked. That is not common in this part of the world. He had on a belt under a furry belly that looked full, fed, and strong, and a kind of—I guess you'd call it—groin cloth. (I was eighteen. I kept a neat beard back then in which a lot of folks said they recognized my Asian ancestors, which is not rare at all in this part of the Yucatán.) He was at least thirty or thirty-five, and his broad bones were heavy with muscle, and that looked kind of threatening. I've seen pictures of the natives who were supposed to have lived in this area a few generations ago, in the local library, with its forty books that anyone can go in and look through (though I gather I am one of about a hundred people in the neighborhood's three thousand who does), and he looked like one of them, though physically a lot larger. He had a beard and was starting to go bald, and a broad, brown nose. He had bright, oddly blue eyes for such dark skin and rough, straight hair.

We are a small enough settlement that we don't get a lot of strangers, but I guess we are on the sort of routes where the ones we get can be pretty varied from one another in this odd world we live in, so that not much surprises us—if they're not toting visible weapons. And he wasn't.

I am a gay man who had had a fair amount of local experience, but I was unprepared for the next thing he did: which was to raise his groin cloth, point to himself, look left and right, then look back at me—which I realized, to my surprise, in that isolated spot, was an invitation to… well, service him. My heart began to pound.

It was not a space where such encounters were common. But I knew of others not far away where they were.

I looked around, and thought, no, this probably isn't a good idea…

Many of the marks on his body were what most of us would call obscenities, which for me oscillated between disturbing and intriguing. Bats, skulls, dragons, as well as male genitals, dogs and mules relieving themselves of urine, excrement, or desire using their fellows... his back was against a rock with lots of foliage on it, and I was on my knees in the fallen leaves in front of him, with his thick (if average length) penis in my mouth, which was pleasantly salty, and pretty much like mine. (That, of course, was when I thought of asking him if he thought this was... But his rough hands held my head, moving it out and in, while above me he breathed harder and harder. And I forgot about all such thoughts.)

When, three or so minutes later, he spilled into me, and I thought I'd better disengage, he didn't release me, but held me to him, finally to let me rise and push against him and, still erect enough to hold aside his clout, with one hand against my buttocks and one behind my head, pressing my face into his neck, he encouraged me to rub against him until—I guess—it was clear to him I too had an orgasm. The upper joints of his left hand bore letters I won't write, but they were now inked out as a second thought; while on the joints of his right hand I recognized a Latino term for excrement.

When finally I stepped away, he held my hand in rough-skinned fingers. Had it been three hours later, I would have had somewhere I had to go. Had it been the day before, while I might have been there on an off hour, I would have had to leave immediately on finishing the first time.

But it was the day it was: He grinned, and without releasing my hand, with his other and his general expressions of humor and contentment, this tattooed giant communicated clearly without any words at all: "That was fun. Let's do it again? No, right *now*...!" And so, with only a little variation, and because nobody else was there, we did. This time his tongue ended up way down my throat, as mine did down his. He was missing a couple of teeth in the back, which my own tongue learned and felt comfortable knowing.

He did not speak to me. When we were done for the second time, I said a few things to him. Where did he want to go? What had he come here for? He listened, looking at me curiously, but did not respond in any way specific enough to make me think he understood any particular word I'd said.

I knew there were people in the world who had once spoken other languages than mine; and I was innocent enough not to be threatened by it as a concept—at least when the results were pleasant, and so far they had been.

It was one of the things I'd taken from my time at the Tolmec Hermitage, supported by things that had occurred on my travels up from Old Mexico through Texas to New Mexico and the northern border to the three-state union that remains, where Canada starts.

I released his hand, and began to walk—and was both curious and surprised when he walked with me.

And somehow I went with him back to the three living units that I shared with some others in the town.

We walked down toward my cabin—and while we were getting to the more populous area I saw Marcus, my friend from work, who basically has little use for gay men at all, though he is a friendly enough work mate—and I reached over to take my big, new friend's hand to make it seem a more normal relationship, at least in Marcus's eyes. But the big fellow pulled his hand away and frowned. So I stepped a little closer and we went on walking.

Moments later, we passed Ara—who had been a Smart Girl back at the same Tolmec Hermit's I'd been at, before all the traveling and disruption, and who had ended up here when Things Settled Down, as the News Pundits say on the Info Dumps that you can go and watch here and there in the streets if you're really interested. Ara and I rarely spoke, but I always assumed there was a kind of bond between us. He blinked at us—and I supposed I understand what he was thinking: My new friend after all was as different from those of us as you might see around the streets and alleys of our town as a movie star or, really, some soldier, either of which, I suppose, he could have been.

Ara had lived a much more common life than I had, for those who had once been Smart Girls in a hermitage. His own travels had taken him way to the south, and rumor had it to Brazil, which was a million miles away culturally—and he had worked for several years in some non-U.S. space program in some South American Union that still had one (though whether he had been to an actual Other World or Other Moon or not I wasn't sure) though now he had returned to Settle Down pretty close to where I had.

Someone else walked by, I believe, and looked, and so I just reached over and took the big fellow's hand, again to make us look more ordinary. And this time he let me hold it, and minutes later we were at the porch of the six-unit dwelling—three on the north side, three on the south: I had the one on the north end. We came in, and he stopped at the door, to look around the circular room where I had most of my stuff, my futon, some pictures that a friend of mine had once drawn, some other things that had been printed that I thought were interesting, some on the door out to the shared latrine in the hall, that hooked up underground to the neighborhood waste disposal system for much of the neighborhood, the only sign for which was the blue band along the bottom of the roll of toilet paper that meant, 'Don't throw it in the hole!' which, I suddenly wondered if my new, nameless (so far) friend was familiar with.

(Apparently he was.)

I asked him a couple of more questions. Didn't get a couple of more answers. (Of course you have to normalize the dialogue; especially in the beginning, and even more especially if some of it is happening in a different language you don't even speak. Though I'd learned a few of those words, I'll leave them out. It's not just literary universalism, it's comprehension.) One of the things he said to me when we got inside was: "First, I think you mean 'means *of* production,'" and explained what it meant, "and, second, arguing over whether the Earth is round or flat is silly when you're living in a geographical union where there's only one sex represented, despite the varieties of genders, for a thousand miles in any direction, and since you were twelve and I was twenty-two neither of us have been allowed to cross a border; some of us are killed by the hundreds every day and others of us are left to die on our own—and the thing I worked so hard for and was in the year before I met you was to escape from one group to the other. It just doesn't happen to be happening right here, right now. Got it? But what either your or my forebears from three generations ago would recognize as ordinary human reproduction is only occurring in two very small republics under conditions of pain, oppression, and physical and emotional abuse."

I frowned. "You," I said, for the first time, "are bat-shit crazy."

"I," he said, "am not going to argue. But have you ever seen or heard of a person bearing a child, or getting pregnant, or birthing a child? How would someone here go about finding out if they were in such a condition—or even could be?"

I said, "I don't know what those terms mean—can you explain them to me?"

He chuckled and shrugged. "Not tonight. But eventually, perhaps you'll see that because I am probably the only person you'll ever talk to who thinks differently—and possibly one or two Hermits in their Hermitages—from the majority is the major proof I'm right."

"Maybe that's something they made me forget in my coming-of-age forgetfulness process."

"Now why would they make you forget that?"

"I don't know. What did they want you to forget?"

"I never had it. It's very expensive. The vast, *vast* majority of people in this union don't. It just removes all sense of personal and social conflict out of the experiences that frighten you out of your preferences for the same sex on the sexual level—which is to say that it assures there are a good number of people like you around who suck good dick and like doing it, and feel it's normal and they're evenly distributed throughout the landscape. That's all."

"Come on. It's got to be more than that. It has to produce a major advantage."

"No, it doesn't. It shifts a 'natural' balance by about three percent, which is enough to restructure an entire society. And nobody ever talks about it." Then he said: "And the other thing they make you forget is just how few of you there actually were. How few a few thousand are who can only be imitated by others in a landscape of millions..."

And that's maybe three years of normalized dialogue, between two people and discussions with whole groups, crammed into the account of a single conversation. Not the whole story at all, nor would it be if I added that part of it came during a shouting argument with some others during an icy morning's breakfast at a conference we were visiting, and another part came with the support of fifty pages transcript read on a secure line in a reader I found in the back of a library when I was browsing in an office while the light through the new windows went from yellow to red in the light outside in the court yard—where there's just been an execution of twenty prisoners.

Hey—what is important to me about our actual meeting was that the next I knew Cellibrex was at my small electric stove and making, first, an acceptable cup of tea (with a laconic "Glad I don't miss coffee..." which bewildered me) and then when we sat on the edge of the futon together, sipping it out of the ceramic cups that I kept over the cooking and washing sink by the stove, he came back in from the latrine, brought over a pot I hadn't washed from the sink, and showed me the white streaks inside it, while I sat cross-legged on the mattress.

"Oatmeal?" he asked.

I was surprised. "Um... yes," I said. "I had it for breakfast. I haven't cleaned the pot yet."

"If I stay, maybe tomorrow...?"

"Sure," I said. "I don't mind. I'll make you some, if you'd like. You like oatmeal?"

He stood above me, dangling the pot. With his other hand, he scratched himself. (His belt and groin clout were all in a pile on the futon's corner.) "You," he said, "are ridiculously talkative. If you shut up, though, maybe I'll stay."

Which surprised me. (And he seemed to think was funny.)

Then he got down on his knees, put his arms around me, and pulled me over and we began once more.

Surprised, I stopped and lifted my head. "Tell me your name."

He had already started in again. "Why? I don't know yours, yet. But you suck some good dick."

And about an hour later, while I was sucking him... well, let me pull a literary curtain over that. I mean it's not like you have to tell everything you do in bed with everybody. (It's not like there are any sexually transmitted diseases left that force you to be honest about all that stuff—as I read about once in the library.) At any rate, it caught me off guard, but I went on swallowing. And when he was finished, I came all over his belly. Taking a big breath, I asked, "How'd you know I'd like that?"

He chuckled. "I took a chance. You can go on calling me Cellibrex. I'll go on calling you Clam. I'll tell you my real name if I'm still here in a week."

I was surprised again.

But he was and he did.

And once out of nowhere he said, "You said your sister told you if you didn't go inside the Hermitage, you would be killed...?"

I looked puzzled. "Yes...?"

"Well, admittedly it would have been ten years earlier, but if you had stayed outside, we—or children very much like us—are the ones who would have swarmed by and killed you. That's who you were fleeing from." He gave a humph. "That's who I was fleeing from when I started my wanderings and was captured by the very gang of ruffians you were fleeing by seeking refuge inside."

"That's who you... defected from?"

He didn't say anything.

"But why—?"

"Because by that time they would have killed me."

When we were together for three weeks, Cellibrex was wearing clothing like mine, and both of us were spending a lot more time barefooted whenever we were in the house, and... well, it was kind of surprising just how much we had changed each other, in so much of what we did outside, and how well we adjusted to what each of us liked to do when, together, we were indoors. (He too sucked some... well, he'd been imitating guys like me all his life. But I don't feel comfortable talking about it, because of some of the trouble I've seen people get into over speaking of it.) "We are such different people, you and me," I asked after three years: "Why are we still together?"

I thought it was probably because you can only feel so threatened by someone who makes tea and likes oatmeal and is good at sex, no matter how different they are from you.

"Because we like each other...?"

"... ARE GETTING USED to each other," was his own regularly repeated answer to that question for more than a decade. By then his tattoos had changed from things that now and then could repel me to things that I wanted pressed all over me, to simply something familiar and that I was glad were there because they were his.

(I don't know what you are used to, so that I don't know what you will assume as to cleanliness, technology, neatness, clutter, and will fill in... properly or improperly, if I don't mention it or leave it out.)

That year they put out a new *Star Wars* (number four of the third tetralogy), and I went to see it on a sensory helmet in a theater.

While I was at a tea and cake shop nearby called La Colombe, pretty crowded that afternoon, I had a glass of water and a blueberry muffin. While I was eating it, a woman about my age come in to stand next to me:

605

she was wearing an ordinary black coat and not the stripes that, these days, the disabled often wear. She must have had some kind of stroke, because one hand hung down beside her with the fingers turned to the back, and when she ate whatever piece of pastry she was eating, she had to lean way, way back and she moved around kind of stiff-legged, and the barista who wore a knitted cap took it all in stride; I called Cellibrex on my pocket phone (the thing was working that afternoon), to tell him, as I walked out of the place, that I was going to stop off and see it.

She and I and about half the others had come in barefoot—which, at that time of year, was a slight but not major surprise.

I enjoyed the show. It had been playing for about a week so there weren't that many people in the theater, a large cinderblock building with decorative black curtains on both sides of the auditorium.

Nobody in the projection looked like anyone I was used to seeing—but I was pretty used to that, too.

Still, the story had made me feel good, and afterward when I was coming home, I gave ten dollars to a homeless mother—at least that's what her sign said, as she sat up against one of the uptown building walls, though she didn't have her kid with her—and I also gave twenty to an old friend I ran into who used to hustle and who said he wasn't homeless, but he was still available for pay. So we wandered over to the same place I'd met Cellibrex and had a very unenthusiastic sexual encounter in which neither one of us got really excited.

I didn't tell Cellibrex about any of this, because (one) he does not like movies of any kind in a theater, and though (two) he does not have a jealous bone in his body, he does worry all the time about money, and we both get our government pensions, at this point. And it never seems quite enough to get by on, though we neither one seem to be losing any weight.

Ten or so years after that, when I was retired and took on a lighter job, I was offered a chance to become a Library Guardian, which meant we got a slightly bigger living unit, if we took in five hundred books which were stored in a separate room which was open to the public two days a week, and nobody ever really came for them, though there was a guy named Bill who came and worked there, and whom we both got to like, and who would fly back to his family up in Houston or holidays, sometimes.

Cellibrex was much more outgoing and talkative by then around people outside, though he grumped to me in private that we would do it my way because we always did, and because that had become so habitual among his complaints about me, if anything it reassured me. And we did. And sometimes he would stand and glare at the young people who used the library, which I would tell him he just could not stand around doing. So he took to not going in that room at all.

THEN, THROUGH BILL, we got an invitation to move to Houston, where I could become a Guardian of an even bigger Library. So we did.

There were the usual private grumps: "We'll do it your way, because that's what we always do. Besides, we'll be working with Bill."

We moved—and it was a disaster. They were planning to disassemble our Tolmec unit on the day we left, so there was no coming back. It turned out that the area of Houston that we were moving to (Pasadena) just wasn't anywhere as sophisticated as Tolmec.

A month after we got there, Bill—it turned out—wouldn't be able to work with us. In our front two rooms, we had three times the books we'd had in Tolmec, and the woman who was assigned the job was Bill's opposite: Ms. Chase was fat, talkative, and the first time I said anything to her she stood up from her desk and said, "If you don't like the way I do my job, see the Hermit." I did not say anything thing to Cellibrex about that one because he would just say, "Do what you want, you'll do it your way anyway," and I would point out how I was always doing what he wanted, as soon as he would say what it was.

The next morning, when Chase came in, I said to her, "I know I'm an old man, but this is not working out. Would you please get me an appointment with the Hermit?" I expected her to look frightened or contrite or otherwise confused. But she surprised me:

"Happily." Fifteen minutes later, she came in to say, "You have an appointment at three o'clock. I'll take you over there myself in an Uber, if you like. Do you want your partner to come with you? You might be more comfortable with him...?" and she waited with uncharacteristic expectancy.

"No," I said. "It'll be simpler if I just go myself."

At twenty of three, she came in. "I meant to get you five minutes ago, but the time got away from me. Take a sweater or a hoodie. You two don't use any air conditioning to speak of, and that place is going to be very cold. I've got a notebook here. I could jot down some of the things you've been complaining about. But the main thing is you want me transferred—and *I'd* like that, too!" I went in where Cellibrex was sleeping in our queen-sized bed. I kissed his bare shoulder through the sheet, which is how I like to sleep, though I have a heavier blanket over my half of the bed. He opened an eye and said, "Did you take your pills…?" and I said, as I often do, "Oops. I'll take them," which is another current of our lives that I can leave behind a traditional literary screen. Then I left and Chase and I went out into the heat of Houston's September.

"MAKE SURE YOU tell them you and I both want me to change my job," Chase said. "Just remember that's what you're here for. The way you two old fellows go around, I wouldn't be surprised if you both forgot."

"Are you going to take me back?" I asked.

"No," she said. "They'll get you home." I was totally unsure of myself, and felt very much the stranger in a strange land, but I started walking in through the interleaved walls. At one point I saw a large desk and an elderly dark-skinned woman in a straight up and down black quilted garment. On her face was a blotch of white skin… that made me frown. I don't know where I got the idea, from, but I suddenly went up to her. "Excuse me. I don't want to bother you. But were you ever the assistant to the Hermit of Tolmec—oh, many years ago. Twenty—no, fifty at least."

"Why, yes," she said, turning look at me. "I was. Why do you ask?"

"Now, that," I said, "is amazing. But age in a small town is always full of such coincidences. Well, I was one of the children you had for an educational program that you were running there."

"Oh, yes. I remember that. We had one practically every year. That was quite a while ago. I was only a youngster myself, back then."

I said, "I'm to report to the Hermit of Houston. I expect that's a room full of booths that you go into and tell them your problems…"

She nodded. "Any place in front of that wall will accomplish the same end."

"Oh." I looked over where she indicated. "Well, perhaps I should go over there and get started."

I leaned on my cane and turned. She said, "Excuse me. Wait a moment."

I turned back.

"I assume you were one of the students who didn't go on to the next level. I used to teach Ms. Chase, who brought you here, back when she was a boy, too, just like you. Well, not *exactly* like you. That's just a way of putting it. But that was a decade after I taught you. But to the extent that there is a Hermit of Houston, these days, I'm it. Because you were in our group at all, probably that means you were pretty sharp. Do you want to come to my office for a little bit? You might find it interesting. There isn't any Texas-Mexico border these days, but given that there used to be one only a generation before you were born, you might find it interesting what... well, *some* of what you might have learned if you'd gone on to the next level."

"I really have to get home to my partner..." She made me feel quite uncomfortable. Not like the assistant I remembered, but like the Hermit herself.

"Well, whether he knows it or not, he's probably a native of Mexico. You look as if you might be one, too." She smiled. "Come this way, if you would... don't worry, I'll make sure you get home safely and on time."

I followed her, and I can't tell you how much I felt I was going down a dangerous rabbit or worm hole. "What's Mexico?" I asked. I glanced at her feet, out of some long-remembered habit, to see what color shoe laces she might be wearing.

But it was just a door. The room behind it was almost identical with my own—I thought perhaps there would be a big chair, like the ornate one I remembered the old Hermit had sat in. But this was a simple chair with a simple console beside it. And the pattern on the walls was an enlarged reproduction of material certificates, except in gray rather than pale blue and gold. The carpet was only a little darker in hue than the one in our own bedroom. She walked over to it. She wore sandals, I realized. And a large ring on her big toe. "How would you feel about making a cup of tea for us...? There used to be a drink called coffee, but we don't have it anymore. Possibly your partner drank a great deal of it when he was much younger in the last gangs that worked in its cultivation—much to the south of here. But, then, you had your coming-of-age forgetting process, so that wouldn't be a problem for you." There weren't any laces at all.

"I suppose so. If you have some tea-bags and a tea-kettle...?"

"I have a tea ball"—she went over to the chair—"and an electric water boiler and robots to make it which are all waiting behind the walls, which can be activated from either here"—and she touched a button on the arm of her chair—"or there"—and a chair that looked notably more comfortable than hers rose beside me. "Please, sit down.

"Sit there, unless you'd be more comfortable standing. And often, even at my age, I am."

"That all sounds pretty unusual for me," I said. But I sat, while she stood.

"The reason there's no Texas-Mexico border is because a generation before you were born a politician who very few people remember today proposed we build a wall between what was then the Republic of Mexico and what was then the Republic of the United States of America. The election of 2020 was the Trump of Doom for the Pence—which is the name they gave to an institution called the Electoral College which was supposed to be a safety net that guarded against the abuse of popular elections—which, from time to time, didn't work. In general, megalithic republics weren't doing too well, either."

I frowned. "I don't remember that word..."

"A very, very large republic. And a republic was a country run by elected officials. Generally speaking, unions worked better. Ships of State. The body politic. Bricolage. In general, smaller groups working together and connecting up according to what seemed necessary, and cutting back when it seemed right to do." She moved in front of her own chair and sat. "It works so much better now that we've separated the sexes and mixed up the genders—given them their proper dignity along with that of the ethnicities. All you have to do is dissociate them from where someone actually comes from and how they got here. Then you can do anything you want with them—thank the Night and the Day. What I have been told and what I operate by is that there is a place called Haven and there is a place called Mars and the moon and the moons of the gas giants. There are many people from other unions already working to exploit these and live on them. They don't always tell—in fact, they almost never tell—the people who were there where they were or how they got there or got back. I think the chances are almost overwhelming that your partner"—she looked down at her chair arm, fingered something there—and a table grew up from the carpet in front of her and another grew in front of me—with a steaming cup, and a teapot,—"spent his time in Guatemala, Belize, or who knows, in those other unions we don't mention anymore... I'm very fond of my robots. Have them for a decade and it's almost impossible not to be. Yes, my information tells me that your partner is likely to have been one of those who was turned loose in our landscape (... oh, there's some glitch right now in the internet!)"—and for a moment she made one of those familiar tight-lidded eye-squeezes that I've only seen people do in films, almost as if she were in pain—"after he was returned from a virtual lunar colony, so I'm not getting an exact figure. That's what *we* call the flat earth. But others interpret it differently." She picked up her cup and sipped.

"But what are they working to accomplish?"

"To control mean production—"

"The *means* of production...?"

Glancing at me, she raised an eyebrow that could have used some trimming, as if surprised I knew the term. "I only wish. No, that's something you might have found on Facebook. This is pure Handbook. It's about the imposing of normative, mean standards. Its critics say that it's both mean—that is, cruel and simple-minded together—and productive only of death... in *huge* amounts! But that's what it's designed for. We assume we'll be able to bring the population below the sustainable level in this particular union in two more generations—at least in this quarter of the globe.

"An analysis of the means of production yields a pretty tight theory that same-sex relations produces a variety in art, child rearing, battle, and even science, that is a benefit in pretty much any social structure humans might take part in. Mean production says they're abnormal and the best thing to do is to stamp them out: What you see here is the most humane way we've been able to come up with for doing it. Now we can just withdraw, sit back, and watch you die. It's not pretty, but at least it keeps you away from the fewer and fewer healthy folk. And you don't have to envy them—or Lesbians or anyone else. You never see them."

I didn't feel comfortable enough to drink at all.

"Do you like your new home here in Houston?"

I didn't think we'd been here long enough to know, but this was certainly an unsettling beginning to it. "Do you really want me—or us—to know all this?"

"I think if you tell too many others who don't already believe or 'know' it, they will decide you are one form or another of bat-shit crazy, which I believe is the demotic phrase that still persists in the English of this area." She smiled. "Something I suspect your partner has a good grasp of. And if my information is correct—and I have been raised to believe that it always is—I doubt very much he will believe it either. We find it pretty easy to manipulate people's memories and worldviews these days. You live with Teddy C. Rodriguez, am I right?"

"I think I'd like to get on home," I said. (That is not Cellibrex's real name, either. But in this account, that's close enough to it, so that it will do. Suffice it to say that she gave a name for him I recognized, and because she knew it, I felt far less at ease than I had been when I'd walked in. I would have expected her to call him, well... Cellibrex, the way I do here. But I thought the other was a secret, at least from such as she.)

"You were in the same class with Ara, weren't you," said the Hermit with a falling rather than a rising inflection.

I nodded.

"If you'd gotten to the second level, you would have learned your birthday and known how old you were for the rest of your life—not just till eighteen. We don't encourage such promiscuous knowledge among the population. It makes it easier to control what you think you think about the world." Then she seemed to remember herself—or perhaps saw something on the small screen on the arm of her chair. "All the children we select are smart. And for the first three levels it's practically a lottery who goes on to the next level, but we have to have some way and we call it testing. Still, it makes differences in what happens to you in your life. It's only at the fifth or sixth condensation, when we're bringing youngsters in from outside the union borders, that the testing can be at all significant." She chuckled. "Though some say it's a lottery all the way to the top. Some of the students who were just pleasant, rather than particularly smart, I keep track of. Like your Ms. Chase. Wonderful boy...! Wonderful boy! As, really, were you and Teddy as well. Go through the door there; there's a man with a pedicab, who will drive you home. It is a shameless indulgence that I use for myself and some of my friends."

"Eh—thank you," I said. "This way...?"

"No..." she said. "Over there. If you want to take your tea-cup and tea pot with you as souvenirs...? I have them made for me—"

"No..." I repeated, because that's what she'd said to me; though later I wished I had, at least to show Cellibrex, to have some proof.

"A last question—have you or your partner ever encountered the rumor of another order of human being? A witch, a succubus, a woman—not as we use the word here for someone you could meet in any public pornographic gathering in any sensory helmet theater, but a different kind of woman—or girl perhaps...?"

I stopped and looked back. "What do you mean?"

"Right now," she said, "that's the *perfect* answer! Every once in a while a man like your partner gets it into his head from somewhere that there *is* an entirely other form of humanity... and given the tasks we have of bringing down the population reasonably and safely, it's not a good rumor to let get out and about. It doesn't usually work, even when he thinks he's found one or a few of them. What I've been told, and I have no reason to believe it isn't true, is that there aren't a lot of them left... anywhere, at this point. They were harder to exterminate than you folks. But... well. I'm just glad that wasn't my department. And by now we have pretty much anyone who might even be mistaken for one under our thumb, thousands of miles away. Good-bye."

I walked forward and two panels in the wall opened that I hadn't even seen. Stepping outside, I saw a man sitting on a bench beside some greenery, looking at a magazine with pictures on the pages that were shifting like the old ones I remembered my sister used to read, back when I'd had a family. Did he still have one, I wondered? (I hadn't seen any of mine since I'd gone traveling as a child.) Did Cellibrex—?

Suddenly I remembered. "I'm sorry," I said, "I have to go back. The reason I came was to tell someone that Ms. Chase wasn't happy with her job, and—" Because I was thinking all sorts of things Cellibrex had said that came back to me: maybe his experiences and travels in the Union, in the world, were indeed broader than mine...

But I also felt it was very dangerous to try to pin them down with a language that had been so carefully tailored to erase the possibility. (I could hear her saying to this same man, "I'm going to take in some porn this afternoon…" Though it's the thing everyone does and talks about, it's not what everyone does and writes about.)

The man looked at something on his wrist, then blinked up at me. "According to this, that was taken care of when you came in. I'm assuming you're ready to return to where you live…?"

"The Hermit has already seen to—?"

"Who?" he asked.

"The Hermit. She said she used you—"

"Oh," he said, "about ten big officers at the Hermitage use me to take their friends around the city. But I don't think there is *a* Hermit anymore. I've got your address here. All you have to do is get in and put the blanket up around you, if you get chilly. But it's a nice day. Watch your cane there."

So that's what I did.

The doors to the back of the Houston Hermitage were glass and blackened bronze, like my childhood memories of the doors at the front of the Hermitage in Tolmec. I was surprised, and, yes, for the first time since I'd arrived, I felt relieved. It was glorious weather.

We drove off, with the young guy pedaling in his sandals. (He was probably forty, at least.) I held the handle of my cane in both hands, looking down where the rubber tip was on the ridged matt across the bottom of the little gondola I was seated in. My driver pedaled us along beside segways and closed vehicles. My cane swayed back and forth, and I looked around at bits and pieces of Houston going by.

Why, I wondered, would anyone want another kind of human being, unless it was just for difference? (Was it possible to have a greater difference between people than there was, say, between myself and Cellibrex? Myself and Ms. Chase…?) He drove through bustling Houston. When you look at things, you do very little panning. Your eye locks on something, and even when you're walking, you follow it until you snap your eyes to something else. When I was a child, I used to wonder if, every time you snapped your eyes, you died and woke up in a new present, but just with memories of the past. As I rode home, looking from one bit to another of the landscape of my new home in Houston, so different from the landscape I had negotiated when I was a child, I wondered if there wasn't something to my old theory.

"CELL...?"

"Mmm...?"

"Does it ever bother you that you're probably a decade closer to dying than I am?"

"No." Cellibrex turned around to face me under the blanket. "I never thought this was going to be a very good life—and it was a lot better than it could have been. Hey, little fellow, hold my big guy."

"Come on, don't joke around now."

"Who's joking?"

"Cell, I keep asking you the same questions every few years. But are you sure you never went to the moon, or to Mars, or to the lunar colonies on Io or Europa, Ganymede or Callisto?"

"And I told you, no. I was in jail. I was in the army. I just don't know where. They were just Earthside testing of behaviors someone wanted to try out on a population in a low gravity landscape—that is, if all the folks who think they're actually putting people on other planets are right. But I never left the surface of our infinite flat world. That's what I know. And I'm never going to believe anything else."

I said, "There're too many people on the planet. We're two men and can't reproduce. Doesn't that make us good people? Or at any rate, we haven't reproduced more than once, between the two of us, as far as *you* know."

"Yes...?" He moved closer to me, and I could feel his breath on my forehead, my beard against his chest. "You say I repeat myself. How many times have you said that?" His arm went around me; no, it's not as strong as it once was. But it's the arm that always holds me, as the other goes up and tries to find a position over my head and I smell the very familiar and reassuring odor of what's under it. "Well, even if you're right—which I'm not saying, now—that's the kind of thing I just wasn't brought up to worry about. And I told you, I may have left one kid back there, somewhere."

"That's what I was referring to." I wondered if I should tell him the Hermit had said he'd been on a "virtual lunar colony." But because it was virtual, perhaps that's what Cellibrex meant about it's being somewhere on the "flat" earth, and from his point of view he was right. "You said you don't feel bad about that one, either. Was that a... a different kind of human being?"

"Naw. It was just some guy who'd had a particular set of operations. Either he had it, or he decided not to. So maybe I'm not quite as good as you." His high arm came down and I raised my head to let it go under my neck.

"We are such different people, you and I. Why are we still together?"

I felt him shrug. "Habit. Great sex from time to time..." He chuckled. "Hell, ordinary sex from time to time, which is easier to find on the other side of the bed than going out and trying to locate an entire older group of guys who like the same sort of things you do. Which, I confess, isn't bad either—when I still have the energy or the concentration for it." He adjusted himself, adjusted me on top of him, against him. "And we're used to each other."

"We've only been here a few days, and I had a dream that I used to have again and again when I was kid. Odd. I was in a testing group, a huge testing group, and we all had to fight each other, no matter what we were doing, to see who came out on top. So I decided to take the most important things I knew: my name, where I was from, and my birthday with me in my head. I didn't even bother with my ID number. I could always get another. And did several times. In the dream, we fought and fought and fought and... then I woke up."

It took a while for him to tell me that, actually, in his short accented sentences. But one of the things I said back to him was, "No. You never told me this before." And another was, "You actually know how old you are?"

"I am seventy-nine," Cellibrex told me in the three-quarters dark.

I said, "I never asked you, because I didn't know how old I was, so I assumed you didn't know either." Then I added, "If that wasn't a dream, and you actually did it sometime when you were a child or a younger man, that was very smart. Especially because you got away with it. So you really were from Mexico?"

He grunted, and moved his beard on the top of my bald spot. That could have been a head signal for a yes or a no; lying there, I couldn't tell, though I looked up to see his face. "Argentina," he said with enough of an accent that he had to repeat it half a dozen times before I realized it was the name of someplace I had actually heard before.

* * *

THERE'S A CODA to the story. Three weeks later, I came home and found Cellibrex dead on our filthy living-room rug. A teacup had overturned on the table. His pocket phone was out, and on, and when I picked it up from where it had fallen maybe a foot from his hand (we both used the same access number), I managed to call up an incomplete, unsent, and mangled text message:

Could you please come home before bat-shit crazy

With the handle of my cane I smashed the phone and a few other things in the room. Then I sat at the table and took great gasps, stood up again, checked to see if he was alive, but he wasn't—I'd been sure of that from the moment I'd seen him lying there.

Then, because that's the kind of mind I have, I wondered: Had he been trying to type "...before I go bat-shit crazy" or even "before these bat-shit crazy men [or whatever]..." *Had* somebody come into the place? But no. It was just some failure of the aged machinery of life...

But now I was convinced that the phone itself had killed him: because it had made me feel I was always in contact with him, when I wasn't. I hadn't been in the same room with him. And I was a wreck, because if there had been a last twenty seconds, a last ten, a last five, I felt a malevolent force had robbed me of them, when they should have been his and mine. The phone itself had lied to me, because it had said I was with Teddy C. Rodriguez when I was not.

Then I had no idea what to do, where to go, who to look for or phone to tell about it. He was in a pair of ragged underpants, and the marks on his body that had been a text whose meanings I had felt totally familiar with among his far more white than black body hair the day before, were now, in a way they had never seemed before, cryptic and incomprehensible. So I sat down in the big, soft, ragged chair.

Then I struggled up again and wandered around the house. Then I sat down once more, stood up suddenly—and walked out of the house. I had a hoodie on, and I just walked, and eventually I decided to walk in the sun, and that was better. In the shade I saw the wall of a building where, perhaps fifty years ago, someone had made a mosaic of tiles and paint and pieces of mirror, and I got to looking at it, and examining it—and after a minute realized I was thinking of Cellibrex's death; but in the course of looking at it, I realized some thirty seconds had gone by where I hadn't thought about him or his death at all, and that was astonishing and scary... and maybe, right.

My own pocket phone buzzed, and I took it out. I coughed—some great glob of phlegm had caught down there, and now came up in my mouth, and I swallowed it, surprised, and wondered why I hadn't spit it out. That's what Cellibrex would have done....

"Hello...?" I said.

A man's voice said, "Just a moment. This is the Hermit of Houston..." While I wondered why, if the Hermit of Houston was in fact a woman, they didn't use a woman's voice, the man told me that I should go to a certain address and ring. Someone was expecting me.

It wasn't that far, actually.

"I don't want to see anyone right—" I cleared my throat again. "... right now."

"I would advise you do. This must be a very hard time for you. From where you are now, it's only perhaps six streets away."

"All right," I said.

"It's what most people do. And it works. You can call us back if you need anything."

And half an hour later, an elderly, very black African was making me a pot of tea and we were sitting at his kitchen table, quietly together. His place was different enough from ours that I felt comfortable, but not so different as— say—the Hermit's, where I'd just felt completely disoriented. At one point as we began talking, I remember saying something that a writer I'd been fond of who'd died before I was born had written: "People are not replaceable..." or something like it.

But he poured me another cup of tea. "Good people will often do similar things for you, however." His name was Hammond. "Each one does it in a different way."

I thought of Cellibrex making tea. I thought of the robots of the Hermit of Houston.

And I stayed there for three weeks. Hammond was younger than Cellibrex, but older than I was. He had been to Mars and remembered it very clearly.

We slept in the same bed. On the second night, he told me, "I can hold you, if you like. If you would like to have sex, we can do that. Or I will just stay where I am, and be near if you want to talk." I chose one, and, on the third night, decided that my choice had been a mistake so chose another. And decided Hammond was an extremely tolerant man—and came very close to crying for the first time. (Later, I actually did. But I guess at some point we all do. At least I think so.) And at the end of two weeks I felt better. Then, somehow it was six months later: I was living by myself again. And life was going on. There'd been a funeral that only about seven people had come to, but Hammond was one of them, but there's no point going into all that.

The *Star Wars* film was in reruns—which Cellibrex *had* enjoyed: where you just went to a small theater with a few hundred people in sensory masks, all sitting around together watching only the sex scenes, sometimes with people observing from their homes, sometimes with people right next to you, which Cellibrex said was the kind of porn he'd been brought up on. And I'd liked going with him and I'd like going with strangers—and, yes, I still did.

Now and then I wondered if Cellibrex had known something that had died with him that might have explained something to me, if only I had thought to ask. Or was he just someone who knew no more of the whole story than I or anyone else? Would I eventually forget how much I thought there might be to know, even as I remembered how much I'd been warmed by knowing and being near him—by being as different from him as I had been?

Sometimes I tried to remember the things that had made Cellibrex another person I had been able to live with and—I guess—love all this time—and often I'd stopped because they were too… confusing? Painful?

With a greater variety in all its social structures, what might life have been like? What might coffee have tasted like, though personally I couldn't remember it at all, in a world of unions without borders?

It was easier to think that this had all been set up by the Hermit of Houston, who I had once known when she was an assistant and knew now as a computer and, I guess, a man.

And I was even thankful for them.

— Philadelphia,

Dec 25, 2016–Feb 3th, 2017

BELLADONNA NIGHTS
Alastair Reynolds

Alastair Reynolds (www.alastairreynolds.com) was born in Barry, South Wales, in 1966. He has lived in Cornwall, Scotland, the Netherlands, where he spent twelve years working as a scientist for the European Space Agency, before returning to Wales in 2008 where he lives with his wife Josette. Reynolds has been publishing short fiction since his first sale to *Interzone* in 1990. Since 2000 he has published sixteen novels: the Inhibitor trilogy, British Science Fiction Association Award winner *Chasm City*, *Century Rain*, *Pushing Ice*, *The Prefect*, *House of Suns*, *Terminal World*, the Poseidon's Children series, *Doctor Who* novel *The Harvest of Time*, *The Medusa Chronicles* (with Stephen Baxter), and *Revenger*. His short fiction has been collected in *Zima Blue and Other Stories*, *Galactic North*, *Deep Navigation*, and *Beyond the Aquila Rift: The Best of Alastair Reynolds*. Coming up is a new novel, *Elysium Fire*. In his spare time, he rides horses.

I HAD BEEN thinking about Campion long before I caught him leaving the flowers at my door.

It was the custom of Mimosa Line to admit witnesses to our reunions. Across the thousand nights of our celebration a few dozen guests would mingle with us, sharing in the uploading of our consensus memories, the individual experiences gathered during our two-hundred thousand year circuits of the galaxy.

They had arrived from deepest space, their ships sharing the same crowded orbits as our own nine hundred and ninety-nine vessels. Some were members of other Lines—there were Jurtinas, Marcellins and Torquatas—while others were representatives of some of the more established planetary and stellar cultures. There were ambassadors of the Centaurs, Redeemers and the Canopus Sodality. There were also Machine People in attendance, ours being one of the few Lines that maintained cordial ties with the robots of the Monoceros Ring.

And there was Campion, sole representative of Gentian Line, one of the oldest in the Commonality. Gentian Line went all the way back to the Golden Hour, back to the first thousand years of the human spacefaring era. Campion was a popular guest, always on someone or other's arm. It helped that he was naturally at ease among strangers, with a ready smile and an easy, affable manner—full of his own stories, but equally willing to lean back and listen to ours, nodding and laughing in all the right places. He had adopted a slight, unassuming anatomy, with an open, friendly face and a head of tight curls that lent him a guileless, boyish appearance. His clothes and tastes were never ostentatious, and he mingled as effortlessly with the other guests as he did with the members of our Line. He seemed infinitely approachable, ready to talk to anyone.

Except me.

It had been nothing to dwell over in the early days of the reunion. There had been far too many distractions for that. To begin with there was the matter of the locale. Phecda, who had won the prize for best strand at the Thousandth Night of our last reunion, had been tasked with preparing this world for our arrival. There had been some grumbles initially, but everyone now agreed that Phecda had done a splendid job of it.

She had arrived early, about a century in advance of any of the rest of us. Tierce, the world we had selected for our reunion, had a solitary central landmass surrounded by a single vast ocean. Three skull-faced moons stirred lazy tides in this great green primordial sea. Disdaining land, Phecda had constructed the locale far from shore, using scaper technology to raise a formation of enormous finger-like towers from the seabed.

These rocky columns soared kilometres into the sky, with their upper reaches hollowed out into numerous chambers and galleries, providing ample space for our accommodation and celebrations. Bridges linked some of the towers, while from their upper levels we whisked between more distant towers or our orbiting ships. Beyond that, Phecda had sculpted some of the towers according to her own idiosyncrasies. Music had played a part in her winning strand, so one of the towers was surmounted by a ship-sized violin, which we called the Fiddlehead tower. Another had the face of an owl, a third was a melted candle, while the grandest of them all terminated in a clocktower, whose stern black hands marked the progression of the thousand nights.

Phecda had done well. It was our twenty-second reunion, and few of us could remember a more fitting locale in which to celebrate the achievements of our collective circuits. Whoever won this time was going to have quite an act to follow.

It wouldn't be me. I had done well enough in my circuit, but there were others who had already threaded better strands than I could ever stitch together from my experiences. Still, I was content with that. If we maintained our numbers, then one day it might end up being my turn. Until that distant event, though, I was happy enough just to be part of our larger enterprise.

Fifty or more nights must have passed before I started being quietly bothered by the business of Campion. My misgivings had been innocuous to start with. Everyone wanted a piece of our Gentian guest, and it was hardly surprising that some of us had to wait our turn. But gradually I had the sense that Campion was going out of his way to shun me, moving away from a gathering just when I arrived, taking his leave from the morning tables when I dared to sit within earshot.

I told myself that it was silly to think that he was singling me out for this cold-shoulder treatment, when I was just one of hundreds of Mimosa shatterlings who had yet to speak to him personally. But the feeling dogged me. And when I sensed that Campion was sometimes looking at me, directing a glance when he thought I might not notice, my confusion only deepened. I had done nothing to offend him or any member of his Line—had I?

The business with the flowers did not start immediately. It was around the hundredth night when they first appeared, left in a simple white vase just outside my room in the Owlhead tower. I examined them with only mild interest. They were bulb-headed flowers of a lavish dark purple colour, shading almost to black unless I took them out onto the balcony.

I asked around as to who might have left the flowers, and what their meaning might have been. No one else had received a similar puzzle. But when no one admitted to placing the flowers, and the days passed, I forced myself to put them from mind. It was not uncommon for shatterlings to exchange teasing messages and gifts, or for the locale itself to play the odd game with its guests.

Fifty or sixty nights later, they reappeared. The others had withered by this time, but now I took the opportunity to whisk up to my ship and run the flowers through *Sarabande*'s analyser, just in case there was something I was missing.

The flowers were Deadly Nightshade, or Belladonna. Poisonous, according to the ship, but only in a historic sense. None of us were immortal, but if we were going to die it would take a lot more than a biochemical toxin to do it. A weapon, a stasis malfunction, a violent accident involving the unforgiving physics of matter and energy. But not something cobbled together by ham-fisted nature.

Still I had no idea what they meant.

Somewhere around the two hundredth night the flowers were back, and this time I swore I was nearly in time to see a figure disappearing around the curve in the corridor. It couldn't have been Campion, I told myself. But I had seen someone of about the right build, dressed as Campion dressed, with the same head of short curls.

After that, I stationed an eye near my door. It was a mild violation of Line rules—we were not supposed to monitor or record any goings-on in the public spaces—but in view of the mystery I felt that I was entitled to take the odd liberty.

For a long time the flowers never returned. I wondered if I had discouraged my silent visitor with that near-glimpse. But then, around the three hundred and twentieth night, the flowers were there again. And this time my eye had caught Campion in the act of placing them.

I caught his eye a few times after. He knew, and I knew, that there was something going on. But I decided not to press him on the mystery. Not just yet. Because on the three hundred and seventieth night, he would not be able to ignore me. That was the night of my threading, and for one night only I would be the unavoidable focus of attention.

Like it or not, Campion would have to endure my presence.

*　　*　　*

HE SMILED AT me. It was the first time we had looked at each other for more than an awkward moment, before snatching our glances away.

"I suppose you think us timid," I said.

"I don't know. Why should I?"

"Gentian Line has suffered attrition. There aren't nine hundred and ninety-nine of you now, and there'll be fewer of you each circuit. How many is it, exactly?"

He made a show of not quite remembering, although I found it hard to believe that the number wasn't etched into his brain. "Oh, around nine hundred and seven, I think. Nine hundred and six if we assume Betony's not coming back, and no one's heard anything from *him* in half a million years."

"That's a tenth of your Line. Nearly a hundred of your fellow shatterlings lost."

"It's a dangerous business, sightseeing. It's Shaula, isn't it?"

"You know my name perfectly well."

He grinned. "If you say so."

He was giving me flip, off-the-cuff answers as if there was a layer of seriousness I was not meant to reach. Smiling and twinkling his eyes at me, yet there was something false about it at all, a stiffness he could not quite mask. It was the morning before the night of my threading, and while the day wasn't entirely mine—Nunki, who had threaded last night, was also being congratulated and feted—as the hours wore on the anticipation would start to shift to my threading, and already I was feeling more at the centre of things than I had since arriving. Tonight my memories would seep into the heads of the rest of us, and when we rose tomorrow it would be my experiences that were being dissected, critiqued and celebrated. For these two days, at least, Campion would be obliged to listen to me—and to answer my questions.

We stood at a high balcony in the Candlehead tower, warm blue tiles under our feet, sea air sharp in our noses.

"How does it work, Campion, when there are so many of you dead? Do your reunions last less than our own?"

"No, it's still a thousand nights. But there are obviously gaps where new memories can't be threaded. On those nights we honour the memories of the dead. The threading apparatus replays their earlier strands, or makes new permutations from old memories. Sometimes, we bring back the dead as physical imagos, letting them walk and talk among us, just as if they were still alive. It's considered distasteful by some, but I don't see the harm in it, if it helps us celebrate good lives well lived."

"We don't have that problem," I said.

"No," he answered carefully, as if wary of giving offence. "You don't."

"Some would say, to have come this far, without losing a single one of us, speaks of an innate lack of adventure."

He shrugged. "Or maybe you just choose the right adventures. There's no shame in caution, Shaula. You were shattered from a single individual so that you could go out and experience the universe, not so that you could find new ways of dying."

"Then you don't find us contemptible?"

"I wouldn't be here—I wouldn't keep coming here—if I felt that way. Would I?"

His answer satisfied me on that one point, because it seemed so sincerely offered. It was only later, as I was mulling over our conversation, that I wondered why he had spoken as if he had been our guest on more than one occasion.

He was wrong, though. This was our twenty-second reunion, and Campion had never joined us before.

So why had he spoken as if he had?

I FELT FOOLISH. We had communicated, and it had been too easy, too normal, as if there had never been any strange distance between us. And that was strange and troubling in and of itself.

The day was not yet done, nor the evening, so I knew that there would be more chances to speak. But I had to have all my questions ready, and not be put off by that easy-going front of his. If he wanted something of me, I was damned well going to find out what it was.

The flowers meant something, I was sure, and at the back of my mind was the niggling trace of half an answer. It was something about Belladonna, some barely-remembered fact or association. Nothing came to mind, though, and as the morning eased into afternoon I was mostly preoccupied with making last minute alterations to my strand. I'd had hundreds of days to edit down my memories, of course, but for some reason it was always a rush to distil them into an acceptable form. I could perform some of the memory editing in my room in the Owlhead tower, but there were larger chunks of unconsolidated memory still aboard my ship, and I realised it would be quicker and simpler to make some of the alterations from orbit.

I climbed the spiral stairs to the roof of the Owlhead and whisked up my ship. For all the charms of Phecda's locale, it was good to be back on my own turf. I walked to the bridge of *Sarabande* and settled into my throne, calling up displays and instrument banks. My eyes swept the glowing readouts. All was well with the ship, I was reassured to note. In six hundred and thirty days we would all be leaving Tierce, and I would call on *Sarabande*'s parametric engine to push her to within a sliver of the speed of light. Already I could feel my thoughts slipping ahead to my next circuit, and the countless systems and worlds I would visit.

Beyond *Sarabande*, visible through the broad sweep of her bridge window, there were at least a hundred other ships close enough to see. I took in their varied shapes and sizes, marvelling at the range of designs adopted by my fellow shatterlings. The only thing the ships needed to have in common was speed and reliability. There were also a handful of vehicles belonging to our guests, including Campion's own modest *Dalliance*, dwarfed by almost every other craft orbiting Tierce.

I worked through my memory segments. It didn't take long, but when I was done something compelled me to remain on the bridge.

"Ship," I said aloud. "Give me referents for Belladonna."

"There are numerous referents," *Sarabande* informed me. "Given your current neural processing bottleneck, you would need eighteen thousand years to view them all. Do you wish to apply a search filter?"

"I suppose I'd better. Narrow the search to referents with a direct connection to the Lines or the Commonality." It was a hunch, but something was nagging at me.

"Very well. There are still more than eleven hundred referents. But the most strongly indicated record relates to Gentian Line."

I leaned forward in my throne. "Go on."

"The Belladonna Protocol is an emergency response measure devised by

Gentian Line to ensure Line prolongation in the event of extreme attrition, by means of accident or hostile action."

"Clarify."

"The Belladonna Protocol, or simply Belladonna, is an agreed set of actions for abandoning one reunion locale and converging on another. No pre-arranged target is necessary. Belladonna functions as a decision-branch algorithm which will identify a unique fallback destination, given the application of simple search and rejection criteria."

A shiver of disquiet passed through me. "Has Gentian Line initiated Belladonna?"

"No, Shaula. It has never been necessary. But the Belladonna Protocol has been adopted by a number of other Lines, including Mimosa Line."

"And have we..." But I cut off my own words before they made me foolish. "No, of course not. I'd know if we'd ever initiated Belladonna. And we certainly haven't suffered extreme attrition. We haven't suffered any attrition at all."

We're too timid for that, I thought to myself. Much too timid. Weren't we?

I WHISKED BACK to Tierce. Campion was lounging in the afternoon sunlight on the upper gallery of the Candlehead, all charm and modesty as he fielded questions about the capabilities of his ship. "Yes, I've picked up a weapon or two over the years—who hasn't? But no, nothing like that, and certainly no Homunculus weapons. Space battles? One or two. As a guiding rule I try to steer clear of them, but now and again you can't avoid running into trouble. There was the time I shattered the moon of Arghul, in the Terzet Salient, but that was only to give myself a covering screen. There wasn't anyone living on Arghul when I did it. At least, I don't *think* there was. Oh, and the time I ran into a fleet of the Eleventh Intercessionary, out near the Carnelian Bight..."

"Campion," I said, his audience tolerating my interruption, as well they had to on my threading day. "Could we talk? Somewhere quieter, if possible?"

"By all means, Shaula. Just as long as you don't drop any spoilers about your coming strand."

"It isn't about my strand."

He rose from his chair, brushing bread crumbs from his clothes, waved absent-mindedly to his admirers, and joined me as we walked to a shadowed area of the gallery.

"What's troubling you, Shaula—last minute nerves?"

"You know exactly what's troubling me." I kept my voice low, unthreatening, even though nothing would have pleased me more than to wrap my hands around his scrawny throat and squeeze the truth out of him. "This game you've playing with me... playing *on* me, I should say."

"Game?" he answered, in a quiet but guarded tone.

"The flowers. I had a suspicion it was you before I left the eye, and then there wasn't any doubt. But you still wouldn't look me in the face. And this morning, pretending that you weren't even sure of my name. All easy answers and dismissive smiles, as if there's nothing strange about what you've been doing. But I've had enough. I want a clear head before I commit my strand to the threading apparatus, and you're going to give it to me. Starting with some answers."

"Answers," he repeated.

"There was never any doubt about my name, was there?"

He glanced aside for an instant. Something had changed in his face when he looked back at me, though. There was a resignation in it—a kind of welcome surrender. "No, there wasn't any doubt. Of all of you, yours was the one name I wasn't very likely to forget."

"You're talking as if we've already met."

"We have."

I shook my head. "I'd remember if I'd ever crossed circuits with a Gentian."

"It didn't happen during one of our circuits. We met here, on Tierce."

This time the shake of my head was more emphatic. "No, that's even less likely. You ignored me from the moment I arrived. I couldn't get near you, and if I did, you always had some excuse to be going somewhere else. Which makes the business with the flowers all the more irritating, because if you wanted to talk to me..."

"I did," he said. "All the time. And we did meet before, and it was on Tierce. I know what you're going to say. It's impossible, because Mimosa Line never came to Tierce before, and these towers aren't more than a century old. But it's true. We've been here before, both of us."

"I don't understand."

"This isn't the first time," Campion answered. Then he looked down at the patterned tiles of the floor, all cold indigo shades in the shadowed light. "This day always comes. It's just a little earlier this time. Either I'm getting less subtle with the flowers, or you're retaining some memory of it between cycles."

"What do you mean, cycles?" I reached out and touched his forearm, not firmly, but enough to know I was ready to stop being mocked with half-truths and riddles. "I asked my ship about the flowers, you know. *Sarabande* told me about the Belladonna Protocol. It was there at the back of my mind somewhere, I know—but who'd bother caring about such a thing, when we haven't even lost a single shatterling? And why do you leave the flowers, instead of just coming out with whatever it is you need to share?"

"Because you made me promise it," Campion said. "The flowers were your idea. A test for yourself, so to speak. Nothing too obvious, but nothing too cryptic, either. If you made the connection, so be it. If you didn't, you got to see out these thousand nights in blissful ignorance."

"They weren't my idea. And blissful ignorance of what?"

I sensed it was almost more than he could bear to tell me. "What became of Mimosa Line."

HE TOOK ME to the highest lookout of the Clockhead tower. We were under a domed ceiling, painted pastel blue with gold stars, with open, stone-fretted windows around us. It surprised me to have the place to ourselves. We could look down at the other shatterlings on the galleries and promenades of the other towers, but at this late afternoon hour the Clockhead was unusually silent. So were we, for long moments. Campion held the upper hand but for now he seemed unsure what to do with it.

"Phecda did well, don't you think," I said, to fill the emptiness.

"You said you returned to your ship."

"I did." I nodded to the painted ceiling, to the actual sky beyond it. "It's a fine sight to see them all from Tierce, but you don't really get a proper sense of them until you're in orbit. I go back now and then wherever I need to or not. *Sarabande*'s been my companion for dozens of circuits, and I feel cut off her from her if I'm on a world for too long."

"I understand that. I feel similarly about *Dalliance*. Purslane says she's a joke, but that ship's been pretty good to me."

"Purslane?"

Something tightened in his face. "Do you mind if I show you something, Shaula? The locale is applying fairly heavy perceptual filters, but I can remove them simply enough, provided you give me consent."

I frowned. "Phecda never said anything about filters."

"She wouldn't have." Campion closed his eyes for an instant, sending some command somewhere. "Let me take away this ceiling. It's real enough—these towers really were grown out of the seabed—but it gets in the way of the point I need to make." He swept up a hand and the painted ceiling and its gold stars dissolved into the hard blue sky beyond it. "Now let me bring in the ships, as if it were night and you could see them in orbit. I'll swell them a bit, if you don't mind."

"Do whatever you need."

The ships burst into that blueness like a hundred opening flowers, in all the colours and geometries of their hulls and fields. They were arcing overhead in a raggedy chain, sliding slowly from one horizon to the other, daggers and wedges and spheres, blocks and cylinders and delicate lattices, some more sea-dragon than machine, and for the hundred that I presently saw there had to be nine hundred and more still to tick into view. It was such a simple, lovely perceptual tweak that I wondered why I had never thought to apply it for myself.

Then Campion said, "Most of them aren't real."

"I'm sorry?"

"The bulk of those ships don't exist. They're phantoms, conjured into existence by the locale. The truth is that there are only a handful of actual ships orbiting Tierce."

One by one the coloured ships faded from the sky, opening up holes in the chain. The process continued. One in ten gone, then two in ten, three in ten...

I looked at him, trying to judge his mood. His face was set in stone, as impassive as a surgeon administering some terrible, lacerating cure, sensing the patient's discomfort but knowing he must continue. Now only one in ten of the ships remained. Then one in twenty, one in thirty...

"Mine is real," he said eventually. "And three vehicles of Mimosa Line. None of the others were present, including all the ships you thought belonged to your guests."

"Then how did they get here?"

"They didn't. There are no guests, except me. The other Line members, the Centaurs, the Machine People... none of them came. They were another illusion of the locale." He touched a hand to his breast. "I'm your only guest. I came here because no one else could stand to. I've been coming here longer than you realise." And he raised his hand, opened his fist, and made one of the ships swell until it was larger than any of Tierce's moons.

It was a wreck. It had been a ship once, I could tell, but that must have been countless aeons ago. Now the hull was a gutted shell, open to space, pocked by holes that went all the way through from one side to the other. It was as eyeless and forbidding as a skull stripped clean of meat, and it drifted along its orbit at an ungainly angle. Yet for all that I still recognised its shape.

Sarabande.

My ship.

"You all died," Campion said softly. "You were wrong about being timid, Shaula. It was the exact opposite. You were too bold, too brave, too adventuresome. Mimosa Line took the risks that the rest of us were too cowardly to face. You saw and did wondrous things. But you paid a dire price for that courage. Attrition hit you harder than it had any Line before you, and your numbers thinned out very rapidly. Late in the day, when your surviving members realised the severity of your predicament, you initiated Belladonna." He swallowed and licked his tongue across his lips. "But it was too late. A few ships limped their way to Tierce, your Belladonna fallback. But by then all of you were dead, the ships simply following automatic control. Half of those ships have burned up in the atmosphere since then."

"No," I stated. "Not all of us, obviously..."

But his nod was wise and sad and sympathetic. "All of you. All that's left is this. Your ships created a locale, and set about staging the thousand nights. But there were none of you left to dream it. You asked about Gentian Line, and how we commemorated our dead? I told you we used imagos, allowing our fallen to walk again. With you, there are only imagos. Nine hundred and ninety-nine of them, conjured out of the patterns stored in your threading apparatus, from the memories and recordings of the original Mimosa shatterlings. Including Shaula, who was always one of the best and brightest of you."

I forced out an empty, disbelieving laugh.

"You're saying I'm dead?"

"I'm saying all of you are dead. You've been dead for much longer than a circuit. All that's left is the locale. It sustains itself, waits patiently, across two hundred thousand years, and then for a thousand nights it haunts itself with your ghosts."

I wanted to dismiss his story, to chide him for such an outlandish and distasteful lie, but now that he had voiced it I found it chimed with some deep, sad suspicion I had long harboured within myself.

"How long?"

The breeze flicked at the short tight curls of his hair. "Do you really want to know?"

"I wouldn't have asked if I didn't." But that was a lie of my own, and we both knew it for the untruth it was. Still, his reluctance was almost sufficient answer in its own right.

"You've been on Tierce for one million, two hundred and five thousand years. This is your seventh reunion in this locale, the seventh time that you've walked these towers, but all that happens each time is that you dream the same dead dreams."

"And you've been coming along to watch us."

"Just the last five, including this one. I was at the wrong end of the Scutum-Crux arm when you had your first, after you initiated the Belladonna Protocol, and by the time I learned about your second—where there was no one present but your own residuals—it was too late to alter my plans. But I made sure I was present at the next." His face was in profile, edged in golden tones by the lowering sun, and I sensed that he had difficulty looking me straight in the eyes. "No one wanted to come, Shaula. Not because they hated Mimosa Line, or were envious of any of your achievements, but because you rattled their deepest fears. What had happened to you, your adventures and achievements, had already passed into the safekeeping of the Commonality. None could ignore it. And no Line wants to think too deeply about attrition, and especially not the way it must *always* end, given enough time."

"But the dice haven't fallen yet—for you."

"The day will come." At last he turned to face me again, his face both young and old, as full of humour as it was sadness. "I know it, Shaula. But it doesn't stop me enjoying the ride, while I'm able. It's still a wonderful universe. Still a blessed thing to be alive, to be a thing with a mind and a memory and the five human senses to drink it all in. The stories I've yet to share with you. I took a slingshot around the Whipping Star..." But he settled his mouth into an accepting smile and shook his head. "Next time, I suppose. You'll still be here, and so will this world. The locale will regenerate itself, and along the way wipe away any trace of there ever being a prior reunion."

"Including my memories of ever having met you."

"That's how it has to be. A trace of a memory persists, I suppose, but mostly you'll remember none of it."

"But I'll ask you to pass a message forward, won't I. Ask you to leave flowers at my door. And you'll agree and you'll be kind and dutiful and you'll come back to us, and on some other evening, two hundred thousand years from now, give or take a few centuries, we'll be in this same lookout having much the same conversation and I won't have aged a second, and you'll be older and sadder and I won't know why, to begin with. And then you'll show me the phantom ships and I'll remember, just a bit, just like I've always remembered, and then I'll start asking you about the next reunion, another two hundred thousand years in the future. It's happened, hasn't it?"

Campion gave a nod. "Do you think it would have been better if I'd never come?"

"At least you had the nerve to face us. At least you weren't afraid to be reminded of death. And we lived again, in you. The other Lines won't forget us, will they? And tell me you passed on some of our stories to the other Gentians, during your own Thousand Nights?"

"I did," he said, some wry remembrance crinkling the corners of his eyes. "And they believed about half of them. But that was your fault for having the audacity to live a little. We could learn a lot."

"Just don't take our lessons too deeply too heart."

"We wouldn't have the nerve."

The sun had almost set now, and there was a chill in the air. It would soon be time to descend from the Clockhead tower, in readiness for the empty revelry of the evening. Ghosts dancing with ghosts, driven like clockwork marionettes.

Ghosts dreaming the hollow dreams of other ghosts, and thinking themselves alive, for the span of a night. The imago of a shatterling who once called herself Shaula, daring to hold a conscious thought, daring to believe she was still alive.

"Why me, Campion? Out of all the others, why is it me you feel the need to do this to?"

"Because you half know it already," he answered, after a hesitation. "I've seen it in your eyes, Shaula. Whatever fools the others, it doesn't escape you. And you're wrong, you know. You do change. You might not age a second between one reunion and the next, but I've seen that sadness in you build and build. You feel it in every breath, and you pick up on the flowers a little sooner each time. And if there was one thing I could do about it..."

"There is," I said sharply, while I had the courage.

His expression was grave but understanding. "I'll bring you flowers again."

"No. Not flowers. Not next time." And I swallowed before speaking, because I knew the words would be difficult to get out once I had started. "You'll end this, Campion. You have the means, I know. There are only wrecks left in orbit, and they wouldn't stand a chance against your own weapons. You'll shatter those wrecks like you shattered the moon of Arghul, and when you're done you'll turn the same weapons onto these towers. Melt them to lava. Flush them back into the sea, leaving no trace. And turn the machines to ash, so that they can't ever rebuild the towers or us. And then leave Tierce and never return to this place."

He stared at me for a long moment, his face so frozen and masklike it was as if he had been struck across the cheeks.

"You'd be asking me to murder a Line."

"No," I said patiently. "The Line is gone, and you've already honoured us. All I'm asking for is one last kindness, Campion. This wasn't ever the way it was meant to be." I reached for him then, settling my hand on his wrist, and then sliding my fingers down until I held his in my own. "You think you lack the courage to commit grand acts. I don't believe a word of it. And even if you did, here's your chance to do something about it. To be courageous and wise and selfless. We're dead. We've *been* dead for a million years. Now let us sleep."

"Shaula..." he began.

"You'll consider it," I said. "You'll evaluate the options, weigh the risks and the capacity for failure. And you'll reach a conclusion, and set yourself on one course or another. But we'll speak no more of it. If you mean to end us, you'll wait until the end of the Thousandth Night, but you'll give me no word of a clue."

"I'm not very good at keeping secrets."

"You won't need to. This is my threading, Campion. My night of nights. It means I have special dispensation to adjust and suppress my own memories, so that my strand has the optimum artistic impact. And I still have the chance to undo some memories, including this entire conversation. I won't remember the phantoms, or the Belladonna Protocol, or what I've just asked of you."

"My Line frowned on that kind of thing."

"But you got away with it, all the same. It's a small deletion, hardly worth worrying about. No one will ever notice."

"But I'd know we'd had this conversation. And I'd still be thinking of what you'd asked of me."

"That's true. And unless I've judged you very wrongly, you'll keep that knowledge to yourself. We'll have many more conversations between now and Thousandth Night, I'm sure. But no matter how much I press you—and I will, because there'll be something in *your* eyes as well—you'll keep to your word. If I ask you about the flowers, or the other guests, or any part of this, you'll look at me blankly and that will be an end to it. Sooner or later I'll convince myself you really are as shallow as you pretend."

Campion's expression tightened. "I'll do my best. Are you sure there's no other way?"

"There isn't. And you know it as well. I think you'll honour my wish, when you've thought it over." Then I made to turn from him. "I'm going back to the Owlhead tower to undo this memory. Give me a little while, then call me back to the Clockhead. We'll speak, and I'll be a little foggy, and I'll probably ask you odd questions. But you'll deflect them gently, and after a while you'll tell me it's time to go to the threading. And we'll walk down the stairs as if nothing had changed."

"But everything will have," Campion said.

"You'll know it. I won't. All you'll have to do is play the dashing consort. Smile and dance and say sweet things and congratulate me on the brilliance of my circuit. I think you can rise to the challenge, can't you?"

"I suppose."

"I don't doubt it."

I left him and returned to my parlour.

LATER WE DANCED on the Fiddlehead rock. I had the sense that some unpleasantness had happened earlier between us, some passing cloudy thing that I could not bring to mind, but it could not have been too serious because Campion was the perfect companion, attentive and courteous and generous with wit and praise and warmth. It thrilled me that I had finally broken the silence between us; thrilled me still further that the Thousand Nights had so far to run—the iron hands of the Clockhead tower still to complete their sweep of their face.

I thought of all the evenings stretching ahead of us, all the bright strands we had still to dream, all the marvels and adventures yet to play out, and I thought of how wonderful it was to be alive, to be a thing with a mind and a memory and the five human senses to drink it all in.

DON'T PRESS CHARGES AND I WON'T SUE
Charlie Jane Anders

Charlie Jane Anders (charliejane.com) is the author of *All the Birds in the Sky*, which won a Nebula Award. Her next novel is *The City in the Middle of the Night*. Her story "Six Months, Three Days" won a Hugo Award and appears in a short story collection called *Six Months, Three Days, Five Others*. Her short fiction has appeared in *Tor.com, Wired Magazine, Slate, Tin House, Conjunctions, Boston Review, Asimov's Science Fiction, The Magazine of Fantasy & Science Fiction, McSweeney's Internet Tendency, ZYZZYVA*, and several anthologies. She was a founding editor of io9.com, a site about science fiction, science and futurism, and she organizes the monthly Writers With Drinks reading series. Her first novel, *Choir Boy*, won a Lambda Literary Award.

1.

THE INTAKE PROCESS begins with dismantling her personal space, one mantle at a time. Her shoes, left by the side of the road where the Go Team plucked her out of them. Her purse and satchel, her computer containing all of her artwork and her manifestos, thrown into a metal garbage can at a rest area on the highway, miles away. That purse, which she swung to and fro on the sidewalks to clear a path, like a southern grandma, now has food waste piled on it, and eventually will be chewed to shreds by raccoons. At some point the intake personnel fold her, like a folding chair that turns into an almost two-dimensional object, and they stuff her into a kennel, in spite of all her attempts to resist. Later she receives her first injection and loses any power to struggle, and some time after, control over her excretory functions. By the time they cut her clothes off, a layer of muck coats the backs of her thighs. They clean her and dress her in something that is not clothing, and they shave part of her head. At some point, Rachel glimpses a power drill, like a handyman's, but she's anesthetized and does not feel where it goes.

Rachel has a whole library of ways to get through this, none of which works at all. She spent a couple years meditating, did a whole course on trauma and self-preservation, and had an elaborate theory about how to carve out a space in your mind that *they* cannot touch, whatever *they* are doing to you. She remembers the things she used to tell everyone else in the support group, in the Safe Space, about not being alone even when you have become isolated by outside circumstances. But in the end, Rachel's only coping mechanism is dissociation, which only arises from total animal panic. She's not even Rachel any more, she's just a screaming blubbering mess, with a tiny kernel of her mind left, trapped a few feet above her body, in a process that is not at all like yogic flying.

Eventually, though, the intake is concluded, and Rachel is left staring up at a Styrofoam ceiling with a pattern of cracks that looks like a giant spider or an angry demon face descending toward her. She's aware of being numb from extreme cold in addition to the other ways in which she is numb, and the air conditioner keeps blurting into life with an aggravated whine. A stereo system plays a CD by that white rock-rap artist who turned out to be an especially stupid racist. The staff keep walking past her and talking about her in the third person, while misrepresenting basic facts about her, such as her name and her personal pronoun. Occasionally they adjust something about her position or drug regimen without speaking to her or looking at her face. She does not quite have enough motor control to scream or make any sound other than a kind of low ululation. She realizes at some point that someone has made a tiny hole in the base of her skull, where she now feels a mild ache.

Before you feel too sorry for Rachel, however, you should be aware that she's a person who holds a great many controversial views. For example, she once claimed to disapprove of hot chocolate, because she believes that chocolate is better at room temperature, or better yet as a component of ice cream or some other frozen dessert. In addition, Rachel considers ZZ Top an underappreciated music group, supports karaoke only in an alcohol-free environment, dislikes puppies, enjoys Brussels sprouts, and rides a bicycle with no helmet. She claims to prefer the *Star Wars* prequels to the Disney *Star Wars* films. Is Rachel a contrarian, a freethinker, or just kind of an asshole? If you could ask her, she would reply that opinions are a utility in and of themselves. That is, the holding of opinions is a worthwhile exercise per se, and the greater diversity of opinions in the world, the more robust our collective ability to argue.

Also! Rachel once got a gas station attendant nearly fired for behavior that, a year or two later, she finally conceded might have been an honest misunderstanding. She's the kind of person who sends food back for not being quite what she ordered—and on at least two occasions, she did this and then returned to that same restaurant a week or two later, as if she had been happy after all. Rachel is the kind of person who calls herself an artist, despite never having received a grant from a granting institution, or any kind of formal gallery show, and many people wouldn't even consider her collages and relief maps of imaginary places to be proper art. You would probably call Rachel a Goth.

Besides dissociation—which is wearing off as the panic subsides—the one defense mechanism that remains for Rachel is carrying on an imaginary conversation with Dev, the person with whom she spoke every day for so long, and to whom she always imagined speaking, whenever they were apart. Dev's voice in Rachel's head would have been a refuge not long ago, but now all Rachel can imagine Dev saying is, *Why did you leave me? Why, when I needed you most?* Rachel does not have a good answer to that question, which is why she never tried to answer it when she had the chance.

Thinking about Dev, about lost chances, is too much. And at that moment, Rachel realizes she has enough muscle control to lift her head and look directly in front of her. There, standing at an observation window, she sees her childhood best friend, Jeffrey.

2.

ASK JEFFREY WHY he's been working at Love and Dignity for Everyone for the past few years and he'll say, first and foremost, student loans. Plus, in recent years, child support, and his mother's ever-increasing medical bills. Life is crammed full of things that you have to pay for after the fact, and the word 'plan' in 'payment plan' is a cruel mockery because nobody ever really sets out to plunge into chronic debt. But also Jeffrey wants to believe in the mission of Love and Dignity for Everyone: to repair the world's most broken people. Jeffrey often re-reads the mission statement on the wall of the employee lounge as he sips his morning Keurig so he can carry Mr. Randall's words with him for the rest of the day. Society depends on mutual respect, Mr. Randall says. You respect yourself and therefore I respect you, and vice versa. When people won't respect themselves, we have no choice but to intervene, or society unravels. Role-rejecting and aberrant behavior, ipso facto, is a sign of a lack of self-respect. Indeed, a cry for help. The logic always snaps back into airtight shape inside Jeffrey's mind.

Of course Jeffrey recognizes Rachel the moment he sees her wheeled into the treatment room, even after all this time and so many changes, because he's been Facebook-stalking her for years (usually after a couple of whiskey sours). He saw when she changed her name and her gender marker, and noticed when her hairstyle changed and when her face suddenly had a more feminine shape. There was the kitten she adopted that later ran away, and the thorny tattoo that says STAY ALIVE. Jeffrey read all her oversharing status updates about the pain of hair removal and the side effects of various pills. And then, of course, the crowning surgery. Jeffrey lived through this process vicariously, in real time, and saw no resemblance to a butterfly in a cocoon, or any other cute metaphor. The gender change looked more like landscaping: building embankments out of raw dirt, heaving big rocks to change the course of rivers, and uprooting plants stem by stem. Dirty bruising work. Why a person would feel the need to do this to themself, Jeffrey could never know.

At first, Jeffrey pretends not to know the latest subject, or to have any feelings one way or the other, as the Accu-Probe goes into the back of her head. This is not the right moment to have a sudden conflict. Due to some recent personnel issues, Jeffrey is stuck wearing a project manager hat along with his engineer hat—which, sadly, is not a cool pinstriped train-engineer hat of the sort that he and Rachel used to fantasize about wearing for work when they were kids. As a project manager, he has to worry endlessly about weird details such as getting enough coolant into the cadaver storage area and making sure that Jamil has the green shakes that he says activate his brain. As a government–industry joint venture under Section 1774(b)(8) of the Mental Health Restoration Act (relating to the care and normalization of at-risk individuals), Love and Dignity for Everyone has to meet certain benchmarks of effectiveness, and must involve the community in a meaningful role. Jeffrey is trying to keep twenty fresh cadavers in transplant-ready condition, and clearing the decks for more live subjects, who are coming down the pike at an ever-snowballing rate. The situation resembles one of those poultry processing plants where they keep speeding up the conveyer belt until the person grappling with each chicken ends up losing a few fingers.

Jeffrey runs from the cadaver freezer to the observation room to the main conference room for another community engagement session, around and around, until his Fitbit applauds. Five different Slack channels flare at once with people wanting to ask Jeffrey process questions, and he's lost count of all his unanswered DMs. Everyone agrees on the goal—returning healthy, well-adjusted individuals to society without any trace of dysphoria, dysmorphia, dystonia, or any other dys- words—but nobody can agree on the fine details, or how exactly to measure ideal outcomes beyond those statutory benchmarks. Who even is the person who comes out the other end of the Love and Dignity for Everyone process? What does it even mean to be a unique individual, in an age when your fingerprints and retina scans have long since been stolen by Ecuadorian hackers? It's all too easy to get sucked into metaphysical flusterclucks about identity and the soul and what makes you you.

Jeffrey's near-daily migraine is already in full flower by the time he sees Rachel wheeled in and he can't bring himself to look. She's looking at him. She's looking right at him. Even with all the other changes, her eyes are the same, and he can't just stand here. She's putting him in an impossible position, at the worst moment.

Someone has programmed Slack so that when anyone types "alrighty then," a borderline-obscene gif of two girls wearing clown makeup appears. Jeffrey is the only person who ever types "alrighty then," and he can't train himself to stop doing it. And, of course, he hasn't been able to figure out who programmed the gif to appear.

Self-respect is the key to mutual respect. Jeffrey avoids making eye contact with that window or anyone beyond it. His head still feels too heavy with pain for a normal body to support, but also he's increasingly aware of a core-deep anxiety shading into nausea.

3.

JEFFREY AND RACHEL had a group, from the tail end of elementary school through to the first year of high school, called the Sock Society. They all lived in the same cul-de-sac, bounded by a canola field on one side and the big interstate on the other. The origins of the Sock Society's name are lost to history, but may arise from the fact that Jeffrey's mom never liked kids to wear shoes inside the house and Jeffrey's house had the best game consoles and a 4K TV with surround sound. These kids wore out countless pairs of tires on their dirt bikes, conquered the extra DLC levels in Halls of Valor, and built snow forts that gleamed. They stayed up all night watching forbidden horror movies on an old laptop under a blanket, on sleepovers, while guzzling off-brand soda. They whispered, late at night, of their fantasies and barely-hinted-at anxieties, although there were some things Rachel would not share because she was not ready to speak of them and Jeffrey would not have been able to hear if she had. They repeated jokes they didn't 100 percent understand, and kind of enjoyed the queasy awareness of being out of their depth. Later, the members of the Sock Society (who changed their ranks over time with the exception of the core members, Rachel and Jeffrey) became adept at stuffing gym socks with blasting caps and small incendiaries and fashioning the socks themselves into rudimentary fuses before placing them in lawn ornaments, small receptacles for gardening tools, and—in one incident that nobody discussed afterwards—Mrs. Hooper's scooter.

When Jeffrey's mother was drunk, which was often, she would say she wished Rachel was her son, because Rachel was such a smart boy—quick on the uptake, so charming with the rapid-fire puns, handsome and respectful. Like Young Elvis. Instead of Jeffrey, who was honestly a little shit.

Jeffrey couldn't wait to get over the wall of adolescence, into the garden of manhood. Every dusting of fuzz on his chin, every pungent whiff from his armpits seemed to him the starting gun. He became obsessed with finding porn via that old laptop, and he was an artist at coming up with fresh new search terms every time he and Rachel hung out. Rachel got used to innocent terms such as 'cream pie' turning out to be mean something gross and animalistic, in much the same way that a horror movie turned human bodies into slippery meat.

Then one time Jeffrey pulled up some transsexual porn, because what the hell. Rachel found herself watching a slender Latin girl with a shy smile slowly peel out of a silk robe to step into a scene with a muscular bald man. The girl was wearing nothing but bright silver shoes and her body was all smooth angles and tapering limbs, and the one piece of evidence of her transgender status looked tiny, both inconsequential and of a piece with the rest of her femininity. She tiptoed across the frame like a ballerina. Like a cartoon deer.

Watching this, Rachel quivered, until Jeffrey thought she must be grossed out, but deep down Rachel was having a feeling of recognition. Like: that's me. Like: I am possible.

Years later, in her twenties, Rachel had a group of girlfriends (some trans, some cis) and she started calling this feminist gang the Sock Society, because they made a big thing of wearing colorful socks with weird and sometimes profane patterns. Rachel mostly didn't think about the fact that she had repurposed the Sock Society sobriquet for another group, except to tell herself that she was reclaiming an ugly part of her past. Rachel is someone who obsesses about random issues, but also claims to avoid introspection at all costs—in fact, she once proposed an art show called *The Unexamined Life Is the Only Way to Have Fun.*

4.

RACHEL HAS SOILED herself again. A woman in avocado-colored scrubs snaps on blue gloves with theatrical weariness before sponging Rachel's still-unfeeling body. The things I have to deal with, says the red-faced woman, whose name is Lucy. People like you always make people like me clean up after you, because you never think the rules apply to you, the same as literally everyone else. And then look where we end up, and I'm here cleaning your mess.

Rachel tries to protest that none of this is her doing, but her tongue is a slug that's been bathed in salt.

There's always some excuse, Lucy says as she scrubs. Life is not complicated, it's actually very simple. Men are men, and women are women, and everyone has a role to play. It's selfish to think that you can just force everyone else in the world to start carving out exceptions, just so you can play at being something you're not. You will never understand what it really means to be female, the joy and the endless discomfort, because you were not born into it.

Rachel feels frozen solid. Ice crystals permeate her body, the way they would frozen dirt. This woman is touching between her legs, without looking her in the face. She cannot bear to breathe. She keeps trying to get Jeffrey's attention, but he always looks away. As if he'd rather not witness what's going to happen to her.

Lucy and a man in scrubs wheel in something gauzy and white, like a cloud on a gurney. They bustle around, unwrapping and cleaning and prepping, and they mutter numbers and codes to each other, like E-drop 2347, as if there are a lot of parameters to keep straight here. The sound of all that quiet professionalism soothes Rachel in spite of herself, like she's at the dentist.

At some point they step away from the thing they've unwrapped and prepped, and Rachel turns her head just enough to see a dead man on a metal shelf.

Her first thought is that he's weirdly good looking, despite his slight decomposition. He has a snub nose and thin lips, a clipped jaw, good muscle definition, a cyanotic penis that flops against one thigh, and sandy pubic hair. Whatever (whoever) killed this man left his body in good condition, and he was roughly Rachel's age. This man could have been a model or maybe a pro wrestler, and Rachel feels sad that he somehow died so early, with his best years ahead.

Rachel tries to scream. She feels Lucy and the other one connecting her to the dead man's body and hears a rattling garbage-disposal sound. The dead man twitches, and meanwhile Rachel can't struggle or make a sound. She feels weaker than before, and some part of her insists this must be because she lost an argument at some point. Back in the Safe Space, they had talked about all the friends of friends who had gone to ground, and the Internet rumors. How would you know if you were in danger? Rachel had said that was a dumb question, because danger never left.

The dead man smiles: not a large rictus, like in a horror movie, but a tiny shift in his features, like a contented sleeper. His eyes haven't moved or appeared to look at anything. Lucy clucks and adjusts a thing, and the kitchen-garbage noise grinds louder for a moment.

We're going to get you sorted out, Lucy says to the dead man. You are going to be so happy. She turns and leans over Rachel to check something, and her breath smells like sour corn chips.

You are violating my civil rights by keeping me here, Rachel says. A sudden victory, except that then she hears herself and it's wrong. Her voice comes out of the wrong mouth, is not even her own voice. The dead man has spoken, not her, and he didn't say that thing about civil rights. Instead he said, Hey, excuse me, how long am I going to be kept here? As if this was a mild inconvenience that was keeping him from his business. The voice sounded rough, flinty, like a bad sore throat, but also commanding. The voice of a surgeon, or an airline pilot. You would stop whatever you were doing and listen, if you heard that voice.

Rachel lets out an involuntary cry of panic, which comes out of the dead man's mouth as a low groan. She tries again to say, This is not medicine. This is a human rights violation. And it comes out of the dead man's mouth as, I don't mean to be a jerk. I just have things to do, you know. Sorry if I'm causing any trouble.

That's quite all right, Mr. Billings, Lucy says. You're making tremendous progress, and we're so pleased. You'll be released into the community soon, and the community will be so happy to see you.

The thought of ever trying to speak again fills Rachel with a whole ocean voyage's worth of nausea, but she can't even make herself retch.

5.

JEFFREY HAS WONDERED for years, what if he could talk to his oldest friend, man to man, about the things that had happened when they were on the cusp of adolescence—not just the girl, but the whole deal. Mrs. Hooper's scooter, even. And maybe, at last, he will. A lot depends on how well the process goes. Sometimes the cadaver gets almost all of the subject's memories and personality, just with a better outlook on his or her proper gender. There is, however, a huge variability in bandwidth because we're dealing with human beings and especially with weird neurological stuff that we barely understand. We're trying to thread wet spaghetti through a grease trap, a dozen pieces at a time. Even with the proprietary cocktail, it's hardly an exact science.

The engineer part of Jeffrey just wants to keep the machines from making whatever noise that was earlier, the awful grinding sound. But the project manager part of Jeffrey is obsessing about all of the extraneous factors outside his control. What if they get a surprise inspection from the Secretary, or even worse that Deputy Assistant Secretary, with the eye? Jeffrey is not supposed to be a front-facing part of this operation, but Mr. Randall says we all do things that are outside our comfort zones, and really, that's the only way your comfort zone can ever expand. In addition, Jeffrey is late for another stakeholder meeting, with the woman from Mothers Raising Well-Adjusted Children and the three bald men from Grassroots Rising, who will tear Jeffrey a new orifice. There are still too many maladjusted individuals out there, in the world, trying to use public washrooms and putting our children at risk. Some children, too, keep insisting that they aren't boys or girls, because they saw some ex-athlete prancing on television. Twenty cadavers in the freezer might as well be nothing in the face of all this. The three bald men will take turns spit-shouting, using words such as psychosexual, and Jeffrey has fantasized about sneaking bourbon into his coffee so he can drink whenever that word comes up. He's pretty sure they don't know what psychosexual even means, except that it's psycho and it's sexual. After a stakeholder meeting, Jeffrey always retreats to the single-stall men's room to shout at his own schmutzy reflection. Fuck you, you fucking fuck fucker. Don't tell me I'm not doing my job.

Self-respect is the key to mutual respect.

Rachel keeps looking straight at Jeffrey through the observation window, and she's somehow kept control over her vision long after her speech centers went over. He keeps waiting for her to lose the eyes. Her gaze goes right into him, and his stomach gets the feeling that usually comes after two or three whiskey sours and no dinner.

More than ever, Jeffrey wishes the observation room had a one-way mirror instead of regular glass. Why would they skimp on that? What's the point of having an observation room where you are also being observed at the same time? It defeats the entire purpose.

Jeffrey gets tired of hiding from his own window and skips out the side door. He climbs two stories of cement stairs to emerge in the executive wing, near the conference suite where he's supposed to be meeting with the stakeholders right now. He finds an oaken door with that quote from Albert Einstein about imagination that everybody always has, and knocks on it. After a few breaths, a deep voice tells Jeffrey to come in, and then he's sitting opposite an older man with square shoulders and a perfect old-fashioned newscaster head.

Mr. Randall, Jeffrey says, I'm afraid I have a conflict with regards to the latest subject and I must ask to be recused.

Is that a fact? Mr. Randall furrows his entire face for a moment, then magically all the wrinkles disappear again. He smiles and shakes his head. I feel you, Jeffrey, I really do. That blows chunks. Unfortunately, as you know, we are short staffed right now, and our work is of a nature that only a few people have the skills and moral virtue to complete it.

But, Jeffrey says. The new subject, he's someone I grew up with, and there are certain... I mean, I made promises when we were little, and it feels in some ways like I'm breaking those promises, even as I try my best to help him. I actually feel physically ill, like drunk in my stomach but sober in my brain, when I look at him.

Jeffrey, Mr. Randall says, Jeffrey, JEFFREY. Listen to me. Sit still and listen. Pull yourself together. We are the watchers on the battlements, at the edge of social collapse, like in that show with the ice zombies, where winter is always tomorrow. You know that show? They had an important message, that sometimes we have to put our own personal feelings aside for the greater good. Remember the fat kid? He had to learn to be a team player. I loved that show. So here we are, standing against the darkness that threatens to consume everything we admire. No time for divided hearts.

I know that we're doing something important here, and that he'll thank me later, Jeffrey says. It's just hard right now.

If it were easy to do the right thing, Randall says, then everyone would do it.

6.

SHERRI WAS A transfer student in tenth grade who came right in and joined the Computer Club but also tried out for the volleyball team and the a cappella chorus. She had dark hair in tight braids and a wiry body that flexed in the moment before she leapt to spike the ball, making Rachel's heart rise with her. Rachel sat courtside and watched Sherri practice while she was supposed to be doing sudden death sprints.

Jeffrey stared at Sherri, too: listened to her sing Janelle Monáe in a light contralto when she waited for the bus, and gazed at her across the room during Computer Club. He imagined going up to her and just introducing himself, but his heart was too weak. He could more easily imagine saying the dumbest thing, or actually fainting, than carrying on a smooth conversation with Sherri. He obsessed for ages, until he finally confessed to his friends (Rachel was long since out of the picture by this time) and they started goading him, actually physically shoving him, to speak to Sherri.

Jeffrey slid up to her and said his name, and something inane about music, and then Sherri just stared at him for a long time before saying, I gotta get the bus. Jeffrey watched her walk away, then turned to his watching friends and mimed a finger gun blowing his brains out.

A few days later, Sherri was playing hooky at that one bakery café in town that everyone said was run by lesbians or drug addicts or maybe just old hippies, nursing a chai latte, and she found herself sitting with Rachel, who was also ditching some activity. Neither of them wanted to talk to anyone, they'd come here to be alone. But Rachel felt hope rise up inside her at the proximity of her wildfire crush, and she finally hoisted her bag as if she might just leave the café. Mind if I sit with you a minute, she asked, and Sherri shrugged yes. So Rachel perched on the embroidered tasseled pillow on the bench next to Sherri, and stared at her Algebra II book.

They saw each other at that café every few days, or sometimes just once a week, and they just started sitting together on purpose, without talking to each other much. After a couple months of this, Sherri looked at the time on her phone and said, My mom's out of town. I'll buy you dinner. Rachel kept her shriek of joy on the inside and just nodded.

At dinner—a family pasta place nearby—Sherri looked down at her colorful paper napkin and whispered: I think I don't like boys. I mean, to date, or whatever. I don't hate boys or anything, just not interested that way. You understand.

Rachel stared at Sherri, even after she looked up, so they were making eye contact. In just as low a whisper, Rachel replied: I'm pretty sure I'm not a boy.

This was the first time Rachel ever said the name Rachel aloud, at least with regard to herself.

Sherri didn't laugh or get up or run away. She just stared back, then nodded. She reached onto the red checkerboard vinyl tablecloth with an open palm, for Rachel to insert her palm into if she so chose.

The first time Jeffrey saw Rachel and Sherri holding hands, he looked at them like his soul had come out in bruises.

7.

WE WON'T KEEP you here too long, Mr. Billings, the male attendant says, glancing at Rachel but mostly looking at the mouth that had spoken. You're doing very well. Really, you're an exemplary subject. You should be so proud.

There are so many things that Rachel wants to say. Like: Please just let me go, I have a life. I have an art show coming up in a coffee shop, I can't miss it. You don't have the right. I deserve to live my own life. I have people who used to love me. I'll give you everything I own. I won't press charges if you don't sue. This is no kind of therapy. On and on. But she can't trust that corpse voice. She hyperventilates and gags on her own spit. So sore she's hamstrung.

Every time her eyes get washed out, she's terrified this is it, her last sight. She knows from what Lucy and the other one have said that if her vision switches over to the dead man's, that's the final stage and she's gone.

The man is still talking. We have a form signed by your primary care physician, Dr. Wallace, stating that this treatment is both urgent and medically indicated, as well as an assessment by our in-house psychologist, Dr. Yukizawa. He holds up two pieces of paper, with the looping scrawls of two different doctors that she's never even heard of. She's been seeing Dr. Cummings for years, since before her transition. She makes a huge effort to shake her head, and is shocked by how weak she feels.

You are so fortunate to be one of the first to receive this treatment, the man says. Early indications are that subjects experience a profound improvement across seven different measures of quality of life and social integration. Their OGATH scores are generally high, especially in the red levels. Rejection is basically unheard of. You won't believe how good you'll feel once you're over the adjustment period, he says. If the research goes well, the potential benefits to society are limited only by the cadaver pipeline.

Rachel's upcoming art show, in a tiny coffee shop, is called *Against Curation*. There's a lengthy manifesto, which Rachel planned to print out and mount onto foam or cardboard, claiming that the act of curating is inimical to art or artistry. The only person who can create a proper context for a given piece of art is the artist herself, and arranging someone else's art is an act of violence. Bear in mind that the history of museums is intrinsically tied up with imperialism and colonialism, and the curatorial gaze is historically white and male. But even the most enlightened postcolonial curator is a pirate. Anthologies, mix tapes, it's all the same. Rachel had a long response prepared, in case anybody accused her of just being annoyed that no real gallery would display her work.

Rachel can't help noting the irony of writing a tirade about the curator's bloody scalpel, only to end up with a hole in her literal head.

When the man has left her alone, Rachel begins screaming Jeffrey's name in the dead man's voice. Just the name, nothing that the corpse could twist. She still can't bear to hear that deep timbre, the sick damaged throat, speaking for her. But she can feel her life essence slipping away. Every time she looks over at the dead man, he has more color in his skin and his arms and legs are moving, like a restless sleeper. His face even looks, in some hard-to-define way, more like Rachel's.

Jeffrey! The words come out in a hoarse growl. Jeffrey! Come here!

Rachel wants to believe she's already defeated this trap, because she has lived her life without a single codicil, and whatever they do, they can't retroactively change the person she has been for her entire adulthood. But that doesn't feel like enough. She wants the kind of victory where she gets to actually walk out of here.

8.

JEFFREY FEELS A horrible twist in his neck. This is all unfair, because he already informed Mr. Randall of his conflict and yet he's still here, having to behave professionally while the subject is putting him in the dead center of attention.

Seriously, the subject will not stop bellowing his name, even with a throat that's basically raw membrane at this point. You're not supposed to initiate communication with the subject without submitting an Interlocution Permission form through the proper channels. But the subject is putting him into an impossible position.

Jeffrey, she keeps shouting. And then: Jeffrey, talk to me!

People are lobbing questions in Slack, and of course Jeffrey types the wrong thing and the softcore clown porn comes up. Ha ha, I fell for it again, he types. There's a problem with one of the latest cadavers, a cause-of-death question, and Mr. Randall says the Deputy Assistant Secretary might be in town later.

Jeffrey's mother was a Nobel Prize winner for her work with people who had lost the ability to distinguish between weapons and musical instruments, a condition that frequently leads to maiming or worse. Jeffrey's earliest memories involve his mother flying off to serve as an expert witness in the trials of murderers who claimed they had thought their assault rifles were banjos, or mandolins. Many of these people were faking it, but Jeffrey's mom was usually hired by the defense, not the prosecution. Every time she returned from one of these trips, she would fling her Nobel medal out her bathroom window, and then stay up half the night searching the bushes for it, becoming increasingly drunk. One morning, Jeffrey found her passed out below her bedroom window and believed for a moment that she had fallen two stories to her death. This was, she explained to him later, a different sort of misunderstanding than mistaking a gun for a guitar: a reverse-Oedipal misapprehension. These days Jeffrey's mom requires assistance to dress, to shower, and to transit from her bed to a chair and back, and nobody can get Medicare, Medicaid, or any secondary insurance to pay for this. To save money, Jeffrey has moved back in with his mother, which means he gets to hear her ask at least once a week what happened to Rachel, who was such a nice boy.

Jeffrey can't find his headphones to drown out his name, which the cadaver is shouting so loud that foam comes out of one corner of his mouth. Frances and another engineer both complain on Slack about the noise, which they can hear from down the hall. OMG creepy, Frances types. Make it stop make it stop.

I can't, Jeffrey types back. I can't ok. I don't have the right paperwork.

Maybe tomorrow, Rachel will wake up fully inhabiting her male body. She'll look down at her strong forearms, threaded with veins, and she'll smile and thank Jeffrey. Maybe she'll nod at him, by way of a tiny salute, and say, You did it, buddy. You brought me back.

But right now, the cadaver keeps shouting, and Jeffrey realizes he's covering his ears with his fists and is doubled over.

Rachel apparently decides that Jeffrey's name alone isn't working. The cadaver pauses and then blurts, I would really love to hang with you. Hey! I appreciate everything you've done to set things right. JEFFREY! You really shouldn't have gone to so much trouble for me.

Somehow, these statements have an edge, like Jeffrey can easily hear the intended meaning. He looks up and sees Rachel's eyes, spraying tears like a damn lawn sprinkler.

Jeffrey, the corpse says, I saw Sherri. She told me the truth about you.

She's probably just making things up. Sherri never knew anything for sure, or at least couldn't prove anything. And yet, just the mention of her name is enough to make Jeffrey straighten up and walk to the door of the observation room, even with no signed Interlocution Permission form. Jeffrey makes himself stride up to the two nearly naked bodies and stop at the one on the left, the one with the ugly tattoo and the drooling silent mouth.

I don't want to hurt you, Jeffrey says. I never wanted to hurt you, even when we were kids and you got weird on me. My mom still asks about you.

Hey pal, you've never been a better friend to me than you are right now, the cadaver says. But on the left, the eyes are red and wet and full of violence.

What did Sherri say? Stop playing games and tell me, Jeffrey says. When did you see her? What did she say?

But Rachel has stopped trying to make the other body talk, and is just staring up, letting her eyes speak for her.

Listen, Jeffrey says to the tattooed body. This is already over, the process is too advanced. I could disconnect all of the machines, unplug the tap from your occipital lobe and everything, and the cadaver would continue drawing your remaining life energy. The link between you is already stable. This project, it's a government–industry collaboration, we call it Love and Dignity for Everyone. You have no idea. But you, you're going to be so handsome. You always used to wish you could look like this guy, remember? I'm actually kind of jealous of you.

Rachel just thrashes against her restraints harder than ever.

Here, I'll show you, Jeffrey says at last. He reaches behind Rachel's obsolete head and unplugs the tap, along with the other wires. See? he says. No difference. That body is already more you than you. It's already done.

That's when Rachel leans forward, in her old body, and head-butts Jeffrey, before grabbing for his key ring with the utility knife on it. She somehow gets the knife open with one hand while he's clutching his nose, and slashes a bloody canyon across Jeffrey's stomach. He falls, clutching at his own slippery flesh, and watches her saw through her straps and land on unsteady feet. She lifts Jeffrey's lanyard, smearing blood on his shirt as it goes.

9.

WHEN RACHEL WAS in college, she heard a story about a business professor named Lou, who dated two different women and strung them both along. Laurie was a lecturer in women's studies, while Susie worked in the bookstore co-op despite having a PhD in comp lit. After the women found out Lou was dating both of them, things got ugly. Laurie stole Susie's identity, signing her up for a stack of international phone cards and a subscription to the Dirndl of the Month Club, while Susie tried to crash Laurie's truck and cold-cocked

Laurie as she walked out of a seminar on intersectional feminism. In the end, the two women looked at each other, over the slightly dented truck and Laurie's bloody lip and Susie's stack of junk mail. Laurie just spat blood and said, Listen. I won't press charges, if you don't sue. Susie thought for a moment, then stuck out her hand and said, Deal. The two women never spoke to each other, or Lou, ever again.

Rachel has always thought this incident exposed the roots of the social contract: most of our relationships are upheld not by love, or obligation, or gratitude, but by mutually assured destruction. Most of the people in Rachel's life who could have given her shit for being transgender were differently bodied, non-neurotypical, or some other thing that also required some acceptance from her. Mote, beam, and so on.

For some reason, Rachel can't stop thinking about the social contract and mutually assured destruction as she hobbles down the hallway of Love and Dignity for Everyone with a corpse following close behind. Every time she pauses to turn around and see if the dead man is catching up, he gains a little ground. So she forces herself to keep running with weak legs, even as she keeps hearing his hoarse breath right behind her. True power, Rachel thinks, is being able to destroy others with no consequences to yourself.

She's reached the end of a corridor, and she's trying not to think about Jeffrey's blood on the knife in her hand. He'll be fine, he's in a facility. She remembers Sherri in the computer lab, staring at the pictures on the Internet: her hair wet from the shower, one hand reaching for a towel. Sherri sobbing but then tamping it down as she looked at the screen. Sherri telling Rachel at lunch, I'm leaving this school. I can't stay. There's a heavy door with an RFID reader, and Jeffrey's card causes it to click twice before finally bleeping. Rachel's legs wobble and spasm, and the breath of the dead man behind her grows louder. Then she pushes through the door and runs up the square roundabout of stairs. Behind her, she hears Lucy the nurse shout at her to come back, because she's still convalescing, this is a delicate time.

Rachel feels a little more of her strength fade every time the dead man's hand lurches forward. Something irreplaceable leaves her. She pushes open the dense metal door marked EXIT and nearly faints with sudden day-blindness.

The woods around Love and Dignity for Everyone are dense with moss and underbrush, and Rachel's bare feet keep sliding off tree roots. I can't stop, Rachel pleads with herself, I can't stop or my whole life was for nothing. Who even was I, if I let this happen to me. The nearly naked dead man crashes through branches that Rachel has ducked under. She throws the knife and hears a satisfying grunt, but he doesn't even pause. Rachel knows that anybody who sees both her and the cadaver will choose to help the cadaver. There's no way to explain her situation in the dead man's voice. She vows to stay off roads and avoid talking to people. This is her life now.

Up ahead, she sees a fast-running stream, and she wonders how the corpse will take to water. The stream looks like the one she and Jeffrey used to play in, when they would catch crayfish hiding under rocks. The crayfish looked just like tiny lobsters, and they would twist around trying to pinch you as you gripped their midsections. Rachel sloshes in the water and doesn't hear the man's breath in her ear for a moment. Up ahead, the current leads to a steep waterfall that's so white in the noon sunlight, it appears to stand still. She remembers staring into a bucket full of crayfish, debating whether to boil them alive or let them all go. And all at once, she has a vivid memory of herself and Jeffrey both holding the full bucket and turning it sideways, until all the crayfish sloshed back into the river. The crayfish fled for their lives, their eyes seeming to protrude with alarm, and Rachel held onto an empty bucket with Jeffrey, feeling an inexplicable sense of relief. We are such wusses, Jeffrey said, and they both laughed. She remembers the sight of the last crayfish rushing out of view—as if this time, maybe the trick would work, and nobody would think to look under this particular rock. She reaches the waterfall, seizes a breath, and jumps with both feet at once.

COPYRIGHT